Haunting at Remington House

Laura V. Keegan

Dedication

This book is dedicated to my sons, Blaine, Kyle and Connor; my husband, Tim; my mom, Elvira and my dad, Richard. You are my joy and my inspiration. Thank you for your constant support in this years-long endeavor.

Prologue

We will begin when we end.
That is the rule of eternity.
The end. The beginning.
The finalization of life, the birth of the haunt.

"Do it! Now!" Gabe mustered all his waning strength to shriek his final words to his sister. "Pull the trigger, Helen!" Closing his eyes, he bellowed. "Now!"

Helen hesitated. Her hand trembled. She sat to her brother's left in a solid low-backed chair turned sideways so she could brace her arm and steady her aim. She drew a long, slow breath, then cradled the thin, bony wrist of her shooting hand with her left. She couldn't miss—it would be unthinkable. Another deep breath. She was ready. Helen pulled the trigger.

Gabriel Lindeman's body pitched violently backwards. His head bounced off the pillow carefully wedged behind him. Helen threw her arms up and yelled triumphantly, "I did it!" She watched her brother collapse sideways onto the hard, cold attic floor. His body slammed the wooden planks, bounced once, then settled in a pool of his own blood. Gabriel died instantly.

Without a moment's hesitation, Helen began the ceremony. She lit the nine black candles, watching to make sure they remained burning in the drafty room. Around Helen and Gabe's perimeter was a circle of highly polished onyx stones.

Helen sat tall and straight, her thin legs crossed, head bowed, eyes closed. She chanted: "Lucifer! Obsecro. Dona vitam aeternam ad hoc impia et diabolica peccator cuius nomen est Gabriel Lindeman." ("Lucifer! I beseech you. Grant eternal life to this most unholy and diabolical sinner whose name is Gabriel Lindeman.")

The hairs on Helen's arms stood on end, her skin prickled as a bone-chilling coldness enveloped her. She opened her eyes. Beside her a black, translucent vapor hovered. Helen repeated the sacred incantation nine times. Her voice, soft at first, became louder and louder until it reached an earsplitting crescendo that echoed off the bare walls of the attic, as if her voice were many voices, all screaming the mantra for rebirth.

Helen focused her rheumy-blue eyes on the flickering candle flames. A swift stirring of cold air assaulted her, dislodging the ivory stick that held her hair in an austere bun. Her white hair blew across her eyes, into her mouth—she was unaware. A high-pitched howling emanated from the mist beside her. Warily she reached her hand into the black fog. Indeed! It had substance—oily and cold. Slowly it began to take form: first the eyes, icy blue like her own; the nose sharp and beaklike; lips thin and pulled tightly over teeth yellowed from age and sickness; and then the outline of the jaw, the chin, the forehead.

Helen continued chanting, not looking at her brother again until he whispered in a soft hiss, "Helen, you've done it. I live!"

Helen smiled, got quickly to her feet. There was no time to waste. She dragged Gabriel's corpse from the inner circle to the bed against the west wall, easily lifting his diseased and withered body onto the bed. She placed the blood-soaked pillow beneath his head, then covered the body with a blue chenille bedspread.

For the next three days Helen sat in the circle of stones with her brother's reborn spirit. Together they chanted endless verses from *The Book of the Occult*. Hour by hour, day by day, Gabriel grew stronger.

On the fourth day, Helen and her brother were ready. Helen took her place with her back to the wall, a pillow behind her to cushion and soften the final blow. Beside her, Gabriel steadied her hand—he was not yet strong enough to hold the gun and pull the trigger with any guarantee of accuracy. She would do the deed herself. A murder-suicide—as planned. A look of profound shock registered on Helen's face as the bullet penetrated her skull. Like her brother, she died instantly.

Immediately, Gabriel began the ritual. He chanted from the sacred book. Flames from the black candles cast undulating shadows on the walls of the attic bedroom. Helen's mist was black and almost formless at first. Within an hour, she too was reborn. For three days, brother and sister remained in the circle of stones until her transformation was complete, her strength renewed. Helen and Gabriel's souls were intact.

In death, as in life, the Lindemans were the essence of evil. They would remain and walk the halls of Remington House. After all, this was their home.

Chapter 1

Tom's wife, Elise, had been dead for nearly two years, years Tom endured the dark depths of desolation and despair, immersed in an illusionary existence, fighting desperately to restore the delicate balance between reality and delusion—he battled to regain his sanity. Over time, with a halfhearted conviction, born out of a necessity to get on with his life and forgo his pain, Tom accepted the truth—he was not responsible for her death. Elise. He loved her madly. He hated her passionately.

It was time to leave Jamestown. Time to start over. On this bleak, sunless October day, Tom was leaving his damnable house and its memories of the tragic and untimely death of Elise. He was moving to Ravenswood.

The wind howled around the great, stone house. Dried leaves, like clouds of gold and crimson, sailed in the strong gusts, tossed higher and higher, then abandoned to float gently to the ground, swept up again and again in an endless, rhythmic cycle. Fog, heavily laden with moisture, drifted across the expansive front lawn forming a curtain that slowly obscured the house.

A cherub statue stared vacantly from the fountain, its half-lidded eyes dull and empty. Tom felt unsettled as he passed the imp-child, its eyes watching, following his every move. He'd be thankful to escape its penetrating gaze. A steady stream of water flowed from the urchin's tiny, stone penis into the icy fountain; clouds of steam formed, hanging heavily in the air. Perched on the statue's shoulder was a large raven, feathers shimmering black and midnight blue. As Tom passed, the impressive bird raised its expansive feathered wings, cawed eerily, then flew into the thickening haze.

Tom quickened his pace, hurrying down the tree-lined sidewalk to the waiting cab. Through a momentary break in the fog, a movement from the upper window of the house caught his eye. The wind stirred the white lace curtain of the room that had been Elise's bedroom. For a moment Tom thought he saw the pale outline of a woman. Then the swirling mist completely shrouded the window. A shiver ran down his spine.

Tom handed his luggage to the cab driver and wrapped his wool scarf tightly around his neck against the cold. How fragile the mind, how easily deceived. But that's all it was—a cruel trick of a tired mind. Elise was dead.

"Let's go," Tom said, slamming the taxi's door. *Finally, it's over.* The car pulled into the street, taillights flickering red as the driver slowed for a curve. Tom was on his way to Remington House, his new home.

***

From the third story window, Elise watched Tom walk down the sidewalk carrying his suitcases. She tried to will him back into the house, back to her. To no avail. She cursed as he climbed into the waiting taxi, stared in disbelief as the cab pulled away from the curb. "How dare you leave me in this dreadful house—this house that has become my prison. I don't think so!" she snarled, her opalescent fists flailing against the cold glass. Fury pierced her soul like a hot knife. Tom would pay for his betrayal. She smiled cruelly as the thick mist rolled in, completely obliterating her view.

Chapter 2

Tom hadn't been away from Jamestown since his wife's death. He'd forgotten the simple pleasure of traveling. Aboard the Eastern Express, a trip that would take about eight hours, he found himself content to watch the passing autumnal landscape of vivid reds, bright oranges and dazzling yellows. Quaint New England towns slipped by, one after another. Tom smiled, was caught by surprise at his reflection in the window. It'd been a long time since he'd felt this calm. *I'm doing the right thing. To the depths of my soul I feel it. I think, at last, I am free.*

The porter knocked on his compartment door. "Lunch is being served in the dining car, Mr. Gardner."

Tom straightened his tie, ran his fingers through the thick waves of his hair. Whistling happily under his breath, he made his way down the aisle. As he entered the dining car, he froze. "Elise!" Her name escaped Tom's lips. She was there, waiting, her back to him, in the first dining booth.

The steward stepped forward to greet him, his smile quickly changing to one of concern. Tom tried to compose himself, sensed everyone staring at him. He struggled for self-control. This couldn't be happening again. A drop of perspiration rolled down his forehead to the tip of his nose, hung then dropped onto his upper lip, the taste of salt bitter as he nervously licked his parched lips.

Tom took a quick breath and focused on the face of the woman now turning toward him. Of course it wasn't Elise. He had to get a grip. Turning to the steward he said, "I'll have something in my compartment. I'm more tired than I realized." Tom turned and strode down the aisle as steadily as his shaking knees would allow.

Irritated, the steward muttered under his breath, "Yeah, you poor rich guys—you don't know what tired is." To Tom's retreating back, he said loudly, "I'll send someone with a tray."

After a quiet lunch, Tom lay down on the sleeping berth, his feet dangling uncomfortably over the end of the too-thin, too-short mattress. He slept until the train arrived at the Ravenswood depot. A cab waited on the street in front of the station, the driver, a man perhaps in his late thirties, tall, sturdy of build, wavy blonde hair sticking out from under a hunters cap, impatiently drummed his large fingers on the roof of the car. "Hey! You Tom Gardner?"

Tom nodded. The man came forward, hands out, to take the suitcases from him.

"Train's running late tonight. Should've been here at six!" The driver hesitated, waited for an acknowledgment from Tom. Getting none he asked, "Have a good trip?"

"I did."

The driver hoisted the heavy leather suitcases into the trunk, then opened the rear door, motioning Tom to get in. "Remington House, right?"

"Yes. On upper Beach Highway Road," Tom said, sitting back in the threadbare, gray-cloth seat. He cracked his window a few inches so the side window would defog. He wanted to see where he was going.

"Get cold, let me know. I'll crank the heat up for you."

"I'm fine. Thanks."

Chapter 3

The drive proved much longer than Tom expected. After passing through the quaint town of Ravenswood, its streets filled with costumed children gathering candy on this All Hallows' Eve, the taxi driver and his fare drove for miles in mutual silence, passing only an occasional house set well back from the road. Lights sparkled in windows creating the only visible light in the shadowy trees. On the outskirts of town the road turned into a two-lane highway. Tom rolled the window down. At once he heard the rhythmic sounds of the ocean pounding onto the shore. The glorious smell of salty ocean permeated and stung his nostrils. He inhaled deeply filling his lungs with the wonderfully intoxicating sea air. After driving for about half an hour on the desolate, winding beach highway, the cab turned off onto a dirt road.

Rounding a curve in the long driveway, Tom had his first view of Remington House. He was finally home. Nestled in a grove of barren, leafless trees, Remington House waited for him. The moon peered from behind an expanse of clouds illuminating the stately three-story, clapboard house. From this angle, he could see three stone chimneys protruding from the broad-hipped roof. A wide verandah ran the full length of the house front, continuing around to the east. The moon slipped behind the thick clouds, shadowing the house in darkness.

"You ever been here?" the driver asked.

"No, I bought it sight unseen. My attorney did the legwork for me."

"Nice place. Too bad you're seeing it in the dark for the first time. It's incredible in the daylight."

The driver stopped in the gravel drive below the porch. While he unloaded the suitcases, Tom climbed the stairs and crossed the verandah. He stopped in front of the heavy double-entry doors, fumbling in his pocket for the key. Several lights had been left on inside, their glow casting eerie patterns across the porch. Lace curtains covered the leaded glass windows, obscuring his view into the house.

"Mr. Gardner, are you going to open the door? You have the key, right?"

"Yeah, sorry." Tom's hand was shaking as he unlocked the door and stepped into the oak- paneled entryway. Directly in front of him was a wooden staircase leading up into the pitch black, second floor. A cold draft blew down the staircase and across his face. A nudge from behind reminded him the driver was still loaded down with suitcases and was trying to get past him into the house.

Tom stepped into the entryway, letting the man go around him. To the left, a doorway opened into a study, dimly lit from the porch lights. "Put the suitcases in there. I'll take care of them later," Tom said. "What do I owe you?"

"Twenty four."

Tom handed the driver the fare, along with a generous tip. "That should do it then. Thanks. Goodnight."

The driver stared curiously at Tom. "You okay?" he asked, sticking his wallet into the back pocket of his jeans.

"Fine," Tom said, turning to open the front doors so the driver would leave.

"You look beat. Least I can do is light the fireplace for you. It's freezing in here. Don't think anyone turned the furnace on. Might need to check the pilot light."

"Not tonight. A fire would be greatly appreciated though," Tom said, following the driver into the room to the right of the hall.

"I'll get some wood from out back. I did some remodeling for the previous owners, so I know my way around. Wait here."

Tom paced nervously waiting for him to come back inside. A few minutes later, Tom heard the slamming of a door from the back of the house. Carrying a canvas sling filled with wood, the driver came in, put the bundle down and threw several pieces of kindling into the fireplace. In a short time, he had a fire blazing. Tom leaned forward to warm his hands.

"Much better," the man said. "It's been damned cold the past few days. All these old houses are cold—poorly insulated, lots of drafts." He stood up. "There's plenty of wood chopped outside. You should be fine for a few days anyhow."

"Thanks . . . uh?"

"Name's Joe. Joe Tilson," he said extending his callused hand to Tom.

Joe's handshake was firm and reassuring in Tom's own shaking hand. He realized his trembling was evident to Joe. Embarrassed, he withdrew his hand, though Joe didn't act as if he'd noticed. "I'm Tom Gardner."

"Yeah, I knew that. Need anything else before I go?"

"No. Thanks."

"Well, if you find anything that needs to be done around here, I'm always looking for extra work to make it through the winter. It's the off-season here. I don't do a lot of driving-for-hire this time of year." Joe threw a few more pieces of wood into the fire and stacked the rest of the cut wood into the storage bin on the side of the fireplace. "I was a contractor in New York—once upon a time. Got tired of the big city and moved out here." He zipped his jacket. "Anyhow, I know my stuff, and I'm reasonable. And honest."

"Thanks. Why don't you check back tomorrow? I'll look around and see what needs to be done."

"Sure, Mr. Gardner. I'll stop by in the morning. Goodnight."

After Joe left, Tom sank down into the couch in front of the crackling fire and surveyed the room. The wall with the fireplace was of rich, earth-hued brownstone that reached to the high, ten-foot ceiling. The mantle was about a foot deep and perhaps ten feet wide, built of solid golden-oak, its underside blackened with soot. Dozens of antique-tin, daguerreotype photos covered the ledge. Faces of lifeless men and women stared vacantly from pewter frames. "God those are creepy! They go in the trash tomorrow."

The hearth was deep-brown, polished granite, inlaid with black stones—maybe obsidian. The inlaid pattern radiated out from a central hub. It looked very primitive—possibly even occult in design.

Built into the wall on the left of the fireplace was a large, wood-storage bin, now half- filled with the wood Joe hauled in earlier. Extending from the floor to the ceiling on the right of the fireplace was a bookcase about six feet wide. Photographs of an old couple filled several shelves. He wondered why they hadn't been packed away. Tom picked up one of the pictures, studying it. *Must be the previous owners.*

The man and woman glaring from the frame were obviously brother and sister, their sharp, well defined features mirrored in their faces. Around their necks they wore heavy amulets, inlaid with dark, sparkling stones. The man's face was skeletal. Wrinkled skin hung off his long thin neck, making his stiffly starched, white collar appear several sizes too large. Protruding cheekbones and deep-set eyes added to his pallid, sickly appearance. Tufts of black hair stuck out from either side of his head.

The woman seemed younger, more vibrant. Her silver hair was pulled tightly back from her face in a pristine bun. The woman's face was deeply wrinkled and covered in heavy makeup, apparent even in the photograph. Her eyebrows were penciled dark brown, her thin lips painted scarlet red. Dots of rouge emphasized the woman's sculpted cheekbones. Diamond earrings hung from her elongated earlobes. Tom imagined she'd been a stunner in her day. Her eyes, though—something was wrong. With icy-malice she glared at him from the tarnished frame. Shuddering, Tom turned the photograph face down on the shelf. *All these pictures go in the trash. Creepy damn things!*

To the right of the bookcase was a single black-mahogany door with an antiqued-brass, lever-set handle. Curious, Tom twisted the lever downward and pushed. The door didn't budge. Turning the handle again, he rammed the doorframe with his shoulder. The old wood creaked, its dry hinges squealing as the door gave way. Tom started to fall forward, quickly steadying himself by grabbing the doorframe. The door opened into a small, bare room under the upper staircase.

There was a half-door to the left that Tom guessed was a storage area. Barely visible in the dim light was still another door on the far wall to the left and still another on the wall to the right. Stepping into the small room, Tom was immediately assaulted by a freezing chill. His breath formed a mist in the damp air. The smell of old, damp wood filled his nostrils. Moving slowly forward, Tom opened the door at the far left. It led into the back end of the study. He found the light switch, flipped it and glanced around the room. The study was paneled in oak varnished to a warm glow. The fireplace wall on the west was tiled from floor to ceiling in deep, amber-colored marble squares. The southern wall facing the veranda was comprised almost entirely of windows hung with heavy, antique lace drapes that Tom hoped would allow sunshine to filter into the room and lighten what was, in his opinion, an oppressive atmosphere.

Several large, floral-patterned Oriental rugs, in colors ranging from tans to deep browns, covered the highly buffed, oak floor. All the furniture in the room was upholstered in varying shades of brown leather. On the east wall, by the door to the entryway, were bookcases filled with hundreds of leather-bound books. In front of the bookcase was a massive oak desk and chair.

Alerted by the sound of creaking floorboards, Tom spun around. In the dark shadows, in the far corner of the room, someone stood. Tom's breath caught, there was a ringing in his ears, sweat collected above his brow. Instinctively he reached up wiping it away with a trembling hand. She was standing there, twenty feet from him. "In the name of God!" Tom yelled. "What do you want?" His voice, low pitched and hollow, seemed to come from someone else, someone behind him.

She stepped out of the shadows. "Oh! I'm sorry. I didn't mean to scare you. I didn't hear you come in. It's okay. I'm supposed to be here. Are you Mr. Gardner?" She was a slight girl, maybe 19 or 20 with long blonde hair pulled back into a ponytail. She took a step toward him.

Seeing her in the shadows he'd thought . . . To hell with what he'd thought. Tom took a deep breath, steadied himself. "I'm Tom Gardner. Who are you, and what are you doing sneaking around here?"

"I'm Mary Stevens. I was hired to clean the house."

Tom said, "Oh! I remember. John Atwood hired you."

"That's right," Mary said. "I've been here since this afternoon. I was dusting the dining room and some of the power went out. I didn't hear you come in because I've been wandering around in the basement—in the dark mind you— trying to find the fuse box. Which I never *did* find. When I came upstairs, the door from the basement into the kitchen was locked. I had to go out the basement entrance and around back to get in the house." She pointed behind her.

"Sounds like you've had quite an ordeal," Tom said.

Mary nodded.

"I've been here about an hour," Tom said. "You've been in the basement that whole time?"

"Yeah. Wow! I had *no* idea that much time had gone by. That's amazing . . . and very strange." Mary frowned, wrinkling her forehead. "Anyway, when I came into the living room, I saw the open door and the light on in the study. I was making sure everything was okay. That's when you saw me. You scared me, too," Mary added.

"I bet I did. Well, tell me, Mary, what can I do to make amends?"

Mary laughed nervously. "Nothing. It's okay. I need to call my dad to come get me, though. My car's in for service, so my dad dropped me off here this afternoon. Then of course, my cell phone died, and your landline's not working. Do you have a cell phone I could use?"

Tom handed Mary his phone. "Sorry I yelled at you. It's been a long day."

"That's okay. I completely get it." She smiled at Tom as she punched in the numbers. "Hey, Dad, you can come and get me now. Yeah, I know, but my phone battery died." She shrugged her shoulders. "Yeah, I'm finished. Mr. Gardner's here now. Hey, Dad, you know where the breaker box is? Some of the power's off." She nodded to Tom. "Okay. We'll find it. See you in a while. Bye." She handed Tom his phone.

"Okay. Show me the way to the basement," Tom said. "Let's get the lights back on." He followed Mary through the living and dining rooms and into the kitchen. Candles burned illuminating the room in a dull, shadowy glow.

Mary picked up the flashlight from the counter and handed it to Tom. "The basement stairs are here." She unlocked the door. They'd just started down the wooden stairs when the kitchen and basement lights came on.

"Well, I guess that takes care of that," Tom said. "Still, I better go down and make sure everything's okay. I don't want the lights going out again tonight. Your dad told you where the fuse box is?"

"He says it's in the furnace room. I never found the furnace room! I got kind of lost down there in the dark, though."

They descended the steep, wooden stairs, Tom in the lead. "I think the furnace room is down that hall," Mary said, pointing to her right.

But it wasn't. They wandered around and around, through room after room, some empty, some filled with boxes, some stuffed with antique furniture. Wispy cobwebs grabbed at their bare arms, clung to their eyelashes.

Tom scratched his head. "This makes no sense. We're going in circles. I can't figure out where we are. I thought we came in from the hallway over there, but where are the stairs?" The lights flickered off and on.

Mary motioned to her left. "Let's try that way. That looks like the door at the bottom of the stairs. It must have swung closed." They walked in the direction of the door. There was a loud pop. The lights went out, leaving them in total darkness.

"Damn! What did I do with the flashlight? Did I give it to you?" Tom asked.

"No," Mary said.

Tom felt for Mary's hand. In the darkness he grabbed it, surprised at how icy-cold it was, how bony and stiff her fingers were. He pulled her after him, moving cautiously toward where he thought the door should be. He crept down the long hallway, his shoes scuffling on the hard cement, at last coming to a door. The knob felt reassuringly solid in his hand. He turned it. The lights flickered on. Tom turned to Mary who was squeezing his hand painfully. There was no one there! He looked down. Red indentations were visible from the tight pressure to his hand. *No one there* registered in his mind, echoed again and again. He glanced around looking for Mary. The lights went out! He stood alone, his back pressed against the cold, cement wall that smelled faintly of mold. Motionless, Tom waited in the dark. Waited . . . for what?

In the distance he heard Mary shouting, fear clearly discernible in her voice. "Mr. Gardner?" she yelled. "Where are you? I'm scared! Please! Answer me!"

He had to get to her! Tom felt in his pockets. What the hell had he done with the flashlight? He hurried down the hall, heard Mary's breath coming in short gasps. "Don't be afraid, Mary, I'm here. Walk toward my voice." He inched forward, trying to forget what had just happened, his hand still throbbing. At last, he felt her warm, outstretched hand.

Suddenly there was the whirring of an electric motor, a flash of lights. The power came on. Tom and Mary were standing in the center of the furnace room. Directly in front of them was the fuse box—open, all switches in the on position. Lying on the floor in front of them was the flashlight. Tom reached down and grabbed it, not wanting to risk darkness again.

Mary was pale and obviously shaken. "I swear, someone ran by me—right after the lights went out. Why did you leave me?" She didn't wait for his answer. "Mr. Gardner, how did we get in here?"

Tom hurriedly looked around. "We must have walked though that doorway in the dark without knowing it." Tom pointed at a doorway to their right.

"I haven't moved since you left me. I *know* I haven't. What's going on?" Mary cried.

"It's okay; it's an odd floor plan, that's all. Especially in the dark," Tom said.

"I want to get out of here! Let's go upstairs." Mary twisted her ponytail nervously in her fingers.

"Let me check the fuses first." Tom found nothing wrong—not that he knew a lot about wiring. But it looked okay to him. He closed the metal box. "Come on. Everything seems fine." Again they wandered through hallway after hallway, room after room. When at last they found the stairs, they didn't hesitate but ran up and into the kitchen. Tom slammed the door.

For reasons better left for each of them to understand, Tom and Mary dismissed their experience in the basement, neither one wanting to admit to the other, or more importantly to themselves, what had occurred. Better to let it be. Better to forget that it made no sense.

"I'll tell you one thing. Before I go down there again, I'll find the floor plans for the basement!" Tom laughed, trying to make light of the situation.

"Hello?" a deep voice called. "Mary, where are you? Hello?"

"We're here, Dad. In the kitchen."

Her dad looked from Mary to Tom. "Mary, are you all right? You're pale as a ghost!"

"I'm okay. The power was out, and we got lost in the basement trying to find the fuse box and then . . . well, I got scared in the dark—that's all. Never mind." Mary took her dad's hand. "Dad, this is Tom Gardner. Tom, this is my dad, Mick Stevens."

"Glad to meet you." Mick pulled his daughter to him, hugging her with one arm. He extended his free hand to Tom. "So, you're the lucky owner of this house? This is a fine place. They don't build them better than this. No sirree! My grandfather helped build Remington House back in the twenties. Meant to stand a lifetime. Solid—that's what this house is."

"Dad, I'm tired, please don't get started talking about how things *used* to be," Mary chided her dad. "Mr. Gardner is tired. Let's go home. Oh, almost forgot— I left a few groceries in the kitchen to get you by."

"Thanks, Mary. Much appreciated. It was nice to meet you, Mick. You have a lovely daughter. Mary thanks for your help." Tom handed her a fifty.

"Wow, that's too much. I was only here a few hours."

"Well deserved, I'm sure. Will you be here tomorrow?"

"I have classes all day, but I can come the day after. I'll be here around eleven. Goodnight."

Tom walked them to the door. "Goodnight."

Chapter 4

For the years following Elise's death, while Tom mourned and struggled to find peace with her death, Elise remained hidden in the Jamestown house. She was weak and uncertain. Nothing more than a thinly-veiled aura. Then Tom began making plans to leave. The reason for her existence became clear. Tom would not leave her behind. That was not even a possibility.

Elise arrived at Remington House in an old, worn-leather steamer trunk filled with bedding. Nate Adams, Tom's friend and business assistant, hired a driver to transport some of Tom's personal belongings to the new house. Thankfully, the trip had been tolerable for Elise—and fast. She arrived several hours before Tom. The driver unloaded the truck, placed everything in the attic. Mary had signed for the delivery. All was done quickly and expediently. Within an hour, the driver was gone.

Wouldn't Tom be surprised! Elise laughed wickedly, actually producing a slight guttural sound, truly delighting her. Leaving the cold attic, she went down the back stairs, intent on exploring the main floor.

In a small room at the bottom of the back stairs, behind the door to the kitchen, Elise's elation quickly dissipated. A black mist gathered, hovering in the air over her head. Horrified, she tried to hide as the dark form materialized. It emitted an ominous groan that shook her to her very soul. Elise's scream was silent; her strength vanquished by her fear.

Dark and oily, the misty thing covered her, petted her as though she were a cat. It caressed her head and back with hands that she could feel but could not see. Bony fingers raked her skin. Recoiling into a corner of the tiny room, she tried to summon her strength. To no avail. She cowered; she didn't have enough strength to make herself transparent. The dark entity continued to twine its icy mist around her. *It's smothering me. This vile thing is trying to make me surrender to it. It's trying to steal my soul!*

Then incredibly, tears welled up and trickled down her cheeks. Elise gathered courage. Her anger intensified. She had waited too long for revenge, would not give up now. She summoned all her strength. Her will to survive was strong— stronger than the will of the entity. The roiling mist continued caressing her with greasy, sinewy fingers.

Elise screamed—the sound barely audible at first—but building. Louder and louder, piercing the dark night. The repulsive thing retreated and vanished.

I did it. I sent it away! Elise shuddered, then started giggling, nearly hysterical. This was her first encounter with the malevolent beings that dwelled in the dark realm.

Needing to escape the confines of the airless room, Elise slid under the door into the kitchen. She collapsed on the floor, catching her breath. Then Elise laughed. This time her laughter was clearly audible to the other side. The young girl stopped and looked around, visibly startled. Then the lights went out, sending the room into darkness. The girl screamed.

Elise was exhausted. Without looking back at the young woman she had frightened, she retreated to her trunk in the attic. She needed rest. Curled up in a tiny ball in a soft, chenille blanket, Elise smiled. As she drifted off to sleep, her last thoughts were how easily she had overcome the vile thing.

Of course Elise didn't know—how could she know—that her next encounters with the dark spirits would not prove to be such easy battles. She'd not yet learned the real strength of pure evil.

Chapter 5

Except for the crackling of the fire, the house was silent. Tom lay on the couch watching the flames die down. Here he was. In Remington House. He'd actually done it, he'd left Jamestown! Chilled, he got up and put another log on the fire; the hungry flames engulfed the dry tinder, shooting brilliant orange spikes high into the firebox. Tom was worn-out. Not wanting to make the effort to go upstairs, he pulled a heavy, blue afghan from the back of the couch. He lay down and covered himself; within minutes he was asleep.

Tom slept soundly and, mercifully, did not dream. He woke the next morning when a sliver of light coming through a slit in the curtain shone brightly across his eyes. Disoriented, he looked around the room, not knowing where he was at first.

It was freezing in the house! The fire had died to a few glowing coals. Shivering he got up, and threw some small kindling and a crumpled up piece of newspaper on the coals, managing to get the fire burning. He lay back down, pulled the blanket up under his chin. Quite contented, he drifted back to sleep. A few hours later the sound of a car coming down the gravel drive woke him. He went out onto the front porch to greet Joe. "Joe, I didn't expect to see you so early. Come on in, I'll make some coffee."

"Don't go to any trouble, Mr. Gardner."

"Call me Tom."

"Have a good night?" Joe asked.

"Slept like a baby!"

"Ocean air'll do the trick. I dropped a few fares off in the area, so thought I'd stop by—see if you needed anything. Won't be another train until late this afternoon—no passengers to pick up, so my day's pretty much free now." Joe followed Tom through the living room, into the dining room, through the swinging door into the kitchen.

Tom soon had a pot of coffee brewing, the rich, pungent aroma filled the air. He found mugs and spoons, creamer and sugar while he and Joe waited patiently for the coffee to finish. "So, Joe, tell me what kind of work you'd be willing to do around here? I haven't had a chance to look around yet, but after we have our coffee we can check the place out. I think you said last night that you'd done some work here?"

"Yeah, I did. For the Lindemans. Some painting, removed a few trees, cleaned up dead vegetation. A few years ago, the last summer they were here, I rebuilt the dock and did some repairs on their boathouse. I did a little plumbing work in one of the upstairs bathrooms, and a few odd jobs around the house. Every few months they'd have something for me to fix. Nothing very extensive. Typical handyman stuff."

"Sounds like you know your stuff." Tom nodded his approval.

"Yeah. Not much to it. There was a lot more I'd like to have done, but the Lindemans didn't really like anyone around. I always thought it was a great house," Joe said. "It definitely needs some upgrades. A lot of the wiring is probably outdated, even dangerous. The furnace is almost obsolete; it's getting almost impossible to find parts for it unless you special order them. We don't have a major hardware store in town, so it can take a week or more to get parts here."

"We better look around then. See what you think needs to be dealt with right away. I need to find out what the delay is with the telephone. I'd like to get that taken care of before I do much, then we can look around. I haven't even been upstairs yet. Odd, huh? I was too tired last night. Slept on the couch. After you left, I found out the power was out in part of the house. Once it came back on, and Mary Stevens left, the girl who is helping out here, all I wanted was to get some sleep." Tom poured them both another cup of coffee, added cream to his.

"Oh, yeah. I heard Mary was going to be helping out here, getting the place ready for you. Nice kid. Her great-granddad helped build this house." Joe stirred three spoons of sugar into his coffee, then topped his mug off with cream. "So you lost the power, but only in part of the house?"

"Yeah, but the fuses were all okay. The power went on and off a few times. Mary said it was on part of the time she was here. Funny thing, she was down in the basement hunting for the fuse box when you and I got here. Poor kid. She lost her way in the dark basement."

"Bet that scared the crap out of her. Creepy old basement— especially in the dark! I'll check the outside wires. This time of year we get a lot the gale force winds blowing in from the Atlantic. Might be a loose connection. Or could be some wires shorting out. I'll get right on it, wouldn't want to take any chances of a fire."

Tom rummaged through the cupboards. Finding a bag of blueberry bagels, he handed one to Joe. Through a mouthful of bagel he said, "I need to make a few calls; I left my cell phone in the living room. Have another cup of coffee. I'll be right back."

Chapter 6

Looking around the kitchen, Joe was troubled that it seemed so unfamiliar to him. He'd been in there many times. Apparently he hadn't paid much attention. He always thought he was very observant. Now he wondered what else he'd never noticed around the place.

The kitchen could be entered from either end of the dining room, though the south door was bolted shut. There was an immense fireplace, probably used at one time for cooking, but now only for warmth and ambiance in the large, drafty kitchen. The fireplace was about ten feet wide in the middle of a brick wall that was painted white, as was the rest of the kitchen. Various cooking utensils hung from the wall and high ceiling—copperware, cast iron skillets, hammered brass utensils and several huge, iron ladles.

In the center of the kitchen was an oak table surrounded by eight ladder-backed chairs. The oak-planked floor was varnished to a high sheen, with braided rugs in shades of blue scattered throughout. The southern wall had built-in upper and lower cabinets running the full length of the kitchen, about 20 feet. It was obvious the Lindemans had spent some money to modernize the room. He wondered who they hired to do the work. The counter tops, with double sinks, were tiled in white ceramic with periwinkle blue tile bordering the edge. There was a restaurant-sized gas stove and a double-door refrigerator with a doublewide freezer below. Joe opened the doors; someone had made sure it was well stocked.

There was only one wall in the kitchen with windows, though they took up most of the wall. It overlooked a forest of beech trees, now rigid and stark in the morning shadows—sentinels to the ocean-side estate. Just beyond the beech trees was a forest of white pines.

Joe snooped around some more. Why not? He'd be spending a lot of time here and better re-familiarize himself with everything. He opened a door into a small room that housed the hot water heater and more storage shelves. The water heater looked new, high capacity, too. Another door opened to a short hallway leading to a bathroom that had been added. Joe peeked inside. A claw foot bathtub was visible through the half-open door. There was a door to the upstairs and another doorway next to the bathroom leading to the back porch.

Joe pushed against the door, the hinges squeaking dryly, swollen from the damp air. He breathed deeply. The cold, biting autumn air proved briskly refreshing after the warmth of the kitchen. Stepping out onto the freshly painted porch, he walked the length to the railing. In the distance he could see the solitary figure of a woman walking along the water's edge. She darted in and out, running from the waves as they crashed against the shore, spraying water over her. Her shouts of glee could be heard even from this far away. He heard Tom come out the door onto the porch.

With his mug of coffee in his hand, Tom stood beside him at the railing. "Amazing view," he said. It was breathtaking. The house was built on a point of land, and from this perspective you could see the ocean to the north and east.

"I'd like to take a look around."

"Sure. I'll grab our coats. It's freezing out. Wait here," Joe said.

Pulling their collars up against the stiff, cold wind, they walked down the steep porch stairs. A patio extended beyond the end of the house and along the east side. Beech trees surrounded the house to the north. Flower gardens, overrun with dead growth, went almost to the edge of the cliff. There was a long path though the middle of the gardens that led to beach access stairs built into the side of the cliff. The beach lay some thirty feet below.

Joe and Tom hurried down the narrow walkway to the cliff's edge. The view was spectacular. Squinting against the bright sun, they gazed far out across the ocean and both would swear, with the sky so clear, they could see the Isles of Westmoor, at least seven miles out.

"Awesome isn't it?" Joe asked.

"Absolutely spectacular. I've missed the ocean. It's magnificent. Untamed nature. There's such a feel of power unleashed with the waves crashing against the rocks. Makes me feel insignificant. Yet, even with all the chaotic wildness of the surf, it makes me feel tranquil."

"You're right. It's mesmerizing," They stood in silence, each lost in his private thoughts.

A gust of cold Atlantic air whistling through the trees interrupted the silence. They decided to finish touring the grounds so they could get back to the shelter of the house. Following another path that led along the east side of the house, they came to a landscaped area thickly planted with withered, berry-covered viburnum bushes and wind-dried flowers. It was easy to imagine how lush and beautiful the garden must be in the warmer months.

The ground sloped gradually uphill as they got closer to the front of the house. The front of the house was only about three feet above ground level, whereas the back porch of the house was about ten feet above ground. Joe explained that since the ground was composed of granite, most houses along the ocean were built according to the rock formation. Many of the homes, like this one, were built into, rather than on, the granite.

Tom had his first view of the house in daylight. It was a splendid home. The three-story house had been newly painted pale gray with charcoal-gray shutters and trim around the windows and white doors. The floor of the veranda was painted dark gray, the porch railings white. The house had a serene and comfortable look about it. All along the veranda, sheepberry bushes grew to shelter the south side of the house from the summer heat.

Joe and Tom ventured to the west side. Like the north, it was planted with beech trees. Beyond them was the white pine forest. Wanting to see the house from a more distant vantage point, they walked down the gravel driveway for about a quarter of a mile and turned to look back.

"It's a great place, really well-constructed. A credit to the architect and contractor," Joe said to a smiling Tom. "Yes, sir, this is a fine house. It's been well cared for, for the most part. So many of these old coastal homes have been let go. Such a shame. Although I see a lot of properties are being bought up and renovated."

"Glad to know things are looking up around here." Tom began walking toward the house.

"I better get to work while the weather's holding," Joe said. "Think I'll start by doing some testing on the electrical connections at the back of the house. Go from there."

"I don't know much about wiring, but I'd be glad to help," Tom offered.

"Naw. Not now. I'm sure you have things to take care of. If I find something though, I'll hunt you down," Joe replied, walking away.

Chapter 7

Tom watched Joe disappear around the side of the house. *Joe's quite an interesting fellow. I'm glad our paths crossed.* Tom returned to the kitchen, his mind full of plans for the rest of the morning. His cell phone was upstairs, so he decided to put off making any calls for a while. He decided to make a list of everything he needed to get done. It was too easy to become distracted watching the ocean and forget everything else.

Rummaging around the drawers, he found a spiral notebook and a pen, poured himself another cup of coffee and sat down at the kitchen table. Outside the window, in the branches of one of the beech trees, a movement caught his eye. High on a limb was a black kitten, its tiny mouth open, its unheard sounds of distress clearly imagined. Opening the window, the mews were piercing. Tom ran out the back door and down the stairs to find Joe.

"Hey, Joe, I need your ladder. There's a kitten stuck in a tree!" he hollered. Joe was in fact high up on a ladder, checking for faulty electrical connections at the back of the house. He clambered down, collapsed the sliding ladder to a manageable size and followed Tom around to the side of the house.

"The kitten's halfway up the tree outside the kitchen window. It's in a panic, doesn't know how to get down." The men braced the ladder, raising it to just below the limb where the kitten clung to the branch, yowling louder than seemed possible for such a tiny creature. Tom slowly ascended the ladder. Never having been that high on a ladder, he recognized how unstable it felt as it wobbled back and forth with every step. He hoped Joe was backing him up. He risked a quick look downward. Nope, Joe wasn't holding the ladder.

Apparently savvy to the desperate look on Tom's face, Joe quickly put his hands on the ladder sides for good measure.

He thinks I'm a wuss. Tom reached for the kitten, tucked it under his arm, and descended the ladder as fast as he dared. "Thanks, Joe. Rescue accomplished. Let's take this little guy in the house."

In the kitchen, the kitten scrambled out of Tom's grip and scurried to hide under the table. Tom found a bowl, poured some milk into in, and lured the kitten from its hiding place. "I need to fatten you up." As he drank, Tom petted his scrawny back. "Joe, more coffee before you go back to work?"

"Sure, don't mind if I do. Take the chill out of my bones. Sit down, I'll get it." Joe poured them both coffee. "I found that the main wire into the house had some breaks. Might be the reason the power was fluctuating last night. Wind was blowing the wires around. I'll take care of it before I look any further." Joe sipped his coffee, then continued, "Surprisingly, most of the old wiring into the house has been replaced. There's a good chance that the interior wiring was replaced at the same time. You'll be lucky if that's the case. Like I said before, the previous owners, the Lindemans, did quite a bit of work on this place over the years. You may get lucky—might not be a lot wrong. I'll finish checking all the outside connections, and then you can show me where you had the trouble last night. Might be a few bad switches, maybe even loose bulbs."

Tom picked up the kitten, setting it in the center of the rag rug in front of the fireplace. The kitten took a quick bath, then curled into a little ball and closed its eyes. "Looks like I have my first houseguest. Kind of hope he sticks around. I could use the company," Tom said. The men sat sipping their coffee. "I think I'm ready to nose around upstairs. Come on. Let's take a quick look around. Then you can get back to the wiring."

"Sure." Joe followed Tom through the house to the front entryway and up the stairs to the second floor. At the top was a long hallway that ran the full length of the house. Joe, already familiar with the layout, took the lead. "The master bedroom's this way, down the hall to the right," Joe said. He opened the double doors into the room and stood aside. The smell of fresh paint and lemon oil wafted out into the hall. The suite was tastefully decorated. There was a fireplace built into the middle of the west wall. It was faced with chocolate-brown, polished marble swirled with black veins. The hearth was black marble. On the right side of the fireplace a door led to a large walk-in closet. Centered against the southern wall was a king-size, four-poster bed with nightstands on either side. A large walnut bureau and dresser were to the left of the bed. The drawer edges and frame of the mirror were intricately carved with numerous, odd symbols that were inlaid with tiny, black, polished stones. The east and south walls had large picture windows; double french doors led out onto to the balcony. Joe opened the drapes, morning sun streamed into the room.

"The view's magnificent," Tom said, again finding himself mesmerized by the ocean. In every direction could be seen the vast, seemingly endless Atlantic. He opened the double doors and stepped onto the balcony. It ran the entire length and width of the house on the east and south, with a glass-brick wall dividing the balcony from the rooms to the west. Joe joined Tom to admire the panoramic view. The air was brisk and cold, smelling pungently of damp earth and autumn decay. They made a hasty retreat back into the bedroom. While Tom looked around, Joe built a small fire to warm the room.

In front of the fireplace were a loveseat and an easy chair, both upholstered in navy-blue suede. A low, walnut coffee table sat in front of the loveseat. By the window in the northeast corner of the room was a small, round dining table and two straight-back chairs.

The walls were wallpapered in navy blue and white plaid. All the wood trim in the room had a fresh coat of midnight-blue paint. The room was carpeted in dark brown, tweed chenille—lush and velvety. To the left of the doorway was a built-in bookcase that took up the entire wall, its shelves filled with collections of poetry—most leather bound, old and well worn.

"Didn't think there were that many books of poems in print," Joe remarked. "Not my idea of good reading, but to each his own."

Tom sighed, thinking, *Elise would have loved these books. . . . Well, no sense in thinking about her likes or dislikes now. I'll move the books to another room one of these days. They're not my idea of good reading either.*

"Ready to check out the other rooms?" Joe asked, turning to exit the room.

To their right was the staircase leading up to the third-floor attic. A narrow open room, about ten feet wide, ran the length of the east wall with another set of double doors leading to the balcony. The only furnishings in the room were a high-backed rocking chair and a large, mahogany cabinet filled with a collection of fine porcelain vases and statues.

Joe found the switch that operated the interior light of the cabinet and clicked it on. "What? Look at this! This statue looks just like you! Check it out." Joe moved aside so Tom could see the statue.

Tom stared at the porcelain figurine. The light shone brightly spotlighting the statuette, as well as a female figurine beside it. Tom had the sense that something unreal was taking place. He reached out to touch the statues—too quickly, too clumsily. His hand knocked one statue, then the other, sending them flying off the shelf where they shattered on the hard, wooden floor. "Damn it! I broke them both. Stupid of me!"

"Guess I'm not the only bull in a china shop!" Joe laughed, then disappeared, returning with a broom and dustpan. As he swept up the broken shards, he let out a soft whistle. "Did you see the face? That statue looked like you, didn't it?"

"No! Not at all!" Tom replied a bit too quickly. He walked away and down the long hallway to the west. "Come on. Let's look around, then I need to get on to other things. I still have to call someone about the phones."

"Well, they're good about taking care of the residents here. Probably send someone out right away," Joe answered, following Tom.

There was a room down the hallway, to the east of the stairs, that had been converted into a library. Most of the west wall of the room was taken up by a massive brownstone fireplace with windows that had built-in window seats on both sides. The south wall was mostly windows with a door in the center opening out to the balcony. The two other walls were lined with bookcases. In front of the fireplace were two loveseats with a small, cherry wood, claw-foot table in between them and an overstuffed chair to the right. The loveseats and chair were upholstered in various shades of dark rose. A large desk and chair, also of cherry, were in front of the bookcase on the east wall. Tiffany table lamps were scattered throughout the room. Tom liked the room. It felt warm and comfortable.

"Sure are a lot of books in this house. Guess the Lindemans like to read," Joe said, running his hand across the spines of a row of books.

"Seems that way. And that's a good thing, I enjoy reading myself." Tom walked across the hall. There were two large bedrooms on this, the north side of the house. A narrow hallway, leading to the narrow servant stairs, divided the two rooms. Both bedrooms were empty but would soon be filled with Tom's own furniture. He'd left most of his furniture in

Jamestown to be sold or given to various charities but was having some of it shipped via Coastal Vanlines. It would be arriving in the next few days.

They went down the hall and climbed the wide, steep stairway to the attic. There were two large rooms on the east side of the floor that had probably housed servants at one time. Now they served as storage for dusty old furniture and trunks. The rest of the attic was divided into many small rooms filled with more old furniture, boxes and trunks, some belonging to Tom and some to the previous owners. A narrow hallway separated two of the rooms, leading as they did in the floors below, to the servants' stairway, its door locked and unused. Except for the boxes delivered late yesterday afternoon, everything was coated with a thick layer of dust. "Been a long time since anyone was up here," Tom said to Joe.

Looking out the window to the north, Tom saw another house about a half mile up the coast. Smoke spiraled out of the many chimneys. "Who lives there?"

"The Harrisons—William, his wife, Vivian, and their two boys, James and William Jr. The Harrisons have owned that property longer than anybody can remember. Probably one of the oldest family names around here. Richest, too. Made their fortune with imports. Family dates back to the late seventeen hundreds, so I've been told. Own one of the largest import businesses on this coast. Anyway, they have homes all over the states. That's one of them. They're usually here for Thanksgiving and stay till after the first of the year. They come and go in the spring and summer—typical vacation dwellers. Not some of my favorite people, kind of high and mighty, if you know what I mean. But they tip well. No complaint there."

"Well, I hope they respect my privacy. At least for a while."

"Don't get your hopes up! As soon as Vivian gets wind you're here, she'll be socializing you up one side and down the other!" Joe laughed. "Not so with me though. I don't fit in their social world! I've driven Mr. and Mrs. for over five years. Neither one of them has ever spoken a civil word to me. Orders, that's all I get from them. Take me here, take me there, pick up this, stop here and on and on. Very important people, yes sir!" Joe's face flushed. He took a quick breath and brought himself in check. "Well! Enough gossiping. I better get back to the wiring. I plan to get into town and pick up a few switches before lunch. If you need anything from town, let me know. I'll pick it up." Embarrassed at having said so much, he walked off, not waiting for further comments from Tom.

Tom was disappointed—he'd hoped to have neighbors he could get to know, maybe spend some time with—but on his own terms. Oh, well. Time would tell. Maybe Joe had the wrong impression of the Harrisons. Tom went to his room and began a series of phone calls on his cell to take care of the phone-line hookup as well as catch up on a few business calls. When he was finished with those, he punched in his sister's number. Tom drummed his fingers impatiently on the table, listening to the rings. One, two, three, four. . . . She didn't answer.

Cassie was six years younger than Tom. She was married to Michael Wellington, who Tom thought was one of the finest men he had ever known. He'd worked for Tom as the district operations manager for the past seven years. They had one young daughter, Lizzie, who was eight.

Tom and Cassie had been close as kids but had drifted apart when he met and, two years later, married Elise. Cassie and Elise had not gotten along. When Elise died, Cassie reached out to him. Tom, angry and grief stricken, refused her help and wouldn't allow her back into his life. That slowly changed when Cassie began visiting him in the private sanitarium.

Their discord over Elise had been damaging. It was painful and difficult to make amends. But they'd been close as kids, and they knew they needed each other now. Both seemed to be getting past the strong emotions that had driven them apart. Cassie was coming for Thanksgiving, along with her husband and daughter. Tom surprised himself. He actually looked forward to the noise and chaos he knew would descend on his house when they arrived.

Looking out the windows toward the ocean, Tom saw the winds were blowing in a huge squall. Witnessing the storm's beginning, he sat mesmerized as the black clouds rolled across the darkening sky. Lightning flashed in electric zigzags from the clouds' dark centers, striking downward into the tumultuous waves far out on the horizon. Even though the storm was still miles away, the sound of thunder boomed and shook the house. The storm was gaining strength and momentum. It wouldn't be long before it reached shore.

Not hearing Joe come into the room, Tom jumped when Joe said his name. "Sorry to startle you, Tom. Quite a storm. It's gonna get nasty real quick by the look of those clouds." He pointed out the window. "Want me to close the shutters? The winds get incredibly strong here, it's best to be prepared."

"I'm sure you're right, go ahead. But leave these bedroom shutters open. If it gets too bad, I'll close them later. I like watching storms. As a kid I remember my mom franticly shouting, convinced that the lightning would strike us, even though we were inside. She'd beg me to get away from the windows. I never would though. I loved the sound of the rain pounding on the roof, the lightning flashing and lighting up the room, the thunder shaking the walls. Poor mom finally gave up trying to save me. She gathered up my sister and the pets and hid in the kitchen pantry for shelter from the 'wrath of the heavens' that threatened to strike us down!"

"Sounds like your mom was sensible to me." Joe glanced out the window, flinched when a lightning bolt hit the water, sending spray high into the air. "I'll leave these shutters open, but I'm gonna close down the rest of the house," said Joe. "After I do that, I'm heading to town—before the rain gets too bad. If the storm doesn't lighten up, I won't be back till tomorrow. The ocean highway's way too dangerous."

"You don't need to come back today, Joe. Don't worry about things here."

"All right then. I have things I can take care of in town. Don't wait too long to close the shutters, that wind can blow the windows clean out, I've seen it happen many times."

"I'll pay attention, don't worry." Tom's phone rang. "Hi, Nate," he said. They talked for about fifteen minutes while Joe checked windows and secured shutters. Tom wandered downstairs looking for Joe, who was coming in the front door.

"Got the place secured. Anything else you want me to do before I go?" Joe asked, slipping his arms into the sleeves of his parka.

"No, I can manage. I have a lot to take care of this afternoon. I'll see you tomorrow, I guess."

"I should be here by nine. I'll finish checking the wiring and look around the basement. Have a list of what you need from town?" Tom pulled a folded paper from his pocket and handed it to Joe. With a backward wave, Joe was gone, the door slamming with a resounding *crash* in a strong gust of wind.

Chapter 8

Tom grabbed a cold beer from the kitchen and snagged the kitten from his blanket in front of the fire. He deposited the kitten on the couch and opened the front door. Bracing himself against the rain and wind, he opened and secured the terrace window shutters to the house so he could watch the storm. He built a small fire in the living room and waited for the full fury of the storm to hit. Sipping from the green, heavy-glass bottle, he listened, transfixed, to the wind howling across the rocky cliffs far below. Pounding torrents of rain, driven by gale force winds, hammered the house. Huge waves crashed onto the beach with immense power, sending spray high into the air.

A bolt of lightning struck a tree not fifty feet away. Tom leapt back, almost falling. *Son of a bitch! That was close.* It was time to shutter the windows again. But the wind was blowing so hard and the rain pouring so forcefully, Tom decided against going out and wrestling with the living room shutters. Picking the sleeping kitten up from the couch, he retreated to the safety of the kitchen.

Tom warmed himself before the kitchen fireplace, drank another beer. "A hot shower might relax me. Maybe the storm will be over by the time I'm out." The kitten opened one eye, curled into a ball and dismissed Tom with a flick of his fluffy tail.

Though the storm had lessened somewhat when Tom came back downstairs, the thunder still rumbled, and the rain continued beating against the windows. Opening another beer, he carried it to the living room. As he stared vacantly into the fire, a horrible sense of despondency settled over him. He was alone—for the first time in his life—utterly alone.

"Well, Tom," he said out loud, "are you going to sit here feeling sorry for yourself?" He downed half of his beer, got up and began pacing the floor. He saw his reflection in the storm darkened, living room window. "You look pathetic." He took another drink. "Man, get over her. Elise is dead. Dead and buried. Dead and gone. Dead, as in pushing up daisies. Dead as a doornail. Dead. Dead. Dead!" He swigged his beer. "Need I say more? Thought not," he chuckled, toasting his reflection with his beer.

"She drove you crazy. Remember? It was a hell of a lousy time. The worst you could conceivably experience. And man, you can't go there again. No more loony bins for you. Face the music, move on. Right?" He argued with himself, alternately angry, then sad.

Tom knew it to be undeniably true. Elise was dead . . . but . . . a part of him was unwilling, perhaps unable, to let her go, to truly believe her gone forever. *"How do I let her go?"* Finishing his beer, he hurled the empty bottle into the fireplace relishing the splintering of glass, the hiss of liquid hitting the hot coals. He stared searchingly into the flames.

Crossing to the bar, he poured himself a shot of vodka from the crystal decanter. Tom turned back to his reflection in the darkened window, watched himself down his drink in one swallow. He spoke to his mirrored image, "You have to deal with the truth if you're ever going to get over her." He pointed his finger at his reflection. "It *has* to come to this, of course—this sad realization. Your love for Elise became your obsession. You wanted to possess her, she wouldn't let you. You broke her spirit, held her soul hostage and made her hate you. You wouldn't—couldn't— let her go. She was your heart. Your soul. You were afraid of losing her.

"When you realized she no longer *could* love you, you killed her—as if by your own, bare hands. You snuffed the life out of her, took away her will to go on living. That's what you did. How can you ever forgive yourself?" He turned from his haunting image, got another drink.

He whispered into the empty room, "Elise—my only love —you hated me so much you would rather die than stay with me. I did that to you. You took your own life—but the blood is on my hands. That is what I have to live with." Tom dropped onto the edge of the couch and stared at the floor. "Forgive me." A brilliant bolt of lightning lit the dark room, followed by a rumbling of thunder that shook the walls and the floor. Tom did not notice.

Chapter 9

On the night Elise died, Tom held her in his arms. His fingers gently stroked her golden curls, caressed her pale cheeks; he gazed into her unfocused, brown eyes. He watched her take her last breath, watched her eyes close for the last time. Begging her to forgive him his selfishness, he pleaded with her to understand, to believe he never meant his love to be a punishment.

Whether she understood, or even heard him, he did not know. She died quietly—never granting him final acknowledgment that she even knew he was there. All night he held her—not able to understand that she was dead, only glad to be holding her so closely. In the warmth of his arms, she was very much alive that long, quiet winter night. Elise, his cherished wife, was his again. He clung to her, praying morning would never come.

But it did come. A cold, sunless January day dawned. No birds sang this day. There were no peals of laughter from the children in the neighborhood, only hushed silence. A heavy snow had fallen in the night, shrouding the world in a blanket of white. Few ventured out, choosing to stay inside, sheltered from the icy cold. The quiet of night continued into the morning. Lily, the housekeeper, discovered Tom and Elise late the next morning. Contrary to her usual high-strung nature, she remained calm and controlled as she ran to get Nate, Tom's right hand man, who was having breakfast in his office, going over a contract. Nate called 911.

Tom cradled Elise, holding her tightly. Nate sat by his side as Tom quietly explained to him, "I won't leave her—not after we've found each other again."

"Tom! Oh, God, no. What happened?" Nate whispered, trying to take Elise from Tom's tightly clenched arms. "Tom, Elise is gone, man. You have to let go." When the EMT's came into the room, Tom screamed at them, "Elise is fine! Leave us alone!" He continued ranting, struggling to hold on to her lifeless body. The EMT's tried to pry him away from her. "Don't take her from me! Get out! All of you. Get the hell away from us! Let me go, you sons of bitches!"

Tom's doctor arrived minutes after the ambulance. Nate held Tom down while Dr. Robeson gave him a shot of a sedative to knock him out. Crying out for Elise, Tom slumped backward onto the bed. The coroner examined Elise's body, pronounced her dead, and she was taken to the morgue. The following week, the autopsy would determine that Elise Gardner had died of an overdose of numerous narcotics ingested in a mixture of brandy and water. No suicide note was found.

Tom had only vague memories of the weeks that followed. Elise had been buried, her funeral attended only by Tom and his family. Her mother could not be located, though his sister,

Cassie, had tried. Tom had vague recollections of Cassie and Nate trying to console him as he literally fell apart. The following months were the easiest for Tom. He resided in a drug-induced fantasy. For several blissful months, he shared all his time with Elise. During these months, she never left his side—the outside world no longer existed. Content, he made plans with his wife. Together, they began to build their future.

Cassie, having a family of her own to take care of, left Tom in the care of Dr. Robeson and returned to New York City. Unfortunately, Robeson's idea of treatment was giving Tom all the drugs he wanted. After pleas from Nate, Cassie finally came back to Jamestown to see for herself why Nate was so concerned. She was devastated, realizing her brother was slipping further and further away from reality, living in a fantasy world shared with his dead wife. Cassie took charge.

For the next six months, the renowned psychiatrist, Dr. Kyle Gerard, treated Tom at Jamestown Psychiatric Hospital. Dr. Gerard slowly reduced the amount of drugs Tom had been dependent on until he was able to exist with only the aid of sleeping pills—to get him through the long nights. The sleeping pills afforded Tom hours of dreamless sleep. Without the pills, his nights were unbearable. Elise came to him—no longer as his lover—but to taunt and torment him. Tom tried unsuccessfully to sleep without the pills, finally gave up. After all, there were plenty of other doctors willing to give him what he needed when Dr. Gerard refused to write him any more prescriptions.

Chapter 10

Elise cried, the sound not much louder than a tiny mew, as if from a kitten crying for its lost mama. The attic room was dark, cold, empty. She shivered, her teeth chattered. Elise thought she'd never be warm again.

This house was not like the Jamestown house—there seemed to be nowhere Elise felt safe or warm. As she wiped her tears away with her nearly transparent fist, she grew angry. She vowed she would not be the one to suffer, not anymore. She went downstairs in search of Tom.

Elise was still surprised by the floating quality of her existence, moving without conscious motion, merely a gentle transference of her spirit from one realm to another. Feeling quite ethereal, she drifted into the living room.

Tom sat in front of the fire absently-mindedly sipping a beer. Unseen, she circled around him, felt his sadness permeate the room like a heavy cloud. Seeing the sorrowful expression on his face, she felt exuberant. She so loved his pain. Elise's ghostly fingers caressed the back of his neck, his shoulders. She laughed a silent laugh, then fled to the study to lie before the warm fire.

Chapter 11

Tom jumped to his feet. Every hair on the back of his neck stood up as an icy gust of air wafted across his body. Damn drafty house! He went back to the kitchen, got another beer and returned to the living room. Listening to the storm still raging outside, he paced the floor and remembered the months following his release from Jamestown Psychiatric Hospital.

***

By August, Dr. Gerard felt Tom was well on his way to recovery and acceptance of Elise's death. After six months of isolation in the private clinic at JPH, Tom was released to the isolation of his Jamestown home. *I played the game very well,* Tom thought. *No one suspected the truth. Not for a moment did anyone believe that I was responsible for Elise's death. No one that is, except me. I will always know the truth.*

For over a year, Tom hadn't ventured out of his house. He saw no one except Nate, and on occasion Cassie, who came when she could. She did her best to encourage him and to help him out of his dark, depressed moods.

Cassie's nature was one of joy and optimism. She simply couldn't understand Tom's inability to get over Elise's death or his refusal to leave Jamestown. "Tom," she pleaded, "you have to stop grieving. You need to get out of this dreary house. Come with me to New York City for a while. I'd love to introduce you to some of my friends there. And there are so many things we could do. I know you'd start to heal if you'd get away from here. Won't you at least try? If not for yourself —for me?" With every visit came the same discussion. She begged him to leave—he refused.

It was Nate who finally convinced Tom that change had to come. Tom was in Elise's sitting room staring absently out the window as the sun set, the sky glowing crimson and orange.

Tom seemed not to notice when Nate came in the room. "Tom, can I have a word with you?" Nate asked. Tom gave a slight nod to acknowledge Nate's presence. "I've worked for you for over ten years—good years—most of them. I've been doing a lot of thinking the last few weeks. I've come to a decision. It's time for me to find another job."

"What?" Tom asked. "What did you say?" Nate finally had his attention.

"I'll find a replacement before I go. I know a few people who you might want to interview. I'd be glad to call them for you, if you like."

"Nate, what's the problem," Tom asked. "Is it your brother again? Take off and do whatever you have to do. Take all the time you need. You don't have to quit, for God's sake."

"No, Harold's not the problem—it's . . . ."

Tom interrupted, "I know you have many responsibilities, you carry a heavy load. Tell me what I can do to help. Are you having financial problems? How much do you need?"

"This has nothing to do with money—or my brother. Don't make this harder for me than it already is."

"What is it then? You've been my friend and right hand for as long as I can remember. Hell, you know I always have your back. Be honest with me."

"I'm trying to. You need to listen to me. This is hard to say. As your friend, I'll tell you—you're not the Tom Gardner I once knew. Since Elise died, you've given up on everything that once mattered to you. You go through the motions of being alive, but that's all."

Tom started to say something; Nate ignored him. "I know you loved Elise, but she's been dead for almost two years. Before your marriage went on the rocks you were a strong, levelheaded man. I admired you. Looked up to you. You were like a big brother to me.

"But if you're going to spend the rest of your life talking to a dead woman, I won't . . . can't, be a party to it any longer." Nate pounded his fist on the back of the easy chair. "Damn it Tom! Don't look so surprised. I hear you whispering and carrying on as if Elise was here with you.

Nate stood his ground, silenced Tom when he started to speak. "I'm not finished yet. When you came home from the sanatorium, I thought, with time, you'd get back to your life. But you haven't. I wish I knew how to help you, but I don't. It's all on you now. If you want to spend the rest of your life mourning, that's your choice. I want no part of it!" Nate yelled, his nostrils flares, his face turned beet red.

Tom was unarguably angry, his hands clenched in tight fists.

Still Nate went on, motioning Tom to be quiet. "We all have problems. You always told me to be a man, to stand up and face my problems. I've tried to do that because I knew you were right. You need to take your own advice. Elise is dead. You need to face it—she died despising you. We both know it."

"That's enough!" Tom shouted, jumping up and standing face to face with Nate. "You don't know what you're saying."

"I wasn't blind, Tom. Sure, maybe she loved you once, but for whatever reasons, Elise stopped loving you years ago. Why you stayed together, I'll never know. I can only guess she stayed for the financial security you gave her. But I saw how she looked at you, how she avoided you. She couldn't stand to be in the same room with you. She isn't—wasn't—worth it. Until you face up to that, you'll never get over her. My advice to you is to get out of this house and forget about Elise. Go somewhere else. Maybe you'll even find someone else, someone who deserves you." Nate turned away and left the room, slamming the door behind him.

Tom's anger was all-consuming. Never in his entire life had he been so angry. He paced the room becoming more agitated with every step. He slammed his fist on the desk each time he passed it. Tripping on the desk's leg, he flew into a blind rage and grabbed a brass bookend, hurling it at the wall. Seeing Elise's collection of first-edition books on the shelves, he began throwing them across the room, smashing the expensive glassware displayed on the credenza. Still not satisfied, he picked up a heavy, antique gold-etched urn. With an animal-like yell, he threw it against the fireplace wall. Nate ran into the room as Tom picked up a tiffany lamp.

"What the hell! Tom! What are you doing?"

"Come on. Help me. This was Elise's favorite room—I'm going to tear it apart. Either join in or get the hell out of here!" Tom was laughing and—for the first time in a very long time—in complete control.

"Now this is the Tom Gardner I know!" Nate yelled.

Elise, merely a puff of energy, felt her first real pang of strength. The seeds of revenge were planted. She retreated to her bedroom and disappeared into the mirror.

An hour later, pouring from a surviving bottle of fine brandy, Tom and Nate toasted, "To a new beginning."

***

Tom smiled. There was comfort in that memory. It seemed such a long time ago—that first day of a long journey leading him here. Nate had been right, of course. He could not let

Elise's memory continue to haunt him. He may be alone, but there was no reason to be afraid of that.

Chapter 12

Elise crept toward Tom, her tiny feet dragging. Although they made no sound, her feet left faint indentations in the velvety carpet. She'd taken a short nap in front of the warm fire in the study, now she was bored. Curling up beside Tom on the leather couch where he sat with his head bowed and resting heavily in his hands, his burden of pain evident by his posture, she relished the image of his pained face, his eyes red and swollen, tortured by countless sleepless nights and salty tears shed for her, his lost love.

Seeming to sense her presence in the lonely room, Tom turned abruptly. He looked right through her.

Elise caught her breath, her moment of joy shattered. The remnants of a smile gave life to Tom's face. She'd presumed he would be racked with grief. The bastard was smiling. Elise snarled and disappeared into the darkness.

Chapter 13

Outside, the storm began to wane—lightning ceased, thunder subsided, rain beat more gently with soft, pattering sounds against the clapboard. In the distance someone ran along the shore playing tag with the crashing waves. Tom watched transfixed, wondering who in the world would be out in a storm like this.

Tom whirled around. From far away he heard a door slamming. Just the wind, right? He must have left a window open somewhere. Looking back out onto the shore, Tom saw no sign of the mysterious person on the beach. He knew he better go and find out where that open window was. He walked up the stairs to begin what would be a futile search.

Chapter 14

Tom wandered about the house pulling curtains, opening shutters. The kitten was awake and meowed to go out. "Do you really want out in this weather, little fellow? Well, okay. But stay out of the tree. Don't go wandering off and forget where you live either." Tom carried the cat to the kitchen. "I'll leave this door open a crack so you can come get back in. With no hesitation, the cat bounded out the door. Tom made a pot of strong coffee, waited impatiently for it to finish, then poured himself a mug to take upstairs.

As the sun broke through the clouds, Tom felt rejuvenated. He decided to spend the rest of the afternoon in his bedroom unpacking his personal belongings. For several hours he unpacked his clothes and arranged the few books he'd packed, adding them to the collection in the bookcases. The kitten found its way back into the house and up into Tom's bedroom. He curled up into a tiny ball in front of the fireplace. "Looks like this is going to be your bedroom, too. Works for me."

When Tom was done unpacking, he went downstairs. Looking out the picture window, he saw it was raining again. Half a mile out a small boat tossed on the turbulent swells. It was late afternoon; the setting sun cast long shadows of the cliffs onto the sandy beach. In the distance an ocean liner sailed toward the eastern horizon, the fishing boat had turned, probably headed to the harbor ten miles north.

Tom added wood to the fireplaces in the downstairs rooms, glad for the extra warmth. The aging furnace failed to adequately heat the many rooms in the house. He looked forward to a light dinner and a good book in front of the fire tonight. His mood of desperation had lifted. The house felt warm and comfortable. A soothing, light rain gently pattered against the windows. He read for a few hours. A well-written mystery kept his mind occupied and free from any kind of reality. A sense of contentment and of *being home* settled over Tom.

At eleven, Tom took a sleeping pill and went to bed. He lay in bed for what seemed like hours waiting for the pill to work and carry him into dreamless oblivion. As he finally started to drift off, he heard sounds from the attic. Someone walked back and forth on the floor above him. He tried to rouse himself, but the pill kicked in. He slept a dreamless, drug-induced sleep, not waking until seven.

Tom got up, dressed and had a light breakfast. As he sipped his second cup of strong coffee, he tried to remember—with no luck—what had been so disturbing to him as he drifted into sleep last night. He poured another cup of coffee and carried it to the terrace. Tom rejoiced in the beautiful day. The sun was shining brightly, the air was crisp and smelled salty and clean, birds sang as the day renewed itself. He, too, felt vibrant and refreshed for a change; he was happy to be alive.

Bundling up in an old fisherman sweater someone had left on the back hook, he headed for the beach. The kitten bounced after him and, although the kitten refused to go in the ocean, he stayed on the beach scampering about, chasing after bits of leaves blowing in the breeze. Tom walked along the sand gathering up shells and stuffing them into his pockets. Bending over, he picked up a handful of flat stones and threw them, watching them skip across the water's surface. Up the beach he saw two children playing tag with the waves. Maybe it was one of them he'd seen last night playing in the tide. The boys chased the huge waves as they rolled in and out. Even from this distance Tom could hear their delightful laughter. When they spotted him, he waved and yelled, "Good morning." They ran down the beach toward him.

"Hey, mister, are you the guy who just moved into the house up there?" The younger of the two boys yelled.

"Sure am. I'm Tom Gardner," he hollered back.

The youngest boy ran up to Tom, his hand outstretched. "Nice to meet you. I'm Jimmy Harrison, and this is my brother, Billy." Jimmy pointed to the older boy who stood some feet back. "Hey, is that your cat?" Jimmy asked, a big grin on his face. "I love cats, but Mother won't let me have one. She says they're too hairy and messy. She hates anything messy—that's for sure. Can I pet him?" Tom nodded, and Jimmy got down on his knees and slowly put his hand out toward the kitten. "What's his name?"

"That's a good question. I haven't named him yet. Just found him yesterday. Rescued him from up in a tree. Any suggestions?"

Jimmy's brother, who hadn't spoken a word, walked over and pulled Jimmy up by his arm. "Come on. We have to get home. Now! Mother will wonder where we are."

"No she won't. She told us to stay out of her way today. She's busy with house cleaning. I'm staying here with Mr. Gardner and the kitten. You go home if you want," he snapped, pulling free from his brother's grasp.

"I'm gonna tell Mother you're talking to a stranger. You know what she'll do to you for that," Billy said as he turned and began walking up the beach. "Are you coming or not?" he yelled over his shoulder.

"You're a pain in the neck, Billy. Besides, Mr. Gardner isn't a stranger—he's our neighbor. Go ahead and tell on me. See if I care!" he yelled at his brother. Jimmy, his face red with anger and embarrassment, said to Tom, "Don't mind Billy. He's always like that, always trying to get me in hot water."

"I don't want you to get into any trouble," Tom said

"Don't worry. I won't. Hey, did you really mean I could help you name your cat?" he asked grinning.

Tom knelt down on the sand beside the boy. "Sure did. Any ideas?"

"Hmm. Let me think a minute. What about Tiger? No. I don't like that. He doesn't look anything like a tiger."

Tom looked away so Jimmy couldn't see him smiling. He didn't want him to think he was laughing at him, but Jimmy was taking the naming so seriously he actually looked distressed.

Jimmy snapped his fingers and grinned. "I know! Wiggins. I had a friend named Bobby Wiggins. He moved away. What do you think?" he asked, very seriously.

"Wiggins! I like it!" Tom scooped the kitten up. Wiggins squirmed to get away. Tom put him down on the sand. Jimmy found a length of fishing line laying on the beach and began playing with the cat, who ran in circles trying to catch the elusive end. Tom watched, amused.

Jimmy was a small boy with a slight build. Tom guessed he was maybe eight or nine years old. His complexion was fair and dotted with pale, reddish- brown freckles. His unruly, red hair fell across his forehead into his hazel eyes. His face had an impish quality, especially when he grinned like he was doing now as he played with the kitten.

"Tom Gardner?" a man shouted from down the beach. "I'm Dick Groden from the phone company. I'm here to check your phone lines."

"I'll be right there," Tom yelled. "Jimmy, I need to go. See you around, kid!"

Jimmy followed, asking, "Can I come with you? I've never been in the Lindemans' house. They were old and sick, and Mother wouldn't let us bother them. I promise I won't get in the way. Please?"

"What about your mom, Jimmy? I don't want to worry her. And I don't want you to get into trouble. Why don't you go and ask. I'll wait here for you."

Dick was walking toward Tom. Tom gestured to Jimmy running down the beach. "I'm waiting for the boy to come back. Give me a minute?"

"Sure," Dick said, extending his hand to Tom. "Good to meet you. Glad someone finally bought the Lindeman house. Nice place." Dick shook Tom's hand.

In a few minutes, Jimmy came running down to the beach from the Harrison house. "Mother said I couldn't go into your house. She says you might be some pervert or something. She says I can't go to your house until she has been 'properly introduced'. Boy oh boy, mothers are a real pain sometimes! Could you come and meet her, do you think?"

Dick laughed. "I'm not in any hurry to get into the house. I need to do some checks on the connection box down the road. I'll go ahead and get started. Probably take me half an hour anyway. I'll be back in a while. Jimmy! How you doin', kid?"

"Hey, Dick! Mr. Gardner let me name his kitten. Cool, huh? I'm gonna take Mr. Gardner to meet my mother. See you later." Jimmy grabbed Tom's sleeve and gently tugged. "Come on. Let's get this over with! Mothers!"

The Harrison's house was a large New England Colonial; three stories high—its floor plan at least twice the size of Tom's house. "Come on this way, Mr. Gardner. We better go around to the back door. Mother's getting the house all cleaned up for Thanksgiving, and if I track any dirt in she'll have my head," he stated matter of factly.

As Tom was led through the rear door, he saw the back of a woman disappearing through another doorway. She turned around when she heard Jimmy and Tom.

"Oh, Jimmy! For heaven's sake. What is it now?" Her eyes met Tom's. "Oh!"

"Sorry to intrude. Forgive me for barging in unannounced," Tom said, trying to keep his tone light and hide his embarrassment at the obvious intrusion.

"Mother, this is Mr. Gardner. He moved in the house next door. This is my mother, Mrs. Harrison."

"Oh! Goodness! How rude I must seem." She smiled, fluffing her stylishly coiffed, blonde hair. "Gardner? Are you any relation to Robert Gardner, from Jamestown, by chance?" she asked, an expectant note in her voice.

"Robert was my father. He's been dead for many years, though."

"Yes, I remember. My dad knew him. We were terribly sad to hear about his death. A hunting accident wasn't it?"

"Yes, it was." Tom glanced around the room. Changing the subject he said, "You have a beautiful home, Mrs. Harrison. I apologize for just dropping in, I thought Jimmy . . . "

Vivian interrupted, her green eyes sparkling, "On the contrary, Mr. Gardner, I insisted that Jimmy bring you. I just didn't realize he was going to bring you right away." She laughed. "I'm so glad you came. Don't give it a second thought. And please, call me Vivian. Would you care to come into the drawing room, and I'll get you something to drink? Maybe a cup of tea . . . or coffee?"

"Thanks, but I have to get back. Dick Groden from the phone company's waiting. Would you care if Jimmy came back with me? I could use the company."

Vivian raised her eyebrows in surprise. "Are you sure you want him underfoot? He can be such a nuisance sometimes."

"Mother!" Jimmy smiled sheepishly, his cheeks and ears blushing crimson.

"I'm certain," Tom said, winking at Jimmy.

"Well—all right. At least that will keep him busy—I have so much to do here. If he doesn't behave, send him home." She reached out, gently putting her hand on Tom's arm. "Are you sure you can't stay a while?" She smiled warmly. "We could get to know each other a little. It can be so isolating here. Perhaps a glass of sherry before you go?"

"Another time. It was a pleasure meeting you. And don't worry. I'll keep an eye on Jimmy," Tom said, heading toward the back door. "Come on Jimmy."

"Jimmy, you be on your best behavior, do you hear? And be sure to get Mr. Gardner's phone number so I can call and invite him for drinks. Do you hear me?" she shouted as they neared the cliff steps.

"Yes, Mother," Jimmy called over his shoulder.

As they walked down the beach, Tom saw that Joe was back and was talking with Dick. As soon as he saw them, Joe walked down the beach to meet them. "Well, well, if it isn't little Jimmy Harrison." Tom didn't care for Joe's tone of voice and shot him a disapproving look.

Jimmy ran over to Wiggins sunbathing on a rock. Lifting him up in his arms, Jimmy started climbing up the cliff steps toward the house. Tom lagged behind, waited until Jimmy was halfway up the stairs, then he said to Joe, "I know you don't like the Harrisons, but Jimmy's a great kid. I don't want you to hold his family against him. All right?"

Joe shrugged his shoulders. "You're right. But if his mother finds out he's here, she'll tan his hide."

"He's here with her permission, Joe. All is well."

After showing Dick where the phones were inside the house, Tom looked for Jimmy. He found him playing on the study floor with the kitten.

"Do you live here by yourself?" Jimmy asked Tom.

"Yeah, just me. And now Wiggins."

Jimmy was trying to tie his shoelace while Wiggins chewed on it. "Aren't you afraid here all alone?" he asked.

"What's there to be afraid of?" Tom asked, somewhat taken aback.

"Well, I don't know for sure. But I'd be scared in a house this big if I was all by myself."

"Come on. I'll show you the rest of this 'scary' old house. You'll see there's nothing to be afraid of. Just a lot of rooms." They spent the rest of the morning exploring. Tom was glad to get to go through the house again. It was a chance to find all the extra closets and hidden stairs that he hadn't yet had time to find.

When Jimmy left to go home for lunch, Tom wrote down both the house and his cell phone numbers for Jimmy to give to his mom. Tom walked down the beach stairs and watched Jimmy until he reached the stairs to his own house. Wiggins followed Jimmy about half way up the beach, then scampered back to Tom. He knew where his home was, no doubt about that.

Chapter 15

"Hey, Tom," Joe said when Tom reached the front porch. "Good news. I stopped by the city offices yesterday. I knew Mick Steven's granddad built this house with a local contractor, so I figured the building plans should still be on file. Got lucky. The clerk was able to find the blueprints, and she's having a set copied for us. They should be done in a day or two." Joe followed Tom into the house. "Jimmy gone?"

"Yeah, he just left. We had quite a time exploring the house. Kind of fun. Glad you found the plans, they'll come in handy. I'm curious about the basement. Odd layout. Didn't take Jimmy down there. I didn't think it was safe. Too much chance of having the lights go out. Any luck with that?"

"No. I haven't had a chance to get down to the basement yet. I will later." Joe picked his tool belt up off the bottom step. "Found a wiring problem at the back of the house. And a few bad switches I need to replace in the kitchen and back stairway."

"Figures. Glad you're making progress." Tom was tired. The trips back and forth going to the Harrison house and climbing the beach staircases had worn him out. He wasn't used to so much exercise. He'd probably walked five miles today. He'd be in tiptop shape if he kept this up. "Hey, Joe. Is there a sporting goods store in town where I could find some workout equipment?"

"Yeah, what do you have in mind?" Joe said.

"For now, just a set of weights. But I think I want to put a gym in the basement. Plenty of room for one."

"Sounds like a good idea."

"I'm thinking maybe a boxing ring, too. Harold, my friend Nate's brother, used to be a small-time fighter. Won a few local bouts. Ruined any chance he had of making a name for himself though. He couldn't keep away from the drugs. Talented kid. What a waste! All beside the point. Sorry. Anyway, Nate, who is also my accountant and my business manager, and I used to spar a bit with Harold. Having a boxing ring would be a lot of fun—

and a hell of a workout." Tom jabbed at Joe who raised his hands defensively. They exchanged a few light punches.

"Sounds like a great plan. I boxed a bit too when I was a kid —at the Boys' Club. I wasn't bad. Yeah, a gym and a boxing ring'd be doable. It'll be a major job to remodel the basement, but I'm up for it. Timing's good. So, when did you say your friend's gonna be here?"

"Hopefully before Thanksgiving. Nate stayed in Jamestown to tie up loose ends and to close up the house." Tom took another jab at Joe, who ducked sideways and jabbed back, hitting Tom's chest with a *thud*. "Good one. I'm really out of practice. You'll have to give me a little slack. I was sick for a long time; it took a toll on me. I'm pretty weak right now—not to mention slow!" Tom laughed. "Have time for a beer? I could use a cold drink. You can fill me in on the electrical problems you found."

Later that afternoon, after Joe had gone back to town, Tom called his sister again. She answered on the second ring, apologizing for missing his call the day before. They made plans for the Thanksgiving holiday. Cassie and her family were coming by train early in the week, several days before Thanksgiving. They planned to stay as long as her husband, Michael, could manage to be away from work.

"I'm so happy you're getting settled in so quickly. You sound genuinely content, Tom." They talked for the better part of an hour, then said their good-byes, promising to talk in a few days.

After dinner, Tom fed Wiggins, then took his coffee out to the front veranda to call Nate. He watched the setting sun— oranges and reds reflected on the ocean from the twilight sky. A single gull flew gracefully across the fiery horizon on its journey to find a roost for the night.

Nate answered the phone on the first ring. "Gardner residence," he said in his deep, resonating voice.

"How are you? How are things shaping up out there?"

"Hi, Tom. Glad you called. I have a major problem here. Harold's gotten himself into a serious . . . ahh . . . situation."

"What happened this time? Anything I can do to help?" Tom was worried; he heard the edge in Nate's voice.

"Thanks. I'm not sure what anyone can do at this point. Listen, I can't talk about it right now. I'll call you when I know more. How about you? Is everything okay at your new place?" Nate asked.

"Yeah, everything's fine. It's a great house. I couldn't be more pleased. Meeting some good people, too."

"Glad to hear that."

Nate sounded distracted. Tom said, "You do whatever has to be done. Let me know if I can help. God knows you've done enough for me. I guess you don't have any idea when you might be wrapped up there?" Tom hoped Nate could get to Remington soon—though he was beginning to feel like he could manage everything pretty well for the time being, especially with Joe around.

"I don't. Looks like I'll miss Thanksgiving, though."

"Nate, do you want me to come to Jamestown?" Tom asked, not convinced Nate could handle Harold's situation by himself. Nate's and Harold's sister, Rosa, had vowed she would no longer tolerate nor lend any support to Harold. She'd had enough of him. He seemed destined to follow a downward spiral, trying to pull all those who loved him down as well. Nate and his sister were constantly bailing him out of trouble. Rosa had finally drawn the line.

"No, Tom. I'll figure something out. Don't worry about it. Hey, I'll call you back, someone's at the door."

Tom didn't like the sound of Nate's voice. He sounded genuinely disturbed. For the rest of the evening, Tom waited for Nate's call. When he hadn't called by midnight, Tom was increasingly worried. Trying to distract himself, he tried reading —to no avail. He couldn't concentrate and ended up reading and rereading the same page. He paced the floor, staring at the phone, willing it to ring. He turned on the stereo hoping music would distract him. Listening to a piano concerto, his head resting on the back of the sofa, he drifted off to sleep.

Chapter 16

Tom woke with a start. From upstairs came the sound of floorboards creaking. He turned the music off and listened. *There! Again!* He heard the faint, though distinct sound of someone walking in the room overhead. The telephone rang nearly giving him a heart attack. He glanced at the clock; it was two o'clock. "Hello?" He whispered into the mouthpiece, holding his free hand over his racing heart. "Nate? Hello?"

The phone went dead. Tom placed the receiver back on the hook and sat on the edge of the sofa slapping his cheeks, trying to wake himself up. *Maybe I was dreaming.* The phone rang. "Hello?" Silence. "Who is this?" he yelled into the receiver. No one answered. The phone went dead. He slammed it down. Wiggins, who had been asleep on the end of the couch, lifted his head, his ears stood straight up, his feline body tensed, ready for flight if necessary.

Overhead, the sound of footsteps echoed through the still house. Wiggins hissed and backed up against the arm of the couch. "What the hell? What's going on? Is there someone up there?" Tom yelled. "Is someone here?"

The house echoed undisturbed silence. Tom grabbed the poker from beside the fireplace, wishing he had his .45 instead. As quietly as possible, he crossed the room. Standing at the bottom of the stairs he listened, all senses fine-tuned to detect the smallest deviance of sound. Silence. The shrill ring of the telephone broke the quiet. He ran back into the living room and stared at the phone. It rang over and over before he finally picked up the receiver. He held it to his ear saying nothing.

"Hello. Is anyone there?" It was Nate. "Tom, sorry to call so late. You told me to call no matter what time it was. Did I wake you?"

"No, I've been waiting for your call. Did you call earlier?"

"No. You sound out of breath. Is everything all right?"

"Yeah," Tom lied. "So what's going on with Harold?"

"Nothing good. Harold's been arrested. The police came while I was talking to you earlier. I got back from the police station a few minutes ago. It doesn't look good for Harold at all. He's in serious trouble. Worse than I ever imagined was possible. Damn him! He's my brother, and I love him, but this time, he's gone too far. I don't know what to do." Tom could hear Nate choking back tears, pushed well beyond his endurance.

"Nate, take a deep breath and tell me what this is about," Tom said.

"Harold killed someone! They arrested him for murder." Nate's voice cracked. "I don't know what to believe. Harold swears it was self defense, drug deal gone bad, but I don't know." Nate sounded as if he were on the verge of hysteria.

Tom needed to calm him down. "Nate, stop it! Listen to me. You know Harold better than anyone. Do you really believe he's capable of murder? From everything I know about him, I don't think so. Get hold of yourself and calm down. You're no good to Harold—or yourself—in the state you're in right now. You need a clear head. Why don't you try to get some sleep? I'll call John Atwood first thing in the morning. We'll get this figured out."

"Thanks, Tom. You're right. I'm beyond tired. I hope you're right about Harold, but I don't know this time. Harold's holding something back. He's genuinely scared."

"I'm sure anyone would react that way. Now get some sleep. I'll talk to you in the morning." Tom, his hands absently petting the kitten, thought about what Nate was going through. Damned Harold was always getting into trouble and expecting Nate to bail him out. As much as he hated to help Harold, Tom owed it to Nate to do all he could to help. Tom fell asleep on the couch and awakened at dawn. . . .

Chapter 17

. . . awakened to the sound of footsteps pacing overhead in his bedroom. he sat up quickly, tried to clear the sleep from his brain. as he listened to the footsteps going back and forth above him, he fought to control the panic threatening to immobilize him. sounds of shattering glass brought him to his feet. he flew up the staircase, down the hall to his bedroom and threw the door open.

no one there. nothing but an empty room, quiet and still. Tom looked for someone, but there was no one to find. he stood in the doorway and knew no one had been here. no one . . . except Elise. she had been here tonight, had been here all along. the wafting scent of lavender lingered. he whispered her name into the still air. it sounded like a question as it floated in the darkness. there was no answer. only the quiet, the silence just before dawn.

the moment passed. from outside came the sound of birds chattering. the first shafts of sunlight glided into the room. it was morning again. she was gone now. he closed the door, descended the stairs, dropped onto the couch, and shut his eyes. . . .

Chapter 18

Tom awakened to the boisterous songs of birds welcoming the first rosy glow of dawn. The sun broke through thick clouds that hung like gray cloaks across the horizon. The ocean was angry today; huge whitecaps were visible as far as he could see. Waves broke on the shore sending spray high into the air. Tom sat in the living room by the terrace window drinking coffee, feeling small and insignificant. In the distance a group of six or seven fishing boats bobbed like toys in the choppy water.

Still troubled about Harold, the phone calls last night and the dream about Elise, Tom sat, his cup of coffee cold and forgotten, gazing out across the sea. Mesmerized by the turbulence and violence of the ocean, he let his mind drift, tried to think of nothing at all. It worked for a while—he let the thunderous pounding of the ocean lull and distract him until he heard Joe's car pull up and stop in front of the house. Glancing at his watch, he realized he'd been sitting there for an hour. "Morning, Joe," he called through the open window.

"Morning, Tom. I brought some groceries. Have you eaten yet?"

"No. How about you?"

"Nope."

Tom helped Joe with the boxes. While Joe cooked scrambled eggs and bacon, Tom fed Wiggins, put the groceries away and made toast. The two men sat in silence, Joe because he was starved and seemed unable to think of anything but food, Tom lost in thought about Harold. And more importantly, he was trying to distinguish between what was reality and what was imagined. His dream last night had seemed so real, so vivid. He swore he'd smelled the faint, lingering scent of lavender when he awoke. The task of separating the real from the imagined so disturbed him that he completely forgot about Joe sitting across the table from him. Tom replayed the late-night calls and his dream—had it been a dream?—of someone —Elise?—pacing the floor in his room.

Joe scraped the last of the egg from his plate. The noise startled Tom. He jerked his head toward the sound, struggled to focus. He realized Joe was talking to him. "Sorry, Joe, I'm distracted this morning. Remember me telling you about Nate's brother? I talked to Nate late last night, and Harold's in serious trouble."

"Sorry to hear that. Anything I can do?"

"No. Thanks. I told Nate I'd call my attorney for him. John should be in the office by now. I better give him a call. Back in a few minutes." He stood up.

"I'll clean up in here, and then I better get started on the wiring," Joe said, a frown on his face as he watched Tom leave the kitchen. The kitchen door swooshed as it swung closed. "I think there's a lot more to Tom's distant behavior than that business with Harvey—or whatever his name is," he said under his breath.

In the study, Tom talked with his attorney for the second time that morning. John Atwood had just called him back with some information. "Tom, I talked to Jim Wood, an associate in our office. He agreed to get in touch with Nate this morning. Good chance he'll be willing to take Harold's case. I'll keep you posted. He's a very competent criminal attorney, Tom— Harold will be in good hands. Don't worry. Damn, my other phone's ringing, and I have a meeting to get to. I'll call you later. Bye."

Tom called Nate to tell him the news but got no answer. He left a voice mail telling Nate to call him when he could.

"Tom!" Joe called from the front doorway.

"What is it, Joe?"

"There's a van pulling up the road. You expecting any deliveries today?"

"Damn it. What day is today?"

"Thursday."

"Yeah. Must be my furniture."

"Looks like there's plenty of guys on the truck to unload it, at least," Joe added as he walked down the front porch steps.

Tom gave instructions to the crew about where to put everything, then left an exasperated Joe to supervise the unloading. Tom went back to the kitchen to escape the hubbub. There was a gentle tapping at the back door. It was Jimmy, with a grin stretching from ear to ear, on his freckled face.

"Come in, Jimmy. You look like the cat that swallowed the canary. What's up?"

"Hi, Mr. Gardner. Joe told me to come around to the back door." He took his jacket off, threw it over the back of a kitchen chair. "They were unloading a piano out front. Wow! Is it yours?"

"Well, technically yes. It belonged to my wife, so now it's mine. Is that what you were grinning about? Looks like I found someone to play it. You do play, right?"

"Not yet! But I've always wanted to learn. Do you think you could teach me? Do you know how to play?" He didn't wait for Tom's reply, "Mother won't let me near her piano. She's afraid I'll scratch it or something."

Tom laughed. Jimmy ignored him and went on to explain, "Once, when I was little, I put a tiny, little scratch on her precious piano. She says she can't trust me with her damn, oops, darn old piano. It's an heirloom, she says, and she doesn't want me to go near it. How am I supposed to learn to play the stupid thing if she won't let me near it? Mothers! How do you figure them?"

"Jimmy, my boy, women—mothers—are a phenomenon not meant to be understood by mere men. In my forty years, I have not been able to figure out even one of them. Once, I thought maybe I could, but well . . . never mind that. So, you'd like to learn to play the piano, huh? I'm a little bit rusty myself, be good for me to brush up. I'd be happy to teach you."

"All right! Thanks. Can we keep it a secret, though? I want to be real good before anyone finds out. I don't want anyone making fun of me. Okay?"

"It's a deal. How about starting tomorrow afternoon? There's too much going on today."

"Okay, cool! Oh! I almost forgot why I came over. Mother wants to know if you'll come to dinner tonight?"

"I don't know. I'm not so sure I'm ready to meet your whole family quite yet. It's been a long time since I've gone out socially, Jimmy. I know you don't understand what I'm talking about, but—it might not be a good idea for me to come."

"It'll only be Mother, Billy and me. Dad's still in . . . hmm, well I'm not sure where he is right now. Maybe New York. Anyway, Mother's not as bad as I make her sound. She likes everything to be just right, that's all. Please come?" Jimmy flushed, his cheeks glowed as red as his hair. His freckles all but disappeared.

Tom reluctantly agreed. He found it hard say no to this kid! Jimmy promised to meet him on the beach a little before seven. When Jimmy had gone, Tom went looking for Joe.

The crew had almost finished unloading the furniture. Tom followed Joe to the second floor to see how things were going. It was comforting to have some of his own belongings in the house. "Everything's looking great." The crew had arranged the furniture in one of the bedrooms. "Works well. Let's go see the other room."

The bedroom furniture had been brought up but not arranged in the room across from the master bedroom. Joe and Tom began moving the furniture into place. Soon two of the crew came in and helped with the heavier pieces. All that was left to be done was to unload a dozen crates containing personal papers, books and etc. While the crew put them in the library, Tom went to his room to call Nate, who still hadn't returned his call. There was no answer. He no sooner hung up the phone when it rang.

"Tom," John Atwood's voice came through the line. "John here. I wanted to let you know Jim Wood has given the thumbs up for handling Harold's case. I just got off the phone with him. He's already been to the police station where they're holding Harold. He hasn't been charged yet. Jim doesn't feel that the DA has much of a case. But he's on it. Not a man to waste any time. Good man." Tom could hear him drumming is pen on his desk. "I haven't been able to reach Nate. Any idea where he might be?"

"I've been trying to reach him all morning myself, John. Doesn't make sense. If he wasn't at the police station, he should be home. I'd better call one of the neighbors and have them go by the house, make sure everything's okay. I'm getting a little worried. I'll let you go. Call you as soon as I hear anything," Tom said.

"Likewise. Goodbye."

As soon as Tom hung up, he called Clint Travis, one of the neighbors who lived down the street from his Jamestown home. He agreed to go right over. After telling him where he kept a spare key, they hung up. Tom hated waiting, found it excruciatingly difficult. He felt helpless as he sat and waited to hear back from Mr. Travis. What could possibly be wrong now? He had no choice, though but to wait it out. There was a knock at the door.

"Sorry to bother you, Tom. The moving crew's about finished. Is there anything else you want them to do before they go? They put all the crates into the library. Did you want any of them hauled up to the attic?" Joe asked, peering around the edge of the door.

"No. They're fine. I'd like to go through them later. Unless you can think of something more, send the men on their way." Tom pulled several bills from his wallet and told Joe to give the money to the crew.

As he crossed the room to take the cash, Joe stopped. "What the hell happened? There's glass all over the carpet. Let me get the guys paid, then I'll clean it up. Back in a minute."

Feeling a shard of glass splinter under his foot, Tom stepped back. Fragments of broken crystal glistened in the sunlight. He was on his hands and knees picking up the larger pieces of glass when Joe came into the room carrying the vacuum.

"Movers must've come in here. I told them to stay out of your room. Thought I was keeping my eyes on them most of the time, too. Damn. Probably one of the guys being nosey. Any idea what they broke? A vase or something?"

"Maybe. Not sure"

"Better look around and make sure nothing's missing, don't you think?"

"What? Missing? No. Not that I see, Joe. Don't worry about it. It's certainly not your fault." Tom looked at an empty space on the bookshelf. He remembered now. In the back of his mind, Tom recalled the sound of shattering glass. When had he heard breaking glass? He knew. He paled, his brow knitted in worry. But that had been a dream. Hadn't it? Tom brought his hand to his face, massaged his temple. Now he knew what the glass was from. It was a perfume bottle. His hands smelled of lavender. He quickly wiped them on his jeans.

A sense of dread spread its icy fingers around his heart. Cold shivers ran up his spine as he tried to remember last night's dream. Surely it had been only that, a nightmare that was still haunting him in his waking hours. Damn, enough of this! A clumsy, nosey mover had been in here. He accidently knocked a bottle off the shelf. That was the end of it. Not even worth the time it took to report it. Let it go. The telephone rang.

"Hello?"

"Tom, this is Clint Travis. I have some bad news," he said, his voice tense with concern.

"What's wrong, Clint?"

"Your damn fool friend took two sleeping pills last night. This morning he was disoriented and ended up falling. He's been lying at the bottom of the stairs fading in and out of consciousness for hours. I called 911. They just took him to St. Andrew's. It looked to me like he broke his leg, but I can't be certain. Damn good thing you had me check on him. He was breathing okay and managed to talk a little. I'll head over to the hospital if you want me to. Make sure he gets admitted and everything. Make sure they treat him right."

"That'd be great. Thanks, Clint. You're a good man. I'll get in touch with his sister, Rosa. She lives close by; it won't take her long to get to St. Andrews. Thanks again. I'll call you later."

Joe watched Tom. "Bad news?"

"Yeah, Nate fell down the stairs, might have broken his leg. My neighbor just called to let me know. He thinks he'll be okay but still . . . I need to call Nate's sister. I'll be down in a minute. I'll grab a couple of beers and meet you on the front porch." Tom sat on the top step and called Rosa. "Rosa, this is Tom Gardner."

"Tom? For heaven's sake, I certainly didn't expect to hear from you. How are you? Enjoying the sea air?"

"I'm doing all right, thanks. I'm calling with some bad news about Nate." Tom heard the quick intake of breath over the phone line as Rosa reacted. "Don't be too alarmed. I'm sure he's going to be okay. He fell down the stairs at my Jamestown house and may have broken his leg. A neighbor, Clint Travis, went to St. Andrews to follow up. I know you'll want to get over there right away."

"I thought Nate was with you in Ravenswood. What's he doing here?"

Nate apparently hadn't told Rosa the trouble Harold was in. "Nate had some things to wrap up for me. And he was dealing with a serious issue with Harold. I know how you feel about Harold, but for Nate's sake, hear me out." Tom explained what he knew about Harold's arrest and that his attorney, John Atwood, and an associate of his were handling the legal ramifications. "Hopefully Harold will be released soon, possibly without charges being filed."

"That stupid, idiot of a man. He'll never change. Right now I could care less about Harold. Nate is the one I'm worried about. I need to get to the hospital. Thank you for calling, Tom." The phone went dead before Tom could say goodbye.

Tom called John Atwood next, filling him in on Nate's accident.

John said, "What a disaster. Don't worry; I'll take care of everything. I'll call Rosa later and let her know what's going on with Harold. Nate sure as hell doesn't need to deal with him for a while."

"Such a relief to know you're on this, John. I know you have everything under control. I can't thank you enough."

"Don't give it a second thought. Besides, you'll get my bill soon enough," John laughed, then said goodbye.

Joe was on the front porch testing the strength of the railings. Tom brought a couple of beers and a bag of potato chips. He handed a bottle to Joe, popped the cap off his and enjoyed the blast of bitter bubbles assaulting his tongue.

"Things are being handled. Wish I was in Jamestown to help out, but John is immensely capable. I couldn't ask for a more dependable attorney. I'm very lucky."

"Yeah, you have lots of people watching out for you all right. You *are* a lucky man! You have it all. Family, friends, education, money. Then there's me!" Joe laughed.

"I don't know about that. You seem pretty together, Joe. Very often I feel like I'm the one who missed the boat," Tom said, his face set in a stern, unblinking stare. "Having it all isn't enough. It guarantees nothing!" He took a drink of his beer, looked out across the property that was now his. "Enough of my whining! Let's get some of the crates from upstairs and take them to the study. I want to sort through most of the boxes before my sister, Cassie, gets here. I need to get things settled, get some order in the house. Give me a hand bringing them down, and then you can get on with what you were doing."

Going through the boxes that contained personal papers was a snap. Nate had already put everything in order. When he was finished, Tom carried the boxes to the attic and stacked them in a small room overlooking the forested property to the west. That was what he'd needed—busy work. Good for his soul.

There were several boxes stacked in one of the other rooms. Tom carried them down the two flights of stairs to the study. Before he had a chance to open them, his cell phone rang. "Tom, it's Vivian Harrison. How are you?" Not waiting for an answer she went on, "I'm calling to remind you about dinner this evening. Come over about seven. Please don't go to a lot of fuss either; we're going to be casual tonight."

"Thanks, I'm looking forward to seeing you and the boys," Tom lied.

"Oh, Tom, is Joe Tilson there by chance? I wondered if you would have him pick up my cousin at the train station. The train comes in at four. I told Sara that Joe would be there. Thanks a million, dear. See you tonight," she spoke quickly without taking a breath.

"I'll be there. I'll make sure Joe's at the station. See you . . . tonight." Tom finished his sentence though Vivian had already hung up.

Tom found Joe on a ladder at the back of the house replacing a small transformer. "Is that what's causing the problems with the power?"

"Hard to tell for sure, but it's definitely in need of replacing. Need some more help moving boxes? I'll be done here in about ten minutes."

"No. But Vivian called and wanted to see if you'd go into town this afternoon and pick her cousin up. Told her you would —was that okay?"

"You bet. That would be Sara Lawson. She's a great lady. She's a lot of fun, very nice—not at all like Vivian. Attractive, too. I hope you get to meet her soon."

"I've been invited to dinner, so I guess tonight's the night. I'm not exactly looking forward to it, but Jimmy wanted me to come. I couldn't refuse."

"You seem to really like the boy."

"I do. He reminds me a lot of myself when I was a kid. Reminds me what it was like to look forward to life—no worries, just living in the moment. What I wouldn't give to be a kid again. Anyway . . . being around Jimmy reminds me of the carefree times."

Joe reached into his tool pouch and pulled out a screwdriver. "You don't sound very optimistic. You should be glad you have this great house. And lots of plans for it—not to mention the means to carry them out. What I wouldn't give to have . . ." He looked down at Tom. "Oh, shit, me and my big mouth."

"Don't worry about it. You don't have to watch what you say around me. I brought a lot of baggage with me; there's no reason you should have to deal with it."

Joe nodded as he put a final screw to secure the transformer to the back wall of the house. "Sure, I kind of figured as much. Anytime you want to talk, let me know."

"I will. Thanks. I'm going to go through some more of the boxes. I'd like to get them sorted and put away this afternoon."

Chapter 19

A lofty tower of cumulus clouds glowed orange and crimson, their billowing edges turning dark gray with the hint of the coming night. Shimmers of color were reflected in the Atlantic. Far out on the horizon waves began their rhythmic ebb and flow and would soon render the calm waters turbulent.

A murder of ravens circled over the water, then landed in the boughs of a stand of beech trees on the bluff. The black birds' resounding caws echoed in the heavy, humid air. It was twilight at Remington House.

Needing some time to relax and unwind before getting ready for dinner at the Harrison house, Tom left the house and walked along the shore. The early evening air was cool and brisk. A full moon, known as the *Snow* moon, was beginning to climb high, reflecting luminous silhouettes across the water. In the distance, the lights from a lighthouse illuminated the dark landscape in eerie, roving patches, its twinkling reflection sparkled in the moonlit water.

Tom remembered a night, some eight years ago, when Elise and he had been vacationing on the San Diego coast. *She did love me then—didn't she?* They'd taken a blanket down to the beach one warm night to watch the full moon rise over the ocean.

"Darling," Elise teased, her voice low and sultry, "show me how much you love me." She seductively loosened the straps of her swimsuit, dropping them around her shoulders. She lay back on the blanket, pulling Tom on top of her, running her hands up and down his thighs.

They stared into each other's eyes. Tom knew at that moment, his soul belonged to Elise. They made love again and again, the moon and stars their only witness. Tom was lost in the silkiness of her body, his needs insatiable. She'd laughed with wild abandon, loving to be so free.

Languid shadows momentarily covered them with darkness as clouds floated across the moon. From far out in the ocean, the peal of a foghorn, lonely and desolate, drifted in the gentle wind. The forlorn note invaded Tom's mind, wrapping its cold fingers around his thoughts. "Elise," he whispered in her ear, "I promise I will you love you forever. Will you promise to love me forever?" He held her closely, waiting. Her body felt helpless and frail in his arms.

"Of course I will, silly man," she said flippantly, pushing him away and running naked into the crashing waves.

He ran after her, yelling, "You'll catch your death, Elise. Come back!"

"Hey, Mr. Gardner, what are you doing? You're getting your feet all wet! Hey!"

With a start, Tom whirled around. Jimmy was running down the beach toward him.

"Jeez, you scared me! I've been hollering at you and you didn't answer," Jimmy panted, trying to catch his breath. "What were you running after?"

"A ghost, Jimmy. A beautiful ghost." Not wanting to frighten Jimmy, Tom put his arm around the boy's shoulder. "Just joking, kid." He could think of nothing to explain his behavior, thought it best not to try. "If you think it's okay, come back to the house. It's too early to go to your house for dinner. I still need to change. You can play the piano while you wait for me."

"Yay! You better change your shoes too. They're all wet. Mother won't like that." Jimmy grinned and ran up the cliff stairs ahead of Tom.

Chapter 20

"Come on. This way, Mr. Gardner." Jimmy and Tom entered the house through the back door. Tom followed Jimmy down a short hallway and into the kitchen.

"Jimmy, where are your manners? What's wrong with you, bringing a guest in through the back? Your mama's going to box your ears for sure," a frail black woman scolded from across the room. She was stirring several pans, all emitted fabulous smells, making Tom's mouth water. He was glad he'd come—at least for the food—not for the prospect of spending an evening with Vivian Harrison. He hadn't had a home-cooked meal in weeks.

"Oh, Mannie. Mother won't even know unless you tell her —she's clear in the drawing room. We came up from the beach. Who the heck wants to walk all the way around the house when the door's right here? It's too cold outside. Who cares what door we come in anyway?"

"Your mama, that's who. Now introduce me to your friend, then get on out of here before your mother comes checking on dinner." She winked at Jimmy, then smiled at Tom.

"Mannie, this is Tom Gardner, our new neighbor. Mr. Gardner, this is Mannie Parker, the best cook in the world!" Tom and Mannie shook hands. "Come on, Mr. Gardner, before Mannie has a cow." Tom followed Jimmy out of the kitchen and down a long hall toward the front of the house. They stopped in front of a set of mahogany, double doors, all the brass hardware buffed to a gleaming shine. "Wait here," Jimmy whispered. He tiptoed to the front entryway and opened the door, then slammed it hard enough to make certain it would be heard behind the closed doors of the drawing room. Tom winked at him in understanding. Jimmy hurried down the hall to Tom. Smiling, he opened the doors and they entered the room.

Vivian stood in front of a black marble fireplace sipping a dark amber liquid from a cordial glass. She looked stunning in a simply cut, black silk dress. At her waist was a single, black velvet rose, accentuating her slim figure. Her pale blonde hair was pulled into a soft chignon, accenting her high cheekbones. Diamond and ruby earrings dangled from her ears. Her green eyes sparkled in the soft firelight.

"Good evening, Vivian."

"Tom, darling. How wonderful to see you. Come here by the fire. You must be freezing." She motioned for Tom to come and stand beside her. "Jimmy, take Mr. Gardner's coat."

Tom handed the boy his coat. "Be right back," Jimmy said, leaving the room.

"Tom, what would you like to drink? I have brandy or sherry."

"Brandy's fine." Tom watched Vivian, trying to guess her age. He guessed maybe thirty five, a few years younger than he. She certainly looked fabulous, obviously spent a lot of time taking care of herself. And probably a lot of money.

Sipping his drink, Tom discretely checked out the room. One thing was evident—the Harrisons had money. The room was furnished in what Tom guessed were authentic Louis XIV pieces, inlaid with gold and ivory. On one wall was a collection of Gainsborough landscapes. *Very impressive.*

"My, aren't you the quiet one, Tom?" Vivian smiled coyly.

"I was admiring your paintings. Gainsboroughs?"

"Yes, aren't they gorgeous? Such extravagant gifts from my husband, William. He bought them for me for my birthday last year. They were very difficult to come by, but somehow he managed to find them. He spoils me, but I do love it!" She laughed. "He's such a dear. Come on, Tom, and I'll take you on a tour of the main floor. That is if you'd like to see it?"

Not waiting for an answer, she took his arm and led him out of the drawing room. The rest of the main floor was just as extravagant; all of the furniture authentic antiques from this or that era— Queen Ann, Louis XVI or Louis XV. Tom was more and more curious as to what exactly William Harrison did to amass his obvious fortune. Another brandy or two, and he just might ask.

The mysterious cousin still hadn't made an appearance. When Tom asked about her, Vivian explained, "Sara's resting; she'll join us in a while." Back in the drawing room, while they waited to be called to dinner, Vivian poured them another brandy. Tom began to relax. Billy came into the room and stood at the fireplace, glaring at Tom. Tom smiled and asked how he was enjoying his holiday vacation.

Billy mumbled, "Fine."

"You'll have to forgive Billy," Vivian said. "He had a big disappointment today." Vivian patted her son's shoulder. His friend George called, and he isn't able to join us for the holiday. Billy was looking forward to having him here. My poor dear is very upset. Aren't you, Billy?" Billy didn't answer, rudely pushing Vivian's hand off his shoulder.

"Sorry to hear that," Tom said, thinking, *Brat.* "Maybe you could invite someone else. It's still a few weeks until Thanksgiving. I'll bet you have lots of friends who'd jump at the chance to spend the holiday here." There must be a punk or two whose parents would love to get rid of them.

"What a good idea, Tom. Billy, I bet Alan would love to come," she said, then explained to Tom, "Alan's an only child, he's probably bored to death. Maybe you know the family? Alan's father is Dr. Raymond James." Vivian's eyes were intent on Tom's.

"I don't know Raymond, but I know his brother, Nicholas. We were at Yale together. I haven't heard from him in years. I heard he's a surgeon in Baltimore. I guess I should look him up sometime." Tom knew he never would. Nicholas was a real jerk. Boring and arrogant as well.

"Billy, why don't you call Alan before we sit down to dinner?" Vivian said, dismissing her son. Tom was greatly relieved to have him out of the room.

"I have some exciting news, Tom. I talked to one of my New York friends today. When I told her who I was having over for dinner tonight, she told me she knows you!" She watched Tom's face. "Aren't you curious who she is?"

Tom could tell by the frown that momentarily shadowed her face that she was expecting more of a reaction. He felt nothing, except perhaps dread.

"Don't you want to know who?" Her eyes twinkled as she waited for his answer.

Not really. Vivian watched him, disappointment registering in her voice at his lack of enthusiasm, though he sensed she enjoyed putting him on the spot. Okay, he'd bite. "Of course I do. Who?" Tom didn't like the games she was playing. He'd get through this evening, then keep his distance.

"Catherine Connors!" She spat the name, almost giggling with delight.

"I don't know who that is."

"Catherine Connors," Vivian said again, obviously frustrated. She was quiet for a second. "Maybe you know her by her maiden name? Let me think. I know I know it. Hmm." She chewed on her bottom lip. "I remember. Balantyne."

"Cathy Balantyne?" Tom took a quick breath. "God, she was just a girl the last time I saw her. We used to compete to be the teacher's pet. *I actually believe Cathy hated me! Her sense of competiveness was all-consuming.* I haven't seen her since grammar school."

"Really? Well, perhaps Catherine was trying to impress me. You know Catherine! She likes everyone to think she knows everyone!"

It didn't sound like Cathy and Vivian were close friends at all. And, if they weren't, Vivian probably knew nothing about Elise's past friendship with Cathy. Several years ago, after Tom found several letters from her encouraging Elise to leave him, he'd contacted Cathy and rather forcefully severed all contact between her and Elise. He had no clue how or when Elise and Cathy met. It'd been quite a shock to him to find out that they knew each other. He could only guess why Elise kept the relationship a secret. Vivian cleared her throat. Trying to smile, Tom asked, "So, how is Cathy?"

"According to her," Vivian said, slightly sarcastically, "she leads a perfectly charmed life. Catherine's married to a prominent New York plastic surgeon, Elrich Connors. They're the toast of the town. I see them whenever I'm in New York. They have fabulous parties!" Vivian winked, laughing.

Tom, though, knew from Cathy's letters to Elise that she was in a loveless marriage, relying on alcohol to dull her pain.

She remained married to the 'dear doctor' to avoid the shame a divorce would bring to her and her family. Not to mention their prenup that would give a huge sum of money to her husband if they divorced.

"I can't imagine why Catherine acted as if she knew you so well. But you haven't seen her since you were kids. I was so excited that we had a mutual friend, and it's not even true. I don't know what game she's playing with me." Vivian sulked, drew her lips into an ugly frown. Tom guessed from the look on her face that she was planning to get even with Cathy for her deceit. She grinned wickedly. Her mood changed immediately.

Tom drained his brandy snifter. *And my sister wonders why I dread these social engagements. Not too hard to figure out.* Tom prepared himself for the task of spending the rest of the evening with the self-centered, childish Vivian. *I hope I'm up to this!*

Vivian blushed. "You must think I'm awful, being upset over something so trivial. I only wanted to be friends with you! I thought having a friend in common would make it much easier. Well, never mind about Catherine. Since she obviously doesn't know you well, I guess you'll just have to tell me all about yourself." Tilting her head slightly, she looked at Tom through her long lashes, her green eyes glistening, a seductive smile on her face.

Oh, great. Now she was flirting with him. Then Tom felt guilty. After all, what did he know about Vivian? She probably was lonely without her husband and friends here. Cassie said he had a bad habit of reading false emotions and traits into people. It ensured that he kept people at a distance. He supposed she was right to some degree; it made it easier to isolate himself. Tom smiled at Vivian and decided to give her another chance. Studying her, he tried to see nothing but the pretty, young woman who was trying very hard to entertain a difficult guest.

"I'm going to check on dinner. I'll be right back."

Tom poured another brandy and entertained himself by nosing around the room looking at the Harrisons' extensive book collection. Vivian returned in a few minutes. Dinner was ready. He followed her to the dining room.

The room was hot and stuffy; beads of sweat gathered on Tom's brow. Trying to be inconspicuous, he wiped his forehead with the back of his hand and loosened his tie. Vivian, the all-seeing, gracious hostess, called for Amos, one of her household staff and the husband to Mannie, to open the window. Tom was moved from his seat in front of the fireplace to the other side of the table. He now faced Jimmy, who beamed at him.

Billy sat to Tom's right. He asked, "Mom, where's Sara? I thought she was eating dinner with us. I have some things to talk to her about."

"I sent Mannie to get her. She'll be down soon." Vivian had barely finished her sentence when the door opened, and Sara entered.

"I'm so sorry. I lost track of time. Did I keep you waiting? Oh, hello. You must be Tom Gardner," she said to Tom's back as he strained to turn around in the chair which had him trapped in its cushy, velvet embrace.

Quickly standing, almost tipping his chair over, Tom offered Sara his hand and a warm smile. Sara sat down across the table, next to Jimmy. While she told the boys about the trip she had just returned from, Tom took the opportunity to study her. She was in her mid thirties and very beautiful. Her dark, chestnut-brown hair fell in soft curls that framed her face—a stark contrast to her pale complexion. Her eyes were deep violet-blue, fringed with thick, black lashes. Her bright red lips were full, and when she smiled, revealed perfect teeth. Naturally high color on her cheekbones gave her a healthy glow. She radiated a sultry, sensual aura, while maintaining an innocent demeanor. He was immediately drawn to her.

Sara talked animatedly to the boys, her eyes expressive and intense. Her hands were as active as her voice. She excitedly recounted several stories about her travels in the Bahamas. The boys were a captive audience. Tom caught her eye. She blushed, her cheeks turning bright red. Smiling back, she continued talking to Jimmy and Billy, who hung on her every word. Her smile caught Tom off guard. It seemed directed straight at his heart. Pure, innocent, real. He hoped the evening would be long.

Vivian interrupted, ending Sara's tale about her encounter with a white shark in the Sargasso Sea. "Jimmy and Billy, that's enough. Sara can talk to you about her trip any time, for heaven's sake. You're being very rude, monopolizing the conversation. Do stop."

Jimmy's face flushed red, Tom was afraid the boy was going to cry. Sara came to his rescue. "Jimmy, we'll go down to the beach tomorrow and have a picnic. I'll tell you all about my trip then." She winked at Jimmy. "Sound like a good plan?"

He nodded.

"You too, Billy. We'll even do some fishing." Both boys agreed, and the awkward moment passed.

For the duration of the dinner, Vivian monopolized the conversation, talking about her remodeling plans for their New York brownstone, a property recently purchased by her husband. Vivian and her boys would stay here at the beach house until the remodeling was complete, probably for the rest of the winter. Sara, who was a teacher, had recently quit her job at a small private school and would be staying here to tutor the two boys. Tom's mood quickly elevated.

While Vivian's high-pitched voice droned on and on about fabrics and wallpaper, name dropping as often as possible about her interior designers, Tom listened quietly, nodding from time to time, saying "sounds great, very nice, impressive, etc." He caught Sara's eye and grinned. She returned his look with a knowing smile, silently toasting him with her glass. Vivian never noticed, continuing her diatribe, thrilled at having her rightful place as the center of attention.

***

Mannie prepared a delectable meal—Cornish game hens stuffed with wild rice and mushrooms; baby asparagus spears in a light wine sauce with slivered almonds; buttered, new potatoes and a fresh spinach salad with raspberry vinaigrette dressing. After dinner, they returned to the drawing room where Amos served fresh peach pie and french vanilla ice cream. Giant mugs of strong, dark-roasted coffee steamed on the side table with an array of flavored creams and honeys. They savored the desert, eating the warm, cinnamon spiced fruit pie slowly, sipping coffee and making small talk.

After dessert, Amos poured each of the adults a glass of cognac, part of a private reserve that Vivian's husband imported from France. "We're so spoiled," Vivian purred as she sat down next to Tom on the sofa.

"Vivian, what all does your husband import?" Tom asked, curious and unable to let the mention of William Harrison's business pass by.

"Almost anything you can think of: antiques, artwork, automobiles, textiles, gemstones. He imports artwork for museums and private collectors, too. His great-grandfather started the business, over the years building a large and varied clientele for his merchandise." She glanced at Tom to make sure he was paying attention to her. "William became vice president of the corporation as soon as he graduated from Harvard. When his father died two years ago, he became president." Vivian sighed. "Tom, you must find this boring. All this talk about business is so dull. Let's talk about something else." She took a sip of her cognac. "You haven't told me about Remington House, yet. I hope you'll invite me over soon, I can't wait to see it! Tell me all about it."

Duty-bound and knowing no way to get out of it, Tom described the house and décor as well as a man could. Sara raised her eyebrows and tried to suppress her giggle with a yawn. Vivian seemed not to notice and told Tom she was ready and willing to take over his redecorating. "Don't hesitate to call me before you make any changes, Tom. I totally know all the ropes. Promise?" He nodded, then glanced at Sara, who was lost in conversation with Jimmy and Billy. Disappointed, he looked back at Vivian.

Leaning forward, Vivian reached her hand toward Tom, gripped his forearm. Very subtlety, her demeanor changed. Staring at Tom with a look of grave despair, her eyes filled with tears that overflowed and ran down her cheeks in glistening rivulets. Her painted fingernails dug into his skin. Then she smiled, abruptly stood and walked over to the piano. She began to play—a melody whose chords sent chills down Tom's spine. Slowly, hauntingly, her pale fingers gliding, stroking the ivory and ebony keys as she played Beethoven's *Für Elise*. Tom had often played the song for Elise—when their relationship was new and they were immersed in their love for each other. The gentle refrains expressed his innermost passions for her. Over time, Elise grew to hate it because he loved it, loved her.

As Vivian continued to play, Tom walked over and sat beside her on the piano bench. She turned to him, her eyes filled with a look so cold and vengeful, it made Tom's blood run cold.

"Vivian! Stop!" Tom's voice was barely above a whisper. She continued playing. Beads of perspiration trickled down Tom's back. He whispered again, "Stop!" He heard no other sounds in the room, only the ethereal sounds from the piano as Vivian continued to play *Für Elise,* the haunting chords reverberating deep in his soul.

Vivian turned to him. In a voice so quiet he had to strain to hear the words, she said, "You bastard!"

Tom stared at her in disbelief.

Vivian's head jerked up. She stared at him, her face registering complete surprise. "Tom, what is it? Is my playing so terrible?" She seemed completely unaware of what had just transpired. "What was I playing? How odd, I can't remember. . . ." Vivian rubbed her temples, gently shook her head. "Come here, Sara. Come play for us."

"What did you say to me, Vivian?" Tom asked, his hand on her wrist, his eyes searching her face.

"Tom, I don't know what you mean. I didn't say anything. I was only asking Sara to come and play for us. Why are you looking at me like that?" She seemed to have no idea what Tom was talking about.

"Never mind," Tom said, scrutinizing her face. "I thought you said something. I thought, well . . . that song you were playing . . . "

"I have no idea what you're talking about," she said, pulling her hand free from his grip. "I don't remember. Sara, come over here and see if you can brighten Tom's mood. You play, and Tom and I will accompany you. Billy and Jimmy, yes, both of you, come over here." She opened a well-worn songbook to the music for *Blackbird*. As Sara began to play, Vivian started to sing. Soon the boys joined in.

Tom was too shocked to do anything more than watch and listen. As Vivian, Sara and the boys harmonized, he tried to make sense of what had just happened with Vivian, decided it was best to forget it. What was clear to him was that Vivian was not who she seemed on the surface. It's possible she had some serious mental issues. He'd have to be on guard.

Vivian, Sara and the boys sang and played half a dozen songs. Prompted by Jimmy's poking him in the ribs, Tom finally joined in, his deep bass voice blending well with theirs. He continued to study Vivian. Her face was flushed with excitement as she sang and played a few verses to accompany Sara. Vivian seemed perfectly fine, genuinely oblivious to what she'd said to Tom earlier. *Maybe I imaged the whole thing. That's the only explanation—too many cognacs. But . . . why did she play Für Elise—of all songs? Or did I imagine that, too?* Tom took a long breath and tried to focus on Sara and Jimmy, their smiling faces a salve for his raw nerves. He began to relax. After several more rounds of the chorus, Vivian sent the boys to bed.

It had started raining again. Huge drops danced off the windows, sparkling in the moonlight. "It's almost eleven. I had no idea it was so late. I should go," Tom said. "Vivian, thank you for being such a gracious hostess. It was a memorable evening." *To say the least.* Vivian smiled warmly at him, leaving him convinced that maybe he had imagined the whole incident.

Sara walked out onto the porch with him, shivering in the cold night air. "Wait a minute," she said. She ran inside, returned wearing a heavy sweater. "That's better. It's cold tonight. Hope the rain doesn't turn to snow."

Tom nodded in agreement. "I'm glad we met tonight," he said softly.

"Me, too. And," she smiled, "I'm very glad you bought the house next door. It's reassuring to know there's someone close by. The winters can be very lonely. It's pretty isolated here." Sara pulled her collar up around her ears. "I'm grateful for Vivian, don't get me wrong. She's been a Godsend, inviting me here to tutor the boys. But she tends to focus pretty much on herself and her own agendas. It'll be nice to have someone else to talk to." She blushed, then kicked at the bottom porch railing, obviously embarrassed. "Listen to me! I talk too much. You must think I'm awful."

"Not at all. I understand. Vivian is everything you said. I'm sure she has a good heart, as long as no one shadows her place in the limelight. I've known many women, and men, like her. Unfortunately, money tends to give them an inflated sense of self-importance." Tom took her hand in his. "Whenever you need to escape—or to talk—come on over. In fact, Jimmy's coming over tomorrow afternoon, come with him. I'll show you around my place. I could use the company, too."

"I'd like that—if I can get away."

"Good. You should go inside now, you're shivering."

"You're right. I'm freezing! Goodnight. Oh, Tom, there's a path on the other side of the rose garden that leads up the hill to your house. It's a lot shorter than going down to the beach."

"Okay, good. I'll go that way, then. Well . . . goodnight, Sara." Tom impulsively brought her hand to his lips and gently kissed it. "I look forward to seeing you tomorrow. Goodnight."

"Nite." Sara smiled, then watched him as he hurried down the walkway toward the garden.

It was raining much harder now. Tom hoped the pathway leading through the trees would afford him a little shelter. By the time he reached his property, the wind was blowing at near gale force. Rain pelted his hands and face like sharp needles. Pulling the collar of his coat up under his chin, he sprinted the last fifty yards on the narrow path to his house.

A darkened Remington House was silhouetted eerily against the stormy sky, the moon oppressively dimmed by the storm. Tom thought he'd left a light on, but maybe he'd forgotten. Or maybe the power was out again. He reached for the light switch inside the front door. The dark entryway immediately glowed with amber light. Good. The power was on.

Dense shadows followed him as he walked through the house. As he turned on one light after another, Tom began to feel at ease. Wiggins, lying on the kitchen rug, looked briefly at Tom, then curled into a more comfortable position and went back to sleep. Tom made a pot of coffee and took it to the living room where he built fire, then turned off the lights. The room glowed in mellow oranges and yellows, the firelight creating a warm, cozy nuance. Sitting at the table in front of the window, Tom watched the ocean's choppy waves erratically reflecting slivers of pale moonlight.

His thoughts drifted—as he hoped they wouldn't—back to Vivian and her disturbing behavior and spiteful verbal attack directed at him. Had he imagined it? Her look of hatred was so real—he'd seen that look often enough from Elise. Elise? No, it wasn't possible! And yet . . .

Tom slept little that night, his dreams filled with visions of Elise, then Vivian, morphing back and forth until he could no longer distinguish one from the other as they chased about his house, alternately playing the piano, then mocking Tom with raucous peals of laughter.

Chapter 21

Tom, unshaven, dressed in jeans and a t-shirt, was talking on the phone with John Atwood when Joe arrived the next morning. Tom nodded and waved to Joe as he passed by on his way to the kitchen. John relayed the news to Tom about Nate's brother, Harold, and about Nate. "The judge released Harold yesterday afternoon without pressing charges—at least not at this time. Jim Wood, Harold's attorney, took him to the hospital to see Nate. Rosa was there visiting. She reluctantly agreed to let Harold go home with her for a few days, until other living arrangements can be made."

"Hope he doesn't drive Rosa crazy. But he's better off staying with her for a while," Tom said. "She'll make him toe the line."

"We shall see. It sounds as if Harold is more obstinate than usual. His dark side seems to have a fairly strong presence. I hope he gets some help. For now, he's off the streets at least." Tom could hear John drumming his pen on the desk as he talked. "Now the news about Nate. The fracture and resulting wound from the bone tearing through the flesh will keep him hospitalized for at least a more few days. The doctor is worried about infection. Nate will likely be out of commission for weeks. He might need to stay with Rosa, too. Or, if it's okay with you, Tom, he could stay on at your Jamestown house—we could hire an in-home nurse to take care of him."

"I think we better leave that up to Nate. I'll do whatever he wants," Tom said. Out his window he watched a gaggle of snow geese fly to the north. He jumped when a raven flew at him, turning before it hit the window glass. It flew in a large circle, then come back to land on the porch railing. Cawing and flapping its wings, it took another dive at the window, then flew away.

"Still there, Tom?"

"Yeah, sorry. Just watching a crazy bird. Keep me posted about Nate . . . and Harold."

"More bad news?" Joe asked when Tom hung up the phone. Tom told him what was going on in Jamestown. Joe expressed his sympathy and left when Tom answered another phone call. He returned in a few minutes with a tray of coffee and plate of fresh donuts. They sat quietly at the small dining table watching the rain as it fell in endless torrents. It was a cold, gray day; the entire horizon was filled with dark clouds.

"How was your dinner last night?" Joe asked trying to lighten the heavy mood.

"Hmm? Oh, last night? Well, the food was excellent, the booze plentiful, Sara was charming, Jimmy was a trooper and Billy was a brat. . . . And then there was Vivian! Thanks for asking. All in all, a crappy introduction back into the social scene for me. Not quite the night I envisioned. I'm glad I kept it foremost in my mind that the kids and Sara were there, or I would have gotten completely smashed.

"And might I add, I'm generally not one to get loaded as an escape. A waste of good booze, to be sure." Tom got up and paced in front of the window. "It seemed like I spent most of the night, between Vivian and Billy, watching my back. Vivian spent most of the evening alternately insulting me, then trying to impress me, always making sure I paid no attention to anyone else. I think she's afraid I might be higher up on the social ladder than she is. Billy is just a brat looking for trouble —at anyone's expense. He tried his best to get a rise out of me."

Joe laughed. "Sounds like a fun night. Wish I'd been there. And to think I spent my evening playing pool with the guys."

"It might sound funny now, but trust me, last night was not fun. Next dinner at the Harrison's, I'll make sure you get invited, too. Misery deserves company."

Joe cleared his throat. "Not my scene. I'll pass. I'm not much for fancy dinners. I'm the quiet dinner-at-the-cafe type."

"I'm serious, Joe. Why should I have all the fun? After all, this is your town. If I have any other social invitations, I'll take you as my guest. You'll see how the other side lives, learn the value of years of proper etiquette learning which fork to use for which dinner course. Critical and invaluable *stuff.* More importantly, you'll see why I hate it. Then you can help me convince my sister, Cassie, that my reintroduction into society is not the right direction to go. Give me a cold beer and a pool table any day. Now that sounds like a good time."

Joe added, "It is. We have a great time in town at the *8 Ball.* A bunch of us guys meet there Friday nights. Glad to have you join us any time."

The two were quiet for a while as they watched the storm, then Tom said, "Don't get me wrong. Wealth definitely has its advantages, but it sure doesn't have much to do with making a person happy."

"Yeah, well I wouldn't mind a bit giving it a try. Been struggling my whole life." The sun broke through the heavy clouds, the choppy waves lit up with mirrored reflections of light. "Oh, well, things aren't too bad. I'm not complaining." Joe stood up. "Storms moving out, looks like there's a break in the rain. I better get up on the roof and check for loose shingles. Wouldn't want any water leaking in the house—that wind was incredibly strong last night, and I don't know how long this roof's been on."

"Mind if I give you a hand? I'd like to get out of the house for a while. I'm feeling cooped up."

"Make sure you have shoes with a good grip to the soles. The roof will be slick after this rain. Have you been on a roof before?" Joe grinned at Tom as he wrenched the rain-swollen back door open.

"Yeah, sure have," Tom lied. "Be right back, I need to change shoes."

There was a light, brisk wind blowing, but the sun quickly warmed the air as it burned through the clouds. Climbing the ladder, Tom smiled to himself anticipating what he hoped would end up being a morning of hard labor. Even though he'd had little sleep last night, he wasn't physically tired, and he craved rigorous physical activity. Looking around the roof they found several areas where roof tiles had lifted from the hard-driving winds and pounding rain.

"I'll be right back; you want to wait up here?" Joe hollered as he backed around the top of the ladder to start down. "I need a few things from the shed."

Tom teetered on the steep slope of the roof, then was angry with himself for showing his clumsiness to Joe. "Yeah, go on." Tom regained his balance and cautiously walked around the roof to a vantage point next to one of the chimneys where he could see for miles in all directions. To the east was the Atlantic, its swells shimmering in the brilliant sun. To the north, high atop the bluff, the Harrison estate rose—austere and proper, easily evident as the residence of someone wealthy and in the upper echelon of society.

Thick woods covered the landscape between his property and the Harrison's. Though the trees were nearly bare now, in the summer they would be masses of green against the azure of the coastal sky, their boughs home to birds and wildlife, a cacophony of orchestrated melodies carried for miles across the ocean on the gentle breezes of summer. Looking far to the west was the town of Ravenswood, a town of perhaps five thousand year-round residents, the majority of whom lived in an area about three miles square. From this distance, the town seemed small and insignificant compared to the expanse of the Atlantic to the east.

Tom realized he wanted to find out more about Ravenswood. About all he knew was that it was founded in the late 1800's as a mill town. It was populated with workers, their families and the businesses necessary to keep the town alive. He wondered if the mills were still operating. Tourism kept the economy alive in the summer, but how did the town survive the rest of the year? He'd have to ask Joe. See if there was anything he could do to help out. He might look into starting, or maybe investing in, a business in town.

"You look a million miles away, Tom. Guess you didn't hear me hollering. Here, grab this." Joe hoisted a wooden handled, canvas bag filled with roofing supplies up over the edge and onto the roof. "Awesome view. The last owners thought it would be ideal to build a lookout up here. I had to ruin their plans. Anything other than a solidly built structure would be pounded mercilessly by the rain and wind—wouldn't stand up for more than a season or two." Joe climbed onto the roof, pulling a small roll of tarpaper he had attached to a rope. Tom helped him leverage it on to the roof. "Set it down right over there. It won't roll off if you set it so it's vertical."

The men worked for hours. Joe alternated between whistling and humming, Tom concentrated on nothing but the work at hand. Old roof tiles were pulled off and new pieces of tarpaper laid. When the heavy black paper was down, Joe brought up a bundle of roofing tiles, and they covered the areas where wind and rain had shredded the roof. An effortless camaraderie, built of sweat and honest work, formed a bond between the men.

When they finished, they remained on the roof, looking out over the ocean. Yet another storm could be seen on the far horizon. Joe pointed to the roiling black clouds. "It looks like it's gonna be another fierce one. This time of year, seems like we get one storm after another. The roof's in good shape now, shouldn't have to do any more repairs this season. I'll keep an eye on it, though."

They gathered up their tools and descended the ladder. "I'm starved. You ready to go in and have some lunch?" Tom asked.

While they ate fried chicken, salad and biscuits Joe brought from the deli that morning, Tom brought up the subject of Thanksgiving. "My sister and her family will be here next week. They'll be staying for at least two weeks. Mary's going to help on and off, but I need to find someone to cook and do some light cleaning while Cassie's here. Do you know anyone who might be interested?"

"Lots of people looking for extra work this time of year. How many people are you looking for?"

"Maybe three to get the house cleaned and in order. There are more boxes that need to be unpacked and all the bedrooms need to be made up, that kind of thing this week. After that, then someone to cook and pick up while Cassie and her family are here."

"I know a real nice woman who used to cook for the Brunsons—they own one of the textile mills. I know Nellie is looking for work—I ran into her the other day. She ran a temporary maid service last year for the summer residents so she has great credentials. She's a fantastic cook, too. I'll give her a call now." Joe called her and started making all the necessary arrangements while Tom sat idly by enjoying the view out the window. The clouds, pushed by the strong winds, rolled in heading for the coast.

"All set. Nellie's good to go. She'll be here in the morning."

"Thanks, Joe. About next week—do you have any plans for Thanksgiving dinner? Care to join us? There'll be plenty of good food and conversation."

"Yeah, I'd like that. Thanks. Since I broke it off with my lady, I seldom have dinner plans. It'd be a good change for me. And—I'm anxious to meet your family."

"Good," Tom said. "Think you'll hit it off with my sister, she's amazing."

Jimmy and Sara knocked on the back door as Tom was finishing loading the dishes into the dishwasher. Jimmy was anxious to start his piano lesson, and they went right to work. Tom found a book of simple songs, and another of scales, for him to start practicing on. While Jimmy worked through the exercises, Tom and Sara sat on the sofa and listened. Jimmy played quite well, managing to play several songs all the way through with few mistakes. Obviously he'd had at least a few lessons in the past. He was very serious as he concentrated on the proper placement of his fingers, chewing his bottom lip when he came to a difficult part. After a few minutes he forgot all about Sara and Tom. They quietly got up and went into the kitchen to make some iced tea, leaving Jimmy to practice scales from a book that had belonged to Tom and Cassie when they were kids.

"So, how did you and Jimmy manage to escape Vivian?" Tom asked.

"Pure luck. William's new car was delivered today. She and Billy went into Ravenswood for the afternoon. I told her Jimmy and I had plans to collect seashells. I think she was relieved not to have to entertain Jimmy or me today. So here we are."

"Want a tour of the house?" Tom asked. After showing her the main floor, with which she was duly impressed, they went upstairs. The library was still filled with packing crates Tom had forgotten about, but the two bedrooms on the north were in fairly good order. Sara was enthralled with the view of the ocean from the balcony.

"I never met the people who lived here before you," Sara said. "Do you know anything about them?"

"No. No one's told me anything about them. I never thought to ask, though. I found a few pictures of them on the shelf in the living room. They seemed odd, something strange about their eyes—cold and . . . I can't explain it. Gave me the creeps." Tom smiled. "But they seem to have taken excellent care of the house and property. That's a positive!"

Sara returned his smile, then said, "Vivian talked about them once in a while. Apparently she tried to get them to come for dinner on several occasions. They had some high-society connections, so she was eager to get to know them. They told Viv they seldom left the house. The brother was too ill."

"Yeah, he certainly looked it in the pictures I found."

"The second or third time they refused her offer, Vivian took it as a personal insult and didn't ask them again. She said she assumed that they felt socially superior, and if that was the case, they were not welcome in her home. I was always curious about the couple, probably because they were so reclusive and because I never got to meet them. I actually only saw the two of them once. They were getting into Joe's taxi at the train station, back from a trip out of the city. Joe was one of the few people who ever spent time with them. I'm sure he told you he worked for them on and off."

"Joe said he worked on the house. He didn't seem to know much about them personally. I got the impression he was on a work-only basis with the Lindemans. No social interaction," Tom said.

"Did you know that they died here—in this house?"

"What? No!" Tom was visibly upset, is brow furrowed, his brown eyes narrowed and focused on Sara. "What happened?"

"Apparently it was a murder-suicide. It was kept very quiet. Mannie, Vivian's cook, was our only source of information. I don't know that she's a particularly reliable source. But she's the best we had! Anyway, she heard the story from the sheriff's sister, so we have to assume it's at least partly true. It seems that Helen shot her brother, then several days later, shot herself. They found both of their bodies in the attic. Helen left a suicide note explaining her brother, Gabriel, was in unbearable pain from his cancer. He begged her to end his suffering. After much agonizing, she did. And then, unable to forgive herself, she took her own life." Sara stared at Tom, her violet eyes guarded.

"Not what I wanted to hear happened in my house. Damn! I didn't know anything about it until now."

Sara twisted a chestnut-brown curl around her index finger. "Sorry to be the one to break the news to you. If it's even true. Personally, I prefer to ignore Mannie's account and take a more romantic view of their deaths."

"How can anyone take a romantic view of a murder?" Tom asked, surprised that she would say such a thing.

Sara smiled and continued, "I like to think they weren't brother and sister at all but lovers who were separated for years. Then one day fate stepped in and their paths crossed. For reasons that shall remain a mystery, perhaps because of their families or maybe because one of them was married, they were never able to be together. Finally, after years of separation, they knew they could no longer be apart."

"You have quite an imagination, Sara!" Tom laughed softly.

Ignoring him, Sara continued, "They moved to this small town, to this isolated house, so they could live the rest of their lives in peace, away from the rest of the world that had treated them so unfairly. Then, when the man became ill, unable to bear the thought of being torn apart again, they ended their lives." Sara looked at Tom, watching to see how he would react to her tale, "Well?"

Tom was uncomfortable. This talk of death was disquieting, especially knowing they died right here in his house. Sara watched him intently waiting for his response. He answered, "I agree your version is the more preferable. Two lovers, beaten once again by fate, laugh in her face and secure their own eternity together. And why not? Didn't they have the right after the lonely years spent apart—never knowing if the other was dead or alive, or happy or living in turmoil? Or— maybe Helen Lindeman did murder him. Perhaps because she realized that she loved him more than he loved her. Perhaps she even laughed when she pulled . . . "

"Tom! Don't. Stop!" Sara exclaimed, reaching out and grabbing his hand. "You're ruining my romantic story. You're as bad as Mannie. Let's go back downstairs and see how Jimmy is doing." She dropped Tom's hand, started to turn away.

"Sara, wait. I'm sorry. I don't know why I lashed out like that. I didn't mean to offend you. I . . . I don't know what I was thinking. Forget what I said." *What the hell is wrong with me? What possessed me to go on such a cruel tirade?*

Sara was standing at the bottom of the attic stairs. Tom let his hand rest on her shoulder. She smelled of delicate roses and sea air. Turning her to face him, Tom gently kissed her. She felt small and vulnerable in his arms, as if she might break if he held her too tightly, as if she might easily be destroyed if she could but guess his horrid sin. Selfishly he held on to her and felt comfort and solace. Quite possibly he thought he felt the beginning pangs of love and passion for this woman. "Sara," he whispered into the soft silkiness of her hair.

Did she feel the same? She hasn't pulled away from him. Her kiss was as passionate as his. Wasn't it? Or would he open his eyes and find he'd only imagined she felt as he did—only inane assumptions of a man crazed, possibly even mad, from guilt? A man haunted and tormented by the agony of unrequited love? But—if he was imagining that moment, it was better than the hell he'd been living, and he didn't mind.

Sara spoke his name softly, her voice floating on the air. Tom inhaled the delicate scent of her perfume, felt her arms around him. As he opened his eyes and looked into her violet eyes, she smiled. *This is real.* Tom smiled back.

"Sara? Mr. Gardner? Are you up there?" Jimmy called from the bottom of the stairs.

"Yes. Tom was showing me around the house. Come on up," Sara shouted. Reluctantly, Tom released her as Jimmy bounded up the stairs and down the hall.

"I've been looking all over for you. Thought maybe you went down to the beach or something. Anyhow, were you listening to me? How did you think I played that last song?"

"You're a natural, kid." Tom playfully ruffled the boy's unruly, red hair. "In fact, you did so well, I think by Christmas you'll probably be able to make your debut. That is, if you promise to come over and practice as often as you can. What do you think about that, champ?"

Jimmy beamed. "You bet I will. I'll figure out something to tell Mother. She's always glad to have me out from under foot anyway. And Billy's friend Alan is coming next week, so nobody will even notice if I'm not around. I promise I won't get in your way. I'll stay in the living room and practice. Okay?"

"I don't mind your being around one bit. My sister and her family will be here next week. I have a feeling they'll be very happy to have you here. In fact, my niece, Lizzie, will be thrilled to have someone to play with, even if it has to be a boy." Tom winked at Jimmy. "Come on, let's go down to the kitchen and have something to drink. I think there are chocolate chip cookies, too."

While Jimmy ran ahead, Sara and Tom stood together for a moment, not wanting to end their time alone. Tom held her for a few moments and whispered, "I don't want you to go, Sara. Won't you stay with me today?"

She pulled away, taking his hand in hers. "I don't want to go either, Tom, but I have to. Don't look disappointed. Now that Vivian has a car, she'll be gone a great deal of the time . . . if William will let her drive his car! She's not the safest driver! Somehow we'll make time to be together—just the two of us— as often as we can."

It was raining again when Sara and Jimmy left. Joe was leaving and offered to drive them home on his way to town. Tom watched somberly as they drove off. *Sara, what have I gotten you into?*

Chapter 22

"Tom, I'm so pleased you're already getting to know your neighbors. Good for you, big brother," Cassie purred. She'd called right after everyone left.

Tom told her about the Harrisons and his friendship with Jimmy and Sara. He carefully avoided mentioning his feelings for Sara.

"I'm certain I've met William Harrison before. Isn't he an antique dealer or something?"

"Yeah, that's the one," Tom said. "Actually, he's in the importing trade. He does extremely well judging by the money he's spent decorating their 'vacation' home. I haven't met him yet. Seems to be a very busy man. He's on the coast pursuing a business deal, according to Jimmy." Cassie was silent; Tom knew what she was waiting for him to say. He would not give her the satisfaction. "You still there, Sis?" he taunted.

"Quit teasing me. You're being much too guarded. What about Sara Lawson? Come clean."

"Very charming woman. I don't know much about her. She's a teacher and plans to stay here tutoring the two boys."

"Tom, you can be so exasperating! You know that's not what I meant! Is she young, old, fat, ugly, married or? . . . What? Quit laughing at me and tell me what she's like!"

"Cassie, you know I'm not good at that sort of thing," Tom chided.

"All right have it your way! I'll have to wait and see for myself, I guess. But you have to promise me you'll invite her over after Thanksgiving. Will you?"

"Sure. Tell you what. If you give me your word that you'll play hostess, I'll do one better. I'll invite the whole Harrison clan over so you can inspect them all at once. What do you think about that?"

Cassie was quiet for a moment. Apparently Tom had caught her off guard. After all, it had been years since he'd shown any interest in seeing anyone socially, let alone actually giving a party. "You know I'd love to. Are you sure you're up to it, Tom?"

"Guess I have to find out sometime, don't I? Can't stay a recluse forever. Besides, there won't be that many people— just the Harrisons and our family. And, of course, Joe. How about the Saturday after Thanksgiving?"

They talked for about an hour until Cassie finally said she had to go. She and Michael had a dinner engagement. Tom hated ending their conversation. It had been so long since they'd talked like this. He felt a need to try to make up for all the years they'd missed. Cassie and Elise had never gotten along, so during the years of their marriage, he and Cassie had little contact. The bond they'd once felt had all but disappeared. There would be lots of time to make up for that now.

***

Cassie and Tom were close as children. He was six when she was born and still, to this day, he remembered his mother holding the tiny baby out to him. "Tom, this is your new sister, Cassie. She's yours as much as she is your father's and mine. I need you to help take care of her. You can see how helpless she is. She'll need a brother like you to look out for her." She handed the bundle to him, and he'd gazed in awe at the tiny red face, the perfect miniature hand with its thumb searching for her tiny, pink mouth.

By the time Tom met Elise, Cassie was on her own, no longer in need of his affections or his guidance. But Elise! How delicate and innocent she was. She needed him. He would love her, adore her, share his life with her. So he'd thought.

Now, looking back, Tom realized the mistake he'd made. Elise had been too young and hadn't realized what she was doing when she entered into a relationship with him. She thought him bold, daring and exciting, her chance for a new life. She was too young and too inexperienced to have made such a serious commitment.

Or maybe his mother had been right, and Elise had stalked and cunningly hunted him—her bait her feigned frailty and innocence. Tom mistakenly believed her weak and helpless, making it easy for her to entangle him in her web of deceit. Maybe.

Or possibly Elise thought she loved him. That's what Tom believed.Then. After all, she'd been very naive and was searching for an escape from an abusive, alcoholic mother. She needed someone to love her unconditionally. Tom promised her he would. Always.

The joyous union Tom thought would last a lifetime was short lived. For three of the eight-years of their marriage, Elise seemed genuinely in love with him. Then something changed. Perhaps Elise simply grew up, tired of her life, tired of Tom.

But Tom would not, could not, let her go. Instead, he became obsessed with her. How could he live with a woman who didn't love him? It was simple. He thought he could make her love him again. Instead—he made her hate him.

Elise's loathing for Tom grew. He refused to see the reality of her abhorrence for him. He decided her unhappiness had little to do with him but with her inability to get pregnant.

"I have absolutely no desire to have a child—yours, or anyone else's," she told him one night when he tried to make love to her, telling her he wanted her to carry his child. "I've been on birth control since we married. Do you understand now?" She'd pulled away from him as he tried to hold her. Breaking free, she ran to her room and locked the door.

Heartbroken and betrayed, Tom created ways to ignore and twist the truth; his descent into a world of delusions began. He carefully constructed a life of lies, denying the inevitable, refusing to see that one day his world would fall apart. The house of cards would come tumbling down. Elise's life, and his carefully planned future with her, would end.

One drizzly, spring afternoon, Elise found Tom in his office reading a contract. "Tom, I had a call from my friend, Catherine. She's going through a difficult time right now. I told her I'd go and stay with her for a while. She desperately needs a friend to lean on right now."

Putting his paperwork down, Tom stared incredulously at her. "No, I need you here."

"Don't say that. And don't look at me like that!" Elise said, her shaking voice giving away her frustration. "Some time apart would be good for both of us. Why don't you go see Cassie? You could use some time away from here, too. It's been a long time since you've been anywhere other than for business." Seeing the wall go up, she spat her words at Tom. "I need to get away! This house is beginning to feel like a prison."

The inevitable happened. The flash of revulsion in her eyes was painful. Tom looked away. The seeds of doubt were sprouting and growing, spreading like a malignancy. He knew he could no longer trust her.

"Please, Tom, let me go. I'll only be gone three or four weeks. I promise I'll call you every day. Let me go."

Tom refused, knowing if she left, she might never come back to him. He cut off her credit making sure she had no money or access to money. He made certain she couldn't afford to leave him. He intercepted her mail and monitored her phone calls. He did, for all practical purposes, in fact make her a prisoner. If she did leave the house, he was at her side, watching her every move, orchestrating her every outing. He let her know, if she left him, he would make sure she was penniless. "I control you, dear. That's how it is. Wealth, after all, has its advantages," he told her.

How could he do this to her? He was making her hate him more every day. Why didn't he let her go? But somehow, Tom *could* not, *would* not. He convinced himself that she would learn to love him again, given time.

And so Elise came to believe the only way to free herself from Tom's control was through death. Her own. But her hatred for him would not die so easily, would tie her to this earth.

Chapter 23

Tom paced the veranda, a half-empty bottle of vodka in his hand. Wind blew the rain sideways into the porch, soaking through his heavy fisherman's sweater. Silently he pleaded for forgiveness for what he had done to Elise, though he knew in his heart, it was not to be. He had punished Elise for not loving him, and now she would punish him for destroying her.

As a flash of lightening lit the night sky, Elise appeared in the doorway, pale and fragile, wisps of golden hair gently blowing across her face. She smiled sweetly at Tom.

Her smile melted his heart. Slowly, not taking his eyes off her delicate form, Tom began walking toward her, reaching out to take her in his arms. He pulled her to him—his arms met empty air. Behind him, shrill peals of laughter cut through the air. He whirled around. There was no one there. "Elise!" he screamed. "Elise!" Her laughter echoed, chilled his soul.

Tom ran into the darkened house, trying to escape her maniacal laughter. In the corner of the room, he saw her. She sat at the piano. Softly she began playing Beethoven's *Für Elise,* repeating the same refrain again and again, each note a mockery of their love. All the while she watched him, staring unblinking into his eyes, smiling gently, sweetly beckoning him to her side. But he did not go to her. He stood frozen, unable to move. Elise threw her head back and howled; then she was gone. Silence filled the room. Tom could see his breath, like puffs of moisture, ballooning out in the frigid, dark room.

The phone rang, jarred him back to his senses. With a shaking hand, he lifted the receiver.

"Tom? It's Sara. Hello? . . . Are you there?"

"Sara?" he whispered.

"Yes. Is something wrong? I can barely hear you."

"I need you. Come right away," Tom said and hung up. The second he placed the receiver on the cradle, the phone rang again. He didn't answer it.

Tom waited for Sara on the front steps. It was raining harder now, the temperature was dropping rapidly. But Tom didn't feel the cold. On this stormy night, Tom, finally— without a doubt— knew his enemy. And more importantly—he knew he no longer loved Elise—was no longer *willing* to love her. He also recognized, with an inevitable sense of horror, that Elise would make him pay for his change of heart. *Go ahead and try. I've done my suffering. I've paid the price for loving you. It must end. Damn you, Elise, it will end!*

Sara—out of breath, soaked, hair plastered to her head— ran up the porch stairs to Tom. Inside the house the telephone continued ringing. Sara's hand trembled as she reached to touch Tom's face. He said nothing, closing his eyes at the gentle touch of her hand. "What is it? What's wrong, Tom?"

He took her hand, led her into the living room and guided her to the couch. They sat for a moment looking at each other. The phone continued ringing, the sound shrill and eruptive in the dark, lonely night. There were no lights; the only illumination came from the glowing coals in the fire. The phone stopped ringing.

Tom awkwardly fumbled with the buttons of Sara's wet coat. Taking it off, he dropped it carelessly onto the floor. He took a bottle of brandy from the liquor cabinet. Removing the glass stopper, he took a long swig and then offered it to Sara. "Glass?" She shook her head, took the decanter from him.

They passed it back and forth several times. The alcohol began to warm Tom as it spread though his body, to his arms and neck. Gradually, he started to relax. The phone rang again. Tom had no intention of answering it.

"Tom, aren't you going to answer it? It must be important if whoever it is keeps calling. It might be Vivian. I left without telling her where I was going." Realizing Tom was not going to pick up the phone, Sara did. "Hello?" There was no one there.

As soon as Sara hung up, it rang again. This time Tom picked it up. The sound of shrill laughter resounded from the receiver. After a moment, the recorded voice of the operator could be heard saying, "If you would like to make a call, please hang up and place your call again." Tom replaced the receiver.

"Tom, I'm waiting for an explanation. You scared me to death tonight. What's going on?" Sara demanded.

He took another drink of brandy while he decided what to say. The last thing Tom wanted to do was make her angry.

Sara watched him, pursing her lips and twisting her hair around her finger, her foot tapped impatiently on the floor. "Well?"

Tom took a deep breath and said, "Sara, I know we haven't known each other very long. It seems unbelievable, because it feels like I've known you for a very long time. There's a connection I feel with you that I've never had with anyone before." He paused and waited for her reaction. She remained stoic. He continued. "There are things you don't know, couldn't know, about me." He took another sip of the liquor and passed the bottle to Sara. She put it to her lips, not taking her eyes off of him. A flash of lightening lit the room followed by the resounding boom of thunder; the storm was on top of them. Sara started to speak; Tom put his finger to her lips saying, "No, let me go on."

Tom said softly, "When I held you earlier today, the void in me was filled. For the first time in years, I felt whole. I thought my reason for living was gone, and then today, I realized that maybe I had another chance at happiness. With you. I'm falling in love with you, Sara."

Another lightning flash lit the room. Sara's eyes filled with tears. She smiled and reached her hand to take his. He drew her into his arms, felt her kiss like the soft petal of a rose on his lips and tasted her tears, salty and cleansing like ocean mist. "Sara, stay with me tonight, I need you. Let me make love to you."

As Sara caught her breath and started to speak, the phone rang, startling them both. "Answer it, Tom." Sara handed the receiver to Tom. "It must be important."

It was Vivian. "Tom, is Sara with you? I'm so worried. She left and didn't tell anyone where she was going."

"She's here, Vivian. I had a small accident and needed her help."

"What? Let me grab a coat. I'll be right there. Have Sara meet me halfway; I hate walking in the dark. It's raining cats and dogs again; I better get Billy to come with me."

Tom interrupted. "Hold on, Vivian, I'm fine. Nothing serious, just a fall down the stairs in the dark." Sara pulled on his sleeve. "Sara wants to talk to you." He handed the phone to her outstretched hand.

"Stay home, Viv. The storm is horrible. I don't want you falling on the slick rocks. The upper path is way too muddy to use. I'll wait out the storm here. Tom will be fine, he just . . . "

Tom pointed to his knee.

" . . . twisted his knee. Don't worry. I'll be home when the storm passes, don't wait up."

"Well, if you're sure. I hate to go out in this weather. And I had my hair done this afternoon, too. I'm sure you have everything under control. You call me if you need anything. Wake me when you get home."

"I wouldn't think of waking you, Viv. I know you need your rest. See you tomorrow." Sara hung up the phone. It immediately rang again. She lifted the receiver. Dead air. "Tom, what in the world is going on with the phone?"

Unplugging it, Tom said, "Must be from the storm."

"You fell down the stairs? Is that why you told me to come over when I called earlier? Because you were hurt?" She studied his face. "There's more to this, isn't there? If you want our relationship to go anywhere, you can't keep things from me. Did something happen? Does it have to do with all these phone calls?"

"I didn't fall. And yes, the phone calls have something to do with all of this but . . . I have so much to explain to you. Trust me, Sara, tonight is not the right time."

Sara squeezed his hand. "What is it?"

"I have some issues I'm still dealing with, having to do with my wife's death. I want to talk to you about her, but not tonight. Can you accept that?"

"Tom, I'm sorry. I had no idea. No one told me. Of course I'll give you time. But you have to trust me, too."

"Elise's death has been a difficult and painful ordeal. I'll tell you everything. In time. In my own way. I promise. But I'm not ready yet." Tom put his arms around Sara, pulled her to him. "Now, will you stay with me, or do you want me to take you home?"

"Of course I'll stay, Tom. I want to be with you, too."

Taking her hand in his, Tom led her up the stairs and into his bedroom. He removed her muddy clothes, slowly without urgency. Sara stood before him, skin white as lily petals, soft as velvet to his touch. He lifted her into his arms, surprised at the lightness of her. He carried her across the room to the bed where he gently laid her on the blankets.

As she watched, he removed his own clothes, then lay beside her, relishing the warmth of her skin next to his as his thighs touched her thighs, his chest melted into her breasts. As their lips met, they forgot all else, save their passion.

Chapter 24

With dawn comes the sound of the awakening earth. The ritual of transition from dark of night to light of day begins. Birds sing, welcoming the amber orb of sun as it rises above the horizon. Today's is truly a magnificent sunrise. Even the pounding of the waves on the beach seems more serene this daybreak. Dawn is a peaceful time. A time of gentle quiet. A time to ponder the wonders of nature. . . . For some.

In the upstairs hall of Remington House, the rooms are still dark; the light of morning has not yet penetrated here. The disquieting shuffle of footsteps can be heard pacing back and forth, back and forth. As the sun begins to cast its light into the attic, we see a woman, slight of stature, delicate of feature, pale as mist. She paces, livid with rage, pounding the air with flailing fists. Her lips are pulled back tightly exposing tiny teeth. Listening, we hear her angry voice spitting out obscenities. As the sun continues its ascent, Elise continues her ravings, vile and bitter. One is shocked to hear such dark words spew from such an exquisite creature.

As we watch quietly, not wanting to disturb her even more, we see two others—a grizzly almost skeletal, old man and a shriveled old woman. They watch Elise from the far side of the hall. Both appear happy to have Elise in their midst. They go to her. Their hands reach out to touch her but are lost in empty air. They smile knowingly to each other. Elise is gone. For now.

Chapter 25

For Tom and Sara, the day dawned clear and quiet. "Morning, Sara. You look ravishing." Tom playfully pulled the covers off Sara.

Sara rolled on top of Tom. "Definitely too early to get out of bed. Good morning, my love."

They made love again. From overhead, Tom thought he heard the creaking of floorboards. Feeling Sara's caresses to his thighs and buttocks, he put the sounds out of his mind and concentrated on Sara's demands to his quickly responding body.

After they made love, as they lay together watching the sun continue its morning ascent, Sara turned to Tom. "I better get back to Vivian's before anyone notices I've been gone all night. I don't think I'm up for the third degree. I don't want anything to spoil our night together."

Tom watched sullenly as she walked naked across the room. "Do you really have to go? I think we can explain to Vivian that this is what we both want. We're all adults, after all. I don't see any reason you can't stay. At least have breakfast with me." Tom followed her across the room.

"Tom, you don't know Vivian. She wouldn't understand how we can feel this way, this soon. We need to be realistic." Sara continued dressing. Tom tried to pull her back toward the bed. "Now, stop. I have to go, Tom." She teasingly stroked his face, then pretended to fight him off as he carried her back to bed.

Tom gently tossed her to the bed and removed the clothes she had just put on. "Not yet. You can't go yet," said Tom.

They said their goodbyes on the front porch. Sara kissed Tom then ran down the stairs and disappeared into the trees. She took the back path to Vivian's hoping no one would see her.

A car came up the drive, taking the final curve just as Sara ducked into the trees. Tom watched the car as it stopped in front of him. A middle-aged woman got out, smiling as she held her hand out to him. Tom had no idea who she was. "Hello, are you lost? Can I be of some help?" he asked.

"Oh goodness, no. Mr. Gardner? I'm Nellie. Nellie Swenson." Seeing he was still unsure about who she was, she added, "I was hired to cook and clean. Joe Tilson called me yesterday. He said you approved my hiring."

"Of course. Yes. Come in please. I'd forgotten you were coming today." Tom held the door open for her.

"What a lovely home. I haven't been in here in years. Not since before the Lindemans bought the house."

"Well, ah... Miss Swenson? Let me show you around."

"Call me Nell. Everyone does. And it's Mrs., although my husband died many years ago. Look at this huge kitchen. What a joy this will be." She smiled at Tom, her eyes crinkling at the corners.

Another happy soul. Must be the sea air. Seemed like all the locals were happy. Maybe it'd rub off on Tom. "Glad you approve. Trust me, for the next few weeks, you'll be very pleased you have this much space. My sister, Cassie, loves to cook, too, so she will no doubt be in here shadowing your every move." Tom turned. Joe was coming up the back steps.

"Hey, Nell," Joe said. "I see you've met Tom." Joe entered the kitchen carrying a box of Nell's spices. "I'll set these here on the counter. Be right back, gonna get the other bags of stuff from Nell's car. Morning, Tom. You look pretty chipper this morning. Hope the sea air is starting to work its magic."

"Something like that, Joe. Can you show Nell around? I need to make a couple of calls, then I'll be back."

"Glad to."

Later that afternoon, as it was getting dark, Tom called Sara and asked her to meet him at the bottom of the beach stairs. He waited for a while, throwing stones into the choppy water.

Tom thought he heard someone call his name. He looked around, but saw no one. Picking up another stone, he hurled it far out into the water, watched it splash as it hit. A few minutes later Sara came running down the long stretch of sand toward him. They hugged. Sara was shivering from the cold sea air. They huddled for a few moments, finding warmth in each other's arms. Tom had brought a blanket and a thermos of hot cider. They gathered driftwood and built a small fire. They sat quietly, lost in their own thoughts. Tom held Sara's hands in his large ones until they were finally warm.

"What are you thinking about, Sara?"

She didn't look at Tom when she answered. "About your sister. I hope she'll understand about us. I mean, you came here to get over one relationship, and now here I am. I want her to like me. I know she's very important to you. Maybe it's best if we keep our relationship quiet for the time being.

"No! You're wrong. Cassie will love you because I love you. Trust me, Sara. I know Cassie. When she sees how happy I am, she'll love you, too. Now stop worrying."

Sara turned to Tom, smiling. "Okay, you're probably right. I want everything to go well. I'm so happy, Tom." Sara stood up. The moon spread a golden aura across the ocean. The evening was still, the only sound that of the breaking waves.

Tom pulled her to him, kissed her upturned face. "Oh, yes. I'm a very happy man. Come on. Let's go for a walk. When you meet Cassie, you'll see how ridiculous it is to worry about her." He pulled her by the hand. Laughing, they raced along the beach trying to stave off the cold wind blowing in from the east.

Chapter 26

In the half-light of twilight, the softening dusk of evening transformed the harsh landscape, metamorphosing harsh rocky cliffs into orange-tinged velvet walls. Shadowy crevices turned to rich earth-brown pallets lush with moss. Sparkling water-diamonds shimmered above the beach as the tiny droplets flew into the air, tossed high from the crashing waves pounding the shore.

Transfixed, Elise watched Tom skipping stones into the high water. Even from this distance, she heard his carefree laughter echoing off the cliffs as he retreated hastily from the crashing, ice-cold waves, running backwards—almost, but never quite—falling and getting pounded by the frigid swells.

***

To the casual observer, one would think this lovely young woman, standing too close to the cliff's edge, was enjoying the scene below. Surely she was watching her lover or her husband with a proud and joyous heart. This lovely young woman, pale blonde curls blowing carelessly in the wind, teeth glistening like pearls in the last light before dark, must be smiling and full of life—like the man she watches. But, one would only be imagining this. Because, in fact, this creature has a heart of stone. If one could look into her soulless, wicked eyes, one would probably turn and run for his very life.

***

Elise, furious beyond reason, suddenly calmed. Something amazing happened. In this collision of day and night, this wonderful twilight time, she found strength, felt a power rising, pressing hard into her throat—at first almost choking her, and then flowing easily through her whole being. A power she had never before experienced. On this glorious night she had found a way to make all her plans move ahead. She knew how to find strength. *Twilight.*

"Tom," she shouted, then quickly silenced her voice. Now was not the time. She'd deal with him later. There was somewhere else she needed to go now. She laughed silently as Tom searched the cliff's edge to see who had called him.

Chapter 27

Peering out the living room window, Vivian noticed Billy walking along the beach. At his side was a woman. Vivian couldn't tell from this distance who she was. Maybe it was one of the Larson's daughters, here for the winter break.

Actually the woman with Billy looked too old to be one of the Larson girls though, even from this distance. Something about her movements—the way she was leading Billy, showed more self-assurance and control than that of one of the Larson girls. She'd talk to him later, she thought, as the doorbell chimed. Right now she had more important things to take care of.

Vivian looked forward to her appointment with the masseur her friend Mila was sending over. Mila had booked the session with Kenneth weeks ago. He was in great demand, and as Vivian opened the door to greet him, she knew why. *Oh, yes, this would be a lovely evening.*

"Hi! You must be Kenneth. I'm Vivian. Come in." She took his arm and led him up the stairs to her room. Yes, she'd talk to Billy later. She had more important things on her mind right now.

***

On the shore, the young woman walked slowly beside Billy. She led him away from the water's edge toward the cliff. He followed without hesitation.

"So you know Mr. Gardner?" Billy asked. "That's funny. He moved here a couple of weeks ago, too."

"Small world. He and I crossed paths once—for a while. He was very interested in me. It wasn't mutual. The relationship didn't go well. It's really an odd coincidence that he's here. I hope you'll let this be our little secret. I'm here to get away from just about everyone and everything. Tom Gardner can't know I'm here," the beautiful young woman said with a sweet smile. She took Billy's hand and brought it to her cheek. "I fear for my safety if he finds out. No one can know about me. Only you. Okay, Billy? Promise?"

"Sure, no problem. I get it," he agreed, feeling his face flush as she squeezed his hand. He managed a weak smile, trying to hide his embarrassment. He was so happy to have her holding his hand. There was no way would he do anything to jeopardize this friendship. Who knew where this might lead?

Elise dropped his hand, running ahead of him up the beach. She disappeared behind a rocky cliff jutting out into the sandy shore. Billy raced after her. *How did she get there so fast?*

Chapter 28

From the stairway leading to the beach, Jimmy watched Billy, glad to be rid of his annoying big brother. Smiling, he hopped off the landing into the soft sand and headed to Mr. Gardner's house. He had another piano lesson tonight. His mom had plans this evening, so he and Tom were fitting in an extra session. Now he didn't have to worry about Billy following him. Further down the beach he saw Mr. Gardner with his cousin Sara. Waving, Jimmy ran to meet them.

Sara said, "Tom, I think I'll take this opportunity to spend some time with Mary. She's helping Nell. I'm sure Nell would like to get home before it gets too late. Do you mind?"

"Not at all. See you after Jimmy's lesson."

Jimmy noticed how Tom smiled at Sara, and how he didn't take his eyes off of her as she walked away. Sara must have been happy; she took the beach steps two at a time. She disappeared from sight when she reached the top and began the walk up the path to Tom's house.

Tom took Jimmy's hand and the two, almost like father and son, climbed slowly up the beach stairs, shivering in the chill air as the sun dropped lower on the horizon. It would be dark soon. They hurried toward the warmth of the house. They set about building a fire in the living room fireplace and then Jimmy warmed up on the grand piano, limbering his fingers running through several sets of scales from the workbook.

Jimmy was making strides and gaining self-confidence. Tom was pleased he could nurture and support the boy. He was a great kid. Jimmy's dad still hadn't been able to tie up his business and join his family in Ravenswood. Tom enjoyed his time with Jimmy and was not particularly looking forward to having William Harrison show up and take over his fatherly duties. Well, he'd deal with that when he had to.

Chapter 29

On Friday, Sara and Tom decided to escape the hustle and bustle at their respective houses and have lunch in town at the Raven Café. They were charmed by the quaint atmosphere. Antique teapots and hand painted crockery were displayed on baker's shelves of stressed, milk-washed wood. Each table was covered with a paisley tablecloth of varying shades of violet and cream. Matching napkins and chunky white pottery vases filled with simple bouquets of fresh pansies adorned the tables. Black and white striped wallpaper covered walls that were hung with ornate silver-framed mirrors that reflected the outside winter landscape of bare trees, every branch covered with ravens.

"Guess I know how the town got its name." Tom smiled at Sara, pointing at the branches covered with ravens.

"Wow, look at those beautiful birds. I read that ravens are considered to be a good omen. The native Indians believed the souls of their ancient ones came back in the bodies of the ravens. They even had a ceremony in the fall, on the beach below the town, and adorned themselves with black paint and feathers. They lit huge bonfires and danced around the fire performing a drumming ritual.

"Sheep were slaughtered, their blood drained, then the natives drank it in hollowed out gourds. Thousands of birds would fly in from the surrounding woods to watch the ceremony. The meat from the sheep was offered to the ravens to feast on. This was the Indians' way of keeping the souls of their ancestors at peace, insuring that the ancestors would watch over the tribe during the hard winter ahead." Sara stared out the window at the blackbirds across the way. "Very poignant." She picked up her wine glass, raised it to the birds. "To the ravens of Ravenswood. May their souls be at peace. Cheers." She made an ugly face at Tom, pretended to choke on the wine.

Tom took a sip of his wine. Imitating Count Dracula's voice he said, "Ahh, blood. Good to the last drop."

The waitress appeared at the table. Clearing her throat to get their attention and trying not to laugh, she asked, "Ready to order?" She stared at Tom. "Are you Tom Gardner?"

"I am," he said.

"Thought I recognized you. I love your boutiques. Are you here to open one?"

Caught off guard, Tom swallowed his wine and answered, "No, I hadn't thought about opening a store here. But, hmm, now that you mention it, you may be on to something. I live here now. Bought a house outside of town. You are . . . ?"

"Joanie. Wow! You live here? That's fantastic. It'd sure be cool if you opened one of your boutiques in Ravenswood. They'd be very popular. There aren't any stores that carry your clothing line anywhere near here." She saw her manager giving her the evil eye and quickly said, "We have two specials today. The soup of the day is clam chowder, and our entree today is cod fillet with sautéed rice and mushrooms. Are you ready to order?"

The two ordered the specials. As soon as the waitress was out of earshot, Sara turned excitedly to Tom. "What boutique? What's that about, Tom?"

"Guess it never came up. One of my family's businesses are the Alexa's Boutiques. They're named after my grandmother."

"I've heard of them. Wow! Tell me more."

Tom continued, "Grandmother had the concept for the store, was even the original clothes designer. She died years ago, but the stores were always very profitable, so my dad kept them going. The hotels are my pride and joy, though. Of the two of us, Cassie's the most involved in the boutiques. They're her babies. And I prefer the financial side of the operations, hands down."

"Cassie must be quite a businesswoman. And very talented," said Sara.

"She is," said Tom. "She studied fashion design at the New Haven Art Institute. She deals with most of the conceptualizing and designing of our line. She used to do a majority of the designs herself, but she's had to cut back a bit since she married and started a family."

"I can't wait to meet her. She sounds fascinating. You must be very proud to have her involved in the business with you."

"I am. I make sure the finances are straight, she does the hard work. The fashion business is very competitive, but it's proven to be worthwhile. Cassie knows the market."

The waitress brought their soup, offering her brightest smile to Tom as she set the bowls in front of them. "Would either of you care for hot bread?"

"No, just crackers for me," said Tom. Sara nodded in agreement. "Joanie, this soup is fantastic. Give the chef our compliments."

A few minutes later Joanie brought their entrees and poured them more coffee. Tom and Sara ate and talked, enjoying getting to know each other. Watching Sara, Tom realized how easy it was to be with her. Not only that but, as he watched her eyes, her lips, heard her words flow and wrap around him, he knew he was in love with her. He thought she might be feeling the same for him. Reaching for her hand lying on the table, he was taken aback when she moved away.

"Oh, no! Don't look now, but there goes Vivian. Duck!" Sara whispered as she slouched down in her chair. Vivian, riding in Joe's taxi, drove slowly down the street. "Good! She didn't see us. Whew! I wonder where she's going? It's odd she'd leave the house this early in the day. Must be meeting someone for lunch." She glanced at Tom. "I'm awful aren't I?"

"You are, but I don't mind!"

Sara giggled as she put the last bite of cod into her mouth. "Mmm, delicious. Now I recommend a piece of their famous cherry pie for dessert. Sound good?" Tom nodded, reached across the table and wiped a crumb of breading off her lip. She smiled, taking his hand in hers.

***

Vivian looked around the nearly empty streets hoping no one would see her. She was on a mission and had made it very clear to Joe that no one was to know that she had used his services today. As far as her household was concerned, she had a headache and was in her room sleeping, not to be disturbed. This errand would not take long. She knew her absence would not be discovered.

"Joe, please pull over at the next building. I'll be back in about half an hour. Go get a cup of coffee or something. I'll call you when I'm ready for a ride."

"Okay, think I'll do that," Joe said, pulling over and parallel parking in front a small, red- brick office building. Its windows were barred with ornate, black wrought-iron and shaded with kelly-green awnings. Stone lions guarded either side of the walnut-stained door. A shiny brass mailbox hung to the right. Below that was a brass doorbell. An oak sign, with the names Kranston and Rivers engraved in black, hung from a wrought iron hanger.

Joe got out of the taxi and opened the door for Vivian. She walked across the sidewalk to the door and pulled to open it. It was locked. She rang the bell, then impatiently tapped her knuckles on the window of the door. A well-dressed man, whom Joe had never seen before, opened the door, smiled and ushered Vivian inside.

***

Joe headed over to the Raven Café for a piece of pie and cup of coffee. He sat at a small table in front of the window so he'd be able to see Vivian when she came out and to be able to see if anyone else came or went from the office. "Afternoon, Joanie. Just coffee and a piece of blueberry pie. Hey, any idea what that new office down the street is about? There are a couple of names on the door but nothing else."

"I don't have a clue, Joe. Let me get you your pie, and I'll check with Mr. Thorn—see if he knows. They moved in last week. I've seen a couple of men go in and out, business suit types, but that's all I know. Be right back." Joanie returned with a huge slice of warm blueberry pie and a cup of coffee. "Fresh out of the oven. Enjoy, Joe." She smiled at him. "Be right back. I'll go ask Mr. Thorn about the new business."

Joe always suspected Joanie was attracted to him. She was a cute girl but a bit young for him, he thought. A little on the wild side too, from what he'd heard. It was nice to be fussed over though. He was lonely since Anna left him and was glad that he'd met Tom. Glad he had plenty of work to keep him busy and tide him over this winter. That reminded him, he better get to Len's today—see if he could order the workout and boxing equipment for Tom's basement gym. That would be quite a project—a very good idea. He was eager to tackle it.

"Joe?" Joanie interrupted his thoughts. "Mr. Thorn said the place is an importing business—diamonds and gemstones. He thinks Mr. Harrison probably owns it—just a guess on his part."

"Makes sense," Joe said.

"Yeah. Mr. Harrison does all that importing stuff. Mr. Thorn said he met the owners but they offered little information about themselves or the business. In such a small town, it won't be long before we all know everything there is to know about it. When I hear more, do you want me to call you or something?"

"Sure. You're right though, in a week or two we'll know all about them. Not a big deal, just being nosy. Small towns bring that out in all of us, huh?"

"Joe. Didn't expect to run into you here," Tom said walking up to Joe's table. "Sara and I just finished lunch. Very good, I might add. Thought you were under Nell's thumb for the day."

"Had a fare. Thank God. That Nell's a slave driver. She and her nieces are a force to reckon with. But I won't be in town long. You guys headed home?"

"Not for a while. We have some shopping to do before Cassie and Michael get here. We saw you had Vivian in your

cab. Don't tell her you saw us. Okay? Sara and I wanted some private time." Tom smiled a bit uneasily.

Sara asked Joe, "Where did you take her? I was surprised to see her in town at all. Especially alone. What's she up to?"

"Not a clue. But be forewarned—Vivian told me I was to tell no one she came to town. As far as anyone knows, she's at home. You didn't see her. You didn't see me. Okay?"

"Very mysterious. My dear cousin, what is she up to now?" Sara asked. "What time are you picking her up? We better be careful so we don't run into her."

"She said half an hour. So about another fifteen minutes. You two better beat it before she shows up. You'll get us all in trouble."

"Where is she?" Tom asked.

"Down the street." Joe pointed. "You two should head uptown," Joe said, putting the last bite of pie on his fork. "Need me to come back and pick you up later? How'd you get here anyhow?"

"Borrowed Nell's car. We don't require your services today, my man." Tom laughed, took Sara's arm and the two left, quickly ducking into The Hallowed Ground, a gourmet coffee shop.

Chapter 30

Vivian examined the brilliant diamond, its intricately chiseled facets gleaming in the light from the chandelier hanging from the ceiling above the table. "It's perfect. I have to have this. It's simply exquisite." Vivian put the stone down on the black velvet pad and looked boldly at the gentleman standing to her right.

The attractive man wore an expensive black, pinstriped Armani suit with a white silk shirt and black calfskin Gucci shoes. A black tie with a single diamond tie tack and white gold cufflinks at his cuffs completed his ensemble. Vivian was impressed by his appearance, as of course she was supposed to be. Anthony Rivers knew how to look the part of a successful diamond broker.

"It's a perfect diamond, Mrs. Harrison." He gave her his loop for a better examination. "Would you like to see the stones we've cut for the accents?" He didn't wait for her response but opened a small, velvet pouch. He poured a dozen smaller baguette cut stones next to the larger, single gem. "Fantastic aren't they? Also the same perfect quality and clarity. I have all the papers here for you to examine as well. These are from the same mine as your last diamond, the one you had set in the cocktail ring with the pink sapphires. Best quality I've found for some time. What do you think? Shall I show you more?"

Vivian's face lit up as she caressed the diamonds lying in front of her. "No, I've made up my mind. I've never seen such a unique cut. This is the one I want," Vivian said. "Set with the baguette-cut stones."

"Let me show you the designer's drawings. I have several renditions for you to choose from, each exclusive of course." He opened a leather portfolio and extracted several drawings. "I think we can do either of the first two necklaces quite easily here in our studio, but the last two designs would take several weeks. We don't have the mountings here, yet. We expect another delivery, but not until after Thanksgiving."

"I'd like to have it as soon as possible. This necklace is perfect." She handed Anthony one of the drawings. "And of course, I must have the earrings, too. When will you have them ready for me?"

"Would next Friday morning be agreeable?" Anthony asked studying the sketch. "I have to check the availability of my jeweler." But he knew it wouldn't be a problem. No matter what other work Caesar had lined up, for the right price, he'd accommodate Anthony.

"I'll pay you in cash. My husband is not to know about this." Her smile gone, she stared icily at Anthony. "This is just between us. Do you understand?"

"Certainly. As you wish, Mrs. Harrison. Shall we discuss the price before you leave?"

"I'll pay you twenty-five thousand dollars. That's a fair price. Don't you agree?" Vivian asked as she began putting her tan, wool coat on. From her suede bag she pulled an envelope and handed it to him. "I'll give you a deposit today of ten thousand dollars. I'll call you in a week. Don't call me. Do you understand?"

"Of course." Anthony wasn't sure what was wrong with Vivian. In the ten or so years he'd known her, he'd never experienced that tone of voice or her rude demeanor. She was almost like a stranger. If he hadn't known better, he'd think she was 'on' something. Her voice sounded harsh; her eyes were glassy. What was going on with her?

"Oh, get that look off your face. My money's good here, isn't it? Can't a woman buy her own jewelry without you men feeling all pussy-whipped for heaven's sake?"

A very surprised Anthony watched her leave the store.

"I'll be in touch," she said as she pulled the heavy door shut behind her.

After getting into the cab, she called Joe. "I'm waiting in the cab, Joe. Hurry up."

"I'll be right there." He handed Joanie a ten. "Keep the change. I'm in a hurry." He took long strides and was at the car in minutes. Opening the door, he asked Vivian, "Where do you want me to take you now, Mrs. Harrison?"

She looked completely bewildered. "Joe? What's going on? Where am I?" Her hand trembled as she grabbed his arm.

"Are you okay, Mrs. Harrison? You hired me to bring you to town. You told me not to tell anyone either. I dropped you off in front of that building across the street." He pointed to the office of Kranston and Rivers. "Did something happen? Should I call Sara?"

"Why in the world would I want you to call Sara? Get in, Joe. I need to get home. Now! Get this piece of junk you call a car moving."

Joe got in, started the car and hit the gas. Vivian's face reflected in the rear view mirror. Joe was amazed. She was smiling. *She's going psycho on me.* He'd warn Sara next time he saw see her. The woman needed therapy. He gunned the car and sped down the street. He wanted her out of his cab as soon as possible and, if it meant getting a speeding ticket, fine.

When they neared the driveway to the Harrison property, Vivian said, "Let me out by the side of the house where you picked me up. Remember, this is our secret, Joe. Here's a little something extra—so you don't forget." She handed him a fifty dollar bill. "And this is for the ride." She handed him another fifty.

"Keep it, Mrs. Harrison. Don't need it. I told you I wouldn't tell anyone I took you to town. I always keep my word." She took back one of the fifties, refused the second. Joe wanted to tell her that her secret was already out, but he wouldn't. Sara and Tom didn't need the aggravation.

Vivian looked quickly around making certain no one would see her. She opened the door slowly, then ran up the back stairs and into her room. After throwing her purse and coat into her closet she lay down on the bed and closed her eyes.

Half an hour later, Vivian woke up. She looked around, puzzled. Something didn't seem right. A vague memory of being in Joe's taxi surfaced. Just a dream. At least her headache was gone. She got up and went to see what her sons were doing.

Chapter 31

The next several days were spent in preparation for the arrival of Tom's family. Mary Stevens was helping Nell and Nell's two nieces, Linda and Gwenn, with some general cleaning. Windows needed washing. Furniture needed rearranging. Floors needed waxing. A household of chores needed to be done so Cassie could relax when she got here. Tom knew

Cassie well—if anything needed doing, she would take over. He didn't want that, he wanted her to have a restful vacation. Besides, Nell and the girls had happily stepped up.

While the women took care of the inside, Tom and Joe worked together on the outside, a needed break for Tom. "Heard any more from Nate?" Joe asked, his ax poised in midair as he prepared to chop more wood.

"Yeah, I talked to him last night. I guess he's not going to make it up here for at least a few weeks. Until he can get around easily, he's going to stay in Jamestown and work from our office there."

"Sounds reasonable. You said your attorney is there, too?"

"Yes, his office is there but it's on a different floor of the Werner Building. It'll actually be good for me not to have to deal with the businesses very much while Cassie's here. I'd like to relax with her and her family for a while. I'd like to spend some time planning the remodel. I want to get the gym built and start plans for remodeling the third floor. Think you have enough time to supervise the work, Joe?"

"You bet. Timing's perfect for me. What are you planning for the upstairs?" Joe asked. "I don't think you mentioned that before."

"I'd like to put an office up there. And Nate will need space for his living quarters. I was thinking there's enough room that we can have a guest suite for Cassie and Michael when they visit. I hope she'll like it here and want to come often, kind of a home-away-from-home. Michael travels a lot, so it would make sense that she could have part of the upstairs to call her own. We'll see. Either way, I want to make it pretty comfortable in the attic. Think we can get it done by late spring? Then maybe Cassie could stay up there this summer."

"Shouldn't be a problem," Joe said. "I'll get with Walt James; he's an architect I used in New York. He loves old houses. He's the most knowledgeable and experienced guy I know. He's the one we need to draw up the attic plans. Maybe we can get him out here after the holiday. I'll give him a call."

Joe brought the ax down with a *whoosh*, splitting the wood effortlessly.

Tom picked up the pieces and threw them onto the pile. "Mind if I give it a try?"

Joe handed him the ax. Tom raised the blade. Making an arc over his head, he quickly swung the ax down into the log, grinning as the wood flew onto the ground in two perfect pieces. "Always wanted to do that. Very empowering isn't it?"

The men spent several hours chopping and stacking wood. Neither saw Sara come from behind the house. She hollered and waved to get their attention. "You guys sure are working hard. I'm impressed. There's enough wood cut to last for months. Tom, I need to talk to you."

"I'll finish up here," Joe said, slamming the ax blade into a log. "Go on. I have to get back to town in a while. I'll see you later this afternoon."

"What's up?" Tom asked, taking Sara's hand in his.

"I wanted to talk to you about Jimmy. Billy's giving him such a hard time, worse than usual. His friend Alan was going to come for the week, but he changed his mind. Billy is seething. I wondered if you could find anything for Jimmy to do around here to get him away from his brother. Vivian always sides with Billy. So unfair."

"What about their dad? Isn't he supposed to be here?"

"He was, but I guess he isn't even going to make it for Thanksgiving. So there's nothing much going Jimmy's way right now," Sara said. "His dad, when he's around, is fair and doesn't take sides, but he's hardly been around these past few months. In fact, Vivian said William left for Amsterdam this morning. She doesn't know when he'll be back."

"Cassie's daughter might be the solution. She'll be the perfect excuse for Jimmy to hang out here. She's eight, so they should have a lot in common. Lizzie is an only child—having someone to play with will be her dream come true. They'll be here tomorrow night. How's that sound?"

"I'm sure that will be great. But I meant today. Jimmy is miserable. Anything you could have him do around here?"

"Hey, Joe?" Tom hollered. "Any chance you could use a hand this afternoon? Jimmy needs to get away from Billy and his mom." Tom and Sara crossed the yard to where Joe was covering the wood stack.

"Hmm. Well I guess he could ride with me into town. Don't have anything for him to do, but he could hang out with me. Think that would be okay?"

Sara hugged Joe. "Let me call him. I bet he'll be thrilled. He likes you so much. Thanks, Joe." She made a phone call on her cell. "Vivian said yes!"

After Jimmy and Joe had gone, Sara and Tom made a fire in Tom's study, away from the hustle of the household. "I feel much better now. Thanks for being understanding about Jimmy."

"You have any idea why Vivian's so hard on him?"

"Sadly I do. Or I think I do. Jimmy was unplanned. I think Vivian knew she wasn't cut out for the parenting thing. Billy was a handful, so when she had to take on the responsibility of two kids, it was too much. She loves them, don't get me wrong, but they do interfere tremendously with her social life. And this town seems to bring out the worst in her for some reason. Not much social life here, I guess. With William gone so much, it's a lot for her to have to deal with the boys all the time. She needs constant adoration—which she certainly does not get from her kids."

"What a selfish women. Such a shame for her boys. At least they're lucky to have you to stand up for them." Tom smiled at Sara and brushed a stray hair from her lips. He pulled her to him, and they snuggled contentedly on the sofa. The fire was warm; the afternoon sun was beginning to shine into the room turning the oak paneled walls a soft, golden brown. "What about your family, Sara? Do you have anyone besides Vivian and the boys?"

"No, I was an only child. Both of my parents were killed in an auto accident when I was twenty two."

"I'm so sorry. It must have been very difficult for you." Tom stroked her hair gently.

"Yes, for a long time I didn't know what to do, but I was always very independent—that helped. They left me enough of an inheritance so I was able to complete my college classes at Boston University and earn my teaching degree. I still miss them terribly, of course, but what can I do? We all have our crosses to bear." Tom massaged her neck as she continued.

"I taught English and Math at a private school. But I hated it." She smiled sadly. "I liked teaching, but felt too confined. Living on everyone else's schedule, teaching only what they wanted me to teach, was too regimented for me." She stared into the fire.

"Hold that thought. Let me get something for us to drink," Tom said as he stood up and then disappeared through the doorway. He returned carrying a tray of coffee and muffins. "Mmm. Nell's been baking. Have one." He set the tray on the table in front of them. "Okay, now tell me, how did you go from teaching in a private school to working for Vivian?"

"I asked the school to terminate my contract. I was involved in a . . . situation." She looked nervously at Tom.

"What happened?" he asked.

"I guess you should hear it from me, not Vivian. That way you'll know what really happened. Vivian tends to put her own slant on things. Makes her life more exciting to add as many torrid, if untrue, details that she can.

"I was having an affair with one of the professors at the school." She glanced quickly at Tom. He frowned slightly.

"Go on," he said softly.

"It was a stupid mistake. And apparently I wasn't his first —he had affairs with several other staff members. I didn't know that at the time. Then I heard that he was dating one of my colleagues while he was seeing me. I reacted quite badly, waited to catch them alone together and confront them. The other woman was the school's principal. She was livid. Like me, she had no idea he was seeing us both."

Tom said, "What a mess. Must have been a pretty painful experience. Was he your first love?"

"Oh, I didn't love him, and no, he wasn't my first. I was lonely . . . and bored. I needed some excitement in my life. He was it. I wasn't all that naïve. I should have known better. Anyway, it all blew up. I chose to keep quiet about the principal's affair. In exchange, she agreed to terminate my contract and give me a good recommendation. It was a good reason to leave. I needed a major change in my life." She took Tom's cup from him. "That's about it. Not very pretty, but a mistake I learned from." She poured him another cup of coffee.

"I've made my share of mistakes, too," Tom said. "Well, we can't go back. Have to move forward, don't we?" He reached out, grabbing her hand. "Are you glad you met me, Sara?"

"Yes! You are my knight in shining armor—as trite as that sounds." She giggled. "I'm growing very fond of you, sir! I've even risked the wrath of Vivian to sneak time with you. Seriously, Tom, you are a joy to me."

Chapter 32

Helen and Gabe Lindeman studied the young woman as she slept curled in a blanket on the old bed that had once been a servant's. They smiled at each other, completely delighted. Helen was the first to touch the woman. She thrilled as her hands made contact with the silky hair, as soft and wispy as a child's. She marveled at the golden color, so like her own had been when she was young. Motioning Gabe to come to her side, Helen whispered, "Gabe, come and feel how smooth her skin is. She can't be very old either, maybe thirty, don't you think? Oh, she is lovely. Come dear, see how much she looks like me when I was a girl. Not quite as lovely as I was but lovely nonetheless. Here, feel her soft skin."

Helen took Gabe's withered hand, pushing it down to make contact with the sleeping girl's throat. "Gabe, she's perfect. I knew someone would come to us. Why, she sleeps so soundly, she doesn't even know we're here. Gently, Gabe, touch her lips." Helen carefully drew Gabe's forefinger across Elise's lips. "See, she doesn't mind. Now, touch her eyelashes. See how silky they feel? Kiss them dear. Softly, don't wake her yet. Let's enjoy her for a while, don't you think?" Helen murmured softly as she caressed Elise's cheek.

Gabe leaned over the girl, running his tongue slowly over her eyelids and down her nose. "I think you're right, Helen. She must be the one," he whispered. "We've waited so long for someone to come to us. Our sweet little Elise. We will take such good care of her, won't we dear?" Gabe ran his fingers delicately down her arm to caress her hand, now clenched into a tight fist. "Let's leave her now. No need to wake her. We'll come back later, Helen. She's tired. Come, we have plans to make." The two held hands and vanished, leaving behind the acrid odor of decaying flesh.

Elise screamed. Bringing her hands to her face, she felt her eyelids, her cheeks. The air reeked of dead flesh, the putrid odor lingering in the air. Shivering uncontrollably, she sat up and grabbed an old blanket, managing to pull it around her shoulders in one quick motion. Looking around the attic room, she saw no one. But she knew. They had been here again. She felt the oily marks left by their hands on her face and throat, smelled their stink around her. These were the same spirits she encountered a few days ago.

Elise had the distinct impression they belonged to this house. She pulled the blanket tightly around her. They would have to go. She had no intention of sharing this house with them. She would find out who they are and why they were here —then she'd get rid of them. Somehow. And soon. Before they spoiled her plans for Tom.

***

Restless, Elise left her room and quietly crept down the hallway. The last room to her left was filled with boxes from Tom's Jamestown house. One in particular caught her eye—a box marked "Elise/Personal." Tearing it open, she was joyous to find some of her old possessions. *Funny that Tom kept anything of mine, I'm flattered. And hopeful. Maybe, after all, I'm not forgotten.* For an hour she pored over every item in the box. She gathered some clothing, personal items and books of poetry, hauling them laboriously to the room she claimed as her own—a dusty, cramped room, not much more than an oversized closet. She felt safe there. It was too small to be of use to anyone but her. As she carefully folded her clothing and placed it in a small, two-drawer bureau, she hummed happily.

Helen and Gabe found Elise brushing her hair with her gold-plated hairbrush. She was immediately aware of their presence. Frigid air enveloped her. She shivered, dropped her brush.

Gabe picked it up and started brushing Elise's hair. He smiled at her. In the small vanity mirror, his reflection was faint but powerful. Elise gagged. Gabe's smell was nauseating. He patted her hair, clumsily drawing the bristles through the tangles.

"Gabe!" Helen said. "Your manners, dear! The poor girl is suffocating."

Instantly the air changed, and the delicate smell of roses permeated the room. "There, there, dear. How is that?" Gabe asked. "Introduction time. I'm Gabriel Lindeman, and this lovely woman is my sister, Helen." He continued brushing Elise's hair, pulling the tangles roughly.

"Elise, we're pleased to have you here. But perhaps we should clear a few things up for you," Helen said. "This is our house. Gabe's and mine. We have lived here for a very long time and plan to go on living here. You must know, if you stay, you will abide by our rules. Do you understand that, dear?" Helen stroked Elise's shoulder.

"For the most part, we've left you alone the few last weeks. But to be very honest, we feel you are beginning to intrude," Helen said. "We have our own plans—you're starting to interfere. Perhaps if you could tell us what you want, we could help you and then you could move on. Or," she put her hand on her brother's shoulder, "maybe, you would like to join Gabe and me. We would enjoy that—on our terms of course. It is our home, after all. But we think you could fit in nicely here. With us."

Furious, Elise flailed her arms at the old ones. Her fists met empty air. The two had vanished as quickly as they had appeared. Once again the room filled with the foul scent of decay. Another subtle reminder they had been there. Elise picked up her cherished gold hairbrush, its finish now dull and discolored. "Well, we'll see who stays here. And whose rules we live by. I'm not afraid of you shriveled, old ghouls."

Helen and Gabe heard her of course. "Well, we'll her give her some time to come around. After all, she needs us, doesn't she, Gabe? And if she can't see things our way, well, we'll deal with her when—if —that time comes."

The two, tired and somewhat dejected, silently dragging their feet, retreated to a small, dark room at the back end of the hallway. "Time to rest, Gabe." Helen held her brother's hand affectionately and closed the door.

Chapter 33

"Tom!" Cassie hopped down the metal steps of the train. "Give me a big hug! You look wonderful, big brother."

Tom released Cassie, held her at arm's length. "So do you, Sis. God it's been a long time. I'm so glad you're here."

"Hello, Tom," William said, as he helped his young daughter down to the platform. "Cassie's right. You look well. The ocean air obviously agrees with you." He firmly shook Tom's hand.

Tom exclaimed, "Is that Lizzie? I can't believe how much you've grown, little lady! Come here and give me a big hug." He wrapped his arms around the child and held her tenderly. "I've missed you guys." He smiled at his sister and her husband. "How was the train trip?"

"Long, but relaxing. Beautiful landscape. A perfectly lovely trip," Cassie said looking around the nearly empty station. Old-fashioned, black filigree street lamps lined the platform. Twinkle lights sparkled in barren tree branches. "What a quaint station. I feel like we stepped back to the turn of the century,"

"Whole town's like that. Very old-fashioned. Come on, Joe's waiting for us. Let me help you with the luggage."

"Is Joe the man who's been helping you at Remington?" Michael asked.

"Yeah. He also drives a taxi, one of two in town. Great guy, you'll see." Tom picked up two suitcases and motioned with his head for everyone to follow. Joe came running and took the suitcases Cassie was carrying.

"Joe, this is my sister, Cassie Wellington, her husband, Michael and their daughter, Lizzie."

"Pleased to meet you," Joe said. When they reached the cab, Joe shook hands, then he and Tom loaded the bags into the trunk.

An hour later, after all the luggage had been carried into the house, everyone gathered around the dining table. Nellie brought in trays of hot chocolate, ham sandwiches, potato salad, and chips. Halfway through her sandwich, Lizzie started falling asleep. The second time her chin dropped to her chest Cassie said, "Time to get you to bed, little one. Come on." Cassie led a worn-out Lizzie to the spare bedroom upstairs and tucked her into bed.

"Mama, leave the light on please. Where's Buster?" Cassie handed her the well-worn rabbit. Lizzie snuggled under the down comforter, the blue bunny tucked tightly to her chest.

"Nite, Lizzy. I love you. Sleep tight"

"Nite, Mama."

Leaving the door slightly ajar, Cassie went downstairs. She poured herself a hot cup of coffee before bundling up in her heavy parka and joining her brother and husband who were out on the terrace watching the evening sky. "Truly lovely. You must be so pleased to have found this wonderful old house."

"Without a doubt," Tom said, focusing his binoculars out on the water. "Something's jumping out there." Tom handed the binoculars to Michael. "See if you can figure out what it is."

"The pounding surf's hypnotic isn't it?" Cassie leaned against the porch wall and closed her eyes. "I can practically hear the waves call my name. I read that the ghost of a woman who drowned off the Isle of Westmoor haunts this coast. Maybe it's her that you see." Cassie opened her eyes. "Stop laughing at me. I'm serious. You both know I believe in spirits."

"Tom! I can't believe it." Michael handed the binoculars back to Tom. "Look, Cass is right, it's the ghost of the mermaid." He burst out laughing.

Cassie stuck her tongue out. "Enough abuse! I'm going to bed. Goodnight." Cassie smiled, gave Tom and Michael a peck on their cheeks, then closed the terrace door.

"I love that woman!" Michael said, offering his flask to Tom. "Whisky?"

Chapter 34

Cassie and Mary spent the morning rearranging the furniture in Cassie and Michael's bedroom. Cassie loved the thought of waking up to a view of the Atlantic. What a sinful luxury, pure indulgence for the soul. She smiled at Mary, wishing the young woman was more talkative and comfortable with her. She felt a little out of place. It seemed like everyone here knew everyone else.

Cassie was dying to have a good chat with someone besides her brother. She wasn't used to the silence that seemed to prevail in her brother's house. Besides the constant roar of the ocean, it seemed little else was going on. Oh, well. For today, she'd settle for getting acquainted with everyone.

Cassie asked, "So, what do you do with yourself here in Ravenswood?"

"I work part time at the vet clinic, and I go to the local college. I'm studying veterinarian medicine."

"Wow, that's great. I love animals, too. I guess you have several years of school left then?"

"Yeah, I still have another four years—I won't be going anywhere for a while. I plan on staying here after I graduate. I love it in Ravenswood. The local vet needs a partner, there's no one to take over his practice when he retires, so he plans on working me in."

"Sounds like a solid plan. Good for you." It took several hours to get everything to Cassie's satisfaction. There was still more clothing to be unpacked, but that wouldn't take long. Cassie could tell Mary was beginning to relax and enjoy herself. A special rapport was building between them as they worked side by side.

Mary lifted one of Cassie's brown-suede suitcases onto the bed. "Your husband is so handsome," Mary said.

"You're sweet. He is, isn't he? And wonderful to boot! I can hardly believe we've been married almost twelve years."

"You're lucky. I wish there were more guys around here. Most move to the big city or go away to school. I hope I find someone special someday," Mary said, smiling as she unpacked Cassie's suitcase. "Oh, wow, these are beautiful chemises. Are they silk?"

"Yes, they are and they're part of my designer collection." She laughed. "You look surprised."

"What did I miss?"

"I bet Tom didn't tell you, did he? We own the Alexa's Boutiques."

"He did *not*! Alexa's clothing is so chic. I've only been to one of your stores though. The one in Concord. I heard the main store in New York is unbelievable. Wow! Do you go in and pick out what you want and say, 'Wrap it up and send it to my place?' Talk about lucky."

"No, I pay for most of my clothes, like anyone else, but I do get a nice discount—after all I design many of them." Cassie grinned realizing what a chatterbox Mary was now that they had found more common ground.

"You're a designer for Alexa's? I'm jealous. Would you show me your designs sometime?"

Cassie was pleased. Though well grounded, she liked it when people fussed over her. "Sure. Let's finish up here; you and I can spend some time later today looking at my latest portfolio. I'm working on the summer line. I'd love for you to give me your opinions. Can you stay for a while this afternoon?"

"Yes. I'd love that. Thank you. This is amazing!" Mary was beaming.

Tom knocked on the door. "Hate to spoil your fun. Mary, I've been instructed to search you out and send you downstairs. Nellie needs your help in the dining room. Looks like you two are hitting it off. No one is safe from your charms, are they, Sis?" Tom gave her a gentle punch on the arm and left the room.

"Go on, Mary. I want to finish unpacking." *An ally. Yay! One down and . . . hmm, how many to go? I like Mary. I know we'll be good friends. She's a darling.* She carried an armful of Michael's shirts to the closet and began putting them on hangers. She didn't get to ask Mary about Tom's neighbors. She'd have her fill her in this afternoon. Mary probably knew everything about everyone in this town. Cassie hummed contentedly. Joe had taken Michael and Lizzie into Ravenswood to get a few things they'd forgotten to pack. She was glad to have them out of her hair for a while, knowing she'd get little accomplished with Lizzie running around.

As she passed the dresser, Cassie jumped. Her hand flew to her mouth. She stifled her scream. Reflected in the mirror was an old woman. She was crying, her eyes puffy and red. Her lips trembled slightly, then parted as if she was about to sob. She raised a boney hand speckled with brown liver-spots, blue veins protruded across the back. Clutching an embroidered handkerchief edged with blue lace, she brought her gnarled hand to her eyes to dab her tears. In that instant, she and Cassie made eye contact. Cassie detected the faint smell of lilac water —and something slightly rancid. She whirled around to face the woman standing beside her, ready to go to her and offer comfort. Her hand reached out to the woman. The room was empty. She ran to the hallway, there was no one there either.

Chapter 35

"Cassie, what's wrong? You're white as a sheet!" Tom ran down the hallway.

"The old woman startled me. Where is she?"

"Who? There's no up here except you. What woman?" Tom asked, trying not to show his alarm.

"The old woman. I saw her in the mirror. She'd been crying. I was going to help her, but I don't know where she went. Who is she?"

"Did you actually see her, Cassie?"

"I saw her reflection in the mirror. I just told you that!" Cassie was getting annoyed with Tom. "Where did she go?"

"No clue. Did she talk to you?"

"No! I told you I saw her in the mirror, and when I turned around, she was gone. You didn't see her?"

"No I didn't and, unless she went into another room, she would have passed me in the hall. Was it Nellie?"

"No, it was not Nellie! I know Nellie. This woman was *really* old. Not anyone I've seen before. Please, let's look around. This is crazy. I know what I saw. Come on." They looked in every upstairs room; their search proved futile. Tom went downstairs to ask Nellie and her nieces, but no one had any idea who it could have been.

Tom went back upstairs to get Cassie. "Michael and Lizzie just got back. I had Michael look around outside, but he didn't see anyone."

"This is so strange, Tom. I saw the woman very clearly. Creepy." Cassie giggled uneasily. "Think you have ghosts in the house?"

"What an imagination you have. Probably just shadows from the tree outside the window or something. Forget about it, Sis. Come on. Lunch is on the table." Tom gently pulled her toward the stairs. Now what? Cassie couldn't expect him to believe there was an old woman roaming around here. He wouldn't put up with her ghost-talk for long. She would upset everyone. She'd always had an over active imagination. He wouldn't encourage her. And he didn't want anyone else to either. As he descended the staircase, he took a deep breath. In the dining room he faced the questioning eyes of everyone with a quick shrug saying, "Ghosts! My sister is seeing ghosts. Better watch out, next thing you know, she'll be talking to them, too."

Cassie shot him her famous "if looks could kill" glares and stuck her tongue out.

Tom suffered through lunch, skillfully leading the conversation away from the topic of the old woman. "Nellie, thank you," Tom said as she began gathering up the dishes. "That was a great lunch. We'll go to the living room now. You too, Mary. We have a few things to talk over. Come on, it won't take long."

Cassie looked at Mary and said, "We'll look at my designs after while then. Tom, don't keep us too long. Mary and I have plans, and Michael and Lizzie want to go down to the beach before it gets too cold."

Chapter 36

Everyone filed through the double french doors to gather in the living room. Nellie followed with a tray of coffee, milk, and chocolate cake. "Mr. Gardner, I'll pick up the dishes in a while, I need to get my nieces started in the attic. You said you wanted them to go through those old trunks in the back room, didn't you?"

"That would be a good place to start. I think it's mostly stuff from the previous owners. Blankets and household things. I'll be up in a while to see if I want to keep any of it. I don't want to store a lot of junk. Thanks, Nellie."

To Cassie, Tom said, "I'm thinking about adding another bedroom in the attic so when you and Michael are here, you'll have your own space. There's plenty of room to have a master suite up there. But . . . no definite plans yet."

"We'll talk about it. I'm happy to stay on the second floor. The room we're in is lovely. Talk about a view! I love this house!"

"Good, I'm relieved—it's so different from Jamestown house, I didn't know what you'd think." Tom stirred cream into his coffee, then took a sip. "Listen, before everyone gets involved with other things this afternoon, we need to make plans for our Thanksgiving dinner. What do you think? Do you guys want a traditional dinner or something else? We need to decide so Nellie can plan the meal. She said she'd prefer to cook for us and spend the day here instead of being home."

"You're kidding. Why?" Cassie asked, taking a bite of cake, after carefully scraping the frosting off first.

"Said her house feels too empty without her husband. And she's not getting along with her sister at the moment, so she has no plans. So what's everyone think; what do you want to have for our dinner?"

Michael jumped in. "I vote turkey with all the fixings. Mashed potatoes, gravy—the regular fare. How about you, Lizzie?"

"Yay! And chocolate cake, too. This cake is yummy. Mommy, can we have it for Thanksgiving?"

"Yes on the traditional food. And chocolate cake for the kid!" Cassie said, laughing.

"Easy enough," Tom said. "I'll let Nellie know so she can plan the shopping list. Did I tell you Joe's having dinner with us?"

"Doesn't he have family he'd rather be with?" Cassie asked.

"No, no family at all. Besides, he's becoming a good friend. I'm lucky I met him. Good sense of humor to boot! Great guy."

"Sounds like it. Seems very grounded too. What about the Harrison family? When do we get to meet them?" asked Michael.

"Glad you asked. The Saturday night after Thanksgiving, we're going to have a party here!" Tom said. "Cassie and Mary are going to plan it. Right?" Tom winked at the two women.

"Gee, Tom. Thanks for the advance notice. Not only do we have Thanksgiving to plan but a dinner party two days later, too?" Cassie got up and punched Tom in the arm. "Tom, what are you thinking?"

"We talked about this on the phone a few weeks ago." Tom was not smiling. "Sorry, Sis. I thought you were up for it. Maybe we should postpone it."

"Have you already invited them?"

"I have. But I'm sure they'd understand if we changed the date," Tom said sullenly. He pictured an angry Vivian, all too eager to use her most condescending tone as she said, "Yes of course. I understand," then slamming the phone in his ear.

"Not on your life. Mary and I can handle it. Not a problem, right Mary?" Cassie looked pleadingly at Mary.

Mary giggled, "Why not? I'm on school break. It'll be fun. I have a friend whose mom has a catering business. What would you think of using her? It would make it a lot simpler. She's really talented and has a great menu. Or she'll prepare almost anything you could want. Simple *or* fancy."

"Sounds perfect. We'll use her then. We better get on it right away. Anything else, Tom?" Cassie asked.

"What was that?" Tom jumped up and ran toward the staircase. "Someone just screamed! Did you guys hear that?" He yelled, "We're coming," taking the stairs two at a time. Michael followed closely behind.

Linda and Gwenn, both pale, their eyes wide with fear, met them on the stairs going the other way.

"What's wrong?" Tom stopped in front of the sisters, blocking their way.

Panting, Nell rushed up from behind. "What happened, Linda?"

"We heard a woman scream. But there's no one up here except us," explained Linda.

Shaking her plump finger at them, Nellie scolded, "You girls and your imaginations. Shame on you. Look! It's just the cat, for heaven's sake." Wiggins came tearing down the attic steps, a blur of fur as he whizzed by and disappeared into the study on the first floor. "Now, both of you apologize for your silliness and get back to work." She rolled her eyes at Tom.

"Sorry," they said in unison, both blushing.

"It's okay, girls. Do you want me to look around the attic?" Tom asked.

"Well," Linda said, "I *would* feel better if you did. I'm kind of nervous. We're so far from everyone up there. I know we're being silly, but . . . "

Tom interrupted. "Don't worry about it. I'll do a quick check, make you feel more comfortable." He walked to the end of the hallway, started climbing the stairs to the attic.

"I'll go with you," Michael said.

Cassie started to say something. Tom stopped her with a cold glare, was annoyed with the frosty look she gave him. He didn't want to listen to any of her ghostly theories. Not now.

Cassie took Lizzie's hand. "Mary, come downstairs with Lizzie and me. We've got plans to make. And I want to show you the summer portfolio I'm working on. Lizzie can help us until her dad's ready to take her for a walk." She stomped down the stairs obviously making sure Tom knew she was annoyed.

Tom turned the doorknob of the first room, discovered it was locked. He jiggled the knob back and forth. "I don't remember locking this. Michael, I have to get the keys. I'll be right back. Go ahead and check the other rooms."

Linda and Gwenn hung back a few steps as Michael went down the hallway looking into each open room. Most were filled with boxes, some half unpacked, but nothing seemed out of place."I know it sounded like a scream to you girls, but honestly, in this setting, a cat howling could spook anyone. Old attic. Dim light."

Linda wrung her hands. "Gwenn, you were as scared as I was. You heard it, too. Do you think it was the cat?" Gwenn didn't answer her sister.

Tom returned with the skeleton keys dangling in his hand. After several tries he found the right one. "Hmm. Nothing much in here," he said looking around the small room. "Besides, it was locked, so Wiggins couldn't have been in here. God, it smells horrible. I'll open the window and air it out. Better have you girls see what might be in these trunks. They reek. God! What a stench." He covered his nose with his sleeve.

Tom glanced at the girls who obviously were not happy at the prospect of finding the source of the smell. "Never mind. I'll bring Joe up here later. He and I can go though these." He wrenched open the window, an old wooden-framed slider that hadn't been opened in a long time. A gentle breeze was blowing; fresh air flowed into the closed quarters. "Better," Tom said. "I'll leave it open for a while."

Tom followed Michael and the girls into a large room to their left, the room he eventually planned to make into a suite and office for Nate. "Looks like you unpacked some of these boxes. I guess I forgot to tell you not to get into the ones marked *Elise*. I wanted to go through them myself."

"We didn't open those. We're working on the crates in the room down the hall," Gwenn said defensively.

"Nell must have, then." Tom slammed the door making everyone jump. "Sorry." He handed the keys to Michael. "Would you finish looking around, Michael? I have a few things to take care of. Told John I'd call him at two o'clock. Almost forgot. Girls, if you're nervous being up here, maybe you better see if Nell has something else she'd rather have you do."

"No," Gwenn said. "We're fine. The cat was probably chasing a mouse or howling to hear himself howl. My cat does that sometimes. I think animals get lonely and like to hear their own voices. Come on, Linda."

"I'll look around a little, Tom. Go on and make your phone call," Michael said.

Chapter 37

Tom waited until Michael and the two girls disappeared into a room down the hall. He quietly turned the doorknob and reentered the small room. Numerous boxes were stacked—all with his personal items from Jamestown. He sank to his knees fingering the torn cardboard on one of the boxes. It was almost empty. It had been full of Elise's books and clothing. He'd watched Lily pack it. Who had been going through her things? What had they done with them? Tom hung his head into his hands. Of course. Elise. She'd been in here.

The door opened. Tom whirled around. Just Michael. Reality check He stared blankly at Michael.

"Thought you went downstairs. You okay?" Michael asked looking into the empty box. He put his hand on Tom's shoulder. "Let her go. Man, you've come too far to let this happen again. Come on. Let's go downstairs." Michael shoved the box away from Tom with his foot. "Now, Brother! Let's get out of this room." He opened the door and waited for Tom to follow.

Halfway down the stairs, Michael said to Tom, "Cassie doesn't need to see you like this. Let's get a cold beer and take a walk. There are a few things we need to talk about—don't you think?" He hollered into the living room where Cassie, Lizzie, and Mary were busy writing in a notebook. "Be back in a few minutes. Tom wants to show me a few things down by the garage."

Michael and Tom walked in silence for a few minutes, swigging from their bottles of cold beer. "I hate to ask, but are you in trouble again? You seemed so shaken a while ago. Anything you need to talk about?"

"No, there's no reason to be concerned. I wondered who'd been in my personal stuff. That's all. Took me by surprise to see that someone had gone through Elise's things. Nell must have moved her belongings to another box or something—looked like that one was torn and damaged in the move. Hey, don't worry. I'm fine, Michael. Really." He sipped his beer, put his hand on Michael's shoulder. "I sure am glad you and Cass are here. You guys seem very happy. And that daughter of yours, what a little monkey. Makes me wish I had a couple of kids."

"Yeah, I'm a lucky guy. I love your sister more than I ever thought possible. We're good for each other. Cassie and Lizzie are my life. Everything I gave up for them is worth it." Tom knew Michael was talking about forgoing his own ambitions to help Cassie and him with the numerous business ventures of the Gardner family.

"So what about you?" Michael asked.

"I'm adjusting. Lots of changes for me right now. But all in all, I'm doing well."

"Pretty fantastic home you have here. Odd place for you to end up though."

"Not really. It's perfect, actually. No one here to bother me. The few people I have met are pretty innocuous. I like that for a change. Genuine, honest, simple. Just what I need. No demands. It feels right."

"Good for you. So Cassie and I don't need to be worried? Those funny looks she keeps giving you are my imagination?"

"Probably not. But you know Cassie. She likes to worry about me. Satisfies her nurturing nature." Tom artfully changed the subject hoping Michael wouldn't notice. "Michael, look over there. What a spectacular view of the seascape. Think I'll build a deck here next spring. What do you think?"

Lizzie hollered and ran down the walk toward them. "Daddy, you promised to take me to the beach. Come on. Uncle Tommy, want to come, too?"

"Sure, let's go."

The three raced to the wooden stairs leading down to the beach.

***

Standing on the second floor balcony, Cassie and Mary watched Tom, Michael, and Lizzie disappear down the beach stairs."

"Mary, you've spent some time with Tom, haven't you? I hate to ask, but . . . well, Tom would never let on to me—I'm such a worrier—but . . . do you think he's okay? Have you noticed anything odd about his behavior?"

"I don't know him well enough to be a good judge. He seems a bit edgy. Maybe it's this house. It seems to get on everyone's nerves. Drafty and creaky. Too many out of the way rooms. Lots of odd spaces. Did Tom tell you he and I got lost in the basement his first night here?"

"What? That sounds really odd. How could you get lost in a house?" asked Cassie.

"We were looking for the fuse box because the power went out. We went down to the basement. The lights kept going off and on. We wandered around for what felt like forever. Probably only a couple of minutes, but you know how it is when you're scared."

"Scared? Of what?"

"I don't really know. We were disoriented in the dark and then somehow got separated. I could have sworn I was with Tom, but when the lights came on, he wasn't with me. He was at the far end of another hallway. Then the lights went out again. It was pretty unnerving."

"I'll bet. How did Tom handle it?"

"Just like a man—very cool and calm. Made me feel like he had everything under control. He made a joke about it, but I could tell he was pretty angry that it happened. But he definitely had a handle on the situation. Me, I was in a panic. Thank heavens he was there."

"I think this house is odd," Cassie said. "I certainly pick up strange vibes. I'll be glad when Nate gets here. He'll put the normalcy back into this place. You'll like him, too." Cassie smiled. "Tall. Blonde. Intelligent. Not to mention that he's drop-dead gorgeous. And single."

"Always a plus! Who is he?" Mary asked. She'd gone to the opposite end of the balcony, was looking toward the Harrisons' house. "We could see a lot more from the attic. We'll have to go up there sometime and take a look. I've always been curious about their house, one of the few places in this town I've never been inside. Oh, sorry you were talking about Tom's friend."

"You haven't heard about Nate?"

"Very little."

"He works for Tom. He stayed in Jamestown to wrap up some things with the business and take care of the sale of the house. He's moving here too. Nate handles much of our family's business, Tom's personal finances, too. He's been with Tom for as long as I can remember. I guess he's having family issues right now, not to mention he broke his leg last week, so he can't travel now. I hope he gets here soon though. Tom could use his calming influence. I agree with you, Tom seems really nervous. That's not a good sign."

"Yeah, he's a bit distracted—like he's thinking about a lot of things all at once. I don't know him well enough to know if that's just how he functions. Lots of people do. It's understandable, given all the things he probably has to contend with having just moved here."

"You're right. But, will you do me a favor? If you notice anything too off, let me know. Okay?" Cassie wasn't yet ready to confide in Mary about Tom's wife's death or his breakdown. But it couldn't hurt to have Mary at least aware that she was worried about her brother.

Mary nodded. "Of course."

Cassie headed down the hall toward the library. "Come on. We can look at the renderings I'm working on for the summer beachwear line. I have some really different ideas that I'd like your opinion on."

Linda and Gwenn clomped down the attic stairs, both smiled politely as they passed them in the hall going back to the first floor.

"Wait, Cassie," Mary said. "Let's go to the attic first. I'd love to look around if it's okay with you? Please? I'd like to get a good look at the Harrison house. I've never been there, and there's nowhere else around here where you can see it. Maybe I could finally satisfy my curiosity. You ever feel curious like that?"

"What woman doesn't? Sure, come on. Then I need to get some work done," Cassie said, "before Michael and Lizzie get back."

Mary led the way up the steep stairs. Her fingers lingered on the beautifully carved banister. "Someone certainly put a lot of expense into this house. The woodwork is awesome. Have you noticed the carvings on all the fireplaces? Someone must have commissioned them—they're so unique. Most likely the Lindemans, the old couple who used to live here. My dad said they had a lot of specialty work done. Guess they were pretty well to do, though that's not unusual around here. Most of the oceanside properties are owned by wealthy families who come for the 'fun in the sun' summers."

"Tom hasn't mentioned anything about the previous owners. Who were they?" asked Cassie.

"A brother and sister. Very reclusive. And old. They died here." Mary glanced at Cassie. "You didn't know? No, I guess by the look on your face, you didn't."

"Oh!" Cassie paled, brought her hand to her mouth.

"Sorry to be the bearer of such tragic news. It does help you understand why this house feels odd sometimes. I feel a lot of sadness here. There are lots of bad memories floating around these hallways, I guess."

"God! How creepy," Cassie said. "And very sad. How did they die?"

"I heard that the brother was deathly ill. Cancer. The sister shot him and then shot herself. I guess they left a note. Terrible, isn't it?"

"That's putting it mildly," Cassie said. "I can't believe Tom would buy a house with that kind of history."

"Well, I'm sure he knows. Sara told me she and Tom talked about it. The Lindemans lived here a long time. They were really odd. Scary even. I remember seeing them in town and being afraid of them. They had this evil-eye look they used to give me. I hid behind my mom whenever we were around them—which wasn't often. They pretty much kept to themselves. Guess this house was their castle, huh? They sure did a lot of elaborate custom work. Really impressive."

Cassie nodded, Mary continued, "Joe worked for them. But I doubt he did any of this. He does more general contracting work, nothing custom like the detailed woodwork that's been done all around the house."

Cassie was visibly upset. "Come on, don't look so dismal," Mary said. "Your brother's lucky to have a house with such an interesting, though sordid, story behind it. I think it makes his living here exciting. Don't you?" Mary laughed and went into an open room to see if she could see the Harrisons' house. "Yep. Just as I hoped. A perfect view. Look, you can see right into the upper floors of the house. Geez, if we had binoculars, we could probably see a thing or two."

"Mary!"

"Just kidding. What a spectacular house. It's gorgeous. I'm jealous."

"Well, don't be. From what I hear from Tom, the Harrisons are nothing to be jealous of. Money isn't everything, after all."

"So they say!" Mary glanced at Cassie. "I'm sorry. I didn't mean for that to sound so rude."

"Forget it. No offense taken," Cassie said, shivering. "Let's go downstairs, it's cold up here." She turned to go. "Wait! Did you hear that?"

Mary stopped and listened. She whispered, "Sounds like it's coming from one of the rooms down there." She pointed toward the end of the dark hall and motioned for Cassie to follow her.

As quietly as possible, the two women crept down the hallway, consciously trying to muffle their footsteps on the wooden floor. From one of the rooms at the end of the hall the sound of furniture being dragged across wood echoed eerily in the dim attic. The whispering of voices floated through the attic. "Listen you wrinkled, old piece of shit. Get that box out of my way. You know I can't lift it."

Another voice quipped, "You worthless old hag. Get up and move . . . " The floor creaked under Mary's weight.

Cassie turned to Mary, the color draining from her face. She grabbed Mary before she bolted. She whispered urgently, "Stop! Wait! Shh. It's okay. We need to know who's in there. They can't hurt us. Come on."

Cassie reached for the knob, shocked at how cold it felt in her trembling hand. She turned it so slowly, so carefully, so sure whoever was on the other side wouldn't detect the movement.

Cassie was wrong, of course. She couldn't know the secrets of the other side. Helen and Gabe slithered under the doorway, leaving only a cold, misty fog inches above the floor. As Cassie opened the door, icy tendrils of air coiled around the two girls' legs.

Elise watched from above the doorway, balanced precariously on the sill and breathed a hot, oily film down onto the two women. She laughed as Mary stifled a scream. Cassie grabbed Mary and ran.

Tom ran to the bottom of the staircase just as the two came flying down, their feet slipping dangerously on the stairs. Tom caught Mary before she fell when she missed the last step. "Cassie! Mary! What's going on?" Tom asked, trying to keep his anger in check, although he had a pretty good idea. *Cassie's stirring things up yet again.*

"You tell me, Tom!" Cassie shouted at her brother.

Michael, who was right behind Tom, grabbed Cassie by the hand and pulled her toward him. "Take it easy, Cass. What happened?"

Cassie blurted out, "There was someone in the attic. Tom, you know what this is about. Don't you?" She glared at him and shook free from her husband's hold. "This isn't something we imagined is it? Well?"

"What do you mean, Cassie? What happened?"

"Oh, I think you have some idea. I've seen and heard people in this house, yet you say you have no idea what I'm talking about. I know you do. I want some answers. When you're ready to talk to me, I'll be in my room." She stormed upstairs. Seconds later the door to the bedroom slammed.

"Daddy?" Lizzie rushed up to her dad, Wiggins tucked tightly under her arm. "What's wrong with Mommy?"

"Come on, Lizzie, let's go find out. I think she's just tired. She's worked pretty hard today. Bet seeing you will cheer her up. Come on."

"Can I bring the kitty," Lizzie asked, reluctant to put him down. It had taken her so long to catch him.

"Sure," Michael said, then turning to Tom added, "Let me spend some time with Cass. Then we all better get together and talk. Don't you think?"

"Go to Cassie. I'll have Nell make some coffee, and I'll see you in the study in about half an hour," Tom said. "Mary, come with me." She followed him as he led her to the kitchen.

Nell was scrubbing the sink, humming softly. She turned when she heard them behind her. "Mary, what's wrong?" Nell asked.

"I'm okay. I think. Scared, but okay."

"Scared? My lord, girl! What has you so shook up?"

Mary wrung her hands nervously and said, "There was someone in the attic. Cassie and I heard them talking and moving things around."

"For heaven's sake! That's pure nonsense," Tom said, turning away.

Nell asked, "Mary, what are you talking about?"

Tom interjected, "Nothing to worry about, Nell. Would you mind putting a pot of coffee on? We're all meeting in the study in a little while. Mary, stay here. I'll go upstairs and look around. I imagine Lizzie left her TV on, and the sound carried upstairs through the vents. As for the other noises you heard, Joe's been working on the roof. He must have forgotten to put the screen back on one of the chimneys. Squirrels have probably gotten in. There's no one is in the attic for God's sakes!"

Chapter 38

Tom didn't go upstairs. Grabbing a jacket from the hall closet he quietly opened the front door and left the house. A frigid wind blew. Dark, turbulent clouds threatened to engulf the blue sky and block the sun. Icy splinters of snow pelted his face. He pulled his gloves and hat from the coat pockets as he started down the wooden beach stairs made treacherous by a coating of ice as the snow began to melt and freeze.

Tom went straight to the Harrison house. He had to see Sara. Before he lost his cool entirely and did damage to his and Cassie's relationship. Sara would help him. He pounded on the back door. Footfalls resounded loudly as someone hurried to the door.

Cautiously the door opened, an unknown face peered through the crack. Not waiting to be invited in, Tom pushed the door open. "Where's Sara? I need to see her!"

"Hold on a minute, mister. You have no right barging in here. Stop now, or I'll stop you myself!" The young man put his hands on Tom's chest and shoved him backwards out onto the porch.

"It's okay. I'm their neighbor, Tom Gardner. I need to talk to Sara."

Vivian came running down the hall. "Tom, what in the world is this all about? It's all right, Tony. Go on back to the studio; I'll be there in a minute."

"Where's Sara? Would you get her, please."

"You're being very rude. What's wrong?" Vivian asked. The young man stood behind her, hesitant to leave her. Vivian dismissed him with a wave of her hand. She took Tom's arm, leading him down the hallway into the living room. "I'm not getting Sara until you tell me what's wrong. What did Sara do to make you so upset?"

"Not a thing. I need to talk to her." Tom walked out of the room, going toward the staircase. "Sara! . . . Sara, it's Tom!" he yelled.

"You're scaring me," Vivian said. "Anyway, Sara isn't here. She's in town with the boys. They won't be back until late this evening. If you won't tell me what's going on, you should leave. Now."

How he detested this woman. "I'm sorry, Vivian. I know I'm acting like an ass. I'm not mad at Sara. But I need to talk to her. It's important. Tell Sara to call me as soon as she gets back, will you?" Tom walked out, slamming the door and ignoring Vivian when she called out to him.

Tom sprinted down the beach toward his property. Joe stood at the top of the cliff waving at him. Tom ignored him, running up the stairway, slipping several times on the ice, cursing loudly each time.

"Tom? What's wrong?" Joe hollered.

"Joe, I want you to go up on the roof and see how the squirrels are getting in the attic. You must have left one of the vents uncovered."

"I'll check, but it's not likely. Squirrels in the attic? You sure?" Joe asked.

"Something's gotten in."

"Hmm. Kind of slick to get on the roof right now. I'll check the attic though. Maybe I can find the problem from there."

"Yeah, sure. Damned animals have all the women running around screaming that someone's hiding in the attic."

"You must be joking. What happened?" Joe asked, the smile on his face quickly fading when he saw the cold look on Tom's face.

"First the cleaning girls heard noises. Then Cassie and Mary played right into their fantasy. Came running down the attic stairs screaming that they heard someone talking and moving things around. Their imaginations are running on overtime. Just check it out, okay?" Tom didn't wait for a response from Joe.

A puzzled Joe kicked the ground and followed Tom into the house. "I'll check right now. Have you seen any signs that squirrels have gotten in?"

"What else could it be? Make sure they haven't done any damage. I'll talk to you about this later."

Chapter 39

After getting his toolbox, Joe slowly climbed the stairs. He was deeply troubled by the way Tom had talked to him. Tom generally treated him more like his friend than an employee. "There's something really troubling about Tom," Joe muttered to himself. "I can't figure him out. His sister seems to have him all riled up. Hope things settle down soon." He opened the door to the first attic room on the right and went in. "Might as well start here. See if I can find out what's causing all the noises up here."

***

Still angry, Tom rifled through the mess on his desk trying to find his cell phone. He usually had it in his pocket but had obviously left it somewhere else. Finally he found it under his jacket, thrown carelessly on the chair. The winter storm blew frozen pellets against the window glass. Tom wondered if Sara would be okay driving home from town. He dialed her number, she answered on the first ring.

"Tom, I've been trying to get hold of you," Sara said. "Vivian called and said you were trying to find me. What's going on?"

"We need to talk, Sara. Can you meet me later tonight?"

"I can try. I have the boys with me. We have tickets to a play. It'll be after ten before I get home. Can't we talk now? The boys are at the arcade. I have a few minutes. What's up?"

"Sara, I need to talk with you. Face to face," Tom said hoping she would make time for him. "I miss you. I need to be with you. It's been days."

"I know, Tom. I'll call you when I get home tonight."

"What about skipping the play? I could drive into town and meet you. Couldn't the boys go without you?" Tom pleaded.

"Sounds more serious than what you're telling me. But no, I won't leave the boys alone. Especially if you won't tell me what's wrong." Sara sounded annoyed.

Damn it! Tom hung up on her. He stared at his phone when it rang; the screen told him it was Sara. He debated a second on whether or not to answer it. "Hello, Sara."

"Don't ever do that to me again, Tom. That was uncalled for. I told you I'd call you when I get home. That's the best I can do. If it's not good enough, I don't know what to say."

"I didn't hang up on you, Sara. Must have lost our signal," Tom lied, angry with himself for being rude to Sara. "I understand that you need to stay with the kids. Sorry for being so thoughtless. Go. Enjoy the play. It's nothing. I'll talk to you tomorrow."

"I have to spend tomorrow with Vivian and the boys. We made plans, and I can't break them. We'll have to wait until Saturday. I'm sorry. Hey," she said softly, "I miss you, too."

"Good!" he laughed. "Have fun with the boys. We'll talk Saturday morning."

After they said their goodbyes, Tom poured himself a glass of vodka, enjoying the burning sensation as it hit his stomach. Much better. He poured himself another, drinking it in one gulp.

***

Elise stood behind Tom, undetected as of yet. She gently massaged his shoulders, then ran her sharp fingernails down his neck. She giggled as he whirled around. She let him see her for just an instant.

Gabe and Helen grabbed Elise roughly, pulling her from the room and back to the cold attic. "Well done, my dear," Helen whispered, then slapped Elise sending her flying into the darkness of the closet. She slammed the door and motioned to her brother to guard it. "Keep her in there for a while, dear. Mustn't let her spoil our plans."

Rubbing his neck, Tom felt lines of welts rising on his skin. *Bitch! You will pay for this.* He shook his head trying to clear his mind. It didn't work. He had another glass of vodka instead. Unsteady, he stumbled into the living room. Mary was already there having a cup of coffee.

"Mr. Gardner, are you okay?"

"Absolutely."

"Here, drink this." Mary poured him a cup of black coffee.

Chapter 40

Joe stuck his head into the living room. "Tom, no signs of squirrels or anything else anywhere in the attic. I checked every nook and cranny. Must have been branches scraping the roof or windows. That would make sense. It's windy today."

Tom looked at him, puzzled. "Just the wind? Don't think so, Joe."

"I'll look around outside tomorrow. Get up on the roof, too. Anyway, I'm on my way out, I have to take a fare into town."

"Who would that be? No one's going anywhere. We have things to discuss. Didn't you know?" Tom said sarcastically, his words slightly slurred. "Things are going bump in the night here. Michael has called a meeting. No one in, no one out. Right, Mary?" Tom smiled coldly at her.

"You want me to stick around? I can probably get someone else to pick up the passenger," Joe said. "By the way—it's not anyone from here."

"It's fine. Go on. No reason for you to stay." Tom nodded to Joe, dismissing him.

"All right," Joe said. "See you tomorrow."

After Joe was gone, Tom said, "Just the wind, Mary. You believe that?"

"No. Not for a minute," Mary replied.

Cassie and Michael came tromping down the stairs. As they walked into the room, Cassie said, "What don't you believe, Mary?"

"Joe thinks all the noises we heard upstairs were caused by the wind. He's wrong though. I know what we heard," Mary said. "There were people talking."

"Who, Mary?" Michael asked. "Who would be up there?"

Tom interrupted. "I need a drink. Anyone else?"

"Yeah, something stronger than coffee would be great about now," Michael said. "Tom, what's your pleasure?"

"Vodka."

"Give me the same—on ice please," Cassie said.

Tom stumbled across the room, obviously inebriated.

"Maybe you've had enough," Cassie said. "Getting drunk isn't going to make this any easier to sort out. Let me pour you another cup of coffee. I don't want Lizzie to see you like this. She might come down any minute."

"You're right, Sis. Sorry, selfish of me. I would never want to upset Lizzie. Coffee it shall be."

Michael poured himself a drink and said, "I guess there's more going on here than you've told us, Tom. Cassie told me about the old woman she saw the other night. And about something happening with you and Mary in the basement. What's the story?"

"Damned if I know. The power was going on and off the night I got here. Mary and I went down to the basement to check the fuse box. We got turned around and had a hard time finding the stairs. That's about that. As for Cassie's 'old woman sighting ' and the noises in the attic— it's simply a case of overactive imaginations. Wind. Shadows. Squirrels. Absent-minded gossip. TV's through vents. It's an old house, that's all.

Lots of creaks and groans." Tom slammed his fist onto the back of the sofa. The girls jumped. "This is my home for God's sake, not some damned haunted house! Enough about spirits! I don't want to hear any more about them. Understood?" He whirled around and stared out the window, not wanting to meet Cassie's stare. His thoughts ran rampant. *Damn you, Elise! You're not going to interfere with my life at Remington. Do you hear me? You will lose this battle. I will win. Again.*

Ignoring her brother, Cassie replied, "I agree with Mary. We both know what we saw and heard."

"What exactly are you saying, Cassie?" Tom asked, turning quickly around to face his sister. He was getting angrier by the second.

"I'm not quite sure . . . yet. But after hearing the tragic history of the house, I believe there are spirits here."

"Enough!" Tom fought to keep his voice even. *They can't find out Elise is here. I'll deal with her. It's not up to Cassie— or Mary. Elise is my tormentor, not theirs.* He took a sip of coffee to calm himself, his hand trembled ever so slightly. "Mike, talk some sense into Cassie, would you?"

Cassie's brown eyes flamed. "It's not nonsense, Tom. You're hiding something from us,"

Tom fumed. "Damn it, Cass! Stop it!"

"I'm sorry, Tom, but something's very wrong here. And you know it is. We've all seen and heard things. We need to find out what's going on. If you have spirits or some kind of entities here, we need to get rid of them." Cassie looked at Mary for support. "I think we should investigate this. I sense others here."

Frowning and drumming his fingers on the coffee table, Michael said, "Cassie, please. I agree with Tom. You ladies are going off the deep end. Squirrels, wind...yeah. Ghosts? Oh, come on!"

Tom jumped in. "Listen, Joe's going to look around some more tomorrow when the storm dies down. So, let's be realistic and accept that this house has some issues. Old houses creak and moan. Sounds carry though vents. Wildlife moves in.

Nothing unusual at all." Tom poured himself more coffee. "Not to mention mirrors and shadows," he said under his breath, just loud enough to be heard. "I have work to do. End of discussion. See you all tomorrow." Tom walked out, leaving them staring at his back.

"Well, that certainly went well!" Cassie shrugged her shoulders. "He's hiding something, and I'm going to find out what it is."

"Let it go, Cassie," Michael replied. "I'm going upstairs to check on Lizzie. You two listen to Tom. He's pretty tense. Give this ghost business a rest."

After Michael had gone upstairs, Cassie said, "I know I saw that old woman. We both heard voices upstairs. There are active spirits in this house. This is not something we're imagining."

"If no one else believes us, I guess we're going to have to deal with this on our own. Any ideas?" Mary asked Cassie.

"I have a few. Let's go upstairs to the library and talk before you have to go back to town. Come on."

Chapter 41

Avoiding his family for most of the next day, Tom secluded himself in his bedroom suite going over papers from John Atwood. For lunch, Nell brought a tray of sandwiches and fruit to his room. He called Nate late in the afternoon and was disappointed to find that he wouldn't be able to come to Ravenswood until late in January. "I hoped you could get here sooner. But you need to take care of your leg, make sure it's completely healed. I understand."

Nate replied, "I wish I could get up there too, but at least I'm able to handle the business side of things from here."

"Well, nothing we can do but accept the inevitable. So, how's Harold doing? John said he thought the charges against Harold would be dropped. What's the date for the hearing?"

"Actually, it was yesterday. Guess you didn't read your email. My fucking brother took off. Can you believe him? Never showed for court."

"Sorry to hear that. Any idea where he went?" Tom asked.

"No. I'm sure his erratic behavior has to do with his drug habit. He's probably somewhere stoned out of his mind. John said he'd get one of the detectives from a firm he uses to track Harold down. John's legal team was able to get the murder charges dropped, but of course, since Harold didn't show up, there's a warrant out. The plan is to get him into a rehab facility. If we can find him."

"Not easy for you. Hope they find him before he gets himself into more trouble. Keep me posted," Tom said. He sipped his cold, bitter coffee and shuddered. "So—what about William Harrison? Heard anything yet?"

"Did you get the faxes I sent yesterday?"

"I haven't read them yet. Been dealing with family. Cassie, Michael and Lizzie are here, so I'm behind on everything. What gives?"

"Harrison is quite the businessman. A high roller to the max," Nate said. "John ran a thorough background check on him, his family and his business ventures. His businesses are all completely above board. Harrison is very powerful *and* very wealthy. Read the report. I think you'll be impressed."

"Yeah, I figured as much. I plan to take the train to Jamestown after Thanksgiving. We need to go over the contracts you and John have ready for the Tempe deal. Then I have a few ideas I want to discuss with the two of you. Something to do with Harrison."

"Care to elaborate?" Nate asked.

"I hear he opened a high-end jewelry store in Ravenswood. I may be interested in starting a little friendly competition. Nothing like competition, is there, Nate?"

"Got that right," Nate laughed.

"Listen, got to go, Nate. Cassie needs to talk to me. I'll call you later." Laughing, Tom hung up. He needed a good distraction.

"Glad to see you're in a better frame of mind today." Cassie smiled brightly at Tom from the doorway. She wore a heavy, red flannel jacket, the collar turned up around her chin. "Just came back from a long walk on the beach. I feel so invigorated. You should try it. It's gorgeous out today. What's up? Haven't seen you all day."

"Had some business I needed to take care of with the hotels. You need something?"

Cassie came in the room and shut the door. "I need to talk to you. I know you don't want to hear what I have to say."

"Stop it, Cass." Angry, Tom whirled around, walked over to the fireplace and threw a handful of kindling into the fire, sending embers flying. "I'm aware of what you think. I'm asking you to drop it."

Cassie backed up to the bedroom door and leaned against it. "Please don't shut me out." She paced the room, then stopped and put her hands on her brother's shoulders. "When we talked a few months ago, I believed you were doing the right thing by coming here. But that's not the case now. Something is very wrong here. I know it. I believe there is someone or something else in this house. I think you know it, too. And you know whatever is happening is beyond your control. Isn't it?"

He threw her hands off his shoulders, grabbed her wrist. "What makes you think I know anything about these fantasies you're having?"

"Let go. You're hurting me." Cassie pulled away. Tom immediately dropped her hand. She rubbed her wrist but didn't back off. "I know what I saw. What I heard. Mary told me about the couple who died here. I think it's them. I think they're still here. Mary does, too."

"You're being silly, Cass. Stop all of this crazy talk about ghosts. I don't have time for it. I know you're worried about me, but you don't need to be," Tom said, gently tousling her red hair. "There are no spirits here. We happen to be living in an old, creaky house. We have a few rodents nesting in the attic; add that to the wind blowing branches against the house and you'll see it all comes into perspective."

She gave him an icy glare. "I don't know why you're pretending you don't believe me. You know something's going on." She continued to stare at him, her eyes cold, her lips pursed. Finally she shrugged and looked away. "I have nothing more to say. When you're ready to talk, let me know. Anyway. . . it's time for dinner—we're eating early. Nell has a meeting and needs to be in town by 6:00. Come down to the dining room. Everyone else is already there." She opened the door and waited for Tom to follow.

"Lighten up, Sis. It'll be okay," he lied again. He would stop Elise somehow. He couldn't involve anyone else. But he had to deal with her himself.

Dinner was strained for the entire family; small talk prevailed. Nell doted on them all, trying to ease the tension. "Such a lovely day today. I hoped we would dry out, but now it's raining again," she said as she served them roast beef and mashed potatoes. "My heavens! Look, it's starting to snow."

Chapter 42

Gabe and Helen were gone for now. *Probably sleeping in the room down the hall,* Elise thought. She waited until she heard no sounds and came out of the tiny closet they had thrown her into. Her lips were bloody and swollen from biting them—the only way she could keep herself from screaming out.

While she'd cowered in the closet, afraid to come out, she began devising a plan. With each passing hour she was becoming stronger but knew she was not yet strong enough to deal with the old crone and her brother. Instinctively she felt that she was smarter and more cunning than they, more devious too. For now, she would do her best to stay out of their way. Let them think she was afraid of them.

There was a small cottage down the beach, not too far from here. As were many properties, it was closed up for the winter —she would be safe there. As soon as she was able, she needed to leave this house. She would concentrate on gaining her strength and cunning, carefully plan her revenge and, when the time came, rid herself of the old couple. Then she could get on with the real issue at hand—Tom.

Chapter 43

After finishing their early dinner, Tom and his family moved into the living room for coffee. Michael cleared his throat and said, "Tom, I got a call today from the New York office. I need to be in Manhattan the Monday after Thanksgiving. Cassie and I talked about her staying here with you for at least a few more weeks, maybe longer, depending on when I can get back."

Cassie spoke up, "There's still so much to do here, Tom. I want to help you get completely settled before I consider leaving. Would you mind if Lizzie and I stayed?" She hugged her daughter as she spoke.

Lizzie chimed in, "Please, Uncle Tommy?"

"Of course you can stay. But I'm leaving that week, too. I talked with Nate earlier today. He and I have some business negotiations to discuss. I'm planning to go to Jamestown for a few days. I'll leave on Tuesday. What do you think about being here with both Mike and me gone?"

"I don't mind at all, Tom. I have so much work to do for the summer collection. We have a show coming up in late January. And I plan to help Nell finish all the unpacking. As long as it's okay with you?"

Pouring another cup of coffee, Tom nodded.

"And when you're busy, Mommy, I can play with Jimmy." Lizzie jumped up and ran around the room. "He said he would show me where to find arrowheads. He said there's a whole bunch of them buried around here."

"Sounds like a good plan, Lizzie. I'll bet Jimmy knows all kinds of interesting things like that," Tom said. "Just promise to watch out for Billy. Okay? He's too old for you and likes pushing Jimmy around. Can you do that?"

"Jimmy hates Billy. He told me that the first time I played with him. We won't play with him. It'll just be Jimmy and me."

"I'm sure he doesn't really hate his brother, but . . . well, never mind. You guys are more than welcome to stay for as long as you want. So, it's all set then," Tom said. "Your parents and I have things to talk about. Boring stuff. Why don't you go to your room and watch TV for a while, Lizzie."

She twirled out of the room, smiling back at them as she did a perfect pirouette.

"She's precious; you guys are blessed," Tom said.

Michael and Cassie nodded in agreement. After putting another log on the fire, Cassie dropped onto the couch next to her brother, fluffed the throw-pillow, then absently threw it onto the floor.

"Was Mary here today? I didn't see her," Tom said.

"She was. She had to leave before dinner. She had homework to do. Said she'll call you in the morning to see when you need her again." Cassie jumped up, began gathering coffee cups and placing them on the tray. Someone had spilled cream all over the side table. Unfolding a napkin, she began to clean up the mess.

Nell came in and took the cloth from her. "I'll finish picking up, dear. Have you made a grocery list for Thanksgiving dinner yet? I'd be happy to pick up the groceries the first of the week."

"Thanks, Nell, but I thought I'd do the shopping," Cassie said. "Mary and Lizzie are going with me. We're planning to make a day of it and have lunch in town too."

"Sound fun! The three of you will have a good time," Nell said. "I'll finish up in the kitchen and see you all tomorrow." Carrying the tray, she disappeared through the double doors into the dining room.

Cassie plopped down on the sofa. "Tom, we need to talk about the dinner party with the Harrisons. Remember?"

"Believe me, I haven't forgotten. I wish I'd never opened my mouth to Vivian about it. But I did. We might as well get it over with. Besides, I want you to meet Sara. I think you two will have a lot in common. You'll like her too, Michael." Michael nodded, then went back to the text message he was writing.

"Nice! It'll be fun. I'm excited. It won't be a lot of work either," Cassie said leaning over and picking the pillow up off the floor, tossing it onto the couch. "Mary's friend said she could do the catering. She'll prepare the food, the flower arrangements and set everything up. Mary and I already planned the menu. I need your help with the seating arrangements though." She glanced at Tom who was pouring himself more coffee, this time adding cream and a shot of whiskey.

"Thought we could put Vivian in the attic." Tom pointed at the ceiling. "Or maybe on the back porch, weather permitting." Cassie didn't laugh as he had hoped. "Sorry, but after you've spent an evening with her, you'll wish we had. Let me think about it."

The room darkened as the sun set on the western horizon. Out the window the pale, salmon-pink sky turned slowly to violet. A light shimmering snow continued falling; the sky glowed with a promise of more to come. Soon the moon would rise, but for now, darkness began enveloping the estate. Tom was beginning to hate the long nights here.

The wind started blowing again, whipping barren branches against the clapboard, the sound echoing throughout the house. Tom got up and began turning on the lamps, relieved to see their warm, yellow glow illuminating the room.

From upstairs, Lizzie yelled something indiscernible and Cassie bounded upstairs to her daughter. Michael asked, "Care for a shot before Cassie calls me upstairs? She hates these storms. They really scare her. " He held the vodka bottle out. "Drink?"

"Sure. Pour me one, too."

The men clinked their tumblers together. "Cheers," Michael said. "There's something I wanted to mention . . . while it's just the two of us."

"What's that, Mike?"

Michael took a swig of his vodka. "I'm not particularly comfortable with Cassie and Lizzie being here when there's not a man around. It's very isolated here. And what happens if the girls start hearing things again? What do you think?"

"Don't worry; I'll have Joe check on them. He won't mind. He's completely grounded too. He won't let them spook themselves. He'll be around most of the time anyway since his crew will be starting work in the basement."

"Oh, that's right. I forgot about that." Michael got up and stirred the fire. "I won't worry now. So . . . what made you decide to buy this place anyway? It seems a far cry from your usual digs in the big city. Who would have thought you'd choose a house that was so far from everything."

Tom replied, "That was the plan. I wanted a fresh start, a new challenge." Staring out the window at the moon floating above the horizon he added, "I saw its potential. It's a great house." He ran his finger around the rim of his glass. The fine crystal hummed.

"Guess a lot of work is what I see. Maybe I would have bought it too . . . if I were looking for a complete change. Which you were." Michael put the almost empty bottle on the table. "What a view of the ocean you have here, that's a fair trade off, makes it completely worth the isolation. Well, I better get upstairs to Cassie." He poured them another shot, drank his and went upstairs.

The banging branches began to unnerve Tom. The resounding caws of ravens calling to each other as they headed for their nests in the hills behind the house filled the night. Then suddenly—silence. Just like that, the birds apparently found their roosts and quieted their noisy cacophony. Thunder boomed, and the room flooded with light. *What the hell was that?* Tom ran to the window facing the ocean and watched a bolt of lightning glancing off the shoreline, randomly striking the cliff at the edge of his property.

It was still snowing—fluffy, iridescent flakes glittered in the radiant lightning flashes. Fascinated, Tom stood transfixed as the bright bolt hit again and again, striking the shoreline four or five times before dying out. Huge clouds of moisture rose and flowed eerily toward the rocky cliff edge, finally merging into the tumultuous waves crashing on the beach. Another strike, farther out on the ocean, produced a wall of light engulfing and illuminating the night sky. The rumble of thunder echoed off the cliffs.

A figure, shrouded in the heavy fog, stood at the edge of the turbulent water. Tom thought it was possibly a woman but she was too far away to be sure. "You fool! What are you doing out in this storm?" As if they could hear him, whoever it was turned to him, then whirled around and around in a crazy circle in the falling snow. Tom stepped back from the window as a final crash of thunder shook the house. He thought he heard a window shatter. Cassie and Lizzie screamed. Racing up the stairs to their room, Tom yelled, "It's okay. I'm coming." He opened the bedroom door. "Quite the lightning show. Not to mention the thunder! Incredible. Guess it scared you guys."

"It always does!" Cassie hugged Lizzie to her.

Tom glanced around the room. "Where's Mike?"

"He went down to the kitchen to get some snacks," Cassie answered. She grabbed Lizzie's hand. "Come on, sweetie, let's go find Daddy."

They met Michael on the stairs, a mischievous grin on his face. "Caught red-handed. Just making a munchie run. Want to join us, Tom?" Michael asked. "What's wrong with everybody? What happened?"

"You didn't hear the thunder? The house shook so hard it just about knocked us off the bed. Didn't you feel it?" Cassie snapped.

"Of course I did. You're overreacting as usual. I've told you not to upset Lizzie like this," Michael said. "You okay, Lizzie? It's only thunder. Come here." Setting the tray of sandwiches and hot chocolate on the floor, Michael scooped Lizzie up and onto his shoulders. "Get the tray, Cass." He galloped down the hallway, Lizzie laughing gleefully. "Let's go pig out. You two coming?"

"Go on, Cass, I thought I heard breaking glass. I better check it out," Tom said. "Poor, Sis. Still afraid of thunder. Don't worry. It's over now. Go and have some fun with Mike and your kid, I'll see you in the morning."

"Nite, Tom." She shuffled down the hallway, the sound of the bedroom door closing echoed in the empty hall.

Tom checked the house top to bottom and found no broken windows. After another shot of vodka, he went to bed, only to toss and turn, listening to the noises of the old house. From the rooms overhead the sounds of shuffling and creaking continued for hours. He went upstairs to the attic several times but found nothing to explain the noises. Another drink of vodka, a sleeping pill and he finally fell asleep. A night of unsettling dreams left him emotionally exhausted. In the morning, though he tried, he could not remember what his dreams had been about. He had a horrible headache and went in search of aspirin.

Chapter 44

The rest of the household was already up and about. Tom entered the kitchen from the back stairway once used by the servants. The voices of Michael, Cassie and Joe drifted in from the adjoining dining room. Nell was making scrambled eggs and bacon. A pan of cinnamon rolls cooled on the counter, their sweet, spicy aroma filled the air.

"Morning, Mr. Gardner. Care for a cup of coffee?"

"You bet I do," Tom answered. "Nell, those rolls smell like heaven!"

"They do, don't they? Go on to the dining room. I'll have breakfast ready in about ten minutes. I'll bring you your coffee in a minute." She hummed as she opened a cupboard door and reached for a mug.

"Thanks, Nell. Need some aspirin as much as I need coffee. Be right back." From the medicine cabinet in the bathroom off the kitchen, he took out a bottle. It looked ancient. Tom hadn't seen a glass prescription bottle in years. Tom picked up another old bottle. It didn't make sense. Why were these still here?

"What's that?" Cassie asked, reaching out to take the bottle from Tom. "Oh my gosh, it's medicine for Gabriel Lindeman, dated September 14, 1945. That's the old man who died here, isn't it? "

"Yeah, I think so," Tom answered, annoyed that Cassie was intruding again.

"I knew it. What else is in the cabinet?" Cassie pushed her way in the door and began taking bottles off the shelves, reading the label on each one, then handing them to Tom. "I thought Nell's nieces had cleaned all the junk out of here."

"Yeah, so did I," said Tom. He picked up the small trashcan and began throwing the bottles away.

"Wait, Tom! I want to see what all's here. Stop." Reaching down into the trash, she took the bottles out and read the labels. "Most of these aren't nearly as old—this one's from 2009." Holding the bottle so Tom could see it, she said, "It's for Lithium. That's for treating bipolar disorder. Wow!"

Tom took it out of her hand and tossed it the trash.

"Wait, Tom. Look, here's another one. For Lithium, too, but in his sister's name—Helen Lindeman." She was quiet for a second, then added, "Mental illness must have run in the family."

"For craps sake, Cass! What difference does it make? They've been dead for years. It's not as if it matters what medicine some old couple was taking. You're being silly." Taking her by the shoulders, Tom moved Cassie out of his way and started to leave the room. "Damn, I forgot the aspirin," he said. He rummaged through the upper shelf, throwing more bottles into the trash. Finally he found some aspirin.

Taking the last bottle from the shelf, he tried to keep Cassie from intercepting it before he could toss it into the wastebasket. No luck.

"Let me see that." She examined the bottle, pointing at the label. "It's so faded, I can't read what it says."

"What are you two up to?" Michael asked. Joe was right behind him.

"We found old medicine bottles from the couple who died here," Cassie explained. "Look at this." She handed the umber colored bottle to Michael. "Can you decipher the label? It's gotten wet, and I can't make out what it says."

"Excuse me, I need out of here," Tom said. He left the tiny bathroom and crossed to the kitchen sink where Nell was filling a glass for him.

"What are all of you looking at in there, Mr. Gardner? Don't mean to be nosy, but I can't help myself. Found something pretty interesting it looks like," Nell said handing him a glass of water.

After swallowing a handful of aspirin, Tom answered her, "Just a bunch of old pill bottles. Thought the girls had thrown all that stuff away, Nell. Good thing I found them—lots of pills there. They need to be tossed."

"Guess Linda and Gwenn didn't get to that room yet. I'll take care of it if you want—after you all have your breakfast."

"Yeah, do that. Wouldn't want any of the kids to find them."

In the bathroom, Michael and Joe were trying to read the handwritten label. Giving up, Michael carefully pried the old glass and cork stopper out of the bottle. "Well, well. What have we here? I think this is opium!" Michael exclaimed. Reaching his finger down into the bottle, he touched the brown gummy substance, scraped a little with his fingernail and cautiously smelled it. "Tom! Come in here," Michael yelled. "Look at this. The old couple was using opium."

Examining the bottle and its contents, Tom said, "Yeah, think you're right. Sure looks and smells like it to me. I don't get it though. Why would all this stuff still be here? If there was a murder-suicide here wouldn't the police have taken most of these bottles for evidence? Especially a bottle full of opium."

"Not when Sheriff Rogers happened to be an incompetent drunk," Joe said. "He probably didn't check the house at all, other than the immediate area in the attic where the bodies were found. It was pretty cut and dried, after all. No reason to spend time searching the house when they knew what happened and why. Helen Lindeman left a suicide note explaining everything. Rogers retired shortly after that and no one was much interested in the Lindemans."

"Well, no sense stirring things up. I have enough to deal with without turning my house into a crime scene." Tom grimaced and shook his head. "Let's keep this just between us," he said to the three huddled together around the bathroom sink. "You too, Nell. Our little secret. Joe, check under the counter, make sure there's nothing more there."

"What do we do with all these pills? . . . And that?" Cassie asked, pointing at the opium bottle.

Tom opened the toilet and started taking lids off the bottles, pouring the contents into the churning water as he repeatedly flushed. He picked up the brown bottle. "Can't flush this. No way to get the stuff out of the bottle."

Nell left briefly, returning with a small, black trash bag. She dumped the trashcan filled with empty bottles into it. "There, I'll take this out to the trash. My goodness! I feel so wicked being part of a conspiracy. Don't worry though— mum's the word." She winked. "Breakfast is getting cold, go on into the dining room, and I'll bring you all some fresh coffee.

"What do we do with the opium?" asked Joe.

"Burn it," Tom said. In the kitchen, he smashed the bottle on the cutting board. The kitchen fireplace was blazing, and he scraped the sticky drug and the glass shards into the flames. The group watched as the substance sizzled, smoked, and was consumed by the fire. "Don't anybody breathe. Let's get out of here." He opened the door to the dining room.

Lizzie was eating hot cinnamon rolls and bacon at the dining room table. The tip of her nose was white with frosting "What's that smell?" she asked, wrinkling her nose. "Disgusting."

"I threw some trash into the fireplace," Michael said. "Forgot about the stink it would make. I'll turn the exhaust fan on and open the kitchen window. Be right back."

Tom was down on the rug in front of the fireplace, petting the cat. "Wiggins, let's get you out of here. Can't be good for you to breathe this stuff."

"Tom," Michael said, "Let's not talk about the opium in front of Lizzie. She's asking what the smell is. Told her it was trash burning." He strained to slide the heavy, wooden framed window open. "Turn that fan on, would you?"

Standing up, Tom flipped the switch. Sparks flew from the wall, followed by a puff of rancid smoke. "Damn! Now what?"

Wiggins yowled, then ran from the kitchen. Michael and Tom covered their noses with their hands. The stink was over powering.

Nell came to their rescue. She had a fire extinguisher in her hand and calmly sprayed the wall. "Good Lord! What in the world happened?"

"Just turned the fan on and the wires shorted out, I guess." Tom pointed at the red tank. "Where did that come from?"

"From Joe. Thank heavens. He bought a case of them to put around the house. Better have him show us where he put them all— this old wiring can be dangerous," Nell said. "Hmm. Doesn't smell electrical to me." Fanning the air in front of her face with her free hand, she added, "What *is* it? Is it from that drug you burned in the fireplace?"

"No," Tom said, "that's cleared out. Maybe the fabric on these old wires is what smells so bad."

"Maybe," said Nell. "By the way, that's not the switch for the fan. That's over there." She pointed across the room. "That one's for the basement stairs." Flipping the fan switch on, she set the canister down on the counter and picked up the coffee pot. "Now go on, you need to eat."

She followed the two men to the dining room and began pouring fresh coffee.

"Joe, the light switch shorted and sparked. Would you check it and make sure it's safe. Nell used the fire extinguisher on it, but you better take a look at it."

"What? Which one? I just replaced two switches in the kitchen."

"Nell, show him, would you?" Tom asked.

Joe followed Nell to the kitchen. She told him, "This one, the one for the basement stairs."

"I just replaced that. Doesn't make sense. I better disconnect the wires for now. Got a screwdriver I could use?" Nell found one in a drawer and handed it to him. He took the scorched cover off and scratched his head. "Hmm. Nothing wrong in here. Look. Not a sign of fire. What in the heck caused the smoke?"

"This old house and its ghosts, I suspect," Nell said shuddering. "You know all the girls say this house has ghosts."

"Come on, Nell. Don't start that up."

"I've heard a lot of tales about that old couple. But I won't say anymore about it to you. Go on and have your coffee with the rest of them." Nell shook her finger at Joe. "I know what I know, Joe. Just be careful. Don't say I didn't warn you."

Joe left the kitchen, the door swung shut behind him. Sitting down at the dining room table, he picked up his coffee cup and took a drink, grimaced when it burned his tongue. "Damn!"

"You okay, Joe?"

"Yeah. Thought the coffee would have cooled off by now."

Cassie licked a dab of frosting from the corner of her mouth. "Guess not." She blew on her cup before taking a sip. "Mine's cool. Hmm. Well anyway, I wondered if you'd take Mary and me into Ravenswood this morning. She's coming over at ten, and we need to do some major grocery shopping."

"I forgot to tell you. I thought you and Michael could use my minivan while you're here," Joe replied. "I don't need it now. I'm using my pickup and my cab most of the time."

"Great. Thanks, Joe, that would be really helpful," Michael said.

"And I found a rental for you, Tom. A Jeep Cherokee. Hard to find this late in the season with Thanksgiving so close. We got lucky. Somebody who had reserved it cancelled their trip."

"So how do we get the cars?" Cassie asked.

"We can all ride to town in my cab later this morning," Joe answered.

"Sounds good. Appreciate it," Tom said. "It's getting close to nine. I have some work to do, so what say we meet back here at ten?"

In his study, Tom sat staring out the window at the cloudless, azure sky. The storm had passed leaving behind a clear, bright day. He called Sara. She answered on the first ring. "Sara, hi. How are you? I'm sorry about the other day."

"Hi," she said. "It's okay."

"It's not but… Listen, I wondered if you'd like to go into town today?" Tom asked. "We could have a late lunch. Joe found a rental car for me; I'll have it later this morning. What do you say?"

"You know that might be a good idea. We have to figure out what to do about Vivian. She's really angry with you," Sara said sternly. "I don't blame her either. You haven't told me what made you barge in and yell at her."

"Let's talk about it this afternoon. I'll make it right with her, Sara. I promise. Will you go to town with me?"

"Sure. Sounds like fun. I need to see you, too," Sara said. "I have an appointment in town this afternoon. Could you take me and then we'll have lunch afterwards?"

"I'll call you when I'm on my way. About one?"

"Perfect. I look forward to seeing you. Is everything going okay with your sister and her family?" Sara asked.

"Yeah. It's great to have them here."

"I bet you're having a wonderful time. I can't wait to meet everyone."

"They can't wait to meet you either," Tom said, then added, "I sure need a break. I have a houseful now. Not a quiet moment. Nell and two of her nieces have been here off and on. Mary, too. Not used to all the hubbub! "

"Poor Tom! An afternoon away should do the trick then. Listen, I've got to go. I'll see you later."

"Bye, Sara."

With that arranged, Tom got on with his business calls and started reading his faxes from John and Nate.

Cassie popped her head in the room while he was in the middle of reading a proposal from a small storefront in Ravenswood. "Hey, Tom. Got a minute?" she asked.

"Sure. Come in." Tom pointed to the brown leather chair across from him. "Have a seat. What's up?"

"I wanted to talk to you about the dinner again, the one for the neighbors. I've been thinking, seems like you're under a lot of pressure. You know, with the move and all the Thanksgiving preparations. Do you think we should put it off for a week? Maybe wait till you get back from Jamestown?"

"Not a chance." Tom started laughing. "Thanks, Sis, but I'm fine. Besides, Vivian is already a bit miffed with me. There's no way I'm going to risk making it worse. And I want you to meet Sara. It might even be an amusing night!"

Chapter 45

Pulling up in front of Kranston and Rivers Jewelers, Vivian surveyed the street, making sure no one saw her. She found a parking space in the small lot across the street from the jewelers. As she got out of her husband's Cadillac, she wrapped a mink-lined scarf around her head, adjusted her sunglasses, and pulled her collar up. Walking quickly, she approached the door to the jewelers, her heels clicked loudly on the cobblestone walk. The door was locked. She read the sign 'FOR SERVICE, PLEASE RING THE BELL.'" She rang the bell and waited.

"Mrs. Harrison, do come in. How good to see you."

"Good afternoon, Mr. Rivers. When I called you yesterday, you said you had my necklace and earrings ready. I'd like to see them," Vivian said, pushing her scarf back so it lay around her shoulders. She placed her sunglasses on the glass counter.

"May I offer you a glass of wine?" Anthony Rivers asked. He led Vivian to a leather chair placed in front of a mirrored showcase that was filled with brilliant sapphire and ruby earrings, pendants, rings and several intricately mounted brooches.

"I'm in a hurry. Just show me my jewelry."

"Certainly, I'll be back in a moment. Can I take your coat?" He tried to assess what he may have done to make Vivian so cold to him. In all of their past business dealings she had been extremely cordial, even flirtatious with him.

"Oh, please!" Vivian snapped. "Just get the necklace and earrings, Anthony."

Anthony disappeared into the back room, reappearing in minutes with two black-velvet boxes.

After carefully examining the exquisitely mounted diamonds, Vivian, said, "Perfect," and handed Anthony the balance of fifteen thousand dollars in cash, picked up the velvet boxes and left. "Don't call me," she said glancing at Anthony. The door swung shut. Vivian was in the shop no more than fifteen minutes.

"What was that about, Anthony?" Darrell Kranston asked, coming from the back room.

"I have no idea," Anthony answered.

"That family's business is vital to us. I certainly hope you won't do anything to jeopardize that."

"Certainly not! In fact, I spoke with William Harrison earlier today. As you and he discussed last week, he's sending another shipment of diamonds to our New York office next week. Everything is going very well," Anthony said. "I would guess Mrs. Harrison's lonely with Mr. Harrison being gone as much as he is. No one to keep her warm at night. Women don't handle that well. In my opinion."

"Don't get any ideas, Anthony."

Fanning the stack of hundred dollar bills, Anthony grinned. "Nothing to worry about. There's too much of this at stake."

Chapter 46

Tom dropped Sara off at Lillian's Salon, then went to the bank to transfer money from his account in Jamestown. Afterwards, to kill time, he walked down Main Street checking out the local businesses. Cold and bored, he decided to wait for Sara at the Raven Café. The waitress, Joanie, brought him coffee. "I'll order later, when my friend gets here," he told her.

A young woman sat at the table across the aisle from Tom, her back to him. Her long blonde hair, the way she tilted her head, the sound of her laughter as she responded to something her friend said, reminded him of Elise—back when they were still in love. *Stop thinking like that. That was eons ago.* Dismissing his ludicrous sentimentality, he began to go over everything that had happened the last few weeks, since his arrival at Remington House. *It's been Elise all along! It was she who frightened Cassie—Elise made herself appear old and frail so Cassie would feel sorry for her. At the dinner party, somehow she manipulated Vivian. She made her go to the piano, made her play Beethoven's* Für Elise—*the song I always played for her. When Vivian looked at me, her eyes were Elise's eyes. When she spoke, her voice was Elise's voice. Her hatred for me was Elise's. She wants vengeance. She wants me to go back to Jamestown. To her. To my prison. To my death.*

It's clear to me now that it was Elise who made the power go out at Remington. Somehow she was able to confuse Mary and me so that we couldn't find our way around the basement. It was her hand I held! How can she be so devious? So alive in death? I feel her presence everywhere. At night I hear her pacing in the attic. Back and forth, back and forth. How tormented she must be.

When I'm alone, she comes to me—taunts me, tries to make me think I'm going crazy again. I almost thought I was until everyone else in the house had experiences with her. She hates that I left Jamestown and began a new life, hates me because I don't care about her anymore. I can't imagine what she might do to Sara if she finds out how I feel about her. I have to get Elise away from Remington. I have no doubt she's capable of doing much more than just scaring everyone. I will stop her.

Afraid that he may have been talking out loud, Tom was relieved to see no one was paying any attention to him, a good sign. Tom picked up his glass of water, knocking the rim against his teeth. He looked around the café. The lunch crowd had thinned. A few late afternoon shoppers, store bags on the seats next to them, engaged in private conversations.

"Tom! There you are. Sorry I took so long. Robin was so slow today." Sara smiled and sat down at the table across from him.

Tom took her free hand and brought it to his lips. "Well worth the wait. You look beautiful." He put his thoughts of Elise out of his mind. Sara deserved his undivided attention.

"Thank you." Sara blushed. "I bet you're starved."

Tom and Sara enjoyed a long and quiet lunch discussing their Thanksgiving plans and making small talk. After Joanie refilled their coffee cups, Tom said, "Sara, I owe you an explanation for my intrusion into Vivian's house the other day." He stirred cream into Sara's coffee, watched the brown liquid turn creamy beige. "I needed to talk to you. I was angry. But not with you."

"That makes no sense. Vivian said you were furious. She went so far as to say she was afraid of you." Sara stared at Tom. "What was it all about?"

"There are things about me that I haven't shared with you —yet. I think it's time." Tom cleared his throat, took a deep breath.

"I'm listening. Go on."

"A few years ago, when my wife, Elise, died, I had a complete breakdown. I'm still working through a lot of conflicted feelings—it's been a long and difficult road. But I'm making progress. I'm beginning to become whole, starting to believe I have a purpose again." Sara started to speak, Tom interrupted. "Wait. I have more to tell you." He put his coffee cup down. "A few months ago I decided the best way to heal was to move away from Jamestown. I needed a fresh start. That's why I bought Remington House.

"The feelings I have . . . that I had . . . for Elise are dead. I'm finally getting past all the pain her death brought me. Meeting you—being with you—has changed me." He took a long breath. "I'm able to deal with the loss of everything I once believed I had with Elise. Our life together was a lie. I don't think she was capable of loving me. She had too many problems of her own. I understand that now. I have tremendous guilt surrounding her suicide, but I'm moving on."

Sara paled. Putting her cup down too quickly, she spilled her coffee. "I didn't know any of this." She absently mindedly dabbed at the spill with her napkin. "I didn't know about your wife's suicide."

"No way could you have. I've accepted her death. I've moved on with my life. You can see that, can't you?"

"Yes. You've been through so much. I wish I'd known. I'm so sorry."

"It's okay," Tom said softly.

With eyes unblinking, her brow furrowed, Sara anxiously studied Tom's face. "There's still more to this, Tom. I can see it in your eyes. What is it?"

"Since Cassie got here, I feel like she's waiting for me to break down again. She's always watching me, questioning my moods. Needless to say, I've been on edge. Yesterday all hell broke loose. It was crazy.

"Nell's nieces, and later that afternoon, Cassie and Mary went into the attic. They said they heard noises and voices. No doubt influenced by the local gossip about the Lindemans, their imaginations went crazy. They convinced themselves there are ghosts in my house."

"What?" Sara quit dabbing at the spilled coffee and looked intently at Tom.

"I'm sure squirrels or raccoons have gotten into the attic, and Lizzie forgets and leaves her TV on—that explains the noises they heard. The cat was up there, too. Wiggins probably howled at the squirrels, and it sounded like screaming to the girls. But they wouldn't accept any reasonable explanations. Linda and Gwenn, then Cassie and Mary, started acting hysterically, making a big deal about things they thought they heard. They were screaming and running around—Mary almost fell down the stairs."

"More coffee?" The waitress startled them. "How about a dish of hot blueberry cobber?" They shook their heads. She filled their cups anyway and left.

Tom waited until Joanie was out of hearing range. "Cassie and Mary insist there are ghosts in the house. I don't know how to deal with their hysteria over these nonexistent spirits. It's getting out of hand."

"What in the world are they . . . "

Tom interrupted, "There are no ghosts—only imaginations running wild. Cassie and the rest of the ladies in the house are having a field day with their rants about spirits. They're getting themselves more and more worked up. Cassie has always believed in the supernatural, so she's encouraging them. Cassie even believes she saw an old woman in her room."

"What!" Sara exclaimed.

"Again, her imagination." Tom tried to keep his tone light. He hated lying to Sara. "Cassie sees what she wants to see. With poor lighting and shadows, it was most likely a reflection from outside caught in the mirror. Not an old woman."

Sara nodded, Tom went on, "The other day was the tipping point, it was more than I could handle. I had to get out of the house. I was angry with everyone there. That's why I went to Vivian's. I needed to be with you. You make me feel normal. Believe me, Sara I was never mad at you."

"I'm beginning to understand." Sara held her hand out to Tom and said, "I've always believed there's a logical explanation—that there are no spirits, no ghosts coming back to haunt us or take care of unfinished business."

"You're dead right," Tom said. "Pardon the pun!" He smiled.

Sara pushed a stray hair off her cheek. "When I was a little girl, right after my granddad died, I thought he came into my room one night. He stood at the foot of my bed and sang to me, the song he always sang when he tucked me in." Sara took a sip of her coffee. "I told my mother about it. She said it was a dream—something to make his death make sense to me, my own way of reconciling, a way for me to say good-bye. Sometimes things we think are real are only stories we make up to soothe ourselves, to have everything make sense. It gives us some closure. Maybe when I get to know Cassie, she'll talk to me about her beliefs. Maybe I can help her understand that she is seeing only what she wants to see. Especially if she *wants* to believe."

"Don't worry! I'll make sure Cassie comes to her senses and stops this nonsense!"

"Don't get mad at her. Just because you and I don't believe in the supernatural doesn't mean Cassie will change her mind. If she believes in spirits, she must have her own good reasons."

"I suppose you have a point, but this foolishness has to stop. She's scaring everyone in the household."

Joanie was suddenly beside Tom. "Foolishness! I don't think so, you bastard!" she whispered into Tom's ear, tipping the carafe, pouring hot coffee all over the table. Tom and Sara jumped up, trying to avoid the steaming liquid.

"Oh, my gosh! I'm sorry. Did I do that?" Joanie grabbed a napkin from the table and began mopping up the mess. "I must have tripped or something. Are you okay?"

"Yeah. Are you, Sara?" Tom looked at her.

"What did you just say to Tom?" Sara demanded.

"What? I said 'I'm sorry', that's all," Joanie answered.

"Before that." Sara glared at Joanie who seemed baffled by the whole ordeal. "Oh, forget it!" Sara threw her coat around her shoulders. "Tom, let's go." She was halfway to the door before Tom caught up with her.

"Hey, hold on a minute, Sara. I have to pay the bill."

Sara snapped, "I'll wait outside."

Damn! I clearly heard what Joanie said. That wasn't Joanie's voice. That was Elise's! Tom threw a couple twenties on the counter and went after Sara.

Sara said, "Come on, Tom. What did Joanie whisper to you? She seemed angry with you."

"I don't have a clue," Tom lied. "I wasn't paying any attention to her. You sure you're okay?" Tom asked.

"I'm fine. Not a single drop of coffee got on me. I needed to get out of there before I lost it—that's all. How could Joanie be so rude?" Sara responded harshly.

"Having a bad day I guess." Tom grabbed Sara's hand.

Sara squeezed Tom's fingers tightly in hers. "Tell me more about Elise. If you want to, that is."

"I will, in time. Not tonight. Right now, I want to be with you. I don't want Elise interfering with that."

Sara stopped walking and dropped Tom's hand. Shivering, she pulled her collar up around her neck. "That's crazy! She's dead. She can't interfere."

"I know. I guess what I mean is, I don't want to think about her—not tonight. Okay?"

Tom bent down and picked up a flyer lying on the sidewalk. Turning it over, he started reading it. His face turned ashen.

"What's wrong . . .what *is* that?" asked Sara. "Let me see." The wind caught the flyer as she reached for it. Tom turned to run after it. Sara hurried over to the Cherokee, angrily jerking at the locked door handle. The car alarm's shrill siren pierced the frosty, evening air.

Tom silenced the alarm, opened the door for Sara. "Go ahead and get in, I'll be right back." He chased the flyer as it fluttered down the street, twirling in a playful wind funnel of leaves and dust. *Got it!* He grabbed it out of the air as it took a downward dive.

Sara watched him as he neared the car, a frown on her face. Tom folded the paper and stuffed it into his coat pocket, then slid in behind the wheel, slamming the door.

"You're acting strange. What's on that paper, Tom?"

"Nothing."

Sara reached into his pocket taking the paper out, smoothing the creases. She read it quietly. "It's an advertisement for a concert."

"Not just any concert—a Beethoven concert. Look!" He tapped on paper. "It says 'With a special appearance by renowned pianist Jonathan Rudman from the Jamestown Symphony Orchestra performing *Für Elise*.' Here in Ravenswood. Quite a coincidence don't you think?"

"This doesn't say anything about *Für Elise*. It says *Beethoven's Symphony No. 9*. Here, look." She handed it to Tom, leaned back and fastened her seatbelt.

Tom glanced back at the brochure. He crumpled it up and, putting the key in the ignition, cranked the engine. "Damn! I must be seeing things. Sorry." He knew what it said. It said *Für Elise*.

Tom reached over and stroked Sara's hand. "I'm sorry you had to see me like this. Must be the stress of the holiday."

"Among other things. Listen, Tom, I think you need to be honest with Cassie. Let her know how you feel about her hovering over you right now," Sara said. "She's adding too much drama to your life."

"You're right." He squeezed her hand, took a long breath, let it out slowly. A puff of vapor formed in the frigid cold. The heater hadn't warmed up yet. Beside him he felt Sara shiver. He added, "I may as well tell you, too, that I have to go back to Jamestown next week."

"Do you think going to Jamestown is a smart thing to do right now? If you're already stressing, what good could going there possibly do?"

If he went back to Jamestown, Elise would follow him. He sensed that's what she really wanted. He needed to leave as soon as he could and get Elise away from here. He would deal with her there. "I have some business to take care of that actually can't wait. Maybe it'll do me good to get back there right now. And I won't be alone—Nate's there. Almost everything's been packed up and the house is being repainted. So seeing the house, devoid of Elise's presence may be what I need."

"Maybe, but it seems like an odd time to go. What about your sister and her family? Are they leaving so soon?" Sara asked. "I thought they'd be here for a while."

"Cassie and Lizzie are staying. Mike has to go to New York on business. Joe will be here to check on Cassie and Lizzie. And Nell and her nieces will be around to help with the house. Jimmy will be over to play with Lizzie. Not a chance anyone will be lonely."

"The idea of you being gone right now is overwhelming. I don't think you should go. Wait until your sister leaves. Then you could go—I could even go with you."

"Don't worry. Nate's in Jamestown. I won't be alone." Tom drove slowly down the street, now almost empty of any traffic.

Tom was pulling the car onto Main Street when he saw Vivian peering cautiously out of the jewelry store. She made a mad rush to a car parked in the lot across the street.

Tom said to Sara, "Did you see her?"

"See who?"

"Vivian. She just came out of the jewelers and got into that Cadillac."

"That *is* her. And that's William's car. He must have given her the okay to drive it again. That's rare."

"I got the distinct impression, from the way she was acting, that Vivian didn't want to be seen by anyone."

"Well, knowing Viv, she has her reasons—most likely involving something completely selfish."

"Well, at least she didn't see us."

"Lucky us."

Tom stopped at the next intersection, turned to Sara. "If you want, we could get a room for the evening. We can tell everyone we went to a movie. Would you like to be alone—just the two of us? We won't have another chance for weeks. I need you, Sara."

***

Vivian sat in William's Cadillac in the parking lot, rubbing her temples. She glanced around. "Where am I?"

"Damn!" Elise said out loud. She'd let her guard down. She wouldn't do that again. She turned the key in the ignition and gunned the engine, startling an elderly couple walking on the sidewalk behind her. She flipped them off and pulled onto the street, never seeing Tom and Sara.

Chapter 47

Sara smiled at Tom. He turned the car around and drove to the Sherwood Hotel on the east end of town. The lobby was empty; from the lounge came the sound of clinking glasses, music and laughter. A clerk, looking suave and polished in a dark brown suit, chocolate brown vest and tie, stood behind the reservation desk. In the button hole of his lapel was an orange carnation.

He greeted them with a warm smile. "How may I help you?"

"We'd like a room." Tom said.

"I'll check, but I believe we're full tonight. It is the Thanksgiving holiday after all. How long will you be staying?"

"One night."

The clerk looked at Tom, started to say something, apparently thought better of it. He typed into the computer screen. "Ahh! There's a cancellation. A queen size room, will that be all right?"

Tom nodded. The clerk handed him the standard form to fill out and took his credit card. Tom declined the need for help with their nonexistent luggage. The clerk handed them the room key, and Sara and Tom went upstairs.

The room was lovely. Pale green and floral striped wallpaper covered the walls. It had quaint Victorian furnishings—an upholstered settee upholstered in dark green brocade, a matching high-backed chair and an ornate dressing table and chair sat at the end of the room in front of a small fireplace with a brass screen. The four poster bed was covered with pillows and a down comforter in green stripes alternating with tiny bouquets of pale pink roses. A balcony overlooked a small park with a fountain, its spray of water now frozen. Ornate benches were placed along the paths that wound around the park. In the ground's center, under a stand of leafless trees, stood a small gazebo, its ceiling strung with tiny, twinkling lights. It had started snowing again. The large, lacey flakes swirled serenely in the twilight.

Tom and Sara stood timidly for a moment, then Tom took the initiative, unbuttoning Sara's coat, tossing it on the chair. Gently, taking her face in his hands, he kissed her open mouth, felt her intense response.

Chapter 48

"Lie still, darling, and I'll rub your back," Sara said, her fingers worked magically on Tom's tight muscles. He began to relax and, with a final mumble of contentment, fell asleep.

In his dream Tom was back in his Jamestown home wandering aimlessly through empty rooms looking for something. What, he did not know. Unusually calm and peaceful, he stood for a while at the doorway to his bedroom trying to recall what had happened to all his furniture. The room was completely empty, even the carpet had been pulled out. Patterned wallpaper showed rectangles of vibrant color where pictures had once hung. A slight breeze blew into the room from an open window. Tom started across the room to close it. The breeze turned into an icy gale, bitter and biting. Flurries of snow blew into the barren room. All around him heavy snow fell; the harsh wind blew drifts almost as high as the ceiling.

The window seemed so far away that Tom didn't think he would ever reach it. He trudged forward, each step more difficult as the snow continued falling, mounding ever deeper. He strained with every footfall, his breath a struggle as ice-cold air burned into his lungs.

At last he reached the window. Outside the sun was shining brightly on the trees, green with newly budded leaves. In the garden the tulips and daffodils bloomed red and yellow against the deep purple of early hyacinths. His mother, sitting on a chaise lounge amid the flowers, looked up and waved. She flashed her warmest smile, then looked away.

The sounds of sobbing echoed through the empty hallway. Tom did not dare turn around to find its source—he needed to close the window. That was his task. That was all he would think of right now. The window frame was stuck. His fingers numbed against the freezing glass. Again and again he tried to free the window and slide it closed.

As he labored, his mother watched from the garden, a parasol shading her from the warm sun. She pointed at him and waved, her lips moving as she talked to someone just out of his view. At last the window came crashing down, hitting the sill so hard he thought the glass would shatter. Teeth chattering, fingers blue from the cold, Tom turned, tried to see through the blinding blizzard and into the hall. The snow had settled now, had packed on the floor, making his journey much easier. When he reached the hallway, the temperature was warm and sultry. Tom sat down on the bare wood floor, began rubbing his hands and blowing warm breath on his icy fingers.

Nate came down the hall. Hampered by crutches, he moved slowly, his broken leg dragging uselessly on the floor. "Good morning, Tom," he said. "Do you want me to have Sloan shovel out your room? I think it advisable. It makes such a mess when it melts." Nate stopped, waiting. "Tom?"

"Yes," Tom said. "Nate…I thought I heard someone crying."

"Yes, you certainly did."

Tom sat on the floor rubbing his fingers, watched Nate walk away.

Nate was halfway down the hall when he turned and yelled, "Oh, I almost forgot. I think you were looking for this."

Tom stood up, his legs stiff and slow to move after sitting on the hard floor. Glancing down, he saw he was standing in a puddle of melted snow. "Would you have someone clean this up right away?" he hollered to Nate.

"I'll get Sloan," Nate yelled back.

Tom stooped over to pick up a book now lying on the floor beside him, gasping when he read the title, *The Life and Death of Elise, A Diary*. He dropped the book. It turned to ashes as it hit the puddle of melted snow. He heard a scream, then again the mournful sound of crying. Tom glanced down the long hallway—instead of Nate, it was now Sara who struggled to stay on her feet as she negotiated the hall on crutches that were much too tall for her. When she was a few feet from him, she reached her right hand out. "Here it is, sir." Her voice was Nate's voice. "Though perhaps it would be better if I kept this for you, so you don't lose it."

Sara held Elise's wedding ring in the palm of her hand. Tom took the gold band, stared dumbly at it. Down the hall, the mournful crying continued.

"That woman has been blubbering all morning—ever since I took the ring away from her." Sara's eyes flashed angrily. She reached out and grabbed the ring from Tom's hand. "I think I'll keep this. You better go to her and make her stop. To be perfectly honest, I don't think any of us can take much more of Elise's sniveling."

Sara twirled around, shuffling down the hall away from Tom. "I'll have Sloan clean this mess up. Spring snow is such a nuisance. As soon as you get one room shoveled out, you have two more waiting. Such a nuisance," she mumbled, still wobbling on the too-tall crutches.

Tom crept quietly to Elise's room, his wet shoes making loud squishing sounds on the bare wood planks. He walked into her room, closed the door behind him. The room was dark, the only light coming from a single candle burning in the far corner. Tom's own shadow undulated grotesquely across the floor and onto the wall, alternately large then small in the flickering candlelight. Standing at the window, her back to him, Elise didn't seem to know he was there. Her shoulders shook as she cried. She seemed frail and defenseless.

Suddenly the sound of waves crashing against the rocky beach below drowned out Elise's wails. Tom glanced around the room. It was not her room. Panic overcame him. One wall of the room was lined with packing crates visible momentarily in a flicker of light. He gazed past her out the window. In the distance he could see twinkling lights from the windows of the Harrison's house. He was in the attic at Remington!

Elise remained still, her back to Tom. Without making a sound, he inched toward the door behind him. He reached behind, feeling for the doorknob. At last his fingers touched the cold knob, curled around it and slowly turned it. Not taking his eyes off of Elise, he backed out and quietly closed the door.

"My God, isn't that woman ever going to shut up?"

Tom spun around, his heart pounding. Sloan stood there, a snow shovel in his hand. "I don't know how you can put up with that, Mr. Gardner. Must be something you can to do make her stop that awful wailing. Enough to make a man crazy." He looked at Tom with disgust, then turned and went back into Tom's bedroom.

Behind him Tom heard the sound of the doorknob turning. Sweat trickled down his forehead. For a moment he remained utterly still, his breath echoing in the hallway. "Elise, my darling," he whispered. "Please don't cry anymore. Forgive me." He turned around, arms outstretched to hold her. There was no one there.

***

Tom opened his eyes. The only light in the room a faint, white glow from the streetlight. It took him a second to remember where he was. Beside him, Sara slept peacefully. He wondered what visions filled her dreams. He bent over and gently kissed her forehead. "I love you, Sara," he whispered. Slipping quietly from bed, he dressed and crossed the hotel suite to look out the window. Fresh snow blanketed the park. The gazebo glistened with snowflakes as the moon appeared from behind the clouds.

"Tom, what's wrong? Come back to bed," Sara said.

"It's past midnight; I better get you home before Vivian calls out the guards."

Chapter 49

Vivian slept soundly with no memory of having gone into Ravenswood that afternoon. She'd taken two sleeping pills and curled up in her bed after finding herself on the stairs, dressed in clothes she didn't remember putting on, her coat and purse in her hands. She was becoming increasingly worried about her blackout spells. She should call Dr. Avery, but not now. The only thing she wanted to do now was sleep. She was sure it was all the pressure. She had too much to handle with the two boys and the holidays without William here to help her. When he got home, she'd make sure he knew how she felt about his long business trips. Screw his business deals. She needed him. She floated into a drugged sleep.

Elise had a difficult time rousing Vivian. She should have stopped her from taking those pills. It took what seemed like hours to get Vivian's body to respond and get her out of the bed. But Elise had no choice; she had to use Vivian to take the jewels to her attic room at Remington house. Elise wasn't strong enough to carry them that far. And—Elise needed those jewels.

Elise and Vivian almost made it to Tom's house. They would have gotten there and safely hidden the jewelry in Elise's attic room had it not taken so long to get Vivian up and moving. Damn Vivian and her pills! Elise struggled with Vivian's body, painstakingly forcing one foot in front of the other, all the while negotiating the rocky path behind the house. Elise had fallen several times leaving Vivian's hands cut and bleeding.

Hidden in the trees, Elise watched Tom driving up the winding road and into the driveway. Damn! Now that she was so close to getting into Tom's house, she was trapped. There was no way to get Vivian into the house without Tom seeing her.

Elise knew where Tom had been. "With Sara, of course," she snarled. "I'll take care of her." But right now, she was losing control of Vivian's drugged body. Using the last of her strength to stay with Vivian, Elise managed to bury the jewel case under a pile of leaves. She marked the spot with a large stone, then dragged a broken branch to cover everything

Elise would find a way to retrieve the jewels tomorrow. Her plan to hide them in her attic room until the dinner party would have to change, that's all. She'd planned to put Vivian's jewelry in Sara's purse when the family came for dinner next Saturday night. Vivian, controlled by Elise, would "accidentally" open Sara's bag and find her "stolen" jewels. Now Elise needed to find another way to make it work. And she would. She knew Tom would turn on Sara if he thought she had stolen from Vivian. He would never tolerate that. And Vivian would never allow a common thief to live in her house. Dear, sweet Sara would be on the first train out of town Sunday morning, with no one caring where she went. Elise's plan might have to change, but not the outcome.

Tom remained sitting in the Jeep in front of his house. Elise was growing tense and frustrated. She needed to leave Vivian's body. Damn it! What was Tom doing? Why didn't he get out of the car and go into the house? Elise saw the light in Tom's car go on—he was finally getting out. She left Vivian and returned to her room in the attic.

Chapter 50

After taking Sara home, Tom sat in front of his house thinking about her and the troubling turn of events in his new home. How could he dare bring Sara into this madness?

The only lights burning inside came from the front entryway. Everyone had gone to bed. The dashboard clock glowed in the darkness. It said two minutes past two. Laying his head against the headrest he asked, his voice barely a whisper, "Elise, what do you want?" He didn't expect an answer.

He opened the Jeep door, struggling to free himself from the seatbelt he had forgotten to unbuckle. As his left foot made contact with the dirt driveway, he started to stand, his right foot poised in midair ready to take his weight. He began to pivot, the downward motion of his right leg beginning as his foot sought the ground—all automatic responses, simple movements done a thousand times before. But this time, maybe because of the late hour, maybe something else, Tom became confused. His reactions weren't swift enough to keep him from tumbling out of the car, his right foot did not find the flat surface of the ground.

He fell face first, the gravel slicing into his forehead. His left shoulder hit next, then his torso twisted and his hips slammed into the driveway full force sliding his body several feet from the car. Pulling his arms out from under him, he rolled onto his back and lay looking up at the black sky.

Huge snowflakes swirled and sparkled in light reflected from above him. Gazing up he saw a light burning in the attic. Someone paced back and forth, the shadow alternately casting darkness then light over Tom.

The front door flew open. "Tom?" Michael yelled. "What happened?" Michael flew out the door and down the steps. "Are you drunk?"

"I wish," Tom answered. "Give me a minute. I'm okay, I think. Caught my foot getting out of the car. I hit my face pretty hard. Think I'm bleeding."

Michael squatted beside him. "Oh, man! You're bleeding a lot. Can you get up?"

Pushing himself forward to his knees, Tom leaned forward, then stood with Michael's help. He bent his head down and spit out a mouthful of blood; his nose was bleeding profusely, the heavy drops made faint, dull thuds as they hit the ground splattering a mix of blood and dirt onto his slacks. He rocked back and forth, unsteady on his feet. He reached for Michael's arm. "Just get me to the porch. Let me sit down. I don't think I can walk any farther than that right now."

Grabbing Tom under his arm, Michael helped him walk to the porch, carefully easing him into a wooden porch chair. He pulled his robe off, wadding it up to put under Tom's nose. "Here, hold this, lean back and pinch your nose, right under the cartilage." Tom did as he was told. "Firm pressure, yeah, that's good, don't let go. I'm going to get some washcloths from inside. We'll try to get the bleeding from your forehead and nose stopped. Then we'll get you into the house. You okay for a minute?"

"Yeah."

"Don't try to get up. I'll be right back." Michael disappeared into the house, flipping the porch light on.

Tom straightened up a little. The bleeding seemed to have slowed. At the turn in the drive, partially hidden in the trees, Tom could see someone standing in the shadows. "Who's there?" he yelled. "What are you doing?"

Michael reappeared with a handful of towels and a large plastic pitcher full of water. "Who are you yelling at?"

"Someone's out there. Look! Down at the curve." Tom pointed a bloody finger down the drive toward a stand of trees.

"Just trees and shadows," Michael said. "There's no one there." He dismissed Tom's concerns and wrung out a cloth. He dabbed at the blood, trying to see how deep the cuts on Tom's face were. "Lots of gravel and dirt imbedded in your forehead. Cheek, too. Might need stitches. We should get you into town."

"No. Just let me sit a minute. I'll be fine once I get my nose to stop bleeding." Removing his clamped fingers from his nose, Tom released the pressure. He put a clean towel under his nostrils, waited a few seconds, and checked. "The bleeding's stopped. Hand me another wet cloth." He cautiously blotted the gash above his brow, wincing when the damp rag made contact with the open flesh. He looked down the driveway. Someone stood in the shadow of the trees. "Hey!"

Tom started to get up. His mind said "yes," his body said "no." Clumsily he sat back down. "Michael, go see who that is."

"That's a tree. There's no one there. Trust me."

"There's a light on my key ring—on the ground over there." Tom pointed. "Shine the light out there."

Retrieving the key ring, Michael shone the flashlight down the drive. The brilliant LED light illuminated the trees, making black shadows long and stark on the landscape. Snowflakes glistened. A startled Snow Bird flew from the branch where it had carefully sheltered itself. "Crap! What the heck?" Michael ran toward the trees.

Tom followed, running awkwardly, both hands at his face, one pinching his nose so the bleeding wouldn't start again, the other holding a towel tightly against his head. "Who is it?" he yelled.

"I don't know," Michael hollered.

"Vivian? Is that you?" Tom yelled at the woman standing beside the tree. She was trembling and began sobbing when Tom and Michael reached her. "What are you doing out here in the middle of the night?"

She screamed when she saw Tom's bloody appearance. Dizzy, Tom sank to his knees in front of her. "It's Tom. And my brother-in-law, Michael."

"What am I doing here?" Vivian clenched her hands into small fists, looked imploringly at Tom and Michael.

"I don't know, Vivian. You tell me! What are you doing hiding here in the trees?"

"I don't know." Vivian's confusion turned to anger. Spittles of saliva, reflecting the moonlight like diamond sparks, sprayed out of her mouth into the dark. "For God's sake!"

"Tom! Michael! What's going on?" Cassie ran down the driveway trying to get her arms inside her robe. "Ouch." She stumbled, twisting her ankle. Luckily she caught herself before she fell. "Tom! What happened? Oh, my God!"

"He took a fall getting out of his Jeep," Michael explained. "I told him we need to get him to the hospital—some of his cuts look pretty deep. And then this. . . . " Michael pointed at Vivian. "It's Vivian. Tom's neighbor. Tom saw her standing out here in the dark."

"This is crazy! Tom, are you all right. No! Don't get up. Let me see." Cassie took the towel from Tom's face. "Oh my gosh! It's bad, Tom."

Michael said, "Stay here, Cassie. I'll drive the Cherokee down. We should consider driving *both* of them the hospital. Mrs. Harrison is *not* okay either."

"Don't be ridiculous, I'm fine," Vivian said, wrapping her arms around her shivering body. "I must have been walking in my sleep. I've been doing that lately. I've been having horrible migraines. I think the medicine I'm taking makes me sleep walk. When I saw you and Tom, I was disoriented, but I'm fine now,"

"We'll see," Michael said, then turned and ran to get the car.

"That doesn't make any sense," Cassie said. "How could you sleepwalk all the way over here in the dark?"

"I did, that's all. Get me to the house. I'll call Amos and have him come and get me. I need to go home," Vivian snapped, then pointed at Tom, still sitting on the ground. "You better take care of him, though. He looks horrible." Then to Tom she said, "You look awful."

Covering his forehead with the bloody rag, Tom said, his voice steady and firm, "I want to know what you're doing here, Vivian. Were you spying on me?"

"Don't flatter yourself. Why would I do that?"

"Who cares?" Cassie said. "We need to get Tom in the car and to the hospital. We'll drop Vivian off on the way."

Michael backed the car down the hill. Getting out, he opened the passenger side and helped Tom, then Vivian into the Jeep. "Come on, let's go."

Chapter 51

From the attic window, Elise watched the scene unfolding down in the drive. She was elated to have caused so much trouble for everyone. She couldn't help but wonder what Vivian had come up with to save face. *That woman is such a bitch.* Elise knew Vivian would never admit having blacked out. Elise giggled as Tom hobbled to the Jeep. Tom was covered in blood and seemed weak and disoriented.

Cassie got in the back seat with Vivian. Michael drove back up to the house and dropped Cassie at the front porch. She ran in the house, returning in seconds with her husband's coat. The Jeep sped off toward the main road. They must be going into town. She smiled. Tom must be hurt worse than she'd thought. Elise paced for a few minutes, then decided to go downstairs.

She went into Cassie's bedroom. She wasn't there, but the child was. The little girl, Elise's niece, was sleeping peacefully. Elise wished she'd been able to be a part of Lizzie's life. She was all alone, just like Elise. Cassie seemed to have forgotten about her tonight. Lying down next to the sleeping child, Elise gently pushed a stray wisp of hair from Lizzie's cheek. *I'll take care of you. Don't be afraid.* Lizzie cuddled close to her and sighed.

The door opened. Cassie tiptoed in. "Sleep my little one," she whispered, gently kissing her daughter on the forehead. Completely unaware that Elise was curled up beside Lizzie, she gathered clean pajamas from the dresser drawer and went to take a shower.

Michael had taken Vivian home, then was driving Tom into Ravenswood to the emergency clinic. He promised to call Cassie as soon as he could, probably in an hour or two.

Cassie turned the faucets on and stepped into the hot shower. A quick shower would take the chill from her bones. Maybe help her relax a little.

Chapter 52

Watching the sleeping child, Elise's thoughts began to drift. She wondered how Tom could do this to her. How could he love someone else? He said he would love her forever. No matter what. How dare he forget her? Her mind went back in time; she remembered when she had been happy—when she first met Tom.

***

Elise was seventeen, still a child really. It was a clear, crisp day in early spring and she'd taken a walk to get out of the house and away from her mother who had awaked in a vile mood, hung over and ill from too much cheap gin. As soon as Elise finished her chores, she tiptoed to her mother's room. She had gone back to bed. Quietly Elise crept out of the house avoiding another battle with her mother. She needed to get away for a few hours of peace and quiet. She hated her mother, always either drunk or hung over. Elise detested feeling the constant degradation, despised the endless parade of men coming into the house, loud and sloppy drunks, pawing at her mother with their dirty hands. But she wouldn't think about that now. For a few hours she was free to do whatever she wanted. She made up her mind a few months ago. The day she turned eighteen, she was leaving for good. She'd get out of this rat-hole.

At Woodland Park, Elise sat at her favorite spot on a bench under the trees and watched the geese float peacefully across the lake, invisible feet propelling them through the murky-blue water. Listening to the sounds of children laughing, she felt her dark mood lift. A collie chasing a Frisbee charged in her direction. When she turned to watch him, she saw Tom. He was only a few feet away. Tall, maybe six foot two she guessed, with deep-set, blue eyes. His wavy, dark-brown hair had fallen across his forehead. Pushing it out of his eyes, he smiled at Elise. She took a deep breath to quiet her racing heart and smiled shyly, embarrassed as she felt the heat of a blush spread across her face.

Tom sat down on the bench beside her. "Hi, great day, isn't it? Are you waiting for someone?"

"No, I'm not. I'm just watching the kids play. It's such a beautiful day," Elise said. She took a drink from her water bottle, then wiped her lips.

"Me, too. I'm Tom, by the way. Do you come here often?" He reached down and patted his collie's head

"When I can. It's kind of my special place, if you know what I mean." She stopped talking and studied the man beside her. Their eyes met and they couldn't seem to look away from each other's gaze. She recognized a kindness in his eyes. She also perceived a sadness that puzzled her. "I'm Elise."

"Hello, Elise." Tom threw the Frisbee again. The collie ran after it, returning at break-neck speed to deposit the treasure at Tom's feet. Tom poured water from his bottle into the Frisbee for his dog, who lapped it up noisily, then dropped down in the grass, stretching out for a nap.

Elise and Tom talked for hours. Their conversation flowed easily from one topic to another. He told her he'd just come back to Jamestown last week after being away for several years, a mixture of work and pleasure. Now he was home to stay. Tom was taking his place in his family's business—he had been summoned. His father and uncle owned several hotels, the Gardner Plazas, in Jamestown, Manhattan, and New York City. "Perhaps you've heard of them?"

"Yes, of course I have. Who hasn't?" Elise said.

"We also own a chain of boutiques—Alexa's—named after my grandmother."

Elise had been impressed, of course. They continued talking about their mutual likes. Time passed quickly. Elise, swept up in the stories about Tom's trips to Europe, his warm smile and his ability to make her laugh. She was disappointed when he said he had to leave. Sadly she watched him and his dog run across the park and disappear.

Elise's mother remained mysteriously sober, and the two busied themselves with spring-cleaning. It was a week before she had time to go back to the park. She saw Tom right away. He was sitting on the same bench they shared before.

When he saw her, he jumped up and walked hurriedly to her, waving and smiling. "Hello," he called. He put his arm through hers as soon as she was close. "I've been wondering where you've been. I've been here almost every day hoping to see you again."

"You have? I've been incredibly busy. I haven't had a chance to get away. Sorry." Elise had been elated.

Leading her to a grove of trees, her heart skipped a beat when she saw he had spread a blanket in the shade. On the blanket was a picnic basket. "Just in case you showed up." Tom laughed when she raised her eyebrows and started to say something. "Actually I've brought a picnic lunch every day. I figured one of these days you'd be here."

"You're too much. I *am* flattered. Every day?" Elise asked.

"Yeah. You can be sure I won't let you go today without getting your phone number." He smiled, motioned her to sit down. "I don't know how I could have talked to you for so long and never have gotten your full name, either."

She laughed and held out her hand. "Elise Phillips. How do you do Tom Gardner?"

"Now that I've found you again, I'm great."

The afternoon flew by. That day was the beginning of the happiest months in Elise's life. She and Tom spent every possible moment together. They were young and in love. It was an enchanted summer.

One evening toward the end of June, having finished a steak and lobster dinner on the Plaza, Tom told Elise his family wanted to meet her. "They want to meet the mysterious woman whose been taking up all of my time." This was not the first time he'd asked her to meet his family. She always made excuses. But this time Tom was adamant that she meet them. "You have to understand how I feel, Elise. I love you and I want my family to love you."

Elise explained to Tom how she felt. She knew his family would never accept her, would never feel she was good enough for him. After all, they were a very wealthy and influential family. She and her alcoholic mother were from the wrong side of town. They would think Elise was only after Tom's money. Wouldn't they? "I would, if I were in their position."

"Elise," he said her name softly, touched her hand gently, "I love you, and they will, too. You have no reason to be afraid to meet them. They're wonderful people. They raised me, didn't they?"

Elise nodded and picked up her glass. "Tom, I don't want you and me to end. This is like a fairy tale. I don't want anything to spoil that. So, please don't pressure me. I know I'm right." She smiled at him.

Tom reached across the table and took the glass from her hand. "I want to marry you, Elise."

Elise never imagined he would want to marry her. Not in her wildest dreams. She just stared at him.

"You haven't answered me. Elise, will you marry me?"

"Tom, I love you, you know I do, but . . ." She started to speak, wiped a tear from her cheek. She didn't want Tom to see her cry. She never wanted him to think of her as weak or silly.

"Our relationship can never work. I'm nobody, Tom. I have nothing to offer you," Elise tried explaining as Tom scowled at her. Pausing, she took a sip of her iced tea, swallowed, took a long breath, then continued. "I have a drunk for a mother and no clue where, or even who, my father is. Your family is from a different world. You're all highly educated and well traveled. You know who you are. I don't. Your parents will never allow me to be a part of your life."

Tom couldn't understand her fears. "You're wrong. You're worrying about something you know nothing about. I told you, my family will love you. Because I do. It's that simple," Tom said, downing his goblet of wine, then slamming the glass on the table. The elderly couple at the next table glanced at Tom, then looked quickly away when he shot them a nasty look.

Frowning at him, Elise went on, her voice low and fraught with emotion, "Tom, these past few months have been the best of my life. But our relationship can never go anywhere." Elise grabbed her purse, stood up and walked away with as much dignity as she could manage.

Behind her, she heard the chair hit the floor as Tom ran after her, not taking the time to push it out of his way.

"Elise! Stop!" Tom grabbed her shoulder.

She shrugged his hand off and continued moving toward the door. Once they were outside, Tom stepped in front of her, blocking her path. "No. You will not end this." Fiercely he pulled her to him and held her. "I will take care of you. Forever. Be damned anyone who tries to stop me!"

"It's impossible—you and I," Elise whispered, but made no effort to leave.

The last day of July, Elise, frightened and miserable, prepared to face Tom's family. Arriving in style in Tom's jet black Jaguar, she judged herself completely out of place. An awkward schoolgirl, not the sophisticated woman she felt sure his family was prepared to meet.

The lavishly landscaped and manicured grounds were spectacular. Climbing the cobblestone sidewalk to the house,

Tom grinned at her, seemingly oblivious of her near panicked state.

With the courage of a soldier going into battle, Elise entered the stately Gardner mansion. The heavily polished mahogany and stained glass took her breath away. The entry hall was probably larger than her whole house. On the opposing wall to the entry doors, a sandstone fireplace covered the entire entry hall; deer carved into the stone gazed out from both sides of the fireplace. On the black granite mantle were two elaborate, pewter candelabras. An antique pewter framed mirror hung above the fireplace. To the right hung a portrait of a group of seven or eight garishly dressed men on a horseback chasing a red fox that ran triumphantly into the forest. "Oh my God, Tom. This is stunning. I had no idea. Your family lives here?"

"Yes, and someday it will be mine. Imagine that, my love. Can you picture little children running around and sliding down the banister?" Tom smiled, his blue eyes twinkling. "I can see you perfectly. Standing over there looking out that window at the gardens."

Elise could not. In her wildest dreams she couldn't imagine herself living in a house like this. She'd never considered having children. For that matter, she'd never planned on marrying. It was impossible to think about those things right now. She shuddered, feeling completely overwhelmed.

Tom and Elise crossed the entryway, walking on an exquisite oval, tapestry rug woven in rich browns and deep blues. Taking her hand, Tom led her into the oak-paneled study where the family waited. Following protocol, he introduced her first to his mother, Jessica, a statuesque woman with graying hair swept up in a loose chignon, ice-blue eyes, and a finely-chiseled, aristocratic face. She wore a pale yellow designer pantsuit of cashmere and suede accented with a single string of creamy, white pearls. From her ears dangled matching pearls hanging from clusters of diamonds. "Hello, darling," she said to Tom. She held her hand toward Elise. "So happy meet you, Elise."

Elise smiled, uncomfortably aware of the careful scrutiny she was receiving from Tom's parents and sister.

Tom's father, Robert, looked very much as Elise had imagined: tall, the beginning of a slight stoop to his shoulders, large boned, strong facial features with thick brows over dark-brown—almost black—eyes. He was not as handsome as his son was, but Elise could imagine he had been quite a ladies' man in his younger years. "How do you do?" he said formally, taking her small hand briefly into both of his, then quickly dropping it.

Elise had been right. She could see it in Tom's parents' faces. Standing in front of them, in their pretentious home, in their designer clothing, she felt shabby and unkempt. She hated them for making her feel that way, hated herself more for feeling inadequate.

Cassie offered her hand to Elise. "Hi, I'm Cassie. I've heard so little about you. Come on," she said pulling on Elise's hand. "Let's go into the living room, and you can tell me all about yourself. My brother has been very closed mouth about you, and I intend to find out why." She looked at Elise, who had turned quite pale, and laughed. "Elise, I'm joking. Honest. Tom, tell her I'm always like this."

"Cass, let's go sit down out on the terrace," Tom said. "Elise, come on. Never mind my sister, she's pushy and slightly insensitive. I can only hope you'll learn to appreciate her, maybe even in time to understand her sense of humor." He gave Cassie a gentle punch in the arm. "Mother, Father? Care to join us?" Tom asked.

"Go on," Jessica said. "I need to check with Lily about dinner. I told her we'd dine at seven." She dismissed them with a wave of her elegant and bejeweled hand.

Elise could hear Jessica talking to her husband as the three left the room. "Robert, please come with me, dear. I've had a very interesting phone call. I need to discuss a few things with you. Now!"

Elise was ushered onto a beautiful red stone terrace with balustrades around three sides. A wide, expansive, stone stairway led to Italian gardens with a croquet lawn in the center.

"Do you play?" Cassie asked as Elise looked out over the grounds.

"Play?" Elise answered, feeling foolish that she hadn't been listening to the conversation and had apparently missed something.

"Croquet, of course. When we were young, Tom and I used to be the champions of the summer set. No one could beat us. Tom, do you remember the time we made the bet with the Randolph brothers? They didn't know our reputation. Yet."

"Of course, how could I forget those high-society brats," Tom replied. He looked at Elise, swatting at a wasp that circled her head. "Their family was from 'old money'; we were 'new money', thus socially beneath them . . . in their minds. The boys were always out to make us look inferior."

Cassie grinned at her brother. "Tom and I purposely played horribly the first game," Cassie continued. "Then we upped the ante a bit. The losers had to run naked through the gardens. We won of course. Unfortunately their parents stopped them before they made their run. Such a shame. We had our Polaroid ready."

"Yeah, you and I could taste the victory. We were so up for seeing them humiliate themselves." Tom laughed then turned to Elise. "Elise, keep in mind we were all of what...? You were maybe six, Cassie, and I would have been twelve?" He nudged Elise and winked at her. "Pretty rotten kids, huh? But we sure had fun."

Cassie and Tom spent the next half hour talking about childhood memories leaving Elise to nod and smile when they looked her way. Finally they heard the tinkling of a bell.

"Dinner's ready. Come on, Elise." Tom stood, grasping her hand.

"Smells heavenly. I'm starved," Cassie said. "You're so quiet, Elise. I hope we haven't bored you to death. Tom, make her sit next to me so we can get to know each other better." She smiled sweetly. Elise looked confused.

"We'll sit on either side of you. Okay?" Tom asked Elise.

The dinner seemed to last forever. The Gardners all but ignored her during dinner. They talked and laughed, asked her questions, then continued on with the conversation before she had a chance to answer. Twice, Tom interrupted, answering for her.

After dinner, as Lily served Jessica a chilled glass of chardonnay and Cassie and Elise raspberry iced tea, Tom and his father went to the stables to check on the new mare Robert bought earlier in the week. "Hank delivered her this morning. Come on, Son. I want you to see her. She's a beauty—sired by Golden Boy. Cost me a small fortune, but worth every penny. "

Alone with Tom's mother and sister, Elise tried not to panic.

"You look uncomfortable, Elise." Jessica smiled. "Do tell me *all* about yourself. Oh, by the way, where's your mother tonight?" Jessica picked up her wine goblet, taking a small sip. "I asked Tom to invite her this evening. You didn't know, did you?"

Elise stared coldly at Jessica. *What is she doing?*

"I bet he didn't even ask her. Tom said he was worried that she would embarrass you—because of her drinking problem," Lily said, smiling smugly at Elise.

"Mother! Tom would never say such a thing."

Jessica smiled; saliva glistened at the corners of her mouth. "Tell me, did Tom buy you that dress? It's a very expensive dress, a little out of your league. Though I admit you wear it well. I know it's from our store. Cassie, look at the label. You'll see I'm right. It's an Alexa original."

"Mother, stop it!" Cassie reached for her mother's arm, accidently knocking over her glass of tea, the amber liquid spilled over onto her mother's lap. "Damn it!"

Elise said quietly, "Thank you for a memorable evening, I'll see myself out." Dropping her napkin on the chair behind her, she smiled and walked out of the room.

She heard Cassie yell, "Wait. Elise! Mother, what did you do? How could you?"

As soon as she was out the door, Elise ran down the front walk and past the fountain where the marble cherub peed endlessly into the water. A black raven, perched on the cherub's head, his black eyes followed her. When she reached the end of the sidewalk, she turned to face the immaculately maintained estate. Elise clenched her fists, seething. "You will regret this! All of you!" She spun around and ran.

Elise wandered aimlessly for hours. As the sun began to set, it started raining. Heavy raindrops splashing onto the hot pavement quickly created a thick mist. She felt as if she was smothering as she breathed the damp air into her lungs. Tiny rivulets of water ran down her forehead and neck. Her soaked hair hung in limp tangles down her back. Finally she sought refuge at the park under the trees. Vaporous clouds rose and rolled across the water on the eastern edge of the lake. Oak branches, heavy and laden with rain, dropped their burden, soaking Elise's clothes as she sat in her silent sanctuary. She began to cry.

When a gentle hand touched her shoulder, Elise turned. It was Tom. He sat next to her on the bench, put his arms around her and gently pulled her close to him.

Tom held her until she stopped crying. "What happened, Elise?" he asked, wrapping her in his jacket to stop her shivering. He pushed wet locks off her forehead.

"I told you this could never work, Tom. I felt so humiliated. They hate me! I told you they would." Elise pushed his hands away. "I'll never go through that again. How could you sit there and let them treat me like that? And then to leave me alone with your mother and your sister—how could you?" She pounded Tom's chest with clenched fists. "I don't want to see you or your family ever again."

Tom grabbed her fists. "You're talking nonsense. No one intended to hurt your feelings or belittle you. My family would never do that. Come on. Let's go back. They were stunned that you left." Pulling her up off the bench, he turned her to face him. "Elise, I need you. I'll make it right. It's just a misunderstanding."

Elise pulled away and yelled, "How can you be so blind?" She began sobbing. "I will never go back to that house! Never!" She turned and ran.

Tom shouted, "Stop! Wait for me." But Elise did not.

It was two months before Elise agreed to see Tom again. She met him at Rivaldi's on the Plaza. They drank wine and ate gnocchi smothered in creamy mushroom and garlic Alfredo sauce. Blushing, Elise laughed, feeling alive again.

After they finished their lunch, Elise said quietly, "Tom, I'm so sorry to hear about your parents. It must have been heartbreaking for you to lose both parents so close together. How are you really?"

"I'm recovering. Cassie has taken their deaths harder than I have, but she's getting better. We're taking it one day at a time. When dad had the hunting accident, it was devastating." His eyes filled with tears. He looked away, embarrassed. "My father was on a safari, big game hunting. Mother didn't go with him. She blamed herself for his death. She said if she had been with him, the accident wouldn't have happened. She couldn't forgive herself. She committed suicide the day after his funeral. Mother died quietly in her sleep—some consolation to us."

The waiter brought the leather folder with their bill. The smell of caramelized onions, peppers and smoky steak permeated the air as another waiter hurried past with a tray of fajitas. Tom pulled several fifties from his wallet, handed them to the waiter, then motioned him to go. When he was out of earshot, Tom continued. "Cassie found Mother. I was home that morning, thank God. Cassie pretty much folded up. Not that either one of us were too surprised. Mother and Father were totally dependent on each other. They were seldom apart. It's been hard, Elise." He put his head in his hands, took several deep breaths. When Tom had himself under control, he looked at Elise and said, "I need you. More than ever. Please, Elise, will you come home with me?"

Tom and Elise were married at the end of October. The wedding ceremony, held at Tom's home, was attended by Elise's mother, Mandy, a few of Tom's close friends and Cassie, who brought Michael Wellington, her future husband, whom she met at the university where she was taking classes in design.

Elise's mother had managed to stay sober all through the summer and fall. Elise had been so proud of her. She looked charming and sophisticated at the ceremony, dressed in an emerald green cocktail dress that Elise bought for her at the Gardner's boutique. When the ceremony was over, Elise looked at her mother and saw there were tears in her eyes. Mrs. Elise Gardner had never been happier.

***

For a while that cold, dark, winter night, curled up beside her sleeping niece, Elise forgot her loneliness, forgot about the woman in the shower, forgot the frenzy she caused a few hours ago, forgot her ongoing battle with Gabe and Helen over control of Ravenswood, forgot about Tom, now on his way to the emergency room. Lost in her lovely memories, she found a peace and tranquility in her solitude, a sensation, if not of joy, at least of quiet contentment. Enveloped in reminiscence of gentler times, the spirit of Elise Gardner faded—for a while.

Chapter 53

Helen and Gabe watched Elise and Lizzie sleep. Gabe was on the edge of the chintz armchair, drumming his fingers on his sister's knee. Helen perched on the arm, her feet planted beside her brother's legs.

"Let's leave her here for now. Come on, Gabe," Helen whispered. She didn't want to disturb the child by waking Elise. "Let's go see about Cassie."

"Wait, let me find our stash. It's here somewhere." Gabe began a frantic search of the bookcase. "I hid the bag behind one of these Longfellow volumes. I know I did. Where is it?"

"For craps sake, Gabe, you withered old piece of horseshit. Not Longfellow— Hawthorne. Here!" Helen handed him an old cloth bag, faded and worn. "Take it."

The two crept slowly down the hall to Tom's room. Gabe took a small, amber vial of opium and a scrimshaw pipe from the bag. He put some loose tobacco from his bag in the bottom of the pipe. Pulling a pocketknife from his threadbare pocket, he dipped the blade into the vial. Spreading a ball of the brown goo onto the bowl edges, Gabe lit a match, touched it to the opium, watched until it smoldered. He put the pipe to his lips, inhaled deeply, coughed, and handed the pipe to Helen. She lit another match, held it to the bowl and waited for the mixture to ignite and become vaporous.

"And they thought they burned it all." Gabe snickered at Helen as she choked trying to keep the smoke in her lungs.

Helen smiled at Gabe and began gently massaging her brother's crotch. "Not now, bitch," Gabe snarled, jerked his sister's hand away and pinched her breast painfully. "Later. Come on. Let's go get the sister."

From the bathroom they heard the shower running. Helen, on Gabe's heels, entered the steam-filled room. Slithering through the vinyl curtain, Gabe motioned Helen to follow. They sat on either side of the shower, behind Cassie.

Cassie whirled around. The sensation of someone watching her was overwhelming. *God my nerves are on edge! I'm way too tired. I'm being irrational. No one is in here. How could there be?*

Simultaneously Helen and Gabe reached their liver-spotted, arthritic hands out and caressed the unsuspecting Cassie's body.

Water pounded her skin. The pressure from the showerhead seemed to have increased. It felt like hands on the back of her legs. She twisted around to turn the water down. Hands massaged her back, her calves, her thighs. She watched in horror as wisps of coarse, gray hair glided along her outstretched arm, tickled her breasts, then moved down her chest toward her naval.

Cassie did not scream. She clamped her to hand to her mouth. Lizzie was alone. She could not risk frightening her. As an invisible hand began opening her thighs, Cassie bolted out of the shower. Grabbing her robe, she threw it around her shoulders and ran from the bathroom to her sleeping daughter.

Helen and Gabe did not follow her. The hot shower felt too good. So soothing, so sensual. The two fondled each other and continued their private ritual.

Lizzie was sleeping soundly, making soft snoring noises, her eyes twitching rapidly as she dreamed. Thank God. Cassie collapsed on the floor beside the bed. She lay shivering, thinking about what she should do. After a few minutes, she got up, pulled her robe tightly closed about her waist and went back to the bathroom. The water, now running cold, pounded the tiled shower floor. Reaching in, she turned the faucets off.

The vile thing that imposed itself upon her had gone. Cassie knew it had been one of the spirits in the house. She knew they had to be dealt with. Soon.

Chapter 54

Michael and Tom argued the whole way to the hospital. Michael made it clear that Tom needed to get hold of Sara and have her find out what Vivian was doing on Tom's property in the middle of the night. "Screw loose. Something's going on with her. We can't have her wandering around your house in the night. Who knows what she might do?" Michael had gone on and on.

Tom didn't want to involve Sara. Not tonight anyway. He finally shut up, too tired and in too much pain to continue fighting. He didn't want to talk or think—just get some painkillers in his body and get the throbbing in his head to stop. Warm blood soaked through the heavy towel he held tightly to his forehead and ran annoyingly into his eye.

In a lucid moment, an exhausted Michael thought to call ahead to the ER. The second they pulled up in front of the emergency room, the automatic doors flew open and a nurse met them with a wheelchair.

Ten stitches. That's what it took to close the wound above Tom's brow. The doctor scrubbed the dirt and gravel from Tom's cheek and coated the abrasions with antibiotic cream and a layer of gauze. A CT scan was done; there were no indications of hematoma, hemorrhage or facial bone fractures, though they kept Tom under observation for several hours, to be safe.

Tom and Michael were at the hospital several hours, arriving home right before dawn on Thanksgiving morning. The house was still dark, Cassie and Lizzie slept soundly in the upstairs bedroom. "It'll be a few hours before Nell gets here. Let's get some sleep. You sure you're okay, Tom?" Michael asked quietly, holding back a yawn. "You look like you're in a lot of pain."

"I am. You don't look too great yourself, Michael. Thanks for all your help tonight. Not sure what would have happened if you hadn't been here to handle all of this. Go on, get some sleep. See you in a few hours." Tom left Michael in the hall and walked quietly to his own room, took a sleeping pill and went straight to bed.

What the hell had happened? It made no sense. Though not much seemed to make sense any more. Tom thought that maybe he was losing his mind. Again. Tom lay back against the pillow, pulled the thermal blankets up under his chin. He had to stop thinking like this. He wasn't crazy. Elise was behind this. He knew she was. He would take care of her. Next week. When she followed him back to Jamestown.

Tom's head throbbed. He let it sink into the soft, down-filled pillow, afraid to move very much, lest the pain increase. Finally he fell asleep and began to dream about Elise.

Smells of saltwater and the pungent fishy odor of seaweed wafted into his nostrils. He was dancing with Elise along the sandy beach, just out of reach of the lapping waves. Sara stood at the top of the beach steps above them. Tom knew she had

been watching them for some time. He stopped in mid-step, motioning her to come to him. She slowly descended the steep stairs and walked toward him, dragging her bare feet in the hard-packed sand. "Darling, Sara, how sad you look," he said. "We'll change that. Have you met Elise? She will cheer you up. Dance with Sara, Elise." He reached for Sara's hand and pulled her toward him. Behind him, Elise laughed, reached her hand out to Sara.

Delighted, Tom watched the women twirling round and round, the waves coming in closer and closer, finally swallowing their feet, their legs. Their pale, silk dresses, soaked and limp floated weightlessly around them. The pounding waves enveloped the two women and swept them out to sea. Tom watched as they disappeared beneath the frothing waves into the black depths of the ocean. Haunting caws of a dozen ravens resonated through the night. Shadows of wings brushed Tom's arms as he reached out into empty air.

Tom woke with a start. Sitting up, he grabbed his aching head. His bandages had come off and there was blood all over his pillow. He felt stiff, achy, almost like he was hung over. Lifting his legs carefully over the side of the bed, he planted his feet gingerly on the floor and slowly stood. On the table by the window lay a small bag, next to it was a small, ivory pipe. "Who the hell's been in here? Now what!"

Cassie poked her head into his room. "What's wrong, Tom?" She carried a tray with two mugs of coffee, cream, toast and strawberry jam.

"That!"

Cassie saw the paraphernalia immediately. Setting the tray down, she picked up the small cloth bag and undid the antique button holding it closed. "Tom, this is the same as the vial we found in the bathroom. Look!" She jabbed it at him. "Who does it belong to? Is this yours?"

"Don't be ridiculous," Tom said, grabbing the small bag. Reaching inside, he took out two more vials, both full of what he assumed was opium.

"What do you have there?" Michael asked, coming unannounced into the room.

"Mike, it's more opium—like the stuff we found downstairs. I found it on the table."

Cassie pulled the stopper out of one of the tiny bottles and sniffed it cautiously. "Who would come into your bedroom?"

"I don't have a clue," Tom said.

"Maybe that's what Vivian was doing last night," Michael said. "Maybe she snuck into the house."

"Makes no sense. Not Vivian's style. Besides," Tom held up the bag, "she would never own something this shabby. And this bag and these bottles are very old. What about . . . "

"It was the old woman!" Cassie whispered, grabbing the bag from Tom. "And her brother. It all makes sense now. Oh, my God! They were here last night. Both of them! While you were at the emergency room."

Michael reached for Cassie's shoulder and turned her to face him. "What are you talking about, Cassie?"

"Last night, after you left, I took a shower. Something . . . someone grabbed me. It was horrifying." Cassie wrapped her arms around herself protectively. "Disgusting."

Michael hugged her close to him. "All the craziness last night got to you. I'm sorry, honey! Why didn't you say something to me this morning? I would have helped you sort this out. Dreams can be very powerful. And so vivid. Especially when you're exhausted."

"Why didn't I say something? Gee! Hmm . . . Why do *you* think I didn't?" She looked intently at Michael. "Because I didn't think you'd believe that spirits grabbed and fondled me. And I'm right, of course. You don't."

Lizzie bounded into the room. "Hey, what's that?" She reached to pick up the pipe. Michael intercepted her before she could and lifted her onto his shoulders.

"Some dirty old pipe your Uncle Tom found. Did you have your breakfast yet, kiddo?" Michael asked, shooting a warning glance at Cassie to make sure she said nothing more in front of their daughter.

"Nope." Lizzie giggled. "I'm starving." She looked at her mom and then her uncle. Her smile quickly changed to one of complete surprise. "Uncle Tommy, what happened to your face? You look horrible."

"You uncle fell last night. Out in the driveway. I took him into Ravenswood to the emergency room. They had to stitch up his brow, but he'll be fine."

"Poor, Uncle Tommy. Did it hurt when they sewed your face?

"Not much. They numbed the skin first."

"Oh. . . . Well, we'll take good care of you. Won't we, Mama?"

"Absolutely," Cassie reassured her daughter.

"Let's go downstairs, Lizzie. I'm starving, too," Michael said. Hesitating at the doorway, he turned to Cassie. "We'll talk about this later. Are you coming to breakfast?"

"Go on. I'll be down in a while," Cassie said. When Michael and Lizzie had gone, Cassie turned to Tom. "It happened," she said. "It wasn't a dream."

"Sit down, Sis." Tom pulled her down onto the sofa, handed her one of the cups of coffee. "Tell me exactly what you think happened last night?"

"Why bother?"

"Oh, come off it, Cass." Her eyes flared in anger at his harsh words. "You're trying to tell me you were fondled in the shower by a ghost? A bit farfetched don't you think, even for you?" He smirked, tried to make her think he did not believe her. But of course, he did. *Damn Elise!*

"Why are you being so insulting to me?" Cassie asked. "I know you're very aware that this house has 'things' going on that make no sense. I can read you like a book. Don't ever doubt that I can't."

Tom looked out the window at the rolling waves breaking far out at sea. "I don't want to hurt you. I don't *intend* to belittle what you think is going on."

"Yes, you do." Cassie stood up, sloshing coffee down her shirt as she paced back and forth before the window. "You do it because it's easier than the alternative—admitting that your perfect plan for a new life is all fucked up."

"No it's not—you're wrong." Tom hurled his cup into the fireplace, watched with satisfaction as it shattered against the back firewall, the spatters of coffee sizzling in midair.

"Such rage! Why? Because you know we aren't imagining all of these strange occurrences," Cassie said.

Tom dropped to the couch, held his head in his hands. "Enough, Cassie!"

"What's going on here is real. Your house is being haunted. And I know you know it!"

"You're wrong. You're creating fantasies. There are no ghosts here. That is complete nonsense!"

A huge raven swooped at the window, thudding into the glass. Stunned, it fell to the balcony floor and lay still. Tom and Cassie hurried to the door, opened it and went out onto the balcony, both kneeling to examine the bird.

Screeching, it righted itself and flapped its enormous wings. It circled twice, then dived at them. It happened so fast Tom and Cassie were barely able to duck and cover their heads as the bird flew at them. The air moved. A chill breeze from the flapping wings brushed the back of their necks. Tom felt the beak, or maybe it was a claw, graze his right wrist. Then it was over. He put his hands down. "You okay?" he asked Cassie.

"Yeah, I'm okay. Oh, my God! That thing was huge! What the hell was that about?"

"Survival. Guess it thought we were responsible for its pain. Shit! It's circling back. Come on. Get inside." Tom grabbed Cassie, slamming the french door just as the raven smashed into it. With a final caw, it turned and flew out toward the cliff, disappearing over the edge.

"Tom, your arm's bleeding!"

"Only a scratch." Taking a napkin from the tray, Tom wrapped his wrist. "Enough excitement for me. I'm done. No more talk of ghosts or frigging birds! Go downstairs. We'll talk about this some other time. Not today! Okay, Cass?"

"As long as you promise me we'll have a serious conversation . . . soon."

"Yeah, sure. Now, go downstairs! I need a hot shower. I feel like hell warmed over. I'll be down in a while."

Reluctantly, Cassie left her brother and joined Michael and Lizzie in the dining room.

The smell of bacon and waffles wafted up the stairs and into his room. "Man, oh man. That smells good," Tom said. Standing under the hot running water, his attitude changed. Cassie was only trying to look out for him. He would do everything in his power to make certain they enjoyed their Thanksgiving. There would be no more conflict. He'd finish showering and join his family with a smile on his face. The rest of the day they'd relax and have fun.

With Michael's help, that was exactly how the rest of the day unfolded.

Chapter 55

"Tom," Cassie said, "yesterday was wonderful. What a perfect Thanksgiving. Thank you for bringing our family together."

Tom was more than relieved that the day had gone off without a hitch. A calm, family day. Everything he hoped it would be. "It *was* good, wasn't it? I'm still stuffed!"

"Yeah, me too." Cassie smiled. "We're very lucky to be together."

Tom smiled at his sister. "It's been a long time."

"Let's make sure we never drift apart again. We need each other. We always will." Cassie gently patted her brother's uninjured cheek and gave him a quick kiss on the top of his head. "Well, Brother, one party down, one to go. Do you think Vivian will still come Saturday night? I was so rude to her the other night."

"I doubt she noticed. She was much too worried about inventing a plausible story to explain why she was wandering around here in the middle of the night. She probably didn't pay any attention to us. I'll call Sara in a while and see how Vivian's feeling today. Sara said Vivian didn't even remember being here the other night. Maybe there's a medical reason for her behavior. Anyway, Sara was going to call Vivian's husband yesterday to see if she's had these blackout spells before. "

Cassie pulled the cord to open the curtains covering the picture window. Sun showered the room. Dust sparkles floated and caught the sunlight, swirling like diamond mist as the air was momentarily disturbed. "Tom, come here. Someone's coming up the walkway from the beach. Who is it?"

"Speak of the devil. It's Vivian. What's she doing here?"

Tom and Cassie watched out the window as Vivian came up the path. Looking around to make sure she wasn't seen, she darted into the stand of trees at the bottom of the driveway and began searching on the ground. She bent over, threw a small branch out of her way and picked something up from under a pile of brush. She glanced around, then turned and hurried back toward the path to her house.

"Now that was weird," Cassie said.

"Vivian told Sara she didn't remember being here the other night. Obviously she lost something and came back to find it. I better call Sara and let her know that either Vivian lied to her, or she's having another one of her spells."

"Should I go after her?" Cassie asked.

"No, I'll go." Tom ran to the front door, grabbing his jacket from the coat rack. He called Sara on his cell as he rushed down the steps and onto the driveway. "Sara, just a heads up. Vivian was here. She's headed your way. I don't know if she's okay or not. I'll follow her and make sure she gets home."

"Didn't she say what she doing?' Sara asked.

"Vivian didn't come to the house. She stayed in the trees. She was searching for something. Looked like she found it, too."

"What?"

"She found something under the trees—in the same spot where we found her before. She acted as if she didn't want anyone to see her. I see her now. Sara. Are you getting close yet? She's at the top of the hill above your house."

"Stay there. I don't see her yet."

Tom listened to Sara's quick breathing as she ran up the path.

"There she is!" Sara said. "Vivian!" she yelled. "Tom, I'll call you later. Bye."

From his vantage point on the top of the hill, Tom saw Sara running toward Vivian. He watched the two women come together, exchange a few words. Sara hooked Vivian's arm into hers, and they walked briskly down the path back to the Harrison home.

Cassie ran up behind Tom. "Well? What was that all about?"

Tom jumped at the sound of her voice. "Not a clue. Yet. Sara said she'll call me later. Vivian obviously lost something important the other night."

"Brrr. Let's go back inside. It's cold. Come on," Cassie said.

***

Sara called Tom later that morning. "I don't know what to think. Vivian said she was taking a walk this morning. She said she only walked to the hilltop and back. To clear her head."

"Really?" Tom shrugged, not totally surprised. "I guess she didn't know we saw her. Oh, well. It's not a big deal."

"To be honest, I'm not sure about that. She seemed very disoriented. But with Vivian, it's so hard to tell, she's difficult to read. For now, I guess I can't do anything except keep my eyes and ears open."

Tom asked, "Did you hear from William yet?"

"He called yesterday and spoke with Viv and the boys, but I never got to talk to him. I sent him a text message last night. I'll let you know if I hear from him."

"Is he usually gone this much?"

Tom heard Sara sigh, then she said, "Right now he's working on a deal that's more complicated than usual, it's taking more time. But yes, he's often gone for long periods of time."

"That's a shame. Oh, well, none of my business. Cassie wanted me to ask if you're still coming to dinner tomorrow night."

"Of course we are. Vivian went on a shopping spree earlier this week. She wouldn't miss showing off. The boys are excited. . . . At least Jimmy is."

"What about Billy?"

"Billy never wants to do anything with the family. He's at *that* age," said Sara. "Me, I can't wait to be with you. It's getting difficult, trying to hide that we're seeing each other."

"Say the word, Sara. It's up to you. We don't have to keep our relationship quiet."

"I know. Just a while longer. I'm not ready yet.'

"I won't pressure you."

"Thank you. Hey, how are you doing? I'm almost afraid to see you all stitched up and bruised."

"Pain's better. But I admit that I look awful. The prize-fighter look. Maybe if you think of me as looking virile and manly, you'll be able to get past the shock."

"Poor baby," Sara sighed.

"Not the image I wanted you to come up with!" Tom laughed.

"My nature! I need to go; Viv's calling. Can I do anything to help tomorrow?"

"I don't think so. Cassie and Mary have everything well planned."

"Okay. Let me know if things change. Bye. Miss you." The phone went dead.

Tom went to find Cassie. He found her in the study with Mary. "Hi, ladies. What are you up to?"

Cassie and Mary looked up from the notebook in front of them. "Working on the seating for the dinner party. Tom, did you talk to Sara?" Cassie asked.

"I did. She said they would all be here."

Mary smiled at Tom, handing him a piece of paper. "Well, here are the seating arrangements. Any changes you want to make?"

Tom studied the paper with names marked on a drawing of the table. Frowning he said, "I will not sit next to Vivian. I already told you that." He pointed to his sister. "You and Michael should sit next to her, one on either side. I think you two can handle her." He shrugged and scratched his head. "No one else has your social skills."

"You think?" asked Cassie. "I kind of thought it would be better if I sat across from her."

Mary took the seating chart back from Tom. "Okay, lets' move Michael to her right, Cassie across from her and Sara to her left. Then you can sit next to Cassie, across from Sara. Does that work?"

"Where does that leave Joe?" asked Cassie.

"Here, now look." Mary handed the paper back to Cassie.

"Okay, that looks fine. The kids are sitting together so they can amuse themselves. Tom, what do you think?"

Tom studied the paper. "Yeah, that should work. Guess you scrapped my plan, huh?"

"Yep. We can't have Vivian sitting in the attic or on the porch or with the kids; it won't work at all!" Cassie laughed, then got up, motioning to Mary and Tom to follow her. She led them into the dining room. "The caterers will be here later today to start setting up the serving tables. Mary and I thought they should go over here." She pointed to the north wall. "We'll move the table closer to the windows, that way it won't be too close to the fireplace, and we'll all have a splendid view of the ocean."

"That's fine, you two work out all the details. As long as I don't have to sit too close to Vivian, I'm fine with anything you plan. The main thing is to be prepared for anything."

"What do you mean by that?" Mary asked.

"You know Vivian," Tom answered, his voice dark and troubled. "I'll be glad to have tomorrow night behind me."

"Don't worry; it's going to be fun. Trust me," Cassie laughed. "Nothing will go wrong. I'll make sure of it."

"I hope you're right." Tom gazed out the window at a fishing boat tossing around on the white caps. "Well, I have work to do. . . . "

Cassie watched Tom leave, heard his footsteps on the stairs. Tom was not the only one worried.

Mary and Cassie stared at each other and shrugged. "Bundle of laughs, your brother," Mary teased.

"Tell me about it. I don't know about you, Mary, but I plan on having a lot of fun tomorrow night. I love parties. Help me move this table so we can put the leaf in it."

Chapter 56

In her room, with the drapes pulled closed to shut out any light, Vivian lay on her bed staring at the swirling patterns in the ceiling. Her behavior this past week left her confused and frightened. Yesterday she blacked out again. Sara found her up on the path above the house. Again, Vivian didn't remember leaving the house.

She felt drained; a headache throbbed in her temples. *I'm unraveling, bit-by-bit. A little more each day.* She pulled the covers up around her chin. She needed to rest. She was exhausted, had been under too much pressure. And tonight was the dinner party at Tom's. Vivian needed to look relaxed. She drifted into sleep while Elise, bored to death, waited impatiently at the foot of her bed. As soon as Vivian fell asleep, Elise gently descended into Vivian's sleeping body.

Elise walked Vivian to the closet and removed the jewel box from her coat pocket, then she crept slowly down the hall, making certain she made no sounds. Cautiously she knocked on Sara's door. No answer. Good. Sara was still downstairs with the boys practicing a song they wanted to sing for everyone tonight at Tom's. Vivian opened the bottom drawer of the dresser, lifted up several sweaters and placed the jewelry underneath them. Smiling, her new plan in place, she went back to Vivian's room.

The downy, feather blanket looked enticing, and Elise was so cold. She snuggled into the still-warm blankets and fell asleep. She too was exhausted.

Her cell phone ringing brought Vivian awake with a start. "Hello?"

"Mrs. Harrison, this is Anthony Rivers. How are you today?" he asked.

"Mr. Rivers? How did you get this number?"

There was a moment of silence. "From you. You gave it to me when you ordered your jewelry."

"What? My goodness, that's been ages ago. If you're calling for William, he's not here."

"No, that's why I called your cell. You said you didn't want Mr. Harrison to know about your purchases. I would never abuse your trust. You left me a message earlier. I'm returning your call. I hope nothing is wrong and that you're pleased with the pieces. They're so unique, so perfectly suited to you," Anthony said.

Elise smiled; all was going as she planned.

Vivian swallowed, sweat beaded on her forehead, above her top lip. "When did you say I got the jewelry?" she asked, her voice barely above a whisper.

"You picked it up the Saturday before Thanksgiving. Don't you remember? Is everything all right, Mrs. Harrison?"

Ignoring his question she asked, "What did I buy?"

"Are you sure you're okay?" Anthony asked.

"What did I buy? Tell me!"

"Of course. You bought a diamond necklace and matching earrings. They were special orders. You picked out the diamonds and the setting design yourself."

"I haven't been to New York. What are you talking about?"

"No, not New York—our new store in Ravenswood. You've been here twice. Don't you remember?"

Vivian took a drink from the glass of water on her nightstand. "Of course. I was sleeping when you called. I had a migraine. The medicine makes me groggy. Of course I remember."

"I'm sorry I woke you. I wanted to make sure you're pleased with the set and to reassure you that I will keep the purchase our secret."

"Why would it be a secret? Didn't William buy them for me?"

"You bought them, Mrs. Harrison. Not your husband. You paid me with cash."

Vivian didn't reply. Anthony waited for her to say something. She did not. "Mrs. Harrison," Anthony said, "I have another call to take. I'm sorry you're not feeling well. I apologize for calling at such an inopportune time. Please call me should you need anything."

"Thank you, I will. Goodbye, Mr. Rivers."

"Have a wonderful weekend. Goodbye."

Vivian sank back into the pillows and pulled the covers over her head. This has to be some ridiculous mistake. *Or am I losing my mind?* Vivian took half of a sleeping pill and fell back asleep. When she awoke, three hours later, she actually felt good for a change, like her old self. She got up and went downstairs to find Jimmy, Billy and Sara

They were having a lively discussion about the Gardner house. Billy was trying to convince Sara and Jimmy that the house had been left to Tom, that he was a relative of the old couple who lived there before him.

"Vivian, tell Billy he's wrong," said Sara. "Tom isn't related to them, is he?"

"Not a chance. Why would you think that, Billy? You know those two had no family."

"I bet they did. We just didn't know. I bet they left the house to Mr. Gardner. Why else would he end up here?" said Billy. "He even looks like old man Lindeman."

"That decrepit old thing? Mr. Gardner looks nothing like him. Anyway, Tom bought the house through a realtor—just like we did. Now drop it and go get ready. You both need a shower. We need to leave here at seven. Get going, boys. Sara, will you drive us over in William's car? I refuse to drive that car, it's so big!"

"But I've seen . . . " Sara stopped, not wanting Viv to know she had seen her driving the Cadillac on several occasions. "Sure, be happy to."

Chapter 57

"I'm so nervous, I can hardly stand it. Tom, pour me another shot of vodka would you?" Cassie picked a nonexistent thread from her sleeve and glanced in the mirror.

"Here." He handed her her drink. "Relax. You look gorgeous. This is not at all like you. You're usually so calm. What gives?" Tom asked his sister.

"I want this evening to be perfect. After all the crazy things that have been going on, I don't have much confidence that this night will be any different."

"There you are." Michael walked into the living room. "Lizzie's been asking for you. She needs help with her hair." Michael pointed upstairs. "Go on, Cassie. You could use a distraction about now. Go!"

"Boy, you are so right," she said. "Michael, would you check and make sure the fire in the dining room doesn't need another log?"

"I'll do it, Michael. Go on and get yourself something to drink," Tom said, going through the double french doors into the dining room.

"Be right back," Cassie said. "Don't drink too much. Save it for later, you may need it!" Cassie winked and left Michael standing in the middle of the room, staring out the window into the night sky.

It was a clear night. Bright stars sparkled like shimmers of ice. The crescent moon wasn't quite bright enough to lighten the sky, but vibrant enough to cast an eerie glow on the ocean waters. Michael felt as if he could see all the way across the ocean, thought he could see the beam of light from the lighthouse on the farthest tip of the Isle of Westmoor. The sweeping, white light warned of rocky shores hidden in the ocean shallows.

"Fire's blazing in the dining room, should burn down to a tolerable level by dinner. I hope anyway," Tom said, wiping his forehead with a white handkerchief. "Must be about eighty degrees in there." His cell phone beeped. "Excuse me, Michael. It's John. I need to take his call." Going into the study where he could be alone, Tom closed the door. "Hello, John."

"Tom," said John, "I have Nate on the line as well. He and I wanted to fill you in on the diamond exchange business you were inquiring about. I received the report a few hours ago— Kranston and Rivers is completely legit. You'll find this interesting, though perhaps not unexpected, it's owned by William Harrison."

Tom laughed. "Really? So who are Kranston and Rivers? Partners?"

"No, just management. Although they've been in the business for ten years. They own one retail store in New York. It too operates under the same name, Kranston and Rivers," John explained. "They've agreed to do the day-to-day running of the business in Ravenswood, and if profitable, will be given stock options in a year. Harrison needed them for their upstanding reputation. They're apparently two of the most highly respected jewelers in the business. I know you wanted to go into competition, Tom, but to be honest, there's not enough money in Ravenswood, even with the tourist business, to make a competitive store profitable in today's market."

Tom paced the empty study, stopped to open the heavy curtains. Looking toward the snow covered woodland area to the west, Tom watched Wiggins chase a ground squirrel up into a pine tree. "Not what I wanted to hear."

"Then you might like this. Harrison is looking for a silent partner," John said. Tom could hear the tap, tap, tap of his pen as John drummed on the edge of his desk, a habit he knew well.

"You have to be kidding." Tom smiled, picturing the scenario. *Wouldn't Vivian have a fit if I were her husband's partner?* "Nate, are you listening to this?" Tom asked.

"I am," Nate spoke up.

"What else did you find?" Tom asked.

Nate answered, "Harrison's temporarily overextended himself with art imports. He needs financial backing for his diamond trade. He's a very savvy businessman, Tom. Nothing even remotely shady about him. You couldn't go wrong being his partner."

"John," Tom asked, "you said silent? Does he want financial backing anonymously or is he willing to take on a working partner?"

"He's only looking for financial backing. He has absolutely no use for an active associate. He has Kranston and Rivers to handle any buying and negotiating," John answered.

Tom knew John was sitting in his office on the fourth floor of the Werner building, his desk piled high with a mountain of paperwork that never seemed to diminish. Yet somehow John always knew where every file or paper was buried. "Sounds like my kind of businessman," Tom laughed.

"I figured as much," John chuckled into the phone.

"Nate, can you set up a meeting next week?" Tom asked.

"Will do. I'll arrange it with both Harrison and his attorney. You still plan to take the train here Tuesday?" Nate asked.

"Yeah, I should arrive in the afternoon around four."

"Want me to pick you up? I'll come in a cab, since I can't drive. "

"Sure. It'll give us a chance to talk. Nate, what do you hear about Harold?"

"Not much at all. I hired a detective to try to find him, but so far, no clues. That's my brother. Things get tough, and he runs. Fucker. Would have been so much easier if he'd just faced the judge."

"Well, it's a shame he ran, but Rogers will find him," John said.

"Nothing more you can do. Harold will surface. Keep your chin up, Nate," Tom said.

"Yeah, I will. I'm gonna say goodnight and let you two talk," Nate said, then hung up.

"John, are you still there?"

"I am."

"Will you have the necessary papers ready when I get to Jamestown?"

"Of course. I'll have them for you next week. Hey, why don't you, Nate and I go out Wednesday evening—to the club for cocktails and dinner?"

Again Tom heard John drumming his pen on his desktop, a sign that he had something on his mind. "Sounds fine with me."

"Tom, how are you doing? Any problems with the house?" John asked. "I saw the email you sent to Monica Ellis, the realtor you bought the house from, asking for information on the previous owners. Monica sent me your email, then called me. She's concerned something was amiss."

"Damn right! She failed to disclose the two deaths in this house."

"What?"

Tom heard the front doorbell chime. "Yeah, a murder-suicide. The previous owners. A brother and sister."

"First I've heard of it. Let me make some calls, and I'll get back to you. We can probably get you released from the contract if it's true."

"I don't know. Find out what you can, but for the time being, I have no intention of getting out of the contract for this house. I have big plans for it. Tell Ms. Ellis not to worry, but tell her I want any information she can get."

"Let me have one of my people look into it. Roger's firm, the one looking for Harold, is the best bet for getting information. I'll fill you in when we meet next week, if that's soon enough."

As he talked with John, Tom mindlessly looked at the books on the over-stuffed shelves of the bookcases lining the room's walls. The girls brought the books they'd found stored in the attic down to the study. "That's fine. See you Wednesday. Thanks, John." Tom ended the call.

A book with no title or author on the black leather spine caught his attention. He carefully pulled it out. The leather was aged, no longer supple but stiff and hard in his hands, the surface split and worn. He opened the thick leather cover. The pages were heavy, linen-type paper, now slightly yellowed and worn on the edges. Holding the book under a lamp, Tom read the name *Helen Lindeman* in elegant hand-written script. Curious, Tom turned the page. Again, in the same handwritten script, were the words, *My Life My Death*. "Well, well. What have we here?" Tom said out loud.

"What did you find, Tom?"

Cassie rushed over to where Tom stood at the bookcase. He didn't want her to know what he'd found, not until he had time to examine the book and see what—if anything of consequence —Helen had written in it. He ignored her question, shoving the diary behind another book. "Cass, I must admit, you look stunning," Tom said. Cassie had changed her clothes again and was now wearing a sleek, form-fitting, dark-gray evening dress —one shoulder bared, the other shoulder with a thin strap embroidered with tiny pearls. Over-sized baroque pearl earrings dangled from her ears. Her red hair glowed a deep, burnt umber, her brown eyes sparkled in the firelight.

"What were you looking at, Tom?"

"I found some old books—one appeared to be a first edition. *A History of the Early Whalers in the Northern Atlantic*"

Cassie shrugged her shoulders. "How boring. Come on, Tom. Joe just got here. The Harrisons won't be far behind." Cassie turned to leave the study. "I thought Joe was picking them up. What happened?"

"Sara said she was driving William's car. Vivian asked her to," Tom said. "I'm sure Joe was relieved. Vivian is *not* one of his favorites, to say the least."

Joe walked into the entry hall from the living room. "I heard my name. Good evening, Tom, Cassie. Am I the first one here?"

"You are. There's a car pulling up the drive. It has to be your neighbors." Cassie ran to look out the window. "Tom, is Sara the blonde or the brunette?" She stepped away from the window as the car doors slammed.

"The brunette," Tom replied. "And just so you know, Sara refers to her hair as chestnut brown!" He winked at Cassie.

"They're both gorgeous." Cassie studied her appearance in the antique mirror hanging by the doorway. "Oh, my God, look at me. I'm so pale!" She pinched her cheeks and made a face when her eyes met her brother's in the mirror. She twirled and hurried out of the hallway and into the living room. "Tom, you let them in." She disappeared as the doorbell chimed.

Lizzie raced down the stairs and was the first one to reach the door. "Uncle Tommy, I can't wait to see Jimmy again," she squealed as she flung the door open. To her disappointment Vivian was standing in front with Sara behind her. "Oh, hello," she said.

"What an adorable child," Vivian said. "Hello, darling. You must be Tom's niece." Lizzie beamed.

Tom stepped forward. "Good evening, Vivian. Hello, Sara." He stepped aside and motioned them to come in. Mary came in from the living room and took their coats, hanging them in the hallway closet. Tom showed them into the living room where he introduced everyone to Michael. Jimmy and Billy waited impatiently for the introductions to end.

Michael asked, "Would you boys would like a tour of the house."

Lizzie said that she would take them herself. "Thank you very much, Daddy. I know all the secret passageways," she told them, winking at Tom. "Come on, guys, let's go." She took Jimmy by the hand and led him, followed by Billy, across the entryway and into the study. "There's a secret room back there," she said, pointing to the back of the study. "Don't be scared. I know my way around."

Tom laughed as Lizzie closed the study door. "Kids. Well, they can't go far. The only way out of the 'secret room' leads into the living room, the study or to the dining room. I'm afraid their adventure will be short."

Vivian grabbed Tom's arm. "Tom, you poor dear. Please tell me the doctor took his time putting all those stitches in your forehead. If he didn't place them just so, you may scar. At least your cheek looks like it will heal quite well. Keep it well moisturized, that's the key."

"I'm sure the doctor did the best he could. Besides, a scar will give me character."

Sara grimaced, "It looks very painful. Is it?"

"Not too bad. Not today anyway. Ladies, can I get you something to drink?"

"I'd love a glass of Chablis," Vivian said. "I have some special moisturizing cream at home. I'll have Jimmy bring it to you. Sara, don't let me forget."

Tom poured a goblet of wine for Vivian. "Sara, what would you like?"

"The same, thanks."

Michael asked, "Where's Cassie?"

"She must be in the dining room." Tom knew Cassie had escaped to the dining room to compose herself before meeting the guests. "Sara, come with me. Vivian, we'll be right back." He led Sara into the large dining room where Cassie pretended to be making a final inspection of the table and rechecking the seating arrangements.

"Sara, this is my sister, Cassie Wellington." The two ladies extended their hands, eyed each other looking for signs of approval from the other. Apparently satisfied, the two hugged.

"Cassie, I've looked forward to meeting you. Tom speaks very highly of you."

"Thank you, Sara. What a pleasure to finally meet you, too. I can't tell you how happy I am that you came tonight. I can't wait to get to know you better. Tom says we have a lot in common. Come on, let's join the others, I haven't met your cousin yet." Cassie smiled at Tom, put her arm around Sara's waist and led them into the living room where Vivian and Michael were chatting in front of the fire. Joe stood beside Michael casually holding a bottle of beer, his drink of choice.

Vivian and Cassie, demurely—as only women can—scrutinized each other while Tom introduced them. Smiling brightly, they appeared immediately charmed by each other. Tom was amused; he'd expected Sara and Cassie to bond but certainly not Vivian and Cassie. *Shows you what I know about women.* Tom laughed to himself.

Mary and Cassie were captivated with Vivian—and Sara apparently had much in common with both Mary and Cassie. Everyone enjoyed a wonderful dinner, the women talking about fashion design and interior decorating, the men adding a few words here and there when necessary, but talking primarily about the work starting next week in the basement. Joe was going to act as general contractor and supervisor of the building of a gym and several other rooms. They discussed the upstairs remodel as well, the consensus being that spring would be the best time to undertake remodeling the attic.

After dinner, everyone went into the living room. The lights had been turned off while they dined, and the glow of the burning fireplace lit the room with a radiant luster of reds, ambers and an occasional bright, white flash followed by brilliant orange sparks. The curtains were open against the black night. In the distance, frothy waves broke on the ocean. Spatters of drizzly rain sparkled as the moon moved across the sky. Soon the temperature would fall and the drops would freeze. Another stormy night promised to descend on Remington House. Tom threw a log onto the fire sending a spray of burning embers bouncing against the interior stones of the firebox. He walked around turning on lights. The room lit up, a stark contrast to the darkness of the ocean view.

"Vivian, Tom tells me you play the piano. Would you play for us?" Cassie asked, pointing to the baby grand in the far corner. "I don't think anyone's played the piano since we got here. Have they?" She looked at Tom; he shook his head. "Isn't that odd?"

Tom winked at Jimmy. "No one's had the time, have they?" Jimmy grinned and nodded at Tom. "Vivian, please. Would you play for us?" Tom asked.

Vivian smiled demurely, replying, "I'd love to. As a matter of fact, the four of us," she swept her arm pointing toward Sara and the boys, "have worked on a few songs we'd like to perform tonight." She looked at Sara. "Did you bring the sheet music?"

"I did. Mary, come with me. I need to get the portfolio from my bag. We'll be right back."

Vivian raised the wooden cover off the piano keys. Sitting straight and tall at the keyboard, Vivian pushed her blonde hair back behind her ears and began playing a series of scales. When she struck the high E, there was no sound. She hit it again, a bit harder. Nothing.

"I had it tuned last week," Tom said. He lifted the cover, exposing the strings. A picture frame lay face down. Vivian reached for it before Tom could stop her.

"What is this?" She picked up the picture, turning it over. "It's a photograph. What a beautiful girl." She held the picture up. "Tom, who is this?"

Cassie pushed in behind Vivian to look at the photo. "It's Elise! How did her picture get in here?" Cassie grabbed Tom's arm before he could pull the picture away.

Tom thought for a moment. "It must have gotten in there during the packing. Maybe the movers put it in at the last minute."

"But, Tom, if you just had the piano tuned, how...." Cassie started to ask.

"Elise? Your wife?" Vivian interrupted.

"Yes."

"She looks so familiar," Vivian said, looking at Cassie, then Tom. "I think I've seen her before."

Tom answered quickly, "Certainly, that's possible. Maybe you saw her in New York City, we were there many times."

"It could be. But it seems more recent than that. Hmm." Vivian looked out the window, stared across the Atlantic searching her memory.

Sara and Mary hurried into the living room. "Why is everyone so quiet? Did something happen?" Sara asked.

"Look." Vivian handed the picture to Sara. "A photograph of Tom's wife. Wasn't she gorgeous?" She handed the picture to Sara who nodded and glanced quickly at Tom. Tom was staring at Vivian who said, "I'm still trying to figure out why she looks so familiar."

"Billy, what's the matter?" asked Sara.

"That's your wife?" Billy blurted out. "I thought you said she was dead!"

"Billy!" Vivian stared at her son. "That was very rude. I'm sure you didn't mean to sound so cold."

Turning away from them, Billy mumbled, "Sorry, Mr. Gardner."

Puzzled at his reaction, Tom walked toward him. "No offense taken. Are you okay?"

"Where's the bathroom?" Billy asked, backing away from Tom.

"I'll show you," Sara said. "I better go with him and make sure he's okay," she said to Tom. "He's acting strange. Be right back." As they climbed the stairs, Sara asked, "Billy? What's wrong?"

"Leave me alone, would you. I need to take a piss." He hurried down the hall opening doors until he found the bathroom. He slammed the door.

Hearing the sound of the tumblers on the lock engage, Sara turned and went back downstairs. *What a spoiled brat. I wanted to make sure he was okay. I should know better by now. Oh, well, he's a big boy.*

Chapter 58

Shimmers of moonlight lit the room casting faint shadows across the ceiling. Billy felt the wall for the switch, blinking as bright light flooded his vision. He unzipped his pants, took a pee and felt much better. Gardner had lied to everyone. His wife wasn't dead. No wonder Elise asked him not to tell anyone about her. She had been hiding from him. Tom must have moved here to try to find her. Well, her secret was safe with him. He knew there was a reason he'd hated the guy the second he saw him.

The bathroom was smaller than the ones in the Harrison house. Billy snickered. He liked knowing his house was bigger and more expensively decorated than Tom Gardner's. Billy started opening the cabinets. He had no qualms about going though Tom's things. Opening the mirrored door over the marble sink, he picked up the various bottles, reading the labels on several prescriptions. He didn't recognize the names, so he put them back. He hoped to find something that might liven up the night.

Opening a small drawer below the sink, he found what he was looking for. Codeine. Removing the lid, he poured two into his palm. He put them into his mouth, bent over, turned the faucet on and swallowed the pills with a gulp of tepid water. He stood up, looking at himself in the mirror. He grinned. "How did you get in here? I locked the door."

"Silly, boy, I have a key!" Elise stood behind him, her pale face in the mirror beside his own. She smiled.

"How did you get a ke . . ." Billy started to ask.

"We have much to talk about, Billy. Come meet me later." She ran her hand gently across his cheek, touched his lips, and teased with her fingers. "Go back downstairs now. Come to me tonight—at the cottage down the beach."

"How can I do that?"

"Oh, I know you'll find a way," Elise whispered, taking his hand into hers. She placed his hand inside her dress, placed it on her breast, leaned in against him. "Won't you?"

He answered, "I'll be there."

"Our little secret. Don't disappoint me. Now go."

Billy kissed her, started to pin her against the door.

"Not now." Elise slipped away. She put his hand on the doorknob. "Go. You mustn't let anyone know I'm here. You promised. I'll explain everything about Tom tonight."

"Think I already figured it out. You divorced him and now he's stalking you. Right?"

"You're such a smart man. Not quite right, but close. Now go downstairs." Elise pushed him gently out the door.

Chapter 59

When Billy came back downstairs, Vivian was entertaining everyone playing the piano and singing. Billy watched from the doorway. His mother looked tired to him, was starting to look old. The codeine was beginning to work a little magic for him. He smiled, sticking his hand into his pocket, glad he had taken five or six more of the pills. He'd slip away later, after they got home, to meet Elise. Maybe she would make this a night he would never forget. His fantasies were interrupted.

"Come on, Billy," Sara called. "Everyone's waiting to hear you and Jimmy sing. Stand next to Jimmy." She motioned him toward his brother. Vivian began to play *Do You Hear What I Hear*, one of the songs they'd been working on the last few days. Billy, completely uninhibited as the codeine delivered a sweet buzz, put his arm around Jimmy's shoulder. The two boys sang several songs, then sang with Sara and Vivian.

Amused, Tom watched the group. Smiling, he tapped his hand against his thigh in time to the music. "Would anyone like some coffee or maybe a drink?" he asked when there was a pause in the music.

"I could use an ice-cold beer," said Joe. "It's getting pretty warm in here."

"Let's go out on the balcony." Cassie opened the door allowing a blast of icy, winter air to blow into the living room. "Brrr. Never mind. It's freezing out. What can I get anyone to drink?" She pushed the door shut. Turning toward Vivian, who was still quietly playing the piano, Cassie said, "Vivian, you play so effortlessly."

Vivian nodded at Cassie, continued to play. "I love this Steinway; I could play it all night. It makes me feel like a concert pianist. You know my father said I had the talent for it."

"And he obviously was right. But you really should take a break. You've been playing for an hour." Cassie sat next to Vivian on the piano bench. "Let me get you something cold to drink. Then I thought maybe you'd like to see the sketches for the summer line that I'm working on."

"There she goes, that sister of mine, wrapping Vivian around her little finger," Tom said to Sara.

"I hope she doesn't regret it. Vivian will take full advantage, if I know her. Before Cassie knows what happened. She'll probably try to get Cassie to give her a clothes line of her own." Sara giggled, then added, "Shame on me!"

"Cassie's a big girl. And I warned her about your cousin. Cassie's trying to make everyone comfortable. That's Cassie," Tom said, pouring himself a gin and tonic. "Want one?"

"No, just a tonic." She took the tall tumbler from Tom. "Tom, I love your sister and her family. You're very lucky. They seem so genuine."

"They are. Tonight's gone pretty well, don't you think?" Tom asked, smiling at Jimmy who was peeking out from behind the curtains while Lizzie searched for him.

Lizzie came running into the room. "Uncle Tommy, I can't find Jimmy, and I can't find Billy either. We're playing hide and seek, but they hid too good. This isn't fun anymore."

Jimmy started laughing, giving himself away. Lizzie screamed, "You're caught, Jimmy. Help me find Billy." The two kids ran out of the room, the sound of their laughter echoing through the house.

"What a wonderful sound that is," said Tom. "I wonder how many years it's been since there was any laughter in this house? That's what this house needed. Laughter."

"Tom, I can't get Vivian away from the piano," Cassie interrupted. "She insists on continuing to play. Maybe you can get her to stop. Please, it's getting annoying," pleaded Cassie. "She seems to be losing control. Sorry, Sara. That sounded so rude."

"No, I agree. She is playing awfully loud. I'll talk to her. She loves being the center of everything. We're not paying enough attention to her, so I guess she's going to keep it up until we do." Sara looked worried. "She's been acting so odd lately. I never know what she's going to do."

"Never mind, then. Leave her for now. Maybe we should go closer to her, so she can see that we're listening." Tom took Sara's hand, Cassie followed.

Vivian seemed not to notice them. She played loudly, brazenly, throwing her whole body into the concerto. Sweat began to bead on her forehead, running down her nose, dripping onto the keys. She seemed totally oblivious, playing to an unseen audience in front of her. Her fingers danced on the keys, her performance becoming more and more dramatic. She threw her head back and pounded the keys. After a final, high-pitched shout, her own self-proclaimed bravissimo, she fell silent. Vivian took a deep breath, her head lolled forward to lie on her chest. She didn't move. She took tiny breaths, her hands hung limp in her lap.

"Vivian!" Sara knelt beside her, touching her cheek.

Vivian snarled. "What?" Sweat beaded on her chest, the cleavage between her breasts glistened, strands of hair clung to her neck.

"Nothing, you seemed . . . well, you certainly played the heck out of that piece. I've never heard you play like that before," Sara said. "I'm impressed." Sara glanced at Tom. "Wasn't Vivian wonderful?"

Cassie and Tom answered at the same time, "Fabulous."

Taking Vivian's arm, Cassie said, "Come on, let's get something to drink. I'm thirsty. Mary just brought out a pitcher of sparkling cider. Let's have a glass. What was that last piece you were playing?"

Vivian looked sideways at Cassie, but said nothing. Her lips trembled as she tried to force a weak smile.

"You're amazingly talented." Cassie led her away from the piano, casting a wary look at Tom and Sara.

"Tom, I'm worried about Vivian," Sara said as she led him away from the piano and over to the window. A violent storm was moving in from the east. Thrashing waves beat the shoreline; spray erupted into the air, mixing with shimmering snowflakes that fell, quickly coating the landscape. "I tried calling William three times today. I don't understand why he doesn't call me back. I even emailed him and told him about Vivian's blackouts."

"It seems odd doesn't it? Confidentially, I know my attorney has been in touch with him—about a business deal. I know he's taking at least some calls."

Sara gave him a surprised look.

He continued, "You're right, it makes no sense that he isn't concerned about Vivian."

Jimmy ran into the room, making a mad dash to hide behind the curtain nearest Tom. As he pulled the curtain around him, he put his finger to his mouth. "Shh. Don't tell Lizzie I'm here."

Tom winked and whispered to Jimmy, "Have you talked to your dad lately?"

Jimmy whispered from behind the curtain, "Yeah, he called this morning. Mom talked to him for a long time. Shh. Here comes Lizzie."

"Jimmy, are you in here?" She smiled at her uncle and pointed at the floor behind him. Jimmy's feet stuck out from under the curtain. "Uncle Tommy," she said as she walked closer, "look at the huge spider on the curtain behind you. You better move!"

Jimmy bolted. He whirled around searching for the spider."Where is it?"

"Gotcha!" Lizzie squealed, racing out of the room.

Jimmy ran after her. "She's tricky. I'll get her back though," he hollered at Tom as he ran by.

"Well, there's your answer," Tom said to Sara. "William talked to Vivian—not you. I'm surprised she didn't say something to you."

Sara, staring blankly out the window, answered, "I doubt if William told Vivian I called him. He wouldn't say anything to upset her. He knows her too well. I imagine he spoke with her, instead of me, to see if something was going on with her."

"So when William talked with Vivian, and she didn't tell him anything, in his mind that was the end of it—he didn't need to talk to you."

"Right. Vivian obviously didn't tell him anything was wrong." Sara sighed. "William and I aren't exactly close. He probably thinks I'm sticking my nose in their business. Still, he should have called me. I guess for the time being, I'll leave William out of this."

Glistening snow whirled and danced in the wind, drifting across the balcony to mound against the terrace doors. "Quite a storm. Look, way out there on the horizon, do you see that ship thrashing about? Looks like a toy doesn't it?"

"Yes. I hope it makes it to wherever it's going," Sara answered.

Tom looked around, saw no one was paying any attention to him and Sara. He put his arm around her waist drawing her close to him. Nuzzling her neck he whispered softly into her ear, "Have I told you how delicious you look tonight? I'm having a very hard time keeping my hands off of you."

"The feeling's mutual." Sara blushed and gave Tom a quick but passionate kiss. "Now we better get back to the party. The kids are apt to run through any time."

"You're right of course. Come on." Tom released Sara. "Let's go find the dessert table. I smell chocolate and coffee. An acceptable substitute, for now." He laughed and took Sara's hand. "Cassie's with Vivian, she seems in control of herself again. She and Cassie are laughing and having a wonderful time. Let's enjoy ourselves. Time for cake!" Tom announced loudly."Everyone into the dining room!"

Chocolate-fudge cake, petit fours and carafes of coffee and hot chocolate had been left on the dining table. Joe put another log on the fire, and everyone loaded their plates with desserts. Michael was involved in a quiet conversation with Mary, Cassie and Vivian. Tom and Sara were talking with Joe.

"Where's Billy?" asked Vivian, looking around the room.

"He went upstairs," answered Mary. "He said he left his cell phone up there."

"Oh," Vivian said, then resumed her conversation.

"Joe, "Tom said, "you know I'm leaving town Tuesday—you said you were starting in the basement next week?"

"Yes, that's the plan."

"So you have a crew hired?"

"Yeah, the guys'll start Wednesday. There's a door around the side of the house that goes into the basement, so the men won't interfere with the rest of the household."

"Good. Hmm, never noticed another door," Tom said.

"It's on the west side. It's been boarded over. That's why you never noticed it."

"Oh, well, glad the workers don't have to come in and out through the main floor. They'd drive Cassie and Nellie nuts going in and out."

"Mommy, can Jimmy and I go play now?" asked Lizzie.

Cassie wiped the chocolate from Lizzie's mouth. "Sure, don't make too much noise though. And please stop running in the house. You're apt to fall or break something."

As soon as Lizzie and Jimmy were out of sight, they giggled and ran up the steps to the second floor. "Can we go up there?" Jimmy pointed to the staircase that led to the attic.

"Well, if we're quiet, they won't know we're up there," Lizzie whispered. "Come on, but be careful, these stairs are very steep." The children had just started up when they saw Billy down the hall.

"Where are you going?" he asked.

"Shh. We're going up to the attic. Want to come?" Lizzie asked. She and Jimmy didn't wait for his answer, but continued climbing the stairs.

"Sure. What's up there anyway?" Billy asked, catching up with them.

"Mary and my mom heard a ghost up here. They think the old people who lived here before Uncle Tommy are still here."

"Ghosts? That's stupid," Jimmy said. "I don't believe in ghosts." He looked at Billy and Lizzie. "Do you?"

"I do," Lizzie said, peering down the dark hallway. She started feeling along the wall for a light switch. "Help me find the switch. It's too dark, I'm getting scared."

Jimmy turned the light on and led the way down the dim corridor. He opened several doors. "There's not much up here —just a bunch of boxes. This is boring. Come on."

"Wait, we haven't looked in all the rooms yet. Let's go in that last room and see if we can see your house from there." Lizzie moved in front of the boys. When she got to the last door on the right, she opened it, felt the wall for the light switch. As her hands reached out, she felt something soft and warm. She jumped back.

Jimmy flipped the switch. A single bulb dangling from the ceiling lit the room. Against the far wall, cowering in terror was Wiggins. The cat yowled and hissed. Digging his claws into the wood floor, he sprang high into the air and bolted past the kids.

Glancing nervously around the room, Lizzie said, "I felt something. When we first came in the room. Something touched me. And it wasn't the cat. Something scared him, too. Wiggins isn't afraid of me."

Billy and Jimmy followed Lizzie across the dimly lit room, cautiously looking around as they went toward the window on the far side of the room.

"Who sleeps up here?" Jimmy asked, pointing toward a bed with a rumpled blanket on the mattress top.

"No one," replied Lizzie.

"Well, it looks like someone's been staying here. Look. There's a sweater on the floor over there," Jimmy said, walking over and picking up the piece of clothing. "Eww. Smells awful." He threw it toward Billy who dodged it and kicked it at Lizzie. She stepped sideways, tripping over a small box. The box tipped, spilling its contents onto the floor.

An old pipe and glass bottle fell out. "What's that?" Lizzie bent down to pick them up. As she reached for the glass bottle, a growl, deep and ominous, reverberated through the room. Startled, Lizzie fell over on to the floor. Jimmy reached for her hand and pulled her up. Billy turned to run, but the door was closed and locked. Grabbing the doorknob, he tried to wrench the door open. It didn't budge.

"What was that noise? Did you hear it?" Lizzie whispered. "I want to get out of here. Come on, Billy, open the door."

She tried to push Billy out of the way; he turned and shoved her. "Stop it!" he snarled. "Don't push me. The door's locked! We need to find the key."

"What's that? Over there?" Jimmy pointed toward the back of the room.

Lizzie and Billy looked to where Jimmy pointed. In the far corner, where it was shadowed and dark, sat a haggard old woman, her skin wrinkled and sagging in folds beneath her chin. She rocked rhythmically—back and forth, back and forth —in an old bent-cane rocking chair. She stared for a moment, then pointed at them with her gnarled finger. She spoke in a low, gravelly voice and said, "You leave this room. You take nothing. You tell no one what you saw." She started to stand. "Now go!" The door flew open. The children ran.

"What's going on?" Tom hollered as Lizzie, Billy and Jimmy raced down the stairs. "Slow down! You'll fall. Stop!" He reached out and grabbed Lizzie as she stumbled on the last step. Her eyes were wild, and she seemed not to notice Tom.

"Lizzie! What's the matter?" Tom drew her to him, felt her tiny body shivering.

Cassie came running from the living room.

"Jimmy! Billy! What happened?" Tom asked again. No one answered him.

Cassie knelt down on the floor beside her daughter. "Where were you, Lizzie?" She looked at Jimmy and Billy. "Someone better answer me."

Billy quickly spoke up. "We were playing hide and seek. We hid in the closet down the hall. Lizzie couldn't find us so we jumped out. I guess we scared her. We're sorry." He reached his hand out to touch Lizzie's hair, patted her head absently mindedly.

"I think your game of hide and seek is over for the night. Why don't you kids go over and sit by the fire, play a board game or something quiet," Cassie said.

"Mommy, I just want to stay with you," Lizzie answered.

Tom glanced quickly up to the attic landing. It was dark— an empty void, as he had hoped it would be. He smiled at Sara who shrugged her shoulders.

"We should be leaving anyway," Vivian said. "It's after eleven. Thank you, Tom, for a wonderful evening. We've had such a lovely time. Mary, can you tell me where to find our coats?"

"I'll get them for you," Mary replied.

"Boys, go with her." Vivian motioned them to follow Mary. "It was wonderful to meet everyone. I hope we can do this again very soon. I'd love to have you all come to my house for dinner. Maybe sometime late next week?"

Michael said, "Actually, I'm leaving Monday afternoon on business. But Cassie and Lizzie are staying here for at least a few weeks. Tom's leaving, too. On Tuesday. I'm sure you ladies can get together without us."

"And we will," said Cassie. "Sara, it was so nice to finally meet you. Vivian, call me anytime. I'd love to spend some time talking about your design ideas. You inspired me with your thoughts on color."

Mary and the boys came into the room, their arms full of coats. "Tom, thank you," Vivian said. "Kids, get your coats on, it's freezing out. Sara, do you have the keys?" Vivian asked.

"I do." She jangled the keys in the air.

"Then goodnight." Vivian smiled warmly at Tom and Cassie. She threw her sable jacket around her shoulders and herded the boys off the front porch.

Tom walked with them down the gravel pathway to the car, opening the door for Vivian, then he walked around to the driver's side and gave Sara a good night kiss. "When can I see you again?" he whispered, his lips gently brushing her cheek.

"Call me," Sara said. "I'll make time tomorrow, I promise. Goodnight." Tom closed her door, stepped back and watched them drive slowly down the snow-covered road. The tires crunched, the sound echoing through the barren trees. The headlights made bright white spots of light on the glistening snow, momentarily illuminating the frozen brush. A deer visible in the light at the end of the drive darted into the car's path. The bright red glow of brake lights briefly lit the ground behind the car. The deer turned and ran, disappearing into the stand of trees.

Chapter 60

The car lights faded as Sara turned onto the main road. Darkness returned. As Tom turned to go into the house, a light in the attic dimmed, faded to black, then come back on. Tom stared at the window above him, troubled. The kids must have left a light on. They'd lied. They did go in the attic. Michael must be up there now. But Michael was waiting inside the front door.

"Anything wrong?" he asked Tom.

"No, I thought maybe you'd gone upstairs. Who's in the attic?" Tom asked, then wished he'd kept his mouth shut.

"No one. Why do you think someone's in the attic?" Michael asked, standing aside as Tom came inside. "Everyone's in the dining room having a snack before bed. What's the matter; did you hear something again?" He started to follow Tom.

"No, it's nothing. I guess someone left a light on up there, that's all. Stay here; I'll go turn it off."

"Okay. I'm going to see if I can find a piece of that chocolate cake before it's all gone. Geez that was good! Want some too?"

"Sure. Be right back." Tom dreaded what he would find upstairs, but he refused to ignore it—whatever or whoever it might be. He knew it was more than the kids leaving a light on. "This is *my* house!" he called out as he entered the dark hallway in the attic. He crept slowly toward the room at the end of the corridor. He switched the hall light on. A pale golden glow illuminated the hall. "Get out! Leave my house!" he yelled.

Tom opened the door, standing still for a moment while his eyes adjusted to the darkness. Across the room, visible in the dim light, he could see an old wooden rocking chair. He looked around and saw an unmade bed, its covers rumpled, and hanging halfway off the mattress. Tom pulled the chain on a shadeless floor lamp beside the bed, turning the room into a mix of dark shadows and glaring light. He heard a thump from behind and whirled around. He sucked his breath in, swallowed and moved slowly back toward the hallway. A huge raccoon hissed, then jumped at Tom. With one fast step backward, Tom was out of the room, slamming the door behind him. He heard the dull thud as the animal threw itself at the door. It scampered away, its claws making scratching sounds as it ran across the plank flooring.

"What's in there?" asked Joe, running down the hall. "What the heck is in there?"

"Fucking raccoon. Scared the crap out of me. The kids were up here. They must have opened a window. They forgot to close it, and a raccoon got in. Lucky the room door was shut, or it might have gotten downstairs." Tom opened the door to the room across the hall looking around for a stick or something to use against the beast. Finding a broom, he went back across the hall and opened the door. He peered cautiously inside. The window that faced the Harrison house, on the opposite side of the room, was closed.

Joe pushed in beside him; he had a bat in his right hand. "Where is it?"

"Don't know." Tom took two steps into the room. He saw a second window; it too was closed. "No windows are open. How did it get in here, and where in the hell is it?"

"Must be over there," Joe pointed the bat at the bed, "hiding under the bed. I'll open the windows, you flush it out."

Tom started beating on the floor beside the bed hoping the raccoon would escape through the open window. Pushing the broom under the bed, he made threatening sounds, trying to frighten the animal. He heard the scuttling of claws as the animal scurried to get its footing. Hissing loudly it ran at Joe.

Joe ran across the room to the window. It was nailed shut. Looking at Tom, he shrugged his shoulders then ran to the window that faced the woods. It, too, was nailed shut.

"Shit!" Joe yelled as the terrified raccoon raced around the room. "Both windows are nailed down!" The raccoon, trapped, turned and ran back toward Tom.

Raising the broom, Tom swung. The critter hissed and scurried back under the bed.

There was a pounding on the door. "What's going on in there? You guys okay?" Michael hollered.

"Yeah, there's a raccoon in here. Don't come in."

"What?"

"A raccoon. And he's not a bit happy!" Tom yelled.

Michael cautiously opened the door anyway. He hurried inside and shut the door. "How did a raccoon get in here?" he asked.

"The windows are closed in here, actually nailed shut, so it found another way in. For now, though, we need to trap it and get it out of here." Joe tapped the bat on the wooden floor as he contemplated their next move.

"Thank God the kids didn't get attacked earlier." Michael nodded at Tom. "Lizzie told me they came up here. Said a ghost scared them. It must have been the raccoon.'

"Probably," Tom responded. "Joe isn't there a trap out in the garage?"

"I don't think so. We wouldn't want to hurt the raccoon anyhow. There's a cat carrier out there though. I'll go get it. Here." He handed the bat to Michael. "Don't use it on the raccoon. Unless of course, you have to. Use it to keep it away from you. Be right back."

He was gone only a couple of minutes. Tom heard him running up the stairs and down the hall. "It's me," he said quietly through the door. Joe cautiously entered the room; he carried a wooden cat crate with wire-mesh sides. On one end was a door with a latch. He had a handful of fruit that he placed in the back of the box as soon as he set it on the floor. "I'll stand by so as soon as it goes in I can close and latch the door. Tom, you watch and make sure it doesn't try to run at us. Keep the broom ready."

The men stood by anxiously waiting for the raccoon to come out. "I'd just as soon kill the son of a bitch," Tom said.

"Nasty little critters when they're cornered, aren't they." Joe looked at Tom. "Guess you know they bite."

"Yeah," Tom said. The raccoon poked its head out from under the bed. The men stayed quiet as it cautiously crept toward the cage and crawled inside to get the fruit.

Joe slammed the small wooden door, quickly latching it. He lifted the cage. "Man, that's a big one! Must weigh thirty pounds." The giant raccoon, hopelessly trapped, began an unearthly screaming that sounded like a child's mournful wail. "Never heard them do that before. Gives me the creeps."

"Need a hand, Joe?" Michael asked.

"I've got it. I'll put it in the truck, drive it down the highway a ways and release it. Shouldn't come back here."

"Maybe you better get on the roof tomorrow, make sure there aren't any openings up there. I'd like to know how the hell the raccoon got in here," Tom said disgustedly.

"Makes two of us," Joe replied.

Tom and Michael walked ahead of Joe down the stairs, the raccoon wailing and hissing the entire time. Tom opened the front door. He and Michael stood watch, making sure the raccoon didn't escape the cage while Joe went back into the house to get his coat and keys.

The rest of the family gathered on the porch to watch. Joe, with Tom's help, lifted the crate into the bed of the truck. "Daddy, please don't let Joe hurt it. Hear it crying? It must have a family somewhere. Please don't let Joe hurt it."

Joe jumped in. "Lizzie, darlin' that's the last thing I'd do. Don't you worry. I'm going to take it down the road a little way and let it go. It'll find its family. Don't worry."

"Okay." Lizzie shivered as the cries from the trapped raccoon continued.

"See everyone tomorrow. Thanks for the great dinner, Tom. Night." Joe got in his truck, started the engine and drove down the road.

"To bed, everybody. It's cold and it's late." Tom held the screen door as everyone hurried in out of the cold.

Chapter 61

Vivian lay in bed, too tired and restless to sleep. It was ten past one. Hearing a door close and the quiet creaking of floorboards, she grabbed her robe and tiptoed into the hall. Someone crept quietly down the stairs. She was pretty sure she knew who it was. She followed, not turning on the lights. She was more interested in finding out where her son was going. She hung back and kept out of sight. He was now at the far end of the house, heading to the back entryway. The door opened; a gust of cold air filled the hall. Vivian grabbed a coat from the coat rack, slipped her feet into her boots, waited a moment, then opened the door to follow.

The moon was bright, casting clear, well-defined shadows. It had finally stopped snowing; the clear winter sky sparkled with stars. Larger than life silhouettes of trees and barren shrubs obscured the ground, making it difficult to find her footing. Vivian stumbled, catching herself before she fell. She pulled her coat tightly around her, dug into the pockets for her gloves. As she stood, hidden in the shadows, her son stopped for a moment, turned his head from side to side, listening to some unknown sound. Vivian didn't dare move or breathe, but continued to watch from a safe distance. Billy raised his hand and waved to someone, then he ran, disappearing down the wooden stairs that led down the cliff-side to the beach. Vivian hunched behind the banister and watched Billy sprint across the sand and down the beach. In the distance, Vivian saw someone standing by the water's edge. Her son threw his arms around the waiting figure. They kissed, then joined hands and walked inland into the darkness.

"What are you doing out here?"

Vivian jumped, screaming as she whirled around. "Sara? You scared me!"

"I'm sorry, Vivian. Are you all right?" Sara, who had no coat on, was hopping from one foot to the other, arms wrapped around herself, her flimsy pajamas affording little warmth against the freezing night air.

"I'm fine. Let's get back to the house. You'll catch your death. I was following someone."

"What?"

"It turned out to be Billy. He met someone down there." Vivian pointed down the beach. "He must have a girlfriend. That explains his sneaking out this late at night." She turned, walking quickly up the path to the house. "I'll talk to him tomorrow. Find out who he's meeting. I saw him with someone a few days ago, but I don't know who she is. Has Billy said anything to you?"

"No, he hasn't. Do you want me to get dressed and go find him?"

"No. He's seventeen. I guess I know what he's up to. I'll find out who she is and give her parents a call. Stay out of it, Sara."

Sara held her tongue. There was no use fighting with Vivian when it came to Billy. He could do no wrong.

"Besides," Vivian said, "now that I know what Billy is up to, I'm more concerned with what you have on *your* mind. I saw how you were acting tonight. You really should exercise a little control and quit throwing yourself at Tom. It was embarrassing to watch, Sara."

As difficult as it was, Sara said nothing. Vivian opened the back door and hurried into the house. Sara glared at her back.

"Trust me," Vivian said, not bothering to turn around. "You have nothing in common with him. Like Billy, he's only interested in one thing. At least with someone like you." She closed the door behind her, leaving Sara standing alone on the back porch.

Counting to ten, Sara waited and then went upstairs to her own warm bed. She pulled the blankets around her shoulders, trying to relax and get warm again. But sleep eluded her. She tossed and turned, finally falling into a dreamless sleep around dawn.

Sara got up early the next morning, needing to get her thoughts together before encountering Vivian again. Sara absent-mindedly combed her hair as she stared at her reflection in the mirror, noting the dark circles under her eyes, the tired frown of her mouth. She desperately wanted to talk with Viv, make it clear that she wouldn't tolerate her demeaning treatment. But, as Sara began to wake up and clear her head, she knew she could not confront her cousin. The real issue was something else altogether, had little, if anything, to do with her. She had to convince Vivian to get help. Her behavior was getting more and more bizarre. Something seriously delusional was going on in her head.

Sara dressed and went downstairs to have toast and coffee. She'd call William later. He needed to know that something was very wrong with his precious wife.

Chapter 62

Late Sunday morning, amidst the cacophony of chatter from a Carolina wren in the red oak outside her window and the painful pounding in her head from another migraine, Vivian lay in bed exhausted. A heating pad covered her face, the radiant warmth beginning to ease her pain. After witnessing Sara throwing herself at Tom at the dinner last night, and then finding Sara following her in the night, she had a revelation. Sara! She was behind this. It all started when she came here. As her head cleared, she began to sort out what had been happening to her the past few weeks. How was Sara doing it? She must have drugged her. There was no other explanation. That's what's causing Vivian's migraines and blackouts. But why?

"Money!" she yelled. "Why the conniving bitch. And to think I let her live in my home; trusted her with my boys. How could she imagine she could get away with it?"

Throwing the heating pad off, Vivian got up and began pacing around the room. She caught site of her reflection in the mirror and stopped. "Oh, my God! Look what she's done to me. I look like death warmed over. Well, her little game is over." Dressing in haste, she left the room, practically running over Billy at the top of the stairs. Grabbing the banister to keep from falling, she reached for Billy with her free hand. "Darling, where are you going?"

"Where have you been, Mom?" Billy asked, dodging her grasp.

"For heaven's sakes, Billy. What's wrong? Has Jimmy been annoying you again?"

"No! I've been waiting for you in the study. You said you'd come down. "

"I'm sorry. I was lying down."

"Why? Do you have *another* headache?" Billy asked, kicking at the top step.

"I did, yes, but it's gone now. Have you seen Sara?"

"Mom! You said we'd talk about getting me a car. Who cares about Sara?" He pushed her aside as he came up the last stair. "What about me?"

"Billy, how many times do I have to remind you not to be disrespectful to your mother? Go to your room! Now!" Vivian moved back a few steps and waited for him to follow her instruction.

Instead, Billy whirled around and bounded down the stairs. She heard him running through the house, and then heard the front door slam.

"Was that Billy?" Sara asked, peering anxiously out of the library doorway.

"Yes. He's angry with me. He'll get over it, he always does," Vivian said. She looked coldly at Sara. "Come up here. Let's talk, Sara. Your little game is over. I'm on to you."

"What?" Sara was bewildered. "On to me? What are you talking about?" She hurried up the stairs.

"I had a call yesterday—a very interesting call."

"And what did that have to do with me?" asked Sara, following Vivian into her bedroom.

"I think you know. The call was from the jeweler. Anthony Rivers. I finally figured out what's been going on." Vivian watched Sara for a reaction. "Anthony's call made everything clear."

"Made what clear?" Sara flopped on the bed, waiting for Vivian to enlighten her.

"I know what you're doing. Although it took me a while to figure it out." She glared wickedly at Sara.

"What are you talking about?"

"You've been drugging me!"

Sara jumped to her feet. "What?"

"Caught you, didn't I?" Vivian stood in front of Sara, started pushing her backwards until Sara fell onto the bed. "How could you!"

"Vivian, stop this. This is crazy. I would never drug you! Oh, my God. What are you thinking?"

"I want you out of my house. Today! Get your things and go. Is that quite clear?"

Vivian turned and ran down the hall to Sara's room. She flung open the closet, removed a large suitcase, and started opening drawers and pulling clothes out. In the third drawer, under Sara's carefully folded sweaters, was the evidence. Vivian grabbed the velvet jewel case and opened it. On top of the necklace and earrings was a bill of sale from Kranston & Rivers Fine Jewelers. "I knew it. But how did you make me do it?"

"What is that?" Sara grabbed the box, stared incredulously at the jewels. "Those aren't mine!"

"Did you hypnotize me? You bitch! You did, didn't you?"

"What are you talking about? I didn't. I wouldn't. You know I'd never do anything like that to you."

"You drugged me, and then you hypnotized me to make me get this jewelry for you!" Vivian pulled at her hair. "God! What else have you made me do?"

"This is crazy, Vivian. I haven't done anything to you. I love you. And I love Jimmy and Billy. Please, stop this madness," Sara pleaded.

Vivian grabbed the jewel box back, waving it in the air, "This explains a lot—all these horrible headaches and blackout spells. I thought I was losing my mind, and all the time it was you. You caused them! I want you out of here! Now! "

"You can't mean that. Be reasonable. Vivian, we have to figure this out. I didn't do anything to you. Why would I?" Sara pleaded.

"You tell me. I loved you like a sister. I let you live in my house, teach my sons. Because that's what families do, take care of each other when they need help. How could you do this to me?" Vivian threw the velvet box at Sara. "Take them. If you want them so badly, take them!"

Sara ducked. The box bounced across the bed landing with a soft thump on the carpeted floor.

"Mother? What's the matter?" Jimmy stood in the doorway. He looked past Vivian to the suitcase and the clothes strewn across the floor. "Sara, are you going somewhere?"

"Jimmy, go back downstairs, I'll be down in a few minutes," Vivian said. "I'll explain everything. And yes, Sara is leaving. Go on, dear." Vivian motioned for him to leave.

Jimmy stood outside the door. "Sara? Don't go!"

"It's okay, Jimmy. Go on. I'll call you later." Sara turned away; it was too painful to see the look on his face. When Sara heard him slam the study door, she turned to face Vivian. She was gone.

Sara dug through her purse and found her cell phone. She called Tom. "Tom, something horrible has happened. I can't explain now, but please come and get me. Vivian just threw me out!"

"What happened?" Tom yelled into the phone.

"It's all crazy. I can't talk now. Just come and get me. I'd walk but I have my suitcases to carry." She was starting to cry and wanted to get off the phone. She didn't want to break down. Not now.

"Be right there. You okay?"

"No, I'm not." Sara shut her phone and began stuffing her things into her suitcases.

"Tom to the rescue?" Vivian stood in the doorway. "Don't expect that relationship to last. As soon as he finds out what you've done, you'll be history, Sara."

"Vivian, you're wrong," Sara said sniffing. "You'll see. This will all get straightened out."

"Just get out. I'll have Mannie pack the rest of your things and get them to you."

Sara reached down, picked up the jewelry box and handed it to Vivian. "I don't know how these got in my room. You have to believe me. Something very serious is happening to you Vivian. I need to help you. Don't do this."

"I have nothing more to say to you. You'll be hearing from William. It'll be up to him if he wants to press charges. I tried to call him, but he's in a meeting. Where is he when I need him!" Vivian walked over to the suitcases and jammed more clothing into them, then shut and snapped the latches. "He'll deal with you. I can't stand the sight of you." She pointed at the suitcases. "Take these and wait outside. I need to go to Jimmy."

Sara picked up the two suitcases and left. Tom found her standing in the middle of the driveway, sobbing.

Tom ran to her. "What in the world is Vivian doing?" Tom asked, putting his arms around Sara.

Chapter 63

"Tom, I think Viv's completely lost her mind. She accused me of drugging and hypnotizing her."

Tom took the suitcases from her, opened the back door of the Jeep, and threw them in. "She what?"

"She has some major problems. I need to talk to her husband. I'm scared to death to leave the kids with her. Who knows what she might do." Sara climbed into the passenger side, wincing when Tom slammed the door. She glanced back at the house. Jimmy was standing on the upper balcony. He waved to her, then turned and went back inside.

Getting in, Tom fumbled with his keys, dropping them twice. He shoved the key into the ignition and gunned the engine. Popping the clutch he sped down the driveway. The Jeep lurched forward, threatening to die as he missed second gear. He corrected the gearshift and gunned the gas pedal.

"Slow down!" Sara grabbed the door handle to keep from being thrown around.

"Sorry," Tom said, but he didn't slow down. Instead he sped up and yelled, "Hold on!"

"What are you doing?"

Tom ignored her and raced down the winding drive approaching the main road. He took the turn onto the paved road, throwing Sara into her door. Ahead, in the middle of the highway was a deer. Tom hit the brakes and hammered the horn with his fist. The deer jumped, and Tom raced past it. "I have to get you out of here." He glanced in the rearview mirror then swerved to the right, skidded around a curve. The back end of the Cherokee spun to the left. He corrected, turning into the skid. As soon as the car was under control, Tom hit the gas. Sara held onto to the door handle, knuckles white as she was bounced back and forth.

The report of a bullet glancing off the rock to the right brought a scream from deep within Sara's throat.

"Are you hit?" Tom yelled.

"God! What was that?"

"Get down!" Tom whipped the car to the left, pushing Sara down with his right hand. She hit her head on the dashboard. A second bullet glanced off the passenger side door. Tom sped up, took a quick turn to the right, rounded a curve onto a straightaway and gunned it. "We're out of range, I think. Stay down, Sara!"

She screamed, "Was that Vivian shooting at us?"

"No! It wasn't Vivian. It was Billy." Tom had his cell phone out. "Here, call 911." He thrust the phone at Sara.

"Billy? Oh my God, what's going on?"

"I don't know."

Sara yelled into the phone, giving as much information as she could when the dispatcher answered the call. Tom pulled the Jeep over to the side of the road, continually looking behind to see if Billy had followed them.

Within minutes the sheriff's car pulled up next to them. The sheriff, a tall, burly, middle- aged man, weighing maybe two hundred pounds, got out of the car and approached Tom's side of the car. "I'm Sheriff Jamison. You the party who called in about shots being fired?"

Tom got out of the car. "Yes. My neighbor's son, Billy Harrison, fired at us."

"Anyone hit?"

"No, but he came close. Look!" Tom pointed at the dent above the window.

Sara got out, turning even paler than she already was when she saw how close it had come to the glass—the glass wouldn't have stopped the bullet. "I could have been hit!"

"I'm calling for backup." The sheriff hurried to his patrol car, radioed for another car. Returning to Tom and Sara, he leaned against the Jeep. "I know the Harrisons. You sure it was their son?" he asked.

"Yeah. It was Billy, the oldest boy," Tom answered. In the distance, the high -pitched wail of another siren cut through the air as another patrol car sped down the back road.

"Why would he shoot at you?"

"I don't know. But right now I'm more worried about his mom and younger brother. They're back at the house. The faster you get to them, the better."

The other patrol car stopped. The sheriff said something to the officer, who sped off, red lights flashing, siren silenced.

"Did you see him clearly? Are you sure it was Billy Harrison?"

"Absolutely."

"I've got two cars on the grounds right now looking for him," the sheriff said. "Any idea where the mother and other boy are?"

"I'm Vivian's cousin," Sara said. "Let me call her and see if they're okay. I'll find out where they are."

"Dial her number, then give me the phone. I'll talk to her," the sheriff said. "What are your names, please?"

"Sara Lawson, and this is Tom Gardner." Sara called Vivian's cell and handed the phone to Jamison.

"Hello, this is Sheriff Jamison. Who am I speaking to?" He tapped his thumb impatiently on the grip of his holstered pistol. Jamison glanced at Sara. "He says his name is Jimmy. Would you verify that this is him?" He handed the phone to Sara.

"Jimmy? It's Sara. Are you okay?" She nodded and gave the phone back to the sheriff. "Yes, that's Jimmy. He says they're fine."

"Jimmy, listen carefully. Are you with your mother? Good. I want you to hand the phone to her, please." He waited. "Mrs. Harrison, this is Sheriff Jamison. We have two patrol cars on your property. Your son Billy has apparently taken some shots at his cousin and her friend. They are both okay. I need to know if you and Jimmy are safe." He paused as she answered. "Good. Does the door in the room you're in lock?" He waited for her answer. "Okay. Lock the door. Is there a closet you can go into?" Pause. "Now take Jimmy and go into the closet."

Apparently Vivian was following his instructions. Even through the phone, everyone could hear her screaming at Jimmy to hurry up. The sheriff motioned Sara and Tom to get in his patrol car. When they were in the back seat he drove off, heading to the Harrison house. Flashing lights from the patrol cars lit up the surrounding trees, whose boughs formed a roof over the driveway.

"Mrs. Harrison, you must stay there. You're safe. I'll keep you on the phone, so I know you're okay." Jamison pulled his car in behind one of the patrol cars. Over the police radio a man's voice reported to the sheriff that they had the boy in their sight and that the boy appeared unarmed. "Mrs. Harrison, we have visual contact with your son. You and Jimmy are to stay where you are. Okay? Good."

The sheriff turned to Tom and Sara. "You two stay here. Don't leave the car. Officer Ryan is trying to talk with the Harrison boy now. At this time, the officer believes Billy to be unarmed. But until we have complete control of the situation, please remain here." Jamison walked slowly down the drive and across the lawn toward the garage, his weapon drawn.

A commotion behind the garage brought angry yells from Billy as he realized he was surrounded. A minute later he was led to the sheriff's car, hands cuffed behind him.

Vivian had not waited but came running out of the house. "Billy! What have you done?" From behind her, Jimmy ran at full speed and punched Billy in the stomach. Billy started to fall forward. Jamison grabbed his shoulders, stopped his fall.

Sara ran to Jimmy, cradling the sobbing boy in her arms. Vivian started to embrace Billy, but was stopped by Sheriff Jamison. "Stand back, please. He's in our custody now. You can talk with him later, at the station."

"Mom, don't let them take me. I didn't do anything. It was just a BB gun. Look, see it over there." Billy pointed to a rifle, visible in a leafless sheepberry bush halfway to the garage. "See? Over there. It's a pellet gun."

Officer Ryan retrieved the weapon and handed the gun to Jamison. "Yes sir, Sheriff, it's a pellet gun."

"I swear I was just trying to scare a deer off the road. Mom, tell them I wouldn't shoot at anybody."

"Mr. Gardner, did you see anyone else? There is no way that dent in your Jeep was made with a pellet. Men, spread out, we may have a gunman on the loose. Call in more cars. We need all units to respond. Mr. Gardner, did you see anyone else?"

"I did not. Only Billy."

"Ryan, take the family into the house. Officer Lyndon, keep Billy in your custody until we're certain about what's going on. Is there anyone else in the house?" Jamison asked.

Vivian answered, "Yes, my household help. There are two other people in the house."

"Make sure they're accounted for, Ryan."

"Mr. Gardner, who do *you* think would be shooting at you? Could this have anything to do with your injuries? The stitches and all the bruising. Were you in a fight recently?"

"No, I had an accident several nights ago. I fell in the driveway."

"Easily checked. I assume you were treated somewhere in Ravenswood? "

"Yes, at the ER."

"By the way, your forehead's bleeding."

Tom touched his head, his fingers came away bloody. A couple of stitches had pulled out. "Damn!" He took a handkerchief from his pocket and dabbed the blood.

"Oh, Tom. You'll have to get that looked at," Sara said.

The sheriff cleared his throat. They looked at him. "Did you see anyone else?"

"You said you saw Billy. Didn't you?" asked Sara.

"Yes, I did. No one else," Tom said.

Sara's phone rang. "Hello? William? Where are you, we need you here. Something crazy is going on."

"It's Vivian Harrison's husband," Tom explained to Jamison. "Sara's been trying to reach him for days. Good timing, I guess."

Sara was trying to explain to William what was going on. They could hear him yelling for Sara to put Vivian on the phone. "She's not with me. She's gone into the house with the police officer."

Jamison had gone over to talk on the police radio. He motioned for Tom. "Mr. Gardner, Officer Swan examined your car. No bullet made that dent. Swan says it's from a rock. He's guessing you kicked up a rock in the road with your tire. That's what hit the window. Makes sense, don't you think?"

"Maybe. I saw the boy with the rifle and saw a bullet hit the side of the cliff. I guess it could have been two things different happening—a pellet hitting the cliff, and when I sped up, I threw a rock. I was so certain I saw the flash of another bullet coming at us. Sara, did you see it?"

She wasn't listening but was still trying to get William to understand what was happening. Seeing the odd look on Tom's face she told William to hold on. "What?"

Jamison asked her, "Did you see anything?"

"No, Tom pushed me down, out of the way. But I heard the bullets hit. One hit the cliff when we saw the deer in the road, and then one hit the car on the turn."

"We're pretty sure the first hit was a pellet and the second one a rock. The kid probably *was* shooting at the deer. So, unless you think someone is trying to shoot either of you, I think I'll have the men take another look around, just to make sure everything's okay. We'll talk to the boy, scare the daylights out of him so he doesn't do this again, then call it a day." Jamison talked into the radio, then led Tom and Sara into the house. "One of the officers will drive your Jeep up here," the sheriff said to Tom.

Sara was still talking to William on her cell. As they entered the house, Vivian screamed at them. "Get out of my house! Don't you dare come in here!" She ran toward them, was stopped by Jamison who stepped between Vivian and Sara.

"Hold on. Mrs. Harrison. I understand how you feel, but under the circumstances, you should consider how they might misinterpret your son's actions. I would have thought the same if I'd been in their shoes," Jamison said.

"Sara knows Billy would never do something like that," said Vivian.

"Well, m'am, you know, he *was* shooting at a deer. I could take him in for that. So for now, let's call it a . . . a misunderstanding." The sheriff glanced at Billy, still in cuffs. "Son, we're gonna leave you here with your family." Jamison took Billy's hands, motioning the deputy to unlock the handcuffs. "I get another call or hear you're causing any trouble around here, I'll have you hauled in. You understand me, kid?"

Billy said nothing. He looked at Sara and Tom, mumbled under his breath.

"I'll have none of that!" Jamison snapped. "You have something you want to say to these folks, kid? Like maybe an apology for scaring the crap out of them?" Jamison lightly squeezed Billy's shoulder. "You say or do anything other than apologize, you better be prepared to spend the rest of the day at the police station. Now, I'll ask you once more. You have something to say?"

Not looking up, Billy said, "Sorry."

Reaching her arms toward Billy, Vivian waited for him to come to her. He did not.

"I want to go to my room." He stared at his mother, waiting to be dismissed.

Vivian shrugged. "Go on then. I'll be there in a minute." She waited for Billy, with Jimmy in tow, to go upstairs. She turned to Sara. "You've done enough damage to my family. Get out!" Vivian walked to the door and opened it. "Don't call me. Don't call my husband and don't call my children! Do I make myself clear?"

Sara pleaded, "Vivian, we can figure this out. Let's sit down and talk—the three of us."

"Chief Jamison, will you get these people off my property? Now!" Vivian glared at Tom and Sara. "We're done here. *Everyone* leave." She twirled around, started toward the hallway, stopping to answer the phone. "William? Where the hell have you been? I need you here!" Turning, she pointed to the door.

The sheriff motioned everyone out. When they were all on the front porch, the heavy wooden door slammed behind them. Startled by the loud noise, Sara jumped and then collapsed.

Jamison, faster to react than Tom, caught her before she hit the porch floor. "Officer Ryan! Get her some water from the cooler in the trunk."

The front door flew open. Vivian appeared in the doorway, her hand clasping at her chest. "Sara? Oh, God. Bring her in the house."

Tom picked Sara's limp body off the porch and followed Vivian who ran ahead and threw open the study door. "Tom, put her here. On the couch. Mannie!" she yelled into the intercom, "Bring a cold cloth to the study—Sara passed out!"

Officer Ryan stomped down the hall. Running into the room, he threw a bottle of water at Tom.

Sara opened her eyes and stared blankly at Tom, who smiled encouragingly at her. "What happened?" she asked, her voice barely a whisper. "I don't feel well."

Tom took her hand. "Drink this. Just a sip. You fainted. Do you remember?"

"No." She swallowed.

Sheriff Jamison asked, "Sara, do you know who I am? Do you remember why I'm here at your cousin's house?"

Sara looked at him, shook her head, lifted the bottle to her mouth and swallowed.

The sheriff checked her pulse. "Pulse is okay. Sara, take a couple of deep breaths," he said. "That's the way. Do you feel dizzy or nauseated?"

"No."

Mannie hurried into the study, a small medicine box in her hand. She handed a wet washcloth to Vivian, who gently placed it on Sara's forehead. Mannie handed the box to the sheriff who opened it and took out a small capsule of smelling salts.

"Take a sniff. Might clear your head," Jamison said, handing the capsule to Sara.

Sara took the smelling salts and gently inhaled. Closing her eyes, she breathed deeply and inhaled again. She coughed, then sat up. "That helped. I'm starting to remember everything—the shooting. What a horrible ordeal!" She paused. "And Vivian," her voice caught, "I remember you throwing me out."

Vivian bit her lip but said nothing. She took the cloth from Sara's forehead, swung it in a circle to get it cold again and placed it back on Sara's brow.

"You had us worried. Are you okay?" Tom asked, gently massaging the back of Sara's neck.

Letting the cloth fall carelessly to the floor, Sara got up, and tested her balance. "I fainted. Hmm. How dramatic," she said sarcastically. "Yeah, I'm fine."

"Are you sure?" asked Vivian. "You frightened me."

"Really?" Sara said, again with sarcasm.

"We've got another call to respond to," said Jamison. "If you're okay here, we need to go."

Tom answered. "We're fine. Thank you." He extended his hand to shake the sheriff's.

"Come on, Officer Ryan. There's been an accident on the frontage road by Mill Lane. Let's go." The two men left, their heavy boots echoing hollowly on the wooden floor. The wailing of their sirens resounded in the still afternoon air as they gunned their engines and sped down the drive.

"Mannie, you may go now. Thank you," Vivian said flatly.

Tom gathered up Sara's purse and sweater. "We better leave," he said. "If you feel up to it?"

"Wait. I want to say something." Vivian put her hand on Sara's wrist.

The *bong, bong, bong* of the grandfather clock announced the three o'clock hour. A pine grosbeak chirped melodically in the leafless, white poplar tree outside the study window. Sara looked at her cousin, waiting.

With tears in her eyes, Vivian sat down, patting the sofa next to her. Sara sat beside her cousin. Vivian said, "You have done things to me that I don't understand. I have always loved you and welcomed you in my home. I trusted you with my sons."

Sara jumped up. "I won't listen to this, Vivian. I've done nothing to you. I don't know what's going on, but you have to believe me when I tell you that nothing you have accused me of is true."

"Something is going on. I will get to the bottom of it!" Vivian responded, her emotions barely under control. "William can't come home yet. He has his damn business to deal with. It's all left up to me. I need some time to think this through."

"Okay, Vivian," Sara said, quickly dabbing at an escaped tear running down her cheek "But you have to believe me. I have *never* stolen from you. God, how could you think I'd ever do anything so low? And I would never, under any circumstances, give you drugs nor do anything that could hurt you. Or the boys. You're my family." She took her sweater from Tom. "I'll go. But I want to talk with you. Soon. Will you call me tomorrow?"

"I will," Vivian said. "Or I think I will. Right now I need to lie down—after I check on the boys. Show yourselves out."

"Can I do anything for you before we go?" asked Tom.

"Tell Mannie to come here. Use the intercom." She pointed to the panel. "Push button number two. Tell her I need her. Then go."

Tom and Sara left Vivian sitting on the couch, head cradled in her hands, elbows propped on her knees—the picture of dejection.

Sara intercepted Mannie in the hall. "Mannie, has Vivian seemed all right to you lately?"

"No, m'am. Something's not right. She sure is acting strange. Think she's missing Mr. Harrison."

"Maybe that's all it is, but . . . I'm becoming increasingly concerned about her. Will you take care of her for a few days? I'll be staying at Mr. Gardner's. Vivian and I had a fight. She asked me to leave. Promise you'll call me anytime, day or night, if anything seems wrong? Or if she has another migraine."

"I will. Lordy, I wish you and Mrs. Harrison hadn't had that fight, but I can't imagine she'll stay mad at you. She's just not thinking clear right now. You go on now. I'll take good care of her."

From the top of the stairs Billy stayed out of sight until everyone was gone. "Damnit, why does everyone have to be so kissy-kissy. Shit! Wish my aim had been better. Next time I won't miss. I'll pop that asshole right in the face." Billy slammed his fist into his palm. He went back to his room, picked up his cell phone and dialed his dad's number. As usual, the call went straight to voice mail. "Where the hell are you, Dad? Why don't you come home?"

Chapter 64

The old ones, tired of having Tom and his entourage of people in the house, had taken what belongings they could manage to carry to the basement. At least no one would bother them down there. They needed some rest, some time alone. Everyone had gone somewhere for a change, leaving Helen and Gabe to the quiet solitude they craved. Everyone, that is, except Elise. They spitefully had locked her in a bedroom closet in the attic, guarded by the little, dark-spirit they kept for such a crisis. It was a vile creature that had roamed the beach until they captured its soul. Now it belonged to them. Helen and Gabe called the little thing Ben. Mostly they let it run loose, but sometimes, like today, they summoned it to them.

Chapter 65

Harold, brother to Nate—Tom Gardner's accountant, business director, and personal friend—handed his ticket to the conductor. He slouched down in the plush seat pulling his well-worn, sweat-stained Stetson over his eyes. Sensing the conductor was still standing over him, he pulled his hat up to expose one eye. That's all it took to get the message across. "Don't even think of messing with me," his brazen glare said.

The conductor nodded. *Handsome prick, but those eyes—ice-blue, piercing, cold. Yeah, I've seen trouble before, and it looked like this kid.* He took the next passenger's ticket and moved on down the aisle.

Harold had a pint of whiskey tucked in his jacket pocket. *It's gonna be a long ride.* He pulled the bottle out of his pocket, twisted the cap off. Harold swallowed two gulps, then two more. *Yeah, that's better. Fucking Ravenswood, here I come. Sorry to hear Tommy's gonna be out of town when I get there, but oh well, his loss is my gain. Ha! Lucky I read Nate's emails. Easy money comin' my way.* Harold snickered.

For the past week, Harold had been sleeping in the basement of Tom Gardner's Jamestown house, hiding right under his brother's nose. Nate never knew Harold was there since he wasn't up to the task of maneuvering the basement stairs with his broken leg. Harold managed to stay out of sight and still have a pretty good time of it.

While Nate slept, Harold snooped. That's how he found out Tom was going back to his house in Jamestown. Harold needed to leave Jamestown pretty soon, and what better place to go than to Ravenswood? Just long enough to get some money from Tom's safe. He'd case Tom's place in Ravenswood and break in when the opportunity presented itself, get fast cash and be on his way. He knew Tom well enough to know there'd be a safe—with plenty of money in it—somewhere in the house. Easy pickings. He'd play his cards right and next week, He'd be out of here—and as far away as he could get. He wasn't planning on coming back to the states either. Hasta la vista and all that crap. He fell asleep, snoring just loudly enough to bother the woman seated in the section to his left. She motioned to the conductor who refused to wake the man, but told the passenger there was an empty seat in the next train car. Grudgingly, she allowed him to relocate her.

When the train pulled into Ravenswood that night, Harold with his one suitcase in hand, descended to the platform. He rudely pushed ahead of the woman he caused to be moved on the train and hopped into a waiting taxi.

Lucky for Harold, Joe hadn't seen him shove past Mrs. Johnson, or he would have asked Harold to find his own way to town. "Here, let me take that." Joe took Harold's well-worn suitcase, easily swinging the heavy case into the trunk. "Where to?"

"Any boarding houses around, or maybe a motel, that charges by the week?"

Joe replied, "There's a pretty nice motel out toward the edge of town. Or a small inn on Main Street, if you want to be in walking distance of everything."

"No car. Staying in town makes the most sense. Take me to the inn."

"Sure, it's only about a mile from here." Joe glanced in the rear view mirror at Harold.

Harold chewed his fingernails. He spit out a sliver of nail, started on another finger. Retrieving a nail fragment from the tip of his tongue, he glanced out one window then the other, taking in the small town. *Not bad.*

Joe pulled up in front of the Night Inn. "Here you go."

"What do I owe ya?"

"Five bucks'll take care of it," Joe answered as he opened the backdoor to let the man out.

Harold handed Joe six ones. "Keep the change, man," he said.

Joe popped his trunk and handed Harold the suitcase. "Nice restaurant down the street, Raven Café." He pointed down the dark avenue toward a line of neon lights. "That's the downtown business district. Down a couple of blocks. The restaurant's on the right. Closed now but they open at six in the morning. If you like a hearty breakfast, that's the place to go."

The man nodded and walked away, pushing instead of pulling on the glass entry door. As he climbed back into his cab, Joe heard him cussing. *Now there's a man with an attitude. Wonder what his problem is?*

Chapter 66

It was after midnight. The house was wrapped in quiet as everyone slept—everyone except Tom. Too agitated to sleep, Tom tossed and turned. The tapestry bag filled with opium, a pipe, and matches had mysteriously disappeared from his room. He'd carefully locked it in his file drawer; now it was gone. No one had jimmied the lock. Tom had the only key. The bag was just gone, disappearing as mysteriously as it had appeared. He was, to say the least, disturbed.

In need of a drink, Tom crept down the long staircase, tiptoeing like a thief in the night. Once he got to the living room, he closed the door behind him very slowly so the squeak of the hinges would be minimal. He held his breath and listened for the sounds of anyone stirring in the house.

The embers in the fireplace glowed orange and blue casting an eerie dance of shadows on the walls around him. Tom stirred the smoldering coals, then dropped several small pieces of wood onto the fire. Flames shot up, then settled down, igniting, and burning the tinder. He poured himself a shot of vodka and added a couple of ice cubes from the ice bucket. Putting the glass to his forehead, he listened to the crackle of ice, the effervescent sound echoing into the darkness. The night was so still it seemed to Tom that everyone would hear the popping of the fire and the ice crackling in his glass.

Extending his glass in a silent salute, he whispered, "Cheers, Elise. Tuesday we go home. Back to Jamestown."

Chapter 67

In a corner of the closet, miserable, cold and furious, Elise waited. The vile little creature was still about, taunting her in its hissing voice, to come out. Every few minutes it stuck its bony fingers under the door. "Come out, my sweet. Come see what I have for you."

Elise reached her breaking point. She wept, tasting salty tears on her lips. She tried to remember what it felt like to be alive. To be warm and safe. Her slender fingers traced the rivulets on her cheeks, felt the wetness of her tears. She touched her fingertips to her soft, warm lips. *I am alive, I am.* Weeping, she hugged her arms around her shoulders, comforted herself, and slept.

***

Benjamin, discouraged and bored, hissed a final warning and slithered out of the window, gliding off into the darkness, away to his own private haunts. He was tired of the old ones, tired of doing their biddings with no regard for *his* needs. He'd had enough. Tonight he felt powerless in the presence of this young spirit, recognized that even though she didn't know it yet, her power was superior to his—almost as strong as the old ones. He would leave—before he was eternally damned to her behest.

***

Helen and Gabe, exhausted and disgusted at the constant threat to their peace, slept intertwined on a pile of dusty old blankets in the damp, drafty basement. With a woof, the furnace kicked on and the two hugged each other closer, sleeping a dark, dreamless sleep—the sleep of the damned.

Chapter 68

Elise startled. She woke up knowing instantly the ghoulish creature was gone. She cracked the closet door, its dry hinges creaking. Slowly pushing it open, she crept into the tiny attic room she claimed as her own. Her skin crawled when she saw the oily tracks the creature left on the floorboards and rug as it paced around the room. She saw the grimy marks left on her bed of blankets where it had lain while it called her to come to it and do disgusting things with it. She shuddered, also remembering Helen and Gabe probing her body with their cold, withered hands whenever they wanted to. She vowed it would never happen again! She would take care of them—soon. She felt stronger now. Every hour, every foul encounter with the other side brought her new resolve. Their hold on her would soon come to an end. But she had other priorities now.

Gliding silently though the house, she found Sara asleep in the guest room where she slept in one twin bed and Lizzie in the other. Cassie and Michael slept soundly in their room overlooking the ocean. Their curtains were drawn open and, far below, the ocean water sparkled with reflections of the stars. Elise entered Tom's bedroom on the second floor. Finding the room empty, she lay on his bed listening to the sounds of the night. From the lower floor of the house, she detected distinct sounds of creaking floorboards, the faint popping of a fire. She giggled. *Tom's downstairs. He can't sleep either.* Elise went to join him.

Tom sat on the floor facing the fire, his back to her, holding an empty cut-crystal glass. She entered silently and sat on the sofa a few feet behind him. *It's so warm. It's been so long since I've been warm. Damn you, Tom, for what you've done to me.* She started to reach toward him, wanting to frighten him, make him aware of her presence. But she changed her mind, withdrew her hand. It was too perfect—the warm fire, the soft couch. The velvety upholstery felt so gentle on her skin. She had a right to enjoy this simple comfort—for a while. Elise lay back.

Tom swirled his glass, irritated to find it empty. He needed another drink. He started to stand, stopped, and whirled his head around to look at the sofa behind him. Nothing there. Just a feeling. His ears strained to discern any sound, any movement. And then, there it was was—the faint hint of lavender. She was here. "Elise," he whispered, "we're going home . . . soon . . . " He finished the sentence silently, *to end this nightmare once and for all. Your reign will soon be over.*

Elise smiled demurely; her tiny pearl-like teeth glimmered in the firelight, though Tom could not see them. Could not see her at all. That was her choice. She loved this power she had over him. She curled up on the warm sofa, bathed in the gentle glow of the firelight, and slept.

Tom stared into the fire. "I will end this, Elise," he whispered. After a few moments, with the scent of Elise's perfume still in his head, he crossed the room, poured himself another vodka, tossing it down in one gulp. Staring out into the night sky he caught the faint reflection in the window glass of a misty figure lying on the couch. He poured himself another vodka, started to take a drink, changed his mind and hurled the glass across the room. It smashed onto the brick hearth, sending sparkling shards of splintered glass into the air.

Tiny fragments of glass prickled Elise's skin. As the tiny slivers passed through her, she shot up off the couch, silently cursing Tom. Disgusted and angered at the interruption to her comfort, Elise fled, leaving Tom alone.

Cassie sat up. *What was that?* Slipping quietly out of bed so that she didn't wake Michael, she tiptoed down the stairs to the living room. Tom was bent over picking something off the floor. "Oww!" she yelped.

"Cassie, don't come in here. There's glass all over." Tom warned.

"Too late, Tom! I'm barefoot. Help!"

Tom picked his sister up and carried her across the room away from the glass. "Stay put. I'll get the broom." Tom disappeared into the dining room. She heard the kitchen door open, then close. Then open again, then close. Tom appeared, broom and dustpan in his hands.

"What happened?" Cassie pointed to the glass littering the floor.

"Dropped my glass. That's about it."

"Looks like more than a dropped glass. The shards are everywhere. Tom, what are you doing down here in the middle of the night? What's wrong?"

"What's right you mean." Tom swept at the pieces of glass stuck stubbornly in the bricks.

"Getting drunk won't make things any better. You should have figured that out by now. Why didn't you wake me?" Cassie studied her foot, looking for pieces of glass.

"Didn't need your advice, Sis. Needed a drink."

Sara heard the voices and came to investigate, too. Sticking her head into the room, she flipped the light switch, making Tom jump, spilling the glass shards all over the floor again."

"Shit!"

"Tom, I'm sorry. I heard voices. What broke?"

"He dropped his vodka glass," Cassie responded coolly.

"Oh, it's you, Cassie!" Sara said. "I wondered who Tom was talking to." Sara looked across the room at Cassie who was picking a sliver of glass from her foot."You're bleeding! What can I do?"

"Not to worry, it's a minor injury." Cassie patted at the blood with a tissue. "Tom's the one who needs your help."

"I'll get the vacuum, hold on," Sara said. She left briefly, returning with a small canister vacuum from the hall closet. "What are you doing drinking vodka in the middle of the night, Tom?"

"Fuck! Leave it alone!" Tom threw the broom down, stormed out of the living room and up the stairs. They heard his heavy footsteps in the upstairs hall, then the slamming of his bedroom door.

"What was that all about?" Sara asked Cassie.

"You can't be serious. You know what it's about. It's this damned house and its ghosts. What else! Tom can't rest. I hear him pacing every night. I hear *them* pacing every night. Something's going to happen. Soon!" Cassie sounded nearly frantic. "We need to *do* something—before everything falls apart," she said, pulling the cushions off the sofa so Sara could thoroughly vacuum the upholstery. "Tuesday, after Tom leaves, we need to talk. I have a plan, Sara. But, I need your help."

"I don't know. I can't think any more tonight; there's been too much going on," Sara said. Finished with the clean up, she wound up the vacuum cord. "Do you think Tom is okay?"

Staring at Sara, Cassie answered, "No. Do you?"

"I don't have a clue. I'll go check on him before I go to my room. The best I can hope for is that he's fallen asleep. Goodnight. See you in the morning." Sara put the vacuum away then left Cassie alone. Despite the faint glowing of the embers, the room was pitch-black.

"Goodnight, we'll talk tomorrow afternoon. Okay?" she called to Sara. Sara was already on the stairs, apparently did not hear her. Cassie limped across the floor, heading upstairs to her own, warm bed.

Sara tapped gently on Tom's door. "Can I come in?" she asked. There was no response. She tapped again, finally turning the doorknob. The door swung open. Tom stood on the balcony, a silhouette against the dark night. She went to him, wrapped her arms around him and held him tightly. They stood for several minutes, clinging to each other, and then Sara pulled away, took his hand and led him to the bed. Holding each other, they fell asleep.

***

At Remington House, this dark and starless night, while those who slept a dreamless sleep tossed and turned, and those who clung to each other for solace, and those who tried in vain to comfort themselves—while they all tried to get some sleep, to find some peace, Elise, cold and furious, began to make plans.

Chapter 69

The dawning of morning brought a renewal of light on glistening seascapes and glowing clouds brilliantly painted in subtle hues of peach and orange and gray-tinted tangerine. Silhouettes of ravens darted across the sky at land's end where the cliffs at the edge of Remington House stood in sentinel over the vast ocean. The ravens' haunting caws were the only sounds audible in the quiet dawn.

At the cliff's edge Elise faced the awakening day, arms stretched toward the rising sun, eyes closed in concentration, lips slightly parted. She tasted the new air—fresh, clean, almost palatable. Her tongue savored the vague tang of salt—whether from her own tears or merely in the mist floating in from the sea —made no difference.

Elise felt empowered. Alive. Vital. She had grown stronger, her mind clearer, her purpose more defined. She laughed knowing that Tom thought he could control her. She now was beginning to recognize that she, not Tom, was the master of their future.

Drinking in the morning sun at the dawning of this new day, she was aware of her growing power, her keenness of mind and soul. She smiled and opened her eyes. Remington House would be hers.

Chapter 70

"Cassie, you need to get up. Now!" Michael said into Cassie's ear, while gently shaking her shoulder. "My train leaves in an hour. We've overslept."

What?" She sat up, threw her legs over the edge of the bed. "Oh, shit, why didn't the alarm go off?" She grabbed the clock. "I know I set it. Did you hear it go off?"

"It doesn't matter now!" Michael was running around the room, scrambling to get his clothes on. He tripped as he stepped on the leg of his jeans, his other leg halfway into the pants. He fell forward onto the bed. "Damn it!"

Laughing, Cassie hopped up and grabbed her clothes from the chair next to the bed. In one minute she had dressed and slipped into her loafers. "I'm ready. Just let me pee and we're on our way. Go say goodbye to Lizzie. Hey, Hon! Grab our coats please." The bathroom door closed abruptly.

Michael went to the small bedroom next door to his and Cassie's to wake his sleeping daughter. "Bye, little angel. I'm leaving now." He tousled her blonde hair, soft and fine like her mother's red hair. He hated leaving the two most important women in his life. He thought he was too much like his father —always traveling with business, spending too little time with his family. After this trip he would scale back and leave the traveling to one of the younger, single associates.

Lizzie woke and reached her arms around her father's neck. "Bye, daddy. I'll miss you." She hugged him tightly.

He kissed her cheek. "You take care of yourself, little one. Be good and mind your mother. Got to hurry, or I'll miss my train. I'll call you tonight. Go back to sleep."

"Bye, Daddy," she said, curling up with Wiggins who had found a true friend in Lizzie. Wiggins stretched, licked one paw, and closed his eyes.

Michael met Cassie in the hallway. They raced downstairs. Tom and Sara were sitting at the table on the front porch having coffee and pastries. The aroma of bacon wafted in the crisp, morning air.

Tom motioned to them to sit down. "Morning. Breakfast is served." He swept his hand to indicate the various covered platters of food. "Nellie has done her morning magic. Sit down, and join us."

"We have about five minutes to spare. I'm *starving*." Michael pulled out a chair, motioned for Cassie to sit down. "I need to eat something to tide me over. Besides, with Cassie driving, she'll more than make up for the time it takes us to eat. Right, Parnelli?" He smiled at his wife as she chewed on a piece of bacon.

"Yeah. I'll absolutely get you to the station on time, dear husband," she answered while spooning scrambled eggs onto two stoneware plates.

"How come you're not having Joe pick you up?" Sara asked. She poured them a cup of coffee, passed them the porcelain creamer and sugar bowl.

"I figured it was easier for me to take Michael. I need to do some shopping anyway. Not to mention it gives Michael and me a little more time together." She smiled at her husband. "It'll make my day less hectic, too. Jimmy's coming over later to play with Lizzie. I thought I'd take them down to the beach. Lizzie wants to collect some seashells to send to her grandmother."

Michael and Cassie shoveled food into their mouths and hurriedly drank their coffee. "We've got to go. Come on, Michael." Cassie pulled at her husband's arm.

"Okay. Bye, Tom. Hope I'll catch up with you in a few weeks. Thanks for letting the girls stay here while you're in Jamestown. I think it's a good break for them." Michael extended his hand to Tom.

Michael nodded at Sara as she took a bite of her sweet roll. "Sorry you're having a rough time. I hope everything gets worked out quickly with Vivian. Don't hesitate to lean on Cassie if you need to."

Sara wiped her fingers and offered her hand to Michael. "Thank you. Have a safe trip. Don't worry about Cassie and Lizzie. We plan on having a good time. Mary's going to be around a lot, too. A girl's paradise."

"See you all in a few weeks. Bye!" Michael hollered as they raced to the car.

As she pulled away, Cassie waved to her brother and Sara. "Back in a couple hours. Don't forget Lizzie's still sleeping. When she wakes up, tell her I'm bringing her a surprise."

"I sure like Michael," Sara said to Tom, watching the car speed down the dirt drive, dust clouds following as Cassie navigated the curving drive to the highway. "I see why he calls her Parnelli!"

To nodded. "Michael's a great husband, perfect father, too. Cassie was lucky to find him. Cassie has always shown impeccable taste in people. A knack she has. Kind of a sixth sense, I guess." Pouring them both more coffee, Tom sat back looking toward the ocean, visible from the porch through the bare-limbed trees. "Beautiful day. What should we do? It is our last day together for a few weeks." Tom took Sara's hand. "I have a few ideas. Care to come upstairs with me, and I'll show you what I have in mind?"

The two went hand in hand up the stairs and into Tom's suite. He closed and locked the door.

Chapter 71

At the Raven Café, Joe was enjoying his usual breakfast of two eggs over easy, hash browns covered in hot pepper sauce, two sausage patties, sourdough toast, a glass of freshly squeezed orange juice and orange pekoe tea with half a teaspoon of honey. Reading the local paper, *The Ravenswood Daily*, he didn't notice he was being watched.

Across the room, behind the artfully placed potted plant, in a corner booth, Harold enjoyed his own breakfast of huevos rancheros with sour cream and black coffee. He watched the waitress bring the cab driver a cup of tea. *She's taking her sweet time. Looks like the little lady has the hots for him. Fine looking broad. Wouldn't mind a little attention from her. Doesn't look like she's making an impression. Good!*

Joe smiled at Joanie when she brought him more tea. He joked about the caption on the front page of the newspaper. Looking up, Joe spotted the man across the room watching him. He thought for a second, trying to remember where he'd seen him before. He nodded at him and resumed his chatter with Joanie. When she left to take care of other patrons, Joe went back to reading the paper. Flipping though the paper, he came across the story about yesterday's crazy shooting. Tom and Sara were named in the article—the shooter was not. Joe was alarmed and surprised no one had called him. He pulled his cell phone from his front pocket and called Nellie. "Nellie, Joe here. What the heck happened out there? I just read that Tom and Sara were involved in some crazy incident yesterday. Are they okay?"

"They're both fine. It was that darned Billy Harrison. Said he was shooting at a deer. With a pellet gun, I guess. Said he didn't see Mr. Gardner's car. No one got hurt, just shaken up. Mr. Gardner and Miss Lawson thought someone was shooting at them. The police got involved and apparently they believed Billy's story. I asked Mr. Gardner about it, but he didn't want to talk about it."

"I bet. Tom must have been really mad. That boy! He's nothing but trouble. Wish his parents would rein him in a bit."

"You and me both. Such a shame. And Jimmy is the complete opposite. He's a sweetheart. Oh! In case you haven't heard, well, I shouldn't be telling you this. If anybody asks, you didn't hear it from me. Okay?" Nellie paused.

"I understand, Nellie. What is it?"

"Sara's staying here. Vivian threw her out. Can you believe that? No wonder Billy is so troubled. His mom is as unstable as they come. Don't know how his little brother ended up so regular. Genes I guess."

"What happened?" Joe steered her back on the subject of Sara.

"Well, I don't know for sure. I heard from Cassie that Sara called Tom and said Vivian was throwing her out and would he come get her. Then there was the shooting, so maybe they're all related. No one's telling me any more than that."

"Hmm. Well, no one got hurt, that's the main thing. I'll stop by the police station and see what I can find out. I'll let you know. Course, you didn't hear anything from me either." He chuckled into the phone.

"No, Joe. Not a word. Cassie's husband just left. She's driving him into town to catch the morning train. Mr. Gardner's leaving for Jamestown tomorrow. You gonna be around while they're gone?"

"You bet, Nell."

"Think you need to be checking on this family while the men are out of town. This house isn't safe, if you know what I mean. Spooky, that's what it is."

"Well, I think I can take care of the gals. As for the spooks —we'll see." He laughed at her silliness. "I'm starting the remodel in the basement while Mr. Gardner's gone. The materials are in, so I'm getting a crew together. We're starting work on the gym this week."

"Glad I won't be here, then. I won't mind missing all the noise and dust. I have the house cleaning caught up, and I'm going to visit to my sister, Meg, in Jersey. Mr. Gardner said it was fine. You keep the mess down, you hear me?"

"Yes, m'am. We're using the back entrance. Shouldn't make much of a mess that way, keep it confined to the basement. The crew won't bother the family that way, either. Listen, Nell, I have to go. I'll call you later if I hear any more about Billy. Bye."

Harold had finished his breakfast. He waited for Joanie to bring him his change then walked over to Joe's table. He was talking on his cell phone. Harold waited until Joe snapped his phone closed. "Morning. Remember me?"

Joe nodded.

"You picked me up in your cab last night. At the train station."

"Yep. I remember."

"Not eavesdropping intentionally, but heard you mention you're doing some work. Wondered if you were hiring?"

"Might be. Sit down and take a load off."

"Thanks, man. Name's Harry." He offered his hand to Joe.

"Joe Tilson. I'm doing a home remodel. Converting a basement in one of the old properties. Putting in a gym with a small boxing ring. With a sauna and shower, steam room maybe, nothing too grand but adequate for in-home use."

"Pretty fancy stuff. Family must be loaded."

"None of your concern," Joe snapped, then added in a less harsh voice, "I'm a contractor, I build whatever the owner wants. You have any experience?"

"Sure do. Worked for a private contractor in Manhattan. Got a letter of reference back at my room if you need to see it," Harold lied, pretty sure it wouldn't be necessary.

"Yeah, I would need to see it. Can't be too careful. You have a phone number I can call to verify your past job?" Joe asked, staring into Harold's hardened face. He had no clue who this man was, but he thought that Harold looked like a man who could use a break.

"Sure do," Harold lied again. Not a problem to come up with a letter. He had a few friends who owed him. He'd get someone to give a phony testimonial as to his reliability and skills.

Harold reminded Joe of his cousin Lenny. Poor kid never did get a break. Ruined him, too. Joe tried to see the good in people, give them a chance to show their true colors before making judgment. "Good deal. Here's my phone number." Joe wrote on the napkin and handed it to him. "Call me when you get a minute and give me that name and number. I'm starting work on Wednesday. That work?"

Harold took the napkin, nodding. "Yeah. I'll call you when I get back to the motel. Job far from here?"

"Yeah, a ways out of town. But the guys who're working with me live close by. They'll be willing to drive you if you put in some gas money. I can pick up the crew too some mornings. Nice thing about small towns, everybody helps everybody."

Harold stood up. "Call you later, Joe. Thanks, man." He offered his hand, shook with a decisively strong grip, then walked out of the Raven Café and down the street. Within two hours he had made arrangements with a guy in Manhattan and called Joe with his phone number. Joe called the guy in Manhattan right away and had gotten a report that made him feel he was hiring an honest, hard-working man.

Harold, in his motel room smoking a joint and drinking a beer, laughed after he hung up with Joe. *Well shit yes! I'm all set now.* He showered and headed to the little bar down the street to celebrate his good fortune. There he met up with Joanie, the waitress from the Raven Café, she was on her short shift today. They had quite a time. Drank all day, screwed all night. What a lucky break. Hot damn! Life was good sometimes.

Chapter 72

Benjamin studied Elise as she sat on the edge of the cliff. She'd been there all day, from the break of dawn until now— the fall of dusk. She now appeared to be a normal woman. Not once in the hours he watched her had she faltered in her ability to hold on to her human form. Had he not been watching her for the past weeks, had he not known what she really was, he would never have thought of her as anything *but* alive. Somehow she was transforming herself—and growing stronger.

Benjamin decided to leave—as soon as Elise went back to the house, so he could safely flee. He'd find another place to haunt. His time here was finished. He hoped he could steal away without being detected. He knew from experience that the slightest noise would be amplified with Elise's keen, heightened sense of sound. He, too, had that ability and, even from this distant vantage point, was careful not to make any excessive noise. He waited patiently, watching the rising of the moon glisten on a calm Atlantic. Hints of gray-tinged lilac appeared over the horizon.

Elise finally stood. Benjamin watched her float eerily above the craggy rocks of the cliff edge, gracefully descending through the heavy, foggy air, floating slowly, so slowly, down to the water's edge. Dropping to her knees, she bent from her tiny waist, her pale fingers reaching toward the waves. Cupping her hands, she scooped the frigid ocean water, filling her hands. She threw the water into the air above her. The droplets, shimmering with moonlight, splashed all around her. She repeated the deed, joyously squealing as the salty water rained down and soaked her flimsy, threadbare dress.

Becoming more and more impatient, Benjamin waited for his opportunity to steal away. He remained hidden behind an abandoned boat mooring, some twenty yards down the beach.

Elise startled. Jumping to her feet, she whirled around to look down the beach. Running toward her, kicking sand behind him with every footfall, was a young man. Elise ran to him, throwing her tiny body against his. She was shivering, almost uncontrollably. The young man took his jacket off, wrapping it around her. She was still laughing, the sound a gentle vibration in the quiet, darkening night.

Her laughter brought to mind the many children Benjamin had seen over the years playing in the waves at this very spot— gave him a rare moment of clarity. He decided she must have died very young. He could understand her not wanting to leave this world. The pleasures of the body are not easily surrendered. Benjamin, too, was robbed of his youth—a very long time ago. Now he wished he *could* leave. He'd tired of this world. This existence had become a worse torture—he was trapped on this wretched earth, knew no way out. He was damned. It was easier to lose one's mind than to accept this fate—he knew that to be true.

Elise's laughter now seemed vile and obscene as it echoed in his head. Joy. Happiness. Pleasures he could never experience now—his life forever dark and ominous. Damned. His life/death loomed eternal.

Benjamin took a last look at the young couple, making sure he would not be seen. Elise was enchanted with her young lover now, dancing around him, teasing him as she spun around and around. Benjamin snarled, then fled. As he disappeared into the darkness, he couldn't help but feel sorrow for Helen and Gabe. Their hell was just beginning. They had no idea of the power behind this woman named Elise.

Trying to stop her shivering, Billy pulled Elise to him. Holding her tightly, worried because her body was cold, and she shook so violently. "What were you thinking? You'll catch your death." Billy hated how he sounded—just like his mother.

Knowing the irony of what he had just said, Elise laughed, pushing away. "Don't worry, my sweet. I'll be fine. Come. Walk with me before I have to leave you."

"I've waited all day to see you; where are you going?" Billy asked and, with the impatience of youth, reached out and turned her to face him. "I just got here."

Elise giggled, pulled away and wrapped her arms tightly around herself. "I'll make it up to you. Later. Meet me at the cottage down the beach at midnight. Can you do that?"

Billy smiled. "You know it." He took her tiny hand in his. The two walked hand in hand through the hard packed sand, waves chasing them farther inland with the rising tide until they were sheltered beneath the cliff.

Benjamin took a final look back at the shoreline. Elise and the boy had parted. The young man was running toward Benjamin. Benjamin recoiled and prepared to jump at him when the boy took a turn and bounded up a wooden staircase on the cliff edge.

From far down the beach, Elise heard a deep intake of breath—raspy and strained. She watched as the creature that had imprisoned her in the attic seemed ready to attack her Billy. Instantly she was beside Benjamin. "Don't you dare!" she snarled. "You leave him alone!"

Benjamin turned and ran.

Chapter 73

Joe carried the last of Tom's luggage down the steps to his cab. He didn't know why, but he felt very uneasy. He hated to see Tom leave right now. The family seemed strained; something was not quite right. He remembered feeling like this when his grandma died. Dread, that's what he felt. Dread that something was about to happen. You sensed it, but you didn't know what to do about it. You told yourself you're being an idiot and hoped the feeling went away. Joe swung the last suitcase into the trunk and slammed it.

"Joe?"

Joe turned around. Tom was standing on the top step. "Yeah?"

"Guess you didn't hear me. Did you pick up my briefcase? It was by my dresser."

"No, didn't see it. Want me to run up and take another look?" Joe started up the steps.

"That's okay; I need to say my goodbyes. Wait here." Tom disappeared into the house, the screen door slammed behind him, echoing through the crisp, early morning air.

Cassie, followed by Lizzie and Sara, filed out of the house. Tom was behind them, briefcase in hand. "Found it," he said smiling. "Well, we better get a move on. I want to get to the station a little early and pick up the *Daily Gazette* to read on the train. Maybe the *Post*, too. Long ride ahead of me."

"Bye, Uncle Tommy. I'll miss you." Lizzie hugged him, then handed him a book. "You can read this if you get bored.

It's my favorite story—it's about a little pony name Jubilee—
and his friend who happens to be named Lizzie!"

"Thanks. You be a good girl and keep out of trouble. Stay
away from Billy. You hear me?" He tousled her hair and kissed
her cheek. "See you in a few weeks."

Cassie was next in line to hug him. "I'll miss you, Tom.
Please be safe. I want you to tell Nate how sorry I am about his
broken leg—not to mention how I feel about his brother Harold
and all the trouble he's causing him and Rosa." Cassie gently
touched her brother's cheek. "Promise to call as soon as you
get to the house in Jamestown?"

"Absolutely. I'll call as soon as I can. Smile, Sis.
Everything will be fine. I'll be back before you know it. You
girls enjoy yourselves. Cassie, I promise to send you the latest
scoop on the Walden family."

"Who are the Waldens?" asked Sara.

Cassie laughed. "I'll tell you all about them over coffee."

"Come to the car with me, Sara." Tom led her down the
stairs. "I love you," he whispered into her ear.

"I love you, too," she whispered back, nuzzling his neck.
"I'll miss you." She gave him a long kiss, then pulled away
smiling. "Don't worry about things here. We'll have a lovely
girls' retreat while you're gone. Promise to call us when you
get there?"

"You can count on it." They hugged a final time, then Tom
got in the cab and closed the door.

As the car disappeared down the winding drive, the three
girls shivered in the cool morning air. "Come on, let's get
inside," Sara said.

"Mommy, can I go to my room? I want to play with my
dolls. I'm making some new dresses for Susie. She's going to a
ball tonight."

"Run along, kiddo. Did you have enough breakfast?"

"Yep," Lizzie hollered as she scampered upstairs.

"She's so cute!" Sara said, watching Lizzie bound away.
"Sounds like she's taking after you, huh? Designing clothes

already. I remember doing that when I was quite young, but not as young as Lizzie."

"Well, her idea of making clothes isn't very advanced. She just takes a piece of cloth and cuts holes in it for arms, then ties ribbons around the waist. But she enjoys it, that's all I care about," Cassie giggled. "Of course, as her mother, it's my duty to tell her how lovely her creations are. At least she's interested in something other than TV or video games. For now!"

Sara followed Cassie into the study. "Why are we going in here?" she asked Cassie.

"I walked in on Tom the other evening. He had a book in his hand, and when I asked what it was, he hid it." Cassie walked across the room to one of the bookcases that lined the walls. "Help me find it. It was over here. In this bookcase. He hid it somewhere on this shelf, I think."

"How curious. So I'm looking for an old book. Hmm. All of these books look are old!" said Sara. "What color was it?"

"Black, I think. It was leather—old and worn. No title on the cover that I could see. Tom said it was about whaling, but I know he was lying. He stuck it behind another book"

"Why would he lie about a book?" asked Sara.

"That's what we're going to find out. God, look at these: *The Life and Times of Gerald Wendell, Horace Lambert—A Biography, A History of the Northern Territories*, and on and on. How boring." Cassie ran her fingers along the spines while reading the titles. "I know it has to be here."

"I'm actually finding some good literature on this shelf," Sara said. "Lots of first editions it seems like. So these came with the house?"

"Guess so. Tom said all his books are upstairs. First editions? Wow. Impressive."

Sara squealed, "I think I found it!"

Carefully Cassie and Sara opened the cover of the aged leather book. The dry leather crackled.

"Oh, my God! It's the old woman's—the one who died here!" Sara gasped.

"Read this. This is so creepy!" Cassie pointed to the words on the inside page written in fancy script. *Helen Lindeman, My Life, My Death.*

"Oh, shit! That's scary," Sara said. "Let's take this into the kitchen where there's better light. How can you have all these books and not have decent lighting? Why is that?"

Cassie responded, "Tommy took several of the lamps out of here and put them upstairs. Come on, let's go to the kitchen." Cassie and Sara went through the back entryway bypassing the living room, ending up in the dining room. The kitchen doorway was to their left. From where they stood they could hear the gentle hum of the refrigerator. They entered the bright, sunlit kitchen. "It's cold in here. I'll start a fire."

"Good. I'll pour us some coffee." Sara laid the book down on the table and poured two mugs of coffee. "I could use a snack, how about you?"

"I'm always hungry. Let's look in the pantry."

Sara rummaged around the small pantry finding the rest of the tray of cinnamon rolls covered with cream cheese icing, left over from breakfast. "Yumm."

"Bring the tray, why dirty any more dishes?" Cassie motioned toward the table. "Grab a couple of napkins. The silverware's over there," she pointed, "in the drawer closest to the sink." She lit some paper she had stuffed in the cracks of the firewood. Tiny sparks popped as the kindling caught fire. It took only a few minutes for the tinder to catch. The fire quickly warmed the room. "Better." She turned and sat down in one of the oversized ladder-back chairs.

"The fire feels amazing. I'm surprised the kitchen's so cold. I never noticed it before."

"That's because Nellie's usually baking or cooking in here," said Cassie. "I think this room's heated by the stove and fireplace. No heat vents. That's how these old houses were built, I guess."

Sara cut and placed two rolls on napkins along with the mugs of coffee. "We better eat first, then look at the book." She looked at Cassie. "Don't want to get the pages sticky."

"Yeah." Cassie stuffed a piece of sweet roll into her mouth. "Mmm, this is so good."

"Low fat too, I'm sure!" Sara giggled, then glanced at the clock. "Tom should be getting on the train about now. I'll sure miss him. I wish he hadn't felt compelled to leave this week. I could have used his advice about now. . . . About Vivian—not Helen."

"What's wrong with that cousin of yours anyway?"

"Not a clue. Let's not talk about her. Sorry I brought the whole Vivian thing up." Picking up the diary, Sara said, "So what kind of person titles a book *My Life and My Death*? Weird huh? But then we already guessed that about dear Helen."

"We did." Cassie nodded.

"Shall we delve into Helen's most intimate thoughts? Here," Sara pushed the book toward Cassie, "you do the honors."

Opening the front cover, Cassie gently ran her fingers over the gilt lettering. "Wonder what she used to write this? It's handwritten, but it looks like she wrote it with gold ink."

"No idea. Maybe we should take the book into that antique bookstore in town. Have them look at it," Sara said. "Go on, turn the page. My curiosity is getting the best of me."

"This is amazing. It's definitely done with a calligraphy pen. I know that much." Cassie turned the page. "Look at this, it's fabulous." She lifted the book, showing Sara the exquisite handwriting—tiny, delicate letters perfectly drawn.

"Beautiful." Sara nodded.

Cassie began to read:

"For fifty years I have lived a life tormented and entangled with impiety. This wicked yet passionate story is my own. Anyone who dares read these words—beware. Or—if you are of like mind, be comforted that you are not alone in this darkness. The first twenty years of my life were but a waste" Cassie turned the page. "A silly girl I was, innocent and desperately bored. Then my brother, Gabriel, a world traveler, a man who had tired of the mundane, invited me to share in his adventures. I was flattered. A few months earlier, he'd gone overseas in search of a lifestyle that most find offensive, evil and vulgar. While in Hungary, Gabe had a chance encounter with an elite and extremely private society of promiscuous men and women. He found what he so desired." Cassie turned the page. "Such tales he whispered into my unbelieving ear. He told me he promised himself, and his cohorts in perversion, to live the rest of his life in honor of this darkness that existed in his soul. The ecstasies he experienced, the pure unadultered pleasures of the flesh, were all that mattered."

Cassie stopped reading and glanced nervously at Sara. "Here, you read the next page. This is giving me goose bumps."

Carefully Sara took the old book into her hands, staring at the intricate writing, smelling the mustiness of the aged linen pages. She flipped farther back into the book pausing half way through, then turned back to where Cassie left off. She began to read:

"My brother and I committed every imaginable, hah! some unimaginable! acts of the flesh. The pleasures were only ours. My precious Gabe's and mine. Selfishly so. Our souls, black and dark, belonged to each other. To support our garish lifestyle, we took our parents money. Parents who died so suddenly that I briefly wondered about the unexpectedness of their deaths. But did I care? Certainly not.

The pleasures in which we partook, the marvelous eroticisms we experienced, were beyond our greatest expectations. We knew no confines . . . for a time. Then we became bored. How could this happen? Well! We would not settle for boredom. Not Gabe and I. We found yet another realm to explore. We consorted with the other side. They were our willing guides—our hosts to yet another world of pleasures." Sara turned the page. "Yet we still craved something more. Once we drew another in, but he was so unimaginative and dull that we cast him aside and vowed that we would never again be subjected to such banality. We would live for each other—only."

Sara turned the page and gasped. Throwing the book, she flew out of her chair, knocking it over.

"What's the matter?" Cassie screamed, jumping up as the book flew past her. She grabbed it, immediately dropping it. It landed on the floor with a loud thud. "It's burning hot! Oww!"

"This is crazy. I couldn't hold it—look, my fingers are blistered!"

"Damn! What just happened?" Cassie looked at her own fingers, now bright red. They both ran to the refrigerator and stuck their hands in the freezer, the skin on their fingers sticking momentarily to the ice as the heat from their fingertips melted into the cubes. Cassie turned to look at the book. It was gone. "I knew it. She *is* here. She took her book!"

"Who? Who is here?"

"Helen! She doesn't want us to read it. Damn! We have to find out what she did with it. She can't have gone too far. Follow me." Cassie slammed the freezer door and ran up the back servants' staircase. Sara followed.

"Where are you going? This is silly."

Cassie answered, "To the attic—to the room at the end of the hall. Remember? The kids said they saw something there. Mary and I heard voices coming from there." Cassie stopped and listened. Throwing the door open, Cassie went in, followed closely by Sara who grabbed hold of her arm.

"Cassie, I thought there were boxes stacked over there." Sara pointed to the far side of the room. "And I remember an old rocking chair was over there."

"Maybe Nell had her nieces move it somewhere," Cassie said. "Tom wanted them to organize the mess up here and clear a lot of the old junk out. They probably got rid of a lot of it. Come on, let's check the other rooms." Cassie closed the door. They began what would be a futile search of the other rooms. Cassie opened the door to a small room close to the stairs. "Looks like Linda and Gwenn were going through Elise's things. They've unpacked the boxes and left her things out. How sad. I'll pack them up. I wouldn't want Tom to see this stuff. I'm surprised he brought her things here. Well . . . maybe

I'm not." Sara helped her repack the boxes and move them into the closet in the small room. "Helen's book doesn't seem to be here."

"No, not anywhere we can find, anyway. We've done a pretty thorough search." Sara wiped her hands on her jeans. "Dusty. Thought the girls would have cleaned up better than this."

"They probably spent as little time up here as possible. Poor things."

"Mommy! Where are you?" Lizzie called from the second floor.

"Stay there, honey. We're coming down." Cassie called to Lizzie, then she whispered to Sara, "We'll search the basement later. After Lizzie goes to the movie with Joe. He's taking Jimmy and Lizzie for the afternoon."

Chapter 74

As soon as Lizzie left with Joe and Jimmy to go to Ravenswood, Sara and Cassie began a complete sweep of the house. Searching for one book in such a large house was a formidable task. Helen's diary was the proverbial needle in a haystack. On their way to the basement, the front doorbell rang.

Cassie was alarmed. "Who could that be? Everyone's gone, either out of the city or into town."

Hurrying to the living room, Sara peaked through the curtain. "It's Mary."

Cassie ran to the entry hall and flung the door open. "Hi! Come in."

"I tried calling but no one answered. Thought I'd come by before I headed back to my dad's—just in case you didn't hear the phone."

"Glad you did. We have the house to ourselves right now. We can use your help," Sara said, leading Mary into the living room.

Mary took off her navy-blue pea coat, dropping it carelessly on the end of the sofa. Her long blonde hair was pulled back, as always, into a ponytail. She had on gray sweats and tennis shoes. "I'm ready to work." She pointed to her togs. "What are we doing anyhow?"

"No cleaning! You can relax." Cassie smiled at Mary. "We have tons to tell you. So much has happened since Tom's dinner party. Sit down; we'll fill you in. Wait a minute though; I'll get us all something to drink." Cassie started toward the dining room. "Be right back. Cola okay with you guys?"

"Sure," Sara said. Mary nodded.

Sara and Cassie told Mary about Vivian throwing Sara out, Billy shooting at Sara and Tom, Tom and Michael leaving and finally, about Helen Lindeman's diary.

"Wow! I missed that much in just a couple of days?" Mary looked solemnly at Sara.

Sara nodded. "Crazy, huh?"

"So Vivian kicked you out, and you're staying here. Probably a good idea," Mary said, pulling the scrunchie out of her hair. She carelessly pulled her hair into another ponytail and rebound it. "What's the matter with Vivian? Sounds like she's gone a little psycho. "

"That's the truth! I hope it's just because she's exhausted and lonely, impulsive and spoiled—well I could go on and on. But I don't want to talk about her," Sara said, taking a drink of her cola.

"So what about Helen's journal?" Mary asked.

Cassie chimed in, "Helen and her brother Gabe were into some pretty perverse and frightening activities, to say the least." Cassie shivered. "We were only able to read a few pages of Helen's diary. The entries alluded to a pretty bizarre lifestyle. We didn't get to read enough to find out how far the two siblings had actually immersed themselves into the occult, but it was apparent they were involved."

Mary nodded. "We may never know. The Lindemans were extremely reclusive. As a kid, all I knew was that the couple preferred their own company. No one except Joe ever had much contact with them. Joe knew them because he did work for them on and off." Mary explained to Sara, "They rarely left the house that I knew of. I seldom saw them in town. I remember hearing about them going on a lot of trips, though. But that's not unusual around here. The local paper always made a big deal out of who was coming and going. Social thing. Of course when I was a kid, I could have cared less about them anyway."

"That would have seemed very odd where I come from, their being so reclusive. Didn't your parents ever talk about them?" Cassie asked.

"Nope. No one even gossiped about them that I can remember. Until they died, of course. This part of the country is a good place to find anonymity. Nothing unusual about them keeping to themselves at all."

"So you really don't know anything about them? Darn! That's disappointing." Cassie hit her thigh with her hand.

"No. They were an old couple who seemed very dull, fit right in here. Who would ever imagine someone as weird as they were lived in this lovely house by the ocean?" Mary twisted her ponytail around her finger. "It does explain a few things though."

"What things?" Sara asked. She gazed into the fire, chewing on her top lip.

"Think about it. All the crazy things that have been happening here since Tom moved in. Well, I think we know now who is behind them—the crazy stuff that happened to me and Tom in the basement, the old woman Cassie saw in the mirror, the voices in the attic—I could go on. There's much more. If the Lindemans were into the occult, maybe they found a way to 'live on' and stay in their house!"

"Stop!" Sara said, her voice high-pitched and nervous. She studied Mary's face. "You're serious?"

"She is! Absolutely!" Cassie interrupted before Mary could answer. "I *know* it's them. I even told Tom it was the Lindemans. He dismissed it of course. But I saw the look on his face. He thinks it's true, too. He believes the Lindemans are haunting his house." She jumped up from the couch. Her face animated as her fears seemed validated. "I'm beginning to understand. Now what the heck are we going to do about them? We have to make this evil, vile couple leave!" She turned, her back now to Mary and Sara and stared out the window. "What do we do?"

A bead of sweat formed on Sara's brow. "I don't know, "Sara said. "I'm not so sure I even believe in anything that has to do with the supernatural . . . nor want to believe any of it."

"I think you're being naive. Maybe you're *afraid* to believe it. But . . . tell me, Sara, where did the blisters on your fingers come from?" Cassie turned, held up her own burned fingers, waving them in the air. "Explain it. And tell me how the book just disappeared."

"I can't." A drop of sweat trickled down Sara's brow; she quickly wiped it with her burned fingers. "Ouch!"

Mary grabbed her hand. "That's a serious burn. Are you telling me that happened when you read the book?"

Pulling her hand out of Mary's, Sara absentmindedly picked up her glass and took a drink. She said very quietly, "That's when it happened, I can't deny it. All this scares the crap out of me. If this house is haunted, or whatever you want to call it, by the Lindemans, what do we do? This is something way over my head, not to mention completely out of my comfort zone."

Mary snapped her fingers. "I have an idea!" she said. "There's a client at the veterinarian clinic where I work. She's a clairvoyant—or a medium—one of those. We could talk to her. Maybe she'd help us."

"Do you think she's a wacko or the real deal?" Cassie asked.

"She's the real deal," Mary answered.

"You should call her; let's at least get her opinion," Sara said.

They all jumped as someone knocked loudly and impatiently on the front door. "Coming! Hold your horses!" Cassie ran to the door while Mary and Sara watched from the living room.

"Who is that?" Sara asked Mary.

"Not a clue. No one I've seen around here before."

Cassie opened the door a crack. She glanced at Mary and Sara to make sure they were watching. "Yes?" she asked the man standing on the front porch, a cowboy hat in his hand.

"Looking for Joe Tilson. He here?"

"Who should I say is asking?"

"I'm Harry," he said, then added, "Harry Jones. I'm with the construction crew. For the basement remodel." *Damnit, broad, don't play dumb with me.*

"Oh! Sorry. Of course. I think Joe said he would be starting tomorrow. You're a day early." Cassie smiled at the man young man. He was tall, maybe six foot one, had piercing light blue eyes. His wavy blonde hair was flattened against his head, victim to his cowboy hat. "Joe's not here right now. He took the kids into town. My daughter and a neighbor, actually."

"Darn! Sorry to intrude on you." He returned Cassie's smile, his ice-blue eyes twinkling.

"Not a problem." She looked down the driveway. "Where's your car? Did you walk from the highway?"

Putting his Stetson back on, he nodded. "No car. Hitched a ride from town. I'll come back tomorrow." He started walking off the porch, then hesitated. "Wonder if I could take a look at the basement. As long as I'm here. Might save Joe some time tomorrow if I went ahead and did some measuring for him."

Sara and Mary came out of the doorway to stand beside Cassie. "Hi," they said in unison.

"You have guests! I shouldn't have bothered you. Excuse me. I'll go on, I can see you're busy."

"Not at all. It's okay. We'll take you around. Joe's using the side entrance. Come on." Cassie grabbed her jacket, passing Harry on the front steps. She turned to make sure he was following. Mary and Sara were right behind him. "Harry, these are my friends, Sara and Mary. I'm Cassie, by the way."

"Afternoon." Harry tipped his hat. *Course I know who you are, Cassie. Been at your family's house in Jamestown the past few weeks.* "Fine house you have here. These old houses were built to last for centuries. They sure don't build 'em like this anymore." He surveyed the house carefully, looking for any surveillance equipment or signs of an alarm system. *Nothing. Far fucking out. Not that any alarm could keep me out. This will be so freakin' easy. A few days and, I'll figure where the valuables and money are. Then I'm on a fast train to Canada, then on to Jamaica. Sand and ladies, here I come!*

Cassie was talking to him; he looked quickly at her trying to catch the gist of what she had been saying. He nodded, figured she has asked a simple question. Wrong response.

"She was asking you where your tape is, Harry," Sara said. "Well?"

He patted his jacket pocket. "Right here." Reaching in, he pulled a tape out. *I'm not stupid.*

"This is the door to the basement. Huh—it won't budge." Cassie turned the knob and was pushing her weight against it. "Joe unlocked it earlier. I know it's open because he's bringing some materials back later today."

"Here, let me." Harry stood in front of the door and gave it a quick hit with his shoulder. It swung open. "Where's a light switch?"

Cassie pushed past him and entered the dark doorway. She felt for the switch and flipped it. A bright white light illuminated the dark hallway. A single high-wattage bulb lit the entire area causing distinct shadows of the four of them on the cement floor and up the walls.

"Do you know which room is gonna be the gym? Could you show me?"

Cassie shrugged and walked down the hall. Harry and Sara followed. Mary, silent until now said, "I'll wait here." *I am not going in the basement!*

"Mary, are you sure?" asked Cassie.

"Yep, I'll wait here."

Mary watched them go down the hallway, then disappear into a room to the right. She heard their voices, thought they sounded very far away. She leaned against the wall, staying close to the door—and the outside. A raven cawed from a stand of trees at the back of the house. There was an immediate response as others answered the caw and began to circle. They swooped down, landing on the ground outside the door. Soon a few birds turned into six, then a dozen.

Nervously Mary reached for the doorknob, watched fearfully as the large, black birds, wings spread menacingly, came closer and closer. When one flew at her, she slammed the door closed. The sound of the bird hitting the door was terrifying. She screamed. She thought she heard the others running down the hall toward her but saw no one. The bright overhead light flashed, then went out. She screamed again and felt for the light switch, flipping it back and forth. Nothing. Birds continued to slam into the door, their beaks and claws scratching as they fought against the heavy wood. Backing up against the door, making sure it did not open, she felt the thud of birds reverberate through her body. Mary slid onto the floor.

"Mary? Where are you?" Cassie yelled. "Turn the light on? Are you okay?"

Mary yelled back, "I'm okay. The light switch won't work. I tried."

Suddenly the hallway was bathed in blinding light. "Found another switch," Harry said. "These old houses have odd wiring. If you turn one switch on, it won't work if the master switch is off. We must have flipped the wrong one down at the other end of the hall." Hurrying over to Mary, he reached his hand out and pulled her up from the floor. "You okay?"

"Why were you screaming?" Sara asked. She put her hand on Mary's shoulder.

"The ravens were attacking the door, and then the light went out! That's why!" Mary shouted.

"What *are* you talking about?" Harry asked. "What birds?"

"The ravens. There were dozens flying outside. I slammed the door, but they kept diving and smashing into it. Damn things. I hate these stupid birds."

"Too late for a nest. Must have food stored nearby," said Harry. "Get back. Go on in the room down there and shut the door." He pointed to the room down the hall that they had just come out of. "I'll get rid of them."

No one moved, the girls just stood there.

"Go!" Harry yelled.

***

The knob felt uncomfortably cold in Harry's hand. He twisted it and jerked the door inward while at the same time letting out a loud whooping sound. Hundreds of ravens took flight, turning the sky black as midnight. Harry shouted, shrill piercing sounds coming from his throat. Running out into the woods just beyond the house, he chased and ran in circles underneath the birds. He took his jacket off and began whirling it over his head, striking out at the ravens. They continued flying in circles, then one by one, dozen by dozen, they began diving at Harry. He swatted at them as they attacked, felt their sharp beaks tear into his skin. As one retreated, another and then another bird flew at him, diving, pecking, screeching.

Harry yelled at the top of his lungs, turned and started running back to the house. Reaching for the knob, he shoved the door open. As he turned to face the angry murder of ravens, he froze. They had retreated.

Upon the hill, barely visible in the trees, stood a woman. She was facing away from Harry, her long blonde hair blowing about her in the winter breeze. Her hands were raised skyward toward the retreating flock. Her shrill screeching echoed the language of the ravens. Slowly she turned to face Harry, yelling words impossible to understand. Then, spinning around, she disappeared into the woods.

Harry whirled around and around, searching the sky for more birds. "Fucking shit! What the fuck was that about?"

"What's going on?" Cassie yelled. Looking cautiously out into the hall, she bolted, running to Harry. "Oh, my God! Look at your arms. You're bleeding. Sara! Mary! Hurry! We need your help."

Harry grabbed her arm. "Don't get all hysterical on me. I'm fine. Get back into the house." He pushed her through the doorway, slamming, then locking the door. Mary and Sara, who were running toward them, stopped and stared at his bloody arms.

"Did the ravens do that? Oh, God! We need to get you into town to the clinic." Sara moved closer to examine his arms.

"Just get me to the bathroom so I can clean up. I'll be fine," Harry said.

"Cassie, can you unlock the kitchen door at the top of the stairs so we won't have to go back outside?" Sara asked.

Cassie dug into her pocket. "Yeah, I can. I have the keys." She dangled them in front of everyone. "I've never been down here, though. I hate to ask you, Mary, I know you had a bad experience down here, but can you show us the way to the stairs?" Cassie asked.

"Okay," Mary said weakly. "I think I can."

"Come on, Mr. Jones, follow us." Cassie took Mary's hand as she started slowly down the hall.

"It's this way, I think. Yeah, there's the furnace room. See, there's the stairs." Mary pointed with her free hand. The lights went out; the basement was plunged into darkness. Mary screamed.

"Hold each other's hands," Harry said loudly. "The stairs are just a few yards further down the hall. Let me get around you ladies, so I can lead." Harry quickly shoved past them, then took Mary's elbow, leading her forward. "Just be careful; we don't want anyone to fall. Oww!" Harry shouted, "What the fuck! There's a wall here. That's not possible. What the fuck!"

Mary whispered, "It's happening again."

"Whatever happens, stay together. Don't let go of anybody's hand," Sara said, her voice shrill, her fear barely under control.

Harry muttered, "Must have turned and not realized it. Come on ladies, don't panic on me." Harry let go of Mary's arm for a second. "I've got a lighter in my pocket. Hold on." No one moved. *Flick, flick.* Sparks flew, but there was no flame. *Flick.* Nothing. *Flick.* Finally a dancing flame dimly lit the immediate area. Harry was alone. Stretching his arm out, he turned slowly in a circle. "Hey, where the hell are you?" Silence. A gust of wind extinguished the flame. "Fuck!" Harry moved inch by inch down the dark hallway toward where he thought the stairs should be. "Where are you? You ladies okay?" he yelled creeping forward. *God damn it! Where the fuck did they go?* A cold hand brushed his cheek. He flinched, instinctively swung his fist, punching the wall. "Fuck!" He felt along the passageway and continued on. "Anybody! Hey!"

Chapter 75

"Harry! Where are you?" Cassie yelled into the darkness. "Mary, Sara, where did you go?" Cassie screamed into the dark and turned to her left. *God! I hate this house!* She stumbled and fell, tried to catch herself before she hit the concrete floor. Her left shoulder hit first. She flung her right arm across her body to stop the fall, saving her head from impact. Her temple hit her left forearm—no harm done. Her shoulder hurt, but Cassie counted herself lucky that her reactions were so fast. Just then, someone tripped over her foot, falling hard onto her outstretched body.

"Cassie? Mary? Who is it?" Sara's voice was only inches from Cassie's ear.

"It's me, it's Cassie. You okay, Sara? Get off of me so we can get up before somebody else trips over us? Where's Mary?"

"I'm here. I'm not moving. You guys okay?" Mary asked.

"I'm fine I think," Sara answered, getting up. As she stood up, she lost her balance and fell heavily into the wall next to Mary. "Oww!"

Mary reached out into the darkness. "Sara?"

"Yes. Hurry! Take my hand."

Cassie groped the air in front of her, felt someone's legs. "Mary?"

"Yeah," Mary answered.

"Help me up! I hurt my shoulder." Grateful to feel Mary's firm grasp, Cassie stood.

"Are you badly hurt? Maybe you should stay here. We'll go get help."

"No way!" Cassie said. "Let's get out of here. If we walk side by side and go this way," she pulled Mary's hand, "I think we can get back to the outside door. You ready?"

The three, arms around each other's waists, crept forward.

"Where's Harry?" asked Mary.

"He's probably already in the kitchen," Sara answered.

"I doubt it. The door's locked, and I have the key. He must have gotten out the side door." Cassie shivered. "I can't believe the birds tore him up like that. It's crazy."

"I've never seen ravens attack before, not like that!" Mary said. "I never heard of anything like this."

"One attacked Tom and me last week. He didn't want anyone to know—he was very angry about it. I wonder if this has anything to do with that? Maybe the birds have nests under the eaves or something, and we keep disturbing them. Better have Joe check," Cassie said.

Sara reached out to unlock the outside door. It swung open as soon as she touched the handle. "Harry must have come this way." Sara took a few steps outside, looked around apprehensively. "I don't see any birds now. Come on. Let's get this over with. Let's go." Sara led the way, Mary and Cassie followed, cautiously looking in all directions as they descended the steep hill on the side of the house.

"Harry! There you are!" Sara yelled, then turned and called to Mary and Cassie, still several yards behind her. "He's on the porch." They quickened their steps and caught up with Sara.

Harry ran down the steps, taking Cassie's left elbow to lend her some more support. "What happened?"

"I fell in the hallway and hurt my shoulder," Cassie explained to Harry. His arm was still bleeding, his shirtsleeve soaked in blood. She shuddered. *I think he's going to need stitches. A couple of the gashes looked pretty deep.*

"Where were you? I couldn't find you." Harry led Cassie up the porch stairs. "I thought you were in the house. The front door's locked; I couldn't get in."

"How did you get by us?" Cassie demanded. She pulled away from Harry's uncomfortable grip on her elbow. "How long have you been here on the porch?"

"One question at a time, if you don't mind," Harry snapped, insulted by Cassie's obvious dislike of his hand on her arm. *Bitch!* "I walked out the side door—that's how. Never saw any of you in the hall. I would have run into you if you were there." He took several steps back from Cassie.

"Well, we were there. You must have gone through another room and gone around us," Sara responded.

"Must have. Anyhow, I just got here. The front door's locked. Somebody locked it when I turned the handle. Thought you were inside. Figured you were locking me out." He looked back at Cassie.

"We wouldn't do that." Cassie opened the screen door, turned the doorknob. It was locked just as Harry said. "I'm not too surprised. Are you?" she looked at Mary and Sara.

"What does that mean?" Harry asked.

"One of the idiosyncrasies of Remington House—that's all," Cassie answered. "We better get inside before anything else happens." She pulled the keys from her pocket. "We should look at your cuts. Might need to take you to the clinic for stitches."

"Won't be necessary," Harry said. "Show me to the bathroom, and I'll clean up. I'm fine. Nothing I can't take care of with a little soap and water, maybe some disinfectant for good measure."

"Follow me," Cassie said leading the entourage through the house to the kitchen. "The bathroom's over there." She pointed to the door at the end of the short hallway. There's soap on the counter and disinfectant and cotton in the medicine cabinet."

"Can I help?" Mary asked. "I work at the vet clinic so I'm pretty good at cleaning wounds. And gentle." She smiled. "I'll be able to tell if you need stitches. If you do, we'll take you into town."

"I was a medic in the Army. Trust me when I tell you I don't need your gentle touch, or your diagnosis," Harry said sarcastically. Walking toward the bathroom he hesitated and said, "Sorry. That was rude. But my arms hurt like hell." He opened the door. "Be out soon." He closed the door.

"Come on. Let's have a glass of wine," Cassie said. She disappeared into the dining room, returning with a bottle of whiskey. "Forget the wine, this is what we need," she said, grinning.

Sara got three glasses from the cupboard, poured three shots. The three downed the shots, shuddering as the vapors from the liquor burned their throats. They sat down in unison at the kitchen table.

"Things are getting serious. Harry is badly hurt—regardless of how lightly he takes his injuries," Cassie said. She poured half a shot of scotch into her glass, then asked Sara. "More?" Sara nodded, held her glass for Cassie to refill. Mary shook her head.

"Mary, you should call the medium. The sooner the better, as far as I'm concerned," Cassie said.

Sara sipped her drink, ran her fingers around the collar of her turtleneck. "This, ah, situation is getting pretty crazy."

"Ya think?" Cassie nodded and smiled.

"I'll call her now if you want," Mary said. "It'll just take a second to look up her number."

"Yeah, but what are you going to say? Do we really know what we want her to do?" asked Sara. "Let's figure that out first. I'm not comfortable talking to someone if we don't have some idea of what we want her to do. Honestly, if we aren't careful, we'll end up sounding as if we're idiots. Cassie, what do you think?"

"Agreed. Mary, do you know this woman well enough to trust her to keep our situation confidential? We can't call her if we can't trust her to be completely discreet. Don't you guys agree?" asked Cassie.

Mary nodded. "I don't know her well, but she has an excellent reputation, and yes, she is absolutely discreet."

"That sounds promising." Cassie rocked back in her chair, the wood joints creaking as her weight rested on the back legs.

"I think we should tell her some of the things we've experienced here—since Mr. Gardner bought the house. Actually even before he got here—with the lights going out while I was cleaning. Then there was the horrible incident in the basement right after Tom, umm . . . Mr. Gardner got here." Mary twisted her ponytail around her finger. An ember in the fire popped, and they all jumped.

"Hmm. I'm not sure we should give her any information," Sara said. "If we tell her too much, it makes it too easy for her to embellish on what we've told her. If she's a real clairvoyant, she should be able to tell us what is going on. Right?" Sara waited for Cassie or Mary to answer her.

"You're probably right. I think we should call her and tell her we have suspicions that something is wrong in the house. Tell her we would like her to come and see what she thinks is going on here," Cassie said.

"Yeah, that makes sense. And when . . . if . . . she comes here, we'll let *her* direct *us*. She can walk around, or whatever she does, and tell us what she thinks is happening," Mary said. "Well? Should I call her now?"

Sara and Cassie both answered, "Yes." Mary called information and got the number for Terese Montagna.

So it was arranged. Sara, Cassie and Mary would meet with her in two days. Ms. Montagna would come to Remington House Thursday evening knowing little about the circumstances that led to them contacting her. She had not been told what she might encounter at the house.

The bathroom door opened. "Mind if I have a drink with you ladies? I could use one."

"Sure." Sara got him a glass. "Are your cuts deep? Do you think you need stitches?'

"No. I'm fine. Taped up tight as a . . . well, I'm fine." He downed the whiskey. "I still want to do some measuring in the basement. Then I'll head back to town." He poured himself another shot.

"Are you sure? Can't you do the measuring tomorrow?" Cassie poured half a shot into her glass. "I think we've all had enough of the basement for today. Don't you agree?" She glanced at Mary and Sara, who nodded in agreement.

"You don't need to go with me," Harry said quickly. "I know where to go. Did you lock the side door when you came out?" Harry asked, finishing his shot in one gulp.

"No, but you don't have to go outside; you can use the basement stairs. That door, right behind you. Maybe you better wait, though, until Joe gets back." She looked at Sara.

Sara chimed in, "Yeah, it might make more sense. I mean, Joe knows we've had some problems with the switches in the house. And there seems to be no sense to the layout. If the lights go out again, it's almost impossible to find your way around."

"You got a flashlight?' Harry asked Cassie. "That's all I need. Don't want to waste my trip out here, and I don't have time to wait around for Joe." He waited for Cassie to answer. *Come on, bitch, I aint got all day.* "Well?" He tapped his hat against his thigh. Then reconsidering, flashed a winning smile at the ladies. *Come on, before Joe shows up and spoils my plans.*

Cassie opened a drawer filled with household junk and rummaged around until she found a flashlight. She flicked the switch. "Batteries are good. Here."

"Be back in half an hour. You don't need to worry about me." He grinned at them as he turned and unlocked the basement door. He switched on the stairway light and shut the door behind him. They listened to the sound of his footsteps as he clomped loudly down the stairs.

"We better stay right here until he comes back up. Just in case." Cassie began pacing the room. "I think we can hear him call if he needs us."

"Mary, you should call someone about the birds and see if they have a clue why the ravens attacked," Sara said.

"I'll call Dr. Elvin. He'll know." Mary hit a button on her cell. "Eleanor, this is Mary. Hi, can I talk to Dr. Elvin? I need to ask him something." Mary nodded and said, "Uh-huh. Sure. I'll wait. Thanks." She held for a second then Dr. Elvin apparently came on the line. Mary wandered out of the kitchen, into the dining room, just out of their hearing range.

Gathering up the glasses, Cassie and Sara rinsed and dried them while they waited for Mary to get off her cell phone.

"He thought I was exaggerating!" Mary shrugged, standing in the doorway, hands on her hips. "He didn't believe there could be that many birds on the attack. Dr. Elvin said they must have a nest nearby that we disturbed. Although he said it makes little sense this time of year—no eggs or young birds to protect. He's never heard of an attack involving more than three or four birds, but said it's possible. I got the impression he was trying to humor me."

"Did you tell him about Harry? About the birds drawing blood?" Sara asked.

"Dr. Elvin said he would call the Division of Wildlife. See if they had any more information than he did. But he said Harry should definitely have a doctor look at him as soon as possible. To be safe." She tucked her phone into her sweater pocket. "What are our chances of getting him to go to the clinic?"

"Slim to none is my guess." Cassie absentmindedly hung the dishtowel on the back of the chair. "Did you hear something?" She whirled toward the basement door. "Shh! I thought I heard a woman's voice! There it is again! Shit!" Flinging the door open, Cassie balanced on the top stair, craning her neck toward the basement. "Oh, for heaven sakes! Shit! Harry's singing. At least we know we can hear him from here if he should need us." She closed the door. "I'm beginning to lose my sense of objectivity, aren't I? Panic first, think later."

The house phone rang. "Hello? Hi!" Cassie whispered to Sara, "It's Tom." Cassie and Tom talked briefly. "He just got to Jamestown and wanted us to know he'd arrived. Here," she handed the phone to Sara, "he wants to talk to you."

Sara covered the mouthpiece with her hand. "Do I say anything to him about the birds?" Cassie shook her head. Sara nodded and mouthed, "Okay."

"He sounded tired," Cassie said to Mary. "I'm glad he got away, but I wonder what kind of rest he'll get in Jamestown. Wish Michael could have gone with him. I hate him being there alone."

"I thought someone was at the house—his business manager lives there, doesn't he?" Mary asked.

"He does. But with a broken leg and some family issues, I don't know how much help he'll be for Tom. But they are good friends. Nate would do anything he could for Tom. Still . . . "

Sara had hung up with Tom. "Nate just picked Tom up at the station. They're on their way to the house. Cassie, are you really worried about Tom?" Sara asked.

"I am. Very." Cassie frowned. "He's so stubborn! He won't listen to me. Nothing new on that front though," she sighed.

Harry opened the door and came quietly into the room. He'd been standing at the closed door, listening to their conversation. *Good! Tom is definitely in Jamestown. Fuck a duck, I'm gonna be home free in a few more days!* He cleared his throat so they would know he was there. "Done. Got all the measurements I needed. It'll save Joe some time. Have him call me when he shows up. Here's my cell number." He handed a scrap of paper to Cassie.

"Harry," Sara said, "Mary talked to Dr. Elvin at the vet clinic. He said the birds may have attacked because they have a nest nearby. He couldn't think of any other explanation. Cassie is going to have Joe check around the house so this doesn't happen again. Dr. Elvin thought it would be wise to have a doctor look at your cuts."

"Just to be safe—maybe give you some antibiotics for infection," Mary added, "and a tetanus shot. What a crazy afternoon! Bet you wish you had stayed in town!"

"Don't worry about it. Don't need a shot either, I'm up to date. Ladies, I'm headed to town. Have Joe give me a call."

"Wait! I can take you. I'm meeting my dad anyway," Mary said.

Harry said, "Well, okay, if you're about ready, cause if you aren't going soon, I'll thumb a ride. I got places to be, too." He looked at the clock on the stove. *Got a meeting with a bottle and a blonde. In that order.* "Don't want to rush you."

"Go on, Mary," Cassie said. "Come have lunch with us tomorrow."

"Sure, and we can talk more about Ms. Montagna. I'll be over as soon as I'm off work. See you guys about noon."

"Call when you get to Ravenswood. Okay?" Sara said.

Cassie opened the front door. She touched Mary gently on her arm. "Don't forget to call, Mary. Harry, I'm so sorry about everything that happened to you today. Promise me you'll go to the clinic if you're in any pain? You can have them bill me. I feel responsible since you were hurt here." Cassie followed him down the porch stairs.

"Not your fault. I'll take care of myself. Not to worry." *Bitch!* He smiled and tipped his hat.

They watched Mary's car until it turned off at the end of the long winding road.

"Let's go in; it's cold," Cassie said.

Chapter 76

With a heavy heart, Tom entered his Jamestown home. Nate, precariously balancing on crutches, unlocked the front door and stepped into the entryway to turn on the lights. A soft glow brought the room to life, but the house felt empty and cold. The cab drove silently away, the frigid winter air muffling any sounds. Relieved to be home, ready to end his ordeal with Elise, Tom followed Nate into the foyer.

"The housekeeper forgot to leave the lights on. Watch your step." Nate cautioned. "Everything's been moved around since you left. You better wait until I turn more lights on."

Tom set his bags down and draped his coat over the elaborately carved banister. "Oh, I think I can find my way around in the dark. I haven't been gone that long." He entered the living room, immediately bumping into a chair. "Long enough, I guess!" Tom laughed.

Nate moved cautiously past Tom, his cast-encased leg hitting the marble floor. *Thump, step. Thump, step.* The hollow echo whispered through the almost empty room. *Thump, step. Thump, step,* then silence as he stepped onto a thick Persian rug. Nate turned on a shadeless floor lamp. Immediately the room filled with stark shadows as the bare bulb illuminated the room. The center grouping of furniture cast giant shadows across the room and onto the bare walls. "The painters moved most of the furniture to the center of the room. They've been prepping the walls and ceiling, should start painting tomorrow or Thursday. Unless you'd like me to tell them to wait until you leave on your business trip."

"Absolutely not. I'll work from my study upstairs; let's not hold up on the painting. The sooner we can get all of this done, the better."

"Okay then. It's good to have you home, Tom," Nate said, leading Tom out of the living room and down the long hallway to the kitchen. "Let's get something to eat. Harriet said she'd leave a hot dish in the oven." The aroma of eggs and ham enticed the men's sense of smell as they neared the kitchen. "Quiche, I'll bet."

The men ate, exchanging small talk and catching up on local news and gossip. Both men agreed that business was off the agenda for the night. Tom planned on relaxing in the hot tub. Later he'd take a sleeping pill—he needed a good rest. Tomorrow morning he'd go over files and charts with Nate, then they'd go downtown to meet with John Atwood. They had some minor preparations to do before their meeting with William Harrison, Vivian's long-absent husband.

Despite having taken a sleeping pill, Tom couldn't fall asleep. At two, he gave up and got out of bed. In the bathroom he splashed his face with warm water and rinsed his mouth under the faucet. Looking at his reflection in the bathroom mirror, he saw the feathering of gray hairs along his temples. His dark brown hair, usually perfectly styled, stuck up in patches like a rooster's comb. Beneath his eyes, bluish half-circles gave him an emaciated look. Dark stubble completed his unkempt look. *I look like hell*

Moonlight shone through the window. Wispy shadows of bare trees danced across the floor, exotic undulating movements, alternately stark then indistinct, as clouds veiled the moon. Tom wandered through the dark house, moonlight illuminating his way through the seemingly endless maze of hallways and empty rooms. Going upstairs to Elise's room, Tom stood in the doorway for a few minutes, giving his eyes time to adjust. A solitary streetlight from down the block provided the only source of light on this side of the house.

The room had been completely emptied. Dust bunnies littered the floor, scattering as Tom walked about disturbing the air. Going to the closet, Tom opened the double doors, sliding them sideways to reveal the walk-in closet—all the shelves were bare, the dresser drawers were hanging open like gaping mouths, hungry for sustenance, their only contents dried up sachets. He picked up one of the sachets, trying to detect its scent—lavender, of course.

Turning the light on, he gently ran his hand over the edge of the shelf where Elise had kept her sweaters—always carefully folded and arranged by color. This bedroom had been hers—painstakingly decorated, meticulously cared for. He remembered how happy she'd been to have this haven, this special space of her own. It meant little to him, but to her this was, at least for a time, her sanctuary.

Tom leaned against the built-in dresser, covering his face with his hands. For several minutes he immersed himself into the deep, dark abyss of his own creation. "Elise, what did I do to you?"

"You didn't do anything to her, Tom."

Tom jumped and turned to face Nate standing at the closet door.

"You've been over and over this," Nate said. "You weren't responsible for Elise's death. Her getting sick, then taking her own life, wasn't your fault." Nate put his hand on Tom's shoulder. "Maybe you shouldn't be here. You'd be better off at the hotel."

Tom took a deep breath, went to stand by the window. "This time you're wrong. I need to be here." He touched his fingers to the cold glass and looked out into the star-lit sky. "You know me better than anyone. You've been a good friend." He glanced at Nate. A movement on the ground below caught his eye. A cat ran across the empty street chasing a blowing leaf.

"Well, for whatever reason you think you need to stay at the house, don't forget why you left—to get away from the memories of Elise that were holding you here. You moved on, Tom. Because you had every right to."

"That's part of the reason I'm here, Nate. A final cleansing of my soul, so to speak. This *will* be my final farewell to her." Tom stared down into the yard at the fountain.

The cherub still watched over the grounds, its concrete hands held skyward. The fountain had been drained for cleaning. It would be checked for cracks and patched before being refilled and turned back on. The entire house and grounds would once again be the quintessence of wealth and elegance. New owners would soon inhabit the house, never knowing the well-guarded secrets that were kept here—how Tom's wife had died in her upstairs bedroom and how, consequently, Tom had, for a time, lost his sanity.

But before any of this would take place, Tom had a final objective—to destroy Elise's spirit. He would not let her hurt his family. Or Sara. He would face Elise's wrath. And end it. *Where are you, Elise? Why aren't you showing yourself to me? I'm here. That's what you wanted—isn't it?* The house echoed in silence.

"I need a drink," Tom said "What about you?"

Not waiting for an answer from Nate, he left the room. Nate followed, crutches thumping softly on the carpet with each step. When they came to the stairway, Tom moved to Nate's side and helped him down the stairs. "You shouldn't have come up here. You might have fallen again," Tom said.

"Yeah, right. Like that would stop me, Tom," Nate laughed. "You know me better than that. I heard noises, thought I better investigate. Checked your room. Saw you were gone, so I knew you'd be in Elise's room. Thought you might need a friend."

"You've always got my back, don't you, Nate?"

"Same as you've got mine."

Tom and Nate stayed up the rest of the night, alternately talking, then silently contemplating their own private demons. Sitting in the study, embers glowing in the fireplace, they stared out the curtainless windows, waiting for the night to end. Finally, the sun climbed above the low ridge of clouds. The horizon glowed amber and orange as the day broke.

Neither man felt at peace though: Nate worrying that Harold was up to no good, Tom with a growing sense of unease that all was not as he expected—Elise had not made her presence known.

At the far end of the house, the skeletal shape of the iron scaffolding sparkled with the bright glow of the emerging sun, reminded the men that soon the work crew would arrive and their day would begin. Both silently cursed their lack of sleep. This would be a long day.

Chapter 77

The offices of Atwood, Gunderson, and Larson were on the fourth floor of the Werner Building. Tom and Nate arrived an hour before their scheduled appointment with William Harrison to go over the proposed contract. John Atwood was going over a final draft, one that had several changes Tom and Nate had not yet seen.

"It's very straight forward, Tom," John said, pointing to three paragraphs he added late last night. "I see no reason to deny him the controlling vote. After all, realistically, you're only acting as a financial backer. Harrison's guaranteeing your investment one hundred percent." He tapped on the last paragraph and underlined the important phrases. "Read this again. There's no possibility that you'll lose one penny on this deal."

"Good. I have no aspirations to be more than a silent partner—as you already know, John."

"I see this as a sound investment," John said. "You're guaranteed to have no financial losses, and you actually stand to gain quite a healthy profit as this business moves forward. According to the financials I received this morning, Harrison and his advising board are well-versed and have already demonstrated a high degree of competency in the diamond importing business. With your investment, the business stands to show a profit within the next year. Not a windfall, but a nice, steady growth in the market here."

"Very good, John." Tom nodded in agreement. He pointed at Nate who was sticking a pencil down the back of his cast, trying to scratch an itch. He looked up and smiled, slightly embarrassed.

"Nate, you'll be managing the finances, at least for the next few months. Do you have any concerns we haven't addressed?" John asked.

"No, if you're both satisfied, I certainly am. I don't see any reason to slow down on this. It's a damned good enterprise. Harrison has certainly proven his expertise in imports."

"Good. Let Harrison take the lead at the meeting, and we'll see what concerns he voices—if any," Tom said. He stared out the window; the silhouettes of the bare trees were stark against the gray sky. Snowflakes drifted past the window, increasing in size by the minute. "It looks like it's going to be a nasty storm. Look at that line of clouds moving in. There's another inch of snow on the ground—just since we got here."

"Time of year for it," Nate responded. "Lucky for you, your flight to Amsterdam isn't until Saturday afternoon. You and Harrison should get out okay. The storm's supposed to move in and out fairly quickly."

"Of course we'll get out. Not many storms shut this city's airport down." He almost hoped the Jamestown Airport would close. Tom hated flying. He hadn't planned on being away from Remington for so long—or even out of the country for that matter. He'd be glad to get this trip over with and get back home to his family. Harrison had decided, only yesterday, that he wanted Tom to see his operation in Amsterdam. Of course Tom understood the importance of going there. Part of the deal.

Dropping his head into his hands, he realized he had only a few days to find and deal with Elise before leaving the country. When would she make herself known to him? He had to stop her from . . .

"Tom?" John interrupted Tom's thoughts. "Something more on your mind? Anything else you want to discuss? My receptionist just called. Harrison and his attorney are here."

"No, let's move on this," Tom said, focusing back on John and Nate.

The meeting with William Harrison went smoothly. Tom and William formed a simple partnership: Tom, as a silent partner, was backing William, supplying the financial support needed to ensure the viability of Harrison's newest diamond and gemstone importing business. The company had actually launched several months before with the opening of its first jewelry outlet in Ravenswood—Rivers and Cranston, the exclusive boutique where Vivian, unbeknownst to William, had purchased her expensive diamonds a few weeks ago.

Tom planned to tell Sara about his business venture when he got back to Ravenswood. He didn't want any secrets between them. He imagined she'd find it amusing that he was part owner of her cousin's business. At least that was what he hoped.

After Harrison had gone, Tom asked John what he'd found out about the previous owners of Remington House.

John pulled a file from his drawer. "Here, you can take this with you. I have another copy. The owners, the Lindemans, did indeed die at the house. They were elderly and, according to the clerk at the county office, seemed unnaturally attached to each other, to the point of having extremely limited interaction with anyone else. The brother, Gabriel Lindeman was a frail man. His sister Helen told the county clerk that her brother had terminal bone cancer and had been treated at a clinic in Germany for a time. The treatment apparently failed, and they returned to Ravenswood, becoming increasingly seclusive. They were however generous to the township. They donated, to the tune of fifty thousand dollars, to The Citizen's for Education, attending one meeting each year, according to the organization's minutes, to hand-deliver their check. They did this for many years, then due to the brother's failing heath, began having the check delivered by their banker. Not a happy ending, as you already alluded to. The sister shot her brother, then killed herself. A suicide note was found, actually penned and signed by both of them; their signatures were verified.

"Certainly a tragedy. Monica has assured me that she had no knowledge of any of this when she sold the property. I don't know that I believe her and certainly am willing to take the necessary legal steps to negate your purchase. Say the word."

Staring out the window at the waning storm, Tom rubbed his chin and sighed. "No. I don't want to do that. A letter from you, stating my disappointment with her lack of knowledge of the property upon sale, should be sufficient. Hard to image a story like that would not be public knowledge, no matter how new Monica was to Ravenswood. Everyone I've talked to knows about it. Everyone! But, I'm at home there. I want to keep the property." Tom stood up. "Nate and I will see you later this evening. Dinner at The Pub?"

"Sure. I'll be there at eight."

Chapter 78

Sara put her magazine down. Someone was pounding on the front door. She heard Cassie yelling, "I'm coming! I'm coming! Hold on," and heard her running down the stairs. Leaning over the banister, Sara watched Cassie peek through the curtain and then open the front door.

Vivian burst into the house. Sara had never seen her cousin look so crazed. Her hair was sticking out from underneath a hideous orange and yellow striped scarf obviously tied hastily around her head. She wore a huge, well-worn, black trench coat Sara recognized as belonging to William that generally hung in the mudroom at the back of the house. On Vivian's feet were dainty, pale pink satin slippers trimmed in matching feathers. Black streaks of mascara were smudged around her eyes, across her cheeks and on the back of her clenched fists. Her eyes were puffy and red, her pupils large, making her eyes look black. She glanced nervously toward the living room, then the study. "Are they here?" she screamed, pushing past Cassie into the living room doorway.

"Who?" Cassie asked. Looking up the stairs, Cassie motioned Sara to come down. "Vivian who are you looking for?"

"My boys! I can't find them anywhere. Are they here?" When she saw Sara, she ran at her. "Where are my boys?"

"Vivian!" Cassie grabbed Vivian's hands as she started to pound on Sara's chest.

"Vivian! They're with Joe. Remember?"

"What?" Vivian collapsed heavily on the edge of the first step. "They're with Joe? The taxi driver?"

"He took them with him this morning—to Westlake. Billy, Jimmy and Lizzie. They all went. They're picking up supplies. You know—for the remodel here; the crew started today, Joe had a special order to pick up. They'll be gone most of the morning."

Vivian stared at her.

"I talked to you last night. Don't you remember?" Sara asked.

"The taxi driver?" She looked blankly at Sara, then at Cassie. Sighing, she dabbed at her eyes with her hands, wiping them on the front of her coat. She then stuck her finger into the corner of her mouth and chewed on her nail.

"Are you okay, Vivian?" Sara asked.

Vivian shook her head. "I took some medicine last night. For my headache. I must have forgotten that you called me, Sara."

"Come to the kitchen, and we'll make some coffee." Sara led the way. "So you had another headache. Does your head still hurt?"

"No, but I feel very odd. You think the boys are okay, then? With that man?"

"Of course. You know Joe, he's always been good with the kids," Sara said, gently guiding Vivian into a chair at the kitchen table. "Sit. I'll fix some coffee."

Sara had the coffee going in minutes, a strong French roast, freshly ground at the local market.

"So Viv, how long have you been taking these pills?" Cassie asked.

"What?" Vivian stared stupidly at Cassie.

Cassie put her hand to Vivian's forehead. "No fever."

Vivian jerked her head away. "Of course I don't have a fever. What's wrong with you? Why are you here?"

"Vivian, I think we need to call your doctor. You seem really disoriented. Maybe you took too many pills, or maybe you're having a bad reaction to them," Sara said.

"Maybe. That could be the reason I feel so awful. I don't know how many I took. Maybe two or three. Who is this woman?" She pointed at Cassie.

"I'm Cassie, Tom's sister. Remember?"

"Oh."

"Do you know your doctor's phone number?" Cassie asked.

"I don't, but it's Dr. Richards; he has an office in town."

Sara sliced some strawberries along with a banana and put them in front of Vivian. "You should eat something. Knowing you, you probably haven't eaten today. I'll call information and get Dr Richards' number. Cassie, stay with Viv. I'll be right back."

"Sure. Use the phone in the dining room." Cassie poured three cups of coffee, got the sugar and cream and sat across from Vivian. "Here, what would you like in it?"

"Sugar."

Cassie pushed the cup toward Vivian.

They sat silently, staring at the walls, sipping coffee until Sara came back. "I called Dr. Richards' office. I had to leave a message, but the nurse said she would get in touch with him right away. He should be calling pretty soon." Sara watched Vivian who had absently picked up a banana slice and was smashing it on the table. Vivian jumped when the phone rang.

Running into the dining room, Sara grabbed the phone. In a few minutes she returned and sat down next to Vivian. "Dr. Richards wants to see you. We'll drive you into town. He said it's very important that we get you into his office as soon as possible. He's concerned. You wait here with Cassie and have some more coffee while I drive over to your house and get you some clothes."

The phone rang again. "That was Mannie. She was frantic when she got back from town and found the house wide open and you gone. She's going to bring you some clothes."

Vivian nodded. Sara went on, "She said you told her last night the boys were going to go with Joe this morning. She was very worried when she couldn't find you just now. She said you were sleeping when she left."

"Well, tell her I'm okay. Tell her to tell the boys I'll be home in a little while."

Cassie whispered to Sara, "We better not wait for Mannie to get here. I'll call her back, and tell her we're leaving."

"Maybe you're right. Let's at least get Viv's face washed. You do that, and I'll run upstairs and get her something of mine to wear. We can't let her go anywhere looking this way. She would never forgive us."

"Viv, go with Cassie into the bathroom, freshen up a little. Okay? I'll be right back." Sara ran upstairs. In the middle of her bed Wiggins lounged in a square of sunlight. He watched her pull clothes out of the dresser then grab a pair of boots from the closet floor. Satisfied he would not be disturbed, he returned to washing his face.

Cassie combed Vivian's hair and washed her face. When Sara walked into the bathroom, Vivian was taking off the heavy coat. She wore only underpants, bra and slippers.

Seeing her, Sara gasped. "Vivian! How did you get those bruises?" Vivian had large black and blue bruises on her upper arms and several red welts on her back.

"Oh, my God!" Cassie exclaimed. .

"What are you talking about?" Looking sideways at her arms and into the mirror at her back, Vivian screamed, "What happened to me?" She burst into tears. Sobbing, she gently touched the welts on her upper back.

"We better get you into town right now. Are you in a lot of pain?"

"No, it doesn't hurt." She looked woefully at Sara. "I don't understand; what happened to me?"

"I have no idea, Viv. But right now, we need to get to Dr. Richards' office." Sara held the sweater and pants out to Vivian. "I'll help you dress."

***

This is too perfect, Elise thought. *Vivian, you make it all so easy.* She got up from the table, couldn't resist knocking the sugar bowl over, spilling granules all across the table and onto the floor. No one noticed.

Chapter 79

Dr. Richards motioned to Sara to follow him to his office. "The nurse is with Mrs. Harrison, taking some blood so we can run a few tests. I'm not at liberty to discuss her condition with you, Miss Lawson. However, I know you are Mrs. Harrison's cousin, so I'd like to ask you a few general questions that may help me determine what type of treatment she may need."

Sara relaxed her shoulders, leaned back in the office chair —one of those orange plastic molded chairs, ugly but fairly comfortable. "Certainly," she said.

"As you already know, Mrs. Harrison has extensive bruising on her arms and back. The marks indicate that the bruising is fairly recent—I'm estimating within the last twelve hours. Do you have any idea what happened?"

"No. As I explained earlier, she showed up completely out of the blue, disoriented and frantic. She was looking for her boys. I never imagined she was hurt. Not until we, Cassie Wellington and I, helped her dress. Vivian seemed totally unaware of her injuries. She was shocked when we asked her how she got the bruises."

"Hmm. Disturbing. She told me she lost track of how many hydrocodone tablets she took last night—for her headache. Obviously that would account for her disorientation. By the way, that's not a medication I prescribed; her doctor in New York prescribed it, not for headaches, but for . . . well. Back to this morning." Dr. Richard shuffled a stack of papers, leafing absent-mindedly through them. He glanced at Sara. "She said her husband is out of the country. Is that correct?"

"He's in Jamestown right now. On business." Sara picked at a thread on her sleeve. "What is Viv taking hydrocodone for? That's a dangerous medication. Can't she get addicted to it?"

"I can't discuss that with you. I'm sorry. Is it possible for you to reach Mr. Harrison?"

"I've been trying for days. He hasn't returned my calls," Sara said. "I'm totally baffled with his lack of concern. It makes no sense. I'm guessing they're having some problems. Though Viv hasn't shared them with me."

"I see. Mrs. Harrison told me that you've been interfering with her marriage. Did you know she thinks that?"

"Why would she say that? Of course I haven't been interfering. I've been worried about Vivian and her erratic behavior these past few weeks. Just a guess, but I bet Vivian told William not to talk to me—he isn't returning my calls."

"That *is* the case. Mrs. Harrison told me she instructed her husband to ignore your calls. And . . . she has asked me to tell you that you are not to contact him again." Dr. Harrison glanced at Sara, then stared out the window at the bare trees. "Do you understand that this woman is very confused right now? She thinks you are trying to harm her."

"That's ridiculous. You don't believe her do you?" Sara stood up, grabbing her jacket off the chair back.

"Sit down," he said.

Sara said, "I called you today because I'm worried about my cousin. If you think I'm doing something to harm her, you couldn't be more wrong. Vivian is sick. I don't know what's going on with her, but it has nothing to do with me."

"I'm well aware of that. Please. Sit down." Dr. Richards pointed to the chair. "Let me make myself perfectly clear. Having spent some time with Mrs. Harrison, it's obvious she's having a difficult time right now. That being said, I have few options. I can do little more than try to find out what is going on. And I have to do that in a very cautious way—the law, you know. As you and I both have observed, in addition to an overdose of medication, someone hurt her. Or she hurt herself. It is possible."

"No! Vivian would never do anything to her own body. No matter what."

"Okay then." He picked up his pen and doodled on the folder lying open on his desk. "I'm trying to assess her emotional state. If you, as a family member, feel her mental stability is at issue, you need to be very honest with me. I can't do much without some of your thoughts and input. I have little to base my opinions on. In the past year, I've seen Mrs. Harrison three times. Two of those visits were with her sons."

"I see," Sara said.

"It's critical that I have your opinion."

The lights flickered in the room, a bulb popped. The room dimmed slightly. Sara looked at the ceiling; the fixture was old, the paint peeling, remains of numerous black insect bodies lay in the frosted cover. She looked back at the doctor. "If she's taking barbiturates, then I can understand a lot of her behavior lately. That could be part of the reason she's been acting so odd. But I can't help but think that there's more to it."

"I agree. I'm concerned about the bruises," said Dr. Richardson. "At first I thought she had done something to cause them herself. But you don't think that's possible. So the alternative is . . . " He rubbed his chin, looked at Sara with concern, "Well, do you have any idea who else could have done this? What about her oldest son? Billy."

Sara stared at her hands for a minute before she answered. "I'd hate to think him capable of hurting his own mother. But it does make sense. He has a lot of anger issues—always has. I suppose he could have grabbed her or something. That would explain why Vivian says she doesn't know how she got the marks—she doesn't want to remember or admit it to anyone. A few days ago Billy shot at my friend and me with a pellet gun. He said he was shooting at a deer; we gave him the benefit of a doubt. But he is a problem child. Vivian favors him, so he gets away with a lot."

"Yeah, I am aware of that. I saw the story in the newspaper the other day—I wondered if it was Billy. So yes, perhaps it was Billy who hurt Mrs. Harrison. Maybe he acted out, not meaning to hurt her, but angry and out of control. Where are the boys now?"

"With Joe Tilson. They're picking up some construction materials. They're making a day of it. Cassie's daughter, Lizzie, is with them, too."

"I don't think it's wise to leave Mrs. Harrison alone with Billy right now. Nor is it safe for the youngest boy to be alone with him—or with Vivian—for that matter. I hate to call the sheriff on this, but if you think it's even slightly possible that this is a case of abuse, I'll have to. Is there someone who can stay with Mrs. Harrison and the boys?"

"Can I talk to Vivian first—before we decide what we need to do?"

"Certainly. I'll get the nurse to take you back to the examining room. I'd like to talk to you again." Dr. Richards stood at the door. "I'll give you a few minutes, and then I'll be back to talk to you both."

Vivian lay on the examining table staring at the ceiling. Her hands clutched the thin blue paper gown, her knuckles white with tension. "Vivian, are you okay?" Sara asked.

Vivian rolled her head sideways, stared blankly at Sara. She said nothing.

Gently touching Vivian's hand, Sara smiled at her cousin. Vivian jerked her hand away. Sara stepped back. "Vivian, it's okay. I didn't mean to startle you." Vivian continued to stare at her. Sara said, "Dr. Richards said you could go home, but he doesn't want you to be alone. Do you want me to come and stay with you?"

"No!" Vivian shouted.

"I'd be happy to stay for a few days. You need someone with you right now."

"Not you! Mannie and Amos are there. And my boys. They can take care of me. Besides, I'm fine. It's these headaches that are causing all the problems. I took too many pain pills. I won't do that again."

"But Viv, I want to help you."

"Help me? I don't think you do, Sara. Your kind of help I can do without. I don't know what you're trying to do to my family and me, but I'll tell you—again—I want you to leave us alone. I don't want you moving back into my house!" Vivian yelled. She flailed into the air with her tight fists. "You stop calling my husband, and you stay away from my boys. Do I make myself clear?"

Sara covered her mouth with her hand to stop from saying something she might later regret. The chilling, glazed look in Vivian's eyes frightened her. She almost didn't recognize the woman before her. What was wrong with her? This was not the Vivian she knew.

"Can I talk to you out in the hall?" Dr. Richards asked from the doorway where he stood quietly listening and observing the interaction of the two women.

Sara whirled around and left the room. Dr Richards pulled the door closed and motioned her to follow him. He stopped in front of a door labeled "Private."

"Well, she's back to her old self," Sara said sarcastically.

"There seems to be some major problems between the two of you that you didn't mention. Not that it's any of my business. I don't see how you would expect to help Vivian if the two of you are on such—ahh—shaky ground."

"This is something fairly new, Dr. Richards. Believe it or not, we were close and getting along famously until very recently. Something has changed, but I can't figure out what. Yet."

"Well, it's none of my business." He looked coldly at Sara. "I've always found Mrs. Harrison to be very warm. I have no desire to interfere in your personal affairs. You may have done something to offend her; she seems to be quite sensitive."

Sara was insulted. *You ass!* She glared at the doctor who, in a matter of minutes, had certainly changed his tune!

Dr. Richards continued, "And with her migraines—taking too much medication for them—well, that may be the real issue here. And her older son—he's at a difficult age. I think it'd be advisable if you let someone else care for her. Isn't

Mannie Parker her housekeeper? She may be the best alternative for now."

Sara stared coldly at him. "Certainly. I'll talk with Mannie. She's at the house now. Better than having her alone with the boys, I guess. But I'm terribly worried—more than you can imagine."

"I have other patients to see. I'll let Mrs. Harrison know she can leave." Dr. Richards walked away leaving Sara standing alone in the hallway. He could almost feel Sara's eyes boring into his back. He hated what he had done, but he had no choice—he had to call William Harrison. After all, he had every right to know that his wife was here and that she may have been abused by their son. Mr. Harrison made it quite clear —in no uncertain terms—to send his wife home and butt out. "Mrs. Harrison," he said with a false calmness walking into the examining room where Vivian waited, "You can get dressed now. Miss Lawson will take you home."

"I don't want Sara to take me anywhere!"

"Mrs. Harrison, please. Let her drive you home. That's the simplest thing to do. You need to go home and get some rest."

Vivian started to speak. Dr. Richards ignored her and continued, "When you get home, I want you to throw out the hydrocodone tablets. You seem to be having a bad reaction to them. Will you do that?"

"Absolutely!" Vivian pounded on the bed with her fist. "I think I finally understand what's been happening to me. It's the pills, isn't it! And I thought I was going crazy, for heaven sakes. Dr. Barnes will hear about this!"

"That's the doctor who prescribed hydrocodone?" Dr. Richards asked.

"Yes. But he never told me they could make me feel so disoriented."

"You may have taken too many; they're very potent. I'd like you to call the clinic, maybe tomorrow. You might benefit from acupuncture for your headaches. We have someone who could even come to your house. I advise you to try a different approach for managing your pain. Acupuncture is quite effective for some people. I recommend that you stay off the pills. What do you think?"

"Certainly, I'll try anything you suggest. Anything to stop these headaches. They're ruining my life. I'll have Mannie call and arrange it."

"Mrs. Harrison, one more thing. I know this is awkward for you." He looked directly at her. "Has Billy done anything to hurt you?"

Vivian sat up. "What?" she screamed at him. "What lies did Sara tell you about my son?"

"That's not the case; she didn't suggest anything."

"He did nothing to me! I'm his mother, for God's sake!" Vivian jumped off the bed, pulling the curtain around the bed. Dr. Richards stood helplessly outside the drape, listening as she ranted.

"Now that the medication seems to have worn off, and you seem to be thinking clearly, I have to ask," Dr. Richard continued. "You have some bruising that you couldn't explain earlier. I know—ahh—sometimes young men have little self-control. I thought maybe Billy hurt you, unintentionally . . . of course. "

"Wait until my husband hears about this! I bet Sara was responsible for my bruises. She must have hurt me. When I was drugged. She's trying to tear my family apart—have Billy sent away and make Jimmy hate me. I've taken care of her for years and this is how she repays me. God! Wait until William hears about this!" Now fully dressed, she threw the curtain back.

Dr. Richards stared in amazement at the woman before him. "Mrs. Harrison, wait . . . "

"That bitch. She's trying to steal my husband!" She pushed past him. Her footsteps echoed on the hard tiles as she hurried down the hall and out the door into the reception room. Cassie, waiting in the reception room for both Sara and Vivian, was already getting to her feet as Vivian bust into the room. "Take me home. Now!" Vivian demanded.

Sara waited at the end of the hall. She had ducked into another room when Vivian stormed out. "What happened?" she asked softly.

Dr. Richards stopped and turned to Sara before going into another examining room. "My hands are tied," he said. "There's nothing I can do. You watch out for her and her boys. Okay?" He disappeared into the room and closed the door.

Later that afternoon, Dr. Richards tried calling William Harrison but got no answer. He left a message hoping Harrison would understand that, as a doctor, Richards couldn't turn a blind eye. He was compelled to go to the Harrison house and make sure Vivian and her other son were safe. If Billy was a threat, he'd find out and take action. To hell with Harrison's threats. The woman needed his help. She'd been abused by her son and her husband knew it. The ultimate betrayal. He'd bet his reputation on it.

***

Sara ran after Vivian and Cassie. "Wait, Viv!"

Vivian turned to face her. She had with no expression whatsoever on her face. "Aren't you taking me home now?" she asked. "I'm so tired, Sara. Take me home. I need to rest."

Cassie opened the car door and helped Vivian into the back seat. She was shivering; Cassie took her coat off and put it around her. "What happened?" she asked Sara as she started the car. Cassie checked in her rearview mirror, saw Vivian had closed her eyes and seemed to be sleeping. "What was the yelling about?"

"I'm not sure. But I'm more than worried. I think we better take Vivian to Tom's. At least for today. I'll let Mannie know. The boys can come over later to see her." Sara glanced back at Vivian, her mouth open, snoring gently. "Cassie, I think she's losing her mind. I'm starting to believe Billy has nothing to do with this."

"Billy? What are you talking about?" Cassie asked.

"I'll tell you later."

***

Vivian slept for most of the afternoon, not waking until dinnertime. Joe, Lizzie and the boys were back from town by then. Billy and Jimmy came to the Gardner house to see their mom. She seemed oblivious to what had happened that morning. Her appetite was good, and she appeared much like her old self. "I think those migraines are at the root of this odd feeling I keep having. And the medication, of course. I think I'll be fine now. I think Dr. Richards was right. I need to stay away from the pills and try another approach."

"That makes sense," Sara said. However, thinking about the bruises, she couldn't help but be worried. When—if—William called, she had to make him understand how serious this was. She tried to remember if insanity ran in their family? Hadn't she heard about great-aunt Ollie having been committed when she was a young woman? Or was it Great Uncle Oscar?

Vivian spoke, startling her. "Billy and Jimmy, we should go home now. I have so much to do. Joe, can you drive us? I don't feel like walking."

"Why don't you all stay here tonight? We have plenty of room. Vivian, I think it would be best if you relaxed and let us take care of you. For tonight anyhow," Sara said, watching for signs of a relapse in her cousin's demeanor. She sighed in relief when Vivian remained calm and smiled at her.

"Okay, but only for tonight. Boys? Is that okay with you?" Vivian asked.

"I'm not staying. I have stuff to do," Billy said. "I'm playing in an online game room. I have a match coming up. I can't lose my place." He grinned at his mom. "I'll walk though. Jimmy you want to come with me? You can watch me beat the Titan 12 level." He ruffled his brother's hair.

Flattered that Billy would include him, Jimmy said, "Sure, Billy. I'll go with you."

"I don't want you boys alone. I think we should all go, then."

"Mannie's there and so is Amos. You stay here, Mom. We'll be fine. You need quiet anyhow. Sara and Cassie won't make much noise compared to Jimmy and me."

"Okay, but I'll be home early tomorrow." Vivian reached for Jimmy and gave him a hug. "Be good. No fighting."

The boys left, promising Vivian they would get to bed early.

Cassie made up the bed in the spare bedroom for Vivian— the room that Lizzie had been using. Lizzie would stay with her mom. Sara called Mannie, asking her to stay close by the boys, just in case.

***

Elise was elated. She would stay with Vivian for the night. She wouldn't be alone.

Chapter 80

Dr. Richards got a call from William Harrison at nine that evening. He was told that William would make arrangements to have Vivian taken back to their house in Boston where her physician would take over her care until William could get back to the states the following week. "Thank you for your concern, Dr. Richards. However, this is a problem that I have dealt with before. I hoped this would not happen again, but it seems I was wrong. I would appreciate it if you would say nothing about this to anyone."

Dr. Richards agreed somewhat reluctantly. "You believe her injuries are self inflicted then? I still don't see how she could have caused that bruising herself."

"And you would be correct. I'm asking for your discretion, Dr Richards. Vivian has been lonely, if you understand what I'm saying. I've been away on business. She finds, uh, let's say *ways* to fill the lonely hours. She has some, shall we say, odd urges. This is nothing new. Then she feels guilty and takes too many pills."

"I see," Dr. Richards said, embarrassed to think he had wrongly assumed she had been abused when in fact, she had a rough lover and was too embarrassed to admit it. "I understand. You can trust me. I'll certainly be prudent. I'll make a note in her file that will indicate her visit to the clinic was due to ongoing medical issues that have been turned over to her family physician."

"I appreciate your discretion. Goodbye." The line went dead leaving Dr. Richards disturbed but accepting.

Chapter 81

Cassie closed the door to the bedroom; Vivian had fallen asleep almost as soon as her head hit the pillow. Cassie's cell phone rang. She answered quickly, not checking the screen to see who it was, hoping Vivian wouldn't wake up. "Hello?"

"Sis! Is everything okay there?"

"Tom, hi! Yes, of course."

"I've been trying to reach you and Sara. Where have you been, and why haven't you returned any of my calls? I left at least four voicemails for each of you."

"Sorry, must be a problem with the satellites. I never got your calls," Cassie said, hating herself for lying.

"Is everything okay?" Tom asked.

"Yeah, we had some problems with Vivian. We took her to the clinic. But she's okay now. She took too many pills—by accident—for her migraine. Gave us a bit of a scare. But she's fine. She's staying here tonight."

"God! The drama!" Tom said, sounding slightly perturbed. "What about Jimmy and Billy? Where are they?"

"Mannie and Amos are with them at their house."

"Oh," Tom said flatly. "What about William? Did you or Sara call him?"

"We did. We talked to him a few hours ago. We told him we were taking care of Vivian here. He said he would make sure Mannie came for her tomorrow. He didn't seem very concerned. I don't like the way he's ignoring her and his kids."

"Nor do I," Tom said, pounding his thigh with his fist. He'd have to bite his tongue and stay out of it. He'd call Jimmy tomorrow and make sure he was okay. William might be a shrewd businessman, but he certainly seemed to be a lousy father. Maybe Tom could talk to him on the trip.

Tom's voice sounded weary. Cassie was immediately worried. "Tom, how about you? Are you okay? How was your meeting?"

"I'm fine. The meeting went very well. Listen, I'm going to have to go to Amsterdam on Saturday."

"Wow! Are you up to it, Tom? You sound so tired." Cassie went into her room and closed the door.

"I don't really want to go, but I need to wrap this deal up. I should be back by the end of next week."

"Okay. Well . . . we'll be fine." Cassie lay back on the bed, staring at the intricate patterns in the plaster on the ceiling. Swirls and strokes twirled in intricate detail, shadows from the moonlight seemed to cause the lines to shift and create waves on the ceiling above her.

"Cassie, are you still there?"

"What? Sorry, Tom. Just thinking. Hey, have you talked to Joe?"

"Yes, I talked to him this afternoon. He told me about the bird attack, said he'd check all the eaves and the trees for nests. Makes no sense this time of year, though. We may need to bring in an exterminator if these attacks keep going on. We'll see what Joe finds first. Listen, one other thing I wanted to remind to do. Keep the attic closed up will you?"

Cassie sighed. "Sure. We'll stay out of the attic. Don't worry." She felt guilty lying to her brother. *And guess what, Tom, we have a medium coming here tomorrow night. To help us find the old people living up there.*

"You seem distant. You sure everything's okay?" Tom asked.

"Yep. Long day. Do you want me to find Sara so you can talk to her?"

"Sure. So she's getting along with Vivian? I'm surprised Vivian's willing to stay under the same roof with Sara. After all, she did throw her out of her house last week."

"Vivian seems to have forgotten all about that, for the time being. To be honest, I think she's losing her grip. I think she needs serious psychological help." Damn, why had she blurted that out? After everything Tom had been through himself. "I'm sorry, Tom. I sounded insensitive, I shouldn't have said that." Cassie walked into the living room. Sara, staring out at the ocean view, turned and smiled at her. Cassie pointed at the phone and mouthed, "Tom."

"Tom?" Cassie asked. "Did you hear me? I said I'm sorry."

"Yeah, it's okay, Sis." Tom forced a laugh. "You don't have to apologize. I agree. Viv is a little loony. Been there, done that!" His voice feigned a light heartedness he did not feel.

"It was thoughtless of me. I mean, therapy is nothing to take lightly. Forgive me?"

"Nothing to worry about."

"Hold on, I'll get Sara." Sara had stepped out onto the porch. A cold breeze circled around Cassie's legs as she followed her out. "Sara's running up the heating bill. She has the terrace doors wide open, and it's freezing in here. Brrr. Tom, before I put Sara on—what time's your flight Saturday? I'll call you before you leave. "

"Eleven."

"Okay, I'll call you at eight. Goodnight. Miss you."

"Night, Sis. Stay out of the attic. Do you understand?" Tom asked sternly.

"Rest assured," she lied, crossing her fingers. "Here's Sara."

Sara took Cassie's phone. "Hi, Tom." She smiled and gestured for Cassie to go. "Tom, I have to talk to you about William."

Chapter 82

Half an hour before Tom called Cassie, William had called Sara. "Sara, it's William."

"Where are you?" she asked.

"Right now I'm still in Jamestown, you know that, Sara," he said. "I'm flying out of the country though and will be gone for another week, maybe two."

Sara interrupted. "Vivian needs you. You have to come home. Now!"

"Don't use that tone with me. I can't come to Ravenswood now. I talked to Dr. Richards today, the doctor you took Vivian to see. I don't appreciate you interfering this way, Sara."

"I've been trying to reach you for weeks. Where the hell have you been, William? Don't tell me I'm interfering. I'm doing everything I can to make sure your children and your wife don't self destruct. How dare you say I'm interfering."

"You are! I want you to stay out of this. Do you understand me?" William took a deep breath, then added, "Look, I can't get away. This business venture is a make-it or break-it deal. Can you understand that? I'm handling the, uh, situation from here. I've talked to Mannie. She'll pick Vivian up in the morning. No sense in disturbing Vivian tonight. Mannie will take Vivian and the boys to Boston next week and stay with them until I can get home."

"Does Vivian know this?"

"No, and you are not to tell her anything. I'll talk to her tomorrow. If I have to, I'll have Dr. Cortland fly in and get her. Do you understand?"

"I do." She cleared her throat, thought for a second, and said, "Maybe it's for the best. But I have a suggestion. Don't leave the boys alone with her. I can stay at your house with them. I don't think Viv is capable of looking out for them right now. Something is seriously wrong with her. Do you get that, William?"

"Let me talk with Viv. Maybe you're right, but I still don't want you to stay at our house. Vivian's too upset with you. I'll make certain Mannie and Amos are there around the clock until the family is ready to leave for Boston. Besides, Viv will probably be fine tomorrow, after a good night's sleep. I think all the pills she's been taking are the problem."

"I rather doubt that. Let me tell you some of the things that have been going on. I think you'll see that I'm right." Sara gave William a quick rundown of Vivian's behavior over the last several weeks, keeping all emotion out.

When Sara was finished, William was silent. She heard a loud pounding as William banged his fist against something, maybe the wall. He said, "I'll call you later," and hung up.

Chapter 83

Elise wrapped her arms around the sleeping woman. Elise had come to care for this pitiful soul. Vivian seemed so much like her. So much to deal with, so little help—abandoned by her husband, laughed at and taken advantage of by her cousin and Tom's sister. Even Tom disliked this lovely creature beside her. She gently touched Vivian's silky hair fanned out on the pillow. *She is so beautiful. So fragile. I must take care of her. I need her as much as she needs me.*

Vivian sighed in her sleep, then let out a small cry.

"Shhh," Elise crooned softly.

The old ones slithered into the room. Elise could sense them before she saw them. She covered her nose, tried to keep from gagging. The smell of old flesh and opium were over-powering. It had been days since they dared to come around her. Elise resented their intrusion. She only wanted to sleep, to be warm and to be needed. Now these fiends had spoiled her respite.

Gabe ran his long, thin, wrinkled hand along Vivian's outstretched arm. Careful not to wake her, he hovered over her and placed his tongue just above her mouth—not quite touching her lips, but sensing their luscious warmth. He motioned to Helen to come join him, ignoring Elise who had jumped up and was standing beside the bed.

Elise snarled at the couple. Gabe and Helen laughed. Vivian sat up, horrified at the visions of the old hag and her brother hovering above her. She started to scream. Before the sound could escape from her mouth, Elise quickly entered Vivian's body and whirled around striking the hideous old man. He was slow to react, had not realized Elise's capabilities. Too late, he tried to avoid the impact. The blow struck his mouth; his yellowed teeth sank into the decaying flesh of his tongue.

Helen grabbed at Elise's arm but was too weak to overcome her physical strength. "Bitch! We'll not forget this," she hissed. "You *are* one of us now. You'll see. We'll make you ours. Soon!" Helen reached for her brother Gabe's hand. "Come, dear one, let me take care of you." Pulling Gabe toward the door to the hall, she glanced back at Elise. "We'll be back. You better beware. Your precious one is not safe from us."

"I'm not afraid of either of you," Elise whispered. "You will not touch Vivian again! Do you hear me?"

"Oh, we hear you, dear. See how we tremble! Ha!" Then they were gone; a gray oily mist coiled and disappeared underneath the door.

Elise stayed inside Vivian's body for the rest of the night. She would take no chance on the old couple returning and catching her off guard.

At least Vivian got some much-needed sleep. Vivian dreamed of Tom. As she dreamed, her hatred of him grew. When she woke in the early dawn, Elise left her body, slipping quietly away. Vivian dressed quickly and left the house, puzzled by her strong feelings about Tom. Why did she feel so hateful toward him? It made no sense. Oh, well, what did lately? She needed to stay away from his house. That much was very clear to her.

Elise followed Vivian all the way to the Harrison house, watched her climb the porch stairs and disappear inside. Vivian would be safe now. Although Helen and Gabe were a strong force, they simply didn't have the ability to leave the sanctuary of their home. Elise needed time to think. She turned and walked to the cliff overlooking the beach.

The morning waves slapped the shoreline, then ebbed dragging driftwood haplessly back out into the ocean. Repeatedly, huge waves rolled back to shore depositing the wood onto the beach. Elise watched the endless game. Huge branches, stripped bare, surface slick and gray, floated in and out like weightless flotsams. Elise was in awe of nature's tremendous might. White caps broke far out on the ocean. The sun cast orange and red reflections on the turbulent waves before they tumbled back into the water and dissipated. A ship's horn sounded, eerie and mournful in the watery expanse.

Elise sat on the edge of the cliff staring off into the distance. Knowing she had to deal with the old couple very soon, she began making her plans. For now, with Vivian out of the house, time was on her side. Elise knew she could protect Lizzie—she would never let the Lindemans harm the child. If the old couple did anything to Cassie and Sara, she didn't care. It would make her work that much easier.

As Elise watched, the sun rose higher, casting a golden glow on the beach below. She tilted her head back, felt the warmth on her pale skin and breathed in the crisp salty air. She smiled; she felt her life force growing stronger. She began to feel powerful and whole.

Chapter 84

"Cassie," Sara called from the hallway, "Vivian's gone!"

"What?" Cassie yelled, opening her bedroom door.

"Vivian's gone. I checked everywhere. She must have gone home. I'll call and make sure she's not out wandering around."

Cassie got dressed and hurried downstairs after Sara, who was putting her cell phone down on the coffee table. "Find her?" Cassie asked.

"Yeah," Sara said. "She said she woke up early and didn't want to bother us. She said she's feeling rested and clearheaded. No headache. She wants to be at her own home, with her boys. She sounded fine. Almost like her old self."

"Good. We'll check on her later. Though I'm still worried about her being around Billy," Cassie said. "I talked to Mannie and she's on the lookout. Said she'd stay close, be on high alert with Vivian and Billy. So, Sara, let's get Lizzie up and have some breakfast. We have much to do today!"

"Yes, we do." Sara looked quickly at Cassie, smiled nervously. "The medium comes tonight."

"Yeah. I'm taking Lizzie to Mary's this afternoon. Mary's little sister, Evie, is having a sleepover and invited her. I don't want Lizzie in the house while Ms. Montagna is here."

"You and me both. What time are you leaving?" asked Sara.

"Around one. I told Mary I'd pick her up, so she doesn't have to drive here alone. She'll stay the night here, then I can take her home tomorrow when I pick up Lizzie. Is Joe going to be around today? I don't want to leave you here alone."

Sara said, "Yeah, he and his crew. Joe's making them use the back entrance to the basement, so they won't bother us. I hope they fare better down there than we did. I hate that basement! I'll be so glad when they tear it apart and clean it all out!"

Cassie drove slowly up the long driveway to her brother's house. She was returning from taking Lizzie into town and picking up Mary. She stopped the car halfway up the hill.

"Why are you stopping here?" Mary asked.

Cassie didn't answer her. She rolled her window down and stuck her head out. She stared at the house.

"What are you looking at?" Mary asked. "What's the matter?"

"I'm not sure. Look at the attic window, the one on the east side." Cassie pointed, not taking her eyes off the house. "I think I see someone standing there."

"Hmm. I don't see any . . . Wait, I *do* see someone. Shit! I can't tell for sure but . . . "

Cassie pressed her foot on the gas pedal, throwing Mary back into her seat. "Hang on. I want to find out who's up there!" Pulling in front of the house, she and Mary scrambled out of the car. Cassie pushed the front door open and ran toward the stairs. Mary was right behind her, almost knocking Sara over.

"What are you doing?" Sara called after them.

"Come on! Someone's in the attic. Hurry!" Mary shouted.

"Wait, I'll get Joe!" Sara yelled as Mary and Cassie reached the second floor landing, turned right and disappeared into the hallway leading to the attic stairs. Sara was torn; she wanted to follow the two to the attic but was afraid of what they might find there. She turned and ran through the house to the basement door. "Joe! I need you up here!" she screamed down the stairs. She heard pounding—the men were tearing down walls today. Someone was whistling, someone else laughing. "Joe!"

She could hear him running up the steps. "What's wrong, Sara?" Joe had a pencil behind his ear and a wrecking bar in his right hand.

"Mary said they saw someone in the attic. I thought I better get you. Just in case. Come on." She ran out of the kitchen, started up the back servant stairs. "Joe! Come on."

Mary screamed first, then Cassie. Footsteps pounded as someone ran down the hallway overhead in the attic. Joe passed Sara and was on the third floor before Sara had a chance to reach the second floor landing.

"Mary! Cassie! You all right?" Joe called.

Sara reached the third floor, stopped to catch her breath. Joe was already out of sight. She heard a door slam; then another door slammed. She flew down the hall, the sound of her shoes on the wooden floor echoed hollowly. "Where is everyone? Joe? Where are you?" Sara screamed.

Behind her she heard someone running. "What's going on up here?" It was Harry.

"I can't find anyone!" yelled Sara.

"Joe," Harry yelled. "Where are you?" Opening one door after another, Harry checked each room as he hurried down the hallway. "What happened, anyhow?" Harry opened the door to another empty room, looked around.

"Mary and Cassie said they saw someone up here. They ran up here, and I ran to get Joe. I heard them scream. Now I can't find them." Sara pounded on the wall with clenched fists. "Why don't you answer me, Cassie? Mary? Where are you?"

The last door on the left, at the east end of the passageway, flew open. "Joe?" Harry called. "That you, Joe?" Entering the room, he motioned to Sara to wait. He turned on the light. "Fuck!"

Sara hurried down the hall, then stuck her head cautiously into the doorway. Cassie and Mary stood against the back wall of the room. Sara's first impression was that they were standing way too still. Joe was bent over something big and furry that stood on its hind legs, hissing. Harry sprang forward. Joe swung the wrecking bar, hitting the animal square on its head as it lunged. A sickening shriek emitted from the giant raccoon as the metal made contact with its skull. Then it was silent.

"Oh, my God!" Mary yelled, rushing across the room to Sara, avoiding the raccoon. Its blood began to pool at Joe's feet.

"No one's hurt are they? No bites or scratches?" Joe asked the women. They shook their heads. "This is the same raccoon we found last week. Stay clear of it . . . and its blood. Doesn't look like it, but it might be rabid."

"How did it get in the house again?" Cassie asked, backing out of the room.

I don't know. I'll check for an open window up here. Damned if I can figure out how it keeps getting in."

"Might be coming down one of the chimneys. Want me to look around?" Harry asked, watching Mary, Cassie and Sara go quickly down the hall to the staircase.

"Yeah, go ahead. I've already checked the chimneys, though. I'll get the coon out of here and have one of the crew take it to the vet's office. Just to be sure it's not rabid."

"I don't see any way it could have gotten into this room. This where you found it?" Harry asked.

"Not sure, but this is where Mary and Cassie were when I got up here. We didn't bother with any pleasantries," Joe said sarcastically. "No time to ask any questions."

Harry sneered, his back safely to Joe. "Don't need to give me a hard time. I'm trying to help here."

"Sorry. I just don't get how the friggin' animal keeps getting in. Pisses me off. I've been looking for weeks." Joe scratched his head, knocking the pencil out from behind his ear. He grabbed it mid-air, catching it before it landed in the blood. "Maybe it's getting in downstairs. One of the bedrooms must have a window open, and the raccoon finds its way back up here—must think it belongs here or something. Damned if I can figure it out." He glanced at Harry. "You look around. I'll get this mess cleaned up and check the other floors."

They searched for an hour. Joe and Harry found no open windows, not even an open vent where the animal could have squeezed through. Puzzled they gave up and went back to the basement to work.

***

Gabe and Helen watched—amused at the chaos they had caused. After all the work they had done to move into the basement and now it was being dismantled—wall by wall, stud by stud. They were angry. Soon they would have nowhere to go but back to the attic. They didn't want to do that. Elise was living there. And she was not cooperating with them—not at all.

Chapter 85

Cassie had her own ideas. She knew what she saw in the window, and it definitely was not a raccoon! She, Mary and Sara sat at the dining room table staring out the picture window at the Atlantic. White caps rolled and tossed, spewing showers of water high onto the rocks. A lone seagull dove again and again. Finally catching a small fish, it flew to the rocks below on the beach edge. It tore into the fish, pecked and chewed, pecked and chewed. After every bite it looked quickly around, glancing in several directions, in case it had to protect its meal from other scavengers.

"It was the Lindemans," Cassie said. "They're behind this."

"I know," Mary said quietly.

Sara twisted her hair around her index finger, the tip changing to bright red with the pressure. Saying nothing, she got up and walked to the double french doors leading to the porch. Watching the horizon, she traced circles on the glass.

"Are you okay, Sara?" Cassie asked.

"Yeah. But this is insane," Sara said. "How are the Lindemans doing all of these things? What's the point? Anyone have a clue?"

"Because they can, I guess," Mary answered. "They'll do anything they can to frighten us. *That's* the point."

"Hey, there you are," Joe hollered from the kitchen. "One of the guys took the raccoon into town. I'll let you know what we find out. It's quitting time for the crew. I'm gonna run the guys back into town." He came into the dining room. "Want me to come back after I drop them off?"

"We're good, Joe," Cassie said. She didn't want him to be here when Terese Montagna, the medium, arrived. It was past four already. "Go on. Now that the raccoon is *dead,* we don't have anything to be afraid of," she lied. *Not from anything living, anyway.*

"All right. Call me if you need me. Don't hesitate."

"Thanks, Joe. We'll be fine. Go on; get your guys back to town. We'll see you tomorrow," Cassie said.

"Okay." Joe paused in the doorway. "Night." A minute later the back door slammed, then his oversized pickup started up, the muffler rumbling loudly in the quiet evening.

Cassie, Mary and Sara watched out the front window as Joe drove slowly by the house. He and the three passengers craned their necks looking up at the attic. Joe shifted gears and headed down the driveway.

"For whatever good it will do, let's make sure all the doors are locked," Cassie said. "Come on. We should stay together."

They spent the next twenty minutes checking all the windows and doors, even though they knew Joe had checked them earlier. Everything seemed fine on the first and second floors. Joe had installed a deadbolt on the kitchen side of the door to the basement this morning, and that was still bolted. At the landing to the attic stairs, the three hesitated.

"I don't think we need to check up there. I mean Joe was thorough with the rest of the house. He definitely would have locked everything up there. That's where the raccoon was after all," Sara said, glancing at Cassie and Mary, then up the steep stairs. "Right?"

"I know he did, but we don't know that Helen and Gabe haven't unlocked a window again. We better check."

Cassie turned on the lights as they checked every window in each room. "We should lock the door from the servant's stairs to the second floor, too." Once they'd inspected everything, they went down to the kitchen to have dinner before Terese Montagna arrived.

"Do we have any idea what we're going to say to Ms. Montagna when she gets here?" Sara asked.

"I did some research on the internet," Cassie said. "The correct course of action is to let the medium do the talking. If she's truly gifted, she should be able to pick up on what or who —if anything—is here."

"I talked to my friend, Lisa," Mary said. "I told her a little about some of the things that have been happening here—in confidence—don't worry," Mary added quickly. "Lisa said Terese has an excellent reputation. She said Terese purposely keeps a low profile. The Concord Police Department often has her work on cases with them. She's the real deal." She paused. When no one said anything, she added, "If there are ghosts here, she'll know. And she'll know how to get rid of them."

Sara shrugged. "We hope." She took a long drink, draining her wineglass. "We'll see. This situation is getting desperate. I never imagined spirits could cause so much physical chaos. I'm starting to believe that if we can't figure out what's going on here, and how to deal with it, we better think about leaving." Sara paused and took a breath. "Or maybe consider having Joe stay here with us while Tom's gone. This is getting more frightening every day."

Cassie filled Sara and Mary's glasses. "I wonder what we did to piss off the Lindemans? I hope Ms. Montagna can tell us."

"They're probably angry because we're here. This was their home—at one time," Sara said. Mary nodded. They continued eating their baked salmon and salad, enjoying a few minutes of quiet.

When their plates were empty, Cassie said, "We better clean up. Ms. Montagna will be here pretty soon." She began picking up the dishes.

Sara opened the dishwasher, putting the dishes in the racks as Mary handed them to her. "There, that's done." Sara wiped the table, then hung the dishrag over the faucet.

Cassie was making a fresh pot of coffee. The front door bell rang. "This is it. She's here," she said, her voice high-pitched, reflecting her nervousness.

Chapter 86

Terese Montagna, her back to the door, smoothed her silver hair from her face, licked her lips and took a slow, cleansing breath. When Cassie opened the door, Terese quickly turned around to face her.

"Hi, I'm Cassie Wellington." She smiled at the tall, thin woman whose dangling moon and sun earrings twinkled like stars in the porch light as she twirled to face her. "Come in."

"Good evening. Oh, my goodness! I haven't been inside this house for years." Terese didn't wait for further introductions as she entered the house. "I'd forgotten how lovely it is." She quickly glanced around, taking in the study to her left and living room to her right. Before her, at the end of the short hallway, was the staircase to the second floor. She glanced up the dark stairs, then looked back at Cassie. "I'm Terese Montagna. As you must already know!" She laughed. "My, my. I can see you have some unwanted guests here."

"No, no. These are my friends—Sara Lawson, and you *must* know Mary Stevens. She works at the Ravenswood Vet Clinic."

"I didn't mean Sara and Mary." Terese smiled, extending her hand to Cassie, then to Mary and Sara.

"Oh!" Cassie said, her brown eyes wide, alert. "Come in. Let me take your coat. Can I get you some coffee?" she asked, leading everyone into the living room.

"Stay here. I'll bring a tray," Sara said. "Mary, come with me. We're *very* glad you're here, Terese. We'll be right back."

Terese talked as she took her wool-tweed coat off and handed it to Cassie. "I was so surprised when Mary called me the other day. I didn't realize anyone was living here. In this small town, that *is* amazing. But, I've been away a lot lately. Out of the loop, I guess." She began pacing the room, touched the back of the couch, stood before the grand piano in the far corner of the room. She lifted the cover, ran her fingers gently along the keys. "How long have you lived here, Cassie?"

"Actually this is my brother's house. He bought it a few months ago."

"Does he know I'm here?"

"Actually, no. He's out of town right now, in New York on business. I'm staying here for a while. Maybe until after

Christmas." Cassie followed Terese around, feeling silly, but she didn't know what else to do. "My husband's traveling, too."

"Your brother has been quite ill, hasn't he?" Terese stated. "Emotionally."

"Well, uhh . . . "

"It's okay, you don't need to say anything. I can feel his pain—it permeates the house." She looked into Cassie's eyes. "I know he lost someone he loved. Do you know much about her?"

"I don't know how to answer that," Cassie said, not wanting to tell Terese she was right on about Tom and feeling she shouldn't give away any information about Elise. She felt confused as to what she *should* say.

"Don't feel uncomfortable. This is what I do." She smiled warmly and continued, "I sense his loss. I also sense deep despair that goes beyond that loss. I recognize his confusion, a mix of love and hate. I feel his torment. I'm so sorry. This is painful for you, too, isn't it? You hoped he'd moved beyond those feelings." Terese laid her hand gently on Cassie's shoulder. "The situation here is very disturbing. There are many emotions unleashed in this house." She paled suddenly. "I need to sit down!" She hurried to the sofa, sat down and rested her head in her hands. She closed her eyes and took a long breath as she massaged her temples.

"Is everything all right?" Sara entered the room carrying a tray filled with coffee, blue china cups, a pitcher of cream and a small plate piled with sugar cubes.

Mary followed carrying a plate of strawberries and melon balls in one hand and a plate of macaroons in the other. "Did something happen? Did we miss something?"

Terese looked at her. "This house is filled with malevolence. I felt it as soon as I turned up the drive. There is much spiritual activity transpiring here."

"What do you want us to do?" Cassie asked.

"Let me catch my breath," Terese answered. "Please, don't look so worried, I've done this almost my whole life. I'm fine.

Sit down, girls. The last thing we want to do is show fear. We are, after all, the ones who are living, the ones who ultimately have control. We should not fear these forces, but rather have pity for them—those who cannot leave this realm. They are jealous of our life-force. It gives them enormous pain to see that we live while they languish in the shadows. Our fear though, well, that gives them *some* joy. Let's not give them *any* joy." Terese smiled, poured four cups of coffee. "Smile. There. That's the way." She handed a cup to Sara. "Sit down. Let's talk for a while."

"Oh, my God! I'm so relieved. You believe us," Cassie blurted out.

"I do. But I need to make a few things clear to the three of you. I sense several spirits in this house. Are you aware of that? We are *not* dealing with one spirit here."

"We know. We . . . "

"Please don't say any more. It's important that you don't misguide me with information. I need to do this myself. I have a few pertinent questions for you, and after we've gotten to know one another a little better, I would like to go through the house. I need to find out the true scope of the haunting. It will take a while to do that. Sometimes the spirits try to hide. They sense I am not afraid of them—therefore, they are afraid of *me*."

From the kitchen, the loud bang of a slamming door made everyone jump—except Terese. "I'm not wanted here, you see," Terese said calmly. She gently put her cup down and walked purposefully toward the dining room. "Stay here! I don't want any interruptions."

Sara, Cassie, and Mary sat frozen. Cassie found her voice. "Through the dining room—through the door to the back . . . "

"Shh. I'll find it." Terese frowned at them, then closed the door behind her.

"Do you think it's safe for her to go alone?" Sara asked. She stood up and ran to the dining room door. Cassie and Mary followed.

"She told us to stay here, we better do as she says," Cassie said.

Sara put her ear against the door. "She's in the kitchen now," she whispered.

Another door slammed. The girls jumped. "Should we go after her?" Cassie asked.

"We better wait. She's used to this, I imagine. She'll call if she needs us," Mary said. "We asked her here; now let her do what she needs to do."

"I hear her on the back servant stairs," Cassie said. "We locked that door not an hour ago! I have the key in my pocket —Terese couldn't have unlocked it."

"That must be what we heard a few minutes ago," Cassie said. "The old couple opened the door and slammed it. To show us we can't keep them out. They must've been really angry that we tried to lock them upstairs."

"I don't hear anything," Sara said, her voice strained. "God, I hope she doesn't go up to the attic alone!" Sara twisted her hair around her finger, a habit that was beginning to reveal itself whenever she got nervous. "We locked that door, too, but I'll bet the Lindemans opened it again."

"Of course they did. Come on, let's sit down and wait. If Terese isn't back in five minutes, we'll go after her," Cassie said picking up her coffee, her hands shaking and rattling the china cup in its saucer. She quickly set it down. *I mustn't show my fear.*

No one sat down though; all three nervously paced back and forth. After several minutes they opened the double doors to the dining room. As soon as they entered the kitchen, they heard heavy footfalls pounding as someone ran down the back stairs. The door flew open.

Terese rushed in, quickly shutting the door behind her and leaning against it. Her eyes were opened wide, her skin glistened with sweat. With a trembling hand she pushed her wavy, silver-white hair off of her damp forehead. "Oh, my!"

"Here, sit down." Sara said as she pulled a chair out from the table and led Terese to it. "Cassie, get her glass of water."

Terese blurted out, "Something stronger would be better, dear. Whiskey if you have any." She smiled wanly. "Don't be too concerned, I'll be fine. I was rather surprised, that's all. I hadn't expected the old couple to be so cunning. I had a nasty encounter with a raccoon on the third floor." She studied the girls' faces. "I sense you know all about this. It's happened before, hasn't it?"

"Oh, my God!" Cassie exclaimed. "Yes, about a week ago and then again today. But Joe and Harry killed the raccoon this afternoon. We saw the body; it was definitely dead."

"There is no shortage of raccoons around here," Terese replied. "One dies and the Lindemans call another here. They're using living raccoons—that makes me a little more comfortable."

"It does?" exclaimed Mary.

"Yes," Terese explained. "I believe it shows the Lindemans have no ability to inhabit a person. You see, some spirits, though quite strong, have limitations. It takes great strength to be able to possess another person. But an animal—that's much easier. The Lindemans appear quite adept at possessing the raccoons, but, so far as I can tell, it seems they are incapable of possessing anything more complex." She stared into the fire and added, "At least that *seems* to be the case." She held her empty glass out to Sara. "Just water this time. I rarely drink alcohol while working."

"Tell us what happened," Sara said. "Is the raccoon still up there?" She looked at Cassie. "We better get Joe out here."

Terese spoke up, "No. I took care of it. I opened a window and chased it out. I locked the window, so it can't get back in. Well, not on its own anyway. Before I leave tonight, I'll bless the property—that will keep the raccoons out. They have a spirit I can easily connect with. I don't think you'll have any more encounters with them."

"So you saw the old man and woman?" Cassie asked.

"Oh, no! They kept well out of sight. But I could sense them. Their presence is quite apparent to me. As it is to you, Cassie." She looked directly at Cassie. "I believe you have seen the old woman. That is what I am sensing from you right now."

Cassie looked startled. "I did. When I first got here. I saw her crying. She seemed incredibly sad. I felt sorry for her. Of course I didn't know at the time she was a ghost. Tom, my brother, said I must have imagined her. I knew better."

"Mary and Cassie, you've had several encounters with these spirits." Cassie and Mary nodded. Terese looked at Sara. "I'm having a more difficult time sensing your interaction with these spirits, Sara. But I do have some strong feelings. For today, I'll go no further with them. I won't give the spirits more insight than I have to. Do you understand?" She waited for the three to nod. "I would like you to walk through the house with me now, take me into every room. I need to see every nook and cranny. Do you feel strong enough to do that?" She studied their faces. "If you're afraid, I can go alone. But having all three of you with me may be helpful. There may be images you have that I'll pick up. They'll be invaluable . . . ," she paused, "in helping me prepare."

"Prepare? For what?" asked Sara.

"The séance," Terese said, then left the room. Mary, Cassie and Sara followed her, each reluctant to go through all the rooms and recesses of Remington House. Each knowing they must.

"I ask that you not speak—at least not to tell me about anything that has happened here. I will perceive those occurrences. However—you *must* tell me if you feel an overwhelming sense of evil. You're all very innocent; you'll feel the evil before I do. I'm somewhat *hardened* to it." Terese turned to look at them. "Agreed?" They nodded.

"Where shall we start?" Cassie asked Terese. "Does it matter?"

Terese replied, "It does. I'd like to start in the attic, and work our way down—floor by floor. We need to run out to my car first; I left my bag in the back seat. I brought flashlights, too. We'll each carry one—in case the lights go out." She opened the front door. "Come with me. We must stay together."

The second they stepped off the porch, the front door slammed. "It's okay! I have the keys!" Cassie said loudly, challenging the Lindemans, who she assumed were the culprits.

"Shh, dear," Teresa cautioned. "Don't engage them. We don't know yet what we're *really* dealing with." She opened the door of her black sedan and removed a large tapestry bag. Unzipping it, she reached in and took out LED flashlights for each of them. "The keys please." She held her hand out to Cassie.

Chapter 87

Elise slammed and locked the door to buy herself time to escape. Almost too late, she recognized that the woman who had arrived at Remington was a spiritualist. She fled out the back door and went in search of Billy. He could amuse her while she waited for the woman to leave. She would stay out of sight as long as necessary. The woman would never know Elise existed. Elise would make sure of that.

Quietly, Elise entered the Harrison house, gliding like a gentle breeze up the winding staircase at the back of the house, down the long hallway and into Billy's room. Her pale complexion, her flowing blonde hair, tiny stature and waiflike smile made her seem entirely harmless and helpless.

Billy smiled and reached his hand out to her. He was mesmerized by her perfume; he inhaled the delicate whiff of an exotic flower he couldn't identify. After all, what eighteen-year-old boy knows the scent of lavender? "How did you get in? The doors are all locked."

"Hmm. Guess someone forgot to lock the back door. We need to leave," Elise whispered softly in his ear. "We can't stay here, someone will hear us. Come; let's go to the cottage down the beach. Where we went before."

Billy grabbed his jacket from the hook on the back of his door. "Let me get you a sweater. Wait here." He quietly entered his mother's room. Even though it was only seven o'clock, Vivian had gone to bed.

She stirred. "Billy? Is that you?"

"Just making sure you're okay, Mom." Pulling the cover around her neck, he bent over and kissed her cheek. "Go back to sleep. I'm going out to check the garage. Someone left the light on. Might go for a walk down on the beach, too. Jimmy and Mannie are here if you need anything." Vivian had closed her eyes again. Quietly, Billy took a sweater from her closet.

Elise was waiting for him at the end of the hall. She smiled sweetly and then sunk her nails into his arm. He winced. "We have to hurry. Your brother's coming," Elise said urgently. They hurried down the back stairs, then ran the entire distance to the stairs leading to the beach. No one saw them. They were down on the shore and on their way to the cottage within minutes. The darkness concealed them, the sliver of a moon still too low to cast any light on the beach. Once they reached the back of the small, white beachfront cottage, Billy turned on a small flashlight. They entered through the backdoor. He had a key. He watched the house for the owners who were in San Francisco most of the year.

While Elise stood shivering just inside the door, Billy lit a fire. As soon as the fire turned a brilliant orange and yellow, Elise, chilled to the bone, lay down on the rug in front of the fire. She was so tired of the seemingly endless cold. She believed she was doomed to never be warm again. The heat from the fire felt soothing on her arms and legs. She began to relax as the numbness in her finger and toes eased. She began to think of other things besides the cold.

Billy lay down next to her. He touched her silky hair and ran his fingers along her cheek, traced her lips before taking her into his arms and pulling her to him.

"Billy," Elise murmured, "are you mine? Are you?" she asked, pushing away and holding his face firmly between her delicate hands. The startled look on his face quickly changed to longing. His blue eyes closed momentarily, his breath came in quick, shallow bursts.

Billy, truly not knowing the full extent of what her words meant, grinned. He only knew that he would soon be screwing a beautiful woman who had made it clear she would be his for as long as he wanted her and would do anything he wanted her to do. "Forever," he whispered into her ear. He rolled her over onto her back and began unzipping his jeans.

"Not so fast, darling boy. We have all night." Elise pulled away. Standing in front of the fire, she slowly began undressing, her skin shimmering in the soft glow as the shadows and fire played across her body. Billy watched mesmerized. Finally she motioned him to come to her. He stood before her, still clothed, waiting for her to undress him. Their night had just begun.

Chapter 88

The attic was pitch black. Not even the moonlight pierced through the heavy clouds. Terese led the way, followed closely by Cassie and Sara. Mary lagged behind, hesitant to go through the attic but afraid to stay downstairs alone. Sara stopped and went back to Mary. Taking her hand she said, "Come on, it's okay."

Cassie turned on the hall light. The low-wattage bulb cast vague shadows on the floor and ceiling. Silently they crept down to the last room on the right. Terese cautiously turned the knob and pushed the door open. The room was empty, the windows still securely closed and locked. There were no raccoons this time to dart out or hiss at them. They entered the room and stood in the center, looking around, uncertain what to expect.

Terese closed her eyes, and spoke in a whisper, "They were here—earlier. I feel a lingering presence. A woman, a man. We have made them exceedingly angry."

The three women waited. Terese's breathing became rapid and shallow. She turned slowly in a graceful pirouette, her arms reaching out, searching. Finally she said, "They have gone, but they are not far away." Opening her eyes, she walked across the room to the closet, turned the knob, pulled the door open. The old, dry hinges squealed.

The three hurried to the closet to stand behind Terese. Sara shined her flashlight into the darkness of the tiny closet. Cassie gasped. On the floor, illuminated in the circle of light, lay a picture of her daughter, Lizzie. She recognized it immediately. It was the framed picture that normally sat on her bedside table. She started to grab it.

Terese stopped her. "Leave it! The girl is safe. There is an aura around her picture."

"That's my daughter's picture. I don't want it here!" Cassie looked imploringly at Terese who was paying no attention to her.

Terese touched the back wall of the closet. Sparks shot out. "There was a struggle here. The energy force is amazing. Even now."

Glancing at Cassie, Terese said, "Your daughter is safe. The force that protects her is very strong. You can be assured no one will harm her."

"Oh God! Is it the old woman? Is Helen Lindeman protecting her?"

Terese closed her eyes again, took several long, deep breaths. "I get no sense of who it is. The energy has dissipated." She closed the door. "There is nothing more here. Let's go to the next room."

"Why does Lizzie need protecting?" Cassie asked Terese.

"I don't know yet. We'll find out, though—in time. Don't worry. Your daughter isn't in any danger. You must trust me, Cassie." Terese took Cassie's hand.

As they walked through the other attic rooms, Terese sensed several spirits, though their presence wasn't as strongly felt as in the first. They continued until they'd investigated every room on the upper floor. On the second floor, Terese sensed the old couple's recent presence. *After all this is their home*, she said to herself. Finally, they returned to the main floor by way of the back servant stairs. Terese was visibly tired, her face pale and drawn.

"Do you need to take a break, Terese?" Sara asked.

"No. I'm okay. I think we should continue. That is, if you three are alright?" Terese studied each of their faces. "We're almost finished, but if you want to stop, I understand."

Mary chewed her lip. She seemed the most frightened of the three. "I don't think I can go into the basement." She paused. "But I don't want to be left up here alone either. Can we just go through this floor and not go downstairs?" she asked hopefully.

"My dear, I completely understand your fears. However, I need to visit each room in this house, especially the basement. I'm sensing a strong power radiating from there. It may be an important key to understanding the haunting." She put her hand on Mary's shoulder. "You don't need to be afraid. I will protect all of you. I am strong, don't you see?" One by one, she placed her right hand on the shoulder of each woman. "Do you feel my strength?" They did . . . and more.

Terese would stop the Lindeman's reign here. But, she knew, with a strong certainty, they would not give up without a fight.

All these things Sara, Mary and Cassie realized as Terese looked deeply into their eyes. With conviction they also acknowledged Terese's strong sense of self. Her spirit was powerful. They had no doubt she could and would prevail.

"Okay, let's go on then," Mary said.

The women, led by Terese, made the rounds of the first floor. Again Terese detected the recent presence of not only the Lindemans, but also of another spirit, one she felt had moved on. "This was a very vile spirit. But weak. Weaker than the old couple who controlled it."

"Can you tell if it was a man or a woman?" asked Sara.

"I have a sense of it being a male entity. I can't tell if it ever was a person though. Perhaps it was a force that lived here before the Lindemans or one that they conjured to be their slave, or perhaps to amuse them."

Cassie asked, "Could it have been a child? Maybe that's why they had Lizzie's picture — they wanted a child around."

"No, this was not a child; there was nothing innocent about this spirit. But it has left this house. I sense it has gone permanently."

It was almost nine o'clock. They had not yet explored the basement. Terese tried to open the door. It wouldn't budge. Terese unlocked it. The lock immediately relocked itself.

"The Lindemans again," Cassie said, nervously licking her lips.

"Indeed it is," answered Terese, who after several useless tries told the women she would ask for assistance from her spirit-guide. Eyes closed, head cocked oddly sideways and upward, Terese spoke in a quiet voice asking for her guide's help. She began moaning and intermittently speaking in a language they could not understand. It sounded oddly familiar, yet no words were recognizable. The syllables seemed soothing and lyrical, like a lullaby heard long ago. All three women had the same sensation. They looked at each other, then back to Terese, who had now opened her eyes.

Terese twisted the doorknob. "Are you ready?"

Mary spoke first, "No, but let's get this over with."

Terese opened the door. They followed her down the steep steps and into the dark basement. There were no lights. Most of the switches had been disconnected and a series of extension cords twisted throughout the rooms.

"Surely we'll find a working switch to end our dark journey," Terese whispered. At the far end of the basement, occasional lights flickered on then off, teasing them.

Cassie tripped on a chord, stumbled and was steadied by Terese's strong grasp. Their flashlights sent bright, white flares of light into the darkness, illuminating piles of wood and debris. They could see where the workers had begun tearing down old walls, could smell the dampness and rot of the old, vacant rooms. Not all the walls had been torn down yet, a job that would probably take several more days. Before them, there seemed to be one very large room with many smaller rooms beyond.

"This most likely will be the gym and the boxing ring," Cassie said, trying to invoke a tone of normalcy to her voice as they entered the largest room.

Sara pulled a string hanging down from the middle of the ceiling; a single bulb suspended on a long wire glowed. Shadows undulated on the cement floor, danced eerily on the walls as the bare fixture swung slowly back and forth. Sara reached up and grabbed the cord that held the dangling light to steady it.

"They are here—the old man and woman. I feel their hatred—dark, vile. You don't need to be afraid, though," Terese said, trying to reassure the three women. "I know how frightened you are of them. I will protect you. I need you to verify your trust in me."

Sara, Cassie and Mary looked at each other, and nodded.

"Good," Terese said. "I am feeling not only their hatred, but their fear. They have lived here for so long. They don't want to leave. This is their home, you see. They are afraid they will lose all of their powers. I have to help them understand that if they move on to their next life, they will be all right, and that leaving here will bring them peace and joy. They don't believe that."

***

Helen and Gabe sneered. *They have their nerve,* they thought in unison. They hovered in the dark recesses of a small room watching the women who had intruded into their basement.

"They will not leave us alone. This has got to stop," Helen hissed.

"Helen, let's get rid of them."

"Patience, dear brother. Let the woman spew her bullshit." Helen laughed wickedly. "Gabe, we must go, go to the light!" She glanced at her brother whose mouth hung wide open. She snarled, "What crap!" In an instant she crossed the room and stood beside Terese. In a voice barely above a whisper, she said, "*We* will not leave this house, Bitch."

Mary gasped and grabbed Cassie's arm. She opened her mouth to speak, but Terese put her finger to her lips. "Shh. Say nothing. You're safe." Then she said to the spirits, "Helen and Gabriel Lindeman, this is no longer your home. You must leave here. I will help you." Terese reached forward and touched Helen's cheek.

Helen, taken completely by surprise, shrieked. No one had ever been able to touch her. No one living, that is.

Mary screamed.

Gabe flew to his sister's defense. He reached up and turned off the light.

"Turn your lights on, girls! Now!" Terese turned on her flashlight.

Though shaken and unsteady, all three managed to do as they were told. Spots of light dotted the floor. Terese shined her flashlight around the room, then down the hallway. The women were no longer standing in the large room but were now at the side door that led to the outside. Terese swept her light around the room, trying to figure out where they were. She must not show her surprise to the girls. Indeed, the old couple had many tricks up their sleeves. She hadn't realized their strength. Beside her, Mary sobbed. Terese gently patted her shoulder.

"What happened? How did we get here?" Sara asked Terese. Sara whirled around and around, the light from her flashlight bouncing crazily off the walls. Terese reached out and grabbed her arm to stop her.

"It's okay," Terese whispered. "The spirit world is very strong. They can deceive us into believing we see what isn't really there."

Mary shuddered, and Sara groaned.

"You're safe with me. I need to hear you say that. Out loud."

No one spoke.

"It's important that the spirits hear your confidence in me. Say it. Now! 'We are safe with Terese.'"

Almost yelling, the three women echoed, "We are safe with Terese!"

"Good. Now keep your lights on and follow me. We must find out where they are living. This way." She began walking down the hallway. In the distance, what seemed to be miles away, a light flickered. Red. Blue. Darkness. Then again it flashed. Red. Blue. Darkness. Again and again. "Stay close," Terese cautioned.

"Count on that!" Cassie said. "Mary, get in front of me. Sara, are you okay?"

"I am but, I think we should find our way back to the stairs. Terese? What do you think?" she asked hopefully.

"Soon. We appear to have a long way to go. Do you see how far away the light is?"

"That's not possible. The basement is *not* that big," Cassie said.

"In reality, you are correct," Terese said. "But we're in an altered dimension right now. I sense you have all experienced this manifestation before. Yes?"

"Yes!" Sara whispered.

"If you'll let me lead you, and trust in me and my wisdom, I'll end this illusion. But first I need to see why these spirits are doing this. I think they are simply trying to keep us from finding where they are living."

"I don't understand," Mary said. "This isn't real?"

"Correct. Soon you will see that," Terese said.

They followed her through the darkness, occasionally stumbling and losing their way as walls would suddenly appear in front of them where none had been before. Terese would stop and tell them to reaffirm their trust in her; the walls would fade, and they would continue on. The flickering light in the distance never got closer. "Don't worry. We are close now." She pointed with her flashlight. "There. You see? Follow me. They have not tricked us, though they tried. Look." She shone her light around a room behind and under the kitchen staircase.

"This is so weird. I still see that light off in the distance. You're sure it's not real?" Cassie asked.

"No, an illusion," Terese said.

All four women shined their lights around, illuminating the small living quarters. The room was about ten feet square. There was a closet at one end, its doors agape. It was filled with piles of old clothes and an open steamer trunk. On the opposite end of the room was a built-in bookcase stacked haphazardly with old leather-bound books coated in mildew and dust. An old bedstead with a brass headboard stood next to the closet.

"Oh, my God. Look!" Sara gasped.

"What is it?" Cassie grabbed at Sara's shoulder, her fingers touching only her sweater when Sara lurched forward.

Sara bent down over the trunk. "Look at this. This is a blanket off of Tom's bed. And look at this. It's my bathrobe. How did they get down here?"

"The old couple, of course," Mary said. She was no longer trembling; her hand was steady as she swept her flashlight around the room.

Terese crossed the room to examine the books. "A diary. Fascinating. I'll need this."

"The Lindemans took that from us! That's the diary Sara and I found," Cassie said excitedly.

Terese reached for the book. She was roughly pushed backward. Grabbing the shelf, she recovered her balance and kept herself from falling. Again she reached to pick up the book. Again she was shoved backwards. Lunging forward one more time, she successfully secured the book. She turned to Sara. "Hurry! Take this." She thrust the diary at Sara.

Sara grasped it, pulled it tightly against her chest.

Terese spun around and grabbed a small, cloth pouch off the shelf. The books on the upper shelf came crashing down, bouncing harmlessly to the floor; dust billowed in the glare of the flashlights.

"I've seen that before," Cassie said, taking the cloth bag from Terese. "It had opium and drug paraphernalia in it. It was in Tom's room—the morning after he got hurt."

"You found opium?" Sara asked, her eyes wide with surprise.

"Tom didn't tell you?" Cassie asked. Sara shook her head. "Of course he didn't. He didn't want to believe it belonged to the Lindemans. He tried to make me believe one of Nell's nieces left it in his room. But I knew it was the old couple's stash. I mean, who else could it belong to? We found some of their drugs in the downstairs bathroom—old prescription bottles with their names on them and old glass bottles with opium in them. We burned the opium—in the kitchen fireplace. The next day, we found this bag in Tom's room."

Terese took the bag. Opening it, she reached in and pulled out a pipe. She sniffed the brown, crusted bowl. "As I suspected. They are very active spirits. They actually imbibe in physical pleasures. I don't see this phenomenon very often. Interesting."

"Are they more dangerous then?" Mary asked. Her hand holding the flashlight started shaking again, the effect being an eerie reflection of light that vibrated on the walls of the dank room.

"Do you really want to know the truth?" Terese asked, staring at Mary. Mary nodded.

"You have to be honest with us," Cassie said facing Terese. "We have to know what we're dealing with. Some pretty scary things have happened here."

"I sensed that—even before I arrived. Yes. They are more dangerous. They are more dimensional than many spirits."

Cassie asked, "Do we need to leave this house? Are we safe?"

"Reasonably," Terese responded. Her hand grasped the heavy pendant hanging around her neck.

"That doesn't sound very reassuring," Sara said. "What the hell does 'reasonably' mean?"

"These spirits are angry. But can they harm you? I don't believe that is their intent. They seem to be running out of places to live, you see? They have been banished from their home where they lived comfortably for years." Terese swept her arms all around. The women listened intently. "When your brother bought the house and moved in, the Lindemans relocated to the attic. Then there was much activity there, so they moved to the basement—to have their privacy. Now, as you know, the remodeling is further limiting them. Once they roamed all the floors of their lovely home." Terese paused, shrugged her shoulders. "Where can they go now? That is their dilemma. They are trying to make you leave."

Terese was confident. For over thirty years she'd dealt with many spirits, some even as strong as these. She hadn't encountered a spirit yet that she couldn't guide into the next realm. "I'll do some research on this family. Next time, with more knowledge, I'll be more prepared to help them on their way. I . . . we, will send them willingly and graciously into the light."

"How?" Sara asked, twisting her hair nervously.

"We'll gather together, we four. In one week we will have a séance and a cleansing ceremony. I will contact these lost spirits on their level. Then together, we will send them away."

***

Helen and Gabe watched and listened. They had much planning to do. But not until they heard the final words that the medium spoke did they realize the difficulty they would soon encounter. Helen grabbed her brother's thin, wrinkled arm. "Brother, what will we do?" Then she laughed and, in true Lindeman form, snaked into a thick, gray mist and wove herself around the ankles of Terese.

***

Terese looked down. She shone her light to the floor, illuminating her feet. Mary screamed and started to run toward the stairs. Terese grabbed her arm. "Stay! You're safe." Terese looked into the eyes of the three women. She commanded, "Say it out loud. Now! 'We are safe with Terese.'"

Cassie, Sara and Mary yelled louder and louder. Releasing her grip on Terese's legs, Helen slithered across the floor and disappeared into the closet. Gabe, now visible to all the women, stared at them, then said each of their names. The names slid off his tongue and into the air like venomous threats.

"Ignore him. Look at me."

"We are safe! We are safe!" they yelled, keeping their eyes glued to Terese's lest Gabe see their fear. Gabe followed his sister into the closet. In a booming voice that resonated throughout the basement, he said, "Good evening, ladies. Until we meet again." He laughed merrily and, with a bow, slammed the closet doors.

The women were violently propelled out of the small room and into the main basement. Grabbing on to each other for balance, everyone managed to stay on their feet. Terese began chanting, her voice loud, lyrical and soothing. Immediately a feeling of calm surrounded them.

The light came on, the bare bulb swung back and forth, back and forth. Shadows danced across the floor and up the bare walls. The basement was once again an old basement filled with piles of wood for construction. Bags of cement lay stacked neatly against one wall. Handsaws, hammers, levels, nails and various tools were scattered everywhere. A workbench with a table saw sat in a corner, a pile of sawdust mounded beneath. All seemed deceptively normal. Their wobbling knees barely supporting them, Sara, Cassie and Mary followed Terese up the stairs. They closed and locked the door though all knew it meant little, the gesture purely one of wishful thinking.

Chapter 89

Sitting at the kitchen table—all the lights on, the fire burning and curtains tightly drawn, the women said little. Mugs of hot tea, a plate of scones and butter sat untouched in front of them. From the basement, sounds from the Lindemans were muffled but clearly audible. They slammed doors, pounded on the ceiling and walls. Their whining screams of laughter echoed up the stairway and through the vents. This continued for about ten minutes and then abruptly stopped.

"They're done now. They're tired. They have expended much energy tonight." Terese rubbed her eyes and pushed a stray strand of silver hair off her face. "I'm tired, too. And you! Look at the three of you. You look like you've seen a ghost!" They laughed. A much needed, soul-cleansing laugh.

"There, you see. It's not as bad as it seems," Terese said, knowing that in the back of their minds, Cassie, Sara and Mary were wondering what would happen next. And when. Teresa spoke very calmly, "They will not bother you again. I'm certain of that. Not until the séance. They'll be on their best behavior until then. They know they have much to fear. They may even leave on their own now that they know they can't stay here."

"I doubt it. Did you see the triumph in the old man's face? He loves this." Sara stood up and threw a small log into the fire. Sparks flew, then settled.

"I don't believe that," Terese said. "That was for show. He has to pretend he's strong. Trust me. I know the spirit world," Terese reassured them. "They are only as strong as we allow. Well, we'll allow no more misbehaving! They may make noises, throw things and knock things over, but I don't believe they will. They *are* afraid." Terese picked up a scone and buttered it.

"So now what? Do we pretend they don't exist?" Cassie asked.

"No, but you don't give them any power over you." Teresa put the scone down. "Should they try to make you notice them, look away. Should they try to touch you, move away. I have something I will teach you. When you are afraid, you will say it out loud."

"What is it? I'm too tired to memorize anything," Cassie said. Sara and Mary nodded.

"It's very simple. You say in a loud but calm voice, looking away from them if they are showing themselves, 'Be gone. I am pure. I am not afraid.' Repeat it over and over until you feel safe. They will not linger. They need your fear to stay strong, don't give it to them." She patted them one by one on the shoulder. "Now, I must go. I'm exhausted. I'll do my homework, and we'll come together next week, next Friday night. At nine o'clock. Just the four of us. Come with me outside while I bless this house—to keep the raccoons away."

A few minutes later, she got into her car, and said her goodbyes. As she started to drive away, she stopped and rolled her window down. "Come here, dears. I almost forgot. I must be tired!" She reached into a tapestry bag on the seat next to her. "Put these around your necks. The stones are red jaspar. Hold them tightly if you need reassurance—or if you are afraid. They have very strong powers." She handed each one of them a silver chain with a dark red stone hanging from the delicate, filigree finding. She rolled her window up and drove off.

"Shall we?" Cassie pointed back to the house. "I vote we go in and show the Lindemans that we're not going to give in to them." She looked at Mary and Cassie. "Agreed?"

"Let's go in then," Sara said, leading the way.

Chapter 90

Bong. Bong. It was two in the morning. The clock's peal echoed in the dark night. "What's wrong, Tom?" Nate hollered down the stairs. From the second floor landing, he'd been observing Tom's odd behavior. Tom was on his hands and knees, his ear pressed to the cold air return. For the past ten minutes he'd crawled across the emptied living room from vent to vent listening intently at each grill. Nate normally would have said something sooner, but there was intensity in Tom's silent, sleuth-like demeanor that Nate knew too well. Nate watched. Finally Tom leaned back, sitting on his heels.

"Tom!" Nate gave in, descended the stairs as quickly as he could, limping noticeably without his crutches.

Tom didn't answer. Nor did he turn to look at Nate. From his pant pocket he pulled a small penlight and swept it along the floorboard. The small beam of light did little to illuminate the darkness. Tom, however, seemed satisfied. He turned the light off and turned toward the doorway into the dining room. His footsteps resounded loudly. He made no attempt to be quiet. As Tom flipped the switch, the room came out of its darkness. He stood motionless, looking into the dining room. Below, in the basement, the *whumpth* of the igniting furnace disturbed the silence. "I've been downstairs," he said. "Someone's been staying down there." He glanced toward Nate. "They've gone. It's been several days at least since he left—not longer than a week."

"What did you say?"

"I found food and a makeshift bed. Magazines, cigarette butts. Pretty sure it was Harold." He looked at Nate. "You never suspected he was here?"

"No! Not for a minute. Oh, shit!" Nate ran his hands through his hair, leaving it sticking out in several directions. "The contractors and workers have been up and down and in and out for weeks. I'm surprised no one else ran into him."

"Your brother's too smart to get caught. Probably stayed away during the day, slept here at night. Anyway, he's been gone a while. Food's dried up. Newspaper's a week old."

"Guess I better let Atwood know. He's had his private eye looking for Harold for weeks. Damn! Right under my nose!" Nate slapped himself on the side of his head.

"Harold must have found out I was coming and skipped. He most likely listened to our phone conversations. At least the calls on the landline." Tom shook his head. "He could hide from you easily enough with your being on crutches and all. It makes perfect sense." Tom looked toward the darkened room beyond the dining room. "Doesn't it?"

"I guess you're right. Find anything missing?" Nate asked, peering into the dining room.

"I don't think so—nothing of value anyhow. Almost everything was already packed and put into storage or shipped to Ravenswood." Tom turned his head, listening and raised his index finger to his lips to silence Nate. He looked toward the back of the house, across the darkened rooms. His hand cupped behind his ear, Tom strained to hear.

Nate whispered, "If Harold is gone, what . . . "

"Shh."

Nate leaned against the wall behind him, his leg was beginning to ache. He listened, too, but heard nothing.

"Go to bed, Nate," Tom whispered.

"Not until you tell me what you're doing. You think someone else is in the house?"

"No one else is here." *No one that you can see.* "I heard water running. It seemed to be coming from the basement, but now I think it's coming from the kitchen. Go on. I'll find it. Maybe the ice maker is the culprit. Wouldn't that be a simple solution?" He waved his hand to dismiss Nate. "See you in the morning."

***

Tom searched all night. "Where is she?" he asked himself over and over. He hunted through all the rooms in the basement, searched the main floor—every room, every closet, every nook and cranny. He found no trace of Elise. Pacing his room until dawn, he finally gave up, lay down on top of his bedspread and slept for a few hours. As he slept, he dreamed of Elise. In his dream she smiled and touched her pale hand to his cheek. She gently kissed his lips and said, "Goodbye." He watched her leave, disappearing into the blackness of the kitchen, beyond the dining room. He woke drenched in sweat.

Where was Elise? He'd been certain she'd follow him here. Now he had to leave for Amsterdam. He had half a mind to cancel the trip. His phone rang. It was Sara.

"Good morning," she said.

Her voice sounded bright and fresh. He missed her. "Good morning. You're up early. Everything okay?" Tom held his breath, waiting for her response.

"It is. Thought I'd call before you left for the airport. I heard the storm is miserable there. Will you be able to get out?"

"Looks like it." Tom looked out the window. The sun was beginning to rise in the east, bringing with it the promise of warmth and melting snow. "I'll call the airport and make sure. It stopped snowing a few days ago, though. Yesterday's melting snow may be a problem. Might be a layer of ice on the streets. I imagine the runways are clear—or soon will be."

"That's good, then," Sara said.

"I'm beginning to think maybe I should forget this trip and come home," Tom said. He stared into the mirror at his reflection. He looked awful. There were black and blue circles under both eyes, his hair was plastered down close to his head, his beard was dark and stubbly. He definitely needed a shower and a shave. "I hate being gone so long. It'll be a week at least."

"Tom, don't worry about anything here. Cassie and I are fine; Joe's working on the basement so he's here most of the time. We're in good hands. Have a good trip and get your business taken care of. When you get back, you won't have to leave again for a long time." He couldn't be at Remington, not until after the séance next week. That was critical.

"You're sure? I can be home by tonight."

"Absolutely certain," Sara said. "Go and don't worry about anything. We're fine."

Outside the sun mirrored itself in a window across the street. Two suns. One orange. One orange and black. Tom watched as a raven flew across the horizon and landed gracefully on a branch of a barren ash tree.

Chapter 91

Vivian awakened late in the morning to the *caw, caw* of ravens gathered in the tree outside her window. She stretched, loving the luxurious feel of the satin sheets against her skin.

There was a knock on her bedroom door. Not waiting for an answer, Mannie pressed the door lever down with her elbow, used her left foot to push the door open. She came in carrying a tray with a carafe of coffee, a china plate piled with melon and a single bagel slathered with cream cheese. "Morning. Did you sleep well?"

"I did, Mannie. I feel like a new woman." She flashed a big smile, "I feel like my old self today." She threw the covers back and got up slowly from the soft feather-bed. "Umm, that coffee smells wonderful. Thank you. You always take such good care of me."

"Well, Child, you know I love you. And those boys of yours. That's what I think about most of the time. You and your boys."

"Where are they? Are they still asleep?" Vivian took a bite of her bagel, chewed slowly while Mannie poured coffee, adding a splash of cream.

She handed the cup to Vivian. "Billy, he's still sleeping. Haven't heard a peep out of him. Jimmy is up and gone. Couple hours ago he blew past me like the wind. Going to the beach he said. To find some special seashells for you."

Viv smiled again. "Hmm. That's nice. Billy must have stayed out late again. I worry about him. That boy, he's so charming and handsome. I think he has a girlfriend. I hope he's careful. I don't know who she is—the girl I keep seeing him with. He won't talk to me about her." She walked to the window, looked down across the beach below. Jimmy was running along the shoreline, a bucket swinging in his hand. A cat ran behind him, seemed to be chasing him. She motioned to Mannie.

"Look at that boy. Not a care in the world." Vivian pushed the curtain open a little farther. "Where did that cat come from? Jimmy didn't bring a stray home did he?"

"No, m'am. That's Mr. Gardner's cat. That boy sure took to it. That cat follows Jimmy around all the time. Never seen anything so cute, have you?"

"Well, just make sure that cat stays out of the house. I don't need cat fur all over the place. You hear me?"

"Yes, m'am. I do. But you have to admit, it's a wonderful sight." Mannie turned away and began making the bed. As she was straightening the comforter, the phone rang. "Hello, Harrison residence." She listened, and then said, "Yes, sir, Mr. Harrison, I'll put her on right away." She handed the phone to Vivian. "It's Mr. Harrison." She began to back out of the room. "I'll leave you alone."

When the door had closed, Vivian put the phone to her ear. "William! You bastard! Where have you been?"

"Calm down, dear. You know I'd have called if I could have. I've been in one endless meeting after another. I flew into New York yesterday, met with a client, and now I'm on my way to Amsterdam to take care of the new partnership I told you about."

"I don't care about that! Why aren't you *here*?" Vivian raised her voice, stopping just short of yelling. She stood up and kicked the side of the bed with her bare foot. *Ouch!* She sat down, massaging her big toe.

"This is all for you," William said curtly. "And the boys. You know that."

"I know no such thing. I know I need you here. Please, William, come home."

He could picture Vivian perfectly—her full red lips pouting, her green eyes rimmed with tears. He wanted her desperately, that much was certain. William wished he could be with her right now. Lay her back on the bed; undress her, maybe not so slowly, maybe he'd be tearing her clothes off and . . .

"William! Talk to me. Don't you dare ignore me!"

Timing. Damn. He felt his hard-on shrink. "Vivian, I have an idea. Why don't you fly to Amsterdam? You could be here by Tuesday, and we could spend a few days together. I'll get the penthouse suite at the Westin Arms. We can be together, just the two of us. I miss you. I want to show you how much."

"What about the boys?" she teased. "Would you like me to bring them, too?"

"Not this trip. You come . . . only you . . . for a few days. Then you can go home to Boston if you like, maybe spend some time with your friends. You must miss them."

"I do. But right now, I miss you. I need you, Willy."

William smiled. "Come to Amsterdam then. I'll buy the sapphire ring I promised you. How does that sound?" He imagined her lovely, sensuous face brighten, sensed her happiness. She did love him. He knew she did.

"Will you, Willy? Show your Vivian how much you've missed her?" she giggled, lying back on the bed.

"I will, darling. You know it! And we'll go out on the town. I'll show my beautiful wife off to the city. Will you come?"

"Yes, yes, yes! I can't wait. Can you have Sally book my flights?"

"Right away. Will you make sure that Sara will stay with the boys?" William asked. Vivian said nothing. "Okay?" he asked again.

"Oh, well . . . " she paused for a second, " Mannie and Amos are here. William, I really would rather Sara didn't stay here while I'm gone. She's been horrid to me. You know that. I won't come if you insist that she stays here." Vivian made certain, by her tone of voice, that William understood this was not negotiable.

"Okay, but at least let her check on them. Promise?" William sighed, knew he was being manipulated, but actually didn't care. Sara wasn't his relative after all. Let Vivian have her way. He needed to get Viv away from the pressures she was under. And—he needed her, too. He loved her. If she was with him, he could see what was really going on with her. Maybe it was nothing but the damned headaches and stress from his being away so long. And if Dr. Barnes was giving her narcotics again, he'd have a serious conversation with the son of a bitch. He knew she couldn't handle them.

"Are you listening to me, William?"

"I am."

"I was thinking about how much I miss you. I was beginning to think you didn't care about me anymore."

"Oh, Vivian, I'm so sorry." He pounded his hand against his thigh. "It's this fucking business deal. It's almost finished, though. I promise you. I'll get it wrapped up in the next few weeks."

"I've been so afraid, Willy. No one understands me like you do. Will you take care of me? I need to know how much you love me. I need to have you hold me and tell me you'll never let me go." Vivian was crying, her voice soft, broken.

"Vivian, it's okay. I'll take care of you. In a few days we'll be together." He waited for her to answer him. She was silent. "All right?"

"William, I was afraid I might be losing my mind."

He caught his breath. "What did you say?" he whispered, holding the phone pressed tightly to his ear, his lips touching the mouthpiece.

Vivian said quickly, "Never mind. It's okay. I . . . "

William paced the floor. Outside his hotel window, the sun began to burn through the gray clouds that had covered the sky for the last several days, blanketing Jamestown with several feet of snow. "You get packed up. We'll have a nice relaxing vacation together and then we'll go home to Boston and send for the boys. Okay?"

"Okay," she said, her voice so subdued, he could barely hear her.

"Are you positive you're all right, Vivian? Maybe you shouldn't come to Amsterdam. I can call Dr. Barnes." He swallowed hard, wiped the perspiration that had gathered on his brow with the back of his hand. "You could go to Boston, maybe check into the hospital again—and rest. I'll take care of my business and be back to the states in a week or so."

"No! I need to be with you. I feel really good today. It's this house, the headaches, being alone. That's all."

"Viv, be honest with me," he pleaded.

William heard Vivian take a shallow breath. In a voice too light and too bright, she said, "I'll be fine. I've had a lot of migraines lately and took too many pills." She laughed. "Silly me. I should know better."

William said sternly, "You *should* know better. You can't let yourself rely on pills."

"Willy, I'm so aware of that now. Dr. Harrison was so helpful," she said. "I had a little relapse, that's all. It won't happen again. I'm better now. Talking to you is so good for me. I need you—that's all."

"I can't wait to see you either. Listen, I have to go now, Viv. I'll have Sally get your flights booked and call you. I need to pack and get to the airport, or I'll miss my flight."

"I know, Willy. Don't worry about me. I'm fine now that I've talked to you. I'll see you in a few days. Will you call me when your flight lands? Please?" she asked almost shyly.

"I will. You get some rest, and make sure you eat. I know you. You don't take care of yourself. I'll see to that myself in a few days. Love you. I have to go."

The line went dead. Vivian smiled and stretched her arms out on the down comforter."I'll be okay now. Willy will take care of me." She dabbed at the tears that trickled down her cheeks.

Elise sat beside Vivian, resting her head on the soft down pillow. She too smiled. While Vivian was gone, she would stay here. She'd enjoy the warm feather bed, the silky satin sheets against her skin. She sighed, but Vivian, lost in her own thoughts, did not hear her.

Chapter 92

The taxi driver raced through the streets of Jamestown, trying to make up for lost time. An overturned truck, victim of the icy road conditions, had delayed traffic for almost an hour. Tom, sitting with William in the back seat of the cab said, for maybe the third time, "Don't worry, Will. We'll be at the airport in plenty of time. The flight's delayed, too. Ice on the runway."

Will muttered something Tom couldn't understand. Will was talking on his cell, had been for most of the cab ride. Will nodded and smiled, covered the mouthpiece, said, "Thanks, Tom." He went back to his conversation with the person on the other end of the phone. "Expect me to take over. As soon as I arrive. Give me a few hours, then tell . . . " Will turned his head away and Tom heard no more of the conversation.

Tom dreaded the long flight to Amsterdam. He sat back and closed his eyes. He was dead tired. He'd spent most of last night wandering through his house in Jamestown searching for Elise. What game was she playing?

***

In the cramped airline seat beside Will, Tom mumbled and jerked fitfully in his sleep. Will studied the sleeping man next to him. Tormented. That was his impression of this suave, well-educated, highly successful man. *I certainly hope his demons don't interfere with this business venture.*

The pilot announced cold weather in Amsterdam, 40 degrees and rainy, with wind gusts of 30 miles per hour.

"Tom! We're here." Will nudged him.

Tom, startled, sat up abruptly, hitting the seat in front of him with his knees. The woman in front turned and glared at him.

"Sorry," Tom said crossly to her. She turned back around.

"Fasten your seat belt please," the stewardess admonished the woman, "We're about to land." She smiled coyly at Tom, then hurried down the aisle to take her own seat.

Looking at William, Tom ran his fingers through his hair, straightened and buttoned his suit jacket. He said, "Hope you hadn't planned on having company this last leg of the flight. I was bushed. Did you get some sleep yourself?"

"I did. I slept for several hours. Though not exactly my idea of a sound sleep. Better than nothing, until we get to our hotel, I guess. So this is your first visit to Amsterdam?"

"It is. I see the weather here looks much like what we left in Jamestown. Look," Tom pointed out the window, "it's starting to snow."

"It won't last long. Kind of unusual, but oh well, we won't be outside much. I've booked a small meeting room at the hotel for tomorrow morning." The men stood up, wrestling their bags from the overhead.

Tom hesitated, turned back around, reached under his seat and pulled his briefcase out. "Almost forgot it. I better wake up. Don't need to lose this baby. Laptop's in it."

"That'd be a nightmare wouldn't it," Will said.

The woman in the seat in front of Tom pushed into the aisle ahead of him, knocking him sideways. He grabbed the seat back and righted himself. She smiled and said sarcastically, "Oh, excuse me," then pushed in front of William.

From the look on his face, William was obviously aggravated, but said nothing. He let her pass and continued down the aisle. When they were off the plane and in the airport waiting area, he said to Tom, "Just got a text message from Jonathan, my driver. He's delayed. Let's have a drink in the lounge while we wait.

Chapter 93

The time passed quickly. Vivian left Ravenswood Sunday morning. She would stay with friends in New York and then fly on to Amsterdam. She would arrive on Tuesday, having been awake for thirty-six hours, with a raging migraine. Being true to her husband, having promised him she wouldn't take any medication, she did not. Instead, she suffered through the migraine, praying for the pain to ebb. She spent her long flight with a cold pack on her neck, her head covered with a wool scarf, staring out the window into the dark, clouded sky. The jet plane cut through clouds that looked like black, roiling smoke.

***

Once in Amsterdam, Vivian would experience some serious, shall we say, *mood changes.*

On that same evening, when he picked her up from the airport, William would find his wife, Vivian, much changed. He would agree with her own earlier comments that she *may be* losing her mind.

Tom would spend several days learning everything he possibly could about the operation of William Harrison's diamond exporting business. Leaving Amsterdam several days earlier than originally planned, he would fly into Jamestown and stay at the family home—certain he would find Elise there. He was wrong, of course. She had never intended to follow Tom to Jamestown. On a Friday night, the night of the séance at Remington House, Tom would realize his error. So tragic to be far from home when you have an emergency. But maybe it was for the best. Who knows what could have happened had he been at Remington House with "the girls."

Billy and Elise would be having a wonderful time at the Harrison Mansion on that Friday evening. They had the house to themselves. It was fun for a while, until Elise realized how tired she was of the situation she was in with her young paramour.

Mannie and her husband, Amos, had gone to dinner in town to meet Sheila, one of their daughters, and her future husband, Marv. They were meeting at the Parker House where steaks, grilled to perfection and spinach salad served with warm honey-mustard dressing, were Mannie's favorite. Her husband ordered his favorite—country-fried steak with mashed potatoes, smothered in creamy, country gravy. They, too, would have a wonderful evening.

Jimmy would stay in town with his friend, Tony. Tony was Mary's youngest sibling. Lizzie, too, was sleeping over at Mary's mother's house with Evie—where Lizzie had stayed last week when Terese Montagna met with her mother, Cassie and "the girls" to discuss "the ghosts." (Of course, Lizzie knew none of this.) The four children were having a blast. Mary's mother had rented *Willy Wonka and the Chocolate Factory* and ordered two extra-cheese and pepperoni pizzas from Gino's, the local pizzeria—a favorite of almost everyone in Ravenswood, everyone who loved authentic deep-dish pizza, that is.

Joe would stop work on the basement at five and take the crew to the Raven Café for a burger and beer. He forgot his cell phone; it was in his jacket on the workbench in the basement of Tom's house. Every few minutes, beginning about nine that night, it would ring and ring, then go to voice mail. So Joe's evening would be fine.

Harold would plan on a quick burger, compliments of Joe, washed down with a tall brew followed by a quick screw in the back seat of Joanie's car while she was on break from her shift at the café. Then long about eight he planned on a quick trip to Remington House to break into Tom's safe, then back to town to meet up with Joanie. He would not finish the final task.

Joanie would plan to meet Harold outside of town on the highway with her bags packed. Harold had borrowed her car and had said "it's none of your business what I want it for!" He said this while they were in the throes of passion, her legs pinned over her head, her boobs flattened by the weight of her new stud. Nobody had made her feel this way. Ever! She couldn't refuse him—could she? He told her he was leaving town. She begged him to take her with him. She promised Harold she wouldn't be any trouble, would do anything he wanted her to do. "Just get me out of this town. Please? Besides," she said, "I kind of like you, and we kind of seem to fit each other, know what I mean?" She had grabbed his butt and thrust him further into her. He said okay. But he never showed up. At midnight she walked back to her sleazy little apartment on Main Street and cried herself to sleep. That car had cost her six months of her tips.

Hidden in the basement, Helen and Gabe would hold a private ceremony to prepare themselves for the ensuing battle.

And at Remington House, the séance, attended by Cassie, Sara, Mary and Terese would begin promptly at nine. Their evening would be a nightmare. Until Terese arrived, they busied themselves lighting a fire in the dining room, taking the leaf out of the table to collapse it to a small, round, intimate table.

Later they would all hold hands, sitting close together around the table with candles glowing and faces rosy from the warm flames of the fire burning as apple logs crackled, cinders popped in explosions of red and bright orange. From the front porch, anyone looking in would think they were having a wonderful evening.

Harold would think that as he peered into the dining room window, right before he headed around the side of the house to let himself in the backdoor. He had a key, made from Joe's set of keys, the day he ran into town in Joe's pickup to get wood and more wood screws. The screws the store had sent with an earlier delivery were too short to adequately secure the thick wood being used for the floor of the boxing ring. Joe wanted to make sure they did it right. Harold had whistled as he inserted the key into the dead bolt and heard the *thunk* as the tumblers released. He pushed the door open and silenced his whistling.

Chapter 94

William sat in the cab waiting for Vivian's plane to taxi to the terminal from the runway. The flight had been delayed because of turbulence over the Atlantic. The plane now sat stacked up behind several other jets. Vivian called him from the tarmac, told him the pilot expected they would be delayed another thirty minutes. Taking a sip of scotch from his antique silver flask, William leaned back, closed his eyes, and let the smooth, perfectly blended scotch do its job. It was times like this he so appreciated what money could buy. He momentarily dozed off, was awakened by the gentle chiming of his cell phone. "Hello?" He didn't recognize the number that flashed on his screen.

"William, Tom Gardner here. Have I called at a bad time?"

"Not at all." William sat up straighter, rested his forehead against the cool of the side window. "I'm at the airport. Picking up my wife actually. Her flight's delayed. Right now I'm sitting in a cab watching strangers flag down taxis. What's on your mind, Tom?"

Oh, shit. No way! Vivian's here? Tom dropped his head into his hands.

"Tom, are you there?"

"Yes, sorry, my phone cut out. I called to see what time you wanted to meet tomorrow. I have some financials I want you to look at."

"Give me the morning, can you? I haven't seen my wife for weeks. I'd like to get her settled. We can get together at the hotel restaurant for lunch, if that works for you. About one o'clock?" William asked.

Tom wiped the perspiration from his forehead, then wadded his handkerchief into his fist. "That's fine. My attorney finished the new contract as well. He added the clauses you asked for, so I'll have the final version for you to sign tomorrow. John's having it shipped by one day express. Will you have time to go over that, with your wife here?" William better have the time. Tom wanted this business finished; he wanted to get back to the States.

"It'll be fine. I'll meet you at one. I'll make a reservation as soon as I get back to the hotel. Maybe Vivian will join us for coffee after we've finished our business. I know she'd be happy to see you."

"So you told Vivian about our business venture? She's okay with you taking me on as a partner?"

"No, I didn't tell her. I seldom discuss my business with Viv. It's really none of her concern." Will laughed and added, "All Viv worries about is my bank account."

"I have to warn you, Will, Vivian may not be too eager to have me as your partner."

"Not to worry. As I said, Vivian has no say when it comes to my business. Listen, I have a call coming in from her right now. Her plane must be in. See you tomorrow."

Tom said goodbye and snapped his phone closed. He leaned back against the plush velvet headboard of the hotel bed. He thought for a minute, then he called Nate. "Nate, book me a flight home tomorrow evening. I have a meeting with William Harrison at one. As soon as that's finished, I want to get back to Jamestown."

"Sure, I'll take care of that. I'll call you back as soon as I get your flight information."

"And Nate?"

"What, Tom?"

"I don't want anyone to know I'm back. I'd like to have some time to myself at the house."

The line crackled, threatened to disconnect, then cleared. "You want me to leave, too? I could stay with my sis for a day or two."

Tom knew from the tone of Nate's voice he was not happy at the prospect. But Tom knew he needed to be alone. "I'd appreciate that. I hate to ask it of you, but what with the house being sold and finalized next week, I could use some time to go through everything. Lay my memories to rest, if you know what I mean." Tom was pacing his hotel room. He had a glass of ice ready and poured it to the rim with vodka.

Nate answered, "Sure, Tom. But I don't know if being alone here is the best place for you to be right now."

"I'll be fine. Listen, I have to go. Call me when you get the reservation made." He hung up leaving Nate speaking to a dead phone.

Nate was saying, "I don't think you should be here . . . " when the phone beeped, signaling the end of the conversation. "Alone," he finished his sentence.

***

Vivian looked horrible. William was shocked when he saw her. She teetered toward him, seeming ready to collapse. He rushed to her, offering his arm for support. "Here, honey, let me help you. Are you all right?" he asked as he led her to a bench, away from the crowds filing off the planes.

She tried to smile, instead began to cry. "I'm exhausted, Willy. I need to get to bed. I haven't slept for days. I've had this horrible migraine. You can't imagine how awful I feel. Please get me out of here."

He frowned, seeing how pale she looked, how delicate. "Let me find a wheelchair or something. You don't look like you can walk all the way to the cab. Stay right here." He ran to the flight check-in counter, barging in front of the line of people waiting for seating assignments. "My wife is ill; would you call someone to help us?"

While they waited, Vivian slumped down in the seat. A paramedic, medical bag in hand, came hurrying down the terminal hallway. He checked Vivian's vital signs and determined she was in no danger. "I believe she's fine—probably dehydrated and overly tired." Pulling a bottled water from his bag, he told her to drink it, then radioed for a wheelchair. After cautioning William to call Vivian's doctor as soon as she was back at the hotel, the paramedic left William to wheel Vivian out. William found a porter and gave him the location of the cab with a promise of a large tip when he brought them her luggage.

William and Vivian sat in the cab waiting for the porter. William massaged her neck and got her to take several sips of water. By the time the porter arrived, Vivian had fallen asleep.

She didn't wake up until they arrived at the hotel. "Vivian, we're here. Wait while I get someone to bring a wheelchair," William said, gently nudging her shoulder. Some color had returned to her face, and he was much relieved.

"I'm okay now. I don't want to make a spectacle. Let me walk." Vivian pulled her scarf up, hiding most of her face. Leaning heavily against William, she walked with him to the elevator. Their suite was on the eighteenth floor, and the ride up seemed incredibly slow. Once he got her into the penthouse, he undressed her and tucked her into bed. William lay beside her for several hours, holding her, wishing he were a better husband. How could he allow this to happen to her? Stroking her hair, he listened to her breathing even out, and in the dim light, observed the deep lines in her forehead diminish. When she began to snore very softly, as was her norm, William got up. Sitting in an overstuffed chair, he sipped a glass of scotch and watched Vivian sleep. When his head began to nod, he got up, undressed and climbed into the bed beside his sleeping wife. William did not wake when, several hours later, Vivian got up and quietly left the room.

The gentle chiming of the phone broke into his dreams. William reached for it on the night stand. "Hello? Who is this?"

"Mr. Harrison. This is Hugo Declercq, the night concierge. I am so sorry to wake you at this early hour, but I have Mrs. Harrison here with me. Could you come right away, to the front desk? I'll have the clerk bring you to my office. "

William threw on his clothes and ran for the elevator. At the front desk, the night-clerk took him down a hallway behind the main counter. He pointed to a closed door, the light visible through the frosted glass. "Mr. Harrison, go right in. Mr. Declercq is expecting you."

When he opened the door, the concierge stood up, extending his hand."Mr. Harrison. Come in." He led William into another office. "This is your wife, sir?" Vivian sat in an overstuffed, wingback chair. Her head lay against the back cushion. She stared across the room not seeming to notice William or the concierge.

William hurried to her. "Vivian, what's the matter? Are you all right?"

She turned her head to look at him. She smiled and her face brightened. "Hello, Willy. Where have you been? I've been looking all over for you. I really would like to get back to the room now. I don't know why you left me waiting so long," Vivian rambled, struggling to get to her feet. "Where have you been?"

"I'm here now, that's all that matters." William took her cold and limp hands into his.

"She was trying to get into a taxi with another couple," Declercq began to explain. "The gentleman was very kind and brought her back into the hotel. As you can see, she certainly is not dressed for a trip to the airport. Thank goodness for that," he pointed at her bare feet and her nightgown, "or she may have succeeded in getting a ride to the airport."

"Vivian, where were you going?"

"To find you. I thought you had gone back to New York. Why did you leave me here?"

"Sweetheart, I didn't go anywhere. I was right there in the hotel room. In bed next to you. Didn't you see me?"

"I don't remember. No, I was never in a hotel room. I'm so confused." She began to weep, covering her face with her trembling hands.

"It's because of your migraine, sweetheart. You haven't been well. Come on; let me take you back to our room." He took her hands from her face, pulled a handkerchief from his pocket and wiped her cheeks. "Thank you," he said to Hugo Declercq. "I would appreciate your discretion. My wife has been ill. She hasn't slept for days. I'm sure you understand." He handed Declercq two fifty Euro bank notes.

"Certainly," Declercq answered, handing the bills back to William. "There's no need. I can see your wife is not well. I would never say anything to anyone about this. I will send the hotel physician to your suite if you like. Yes?"

"Thank you. Yes, send him right away."

Several hours later, around four am, Vivian had been examined by the physician who also arranged for a private nurse to be sent to help care for Vivian so William could get some sleep.

By morning, Vivian had shown little improvement. Her headache had lessened somewhat in severity, but she remained confused as to where she was or who was around her. The hotel physician called at eight. After hearing of her continued distress, he made arrangements to have her admitted to the hospital for testing. The nurse gave Vivian a warm bath and hot chamomile tea, followed by a neck and back massage. Vivian finally slept, though fitfully.

***

William called Tom at nine. "Tom, listen, I have a problem. Vivian's not well. I wondered if we could cancel lunch today, maybe just meet for coffee, and sign the contracts. If Vivian's better tomorrow, we'll have lunch then."

"I'm sorry to hear she's sick. Anything I can do to help?" Tom asked.

"No, she has a history of migraines, and this one seems to be a real doozy. I think everything will be fine in a few days, though. I worry because she's pretty near exhaustion."

"I'm very sorry. If it'd be easier, come to my room later. I'll make sure the papers are all ready, and we'll settle our business quickly. What time works?"

"Let me call you back in a while. I'm taking Vivian over to the VU Medical Center. I'll call you as soon as I have her settled. They're going to try a caffeine drip and see if that helps before they do anything else. They prefer I not stay with her, so she can get more rest. If there's no improvement, they'll do tests."

"I've never heard of a caffeine drip before. Interesting," Tom said.

"Me either, but . . . We'll see. If it helps, it's much easier on Vivian; she's so frail right now," William explained. He couldn't tell Tom about Vivian's history with drug abuse because of her headaches. But Dr. Hendrickx understood and agreed to treat her without narcotics, to try alternative treatments.

"Call me when you're on your way," Tom said.

"Thanks, Tom. I'll talk to you later."

Before he could hang up, Tom quickly added, "William, something came up this morning with a real estate deal, and I have to take care of it as soon as possible. I need to get back to Jamestown. I'm taking a flight out this evening. You need to be with Vivian—you'll be relieved not having me around." Tom was thankful he would escape without seeing Vivian, though he felt horrible that she was still having so much trouble with her migraines.

"Well, we've taken care of most of our business anyway— once we sign the final papers this afternoon. I'll be back in Boston in a few weeks, we'll talk more then," William said.

"Absolutely."

"I'll call you later," William said, then hung up.

Chapter 95

Once checked in and settled into a room at the VU Medical Center, Vivian became more and more agitated. "God! What did she do to me? My head! Oh, it hurts so much. Willy, why did she do this?" Vivian pulled at her hair, tears streamed down her cheeks. "Why won't it stop?"

William pushed the call button hanging from the chord on the edge of the bed. "Vivian, honey, try to relax. You'll be fine. I swear to you that the nurse didn't do anything. She's trying to help you."

Vivian pulled at the IV taped to her hand. William took her free hand. "The IV will help hydrate you. Give it a little time; it'll make you feel better. They've added caffeine to the fluids, that's why you feel so jittery. It's supposed to help with the pain. Roll over on your side and I'll rub your neck." Vivian refused, so William massaged her shoulder, hand and arm.

"Make them give me something to stop the pain."

"I can't let them give you any drugs. You know that." As he continued his massage, William was acutely aware of the tension in her frail body, it felt like a tightly- strung bow.

"Why is she doing this to me? What did I ever do to her?" Vivian grabbed William's hand, her nails dug painfully into his skin.

"The nurse didn't do anything to you, Vivian. She's trying to help you."

"Not the nurse! Sara!"

"What are you talking about, Vivian?"

From the doorway, the nurse cleared her throat. "You needed something?" She walked in, her rubber-soled shoes squeaked on the hard vinyl tile.

Vivian shouted, "I need something for the pain. I can't stand it anymore! I'll go crazy if you don't give me something." She pushed William's hand away. "Willy, you have to find out what Sara did to me. She gave me something! And that damned woman, Elise. She kept sneaking into our house. She didn't think I knew, but I did. They've been giving me drugs. I know it!"

"Vivian, what are you talking about? Who is Elise?"

"Tom Gardner's wife. He said she was dead. But she's not. She's helping Sara drive me crazy."

"What! Why would they want to do that?" William asked, keeping his voice calm and soothing. He gently pushed the hair out of her eyes.

"I don't know why!" she screamed and grabbed William's hand.

The nurse took Vivian's blood pressure. "Take a few deep breaths, Mrs. Harrison. You need to calm down" She removed the cuff and gently patted Vivian's arm. "I'll go find Dr. Hendrickx. I'll be right back."

William sat on the edge of the bed holding Vivian's hand. She sobbed loudly, inconsolably.

Dr. Hendrickx, followed by the nurse, hurried into the room. "Mr. Harrison, would you wait outside please," he said briskly, dismissing William with a flick of his hand. The nurse closed the door behind Will.

William paced the hallway, turning every time he heard a door open, anxious beyond belief about his wife. *I'm afraid she's losing her mind. There's no other explanation.*

"Mr. Harrison, Dr. Hendrickx would like to talk with you." The nurse took a few steps toward William. "You can wait down there." She pointed down the corridor to a sunroom filled with black plastic chairs, faux wood tables and several tall potted ferns. William did as he was told. A coffee pot sat empty. The odor of burnt coffee hung in the air. William slumped down in the chair, head in his hands, his body molding to the shape of the hard plastic.

The doctor didn't keep William waiting long. William stood as Dr. Hendrickx extended his arm, shook his hand with a firm grip. "Mr. Harrison, let's sit down shall we?"

"Is Vivian all right?" William's face was tense, his brow furrowed with worry, his jaw clenched.

"I had the nurse give her a mild sedative. Mrs. Harrison was so anxious that I had concerns she would spiral completely out of control." He flattened a tuft of unruly hair on his graying temple and smiled. "Mr. Harrison, I think your wife will be fine. I've scheduled some tests, as you already know. The orderly will be coming to take her downstairs any time now." He looked down the hallway as the elevator door opened. "Yes, that's him now."

"What do you *think* is wrong with her?" William asked, watching the orderly wheel a gurney into Vivian's room.

"Based on the information I have thus far—and after spending a few minutes with her—I suspect she's going through withdrawal from her pain medications. The severe migraines she's having can be a result of this. Her confusion, agitation, all these things tell me her dependency was likely greater than you realized."

"I never suspected she was taking narcotics again, or certainly I would have done something. She's been through this before—to a lesser degree—but she never hallucinated or showed this kind of paranoia." William unbuttoned the top button of his shirt, rubbed the back of his neck. "I've been traveling on business for the last eight weeks. Regretfully, I had no idea she was back on prescription drugs. I should have picked up on it."

"Well, the important thing is that she's here where we can take care of her. We'll run a fairly extensive series of tests today. There are a few things that need to be ruled out. Then if my suspicions are correct, we will begin treatment for her drug abuse." He glanced down the hallway toward Vivian's room. "Right now the best thing you can do is to reassure her before they take her downstairs." Dr. Hendrickx stood up. "There she is now. Let's do what we can to calm her."

Vivian was actually quite relaxed; her eyes were half closed, her hands limp on the gurney. William took her hand in one of his, with his other hand he stroked her hair. She managed a slight smile.

"Hi, darling, are you feeling a little better now?" William asked.

"A little. They gave me a shot, and my headache is starting to go away. I'm going to go with this handsome young gentleman," she smiled demurely at the orderly, "to have some tests done. Are you coming with me, Willy?"

William looked at Dr. Hendrickx, who explained, "Mrs. Harrison, your husband can't come with you, but as soon as we've finished the tests, he'll join you back in your room."

"Mr. Harrison, the tests will take several hours. I suggest if you have something to do, you go on about your business. We'll call you when your wife is ready to go back to her room."

"Willy, I'm interfering with your work, aren't I? Don't worry about me. I'll be fine." She smiled coldly at him. "By all means, Willy, take care of your business. Go."

"I'd stay with you if I could." William squeezed Vivian's hand. "I have my phone with me if the hospital needs to get hold of me. I'll be here when you get back." He leaned over and gently kissed her forehead. "I know Dr. Hendrickx will find out what's causing your headaches and all your confusion. A day or two of rest, and you'll be fine. I can't wait to show you the sights in Amsterdam."

The orderly wheeled Vivian into the elevator. "Bye, darling, don't worry about me." She lifted her head and glared at William.

William stared at the closing doors.

"Mr. Harrison, we'll get to the bottom this." Dr. Hendrickx was paged over the loud speaker. "I have to go. If we need to get in touch, we'll call. Most likely you won't hear from us until Mrs. Harrison is back in her room."

"Okay. Sure." William still stared at the elevator doors.

"I'd like to keep her here tonight, so we can continue to hydrate her. I'll administer a mild sedative to keep her quiet and relaxed. She really needs rest. If that is agreeable?" Dr. Hendrickx waited for William's response.

"Of course. Is it safe to give her more drugs?"

"Completely. These are non-narcotic. She needs sleep." Dr. Hendrickx patted his shoulder, extended his hand to William, then turned and walked to the nurse's station to answer his page. William went in the other direction toward the elevator.

William's cell phone rang. It was the concierge from the hotel. "A package was delivered to the front desk. I'll have it sent up to your room right away if that's what you wish."

"I'm not at the hotel right now. Could you tell me who the sender is?"

"Yes." There was a pause. "Here it is. It's from Jonathan Atwood, Attorney at Law. His address is in Jamestown, New York."

"Listen, would you call Tom Gardner? He's in room 508. Tell him I asked you to have the package sent up to him.'

"Yes, Mr. Harrison. Should I call you when I've reached him?"

"No, I'll be in touch with Mr. Gardner later. Goodbye."

Chapter 96

The meeting between Tom and William was over by two that afternoon. William returned to his room to make some business calls. Tom's flight wasn't until early evening so he packed his suitcase, called a cab and spent the next several hours at the airport lounge. His flight was fairly uneventful, though he was surprised to see the woman who had so rudely stepped in front of him when he left the plane in Amsterdam. She sat across the aisle in the window seat. Occasionally, she caught his eye, and she glared at him. Several hours into the flight, Tom fell asleep. Later, when he awoke, the woman was sitting next to him.

"You don't remember me, do you?" she asked when he turned to look at her.

"I do. We were on the same Amsterdam flight last week. Small world." Tom pulled the blanket up under his chin and closed his eyes. He wanted nothing to do with this woman.

"Not what I meant!" She scowled at Tom when he opened his eyes and looked at her, dismayed at her intrusion. "Not surprised," she snarled at Tom when he didn't say anything. "I find this charade very distasteful. I don't know why I expected anything different. Why would I expect a man to like you to change? It's always been about you. Hasn't it?" She pushed Tom's elbow off the armrest.

Oh, God! Another psycho. Heaven help him. Tom pulled his arm in to his side, turned his head away, ignoring her. He covered his face with the blanket letting the sound of the overhead air flow fan lull him. The woman's voice became soft and lyrical. She talked continuously. He tuned out the words and let the monotonous tone of her voice mesmerize and tuck him into a deep sleep. He slept for several hours.

Ding, ding interrupted Tom's sleep. The steward was announcing the end of the flight. Tom sat up and stretched his shoulders and neck. The woman had moved back to her seat across the aisle. She stared at him for several seconds, her eyes hard and unblinking, then she turned away to look out the small window into the dark night sky. Tom avoided any further contact with her. He lagged behind getting his luggage from the overhead, then watched her leave the plane.

Outside, on the nearly empty sidewalk, Tom flagged a cab. As he neared his Jamestown home, he reached into his coat pocket for his keys. He fingers touched a folded paper stuffed into the pocket of his jacket. He took it out, looking at it curiously. *Tom Gardner* was written on the outside of the envelope in a large, scrawling, almost childlike script.

The cab pulled in front of Tom's house. He stuffed the envelope back into his pocket. The cherub boy, its wings cloaked in snow, smiled blankly at him with its hooded eyes. The cement fountain was layered in clear ice. Nate had turned the fountain's water back on and for some reason had failed to turn it off. A stream of water flowed from the male's tiny genitals, a frozen waterfall in the making, as the water formed a glistening stalagmite. The house security lights flashed on as Tom opened the car door. The driver opened the trunk, setting Tom's bags on the ground. He paid the driver, then carried his leather suitcases up the long stone-inlaid walk. Automatically he glanced up at the second floor window where Elise had so often stood watching him.

I will find you, Elise. I know you are here. Waiting for me. We will end this. Of course—she was not there—as Tom would eventually discover.

Unlocking the door, Tom, entered the silent house. Nate had left several lights burning. Shadows, stark and eerie, carpeted the floors. The painters had finished their work while Tom had been in Amsterdam. The house smelled new and clean, no longer had the familiar smells of home. Most of the furniture had been sold and moved out. There was nowhere for Tom to sit, no place to lay back and relax. In a few weeks, new owners would occupy this house—a new legacy would begin. He wandered through the empty house trying to make himself feel like he still belonged. It was no use. Echoes of his life here bounced off the walls, dissipating into hollow, meaningless whispers.

It was almost midnight. Tom was tired, defeated. "Talk to me, Elise. Damn it! Come here! I want to see you!" He pounded his hand on the wall, kicked the bottom step of the first floor landing, and yelled, "Elise! Where are you?" He heard the sound of footsteps on the floor above. "Elise!" he said, whirling around.

The light from the above landing suddenly illuminated the dark. "Tom? What are you doing down there? You okay?" Nate hobbled down the stairs, holding the railing to keep from falling, his cast reverberating on each step as he hurried down the stairs.

"Nate! God damn it! You scared the shit out of me."

"Sorry, I thought I'd hear you when you came in. Guess I fell asleep. You look beat. How long have you been here?"

Ignoring the question, Tom stood. "I'm glad to see you, Nate." He reached out and cuffed Nate on the chin. "This house is so empty. I didn't think it would be like this. Guess I should have known you can't go home again."

Nate shook his head. "It is pretty empty. Most of the furniture was picked up today. There's still furniture upstairs in the two bedrooms and the study, but other than that, it's ready for the new owners to move in. You hungry? Want me to make some coffee?" Nate began walking down the long hallway toward the kitchen.

Tom followed him. "No coffee. No food either. What I could use is a shot of vodka. Still have the bar stocked?"

"No, I emptied it out last week, but there's still a bottle stashed in the freezer." Nate opened the door of the side by side and pulled out a frosty bottle. He took two glasses from the dishwasher, opened the bottle and poured them each a drink. Neither spoke as they silently raised their glasses in a toast, then swallowed the fiery liquid.

Tom held his glass out for a refill. "Excellent. You're a good man, Nate. Always watching out for me aren't you?"

"That's what friends do. You could use some sleep. Let's call it a night. "

"You're right. I'm exhausted. A hot shower and sleep, that's what I need. Hey, Nate," he said as he followed him up the stairs, "what are you doing here? I thought you were going to stay at Rosa's for a few days."

"Oh, well, guess I figured I'd make sure everything was okay. John Atwood called this afternoon, said he was trying to reach you and couldn't. He had some information he wanted you to have as soon as you got back. I told him I'd make sure you got the message. And I had some trouble with the plumbing, so figured I better stick around. Found your drip! Plumber's coming in the morning."

"Well, whatever the reason, it's sure good to have you here."

"Glad you're okay with it. We'll see what happens tomorrow. If you still want me to, I'll go to Rosa's tomorrow afternoon. See you in the morning."

"Goodnight. We'll talk tomorrow." Tom showered, got into bed falling almost immediately to sleep. He did not dream. He woke at ten when, in the distance, he heard the front doorbell ring. He dressed and went down to the kitchen. Nate was there showing a man to the back stairs. From the logo of a water spigot on the back of his shirt, Tom surmised he was the plumber.

Nate was telling him, "Go down the hallway to the right. The bathroom is the first door on the left. The leak is in the pipe under the sink." The plumber, tool bag in hand, disappeared into the basement.

"Morning, Nate."

"Hey, Tom. I just made a fresh pot of coffee. I'm making an omelet, too. Damn! I better get to it before it burns." Nate hurried across the room and pulled the pan off the burner.

The plumber hollered from the bottom of the stairs, "Hey, I need to turn the water off for about half an hour. You okay with that? I'll give you a few minutes if you need to use the plumbing. Ha! Ha!"

"We're okay, thanks. Go ahead," Tom yelled back.

Nate had set up a small oak dining table and two cane back chairs in the kitchen nook. They ate and drank coffee while Tom filled Nate in on the final details of the business deal with William Harrison. "Sounds like it went well," Nate said. "You've made a good choice of business partners. Harrison's never failed in any of his ventures. Wise move, on your part, Tom."

"It seemed to drop into my lap. Right place, right time, I guess. We'll make a profit within the first two years. That's what we're after." Tom shrugged and took a sip of coffee. He put his mug down on the table, picked up his toast. "You said John needed to talk to me? Any idea what about?"

"Said it had to do with the house in Ravenswood. He didn't elaborate."

"Hmm. Well, I better give him a call," he said standing up and carrying his dirty dishes to the sink. He turned the faucet on to rinse them. "Forgot. No water."

"I'll get them later."

"I'm going to call John and then check in with Cassie and Sara."

***

Tom stared out his study window, phone to his ear, waiting for John to answer his call. "John, it's Tom."

"So you're back. Sorry to hear about Mrs. Harrison's illness. But the deal is complete. The papers were delivered this morning. Congratulations."

"Thanks. I appreciate your addressing all of Harrison's issues. I'm glad to have it finished. I'd rather have stayed here and signed all the papers to begin with. Oh, well. It was important for William to give me the royal tour of his offices and several of his stores. So . . . Nate said you called. You have information on Remington House?"

"I had my research assistant do some digging on the former owners. The Lindemans, as you already know, died in the house. Cindy found a couple of newspaper articles about their deaths. The brother was terminal—bone cancer. The brother and sister were quite private. Apparently they spent years traveling abroad before Mr. Lindeman became ill. During the last years of their lives they seldom ventured out of their house. The Lindemans were apparently a generous couple though, donating large sums of money to a scholarship fund."

"Sounds to me like a pretty innocuous pair," Tom said, staring out the window. Patches of sun appeared through the clouds, beginning to melt the snow. In the street below, a young boy, followed closely by an older girl, walked in front of Tom's house. The boy stopped in front of the fountain, bent over and gathered a snowball into his hands. He threw it hitting the cherub in its face. Glancing up at the window where Tom was watching them, the girl grabbed the boy's hand and pulled him down the street.

John continued, "The murder-suicide was downplayed. It was reported to be the final, desperate act of a loving sister, overly distraught by the suffering of her dying brother. A suicide letter was found that apparently reaffirmed that, though the actual letter was not made public.

"We found nothing further about the two other than social columns indicating they were quite active in New York's high society. They lived there, as well as in Europe, for most of their lives, until they retired to Ravenswood. There were no marriages for either one, no illegitimate children surfaced to claim inheritance. Their will left the bulk of their estate to a religious organization in Germany. We stopped the inquiry there. I thought you might feel better about the house in Ravenswood if you knew the story behind the deaths."

"You're right, of course. Thanks for the follow-up. I'm disturbed and certainly wish you and I had been told about the deaths."

"As I told you before, Tom, if you want, I can begin proceedings against the realty firm for failing to disclose the murder. Just say the word."

"No, I want the house. I've already started some remodeling. A letter expressing my displeasure with the firm's failure to disclose the tragedy will suffice."

The boy had returned alone. Tom watched him scoop snow from the yard, shoveling it with his gloved hands into the fountain. Tom tapped on the glass. The child grinned and waved.

"I'll take care of that this week," John said. Tom could hear him drumming his pen on his desk. "Nate said your Jamestown house is about emptied out. The new owners will be moving in soon, I imagine. Bittersweet for you, I'm sure."

"It's hard to leave the home you've spent most of your life in. But I know I've made the right decision." The boy threw a snowball hitting the window with a loud thump. Tom jumped. The snowball slid down the glass pane. Like a giant slush-slug, it left a trail as it melted and fell to the sill.

"Tom, when are you leaving for Ravenswood?"

The boy laughed when Tom tapped harshly on the window. The child threw another snowball, then ran. Farther down the street, Tom saw the boy's sister walking toward him. She was yelling, her words not audible to Tom behind the double glass pane. It reminded him of when he was a boy. Wait till the boy's mom got a hold of him! No doubt the sister would rat on him! Tom remembered well how his mother dealt with him when he misbehaved. She would have marched him up the street and made him apologize.

"You still there, Tom?"

"Sorry, John. Lost in thought. What'd you say?"

"When are you going back to Ravenswood?"

"I'll be here for a few days, a week at the most. I still have quite a few papers to go through. Nate found more boxes in the attic. I'd rather do it here than ship them all back to Remington."

"Makes sense. Hey, if you don't have plans, why don't we plan to have dinner at the club tonight. Bring Nate, too."

"Sounds good. Sure."

"Very good," John said. "Before we hang up, I wanted to tell you, my associate assumes Harold skipped the country. The firm's run into a dead end. His trail went cold. Nate said Harold even hid out in your basement for a time. Disturbing."

"Sure is. Harold's probably better off out of the country. He's shown a pattern of poor judgment. More than anything, I feel bad for Nate and Rosa. To be honest—Harold's a loser. He'll no doubt die one."

Chapter 97

Tom called Sara. She seemed rather distant, but Tom was tired and glad to keep their conversation short. He didn't tell Sara, nor Cassie, when Sara handed the phone over to her, that he was back in New York. He'd call them in a day or two and let them know when he'd be back to Ravenswood. He and Nate spent the next hours going through cartons of business papers.

"That's the last of the boxes from Gardner Enterprises," Tom said. "Damn! My dad saved a lot of useless documents." Tom closed the lid on the last of the storage boxes. "Down from ten boxes to two. Not bad." He tapped on the lids. "Nate, I want these sent to Remington."

"Sure. I'll have them picked up later today." Nate pulled two smaller, dark-brown leather suitcases out of the closet. "These are locked. Any idea what's in them?"

"Personal stuff, I imagine. My mother packed those and put them away after my dad died. I'll look at them later." Tom sat down in the leather chair that had been his grandfather's, then his father's and, for the last decade, his. Leaning back, he rested his head on the firm headrest. He looked up at the pattern of intricate swirls in the ceiling

While Nate dealt with the plumber, who had inadvertently broken another pipe, Tom returned to the study to go though whatever his mother had so carefully packed away in the cases.

Several hours later, Nate poked his head in the study door. "Tom, the plumber's gone, and everything is back to normal." Nate stood in the doorway of the study. "You finished going through those already?" He walked over to the suitcases, tried to open one of them. It was locked. "Want them shipped to Remington with the rest of the papers?"

"Put them back into the closet." Tom stood up and left the room.

***

Tom was the first to arrive at the Jamestown Men's Club, where he was meeting Nate and John for a late dinner. He'd been in the city for the past several hours, buying gifts to take home to his family and friends in Ravenswood. He sat drinking vodka at the antique cherry table, its top polished to a high sheen. He remembered why, and how much, he detested these pompous asses, these greedy businessmen cloistered together around the room. Many of these men had made their fortunes in this very room. They laughed and clinked leaded-crystal glasses of fine aged scotch, no doubt toasting yet another poor chump they'd just swindled. All in a day's work. Right? Unctuous old men! Screwed their neighbors and padded their own bank accounts. Tom lifted his glass to a table of fat, cigar-smoking men across the room. "Here's to you," he said, then added silently, *you jackasses*. The entire table of eight business men looked his way, directing a toast to him. Tom muttered under his breath as John Atwood came up behind him. "Cheers. Here's wishing you many rotten days to come." Tom lifted his glass toward the men at the table across the room.

"Aren't you cynical tonight!" John Atwood pulled out a chair and sat down across from Tom. "You should have told me you didn't want to meet here; I'd have found a more agreeable place for dinner." He frowned at Tom. "What's got you so pissed off?"

"Sorry, John. I went through my father's papers today. Ten boxes filled mostly with junk. I got through those quickly enough. Then I found the dirty little secrets that my mother saved. In two suitcases she carefully packed away the family's secret ledgers. She must have been horrified to find out her husband and his father before him, were crooks. Did you know that?" Tom flagged the waiter, pointed at his empty glass.

"Of course not! What makes you say that?"

"I found the *hidden* ledgers. Why in God's name did my mother keep them?"

"No idea. But Tom, you're wrong. The ledgers you found belonged to the Ballantyne family, not yours. Damn! I wish I'd known those ledgers were still around! They should have been destroyed a long time ago." He paused and took a drink. "Your grandfather found out the Ballantyne and the Standish families were doing private deals for the New York crime bosses. This was back in the early twenties. At that time there was only one hotel belonging to the Gardners. Bernard Ballantyne and Amos Standish worked for your grandfather. They ran the lounge at Gardner Arms. But more than that, they helped build the second hotel.

"Ballantyne and Standish were almost blood to your grandparents. Your grandfather saved them from a scandal. Remember, the mob ran the city back in the 20's and 30's. The two men were in over their heads. Your grandfather bought them out of their troubles. He paid off the debts they owed to the gangsters, giving both families a fresh start."

"Well, shit! Who knew? So, now I have *two suitcases* filled with *incriminating evidence* stashed in a closet at the house. What am I supposed to do with them?"

"Let me take care of them. I'll make sure they're properly destroyed. I'll drop you off tonight and pick them up," John said.

"I'll gladly turn them over to you," Tom answered. "I can't imagine why anyone kept them."

Thoughtfully John said, "Insurance, I imagine."

The waiter silently placed drinks in front of the men and pulled a chair out for Nate, who hobbled to the table as John and Tom raised a glass to each other. "Sorry I'm late. Must be a convention downtown. I had to wait an hour to get a cab!"

"What can I get for you this evening, sir?" The waiter stood patiently by as Nate removed his coat. "Oldcastle, thanks."

While the waiter got his beer, Nate asked, "What have I missed? You two seemed to be having a pretty serious conversation. What gives?"

"News about my family. Good news actually." While they waited for their food to be served, Tom related the story about the double ledgers he found and the mob activity in New York when his grandfather was starting up the hotels.

As Tom was winding up his tale, the waiter appeared with a huge tray. Large portions of pork tenderloin wrapped in asparagus spears and smothered in apricot sauce, stuffed portabella mushrooms and green beans with slivered almonds kept the men busy for a time.

Tom cut a bite of pork, dragging it through the apricot sauce before he put the succulent meat in his mouth and chewed. "For some reason the name Ballantyne keeps popping up. I've heard it recently—actually several times. Can't be a lot of Ballantynes around."

"You're probably right. Your dad severed ties with the Ballantynes and the Standishs as soon as your grandfather died. But, the reason you know the name, is that you went to college with one of the granddaughters. Catherine was her name."

"Right! Vivian Harrison brought her up—the first time we had dinner together. What kind of a coincidence is that! Vivian said she was a friend of hers. And somehow Cathy managed to work her way into Elise's confidence. Until I put an end to that. I never trusted that woman."

"Like grandfather, like granddaughter, maybe. Small world. Any idea where she is now?" Nate asked. The waiter brought another round of drinks, his tray heavily loaded with glasses and bottles as he made rounds to the nearby tables.

"Damn! Nate, remember the woman I told you about on the plane?"

"Yeah." He nodded, taking a drink of his beer.

"Guess who that was? None other than our Catherine Ballantyne! I thought she looked vaguely familiar. I haven't seen her in maybe twenty years. She was obviously angry with me about something. Think she found out about her family and who she owes her fortune to?"

"I guess it's possible. Maybe someone in her family spilled the beans."

Tom took a drink of his ice-cold vodka. "I completely forgot. I found a letter in my pocket—on my way back home from the airport. I bet it's from her."

"What did it say?" John asked, wiping his mouth with a fine linen napkin. "What does she want?"

"Never read it. Cab dropped me off right about then. I stuck the envelope back in my coat pocket and never gave it another thought. I'll have to find it when I get home."

"Very odd," John said. "Maybe she was angry because you didn't recognize her."

"Hmm. Could be." Tom looked around the room. He picked up his drink. "Cheers! To old acquaintances. Let them stay forever at bay." Tom took a sip, then added, "Trouble. Cathy was always trouble."

Chapter 98

The security lights came on, illuminating the front yard as John's car pulled in front of Tom's house. "I'm certainly going to miss all the Christmas parties you used to throw here."

"Won't we all," Tom said unemotionally. The three men walked up the sidewalk, past the cherub who was now completely surrounded by a pool of ice. Water trickled in a sparkling rivulet down its leg into the surrounding fountain. "You really need to shut the water off. The fountain's about ready to overflow. It'll break the cement."

"The valve won't shut off all the way. The guy from Acers Plumbing is coming back tomorrow to fix it." Nate turned the key in the lock of the heavy front door, pushing it open with his cane.

"I'll go upstairs and get the suitcases," Nate said.

"We'll give you a hand. Come on, John." Tom led the way up to the second floor study. Still hanging across the back of the desk chair was his suit jacket. Tom reached into the pocket and pulled out the envelope. "I might as well read this while you're here, John. I know you're as curious as I am."

"Want me to get us some coffee?" Nate asked.

Tom waved the envelope in front of him. "Don't you want to know what's in this?"

"Damn right I do!"

"Looks like a child's handwriting to me." Tom tore the end off of the envelope. He pulled out and unfolded a letter. It was written on pale blue stationery with an elaborate silver monogram engraved in the upper left-hand corner. "Odd. The handwriting isn't the same as the writing on the envelope." Tom silently read the first few paragraphs. "What the fuck!"

"What is it?" Nate asked.

"It's nothing," Tom lied. "A sick joke. I think Catherine is as sick as Elise was." Tom crumpled the letter into a ball and jammed it into his pants pocket.

"What did it say?" John asked. "You look really pissed off."

"I suspected there might have been another man in Elise's life. I was wrong." Tom smashed the desktop with his fist. "Not another man—Catherine Ballantyne-Connors!"

"Oh, man!" Nate said.

"Let's not make a big deal out of this. Elise played me, but she got her just reward. Let her rot! Nate, get the suitcases out of the closet and get them the hell out of here! I'm sick of this house and its poisons. Damn this place!"

"You better let me have the letter." John stepped toward Tom. "I can't imagine why Catherine would bring all this up now. It's been over two years since Elise died. You sure there isn't more to this? Is Catherine trying to blackmail you?"

"I'll deal with her if I have to. I think she's done all she wanted to do. She hates me. She probably started thinking about me when she talked to Vivian last month. Stirred up old feelings. Forget it! It's over."

"All right. But if she gives you any trouble, let me handle it. I'll call her bluff. Or I'll give her granddad a call. He'll deal with her. All I have to do is mention the contents of these suitcases. Maybe I better hold on to them for a while."

"No, burn them. Catherine won't be a problem." Tom started walking out of the room. "I'm tired. Nate, will you help John take the suitcases down to his car? I'll call you tomorrow, John. I'm about finished here. A couple more days then I'm headed home—to Ravenswood."

Tom sat in the dark in his room, waiting for Nate to close up the house. When he heard the bedroom door down the hallway close, Tom crept down the back stairway to the kitchen. He found the bottle of vodka in the freezer and unscrewed the lid. He swigged several mouthfuls, took the opened bottle with him and sat at the small, oak table. He pulled the letter out of his pocket, smoothing it on the hard surface. He swallowed another mouthful of vodka and began to read:

Dearest (sic) Tom, my Husband, my Tormenter,

Catherine is but a messenger. She loved me as I wanted you to love me. To her deep sorrow, I did not love her in that way —could only love her as a friend. She pledged her undying affection and promised to help me make certain that you suffered for what you did to me. She loved me unconditionally. She loved me as you should have.

If you are reading this, then two years have passed since my death. I have given this letter to Catherine, who tried to help me stand up for myself and leave you. She is delivering this on the condition that once she hands it over to you, she will have nothing more to do with you. You will not torment her as you did me. Do you understand? The consequences will be grave!

Perhaps you are no longer thinking of me? Perhaps you have gone on with your life? Well, I have no intention of letting that happen. You will never find peace from the memory of my life and death.

You were to have been the love of my life, my salvation my soul-mate. But you failed me. Never did I imagine I could hate someone as I learned to hate you. Not a moment of the last years of my life passed without me praying you would let me go. So many times I tried to leave you, but you always brought me back and made me believe your lies.

But you didn't love me. You wanted only to possess me. You sucked the life out of me. You stole my soul and destroyed my love for you. I pray your life will be as painful as was my life with you. You were my jailer, my isolator, my stalker. You drove me to my death.

I write this letter so you may know that whenever you think you will be free from my memory, you will be wrong. I will always be here. I will always haunt you and will make your life a living hell. Perhaps as you read this, you will know I already have.

I will never allow you to love or be loved by anyone. As long as there is a breath of life in your body, you will curse the day you betrayed my love. I hope this hurts you deeply.

Oh, and Tom! Don't look behind you!
Your darling (oh, don't you wish it were so),
Elise

"Bitch!" Tom kicked the empty chair beside him, knocking it sideways. It crashed into the floor lamp that Nate brought in from the now-empty living room. The glass shattered as it hit the floor. The bulb flashed and popped. Exploding shards of the globe flew and landed about Tom's feet.

Tom wadded the letter into a ball, then took another drink of vodka. He stared at his hand, which was clenched into a tight fist around the letter. So this was how Elise wanted it. Game on, bitch! He tipped the bottle and drained it. "Show yourself! Where are you?" He threw the bottle onto the floor, watched it bounce several times and shatter. He sat in the kitchen until dawn waiting for Elise. She did not come. Six hundred miles away, she was sleeping restlessly, hidden in the attic at Vivian Harrison's house.

Chapter 99

Tom woke stiff and sore. His tongue felt like sandpaper, his head ached. He'd gone back to his room around seven after sweeping up the glass from the lamp and bottle. He made it as far as the bed before passing out. He slept fully clothed. Two hours later he got up, took a cold shower, then put on jeans and a flannel shirt. Chewing a handful of antacids and three aspirin, Tom went to find Nate.

"Morning, Tom. Rough night?" Nate asked, pointing to the glass-filled trashcan. "What happened?"

"Not much. Couldn't sleep. Thought a shot of vodka might help. Didn't though. Then to add insult to injury, I knocked over the lamp in the dark. Dropped the bottle to boot!"

Nate frowned. "You all right?"

"Yeah. I need some coffee." He poured himself a cup, added a spoon of sugar.

"Thought you always drank it black."

"Sugar's for my hangover," Tom smirked, rubbing his temple.

"Thought you looked a little green. Sit down, and I'll get you some toast and jam."

Nate put slices of bread in the toaster, pushed the lever down. "Plumber's here. He got here at eight and said he'd be done by noon. Want me to help you go through the last few boxes of photos in the attic?"

"No. I'll take care of them. I don't think they're my family's—I think they're Elise's. Not sure what to do with them. Toss them maybe! Better yet—burn them!"

"Something on your mind, friend?" Nate buttered the toast, put it on a plate and handed it to Tom.

"Coffee tastes good." Tom sipped from the black china mug.

"What gives?" Nate sat down across the table from Tom.

"I want to get finished here. I need to get back to Remington. And to Sara. I miss her and my family. I'm tired, too. That about sums it up."

"I can see that. I'm guessing Elise is your problem. This place reminds you too much of her. That letter you got from Catherine didn't do much to help. Yeah, you need to get away from here. The sooner the better."

"You got that right." Tom stood up and reached for the coffee pot. "I think a couple of days, maybe by Sunday or Monday, and I'll be done here. More coffee?"

Nate nodded. "What can I do to help?"

"I'd like to be alone here for a few days. I think you better stay with Rosa. I'll go through the last few boxes and finish any business about the house with John." Tom leaned back in the chair, tipping and rocking precariously on the back legs.

"All my stuff's already there. Rosa sent Larry over for it Monday. She's happy to have me stay with her."

"I'll bet. She needs to enjoy some time with you. Before we know it, it'll be Christmas and then the New Year and then you'll be leaving here and coming to Remington."

"My leg's healing well, so that's the plan. I'm anxious to see your new place. And I look forward to meeting Sara and seeing Cassie and Lizzie. I haven't seen them for at least a year."

"It's sure been good having Cassie and Lizzie around." Tom lowered his chair back to the floor. "Well, I have things to do . . . "

"I'm all wrapped up down there," the plumber interrupted, standing in the doorway of the basement. He nodded to Tom. "Replaced the pipe I broke the other day, put in PVC this time. Headed out to the pump house next—to change a couple of leaking valves that feed the fountain. Nice place, bet you hate selling it."

"Not really. Too much house for one man." Tom stood up. "I have a few calls to make." He left the kitchen, wandered through the empty hallways, then went to his bedroom.

He found the letter from Elise in his pants pocket. He built a small fire and threw the balled-up letter into the flames. "Wish I could do that to you, Elise. Burn you and be done with you. We'll meet again. Soon! I promise you that! I will find you—wherever you're hiding. I *know* you're here!"

Nate knocked on the door. "Tom?"

"Yeah, come in."

"You talking to someone?"

"Yeah, I was on the phone."

"The cab's here. I'm on my way to Rosa's. Call me if you need anything."

"I'll be fine," Tom said.

"There's plenty of food in the pantry. Refrigerator's well stocked. You should have all you need for the next few days."

"Thanks, Nate. I'll be fine, I won't starve." Tom laughed and cuffed Nate on the shoulder. "I'll call you in a day or two. Take it easy. Tell Rosa hello for me."

For the next several hours, with a bottle of vodka in hand and a roaring fire in the study fireplace, Tom looked through Elise's family pictures. There were two boxes, one filled with loose photos, the other carefully packed and filled with albums. Judging by the clothing, the oldest pictures dated back to the turn of the century. Men, women, children—even a German Shepherd, posed stiffly, frozen in time in sepia tones and faded black and white stills. Tom saw a family resemblance to Elise.

Tom tossed one picture after another into the fire. He tore the albums apart, one page at a time and threw them into the flames, relishing the charring of the faces as they crinkled and withered into soot and ash.

Chapter 100

Joe was on his way out the front door. "Cassie, if you don't need me for anything, I'm going. My crew and I are meeting in town for dinner. See you in the morning; we'll start back to work bright and early." A sense of foreboding swept over Cassie as she watched Joe drive away. She thought back to the last hours, before Joe and the crew left, before Terese arrived for the séance.

Earlier that afternoon, after taking Lizzie and Jimmy into Ravenswood for a sleepover with Mary's brother and sister, Mary followed Cassie back to Remington House in her red sedan, not wanting to be without her car. Mary wanted be able to leave if she thought she needed to. There was, after all, no telling what could happen tonight at the ceremony.

Catching site of her own face in her rearview, Mary giggled nervously. She parked behind Cassie who was talking animatedly on her cell phone. Mary waited for her on the porch. Cassie nodded at her and indicated, with a slice into the air, that she was trying to cut off whomever she was talking to. It was a few minutes past two. Mary was perspiring. Sweat trickled down her back. She looked out over the property, surprised at the seeming normalcy of it all.

Another car had driven up the long winding road to the house. When the car got closer Mary saw it was Harry driving Joe's truck. She waved as he passed by headed around to the back of the house. He smiled, tipped the brim of his cowboy hat and disappeared.

"Sorry about that." Cassie walked onto the porch and unlocked the front door. "That was Mannie letting me know she and Amos were going to have dinner with family this evening. Billy is with friends, too, so looks like the Harrison house is empty for the night." She stood aside and motioned for Mary to go in.

"Where's Sara?" asked Mary.

"She went to town a few hours ago to do some shopping for tonight. I don't think she wanted to stay here alone. She should be back pretty soon. Terese called yesterday with a list of stuff we needed for the séance."

"Are you nervous about tonight?" Mary took her coat off and hung it in the hall closet. Cassie handed her coat to Mary, who was holding another hanger.

"I'm scared to death! What about you?"

"I feel the same way." Mary chewed on her lower lip. "Nothing has happened this past week has it?"

"Not a thing. It's been quiet here. I keep hoping that maybe the old couple left. But fat chance of that, I'm sure." Cassie rolled her eyes and shook her head. "I imagine they're here somewhere. Waiting. I can't envision them leaving without a fight. I think we're in for a battle tonight. I pray we're strong enough for it."

"Strong enough for what?"

"Oh, Joe! You scared us," Cassie and Mary said simultaneously.

"What are you girls so jumpy about? No more raccoons scooting around are there? You hearing noises in the attic?" Joe leaned against the banister and looked up the staircase.

"No, it's been very quiet. I think the raccoons gave up and found somewhere else to live." Cassie tried to smile to hide her nervousness. "How's the construction going anyhow? Seems like you guys have been putting in a lot of hours."

"We have. I'd like to get it wrapped up as soon as possible."

"Yeah, I bet," Cassie said. "Tom called this morning. He's getting pretty excited to get home and see your progress. Hey, Joe, show Mary and me around the basement before you go. We haven't been down there for a while."

"Yeah, come on. We've got the boxing ring, the workout room and the bathroom almost finished. Figure about two weeks and most of the basement will be finished–except the two rooms on the other side of the stairs. Not sure what Tom wants to do there. Looks like the Lindemans used to use one of them as a spare bedroom. We moved most of the storage boxes into the larger of the two rooms."

Hesitantly, Cassie and Mary descended the basement stairs behind Joe.

"What an incredible transformation!" Cassie blurted out. "Amazing!"

"Oh, my gosh, Joe. This is like being in another house!" Mary looked around. Most of the walls had been taken out and replaced with support columns. In the far end of the room, the cement floor had been covered with oak planks polished to a high sheen and heavily varnished. There was low-nap carpet in the rest of the room. The boxing ring was not elevated but sat at floor level surrounded by heavy white and red roping. A full-sized punching bag and three speed bags hung from the ceiling from steel beams. Inside the ring, boxes of other equipment—gloves, a timer, sat out of the way.

"It looks great doesn't it? I must say I'm impressed myself with how it's turned out," Joe said smiling. He pointed to his left. "That's the shower and bathroom. And there's a sauna still to go in over there. The bathroom still has to be tiled but all the plumbing is in and all the lights are wired."

Joe motioned to the far side of the room, to the right of the ring. "That area will be weight equipment and a maybe a treadmill or something. Tom hasn't gotten all that ordered yet."

"Impressive. Tom will be so happy," Cassie remarked.

"I feel pretty proud. The crew has worked hard and surprisingly fast,'" Joe said as he led the way back up the stairs. "I'm gonna wrap up here. Should be out in a few hours. Then off to town for dinner with the guys." He closed the door; Cassie could hear him clomping down the stairs hollering to one of his men to "hold on a minute, I'll help you move that. Don't want to scratch that new flooring."

Chapter 101

Terese rang the bell. No one came. She pressed the button, heard the bell chime in the house. Still no one answered. "What in the world! Where is everyone?" Closing her eyes she allowed herself to relax and tune in to the atmospheric anomalies. "Nothing amiss. Not yet anyway." She knocked, then gave up, turned the knob and walked into the house. "Hello? Cassie, Mary?" she called. She observed that the study on her left was quiet. To her right, the living room, too, was vacant.

A fired burned brightly, offering the only light in the room. The orange and red flames crackled, dark shadows danced on the floor. She crossed to the opposite side of the room. The windows, with the curtains drawn open, revealed the dark sky. Stars twinkled brilliantly, the heavens sparkling with their flickering light. The moon, shadowed in luminous clouds, partially lit the beach where a couple walked hand in hand. A young man and woman, bundled against the cold, caught her attention. Terese watched them, sensed something amiss. They were too far away for her to discern if she knew them. She thought she did not.

"Terese?"

Terese jumped and whirled around. "Cassie!"

"I didn't hear you come in," Cassie said.

"You didn't hear the doorbell? I rang three times."

"No. Sorry. I'm glad you came on in. We're all in the kitchen. Guess we should have paid more attention to the time and have been waiting here for you." Cassie turned on the light. The bulb glowed then popped loudly and went out. She jumped. "Damn!"

"It begins," Terese said. She unbuttoned her coat.

"I'll get another bulb."

"Don't bother, dear. It won't make any difference. It's not the bulb."

"Oh!" Cassie shuddered.

"Let's go to the kitchen. We should all talk and relax for a while." Terese stopped in the dining room. "We must set up the table. But first we need to have some time together. There are things I need to tell you before we begin the séance." She led Cassie toward the kitchen doorway.

Sara, a glass of wine in her hand, nervously paced the floor. Mary sat staring into the fireplace. Too many logs had been thrown in making the room temperature almost unbearable. Cassie wrenched open the window and drew a long breath of the cold, crisp winter air.

"Good evening," Terese said, smiling at the girls.

"Hi, Terese," Sara said, trying to look cheerful. "Here, let me have your coat." She reached out, took Terese's colorful tapestry jacket, and hung it carefully on the hook by the back door. "You look so calm."

"And you look very tense."

"I am," Sara answered. She shrugged, then took another sip of her wine.

Terese glanced at Mary who sat stiffly at the table, her eyes locked on Terese. "And Mary, you look like you would rather be anywhere but here. Are you okay with doing the séance? Are *all* of you okay with going ahead with this tonight?" Terese looked at the women, carefully assessing each. They were nervous, but she could tell they were also strong and determined to do this.

"Ready as I can be. I don't know what to expect, that's all," Sara answered.

"Me, too. I'm *so* scared," Mary said. She shivered, wrapping her arms tightly around herself.

Terese nodded. "I expected that; it's perfectly normal. Before we go any further though, I have more information to share with you. Then you can decide if you feel all right with continuing tonight." Terese pulled a chair out, sat down and reached into the large tapestry bag she'd brought with her. She pulled several photos out and sat them in front of her on the table. "Come, Cassie and Sara, sit down with us."

"What are those?" Mary asked. She looked over, glanced at the old sepia photos. "The Lindemans!"

Terese said, "Oddly enough, I found these at the Historic Society, along with a few other pictures and some information about the Lindemans. The brother and sister were quite generous and endowed the city with money to build a small museum. One of the rooms was even dedicated to the couple by the Citizens for Education, a small but influential group of men and women committed to the now-defunct charity. The group spent most of their money and efforts on the local schools, each year offering several scholarships. Apparently, at the time, the schools were on shaky ground, sorely lacking funds and direction. But that changed, thanks to the Lindemans. They likely contributed to enhance their image and standing in the community, not because they cared about the children. And more importantly, perhaps it was done to buy their privacy."

"That *would* make sense," Cassie said.

Terese continued, "For a few years the Lindemans attended one meeting a year, giving a rather sizeable donation. Then, a year before they died, Helen Lindeman requested that a statement be recorded in the meeting minutes. She explained that she and Gabe planned to continue their donations but would be unable to attend any future meetings, due to their delicate health.

"Ill health seemed to be a constant theme with the couple in the later years, though I found no records that they'd been treated for anything here in Ravenswood. Perhaps they were under the care of a private physician, or perhaps all of their treatments were done out of the city at larger facilities. I didn't really pursue that avenue.

"They continued sending money and publically receiving recognition as upstanding citizens of Ravenswood. However, their private life was an entirely different matter!" Terese pulled several handwritten pages from a large manila folder. "These were harder to find. But when I began researching, Harriet, the librarian, offered to help and came across one of the ledgers from the Citizens for Education. Looking through it, I found this letter, which I discreetly pocketed. Apparently it'd been tucked away all these years in the ledger.

"The letter is from Lisa Shepherd, one of the board members of the Citizens for Education." Terese began reading from the letter:

Dear Jeremy,

I write this letter reluctantly but find, under the circumstances, I must bring a matter of great concern to your attention. As you know, I returned from Germany last week. On my tour, I had a chance encounter with a priest at the Cathedral of St. Augustus. I met the kindly cleric during a tour of the church while visiting with a group of architects and artists. We were there studying the exquisite structures.

When Father Lukas heard I was from America, specifically from Ravenswood, his face darkened. Puzzled, I asked him if something was wrong. He asked to speak to me in private. He said he knew the town I was from was very small and inquired if I might know a couple named Lindeman? "Of course," I told him, pleased he knew of the Lindemans. He, however, frowned and lowered his head.

I explained to him what a kind family they were, of their generosity, how every year they donated a large sum of money to a scholarship fund for our school children.

"Indeed? And do you see them often? Do you know this family well?" he asked.

I told him Gabe suffered from ill health and that his sister, Helen, took care of him, so no, they were seldom seen in Ravenswood anymore. Father Lukas said nothing. He seemed very nervous and excused himself, asking me to wait for him while he went to find something he thought I should see. The rest of the tour group went on ahead. I told them I would catch up with them.

Upon returning, Father Lukas handed me several pictures that showed the Lindemans with a group of men and women. The pictures were taken at the altar of a fourteenth century church. However, the ceremony portrayed in the photograph was not to worship our Lord but was rather a satanic ceremony. Shockingly, the crucifix hung upside down and several holy statues were adorned in black hoods.

Black candles burned on the altar. A young woman was bound to a table, her face covered with a hood. She was surrounded by several dozen men and women—all wearing ceremonial, black robes. The Lindemans appeared to be the High Priest and Priestess. Both stood at the head of the altar. As you can imagine, I was horrified.

Father Lukas handed me another picture, this one of the Lindemans in the living room of a large mansion with many of the same people. It was, to my complete shock, an orgy. As before, Gabe and Helen seemed to be the center of the party. Dozens of naked men and women were coupled around the Lindemans in various performances of lewd acts. To this day, I cannot get those images out of my mind.

I will say nothing about this to anyone except you. We must not let anyone else know of this matter. For obvious reasons, I trust you will help me find a way to extricate the Citizens for Education from these evil people. We must do so with extreme caution. I was told by the priest that this group is not only corrupt but also extremely dangerous. Father Lukas cautioned me to be very careful. The Father said, due to our chance encounter, he felt it was God's design, and thus his obligation, to reveal the true character of the Lindemans.

I will speak to you when you wish, so we can decide what the best course of action should be. Discretion certainly is paramount.

I remain your colleague and friend,
Lisa Shepherd

Cassie gasped out loud. "They're dangerous? Oh, God!"

"We knew they were," Sara said quietly.

Terese looked intently at the three women. "Don't let this make you more frightened. They're not as strong now. They've weakened since their deaths. I can feel it—even since I was here last week—they have lost strength. When we meet them in a little while, we will overpower them. We will cast them out. Do not doubt that!"

Chapter 102

The occasional creaking of the ceiling overhead unnerved the old couple as the women walked about the kitchen. Gabe and Helen listened, holding hands. A black candle burned on the jet-black cloth of the makeshift altar laid between them. Surrounding the two was a circle of stones made of fire opals the two had collected from the desert in Yawoh, a circle that they hoped would prove impenetrable. The brother and sister chanted passages from *The Book of Belial* and called upon the spirits of their legion to come to them, to join them in their battle with the four women who threatened to banish them from their home.

"Soon," Gabe whispered to Helen. "We will be ready." Gabe licked his lips, his tongue momentarily sticking, dry from nervous anticipation.

Helen pulled her hand free from her brother's and thumbed wildly through the book, searching in vain for a desired passage. Sweat beaded on her wrinkled forehead, trickled down the bridge of her nose and dripped onto the page; a puff of smoke rose where the droplet hit the well worn paper. She swallowed and read a passage. Not the one she wanted, but at a loss of what else to do, she read it passionately, seeking strength. She was afraid. Then looking at Gabe, she saw his defiance. He smiled a toothy grin, teeth glistening in the flickering light from the candle.

"My dear, Helen. This is what we live for," he cackled loudly.

Helen laughed. "Of course, you're right, dear." Nonetheless, she shivered.

Overhead, the sound of chairs scraping across the floor startled them. Helen jumped. Gabe slapped her very hard—her lip began to bleed. Lifting her hand to her mouth, Helen wiped the blood from her lip onto her gnarled finger and stared at it, then at Gabe. She spit on him and then the two laughed.

Chapter 103

The *gong gong* of the grandfather clock pealed loudly, reverberating throughout the kitchen. It was eight o'clock. Terese stood up. "It's time. We need to prepare." She led the way into the dining room, her bulky tapestry bag in hand.

"Sara, dear, where are the supplies I asked you to get for our ceremonies?" Terese spoke in a voice she purposely kept light and cheerful.

Sara opened the door of the oak buffet. On one of the lower shelves were several canvas shopping bags and a heavy cardboard box. She handed the bags to Cassie and Mary. She carried the box herself, setting it on the wood floor next to the table. It was heavy and thumped loudly against the hard floor in the quiet room. "This is everything. Should we start taking things out?"

Terese touched Sara's hand. "Not yet." Terese turned to Cassie. "First we need to say a blessing, and we need the roses. Where are they?"

"I'll get them. They're on the back porch. It's so cool there; I thought they'd stay fresher." Cassie said, then took Mary's hand, pulling her into the kitchen with her. She whispered, "I think we should stay together. Don't you?"

Mary nodded and said very softly, "Cassie, I'm so scared." Cassie opened the door to the porch. A blast of cold air swooshed into the kitchen. "Let's hurry." Cassie didn't bother with the light. She grabbed the gold-foil covered box filled with thirty white roses, then whirled around, slamming the door with her knee. She flipped the deadbolt and practically ran back into the dining room with Mary right behind her.

From her bag, Terese pulled a white linen tablecloth. She gently smoothed it as she spread it onto the round dining table. In the center of the cloth was an embroidered circle, maybe a foot in diameter. Inside the circle was an intricate pattern of triangles, radiating out from a single, larger triangle in the center. The design was hand-stitched in narrow, white satin ribbon.

"Sara, I need the candlesticks now." She nodded to Sara. "And the candles."

Opening one of the bags, Sara handed, one by one, ten candles and ten lead-glass candle holders to Terese. Terese placed the ten candles in the triangles on the cloth, leaving the center triangle empty.

"Now, I need the vases."

"I think there are some vases in the kitchen," Cassie said.

"Wait, Cassie, I have them. These are the ones Terese wants." Sara took the lid off the large box. Inside were three lead-glass, three-sided vases.

"Perfect," Terese said. "Sara, can you get a pitcher of water, please."

Sara started for the kitchen, then turned and grabbed Cassie's hand. The two disappeared into the almost dark kitchen. The fire had died down to vibrant embers; a red-orange glow illuminated the walls with eerie flickers of light. The door swung closed. Hurrying, Sara opened and slammed cupboards searching for a pitcher. She turned the faucet on. It sputtered; air had apparently gotten into the pipes. Startled, she and Cassie yelled as cold water splashed into their faces.

Cassie put the pitcher under the running water. The tinkle of glass told them both what had happened. The bottom of the pitcher had cracked and fallen into the sink. A moan escaped Sara's throat. She grabbed another pitcher, this one plastic, from under the sink and handed it to Cassie to fill.

Minutes later, the kitchen door swung open. With shaking hands, a pale Cassie passed the pitcher to Terese.

"You all need to relax. You're safe, trust in me. I'll keep you out of harm's way." Terese smiled warmly, touched each woman's cheek and turned back to her task. "Before we put the roses into the water, I want each of you to take a vase and one of these." Terese reached into her bag and pulled out three long, white tapers. They each picked up a vase and took a candle from Terese's hand.

"Now, as I fill the vases, I want you to repeat what I say."

They nodded. With a lighter taken from her pocket, Terese lit the tapers. The flames flickered, burned brightly, reflected in each woman's eyes.

As she began filling Cassie's vase, Terese spoke softly, "We ask for purity and cleansing of this room, of this house." She nodded to the girls. They repeated the phrase three times as Terese filled each vase. "You can blow the candles out." The pungent smell of smoldering wicks permeated the air, contrasting with the sweet floral scent of the roses.

"Now set the vases around, one at the center of the table, the other two vases on the buffet. Make sure you put exactly ten roses into each vase."

"Why ten white roses?" Mary asked.

"The number ten is an all-encompassing number. It means the ideal, the return to oneness. It represents order, law, and control. It symbolizes perfection, the return to unity. And that is what we will strive for at this séance." Terese absent mindedly smoothed her silver hair as she spoke. "And ten is an axis symbol. That is why there are ten candles and ten white roses in each vase. I use the symbolic ten in many of my rituals. And, the white roses will help us attract the spirits.

"We need to allow the Lindemans to understand they will find completion of their journeys by the uniting of their souls with those on the other side. They need to be shown the perfection of life beyond this earth." By explaining all of this to Cassie, Mary and Sara, Terese tried to put their minds at ease and allow them to impart their innocence into the room. "We will try to reach the old ones and send their lost souls into the light."

Sara stared at Terese and asked in a shaky voice, "And how do we do that?"

"Follow my lead during the ceremony. Once I know exactly what is keeping them here, we will proceed. I won't know that until I connect with their spirits." Terese walked slowly around the table. "You see, I need to know why they won't leave this earth. There are many ways I, *we*, can help them pass. The ritual I lead you through will aid us with that." Terese smoothed the tablecloth again. It still smelled of the hot iron and starch.

"What does the pattern on the cloth mean?" asked Sara, fingering the satin embroidery. "It must have some significance since it's so intricately detailed."

"If you look closely, you'll see that the pattern begins in the center with a single triangle, then radiates out with all interconnected triangles. The number three represents birth, life and death. A complete cycle. The beginning, the middle and the end. The vases, as you see, are also triangles," Terese explained. "And there are three of you. All of these triad symbols give us power to reach the spirits. We have much strength here in this room. I can feel it."

"I can, too," Cassie said, re-centering the vase slightly. "What do we do now?"

Bong! The clocked struck the half hour.

"We'll light the incense now. Sara, will you get the incense burners?" Terese asked.

As Sara got the ceramic burners from one of the sacks, Terese took three silver boxes from her bag. "We have spicy cinnamon which fills the air with warmth and energy, frankincense to expand consciousness and help me ease into a deep meditative state, and last we have earthy sandalwood to help the three of you remain focused."

"*Everything* has a purpose," Cassie said."This is *amazing*. I had no idea,"

"Here, place the three burners around the room." She handed them out, then gave each of them a differently scented incense cone from each silver box. "Here are matches; light the cones as well." Terese checked the clock. "It's too soon to start. We'll begin as the clock strikes nine." Terese put the silver boxes away into her tapestry bag.

"Why nine o'clock?" Mary asked.

"Nine is the number of completion: attainment, the beginning, the end. And most importantly, it symbolizes the Triple Triad, composed of the all-powerful three times three."

"Fascinating," Cassie said as she put another log on the fire. Embers popped and crackled as the wood ignited.

"I brought music, *Celtic Harps* by Angeline O'Hara. Here, Mary, will you put this in the CD player over there?" Terese pointed across the room. "Don't turn it up very loudly." No one said anything until the music began to play.

"We will begin very soon. Let's all go and have a drink first. Nothing alcoholic, of course!" Terese kidded and laughed.

They followed her into the kitchen. Cassie opened the refrigerator and handed each one of them a bottle of water. They drank in silence, then one by one used the bathroom—leaving the door slightly ajar. Cassie, Mary, and Sara avoided looking into the mirror above the sink as they washed their hands. They were afraid of what the mirror might reflect—their own haunted faces, or those of the Lindemans'.

Tick tock. Tick tock. The ticking of the clock a constant reminder to all that time was passing. Soon something would happen that each of them, Cassie, Sara and Mary, wondered if they were truly prepared for.

Tick tock. Tick tock. Tick tock . . .

Chapter 104

"Come. It's time to begin," Terese said, opening the door into the dining room. "Sit down, relax." She pulled her lighter from her pocket and began lighting the candles on the table. The smell of the incense was pungent. A smoky veil floated delicately in the room, wafting and undulating in tiny air currents, stirred by the movements of the women as they took their places.

"Should we hold hands?" Mary asked, reaching her hands out to either side, toward Cassie and Sara.

"No, it's not necessary. If you feel like you want to, go ahead though; it might help you relax."

The three held hands.

"I always record the sessions. I'll start my recorder now," Terese said quietly, clicking it on.

"Now, I want you all to breathe deeply. Slowly. In and out. In—one, two, three. Out—one, two, three. In—one two three. Out—one, two, three." She listened to their breaths whooshing in and out in an even, controlled rhythm. "Now close your eyes. Clear your minds. Breathe. In and out. In and out. Now, imagine the room is filled with white light. Pure. Bright. Innocent. You can open your eyes if you like. Or if you feel more connected and stronger, keep them closed. The spirits do not care. They know we are here. They know *why* we are here."

"Oh, God!" Mary whispered. She squeezed Sara's and Cassie's hands tighter.

"We ask if there are other spirits here, spirits who can help us, spirits who are virtuous and pure, come and surround us. Help us with the tormented souls of Helen and Gabriel Lindeman, who have yet to go into the light. Help us reach them and communicate with them so they can find their eternal peace."

Sara opened her eyes, looked around the room. Cassie and Mary had their eyes closed. Terese stared at the roses in the center of the table. The roses began to droop, petals began to fall. The candles flared, the flames tall, thin, reaching well over a foot into the air. Sara gasped, then became silent when Terese looked at her, putting her finger to her lips.

"We are not afraid. We are strong. We are protected by the divine and innocent spirits who are with us." Terese paused, inhaled quickly, looked around the room. "The spirits of Helen and Gabriel will not be allowed to harm us."

The door between the dining room and kitchen swung open, slamming against the wall. A heavy smell of opium and foul, decrepit bodies enveloped them.

"We are not afraid. We are pure. We are innocent. Please ladies, say this out loud with me."

The four women chanted. Mary, Cassie, and Sara stared at Terese and then at the door as it continued to slam into the dining room wall. Over and over. *Bang! Bang! Bang!* Shrill laughter pierced the putrid air.

Then, directly behind Terese, Helen and Gabe appeared, their eyes black and empty, teeth glistening in the bright candlelight. They squealed as they caressed Terese, their tightly puckered lips blowing kisses, their black tongues darting in and out, seductively taunting the women. They ran their hands through Terese's hair, gently at first, then suddenly and viciously, they yanked. Terese's head snapped back.

Terese gasped and then quickly regained control.

Helen and Gabe laughed.

Terese said loudly, "You cannot harm us. You cannot frighten us. You are nothing but smoke and mist." She turned to them, blew hard into the air at them. The quick gust of air caused the old ones to begin dissipating. Terese said in a loud, steady voice, "You *will* tell me why you have chosen to stay in this house, on this earth."

Helen and Gabe floated around the table, away from the disturbance of moving air. Their laughter pierced the night. Gabe reached out and pinched Mary's cheek. She screamed. Red welts appeared. A tear ran down her cheek. She swallowed, sat up straight but did not touch her face.

Cassie held Mary's hand tightly and joined with Terese in asking, "Why are you here?" Mary and Sara stared, eyes filled with fright as the old ones gyrated around the table, stroking each other, then running their gnarled, wrinkled hands through the women's hair, down their backs, across their breasts. The old ones groped and prodded desperately trying to frighten the women. The women glared, did not falter.

Terese bent over, reached into the tapestry bag by her side. She pulled out a dried bundle of sage, the end wrapped with twine. She stood up slowly and lit the end of the herb bundle from one of the burning candles. The smell of sage filled their nostrils. She reached her hand out, well above the heads of the three women, circled the table, covering them with tendrils of white smoke.

Helen and Gabe retreated, backing away toward the kitchen doorway.

"You must be very calm, all of you. We are safe. There are spirits here with us who are protecting us. I can see them. Don't be afraid," Terese whispered.

"Sara, take this." Terese handed the smoldering sage to Sara. "Stay behind me. Keep your arms out—with the sage in front of you.

"Cassie, take this." She reached into her bag and brought out a small black tin. "This is filled with sea salt."

Cassie took the tin and stood beside Terese.

Terese pulled an atomizer from her other pocket. "This is filled with holy water." Terese motioned to Mary. "Come stand with us."

"Again, I ask you—Helen and Gabriel Lindeman, why are you here?"

Hovering eerily in a quivering, brown mist of buzzing flies, Helen shouted, "This is *our* home. *You* are intruders here. We want *you* to leave!"

Terese misted the air in front of her with the holy water and took several steps toward the old ones. Mary, Cassie, and Sara followed, close behind.

"*You* leave *our* house or *you* will be forever sorry!" Gabe yelled, moving backward. His legs were no longer visible, his body slowly becoming a pale, gray mist. "Leave or we will make you ours forever!"

Terese inched forward leading the women closer and closer to the pair, who were now visibly horrified. She again sprayed a fine mist of holy water. "Spirit to Water. Water to Spirit. Leave this house! Be Gone! Cassie, throw the salt. Now!"

Cassie poured the crystals into her hand, flung them at Helen and Gabe.

"Go! This I command you. You are not welcome here," Terese calmly and sternly demanded. "Leave this house. Now!" She sprayed the air before her yet again.

Gabe shrieked as the salt passed through him. Helen writhed in agony as the holy water touched her. Then they were gone.

"Is it over?" Mary screamed.

"No." Terese turned to them.

"No?" Cassie and Mary yelled in unison.

"No. But we *have* made progress." Terese tried to smile, but was certain her feeble attempt to make light of the situation was obvious. *They are much stronger, this couple, than I ever imagined. This will not be easy. I need to rest for a while.* "We'll take a break. Don't worry, dears. I promise you, the Lindemans will be gone before the night is over."

Mary collapsed into a chair and cried out, "I hate them!"

"We mustn't hate them. Though certainly it's easy to do. We need to keep our emotions in check. In order to banish them for good, we have to remain strong and stoic. We have to let them know we—not them—are in control. We must convince them that they can find safety on the other side. They may be afraid to pass over, afraid they will go to hell for eternity. At least here they have what they think is a 'life.'"

"They deserve an eternity in hell!" Mary said loudly.

"Mary, are you okay?" Terese asked. "Can you do this with us?"

"I'm sorry for the outburst. It won't happen again." Mary shrugged and continued, "I can do this. Absolutely I can. I made a promise to you, and to myself, to follow this through to the end, and I will! I'm mad as hell. I want them to leave." She brushed her hair from her eyes. Cassie sat down in the chair beside her, gently massaged her shoulders.

Turning on the lights, Sara asked, "What should we do, Terese? How can we help you? You look exhausted."

"We all are. I'll be fine in a few minutes." Terese began blowing out the candles, picking the fallen petals off the table and making a small pile of them. "White. Pure. These will still be effective. Come on, let's go into the kitchen. We need tea and chocolate!" They all laughed.

As Terese opened the kitchen door, Cassie hesitated. "Where are they now?"

"In the basement," Terese said flatly.

"Oh!" Sara exclaimed. She turned the light on, and the four women filed into the kitchen.

Terese picked up several pieces of kindling, throwing them into the fireplace. They crackled for several minutes, then finally, flames appeared illuminating their faces alternately from orange to yellow. In unspoken camaraderie, they huddled around the fireplace, shivering. "We need to relax for a few minutes," Terese said, her voice gentle and soothing.

Sara asked, "Will they be stronger next time?" She backed away from the fire, pulled a chair out from the table. The wooden legs scraped the floor like fingernails on a chalkboard.

Collapsing in the chair next to Sara, Terese cleared her throat. "Possibly. But, to be honest, I've never observed spirits get stronger. They are what they are. They reach a level of *growth,* I guess I would call it, and they stay at or below that stage. I expect them to try to make us believe they are more ominous than they actually are. As I've told you before, they work on our fears. Do you all understand the repercussions of letting them see any weaknesses we may have?"

No one answered her, so Teresa explained, "If we allow them to see our fear, they'll use it against us." She hesitated to make sure they understood. They nodded, and she went on. "They'll recognize any indication of fear or panic on your face or in your voice. They'll use it to their advantage. They can conjure incredibly realistic manifestations; make us hear voices and noises that do not exist."

"I thought you said they couldn't get stronger." Cassie put her cup down too quickly; tea sloshed over the sides splattering her shirt. Mary handed her a napkin.

"They aren't getting stronger; they already have all these capabilities. You've experienced them. All the things that have happened to you in this house are proof that they can do a lot of damage, but only when they know you're afraid. Or if they catch you unaware. If you let them into your minds, they will indeed create mayhem. But . . . you saw tonight, when we showed them we would not back down, they left. We'll do that again—in a little while."

Cassie filled the teakettle, turned the burner on the stove to high. "How are we supposed to act like we're not afraid? How do we do that?" She turned, wrapped her arms around herself.

"You remember that they're evil. They don't belong here. You understand that when they leave here, they will face their maker, get their just rewards!" Terese said emphatically. Then in a very quiet voice added, "We can't let them know *that* though. They must believe they can leave this earth, go into the light and be safe. Find their eternal peace."

"But if they knew their punishment was an eternity in hell, wouldn't that be their idea of eternal joy? Wouldn't they want to leave here?" Sara began shredding a napkin into tiny pieces, gathering the scraps neatly into a pile in front of her. The kettle boiled, spit water in tiny sizzling puffs onto the burner.

"No! They believe, to some extent, they are alive. They're terrified that if they leave and go into the hereafter, they will lose everything. They're very content here. *We're* the intruders into *their* lives," Terese explained. "We're threatening to take away everything they hold sacred."

"Despicable as it is!" Mary said disgustedly.

Cassie took four mugs from the cupboard, poured the hot water into them, then added tea bags. Carrying them two by two, she set them in the center of the table. "Sugar or cream, anyone?"

"Yes, both please," Mary said.

Cassie sat down across from Terese, pulled a cup of tea toward her, and dunked the teabag up and down, up and down.

The lights flashed off, then back on. A door slammed somewhere on the second floor. "I thought you said they were in the basement," Mary blurted out.

Terese nodded. "They are. They're trying to frighten us. They'll do everything they can to distract us and delay what they now must realize is inevitable—we are going to send them into eternity." Terese paused to let that sink in. She sipped her tea, then asked Cassie nonchalantly, "Where's the candy? I was serious, we need chocolate."

Cassie giggled. She got up and rummaged through the cupboards. "Aha! I found Nellie's secret stash!" She giggled again as she pulled out a canvas shopping bag. "Look, milk chocolate with almonds, chocolate covered peanuts, and my favorite, toffee!" She poured the candy into the middle of the table. For a few minutes they ate the confections in silence.

"Ahh, much better." Terese gathered up the empty wrappers, tossed them into the fire, then took a sip of her tea. "It's time to get serious again. It's almost ten. What you need to do now is clear your minds. I want you to focus on pleasant things, things that make you happy. It may help to think of how calm and peaceful your lives will be after tonight. It'll help give you strength. And you—we—will need every ounce of it very shortly."

Terese opened the door between the rooms. "I need to go into the dining room; I have a few things to do before we continue the séance. Stay here. Relax. I'll be back in about ten minutes." She walked away, hesitated and stuck her head back into the kitchen. "You're safe. Believe me."

Terese shut the door knowing she had done all she could to give them some peace and sanguinity. It wasn't easy for them, she realize that. But she knew those three women were up to the challenge before them tonight. And so was she. It was going to be difficult, but they would send the Lindemans away.

Chapter 105

Harold was dismayed to see a strange car parked in front of Tom's house. "Shit! Guess I better see who's here," he mumbled as he walked up the driveway, carefully staying in the shadow of the trees. He'd parked Joanie's car in a stand of white pines, well hidden in case anyone drove up the road. Cautiously he climbed the steps to the front porch. The living room was dark. He crept quietly to the side of the house. Pale, white squares of light coming from the dining room danced on the porch floor. He peered in the window, saw Cassie, Mary, Sara and a fourth woman he thought he'd seen in town, sitting around the table. Dozens of candles were lit, faint sounds of music floated in the night. Good. They were having a ladies night. They wouldn't bother him at all. Retracing his steps, he left the porch and crept to the west side of the house. Taking out a small flashlight, he shone it on the door and inserted his key.

Earlier in the day, he'd hidden his tools underneath the workbench. Turning the light on that illuminated the boxing ring, he looked around. No signs of anything out of order, no one had moved his tool bag. Good. Now, the easiest way for him to get upstairs was to go up the back stairs into the kitchen. He patted the sweat off his forehead with a handkerchief. *When I get to the kitchen, I'll just have to be very quiet. I can sneak through easy enough and then take the back staircase to the second floor. They'll never know I'm here.*

Harold gathered his tool bag and checked to make sure he had all his keys. The broads seemed to enjoy locking every door in the place. He turned the light off and went quietly up the back stairs, through the kitchen and up to the second staircase. Once on the upper floor, he shined his flashlight into the long, dark hallway. Several doors down and to his left was the library—that was where Tom's safe was.

Being a trusting man, Tom hadn't bothered to hide his safe. It sat plainly in view beside a low, mahogany side table. Harry had already been upstairs several times nosing around, searching for the safe, determining how to open the lock—which it turned out, would be a simple job for him. It took him all of ten minutes to open it. He had his black carpetbag filled with jewels and cash in about two minutes and was ready to leave. Visions of himself lounging on the beaches of Puerto La Cruz, Venezuela sipping icy mojitos, flashed through his head.

Harold pushed on the safe door—it wouldn't close. He turned the cylinder around and around. *Fuck*! He had to get the door closed. No one could know he'd been in the safe. With Gardner out of town, it would be days before anyone found out that it had been broken into—time Harold needed to get out of the country. He kicked the door with his boot. Shit! The *slamming* echoed like a clap of thunder through the quiet house. At least he got the fucking door closed. Harry froze. Did the ladies hear that? He waited behind the door, pistol in hand. No one came. Like a ghost he crept down the back stairs and peered into the kitchen from the doorway. *Fuck!* All four women were in the kitchen. Closing the door, he sat down on the steps and waited.

Chapter 106

Helen and Gabe huddled inside the safety of their powerful ring of stones. "Gabe, do you believe they can make us leave?" Gabe didn't answer her. Helen snarled. "This is our house, not theirs! I refuse to go." She poked his shoulder when he still didn't answer her.

Gabe reacted, "I'm thinking! Keep your fucking hands to yourself, bitch."

Helen gasped. Gabe had never called her a name before. She didn't like it. She poked him in the shoulder again. "Don't you call me names, you son of a bitch!"

Gabe grabbed her thin, frail arm. "Don't you ever call me that, you old hag!" Gabe glared, dropped her arm and shoved her. Helen fell backwards hitting her head on the floor with a hard *thunk*.

Recovering quickly, she leaned forward and flung both fists at her brother. He ducked sideways, laughing. "Feeling a little better are you, woman? Good, now let's have a little snort and go send those bitches the hell out of here!"

"You sly bastard." Helen's eyes twinkled as she realized what her brother had been doing. Then he took something from his pouch. She licked her lips as her brother pulled out a little silver tin and a small oval mirror. "Where did you find that?"

Gabe said, "Stole it off one of the workers. Harry. The one who keeps sneaking around the house." Gabe carefully poured, then cut the powder into two thin lines. Leaning over, he snorted the powder into his left and then right nostril. He tapped the tin to pour out more cocaine and cut it into two lines. He handed the mirror to Helen. She snorted, then inhaled deeply, let out a long sigh. Her foul breath caused Gabe to turn away.

"What's the matter, brother? Do I offend you?" Helen squealed. She drew her hand back and slapped Gabe across his face. "See how *you* like it." She grabbed his hand as he swung back at her. "I don't forget the things you've done to me. You better remember that." From upstairs they heard footsteps. Heard music. Smelled a faint hint of smoldering sage. "They're getting ready for us again. Get your damned hands away from me, Gabe! We need to prepare. They aren't playing games here; they're dead serious. Get our *Book of Belial* and read that passage I marked. Get it now!" she snapped.

Gabe started to say something, thought better of it. Getting up, he retrieved the book from the dresser top. With bony, arthritic fingers he thumbed through the book and found the page his sister had marked with a thick, black, grosgrain ribbon. Helen lit the black, ritual candle.

They bowed their heads. Gabe read the passages. Helen repeated them. Over and over they chanted, never looking up, never seeing Harold as he came back down the stairs from the kitchen.

Chapter 107

Harold listened, waiting for the women to leave the kitchen. He heard the door to the dining room close. He'd put a piece of duct tape over the bolt so the door couldn't lock. Not yet anyway. He pushed the door open an inch and peered through the crack in the door. The older woman went into the dining room leaving the other three in the kitchen. Closing the door very slowly, he sat down again, leaned against the staircase, wishing he could light up.

After what he figured was maybe fifteen minutes, everyone filed into the dining room, shutting off the kitchen light. Good, that meant they wouldn't be back—for a little while anyhow.

Harold waited for maybe half a minute and then pulled the tape off the door. He shut and locked it, then quietly crossed the kitchen. Creeping slowly downstairs, he carefully avoided stepping on the third and eighth rungs—he knew they creaked. When he reached the last step into the basement, he heard voices. *What the fuck! Who the hell would be down here? Now what?*

Harold crept slowly toward the room behind the stairs. Staring into the dark, waiting for his eyes to adjust, he was careful not to make a sound. On the floor, surrounded by a circle of rocks, were an old man and an old woman. The old man had a book in his hands. He read by the light of a black candle flickering on the floor in front of them. His voice was deep and nasally. The old woman, a shriveled old hag if Harry had ever seen one, repeated everything the old man said. Holy shit, they were talking devil worship crap! He wondered what loony bin those two escaped from? Harold snickered.

Helen and Gabe were on him in seconds. His reaction time was slow; he wasn't prepared for this turn of events. The insanely-loud beating of his heart pounded in his ears. He dropped his duffel bag filled with the stolen money and his tools and prepared to fight.

That wouldn't be necessary. Helen twisted and wrapped her vile, black-misty form around him. Distracted by the nauseating smell of old rotting flesh mixed with an ancient, sour perfume—not to mention his complete shock at seeing this old woman transform into mist— Harold was momentarily stunned. Gabe came at him. Harry backed up, tripped on a bag of cement and fell backward. Slamming his temple into a cinderblock left haphazardly on the floor by one of his compadres, he never knew what happened. He died an hour later, never regaining consciousness.

Helen and Gabe pushed and shoved, finally managing to roll the body away from their sacred circle. Helen threw an old, gray blanket over him, and they went back to their chanting. They had little time left. They felt their spirits being pulled upstairs.

"Helen," Gabe whispered, "we have to go now. We know what we have to do." He slithered and floated up the stairs and through the door. Helen hesitated, then followed behind him.

Chapter 108

Terese relit the candles and incense. Methodically she walked through the room making certain everything was ready. Turning the music on very quietly, she felt soothed by the melodic resonance of the harps, the gentle, angelic voices singing in unison. She sprinkled salt in all four corners of the room, under every window, in front of each doorway, then poured a thick circle around the perimeter of the round, oriental rug where the table was centered. She wanted to keep the Lindemans outside of this boundary. The old couple was strong, but she knew ways to keep them from the girls. Next she sprinkled holy water on the table, on the chairs. She pulled two more sage bundles from her bag lighting only one of them, the other she laid on the table. *There, we're ready now.* She laid the burning sage on a crystal plate on the side-table.

"Ladies," she said, opening the door into the kitchen, "it's time to begin." She held the door as they filed into the room. "Sit down and relax. Here, hold these in your right hands." She gave each one of them a large, pale-blue Celestite stone, icy to the touch and polished to a high gloss. "These will help us communicate and connect with the spirits of light during our ceremony."

Around her neck Terese hung a polished silver amulet that hung on a heavy silver chain. In its center was another Celestite stone. It glimmered, reflecting the dancing candle flame. "I'll summon the Lindemans soon. When they come, they'll try to frighten us. We can't let them. I have, and will again, called upon some very strong spirits to help us. I know you could not see them, but I could. Right now, they too are preparing to help us. Trust in them and call to them if you feel yourself becoming afraid. The stone will help you reach them.

"The Lindemans will feed on any weaknesses we show. But they are not demons, and they have limited powers. I won't lie to you—they are very powerful. But we and the *other* spirits are an exceedingly strong force. In my communications with these spirits, they indicated to me they had been waiting for a long time for someone to come here and banish the Lindemans from this house. They have tried to protect this house and its occupants.

"Helen and Gabe are evil, as we already know. But truth and light will prevail. We've placed talismans and protections throughout this room to keep them at a distance from us. Once they come in the room, I will trap them here. They will not leave this room—except to cross over."

"What should we do?" Sara asked, rubbing the stone around in her hand, kneading the smooth surface.

Terese continued, "No matter what happens, stay seated. Don't make eye contact with either of them. If you want to leave during the séance or during the banishment ceremony, I have to be honest—you can't. We have to see this through. If you aren't all okay with that, we can quit now." Then Terese added emphatically, "Once the Lindemans are here, we won't be able to stop."

Cassie stared out the window. The sky was a deep indigo. Stars sparkled across the expanse of the heavens, the moon glistened brightly on the jet-black water, white waves moved in and out rhythmically. Far out on the horizon a ship passed, bobbing eerily up and down. Occasional sparks of light flashed as the moon reflected off the ship's tall smokestack. Cassie studied the faces of her friends, then asked Terese, "Why can't you stop the séance? What if something goes wrong?"

"Nothing will go wrong," Terese said. "I've done this hundreds of times. These entities are formidable, but I have no doubt, I—we—are going to do this." She paused, then asked, "Well?"

One by one Cassie, Sara and Mary nodded.

"You said a banishment ceremony? What's that?" asked Sara.

"Once their spirits are here with us, follow my lead as you have before. I'll guide you and ask for your help when I need it," Terese answered, taking her place at the table.

The clock began its ritual chiming. It was ten o'clock. "Take a few deep breaths, in and out. That's good." Terese watched the women, made certain each of them was all right. "It's time." She turned the tape recorder on.

Chapter 109

"Where are you, Elise?" Tom shouted up the stairway, his voice echoed, bouncing hollowly off the low ceiling. He'd begun searching in the basement, methodically going from room to room, looking for a clue to where she was hiding. Every closet door was thrown open, each storage cupboard checked. He did the same on the main floor of the house, wandering from kitchen to living room to dining room. Nothing.

On the second floor Tom again went from room to room searching. He'd not heard even a whisper nor seen a fleeting shadow thrown across the floor. The attic was his last hope. And again, not a single sign that Elise was or had recently been in the house.

Giving up his search, at least for a while, Tom took a cab into town and had the driver drop him at a small diner on Linden Street. He sat at a booth next to the street, his image, mirrored in the window, his only company. He felt invisible and alone, enjoying his solitude. No one gave him a second glance.

Slowly he savored a mushroom burger, read the evening paper and enjoyed the obscurity of the poorly lit diner. He ordered a final refill of black, syrupy coffee and a piece of homemade chocolate cake thick with rollup icing. After paying his bill, he wandered down the atmospheric street toward the plaza. Christmas lights twinkled from every window and streetlight. A towering Christmas tree in the center of the plaza was adorned with myriads of lights—blue, green, red, white. Snowflakes, almost the size of quarters, danced and fluttered down from the heavens like sparkling angels. Indoor lights began to turn off as stores closed for the night.

Tom flagged a cab and returned to his empty home. Security lights flashed on the dark porch as Tom searched his pocket for his house keys. Letting himself into the foyer, he walked cautiously in the dark, groping the walls as he went down the hallway toward the kitchen. He flipped on the switch. The room glowed. Stark. Empty. He made a pot of coffee, filled a mug and laced it with brandy and milk. He turned the light off and went upstairs to his bedroom. After a couple of minutes, he picked up his cell phone and called Sara. There was no answer, so he tried calling Cassie. The call went to voicemail. "Cassie, it's Tom. Call me."

He called Joe's cell number. Again no answer. "Damnit! Where is everyone?"

Chapter 110

Billy was playing some distracting video game. The blaring music and the nonsensical patterns of sounds pounded in Elise's head, making her anxious and irritated. And she was bored. Billy was such a child, someone to fill her hours and help her learn more about Tom. She longed for the company of an adult, was tiring more and more every day with Billy's spoiled-child antics. "Billy," Elise said loudly over the racket of the game, "I'm going out. I need some fresh air."

A slight nod of his head was the only acknowledgement that Billy heard her. His thumbs frantically pressed the controller as he fired his assault rifle at the imaginary enemy on the screen. Graphic blood spurted, and an enemy soldier dropped. Another explosion shook the air. Billy hooted. He had struck down another enemy.

It was late. A frigid winter-wind blew in from the ocean chilling Elise to the core. In the distance, lights glared from a window in Tom's kitchen. Climbing the hill above the Harrisons', she followed the path through the back woods. *The séance is tonight. I wonder if they've started yet."* Elise neared the back of Remington House, branches waved in the strong breeze, their shadows like elongated fingers, played on the ground beneath her. *I know I should stay away until the séance is over. I'll go see what's happening, then leave. I can't let the psychic know about me.* She flittered around to the back porch, peered into the entry toward the kitchen. She saw two women; one was Cassie, the other Mary.

Making her way in the dark to the side of the house, she entered the basement. A dim light burned above a newly-constructed boxing ring. It was cold down there. Elise was so tired of being cold. On a nearby bench lay a jacket. She grabbed it, throwing it around her shoulders. It smelled of aftershave, dark and musky. Her thoughts drifted momentarily as she tried to imagine the man who might have worn this coat. Pulling the collar close around her neck, she breathed deeply. It smelled so good, so alive.

Elise stumbled and snapped back to high alert. Much had changed. She hadn't been in the basement for weeks, not since the old couple had moved down here. Suddenly she felt their presence, smelled their evil stench. She shivered. The cold permeated the jacket; she pushed her arms into the sleeves.

The old ones were chanting. *Preparing for the confrontation, no doubt. The séance must be about to begin.* As she neared the room where the brother and sister sat in their circle of stones, Elise smelled blood. A pool of crimson seeped from beneath a blanket on the ground, not far from Helen and Gabe.

The old couple mumbled to each other, then floated, one after the other, up the stairs and through the kitchen door. They had not felt Elise's presence.

Their spirits had been summoned. Elise needed to protect herself. She had to get out! Elise felt herself drawn up the stairs. Fighting the allure of the comforting psychic's incantations, she ran to the blanket. Lifting it she saw the body —still alive, though barely. She touched the face. It was Harold, Nate's brother. There was little time for her to think; she was dizzy and confused. Harold twitched. He drew a shallow breath, not his last, but certainly close to it. Elise watched as his soul abandoned his body. It was black and ominous, though it still retained its human form. She saw its eyes, clearly bewildered as it hovered above its living, near-dead corpse and gazed on its body. Harold had obviously not expected to die this night. Elise reached out, drew the spirit to her, felt its warmth connect with hers. Its close presence was so comforting.

No time! She had to get out. "Come with me! Now!" she yelled. Not looking back, Elise flew out of the basement door and into the woods beyond the house. She did not stop. The lure of the women gathered in the house, calling all the spirits, offered her comfort and warmth, an end to the loneliness of this world. She almost succumbed to the enchanting calls. Almost. But once she reached a safe distance far from the house, she turned and circled the property, heading for the cliff overlooking the ocean. The roar of the waves and the electric snap of cold spray being flung high into the air above the rocky jetties had a much stronger draw for her.

Looking around and into the darkness behind her, she felt disappointment. Harold had not followed her. Distraught, she sat on the edge of a wooden chair that overlooked the water. Billy had brought the old, wooden rocking chair here from his mother's house when Elise complained about sitting on the cold ground.

A low wailing erupted, emanating from deep in her soul. Elise cried, not caring who might hear her. She was desperate. Loneliness surrounded her like a living presence. Tom, her reason for being here, was not even in the country. He was far, far away. So distant she could not reach him. Vivian too had gone, unable to stand Elise's constant manipulations of her body. Elise had enjoyed the physical sensations—the true warmth, the ability to talk, the sensual pleasure of playing the piano, the taste of food and the satisfaction of drinking the wine that was served so freely at Vivian's and Tom's houses.

Her numinous spirit was too weak to do all the many things that had given her pleasure. Her manifestations into a near physical presence when she was with Billy left her aching for true sensations. She did feel something. It was certainly better than the alternative of being dead and no longer in this realm. But it wasn't enough.

The quick staccato of salsa music made Elise jump. A vibration alerted her to an incoming phone call. She stuck her hand into the pocket of the jacket. She had someone's cell phone! The screen lit up. The caller ID said the call was from Tom Gardner. Elise laughed. It was the contractor's coat she was wearing! She had Joe's phone! And now she had Tom's cell phone number!

You're not so far away now, Tom, are you? She giggled, watching the moon rise higher, now almost overhead. It sparkled, its reflection undulating on the gentler waves far out on the horizon. Elise relaxed. She rocked back and forth, stared serenely at the ocean. Far away, from the stand of trees behind Remington House, a single raven cawed.

Chapter 111

Candles flickered. Shadows danced across the table and onto the walls. Flames in the fireplace burned brightly, popped and crackled, exploding in brilliant plumes of orange and blue. Through the open curtains, shimmering moonlight reflected on the Atlantic. All of these things gave a false sense of warmth and serenity to the room.

Terese bowed her head. "Gabriel and Helen Lindeman, spirits that dwell in this house, you are summoned." With dizzying speed, Helen and Gabe Lindeman flew into the room. Terese continued, "I am not alone tonight. With me are many spirits, many who have already passed. They have returned to show you the way to the light." She paused, took a slow breath, then continued, "And there are three women here," she glanced around the table, appreciating the strength reflected in the women's faces, "and they understand that you are trapped here." Terese tapped the table three times with her index finger. The powerful number three representing birth, life and death, a complete cycle, beginning, middle and end. "We know you are afraid to leave. Trust us. We'll help you find your final peace."

Bewildered, the brother and sister darted back and forth around the table, trying to penetrate the thick, salt barrier. Gabe backed into the side table, inhaled the smudge of sage burning in the crystal dish, and slumped to the floor. Helen glided to his side, bending over his slimy, misted form. She felt his temple. Her finger penetrated his vaporous body. Screeching into his ear she implored him to stay with her. "Gabe, this is *our* home! Don't let the bitches take it from us."

While the two old ones were distracted, Terese ran to the closed door between the kitchen and dining room. She poured a thick line of salt in front of it, blocking the Lindemans' only exit.

Too late, Helen saw what Terese had done. She grabbed her brother's arms and pulled. She whisked him up, fleeing to the door to escape. It was no use. They were trapped. In a panic, she shrieked. She dragged her brother by the arm and raced around the room trying to find a way out.

Terese spoke calmly to them. "We understand your fear. You're afraid to leave this world. You must trust us," she said, sweeping her arms and pointing around the room at the spirits only she and the Lindemans could see. "These gentle spirits are here to help you go into the light. You have no choice. You *must* go. You are not welcome here!" Terese lit the second sage bundle and walked in a circle around the table. "This is not where you belong. Your bodies are dead, only your spiritual selves live. You both must seek the solace of the afterlife. Leave!" She sat down and spoke quietly to the three women. "Repeat after me." They nodded. "Spirits of eternal life, we ask you to take Helen and Gabriel Lindeman into the light." She waited while Cassie, Mary and Sara repeated the phrase. "Spirits, Helen and Gabriel Lindeman are afraid to go. You need to reassure them and guide them from here." Terese waited while the women repeated after her.

Cassie closed her eyes and spoke loudly; Mary and Sara recited in a monotone, brows furrowed, both gripping each other's hand. Terese, head bowed, hands gripping the table edge, continued, "You *can* be forgiven for your sins. You need only ask for forgiveness from your higher power."

Terese lifted her head, looking at Helen and Gabe. She stared into Helen's eyes. Helen quickly turned away. Not waiting for the others to respond, Terese continued staring at the old couple and commanded, "Go! Leave this house!" Her voice raised an octave, sliced through the charged atmosphere like a knife. "Go! Be gone from Remington House! You're not welcome here!"

Helen howled. Gabe covered his ears with his ancient, gnarled hands. Then he laughed. He glared at Terese, his eyes glazed with malevolence. Terese returned his stare, unmoved, unafraid.

Gabe shifted his attention to Sara and Mary. They looked to Terese for strength. She was not looking at them but rather at Gabe. They joined Terese in glaring at Gabe, muttering a prayer. Cassie squeezed her eyes tightly closed, sat rigid and unmoving. Gabriel snarled. Startled, Cassie opened her eyes to meet Gabe's unblinking gaze.

Glasses, plates, and vases flew off the shelves of the sideboard, crashed and shattered on the oak floor. Shards of glass sliced into Terese's legs. She winced, nothing more. Quickly she poured salt into a small open space. Apparently she had disturbed the ring of salt when she ran across the room. Spared by their heavy blue jeans, the others escaped being cut by the slivers of glass. Mary gasped, pulled her hand from Sara's and grabbed the polished Celestite stone from where it lay on the table in front of her. She threw it at the Lindemans. Passing through them, the pale blue stone glanced off the wall and fell to the floor with a dull *thump*. Sara jumped out of her chair, her eyes wide in horror. Helen rushed toward her. Sara froze.

"Helen and Gabriel, I said *leave!*" Terese enunciated each word, speaking in a steady, commanding voice. She motioned for Sara to sit down.

"Get out of here!" Mary shrieked, incensed at the Lindemans' destructive behavior.

"We are not afraid of you." Terese reached into her pocket, pulled out her bottle of holy water. She sprang to her feet, dousing the couple with the clear water. Steam rose as it touched the old ones' decrepit, translucent skin.

The Lindemans backed away, then turned and scrambled out of reach of Terese. Becoming a black mist, they slithered behind the china cabinet.

Smoke filled the room. "Oh, God! What have they done?" Sara yelled. The Lindemans had closed the flue on the fireplace. Gabe howled with delight.

Burying her nose and mouth into her sleeve, Terese calmly walked to the fireplace. Grabbing the poker from the hearth, she pushed the flue open again. She rushed back into the safety of the circle. Above the table, she pulled the hanging chain. The ceiling fan blades whirled, slowly dispersing the smoke. The flames of the dozens of white candles danced crazily, threatening to smother in the churning air, defiantly flickered and burned triumphantly. Tiny sparks of hot, burning wick popped and floated. They were extinguished by the rapid movement of air from the overhead fan before they could char the white embroidered tablecloth. Once the smoke had cleared, Terese turned the fan off and sprayed the chain with holy water.

"The only way you can leave this room is by following the spirits into the light. You must realize that now. Go! Find your eternal peace! Follow the spirits into the light," Terese said.

"We'll see about that!" screamed Gabe. A black, murky fog seeped from beneath the china cabinet. Gabe was no longer recognizable as a man. The voice was the only clue as to the identity of the thick, dank vapor. Then, for an instant, Gabriel appeared as a human. He hissed and swirled, exploded into thousands of black, sparkling, diamond-like stones, tumbling and bouncing around the room, pelting the walls and the oak floor with tiny, jagged shards. None penetrated the circle of salt.

"Oh, my God!" Cassie was on her feet, ready to run.

Terese reached her before she could leave the safety of the ring. "Sit down! You're safe." Terese gently pushed on Cassie's shoulder. "Sit down!"

On the floor just beyond the Persian rug, perhaps two feet from Terese, lay Helen. She smiled wickedly. "You whores! We are not going anywhere!" She scrambled onto her hands and knees. With craggy, gnarled hands she grabbed handfuls of the tiny glass stones and began stuffing them into her mouth. The scattered stones sparkled, undulating in waves, and gathering together. Helen continued stuffing stones into her mouth, gagging as she swallowed more and more of them. After a while, she choked, and vomited the abomination of bile and shards on the floor in front of Terese. Helen screeched and laughed, began dancing in a circle around the table.

The disgusting pile of slimy, putrid stones began writhing and shifting, finally forming a huge rat. Its sharp, yellow teeth sparkled. Its nose twitched. Smelling the blood on Terese's legs, the giant rodent lunged. Terese jumped sideways as the rat penetrated the circle, almost biting her. When its front paws touched the floor and made contact with the salt, it squealed and jumped back. With her right hand, Terese reached into her shirt and pulled out a large silver amulet. In the light, the women could see there was a crucifix on one side. Terese turned it, and they saw the face of Jesus on the other side. She pulled the amulet over her neck and thrust it at the rat. Too late, the rat realized its error. The silver medallion burned into the rat's neck. It shrieked and exploded, once again regaining the form of Gabriel, his eyes wide in horror. He crumpled on the cold, wooden floor. Helen collapsed beside him.

Terese was relentless. As Helen and Gabe gathered together to become one black cloud of mist to again escape beneath the china cabinet, she poured holy water on them, then grabbed the smoldering sage and jabbed at them. Sparks of red-hot, burning sage showered down on the hovering mist. "It is time! Go with the spirits of light! Seek your forgiveness. Go!"

Brilliant, white light flooded the dark room. Dancing, twirling forms, luminescent and radiant encircled the old ones.

Then suddenly, stillness enveloped the room. The air was sucked out as if by a giant vacuum, leaving an empty void. Nothing. No sound. No smell. No movement. Dozens of candle flames stood straight, growing taller and taller, drawn into the void. Bright, yellow and blue, they stretched into the endless radiance, moving toward an emptiness that could be felt in the souls of the women who now clutched at the solidity of the chairs, the table, the hands of those beside them. Other than the slight rise of their chests and visible palpitation of blood surging through their carotid arteries, they were like statues.

Screams! Terrified sounds of humans, tortured and tormented, echoed from beyond the room, beyond the earth. The four women huddled in the safety of their holy circle and watched in horror as the ceiling opened. Blackness, and at the same time, an intense all-consuming fire of vibrant bright red and orange flames swirled in an opening that revealed an eternity of more and more flames. Then glimpses of crimson blood, clotted on exposed and ulcerated, writhing limbs, were visible as the tortured reached into the room, searching out their own. Evil recognized evil, sought more black souls to feast upon, to join with them in their eternity of the damned.

In seconds, thousands of hands grabbed at the stunned souls of the Lindemans. Helen screamed as a dark, black vapor surrounded her. Gabriel grasped her hand. Then fire consumed them. A final terrified scream escaped from both brother and sister as they were pulled into the fiery void, taken to their final eternity. The flames were sucked back into the blackness as it closed and sealed over itself.

A canopy of white light radiated across the ceiling above the dining table. Brilliantly luminescent, it pulsated and grew brighter, encompassing the entire ceiling. A clap of thunder shook the room, a bolt of lightning flashed from ceiling to floor. Cassie and Mary screamed. A final flash of blinding light dissipated into a shower of sparks, leaving the smell of fresh earth after a cleansing rain. Sound returned. The gentle lulling melody of voices singing filled the room as the CD continued to play softly. Flames crackled as logs burned and popped, wind whistled through the boughs of barren trees outside the house. Loudest of all was the joyous shrieks of the four women who were at last free from the torment of the Lindemans' nefarious presence.

"To hell! They have gone to hell!" Terese screamed, vindicated.

"They're gone! We did it!" Cassie yelled.

"Do you feel it? The lightness of the air?" Sara took a deep breath. "Everything smells fresh and clean." Sara stood up, looked around the room. Her face turned white. She ran to the Terese who was slumped over the table. "Are you all right?" Sara gently placed her hand on the medium's shoulder. "Terese?"

Chapter 112

"I'll go get some water. Mary! Come with me!" Cassie ran toward the kitchen, pausing in the doorway to wait for Mary. When Mary was by her side, Cassie shoved the door the rest of the way open, and the two of them disappeared into the kitchen.

Sara checked Terese's pulse. It was weak and slow, her breathing shallow and quick. "Bring a cold rag, too," she yelled.

"Should I call 911?" Mary asked as Cassie ran into the room and put the cool rag on the back of Terese's neck.

"No!" Terese groaned. "I'll be all right. Help me sit up straight."

"What happened?" Mary asked. "Did you faint?"

Terese laughed. "Not exactly. Let me catch my breath." She stood up. Her legs were shaky; she grabbed the table to steady herself. "That was the most difficult banishment I have ever done. Damn! But, ladies, we did it! The Lindemans are gone!"

They all cheered.

"What do we do now?" Cassie asked, watching Terese carefully.

"We get the heck out of Dodge," Terese quipped. "Let's go back to Ravenswood. You can all stay with me tonight. We'll let this house breathe."

"I don't know that I can ever stay here again." Mary wrapped her arms around herself and shivered.

"Don't worry. In the light of day, you'll feel differently." Terese patted her gently on her shoulder. "But before we go, I need to do a final cleansing—if you'll all help me, that is. I don't think I can do it alone. I'm exhausted."

"Let's do it and get out of here!" Sara said.

"Come with me." Terese began turning on the lights in the dining room. She handed each of the women a bundle of sage, lighting each with a white candle she'd ceremoniously blessed. First she led them to the back staircase and up the two flights to the attic. Every light switch was flipped. Every bulb set aglow.

Smudgy smoke from the smoldering sage floated heavily in the air. Next they headed to the second floor, where the procedure was repeated. Terese led them down the main staircase to the first floor. They paraded, one behind the other, through the rooms, chanting words of grace, tiredly waving the sage and filling the rooms with the sweet stench. Terese stopped in the kitchen, sat down heavily into one of the chairs. "I need to rest." She began massaging her temples. Cassie, Mary and Sara leaned against the counter. A continual drip of water falling gently into the empty sink from the faucet made a dull *throp, throp throp*.

"Can we go now?" asked Mary

"What about the basement? We haven't been down there yet," Sara said, looking at Terese. "Do we have to go down there?"

"God! I don't want to go to the basement again!" Mary sat down, looked around at all the faces of her friends. "Can't we do it some other time?"

"We have to. We have to cleanse the whole house." Terese tried to smile. "It's okay, Mary, you can stay here. You all can stay here. I can do it alone. I'm fine now."

Mary abruptly stood up. "Shit! Let's get it over with. You won't go alone. Not on your life! Come on!"

"I need to get more sage. We have to do this right." Terese disappeared into the dining room, returning minutes later with her tapestry bag. She took more bundles out. She blessed another white candle, lit it with a wooden match, and ignited the sage bundles.

Terese unlocked and opened the heavy wooden door to the basement, turned on the light. Slowly she descended the stairs, Cassie, Mary and Sara close behind her. As Terese reached the basement, she pulled the dangling chain from the light fixture. *Pop!* Darkness enveloped them. The fuse in the basement had blown, overloaded with the power drawn from having almost every light in the house on. "Damnit," Terese whispered under her breath.

"The fuse box is down here somewhere," Mary said. "But I don't know where! Please, can't we forget about this?" In the pale illumination from the kitchen light down the stairway, Mary's pallor was white, her face drawn.

"Go upstairs. Now! Get Mary out of here. I have a candle; I'll bless the basement alone." She motioned for the girls to go upstairs. "Go!" They did as she said.

Terese stumbled through the basement, the candle barely penetrating the heavy blackness. She walked as quickly as she dared through the maze of rooms, sage in one hand, the candle, now a mere stump in her other. Recognizing the significance of the circle of stones, Terese stopped briefly to kick and scatter them. Her candle went out. She groped for the wall, missed by inches stepping in the congealed blood from Harold's cold body where he lay swathed in the old, mildewed blanket.

A square of light illuminated the bottom of the stairs. Terese ran toward it. Hurrying up the stairs, she closed and bolted the door. She leaned heavily against it catching her breath. "We're done! Let's get out of here!"

Sara and Mary led the way in Mary's small sedan. Terese and Cassie followed, each in their own car. Terese stopped at the end of the driveway, Cassie pulled in behind her. Getting out of her car, Terese stood next to a grove of trees. Shadows, undulating like dancers, played on the ground before her as clouds passed over the moon.

"What are you doing?" Cassie asked, rolling her window down. She saw Mary's brake lights up ahead as Mary stopped her car, waiting for them.

"A final look back, that's all. How serene the house looks now. Look!" Terese swept her arm into the air and pointed to the house. It was lit up like a palace, showcased against the black night. She smiled at Cassie, then got back in the car. They followed each other down winding road to the highway.

Chapter 113

Elise waited until their taillights faded. Turning, she stepped from behind the trees and flew quickly up the driveway and onto the porch, immediately backing away. The stench of sage filled her nostrils. Elise could not go in. On the front porch, next to a wrought iron bench, was a basket filled with firewood. Beside it was an ax. She picked it up and systematically, window by window, smashed the glass in the living and dining rooms. A cold wind blew. The curtains fluttered as the frigid air cleared the putrid smoke from the rooms and out into the night.

Elise sat down on the bench, patiently waiting. Pulling Joe's coat closely around her narrow shoulders, she remembered the treasure in its pocket. "One missed call" the screen said as she opened the phone. She hit the call button.

"Hello, Joe?" Tom said.

Elise laughed.

"Joe? What the . . . Who is this?" Tom asked.

"Hello, Tom."

"Who is this?" Tom demanded

"Your worst nightmare, darling. You better come home," she screamed into the phone, "your family needs you!" Elise laughed hysterically, then closed the phone, abruptly ending the call.

Chapter 114

Tom stood on the sidewalk watching anxiously for the cab. At the airport, a small private jet was fueling up and waiting for him. From a block away, headlights gleamed. Tom waved impatiently as the cab drove slowly down the street toward him. As it pulled up next to him, he grabbed the handle, flung the door open and jumped in. "I'll give you an extra hundred dollars to get me to the Jamestown airport as fast as you can." He slammed the door. "Go!"

The driver turned around and sped down the street. Snowflakes, heavy and wet fell in clumps on the windshield, swept away by wipers set on the fastest speed. "Nasty storm." The driver glanced into his rearview mirror at Tom. "I'll do the best I can."

Chapter 115

Elise was getting impatient. She wanted to go into the house where it would surely be warmer. Her teeth chattered. She pulled the jacket tighter around her body.

She waited half an hour, then stuck her head into the front doorway. The smoky sage had cleared from the house. The horrible stench was gone. Elise walked through the living room, pausing for a few minutes to warm herself before the dying embers in the fireplace. Curious about the séance, she moved to the dining room doorway and stopped. Salt and holy water kept her from going into the room. Backing away, she stood at a safe distance and peered into the room, absorbing all the details of the ceremony where the Lindemans had lost their battle. She shivered, realizing that could have been her fate as well. She turned and retraced her path back to the front entryway, then up the main stairs to the second floor. She wandered from room to room opening and closing drawers and closets, careful not to disturb anything. She must leave no trace.

Elise was exhausted. She found the room where the little child, her niece Lizzie, had slept. Lying down on the bed, wrapping the downy comforter over her cold body, Elise drifted into a deep sleep.

Elise slept peacefully—clear of mind, clear of her task. She had much to do when Cassie, Sara, Terese and Mary returned tomorrow. She intended to make sure they did not leave Remington House alive.

Elise didn't know that, as she slumbered like a child, Tom was on his way to Remington House. When she'd called him earlier this evening, she'd assumed he was still in Amsterdam.

Chapter 116

Half an hour later, Tom climbed aboard the Cessna. The small aircraft landed on a private airstrip outside Ravenswood at two in the morning. Tom ran to the rental car that had been pulled around. Forty minutes later he turned off the deserted highway and drove up the winding road to Remington House. The house was ablaze with lights. Pulling up to the front porch, Tom saw with a sickening dread that all visible windows on the first floor were broken out. The curtains fluttered and flapped eerily casting long, waving shadows over the porch.

He sprinted up the five steps onto the porch, ran around the veranda and peered into the windows. Nothing seemed out of order in the living room. Looking into the dining room, he saw the table with chairs circled around it, dozens of white candles and vases filled with white roses. Everything was arranged for a séance. *Cassie, what have you done?*

He brushed the glass away from around the window and climbed in, careful not to cut himself. Scattered around the floor and the two doorways was a white, crystalline powder. He picked up a bit of the substance and cautiously licked his finger to taste the grains. Salt! What went on here? Desperate, he called Cassie's cell again. His call went straight to voicemail. He tried Sara's with the same result. "Shit!"

Pushing the door open, Tom entered the kitchen. Immediately he saw the door to the basement was locked, a chair pushed up against it. Shoving the chair aside, he unlocked the dead bolt, and flipped the light switch. Nothing. "Damn!" He grabbed a flashlight from the kitchen drawer and took the steps two at a time into the basement, sweeping the light from side to side.

Tom walked vigilantly throughout the basement. In spite of the circumstances, he found himself impressed by the nearly completed boxing ring and fitness room. He continued to the back of the basement, down another hallway. Nothing appeared to be wrong down there. Finding the fuse box, he immediately spotted the popped fuse for the basement and flipped it to the left. A single bulb from the far end of the basement was the only light that came on. He pulled a dangling chain from the ceiling in the hallway.

The bulb illuminated, casting wispy shadows that crawled and climbed the walls. The hanging light fixture swung back and forth. Darkness, mixed with silvery moonlight and the undulating lamp, dimly lit the back of the gym with whirling patterns of light that swayed across the floor, twirling around and around. Tom crossed back through the gym toward the room behind the stairs. He swept his flashlight into the shadows; the bright light instantly illuminated the pool of congealing blood.

With sickening dread, he shone the flashlight on the blanket covering what he knew must be a body. Flashing his light around the room to see what other revelations awaited him, making certain no one hid in the shadows, he was puzzled by the polished rocks scattered all over the floor. Then he saw several half-burned black candles and an old leather book lying on the floor, its cover embossed with satanic symbols. *What the hell happened down here?*

With a trembling hand, Tom leaned over, grabbed the corner of the blanket and slowly pulled it away from the body. "Who is that?" He leaned closer, sucking in his breath. "Harold?" What was he doing here! He felt the throat for a pulse. Harold was dead and had been for some time. His skin was cold and felt oddly elastic. Tom needed to be certain. Again he tried to find a pulse. Nothing, Harold was definitely dead! Tom took his cell phone out of his pocket, pressed 911. There was no signal. Shit. He'd go upstairs to call the sheriff. He got almost to the stairs, then turned around and went back to the body. What would Nate do when he found out his brother was dead? Tom gently pulled the blanket over Harold; he didn't want to see the vacant stare from those eyes again. "Better luck in your next life, kid."

Back upstairs in the kitchen, Tom paced the floor. *What should I do?* He mopped his brow, stared out the window at the radiant, half moon. Harold was dead. There was no help for him at this point. Tom had to be logical. What had gone on here? And why? Where were Cassie and Sara? He called both of their cell phones again. Both calls went straight to voicemail. *Damn, where are you? Think, Tom. I know—Mary!* Tom looked up her parents' number. Her mother answered on the second ring, her voice apprehensive.

"Hello, Mrs. Stevens?"

"Yes."

"This is Tom Gardner, I apologize for calling at this insane hour, but I can't reach Cassie or Sara. I'm quite worried. I wondered if Mary might know where they are?"

"It's the middle of the night, for heaven's sakes. Of course you can't reach them," Mrs. Stevens laughed kindly. "Mary, Sara and your sister are having a lady's night at Terese Montagna's. Lizzie and Jimmy are here, having a sleepover with my kids. So, you can relax, everything is fine. How is Amsterdam, Mr. Gardner?"

"Good. Thank you. Sorry to bother you, but glad I did."

"I understand completely. Good night."

Who the hell was Terese Montagna? Didn't matter. The girls were okay. That's all that Tom needed to know. He glanced at his watch. It was ten past three. What the hell should he do with Harold? He had to do something with him. He wondered, only briefly, what Harold was doing in his house. Up to no good obviously. He must have walked in on Elise performing some sort of prayer ritual . . . so Elise killed him. That made sense. Tom knew what he had to do, it was quite clear. He did not call 911. He dialed Joe's number. He had to find Elise. It was time to face her and end this.

Chapter 117

Terese made certain everyone was tucked in and comfortable after they all had a mug of hot milk laced with brandy to help them sleep. She had a small but cozy house and was happy to share it with her friends tonight. Cassie and Mary slept in the guest bedroom, Sara on the couch and Terese in her own room. By two in the morning, they were all asleep. Completely exhausted, they slept soundly.

Chapter 118

Elise was sound asleep. She had not slept this well for a long time. She was warm and safe. Her dreams were gentle, filled with soft colors and the lusty smells of spring. She was alive. Elise held a small child in her arms. The daughter she'd always wanted. She set the child down and they kicked their feet in the warm water, frolicked on the cool sand. Frothy waves lapped around their ankles. They held hands and ran along the shore laughing. Their hands delicately scooped water to throw at each other. Delighted, they ran in and out chasing the tide.

In the distance she heard a phone ringing. Confused, she looked around, then quickly woke up. Her dream was over; Joe's cell phone was ringing.

Elise put the phone to her ear. "Hello, Tom."

Chapter 119

"Elise! Where are you?" Tom's voice was incredibly angry.

Elise shook her head from side to side, trying to wake herself up. She rubbed her temples. "At this very minute, I'm lying comfortably on the bed in your niece's bedroom. In your house, Tom." She smiled. "Waiting for Cassie and Sara to come back. Too bad you're so far away. I'll have such fun with them."

"Shut up, Elise!"

Elise ignored him. "Your sister did the dirty work for me tonight. The Lindemans were incredibly strong spirits. I didn't know how I'd manage to get them out of this house! But dear Cassie, and her partners," she laughed, "they had the most fabulous séance! They managed to drive the old couple away."

"Who are you talking about?"

Elise ignored his question. "Helen and Gabriel are . . ." she paused for effect, "gone!" Her laughter was so loud that Tom had to hold the phone away from his ear.

Tom yelled, "What are you talking about?"

"Why, Sara, your new love. And your sister and Mary—the little twit!—along with some small-town medium! They held a very intimate ceremony this evening. I was unable to attend, of course," she laughed, "so I can't tell you any of the details, but they did it! The Lindeman are no longer on this earth!" Elise had gotten up and was flitting around the bedroom. She was no longer laughing. "I hid myself so well. The medium never knew about me! And you—you so underestimated my abilities. Now, it's payback time, Tom. I can't wait until you get here and see what I've done to your sister and your girlfriend!"

"I *am* here!" Tom kicked the bedroom door open, stood not ten feet from Elise.

Elise paled and flew backwards. Hitting the mattress edge, she fell onto the bed.

Tom rushed at her. His hands encountered a cold mist, then warm flesh, smooth velvet skin, fine silky hair. He pulled his hands back, not understanding what he'd felt.

Quickly standing up, Elise smiled, reached out toward him. "I'm lonely, Tom. Can't you see that?" Her willowy fingers caressed his arm, his shoulder, finally his cheek. "Hold me, Tom. I have missed you so."

Tom tilted his head into her tiny hand, felt the warmth of her skin on his cheek, smelled the fragrant lavender of her perfume. "You were always so delicate, Elise. And helpless. Beautiful. Precious." He pulled her into his arms, gently laid her back onto the bed. He stroked her soft dewy skin; her flaxen strands of hair were soft like delicate silk. He ran his finger along her perfect teeth, over her lips, now pouty and parted, her tongue gently probing his fingertip. "You were my love."

She watched his face, her eyes wide, pupils large and dilated in the dim light. "I followed you here, Tom. To be with you."

"I know that, Elise. You came to Remington with me, didn't you?" He stroked her cheek. "But not because you loved me!" He laid heavily on her tiny body, crushing her into the soft, down comforter. As she struggled to get away, he held her down with his knees. With his free hand, he reached into his shirt pocket and pulled out a glass vial. A delicate stopper sealed the narrow bottleneck, kept the precious contents from spilling out.

With his teeth, Tom pulled the stopper from the bottle. "Good bye, Elise." He poured the holy water onto her horrified face. "Die knowing I do *not* love you. I do *not* want to be with you. Not in this life, not in eternity."

Elise screamed. Tears, salty and warm, washed over her cheeks, down into her ears, tickling her—a final insult. She had become almost human again.

"Leave! Now! Get out of here!" Tom stared as Elise's essence faded into a cold, white mist. Then there was nothing left, she simply vanished. There was so much less fight in her than in the Lindemans—though Tom would never know that, never know how valiantly Helen and Gabe had fought for survival.

So simple. He'd killed her. . . . Again. Tom studied the bottle he still held. He'd picked it up off the dining room table —an afterthought. Just because. And that was all it took to end her reign—a tablespoon of holy water. He crushed the vial in his hand, unaware of the glass slicing into his palm. Elise was dead! He glanced down, registered that he was bleeding. Pulling a handkerchief from his pocket, he wrapped it around his hand. He sat on the bed, his face buried in his hands. How could this have ended this easily? He got up, smashed his fist into the wall, wishing he felt the pain. He did not. He was numb. "Fuck it! It's over." He walked out of the room, slamming the door.

Chapter 120

Tom returned to the basement. He zigzagged through the rooms, then ran down the long hallway to open the back door used by the contractors. He saw a car parked behind the trees about a hundred yards down the road. Going back to the body, he searched through Harold's pockets, found a set of keys on a ring adorned with a tiny, red flip-flop. He ran down the driveway. The keys were indeed for the car. He started it up and drove it to the door of the basement. In the dim light, he tripped over a bag on the floor. Opening it, he found the tools Harold had used to break into Tom's safe. He also found several thousand dollars and the Gardner family jewels. *Harold, you son of a bitch! You broke in and robbed me.* He rolled Harold in the blanket, and lifted the heavy load over his shoulder. Tom was covered with sweat by the time he got the body out the door and loaded it into the car. It was now four in the morning.

Returning again to the basement, he picked up the bag with the tools, jewelry, and money. He threw them into the car with Harold. He wrestled the blanket off the body and took it back into the laundry room. Out of breath, but with no time to rest, he made his final trip out to the car.

Half a mile behind Tom's house was a narrow road along the bluff. He drove the car along the winding road to a wide area at the top overlooking the ocean. He got out, positioning Harold in the driver's seat. *Who killed you, kid? Elise? The Lindemans? Not that it matters much.* Tom carefully wiped any trace of his fingerprints from the car. He leaned in the door, pulled his sleeve over his hand and put the car in gear. Slamming the door, he jumped clear. The car rolled forward gaining speed as it went downhill several hundred yards before coming to a turn in the road. The car plunged over the edge, launching into the air. Tom watched it as it flew airborne for several hundred feet. Falling, falling, then crashing head-on against the rocks, the car bouncing several times before landing in the ocean, sinking quickly as huge waves washed over it. Satisfied, Tom cut through the woods and back to Remington House.

Tom spent an hour cleaning up the blood on the basement floor. In the laundry room, he washed the bloody rags and the blanket, then put them in the dryer. It was now five thirty.

Going back upstairs, Tom turned off the dozens of lights that had so brilliantly lit the house against the dark night. He walked through the rooms, making sure everything was in order. He showered in two minutes flat. Ten minutes later, he returned to the basement and threw his dirty, blood-stained clothes into the washer. He folded the now-dry rags, returned them to the workshop and put the blanket into the closet in the cold, dank room where Harold had died. He gathered up the black candles, fiery opals, and the satanic bible.

Tom turned the basement lights off and went upstairs to the living room. He threw the book and candle into the fireplace and lit a fire, watching while the flames completely consumed the book. When he was certain the book was destroyed, he stirred the ashes with the poker and threw another log onto the dwindling flames. He opened the front door and hurled the stones, one by one, out into the trees, each in a different direction. Finished, he downed a shot of vodka and checked the house one last time to make sure he hadn't missed anything. He didn't think he had. Then back to the living room. Tom threw another log on the fire, had a second shot of vodka, and collapsed onto the sofa. Within minutes, he was asleep.

Chapter 121

Someone pounded on the front door. Tom stirred, then quickly sat up, stiff from sleeping curled in a tight ball on the couch. The pounding continued. Tom pulled the curtain on the front door aside. A big man, well over six foot four, lanky, well muscled and wearing a badge that said "Sheriff" glared at him.

"Open the door, sir. I'd like to talk to you." He stood tall, hand on his gun. "Now!"

Tom opened the door, stepping out onto the porch. "What's going on?" he asked.

"Good morning, Mr. uhh, Gardner isn't it?"

"Yes, Tom Gardner." He motioned for the sheriff to come in. The sheriff did not. Tom said, "I flew in a few hours ago. You here about the break in?"

"What? No, sir. We found a car in the ocean this morning, at the beach edge actually, below your property. Jogger called it in."

"What?"

"Someone drove off the cliff road."

Trying to wake himself up, Tom shook his head, rubbed his eyes with the fingers of his open hands. "Someone drove off the road? They okay?" He kept his voice controlled and flat.

The sheriff ignored his question and swept his hand around, pointing at the broken glass littering the porch. "What happened? Someone break in?"

"Got home in the middle of the night. Found the windows broken." He let his voice show agitation. "Darn neighbor kid."

"Yeah, I remember. You had trouble with Billy Harrison a few weeks ago." Staring at Tom, Sheriff Jamison shifted his weight squarely to both legs, crossed his arms. "You call it in? I didn't get a report."

"Not yet. Thought I'd call this morning—since it seemed like simple vandalism—and I thought I knew who was responsible."

"Well, I'll send an officer up later to make a report. . . . Anyway, I'm here because of the car. And because we found a body in that car."

"What!" Tom said, sounding shocked, thinking he did a convincing job of it.

"Yeah, you heard right. Driver's license says his name's Harold Adams. Know him?" Jamison watched Tom's reaction.

"Yeah, I do! Brother of my associate, Nate Adams. Oh, shit!" Tom took a quick breath. "Harold's been on the lam.

There's been a search warrant out for him. We've had a private eye looking for him. No luck. We thought he left the country." Tom looked away, beyond the broken glass on the porch, toward the ocean. "I wish he had."

"They're pulling the car out of the water now. I need to get back. Wondered if you heard anything last night?"

"No. Been asleep." Tom looked at the sheriff. "You sure it's Harold?"

"No, but we'll know soon enough. We'll get the body into town and run the fingerprints. If it's Adams, and he has a record, it won't take long to make an ID. I'll need to get a statement from you later. Probably need Adam's brother's contact information from you, too. I better get back down to the beach. I'll send one of my officers up. We'll need to look around. Know if anything's missing?"

"I don't know." Tom massaged his temple. "I saw the broken glass, just figured it was Billy Harrison. I looked around a little, nothing else *seemed* wrong."

"You live here alone?"

"No, my sister and her daughter have been here for a few weeks. And Sara Lawson." Tom pointed down the beach, toward the Harrison house. "You know, Sara, Vivian Harrison's cousin, she's been here with my sister while I was out of town. They stayed in town last night, though. With a friend."

A silver minivan sped up the driveway. Cassie threw the car in park and yelled out her window, "What's going on?" She, along with Sara, Terese and Mary, jumped out of the car.

"Tom! What happened?" Visibly shaken, Sara ran to Tom "Are you okay?" she asked, her face drained of any color. Tom hugged her tightly.

"I'm fine. Where have you been? I called and called! No one answered their god-damned phones!"

"We had them turned off," Sara said.

"We thought you were in Amsterdam. When did you get back?" Cassie asked, and then added. "We stayed at Terese's last night."

Tom looked puzzled, glanced at Terese and made the connection. The medium! "I was going to surprise you." Tom shrugged. "No one was here though. I finally called Mary's mom, found out you were in town. What a crazy night. Someone smashed the windows here. I thought it was vandals —you know—Billy. Then the sheriff showed up a few minutes ago." Tom took one of Sara's hands in his, put his other hand on Cassie's shoulder. "Uhh . . . there's been a development—a car drove off the cliff road. They found a body in it. They think it's Harold, Nate's brother."

"What? This makes no sense." Cassie sat down on the porch bench. Mary and Terese hesitated, then climbed the steps to stand beside her. "Oh, my God!" Cassie blurted out, "I thought I recognized that man!"

"What man?" Tom asked.

"One of Joe's crew. He always acted so weird. We were all a little leery of him. It was him, Tom—it was Harold! He's been working here since you left."

The sheriff said, "It's all starting to make sense. Adams must have broken in here last night. Then he drove his car onto the back road so no one would see him. It's narrow and winding, he probably was driving way too fast and lost control." Jamison started down the steps. "No one touch anything. I'm calling for backup. We'll need to search the house."

Jamison returned to his patrol car and made a call on his radio. A raven dived at him as he got out of his patrol car. Nonchalantly, he slapped at it, sending it flying the other direction where it landed in a tree and began squawking and scolding. Four more birds flew in and landed on the tree branch. They stood side by side, swaying in unison, flapping their wings menacingly. Taking long strides, Jamison was back on the porch in no time. He nodded to Tom. "We better look around, Mr. Gardner. See if anything's missing. You ladies wait here, please. Or better yet, why don't you go sit in the car where it's warm. Chilly morning." He waited as they filed, one after the other, down the driveway and into Cassie's van.

***

And so the day proceeded quite logically—the desired outcome achieved—as Tom had desperately hoped. Sheriff Jamison and Deputy John Hanson scoured the house, quickly determining that the upstairs safe had been opened, its contents of cash and jewels taken.

Later that morning, said cash and jewels were found in a duffel bag in the car that everyone, except Tom, assumed Harold had driven off the road, ultimately crashing into the Atlantic.

They found no trace of blood in the basement; Tom had cleaned up thoroughly, though there was no reason for the sheriff to suspect that foul play had occurred there. The girls were questioned briefly about the séance. They explained it was all in fun and that they had frightened themselves, so they decided to leave Remington and stay at Terese's. Sheriff Jamieson nodded his understanding.

Fingerprints of the body were taken. The body was positively ID'd as Harold Adams. His prints would later be found to match the fingerprints taken from the safe and several doorknobs at Remington House. Case closed.

Later, after everyone was allowed back into the house, Cassie asked the sheriff, "Why did Harry break the windows? It doesn't make sense."

Jamison responded, "Criminals do strange things, especially when they're amped up on drugs and booze. Often they have no reason other than rage." He looked at the girls. "Thankfully you ladies didn't have to experience his rage. You weren't here when he broke in. Spooked yourselves with your silly séance. Lucky break for you."

The sheriff took Terese aside into the study. "I thought we agreed you'd let me know when you had one of your ceremonies. I worry, Terese. You take too many chances. I'd never forgive myself if something bad happened to you." Jamison made sure no one was watching and gave Terese a protective hug.

"Why, Sheriff Jamison, you know I can take care of myself." Terese risked a quick kiss. "It's okay. We cleared the house. I'll tell you all about it tonight."

Chapter 122

Gathered in the dining room, everyone began helping Terese put her paraphernalia away. The flowers were gathered and put into a single, lead glass vase and placed on the side table. Everything else was carefully packed, returned to its box and carried out to Joe's truck. Joe would take Terese and Mary home after dinner.

Joe was on the terrace drinking a bottle of beer, obviously working on a buzz after learning about Harold's death. He had a six-pack on the porch floor by his feet.

Tom wandered outside, his crystal tumbler filled with club soda. "I tried to call Nate to tell him about Harold. No luck, so I called John. He said he'd go over to Nate's sister's house himself. He'll call me as soon as he leaves Rosa's." Walking over to the railing, Tom gazed at the ocean, the waves like foaming black ink. "Joe, let it go. There's no way you could have known who Harold was. I never expected him to show up here, so how could you? Thank God, no one except him was hurt last night."

"Yeah, I know. But damn, what a fucking tragedy. I don't know Nate, but I feel his pain." Joe grimaced, pounded the railing. "I could have stopped this whole mess before that hard-ass Harold got himself killed. I took all the guys to dinner last night. I should have noticed there was something wrong with Harold's behavior."

"How could you, Joe? Harold had it all planned. He'd probably been in the house several times checking things out. They found a key to the basement door in his pocket. He used it to get in last night, then broke the windows out because he was so angry. Kind of his final statement to me."

"Yeah, I get that. Just wish it had gone differently. I'm relieved Joanie didn't end up getting involved in the burglary. Poor kid, she thought Harold was her ticket out of her dead-end job at the cafe. She'll have a hard time living this down." Joe twisted the cap off another beer and took a long drink. "Want one?"

"Sure. Thanks," Tom said, "Club soda isn't what I need. Cassie said I better stay focused. Yeah, right. I say fuck it! Who wants to focus?" He drank half the bottle in one, long gulp.

"Tom!" Cassie yelled, opening the french doors to the veranda. She had a tray of cheese and crackers balanced in one hand. "Hey, I thought you promised to lay off the booze, brother." She put the tray down on the table, pointed at Joe, then at the four bottles of beer on the floor. "Better have some cheese. A handful of crackers wouldn't hurt either."

Sara came next, followed by Terese and Mary. "Brrr. It's cold out here. I'm going to get some sweaters." Sara disappeared back into the house.

The sun had set, the salmon-colored clouds were beginning to lose their soft glow, turning dark gray and black. The moon was rising, a silver crescent on the horizon against the blackening sky. Down the beach, maybe a mile away, a lone figure walked along the edge of the surging tide.

Sara returned with an armful of sweaters. She was watching a passing ship when she noticed a man walking on the beach. "Hey!" She pointed. "Who's that?"

"Don't recognize him. He's too far away. I'll get the binoculars," Joe said, draining his bottle of beer. He went into the house, returning with two pairs of binoculars. He handed one set to Sara, put the other pair up to his eyes. He fiddled with the focus. "Hmm. Not sure. I've never seen him before. What about you, Sara?"

"Don't think so. Must be someone staying at the Shelton's beach house. I'll have to ask Billy if they rented it out."

"Why would he know?" asked Tom.

"Billy's kept an eye on the Shelton's house for a while. He had a 'thing' for their daughter, Millicent." Sara smiled. "Gave

Billy a reason to call the family and talk to Millie when they were in San Francisco."

Tom reached for the binoculars when Sara offered them to him. He looked down the beach, quickly losing interest in the man, focusing instead on the ship. "Joe, that's one of the new *Maersk Eindhovens*. Look at that baby would you! Man, oh man!" he whistled.

Joe turned to watch the ship. "Geez. That thing's massive. Brand new, too. Clean lines. I'd sure like to get a closer look at it. Wonder what it's hauling?"

"I think we can read the name when it crosses in front of us. Then we can google it." They watched intently as the ship crossed the horizon. "Got it!" Tom said.

Tom and Joe forgot the man walking down the beach. They'd turned their attention to writing down the ship's name flag before they forgot it.

Chapter 123

That odd, little man was no mortal man at all. He was Benjamin. That despicable soul, doomed to wander the shores of the Atlantic. You may remember him. He'd lived at Remington House—a captive of Helen and her brother, Gabe.

Much to his surprise, he escaped from them—actually quite effortlessly. He would have left them much sooner had he realized how easy it would be. He even got away from Elise, a formidable opponent, from whom he'd fled, in fear of his very existence.

Now however, he was on his way back to Remington House to find Helen and Gabe. He was lonely. His existence was unbearable. Somehow he would make them take him back.

Benjamin did not yet know the fate of the pair—not that it would have mattered. He would not make it to Remington House. Not tonight, anyway.

Chapter 124

William watched Vivian sleep. Finally she seemed to be at peace. Her color was good, her face relaxed. Gently, so as not to wake her, he kissed her forehead, then covered her with the white thermal blanket, hoping she'd sleep for several hours. William had work to do and would trust the nurses to watch over her.

Back at the hotel, William took a hot shower and called room service for a light lunch. As he ate a turkey club, he looked over the final contract with Gardner Enterprises he'd received earlier in the week. He poured a glass of scotch. "Cheers!" He smiled and toasted himself. He picked up his phone and dialed his house in Ravenswood. Mannie answered on the first ring.

"Mannie, William here. Is everything going all right there? Any more trouble since the incident with Harold Adams?"

"No, Mr. Harrison. It's been very quiet here. Not a thing going on. How is Mrs. Harrison?"

"Good. She's doing much better. The doctor said she was having a drug interaction —caused by taking several over-the-counter medicines, mixed with her prescriptions. We'll be coming back to New York next week. I'd like to have you and Amos close the house. I'll spend a couple of days in New York with Vivian, then we'll come to Boston"

"When will you be in Boston, Mr. Harrison? When do you want Amos and me to have the boys there?"

"A week from Monday. I'll have Lydia get tickets for the train. I want all of you to be in Boston when we get there.

"Okay, Mr. Harrison. Amos and I will get everything ready here."

"Thanks, Mannie. Are my boys around?"

"Yes, sir, hold on a minute."

He heard Mannie hollering to the boys. William waited patiently, poured himself another scotch.

"Dad! Where are you?"

"Hi, Jimmy. Still in Amsterdam. Your mother and I will be in New York next week. We're all going to spend some time in Boston."

"Yeay!" Jimmy blurted, then quickly added, "Is Mom okay?"

"She's much better. She can't wait to see you and Billy. She's still at the hospital, but they should release her tomorrow. We'll spend a couple more days here before we fly into New York."

"What was wrong with her, Dad? She was scaring me."

"Jimmy, don't worry. Nothing serious. We'll talk about it later."

"Okay. I guess. But . . . "

Billy grabbed the phone from Jimmy. "Dad?"

"Hey, kiddo. You ready to come to Boston?"

"Boston? You better believe it! When?" He punched Jimmy's shoulder, shoved him when Jimmy made a fist.

"Next week. You help Mannie and Amos. The house needs to be closed up. Make sure the pipes don't freeze and the mice don't get in. You hear me, Billy?" *Not that you'll do anything other than order everyone around. I know you well, son.*

"Sure, Dad."

"I miss you boys. I can't wait to see you." He paused, waited for Billy to respond.

"Yeah, miss you too, Dad."

William smiled. "Put Jimmy back on." William waited for his youngest to get back on the phone. "Jimmy, you help your brother and Amos close up the house. Okay?" William sipped his scotch, imagined the boys working together as a team, knew it would never happen. Oh, well. A father could dream!

"Sure dad. Oww!"

"What's wrong?" William asked, though he had a good idea.

"Nothing. Will you have Mom call us?"

"I will—in a few days. I need to talk to Mannie again. I love you, Jimmy."

"Love you, too. Bye."

While he waited for Mannie, William took another sip of his scotch, looked out the hotel window at the brightly lit skyline. Lights twinkled on the buildings; crowds of people, like tiny ants, hurried down the sidewalks to the restaurants lining the busy avenue. He felt incredibly lonely. He wanted to be home with his boys.

***

Jimmy went to his room and lay down on his bed. He called Lizzie to tell her his news.

"I'm leaving, too. Next Saturday," Lizzie told him. "I'm going to spend some time with my grandmother in Connecticut. I don't know when I'll see you again." She started to cry.

"Silly," Jimmy said. "You'll be here all week. You'll see lots of me. Hey, you want to go down to the beach and look for some more seashells?"

"Sure. I'll see you in a little while." Hanging up, Lizzie grabbed her coat and ran downstairs."Mom," she yelled, "I'm going to play with Jimmy."

Cassie was in the living room reading a book in front of the fire. "Okay. Stay warm. You check in with me in an hour."

***

Sitting at the small dining table in his bedroom, Tom sipped his vodka and thought about Elise. She'd given up her fight so easily, had succumbed to the dousing with holy water and vanished, dissipating into nothing before his eyes. He was still amazed. A deep sadness settled over his heart. *I did love Elise once—though it seems like such a long time ago. Much has changed—Sara has come into my life. Maybe she and I have a real chance now.*

In his left hand he held an eight by ten photograph in an elaborate, antique silver frame. Elise smiled coyly at him, her dark-brown eyes twinkled, her rose-colored lips parted showing perfect white teeth. Long blonde hair, in wisps and waves, flowed around her shoulders and over her delicate breasts. She'd just come from the pool and wore nothing. Her milky skin glistened in the afternoon sun. She held a bouquet of lavender teasingly toward the camera, a gift from Tom, picked from their garden.

Tom held the picture closer, saw for the first time, in the window of the living room behind her, a face staring out into the yard. *Who was that?* He stared at the face. *It looks like Elise. How the hell can it be Elise?* His phone rang. He jumped.

"Tom? It's William. How is everything?"

"Fine." Tom caught his breath and put the picture down "How is Vivian? Is her treatment coming along?" He swirled the ice around in his glass, then swallowed the last drink. He held the cold glass to his left temple. A trickle of sweat ran down the back of his neck.

"She's much better. Thanks for asking. We'll be coming back to the states next week. I'm having the boys and Mannie and Amos meet us in Boston. We'll be there for the rest of the year—maybe until the end of January. Wanted to let you know the beach house will be closed up. I hate to cause any ill feelings with you, but I wondered if you could talk to Sara for me. She's not taking my calls."

"She's not?"

"The last time we talked, I said a few things that upset her. I told her Vivian was still angry, and I thought it best she stay away from her for a while. Maybe wait until after the new year, let Vivian get completely well. Sara didn't take it very well. She hung up on me, and I haven't been able to talk with her since," William explained. "Such a shame, really. But when Viv's feeling better, they can reconnect."

"I think you're right. Though I understand why Sara's upset. But it's your decision, and Sara will have to be okay with it. I'll talk to her. She can stay here at Remington. Cassie's still here. She and Sara have become very close, so it should all work itself out."

"Good," William said. "Listen, Tom, I spoke to your attorney, and he said everything has moved ahead—the contract and all the legal proceedings involving the new company have been filed. Thank you again for your part in creating this partnership. You'll not regret it. You should have your investment back—and then some."

"I'm sure of it. We'll all do well."

"I have another call to take. Talk to you later. Goodbye." William hung up, not waiting for Tom's reply.

What an arrogant SOB. Well, it makes for a successful businessman, I guess. He picked up Elise's picture. Tom turned the lamp hanging over the table on and stared at the picture. The face in the window was gone. He poured himself another glass of vodka.

Cassie knocked softly on his door. "Tom, have a minute?"

Tom opened the drawer of his nightstand and put Elise's picture into it. "Sure. Come in. What's up, Sis?"

Chapter 125

Cassie glanced at the bottle of vodka, started to say something, thought better of it. Tom's brows were drawn together, his forehead lined in deep furrows; he looked incredibly stressed. She knew that look well and didn't want to do battle right now. "I wondered what you wanted to do for lunch. I thought we could drive into Ravenswood and have a late lunch at the café or something. Sara and I are getting stir-crazy. Lizzie and Jimmy already had lunch; they ate leftover ham and potato salad. Thought we'd drop them at the movies while we have lunch and shop. What do you think?"

"Sounds like a good idea. I need to call Nate first. Let him know I'll be there for Harold's funeral. I'll just be a few minutes."

"Give him my love, will you?" Cassie walked to the door, paused, and turned to Tom. "See you downstairs then."

***

Tom nodded as Cassie closed his door. Outside, the sun shone brightly casting glimmers of light on the ocean. Waves crashed and broke sending sprays of water high onto the beach. Tom saw the little man again, this time he was walking away from Tom's end of the beach going toward the north. While he called Nate, Tom watched the man walk beyond the Harrison's cliff stairs, finally disappearing behind a precipice jutting out onto the shore.

"Hello?"

"Nate. It's Tom." The two discussed the funeral plans and made arrangements for Tom's stay in Jamestown on Monday.

***

Cassie stood outside Tom's bedroom door listening. She chewed her lip while she cupped her hand around her ear trying to hear what Tom was saying, hoping he would reveal something to Nate about what was bothering him. Since his return from Amsterdam, Tom was increasingly distracted and dependent on the ever- present bottle of vodka. Harold's death, and something she couldn't put her finger on, had Tom tied in knots. She was so afraid he'd lose control again. She couldn't let that happen. He was exhausted; he hadn't had a day of downtime since moving here.

Not hearing Tom talking anymore, she hurried quietly down the hall. She hated that Lizzie had to see Tom like this. Lizzie could certainly sense something was wrong. Cassie would see if Lizzie could spend the evening with Jimmy. She went into her room and called Mannie.

"Sure Lizzie can stay here. You know I love having her around!" Mannie said. "She and Jimmy can help me bake cookies. You send them both over when you get back from town."

"Thanks. What's Billy up to? You think he'd like to go into Ravenswood with us?" Cassie felt she had to ask.

"No, he has plans. He's got his dad's car. He going to a friend's house—said he's spending the night there."

"Okay. I'll call you when we get back from town. Bye."

Chapter 126

Lizzie had gone with Jimmy to spend the evening at his house —it was late afternoon. Cassie and Sara were downstairs in the kitchen talking with Joe. Tom was upstairs seeking quiet. The trip into Ravenswood had done little to lighten his spirit. His mood was dark.

It was dusk. The sun glowed orange as it passed through low-hanging clouds. Black trees, like massive waving skeletons, bent in the northeaster, their limbs seemingly close to their breaking point. Hundreds of ravens swirled like giant, moving ribbons, undulating in and out of the sky above the trees. The cacophony of caws was deafening. The ravens called back and forth to one another as the multitude of bodies swarmed over Remington House. They circled for several minutes, casting long, rolling shadows on the winter landscape, then, as if on a silent command, settled into the trees. The branches were suddenly alive with birds, wings flapping as they fought for space on the crowded limbs.

Tom sat in a white Adirondack chair on the balcony outside his bedroom watching the moon rise. A single raven, its wingspan close to three feet, circled the sky above Tom and then landed on the railing in front of him. Folding its wings, its body swaying from side to side, it stared at him. Tom got up and took a step forward. The raven flapped its wings and cawed but did not take flight. A second, then a third raven landed. They watched Tom from their perch, unafraid when he took his jacket off and waved it at them. "Shoo! Go on! Get!"

Angry, Tom ran toward them. They flew out of his reach to settle farther down the railing. Tom heard the *swooshing* of many wings behind him. Too late, he tried to make it to the door and into the safety of his bedroom. Several ravens, talons extended, landed on his arms and shoulders. "Oww! Son of bitch!"

Tom tried to protect himself, flailing his arms at the huge birds as they dug their beaks into his biceps. He covered his head with his coat and backed into the bedroom slamming the double doors. Several birds hit the glass, circled back and flew again at the french doors. "Damnit! What the hell!" He stared, amazed, and watched as one bird after another hit the glass. As suddenly as they appeared, the birds abruptly turned and flew away to roost in the beech trees with the other ravens.

Someone pounded on his bedroom door. "Tom!" It was Sara.

"Sara! Wait!" Tom ran to the balcony door to make sure the birds were gone. He glanced at his right arm, saw the torn fabric and blood soaking into the sleeve of his shirt. He grabbed his jacket from the floor and put it on.

"Tom! What's going on?" Sara continued to beat on the door. "You're scaring me. Please open the door!"

Tom pulled the door open, and Sara stumbled in. He caught her, wincing when she fell against his shoulder.

"Sorry," she said, "I didn't mean to hurt you." She stood away from him. "You're pale as a ghost. You're bleeding!"

"Shit, Sara! The damned ravens attacked me." He pointed outside. "I was on the balcony. I can't believe it."

"Let me see." Sara pulled the collar of his shirt away from his neck. "It's not too bad. Sit down. I'll get some soap and a washcloth."

Tom didn't sit, instead followed her into the bathroom. "They got my arm, too."

"Where? Take your coat off." Sara helped him pull his arms out of his shirt. "I don't understand this." Nervously she twisted a wisp of hair in her fingers. "Why do the birds keep attacking?" Before he could say anything she added, "Don't be mad. Cassie told me they attacked you once before. What you may not know is that they attacked Harry, too!"

"What?"

"While you were in Amsterdam. I'll tell you about it later. Oh, Tom, these are really deep." She dabbed gently with the cloth. "Sit down. Let me see what they've done to you." Tom sat on the edge of the claw foot bathtub. "Luckily they're not as deep as I thought," Sara said. "Why wouldn't you let me in? Why did you try to hide your cuts from me?"

"Didn't want to scare you. And I had to make certain the birds were gone, too. Damn it! I have to make sure everyone stays in the house until the friggin birds fly a . . . " The sound of shots being fired stopped him in midsentence.

Tom and Sara ran to the balcony door. Outside, hundreds of birds took flight, a mass exodus of black bodies and madly fluttering wings. A dozen birds dropped to the ground as Joe fired round after round at the fleeing murder of ravens. The black swarm covered the moon, momentarily creating an eclipse until the cloud of birds disappeared behind the distant bluff.

Tom hollered down at Joe, "Nice shooting. What the hell's going on with the ravens?"

Joe dropped the rifle down to his side. "Something's on over there in the trees." He pointed to the stand of trees to the west of the house. "Come on, we need to check it out!"

"Be right down." Tom grabbed his jacket and gave Sara a hug. "Would you go check on Cassie? Make sure she stays in the house."

Sara followed Tom as he took the stairs two at a time. "Be careful!"

Tom didn't answer but raised his arm in a backward wave as he crashed out the front door. Joe handed Tom a .357.

"Just in case," Joe said. "Safety's off." He led the way across the property toward a grove of barren hickory trees. A single raven cawed, then took flight as they neared the stand. It circled them, calling shrilly, more and more agitated the closer they got to the trees.

"There's something over there." Joe ran, stumbling on an exposed root, nearly falling face-first into a boulder. He went down on one knee, catching himself before his face hit. "Shit!"

"What is that?" Tom ran past Joe, going further into the trees. Quickly catching up with him, Joe raised his rifle and pulled the trigger. A deer, its side cut open, exposed entrails spilling out, shuddered then closed its eyes.

"A mountain lion must have gotten it. Guess the ravens attacked and scared the cat away. I'll take the carcass into town. Have Dave at the Division of Wildlife take care of it. Kind of odd to have the ravens attack a mountain lion like that. Don't get it at all."

"They attacked me on the terrace a little while ago. Sara said the birds attacked Harold, too. Did you know about that?"

"Yeah. But I asked Harry . . . ah, Harold about it, and he said it wasn't big deal. I cleared a few nests out from under the eaves. Thought that was the end of it," Joe said, pushing dirt over the blood-soaked ground with his boot.

Tom kicked mindlessly at the hickory nuts lying on the ground. "The ravens are behaving strangely. Don't you think?"

"Yeah. You get hurt?"

"Scratches mostly," Tom replied, shrugging.

"I think we'll have to poison them or something. I'll talk to Dave when I take the deer in. This is crazy. I've never seen so many ravens." Joe handed his rifle to Tom, took his coat off and wrapped it around the deer's head and side. He bound the feet with his belt.

Joe swung the deer over his shoulder, making sure his jacket protected his shirt from getting bloody. "I'll load this in the truck. You coming?" He looked oddly at Tom, who hung back, looking toward the cliff.

"Someone's on the bluff." Tom pointed to the east. The sun was down now, the moon just beginning to cast a glow on the landscape. "See?"

"Lots of people take walks around here at night. Could be anyone. This stag's heavy. I'm heading back."

"You're right." Tom followed Joe, keeping his finger on the trigger of the revolver.

***

Sara, Cassie and Tom watched Joe drive away, his headlights illuminating the landscape of boulders, pine trees and winter-bare beech and hickory trees lining the road to the highway.

"Come on, let's go inside, it's cold out here," Tom said. He threw several logs onto the fire. Cassie went into the kitchen, returning in a few minutes with a tray of hot chocolate and brownies. "This will warm us up," she smiled and poured each of them a mug of cocoa.

"I talked to William today," Tom said.

"You did?" Sara asked.

"Yeah. He said Vivian's beginning to show improvement. He's bringing her back to the states soon. They're going to stay in Boston for a while. At least until the holidays are over." Sara put her mug down and began picking the walnuts out of her brownie.

"Mannie and Amos are taking the kids to meet them." Tom watched Sara, waiting for her reaction.

"I know. Without me." Sara got up; a tear ran down her cheek. She dabbed it carelessly and asked, "Do they want me to stay at their house then?"

"No, but," Tom quickly added, "I thought you'd want you to stay here. With Cassie and me."

"I don't know, Tom," Sara said curtly. "I never intended to be here more than a few weeks. You have so much going on. You don't need me getting in your way."

"Sara," Cassie said, standing up and taking Sara's hand. "It'll be too lonely if you leave. You have to stay!" Cassie's cell rang. "It's Mannie. Hold on. Be right back." She went into the dining room to talk.

"You don't need to feel like you have to ask me to stay here," Sara said. "I thought, once Vivian was better, I'd stay with her and the family. I never imagined they'd go to Boston. That was never discussed." She clenched her hand into a fist. "This whole situation is unbelievable. I'll have to go back to New York and find work. I can't stay here if I don't have a job." She stared at him. "You get that don't you, Tom?"

"Sara, I want you to stay here. With me. Don't leave." Tom stood, tried to hug her to him.

Sara kept her arms straight, tucked closely to her body. "I need to think about this. I don't want to be dependent on you."

Cassie cleared her throat as she came back into the room. "Listen, I need to go pick Lizzie up. "Can we talk about this tomorrow? There's no need to make a decision tonight, is there?"

"You're right. I'm too upset to think clearly. I need some time." Sara pulled away from Tom. "Cassie, want me to ride with you to get Lizzie?"

"Nah. You and Tom need time alone. I'll be back in a while. Then it's straight to bed for Lizzie and me." She pulled her coat on. "See you guys."

"You taking the back road?" Tom asked

"Yeah, it's so much quicker."

"Be careful, Sis. You know that's the road . . . "

Cassie interrupted, "I know. The road Harry drove off. Have no fear. I'm not in a hurry." Cassie hugged Sara, then left. Tom watched her get into her car and drive slowly down the road.

Sara said, "I'm going to take a hot bath and go to bed. Goodnight."

"I'm sorry, Sara. I shouldn't have told you about Jimmy and Billy leaving. I didn't mean to spring it on you like that." Tom walked over to Sara, put his finger lightly across her mouth as she began to speak. "We'll talk tomorrow. Don't say anything. Come on. I'll wash your back." He led her up the stairs.

Chapter 127

Billy sat on the top of the bluff. Long shadows darkened the beach below. It was almost dusk. He rocked silently in the chair he'd thoughtfully brought here for Elise. The chair creaked faintly when he shifted his weight. He hadn't heard from Elise for days, and he was getting increasingly angry. She'd walked out on him several nights ago. They'd fooled around in his room for a while—tested every bed in the house actually—when everyone else was in town. Then Billy fixed a pizza. She wouldn't eat though. She never wanted to eat.

He figured they could play his new video game. *But hell, no! She never wants to do anything with me.* He'd been in the middle of an ambush, and Elise hadn't even bothered to say goodbye. She just left. He didn't know what the fuck she expected! She was a good lay—but not that good. Anyway, she was getting boring, always wanting him to herself. Billy wanted to hang out with kids his own age. Elise was too old for him—that was pretty fucking obvious. "Well, screw you!" he yelled. "I'm not wasting any more time waiting for you!" He jumped up. Picking up the rocking chair he'd hauled there for Elise, he hurled it over the cliff edge, watched it bounce off the rocky crags and crash into the ocean below. "I don't need you anymore!" He felt better now.

The sun was setting. Billy looked up and saw a huge, sky-darkening, flock of ravens heading toward him. He sprinted to the car parked on the shoulder of the road, hopped in, slammed the door and started the engine. A dozen birds dove at the car, their bodies bouncing off the windows. "What the fuck!" he screamed. Throwing the car into gear, he gunned the engine and drove like a bat out of hell.

Billy drove the back road for several miles, glancing out the windows and into the rearview every few seconds. A dozen ravens followed for a time, then circled back around and flew to the west. Satisfied that the birds were no longer after him, he headed for his new friend Arnie's house. He met Arnie a few days ago at the arcade. They'd bonded instantly. Yeah, he needed his freedom. Bye-bye, Elise. Billy had accomplished what he was after. He got his experience. He got laid and learned a few tricks. Elise was a good teacher. He turned the CD player on full blast and rolled down the windows of his dad's caddy. Besides, in a week he'd be in Boston. He felt liberated.

Chapter 128

Terese knocked on the front door of Remington House. She paced back and forth, then knocked again. "Hello!" she yelled. She tried the door. It wasn't locked. She opened it and stuck her head in. "Cassie? Hey, it's Terese!"

"Hi. Coming. Hang on," Cassie hollered from upstairs. "Be down in a second." She had just gotten out of the shower. "I need to get dressed. There's a fresh pot of coffee in the kitchen. Help yourself."

Instead of going to the kitchen, Terese walked slowly into the study and looked around the dark room. She pulled the curtains back, letting the sun flood into the dark corners. Standing in the center of the room, she closed her eyes and took five very quick, shallow breaths. Next she lifted her arms toward the ceiling and slowed her breathing, concentrating on the sounds and smells in the room. *Nothing here. Oh, thank God!* She saw the door at the back of the room and quickly crossed the length of the study. The brass knob was cold in her hand as she turned it and pushed the door inward. She shone her tiny flashlight into the darkness of the storage room. Again —nothing. Across the storage room was another door. She pulled it toward her and entered the dining room, where only a few days ago, they had exorcised the house of the Lindemans.

Closing the door softly behind her, Terese turned and considered the empty room. The table sat bare of any décor except an heirloom, linen tablecloth with elaborate tatting around the scalloped edge. There was no fire in the fireplace, the room was intensely cold. Terese shivered. She repeated her breathing technique—five quick intakes—then she lifted her arms and began taking longer, shallow breaths. She closed her eyes and focused on the atmosphere of the room.

"Terese, is everything all right?" Cassie stood in the doorway. "Do you think the Lindemans are back?" she lamented, her voice high pitched with fear.

Terese opened her eyes and whirled to face Cassie. "No, that's not the sense I have, dear. Terese dropped into a chair. "I was making sure the house is cleansed. Thankfully I don't sense anyone here."

"You're sure? You looked so strange a minute ago."

"I had an odd feeling this morning. It happens sometimes. All I could think was that I better make certain that we'd achieved a total cleansing. We did. I don't detect any spirits in the house now."

"Thank God! You scared me." Cassie began throwing kindling into the fireplace. "It's so cold in here." Terese crumpled up several sheets of newspaper, cramming it around the wood. Cassie pulled a wooden match from the hearth box and lit the paper. As soon as the fire began to burn, Cassie said, "Come on, let's have some coffee."

The kitchen was warm and bright in the midwinter sun. Wiggins was curled contentedly on the rug before the fire. He opened one eye to look at Terese and Cassie, then covered his face with his paw.

Terese bent down, gently petting Wiggins. "Besides, if anything was wrong, the cat would let us know," she said. "Animals have a strong connection to the other side."

"I'm sure you're right. Wiggins was acting very odd and skittish. And voilà, now that the house has been cleared, he's back to normal." Cassie poured two cups of coffee and put a plate of cookies on the table.

"Where is everyone?" asked Terese.

"Tom and Sara drove over to the Harrisons' to pick up the rest of Sara's things. She's staying here with us, at least for a while." She smiled at Terese. "Lizzie went with them, hoping to see Jimmy, no doubt. Did I tell you Lizzie's going to visit her grandmother?"

"That sounds like a good idea."

"Yeah, it'll give me some time with Tom. Well, at least once he gets back from Jamestown."

"He's going there for the funeral?" Terese stirred her coffee and picked up a cookie.

"Yeah. He's leaving tomorrow, just planning to stay for a few days. He didn't want to go but felt like he had to. Nate and Rosa are heartbroken, he needs to be with them."

"I'm sure. What a nightmare for them," Terese said.

"Tragic."

"Cassie, I have something else on my mind," Terese said.

"You look serious."

"I am."

"My nerves are about shot. Hold on." Cassie opened the lower cabinet door and rummaged around. "Here it is." She opened a foil-covered box. "Chocolate! Remember?"

"I do! It got us through the séance!" Terese laughed.

Cassie sat down and picked up a milk chocolate, the top swirled with a squiggle of white. She popped it into her mouth and chewed. "Mint cream. Yum." She grinned. "Okay. I'm fortified now. What's on your mind?"

"The séance—well, its aftermath. We left everything we used in the ceremony out in plain sight that night. The candles, burned sage, white roses, salt all over the floor. Everything. Your brother obviously knew we'd held a séance. He never said a word to me. Did he ask you about it?"

"He did. And he asked Sara, too. He was very upset with us. We lied and told him nothing much happened and that we thought we made contact with the Lindemans. We told him that the spirits were benign and that you sent them on their way. I told him we'd scared ourselves and decided not to stay here that night. I knew he couldn't deal with the truth."

"And he settled for your simple explanation?" Terese asked, obviously skeptical.

"Tom said he never believed there were spirits here," Cassie said. "Basically he dismissed me . . . and Sara. He said he didn't want to have any more discussions about ghosts. So we let it go at that."

"You sound uncertain. What are you thinking?"

Cassie picked another chocolate and took a bite. "Tom's lying. I think he knows the Lindemans were haunting this house. I think he hates himself for not believing me weeks ago. And he feels guilty for leaving us here to deal with them."

"I got the same feeling from him," Terese said. "But I sense there's more. Your brother's aura is troubling me."

"What do you mean? You can see his aura?"

"I can see almost everyone's aura—if I choose to. Most of the time I have to concentrate to see it. Not so with your brother. He's in a distressed state. Something serious is on his mind. He was visibly radiating. His aura was gray—the color surrounding a person in a dark and depressed state."

"Terese, I should tell you some things about my brother." Cassie moved her chair closer to Terese's. "You already know his wife died a few years ago. It devastated him. He fell apart and was under the care of a private psychiatrist for a long time after Elise's death. He's never completely gotten over her. Maybe he never will.

"He tries to put on a strong, stable front. But he doesn't fool me. He's definitely better than he was, even a few months ago. But so much has happened this past month: dealing with the move here, all the crazy stuff that's gone on in the house, having to fly out of the country—he hates to fly!" She smiled trying to lighten the tone a little. "Then add the turmoil and pain of Harold's death. It's almost more than Tom can handle. I completely understand why he feels dark and depressed. He must feel like he completely failed us—and himself."

"Maybe." Terese got up, poured them more coffee. "That might be it, but . . . "

"That *is* it, Terese. Tom needs time to learn to live like a normal person again. That's why he moved here."

"I'm worried. I get the feeling there's more. But . . . certainly you know your brother better than I do. It's good you're staying here. With you and Sara both around him, he'll be well cared for."

"Absolutely. Tom doesn't stand a chance at being miserable!" Cassie pushed her chair from the table. "Got to hide the chocolate. Somebody's coming!" She grabbed the box and shoved it in the cupboard just as Tom and Sara came in the kitchen. She flashed a smile at Terese.

"Terese!" Sara rushed over and hugged her. "It's so good to see you."

"Sara, Tom, Lizzie! Hi to you, too."

Chapter 129

Terese turned her car radio off, annoyed at the constant barrage of commercials. "I've been in the car for five minutes and not one lousy song. Screw you WBYO!" she yelled. She drummed her left fingers on the armrest. She felt restless and increasingly nervous remembering with clarity the deep gray hue surrounding Tom again today. He appeared close to a breakdown. She saw the signs. Something was very wrong.

A light snow fell. Terese fiddled with the windshield wipers. Either she had to put up with the squealing of rubber on glass or let the snow form a light veil on the window before the blades wiped it away. She tried one last adjustment, changed the defrost level, then cranked the blower fan to high.

On the side of the road, a deer and its two yearlings stopped chewing the soft, brown underbrush and watched Terese pass. As she rounded the next curve in the desolate road, she had a vision, then a flash connection with a spirit, too brief for her to determine if it was a male or female. A sense of deep sadness overwhelmed her. Before she realized what was happening, tears streamed down her cheeks. She pulled over, put her car in park and wept uncontrollably. After several minutes, she leaned back, closed her eyes and searched her mind for clues to the source of this intense pain. She was puzzled, it was indeed rare for her to have no idea what was happening around her.

Just as suddenly as it began, the episode was over. Terese felt nothing. Empty. And she was tired. Taking a deep breath, Terese wiped her tears away with the back of her hand. She glanced out the side window. On the bluff above the ocean, a hundred yards to her left, surrounded by a wispy layer of fog, a solitary figure walked. "What are you doing out in this cold without a coat on?" Terese yelled out, though the woman couldn't possibly hear her.

Terese watched her. The woman appeared to be fairly young judging from her stature and her long, blonde hair whipping around her face in the icy, winter wind. *It's freezing out! What are you thinking?*

On the cliff edge, a man appeared. He was shorter and, even from this distance, seemed much older than the woman. Terese noted that he appeared to be bald and had a pronounced stoop to his shoulders. The man held something and handed it to the woman. It was a coat. He helped her put it on, then touched her face and patted her on the back as if to comfort her. She pushed his hand away.

As Terese watched, the woman turned toward her. When she saw Terese, she grabbed the hand of her companion and ran. Terese shuddered, put her car in gear and pressed the gas pedal. *I need to get home*. She felt increasingly vulnerable and unsettled.

Chapter 130

The shock of her violent encounter with Tom had devastated Elise. He'd gotten the upper hand, had nearly destroyed her. But she survived, would always survive! He thought he could kill her. He would pay dearly for that. She wouldn't let her guard down again.

Since Tom's arrival back at Remington House, Elise had stayed in a vacant house down the beach from the Harrisons'. She was weak and needed time to recover. She was so lonely she didn't think she could stand it. But she knew she'd be safe there. She had nowhere else to go.

Tonight, sitting in front of a small fire, all she dared to have lest someone see the smoke, she studied her face in a hand mirror she'd found in an upstairs drawer. There were still red marks on her face and arms where the holy water had touched her skin. But the marks were fading and her complexion was returning to its normal, pale luminescence.

She'd experienced genuine pain at Tom's hands. "Never again!" she hissed to the mirror. She smiled at her reflection, gently touched the wisps of hair framing her face. Her hair shimmered like gold in the soft firelight, her brown eyes almost mystical as the fire reflected in her enlarged pupils. "I am forever young. Forever beautiful."

The dancing flames warmed and lulled her. As she closed her eyes, her head began to droop—she was exhausted. Elise lay back against the soft cushions of the sofa, pulled a heavy cashmere throw over her small frame and slept, comforted that she was no longer alone. In the basement of the beach house, in a small, dark room without windows— just to his liking— Benjamin had taken up residence. He and Elise had formed an alliance. They needed each other.

It happened a few days ago. Elise had been basking in the final moments of twilight, drawing in the powers from the setting sun. From the safety of an outcrop of rocks along the beach, carefully hidden in the evening shadows, she watched Tom's house. It was then that she saw Benjamin hurrying down the beach.

Once, she would gladly have killed that gnarly creature that held her captive in the closet at Remington House. Now, out of desperation and loneliness, Elise knew she needed Benjamin. She waylaid him before he had a chance to escape from her, though in her weakened and vulnerable state, he could easily have gotten away. He had not. She recognized that he was as lonely as she was. She took him back to the beach house. The two began their odd, but comforting, friendship.

Earlier today, she and Benjamin had been spotted up on the bluff. But Elise was not worried. The medium had not been able to penetrate her psyche. Elise was becoming extraordinarily strong. For the past few days she and Benjamin had been reading books from the occult underground that the Lindemans had hidden in their basement closet, behind a loose board. Benjamin snuck into Remington House a few evenings ago and collected as many books as he could carry while everyone was distracted by the flocks of ravens—the ravens that were now perched, by the hundreds, in the woods behind the beach house, waiting their next summons from Elise.

Chapter 131

Cassie and Sara were bored. Tom had gone to Jamestown for Harold's funeral. Lizzie, accompanied by a hired nanny, left this morning to make the train trip to her grandma's house in Connecticut. The Harrison house was closed up. Billy and Jimmy were now in Boston with Mannie and Amos.

From the basement came endless pounding and the annoying ringing of the band-saw as it cut through numerous two by fours. Joe and his crew were back to work.

Cassie smiled. "I know! Let's go through the boxes in the attic. There must be something to pique our interest there. The room at the end of the hall is still filled with old trunks. They must have belonged to the Lindemans. We should get rid of some of that stuff. It's a fire hazard."

"That's as good an excuse as any to nose through their stuff. Let's do it!" Sara said, jumping up off the couch.

Dazed, confused and unaware of how much time had passed, Sara opened her eyes, putting her hand to her head. She began massaging her temples. She had a horrible headache. On the floor across from her lay Cassie. Sara crawled to her, shook her shoulders roughly. "Cassie! Wake up! Cassie!"

Cassie groaned and rolled over onto her side. "Sara?"

Unable to stand, Sara crawled to the window. "We need to get out of here. I think the air's bad." She coughed as she struggled to open the window. Finally it gave way and fresh, cold air swept into the room. She breathed deeply, then grabbed Cassie by her arms and dragged her to the window. "Take a deep breath. Do it, Cassie!"

The window overlooked the west side of the house. Three stories below, Sara saw Joe carrying a load of insulation into the house. "Joe!" she screamed. "Joe! Help us!"

Joe looked around, finally spotting Sara. He dropped the rolls of insulation and ran. In less than a minute, Sara heard him, followed by several others, running down the long hallway. The door was closed. Joe jiggled the handle. It was locked. Realizing the door wouldn't open, Joe kicked it in.

"Help me get them out of here!" Joe yelled to the four men who had followed him up. Sara and Cassie were carried downstairs to the living room and laid carefully on the floor before the fireplace. "Grab those couch cushions!" Joe barked. "We need to elevate their feet." He lifted first Sara's, then Cassie's feet. All the windows and the doors in the living room were opened and a cold wind blew through. Billowing curtains danced crazily, magazine pages flipped and ruffled on the coffee table. Joe took their pulses and watched their color improve as they breathed the fresh air.

"Here, drink some water." Ralph, one of Joe's men, had gotten two glasses of water and held them out to Cassie and Sara. Both of them were breathing normally now and trying to sit up.

"Cassie, are you okay?" Sara asked, taking her hand.

"I think so." She sat up, rubbing the back of her neck. "Except my head. God it hurts!"

"Ralph, call 911," Joe said.

"Already did. They had a call down the highway, so the fire truck should be here soon."

"Joe, I think I'm fine. Help me to the couch." Joe took Sara's arm and helped her get up off the floor.

The wailing of the sirens could be heard as the fire engine, followed by the paramedics, flew up the drive. Ralph was helping Cassie to the couch when the rescue team rushed in.

***

Cassie and Sara proved to be fine. They were both given oxygen, their vital signs taken and recorded and pronounced okay. Joe took the firemen to the attic to test the carbon monoxide levels. They were normal. The rest of the house was checked. No other chemicals or leaks were found—nothing to explain what had happened to them. Joe drove both the girls into town to the clinic for blood work. Just to be on the safe side.

Per Joe's instructions, Ralph went to Terence Hardware Store and picked up a half a dozen CO_2 detectors. He returned to Remington where he and the crew installed them all over the house. Though it was only mid afternoon, they packed up their tools and called it a day. They all knew Joe would have them make up their time.

***

Tom repeatedly called Sara's and Cassie's cell phones as well as the house phone. He finally tried calling Joe, who once again had left his new cell phone in the basement on his workbench. In Remington House, the sound of ringing phones echoed through empty hallways.

In Jamestown, the funeral service was over and everyone had gone to Rosa's house to commiserate, eat and half-heartedly toast the deceased. "May the poor man be in a better place." They all hoped, but had little faith, that a "better place" was in store for Harold. They made a final toast as the sun began to set. "Rest in peace. May the devil forget your name. Slainte."

Nate went in search of Tom, noticeably absent at the final toasting.

Tom sat, phone in hand, on the front porch of Rosa's house, rocking back and forth on the porch swing. "Tom, what's wrong?" Nate asked.

***

The sun was setting. A peach and rose glow filled the western sky. Minute by minute as the orb of the sun dropped lower in the horizon, the once vibrant white clouds turned gray, then black.

Twilight. A time when the heavens renew. The day ends. Night begins. Stars glisten in the midnight blue sky, the earth rests. Then dawn renews the land as the golden light of day breaks across the horizon. A pattern of renewals and endings. Twilight. Dawn. Again and again.

Chapter 132

Elise and Benjamin sat quietly, side by side, on the upstairs landing of Remington House. They were tired, but exhilarated. It had been quite an ordeal to take over Cassie and Sara. For two hours Elise and Benjamin possessed their bodies.

Elise gently took Benjamin's hand in hers. "We should go now. Before they return. We can't come back here—not for a long time anyway. It's too risky. Besides, we have plans to make."

Benjamin nodded, tenderly stroking Elise's tiny hand.

"This is all so perfect! Tom still believes I'm dead. The fool!" Elise stood up and began gliding down the stairs. "We have much work to do. Come."

Chapter 133

Tom ran down the tarmac and into the waiting rental car. Déjà vu. He had to get to Remington House. Before something horrible happened. Again. Last time Harold had died. What the fuck was going on now? Where the hell was everyone? He tore out of the small municipal airport and hit the highway at eighty mph, weaving around the few cars in his way. No stars shone in Ravenswood tonight through the cloud-covered sky. A heavy fog rolled in from the Atlantic. Tom could barely see the highway in the glare of his headlights against the thick mist.

Gripping the steering wheel with one hand, Tom pulled his phone from his coat pocket with his free hand and called Sara's cell again. She answered on the first ring. "Sara?"

"Hi, Tom. I just got your messages. I haven't had a chance to call you. Sorry. Cassie and I got sick. Joe took us into town to the clinic."

"Sick? Are you okay?"

Sara said, "Yeah, we are. We're back home now. Joe's with us. He's checking on a few things."

"What *things*?"

"We passed out. We thought maybe it was carbon monoxide poisoning. It wasn't. We can't find anything wrong."

"Oh, God! I'm on my way. I should be there in half an hour."

"You're here? I thought you were staying in Jamestown for a few more days," Sara said.

"Sara, I've been calling for hours," Tom said. "I couldn't get hold of you or Cassie, not even Joe. So I panicked and booked a private flight home. Look, I'll be there shortly. You can explain everything then."

Tom snapped his phone closed and dropped it onto the seat so he could put both hands on the wheel. He braked when he saw taillights ahead of him, then jerked the wheel and passed the car on the right shoulder to avoid oncoming cars invisible in the blinding fog. His tires slid briefly in the loose gravel, then found solid pavement as he steered back onto the highway. He passed through the town of Ravenswood, slowed to twenty five mph, then accelerated up to fifty five when he reached the edge of town. Finally the fog cleared. Tom clutched the wheel as he maneuvered the winding beach highway. Within twenty minutes he was turning on to the road leading to Remington House.

He was home. Everything would be fine now. He parked the car in front of the house. Tom took the steps two at a time. Throwing the front door open, he yelled, "I'm home. Hello?" Walking slowly into the living room, he passed the fireplace, embers glowing orange. Sparks flew and popped as the burning kindling broke into small pieces and fell through the grate. Other than the faint glow from the smoldering coals, the room was dark. Tom turned the table lamp on and hurried into the dining room. "Hello!" he yelled. "Sara! Cassie! Where are you?" Silence.

Tom shoved the kitchen door open, flipped on the light. No one had been in the kitchen in some time. There were no dishes in the sink, the stove was cold. There were no dying embers in the fireplace. He glanced at the door to the basement. Sweat trickled down his forehead. He turned the knob. The door was locked, the dead bolt engaged. His fingers twisted the thumb turn and pushed the heavy wooden door open. "Joe? You down there? Anyone?" He heard footsteps from the floor above. *They're upstairs! No wonder they didn't hear me!*

Throwing the back stairs door open, Tom hurried up to the second floor. "Hello?" Tom heard Cassie's voice. They were in his bedroom. He saw Joe first. He was holding Sara up. His calloused hands looked large and clumsy as he maneuvered Sara's limp body gently onto the bed.

Cassie was frantically dialing her cell. "Where is he?" she screamed. "Tom, answer your phone!"

"Cassie, what the hell's wrong?" Tom ran over to Sara, who was deathly pale. She sobbed softly. He touched her tear-streaked cheek.

Her eyes flew open. "Tom! You're all right." Sara's hands shook as she grabbed Tom's hand.

"Of course I am. What's wrong?"

Cassie collapsed on the bed next to Sara. "We just got a phone call saying you'd been in an accident!" Cassie explained, her voice wrought with emotion. "The woman said you hadn't survived the crash!" She stood up and hugged Tom to her. "The woman said she was with dispatch and that the sheriff asked her to call me. I didn't believe her. That's why I was calling you. When you didn't answer . . . " Her voice broke.

Tom pounded his fist on the dresser. "Shit! I left my phone in the car!" He studied Sara. Her breathing was fast and shallow. He dropped down beside her. "Are you okay, Sara?"

"I am now. God, Tom! I was so scared. I thought we lost you!"

Tom pulled Sara to him. "It's okay. I'm fine." He wrapped his arms around Cassie and Sara. "Who would do something so despicable?"

"That's what I want to know. Let me see your cell phone, Cassie." Joe reached for it, flipped it open, looking for the caller ID from the last call. "The number's blocked. Damn!"

"You're certain they said my name? Maybe it was a wrong number," Tom said.

"No, the woman said it was you! Tom Gardner!" Tears filling her brown eyes, Cassie said, "Oh, thank God you're all right!" She grabbed Tom's face, gave him a big kiss on the forehead. "Come on. Let's go downstairs! We need a drink." She leaned forward so she could see Sara sitting on the other side of Tom. "You okay?"

"Yeah. What a horrible day this has been." She choked back a sob.

Tom stroked her hair. "Let's go downstairs. I want to hear everything that happened today. You sure you're both okay?"

"Yeah. We had horrible headaches," Cassie said, "but nothing aspirin and fresh air couldn't cure. Emotionally, though, I feel like I've been dragged to hell and back." She led the way down the back stairs. "Go on into the living room, I'll bring a tray. Joe, could you light the fire? It's cold in the house."

In the living room, Tom pushed the sofa closer to the fire. They huddled around the fireplace. Joe and Cassie told him what had happened in the attic and the ensuing rescue. Tom was seriously disturbed, especially when he discovered there was no explanation for what made Sara and Cassie pass out. "It might have been some chemicals your crew was using in the basement. Maybe the fumes floated up through the heating ducts and got trapped in the attic. You must have breathed in enough of the fumes to put you out. Thank God you woke up when you did, Sara. Luckily you were alert enough to open the window to let fresh air in. Who knows what could have happened. No clues from the firemen?"

No," Cassie said. "They didn't find anything wrong. The firemen checked the whole house."

Joe nodded. "Everything seems to be okay. So maybe you're right, Tom. Whatever was in the room aired out."

"I didn't smell anything odd when we got up there," Cassie added.

Joe scratched his head. "It makes no sense to me. But there seems to be no other logical explanation. One of those mysteries we may never unravel."

"Maybe. I'll make a few calls, too, and get someone out here to take some more air samples. Just to be safe." Tom poured another glass of brandy. He swallowed the amber liquor —warm and soothing. "As for the phone call—that had to have been a nasty prank." Sara was watching him. He looked away, afraid she would read his thoughts. The call was more than disturbing. Tom couldn't shake the feeling of dread he was having. He shuddered and took another sip of brandy, looked out the window to avoid Sara's eyes.

Clouds, black as midnight, covered the sky. There were no stars. No moonlight. Not this night. Far to the east, sparks and a thin, white billow of smoke rose into the sky drifting out and over the ocean. It was coming from the house down the beach. Someone was living there. He knew it! "Joe, any idea who's staying at the house beyond the bluff?" Tom pointed at the thin line of smoke.

"No one should be. Last time I checked with Mandy, the property manager, she said the house was locked up. The house isn't being rented out this season. Guess the water's shut off— pipes froze—so they can't lease it right now."

"You sure about that? There's smoke coming from somewhere down there. Has to be from the Shelton house." Tom poured another drink, then handed the bottle to Joe.

Joe took it, poured himself a drink. "I'll call Mandy. Could be her kid's in town. He stays at some of the vacant rental properties when he's here. Supposed to be a secret. But we all know about it! I don't want to get her, or her boy, in trouble. Mandy can call the sheriff if that's not the case." Joe called her and left a message, then got up and threw a couple pieces of kindling on the fire. "Think I'll head back to town. Long day!"

"Yeah, I'll bet you're tired, Joe. Thanks for everything you did today," Tom said. He stood up and lightly punched Joe on the shoulder. "I don't know how I'll make it up to you, but I will."

"Just watching out for my friends." Joe smiled at Sara and Cassie. "Anyhow, I'm out of here. I'll be back in the morning. My crew starts at eight. You all get some rest—you need it! What a fucked day this has been! Oops, sorry ladies! Well, goodnight," he said. They heard his truck start. The tires crunched on the gravel driveway as he drove slowly away.

"I'm going upstairs to take a hot shower. Then I'm going to bed. I want this day over!" Cassie said. She got up and hugged Tom, then Sara. "Goodnight." She stopped in the doorway and said, "I love you, Brother."

"I love you back! Night, Sis. Sara, I'm going out to the car; I need to get my phone," Tom said. After he'd checked his phone messages and sent a few texts, he added more wood to the fire. He sat down beside Sara on the sofa, cradled her in his arms. They didn't talk, comfortable in their silence. Within minutes, both were asleep.

Chapter 134

Benjamin recovered quickly from their visit to Remington, though it had left Elise exhausted. He laughed remembering the chaos he and Elise had caused. Carbon monoxide poisoning! Ha! Now he was bored and restless. He needed to get out of the beach house, far too small and confining for his taste. He checked on Elise before he left—made sure she was still asleep. Finding her on the couch, he carried her to her room and gently laid her on the bed. He covered her with piles of blankets—she was always cold.

Benjamin promised her he'd stay away from Tom's house, never go near any of the family unless she was with him. But he was restless; he needed to be doing something. He needed to get out of the cramped bungalow!

Tom and Sara were asleep on the couch in the living room. At some level both seemed to have felt the dark energy of Benjamin when he came into the house—though they didn't fully wake up. They shifted slightly—Tom pulled the afghan closer; Sara tucked her head into Tom's shoulder and sighed.

Benjamin hovered for several minutes watching them sleep, then curled up beside the sleeping pair, watching the flames in the fireplace burn down to coals.

He missed the Lindemans. At least life with them had been exciting. He sighed. Sara stirred. He wondered if Gabe left any of his stash and decided to take a look around. Excited at the possibility, he smiled and left the sleeping couple, both snoring softly.

There was nothing the cabinet in the bathroom off the kitchen, everything had been cleaned out. He found nothing in the attic or in any of the hiding places on the second floor. As much as he disliked the basement—where the Lindemans often locked him in a closet—he knew where they'd hidden their hashish. He slipped through the locked door, down the dark stairs and into the Lindemans' bedroom.

Getting down on his hands and knees on the cold cement floor, he felt around for the loose section of baseboard on the right side of the closet—one of several such hiding places. Benjamin pulled the board away and reached into a small cubby. His fingers felt a leather pouch, old and stiff. He pulled it out. The brittle, leather loop securing the flap broke off when he lifted it from around the ivory button.

"Pay dirt!" Reaching into the bag, Benjamin extracted a small ceramic pipe, the bowl carved into the shape of a talon. It smelled strongly of burned hashish—sweet and pungent. He pulled out a small glass bottle stoppered with a wide cork. Prying the dried up cork off, he brought the bottle to his nose, cautiously sniffing the contents. "Fucking fine! Gabe, you old bastard! Fucking fine!"

For the next hour, Benjamin stayed in the cold, dark basement enjoying the hashish. He felt giddy yet calm at the same time. It'd been a long time since he'd felt that good. Leaning back against the wall, he breathed deeply, closed his eyes and enjoyed the feeling of being buzzed. His thoughts drifted back to when he was alive. He laughed. Living sucked. This was so much better. The blessings of suicide. He hummed a song he remembered from his childhood—from the good days—the days before his mom took her life. Her life had sucked, too. Life was hell after she died. Forty years of hell. Suicide was his end, too. Emaline taught her son well. *Better off dead. Yeah. She got that right—I am.* He wiped a tear that dripped down to the end of his nose. *I'm not gonna get all sad. Fuck that.* He took another hit of hashish, relaxed. Then he laughed again. This was living. He had Elise now! He would make her his.

Moonlight filtered through the curtains lighting up the dark recesses of the room. Bored, Benjamin got up and began rummaging around the Lindemans' closet, rifling through the trunks, forgotten by Tom—at least for now. In their bureau he found bottles of painkillers and two amber, glass vials, both filled with what Benjamin believed was once laudanum, the tincture long since dried up, leaving only the opium. Damn the stuff was old! Later he would break the glass and carefully scrape out the opium.

In the back of the closet he found a handmade, tapestry satchel that was lined with black silk. It was filled with what remained of the dozens of carefully selected and polished stones the Lindemans had used over the decades in their satanic ceremonies. He placed the leather pouch filled with drugs and pills on top of the stones. He'd take these back to the cottage. He was floating quietly up the stairs to the kitchen when he heard a high-pitched screech on the other side of the kitchen door. Damned cat! Overhead, running footsteps pounded the ceiling. Benjamin heard something crash to the floor in the kitchen.

"Wiggins! What the hell!" Tom yelled.

Benjamin heard the cat hissing from behind the door. It yowled and began to claw at the door. Benjamin flew down the stairs, through the rooms under construction and down the long hallway to the back entrance of the basement. He could have escaped without opening the door, simply passed through it, but he refused to leave the satchel behind.

Struggling to open the lock, he heard Tom running down the stairs. From behind him the cat howled. Benjamin opened the door, threw the bag out ahead of him and slammed the door. The cat's body hit the door with a loud *thwack*. Benjamin grabbed the bag and ran. When he neared the bluff, he jumped off, sailing through the air and landing in the sand. The bag hit with a *thud*, bouncing several times. He grabbed it and hurried into the dark shadows of the bluff. He ran down the beach, arriving minutes later at the cottage.

Benjamin opened the door. Elise was waiting for him. He'd forgotten the might of her fury. This tiny, elflike creature, of whom he was so enamored, proved a menacing force. And now he had to reckon with her anger. He had betrayed her, had broken his promise. This night he would regret those indiscretions.

Elise entered his mind, showed him her inner darkness. Afraid and thrilled at the same time, Benjamin succumbed to her will, allowed her to take his mind to dark places that he imagined even the Lindemans would be in awe of. For hours she tormented him. Finally, just after midnight, she left him. He did not follow.

Benjamin would spend the next months demonstrating his loyalty to this woman. Still, things were good—he had been lonely—now he was not. Elise would make his life exciting again. And he would prove himself to her—over time.

Chapter 135

"Who's down here?" Tom raced through the dark basement, searching for a light switch as he ran. "Damnit! Where the hell is the light switch?" He stopped when he reached the doorway at the far end of the gym. He knew there was a switch there. He flipped it on, then ran down the hallway toward the back door. Wiggins sat on the floor staring at the closed door. When Tom got close to him, he ran to Tom and hissed. "You okay, kitty?" Tom reached down and petted the cat, then opened the back door. "Who the hell was here?" Wiggins bounded out the door. In the distance, Tom saw a man with a bag in his hand running toward the stairs that led down to the beach. Tom took off after him. When Tom reached the stairs and looked down, the man was nowhere to be seen. Tom searched for few minutes, finally giving up. It was too dark to see anything.

"What's going on?" Sara stopped, held her side, out of breath and panting. "What's wrong? Who were you chasing?"

"That man we keep seeing—the guy on the beach—he was in the house! Fuck! I'm pretty sure he took something. I need to find out what! Come on!" He took Sara's hand and they ran back to the house.

Tom searched the house from top to bottom, but found nothing missing. The grandfather clock struck midnight. Sara had gone upstairs to bed; Cassie was sitting in the living room, staring into a dying fire. "Sorry I woke you, Sis."

"This house. God damn it! Something is always wrong. Tom, maybe you should consider moving." Cassie looked at her brother who was pouring himself a double shot of vodka.

"Want one?" he asked.

"No!" she scowled. "Tom, I'm serious."

"I know you are. But this is my house. I intend to stay here. No petty thief will drive me away. Things will get better." He downed his vodka. The two sat in silence for a few minutes, the *tic toc* of the grandfather clock echoed in the quiet. "Did I tell you Nate's coming at the end of the month? His being here will make everything better. It'll be like old times, you'll see." Tom poured another vodka. "Besides, where would I go?"

"I don't know." Cassie stood up, shrugged her shoulders. "I'm tired. I'm going to bed. We'll talk about this tomorrow. Okay?" She gave him a hug and went upstairs.

Tom locked the house, checked all the downstairs windows a second time and then went upstairs. Getting his .45 from his safe, he put it in the top drawer of his nightstand. After tossing and turning for hours, he finally fell asleep. He dreamed Elise was there with him, his arms entwined around her shoulders, her delicate body curled against his. He held her all night, woke saddened in the morning to find her gone. Sitting on the edge of his bed, he cursed himself for allowing a dream to intrude on his waking life.

There was a knock on his door. "Tom? Are you awake?"

"I am."

Sara pushed the door open and came into the room carrying a breakfast tray. "Morning." She sat the tray down on the table.

Tom took her hand and led her back to his bed. "Good morning." He pushed her gently onto the bed.

Chapter 136

Never again would Elise show Benjamin any signs of weakness. She was regaining her strength since her near demise at Tom's hands. Her hatred for Tom and his family was growing more intense. She would carefully nurture those feelings until she was again ready to face Tom. For now, she'd stay away from him. She had plenty of time.

Right now, Elise needed to find somewhere else for Benjamin and her to stay. Someone might find them here at the beach house—now that Benjamin had been so foolish and made his presence known at Remington House.

Elise stood at the crest of the bluff overlooking the turbulent ocean. Stars sparkled in the midnight-blue sky. The moon glided behind a bank of clouds, shadows enveloped the beach.

Waves crashed onto the shore throwing sprays of water high into the air. She listened to each droplet of water land on the beach. Elise marveled at her heightened hearing—Benjamin taught her how to enhance many of her senses.

Far out on the horizon a freighter passed. Its horn blasted repeatedly as it skirted the Isle of Westmoor. She remained on the bluff until night ended and the cycle of life-renewing dawn began. After witnessing the brilliant oranges and dusty-gray mauves of daybreak, she returned to the cottage.

Elise told Benjamin to gather their belongings—they were leaving. He followed her through stands of pines and beech trees. Loaded down with a trunk filled with blankets, clothes, books and the things Elise had gathered over the past weeks, they climbed a steep path to the top of a hill, then Elise led Benjamin down into a clearing leading to the Harrison house—vacant and boarded up for the winter.

Elise stopped and pulled her coat tightly around her against the icy Atlantic wind. Her blonde hair swirled around her shoulders. Her velvet brown eyes sparkled. "Benjamin," she swept her arms toward the house, "this will be our home." She laughed and ran down the path.

Benjamin hurried after her, the trunk light in his strong arms. When he caught up with her he asked, "This is where that boy lived, isn't it? The one I so often saw you with."

"It is." Elise followed the path around to the back of the house. "Benjamin, go check the garage." She pointed to the building to the west. "Make sure Mannie's car is gone."

Benjamin put the trunk down. "What car would that be?" he asked.

"A white van—a Ford I think."

Benjamin peered into the dark garage. "Not here. Just a Cadillac."

"Good. Come on. Let's go inside." Not waiting for Benjamin, Elise disappeared through the back door. She was already in the kitchen when he caught up with her.

"Will that couple be back then? The one who looks after the house for the family?"

"No, they went with Billy and his brother to stay with their parents in Boston. If their car isn't here, they're gone." She smiled. "And we, dear Benjamin, have a new home. We'll be safe and warm here for months." She glanced at Benjamin. "Don't look so sour. We can come and go as we please. We only have to stay away from Tom's house. And of course, make sure we stay off the beach where we could be seen. When we want to go down to the ocean, we can go farther up, to the other side of the bluff."

Benjamin nodded. "Are you cold? Should I light a fire?" he asked.

"No, just find the thermostat and turn the heat up a bit. A fire would be too obvious. Then take my trunk upstairs. I want it in the master bedroom, the room at the end of the hallway."

The outside shutters had all been carefully closed and latched; the curtains had all been drawn. Elise could turn on every light in the house if she so chose. She was sick of living in darkness. "Benjamin, I need to be alone for a while. Go and choose a room for yourself. You can stay anywhere you like. Leave me for a while, please." She watched Benjamin walk down the hall and disappear down the basement stairs.

Elise took Joe's cell phone from a soft, red leather purse Elise had found at the beach house. She plugged the phone into a charger she found in Jimmy's room. She found another phone and charger in Viv's room. She needed to transfer some numbers from Joe's phone into Vivian's old phone, then she'd throw Joe's away. In a few hours, she would have a new connection to Tom. Laughing she laid down on her bed, pulled the warm comforter around her shoulders and took a long nap.

At dawn, Elise returned to the bluff above the ocean. Dangling her legs over the edge of the precipice, she watched the sunrise. A warm cable knit sweater, scarf, thick tights and wool gloves, all belonging to Vivian, kept her warm. Daybreak gave her intense joy and strength. One of a dozen ravens that settled in the bushes around her flew to her, perched on her shoulder and cawed as the sun rose. She stroked the raven's silky feathers.

Elise sat quietly, breathing in the cool salt air and began making her plans. She and Benjamin would stay at the Harrison house until they were ready to make their move. She smiled and felt soothed as the sun warmed her face.

***

Benjamin chose to move into the basement. He took the satchel filled with ceremonial stones, his stash, and a set of books he'd gathered over the decades down the two sets of stairs. Things would be good here. At least for a while.

When dawn broke, Benjamin, too, left the house, traveling miles down the beach to the cave where he'd been living before meeting Elise. He took a pipe filled with hashish and several of the Lindemans' books of the occult with him. He'd make certain he'd be a worthy cohort for Elise, make sure he was as strong as she was.

After years spent being a slave to the Lindemans, he would never allow anyone to dominate him again. He was already recognizing that tendency in Elise and would make certain he was up to the challenge should the need to overpower her arise. It may never happen. She may learn to consider him her equal. For now, he'd make himself indispensable to her, enjoy himself while he learned to become a real man again. He'd been studying *The Ancient Book of Transformation* and would spend the next weeks immersed in the ritual of change.

***

All alone, Elise climbed the stairs to the attic. No shutters blocked the view out this window. Looking to the south she could see Remington House. She'd carried Jimmy's telescope up here earlier in the day. Now, at dusk, Tom and his family began turning on lights. From her vantage point, Elise could clearly see into the dining room on the lower floor and into Cassie's room, Sara's room and the east hallway on the second floor. She settled in to watch the house for a few hours, saw Cassie and Sara leave around six. Taking the phone she'd found in Viv's room from her pocket, she called one of the numbers she had transferred into it earlier. Elise smiled when she heard the voice on the other end answer.

Chapter 137

For a change, the day at Remington had been uneventful and routine. Other than the constant pounding of the construction from the basement, all had been quiet. Cassie and Sara went for a long walk on the beach. Tom spent most of his day working upstairs. By evening, everyone had put the events of the past few days behind them.

After dinner, Cassie and Sara went into town to meet up with Mary and Terese to see a movie. All alone now, relishing the calm, Tom went upstairs to read through some papers. His phone rang, startling him. "Hello?" Tom answered after the first ring. The incoming phone number wasn't familiar.

"Tom Gardner?" a feminine voice asked.

Tom didn't recognize the voice of the caller. "Yes. Who's this?"

"Tom, it's Rosa. Am I calling at a bad time?"

"No, not at all. Is everything all right?"

"I've had the strangest call. I don't know what to do or what to think. I can't talk to Nate, about this. He's so upset already. He's taken Harold's death so hard."

Tom waited for her to say more, but heard only silence. "Rosa, are you there?"

"Yes. I'm here. I thought you could help me deal with this. I don't know what to do. Maybe I'm losing my mind," Rosa sobbed into the phone.

"What's wrong? Has something happened?" Tom asked. He began pacing the floor of his room, leaving a trail of footprints in the plush carpet.

"Someone called me." She paused. "He said he was Harold!"

Tom heard a gasp, then a rush of static on the phone line. "Rosa? Hello?"

Dead air. Then more static. Tom flipped his phone closed and waited for a return call. *What the hell? Harold! What!* After ten minutes he dialed the last call-received number. A male voice answered. "Casey Howard here." Tom repeated the phone number, was told he had the right number, but there was no Rosa there. "What the hell is going on?" Tom muttered as he dialed Nate's number.

"Hello?"

"Nate!"

"Tom? How are you?"

"Good, hectic here, but we're managing. Nate, how are *you*?"

"I'm all right. Rosa and I have been going through Harold's things over the past few days. Rosa is pretty devastated. Her son Dom's been a huge help though. She's been staying with him at night. He takes her to church each morning, then brings her back here to her house. I still have this damned cast on, so I can't drive her anywhere."

"She's not with you?" Tom asked. He'd poured himself a glass of ice water and twirled the ice cubes, watching the resulting funnel in his tumbler.

"No. She's with Dom and his family. Why?"

"She just called me. We got disconnected, and when I called her back, it was a wrong number. Some guy name Casey answered. I thought I better call you; see if everything was all right. Rosa said she was worried about you."

"Huh! That's odd. She's worried about me? I'm really doing okay. Funny she'd call you. So—what number do you have for Rosa?"

Tom had him hold while he looked up the number on his call log.

"No clue who that number belongs to," Nate said. "Thought maybe she'd called from Dom's phone. But that number isn't his—or Rosa's."

"Rosa seemed upset. We got cut off before she could explain." Tom saw no reason to tell Nate who Rosa said had called him.

"I'll call her right now," Nate said. "Call you back in a few minutes." The line went dead.

Tom paced the floor while he waited. He wandered out of his room and into the wide hallway that ran along the east side of the house. Out the window to the north, in the distance, he saw the dark outline of the Harrison house. It looked lifeless. A glint of light from the cloud-covered moon sparkled in the upstairs attic window, the only one apparently not covered with shutters. He thought he saw movement in the window, decided it was the reflection of branches swaying in the night breeze. His phone rang, and he forgot about the distraction.

"Nate. Did you talk to Rosa?" Tom asked.

"I didn't. I talked to Dom's son, Chris. He said Dom and Rosa had taken the dog to the park. Rosa didn't have her phone with her. I think someone's playing a joke on you. I can't think of any other explanation."

"Who would do that? What's the point? Damn! That's the second call our family's had that's sent us on a wild goose chase."

"You're kidding me. What happened?"

"Sara got a call day before yesterday saying I'd been killed in a car accident!"

"What?"

"Yeah, thank God I got home right after the call. She and Cassie were hysterical. And now this. It makes no sense."

"Sure doesn't. Who the hell would be doing this? And why?"

"I'm at a loss." Tom stared out the window at the Harrison's attic. His own house's lights seemed to reflect and glisten off the attic glass.

"Someone's having fun at my expense. Who even knows I know your sister?"

"No one I know who would harass you like this. What about Harrison's wife?"

"That's a possibility. Makes little sense though. She's out of the country. Hold on. . . . I think I just figured it out. Catherine Ballantyne! Has to be."

"You might be right, she seems like a bit of a wacko for sure. Sounds almost like she's stalking you. She's probably the same caller who told your sister you had an accident. You should call John and have him get one of his detectives to track her down. She could be dangerous."

"Yeah, I'll do that—if she keeps bothering me. Maybe she'll quit if we ignore her. Listen, Nate, do me a favor, will you?"

"What's that?"

"Get up here as soon as you can. This house could use another male under its roof."

Nate laughed. "Better not let Cassie hear you say that. I bet she loves having you to boss around!"

"You got that right. Trouble is, she wants me to sell this place.That's how well things are going here."

"Why?"

"I told you things have been hectic. But it's more than that —odd things are happening. Cassie and Sara passed out in the attic after inhaling something toxic, but no one knows what. And several nights ago, someone broke into the house. Came in through the basement door, I guess. He got away. I'm pretty sure he took something from the house, but I don't know what. I couldn't find anything missing, but he was carrying a small bag when he ran out."

"Did you call the police? Could that have been Ballantyne too? I think you should call the cops. This is sounding serious."

"No. I don't want the cops around here again. I'll take care of it myself. I think I know who broke in. Not Catherine. Some transient. I believe he's living in a vacant house down the beach. I'll take Joe with me tomorrow, pay the guy a visit and scare the crap out of him."

"Well, you know what's best. After everything that's happened, I think you're right, though. I better plan on getting to Remington sooner than later. I don't need to wait to get the cast off. We're pretty well wrapped up here in Jamestown. Let me see what I can do. Any more business can be handled from Ravenswood. Your computers are working, right?"

"Yeah, for the most part, we're functional. So when do you think you can be here? Maybe by Christmas?"

Tom heard Nate drumming his finger against the phone. "I think I can be there by the nineteenth. If something comes up, I can always fly back to Jamestown. I'll get Rosa squared away, make sure one of Dom's boys can stay with her for a while. She's a tough cookie. She'll be fine. Sounds like you need me more up there."

"Do the best you can. I won't hold you to it," Tom said. He was watching the Harrison house again, swore he saw movement in the attic. *Fucking nerves.* Tom turned around and went back to his room.

"I think it's doable," Nate said. "I'll talk to Rosa in the morning. I'll give you a call tomorrow. Night, Tom."

"Night." As soon as Tom hung up, Wiggins bounded into his room. The hackles on his neck and back stood straight up. He ran past Tom and under the bed. From downstairs, a resounding crash echoed through the house. Tom ran down the back stairs, stopping in the kitchen to grab a butcher knife and a flashlight from the drawer. He felt a cool breeze brush his cheek. The back door was wide open. He flashed the light around. The door to the basement was closed and bolted. The door into the dining room was closed but still swinging slightly.

Putting his ear to the door, Tom listened. He heard sounds coming from the front of the house. He quickly latched the dining room door and crossed the kitchen to the door leading to the small room between the living room and the study. Slowly he opened the door, holding his breath, waiting for a telltale squeak of old, dry hinges.

From his left—a loud slam—the door into the living room flew shut. He shoved it open, flashing his light around the dark room. The lace curtain blew inward. The side door to the veranda was open.

The phone rang. Tom jumped, his nerves on edge. Ignoring the ringing, he ran across the living room as a figure ran across the porch, hurdled over the banister, and took off down the driveway into the woods. He had something, a bag—maybe two—tucked under his left arm.

Something about him was familiar. Tom assumed it was the same man he kept seeing on the beach, the one who'd broken into the house several nights ago. But this man seemed taller, his movements more agile—those of someone younger. *What the hell are these men after?*

The house phone rang again and again. Tom slammed the door, locked it, then grabbed the phone. "What!" he yelled.

"Sorry. Wrong number." The phone went dead.

Tom slammed the receiver down. "Fuck!" He walked through the house turning on lights, closing and locking doors, looking to find anything out of place or missing. Once again he found nothing unusual. Glad Sara and Cassie were staying in town for the night, he built a small fire and slept in the living room, his .45 by his side.

Chapter 138

Elise waited impatiently for Benjamin on the front steps of the Harrison house. He finally appeared around the bend of the path, barely visible in the darkness. Trees, like sentinels, surrounded and cast dark shadows on the path as Benjamin ran to her carrying two cloth bags, the handles of both clutched in his left hand. He cradled a small box in his right.

Elise ran down the path to meet him. "Benjamin, did you find them?"

"I did," he called, triumphant.

Elise had a hard time containing her joy. "Take them to my room. Then we need to go to the beach house—one last time, just as we planned." She led the way up the dark path to the Harrison house. She waited while Benjamin took the bags inside. He returned and handed her the small wooden box. She smiled. "Benjamin, what is this?" Opening it, she saw Tom's wedding ring. She gasped. "You're brilliant, Benjamin!" She hugged him, then recoiled, embarrassed at her display.

Elise had been shocked to see the changes in Benjamin when he returned after having been gone several days. He stood much taller now. His movements were quick and decisive, his shoulders much broader, the muscles in his arms obviously strengthened. He was taking on his former youthful appearance—tall, dark and broodingly handsome. For a brief moment, Elise was afraid of Benjamin.

Benjamin slipped his hand behind her back and roughly drew her to him. He pulled her face to his, gave her lip a sharp bite, then let her go. "Come on," he said, laughing. "Back to the beach house." Elise stayed several yards behind him as they maneuvered the dark, shadowed path to the beach house.

Even though he had the house key in his pocket, Benjamin hit the back doorknob with a large rock to make it look like a break-in. Inside he started a fire in the fireplace and began burning stacks of magazines he'd found on a shelf. He scorched the covers he had torn off of several books he'd stolen from Remington House. He placed those on the hearth. He threw blankets and pillows haphazardly onto the floor. Then he placed one diamond earring on the floor, letting it rest just under the edge of the couch, visible to anyone looking around. It was one of many pieces he had taken from Cassie's jewelry box several days ago, when he and Elise had been in the house.

"There. It's done. Let them think John Darby has been staying here."

"Did you take care of him?" Elise asked.

"Yeah. I left Darby down by the highway. Drunk and drugged. He had no clue what I was going to do with him. So gullible. He was an easy target."

"Now let's get out of here," he said to Elise. She'd been in the bedroom and kitchen ransacking the few belongings that had been left in the house. Benjamin grabbed her by the arm, trying to hurry her out of the house.

Elise shook his hand off and glared at him. She ran ahead, leading the way along the back path to the Harrison house. Once they were inside, she closed and bolted the locks. Benjamin went immediately to the basement.

Elise searched for the bags Benjamin had stolen from Remington. When she couldn't find them, she gave up and floated down the basement stairs. Benjamin sat in the center of a circle of stones, his head bowed, a large book opened in front of him. Three black candles burned on the floor before him. Shadows of demons undulated crazily around him. Elise turned to leave before he noticed her.

"Join me," Benjamin said. Though she hesitated for a moment, in the end, Elise came and sat beside him, inside the circle. Benjamin put his arm around her and drew her close to him. She shuddered. He held her tighter. "This will bind us together. Make us stronger. I will be with you. Relax." Benjamin began to chant in an ancient language she thought was Latin. "Daemones noctis hora intra circulum. Ostendunt tenebrarum nos participes tui. Tecumque erimus in ista nocte. Nobis tua. Nos unum cum te." ("Demons of the night, take us inside your circle. Show us the darkness. Share with us your power. For this night we will join you. Give us your power. Make us one with you.") Elise closed her eyes.

Together they joined in mind and body with the demons. There was no sense of time, no sense of anything. Elise remembered little of what had actually happened. For that she was greatly relieved. Somehow she knew she had been repulsed by the darkness she witnessed. She sensed Benjamin had not.

When dawn came, Elise carefully removed Benjamin's hands from her and quietly left the basement. She returned upstairs knowing with certainty she would never be a part of that demonic underworld. *I have to be careful. Benjamin is becoming stronger and seems increasingly drawn into the darkness he shared with the Lindemans.*

Elise slept for hours, not waking until Benjamin entered her room at dusk. He had the two bags in his hands. "Here." He set them down on the floor beside the bed. "I'm going. I'll be back in a few days. I have some things I need to take care of." He didn't wait for Elise to respond, but turned and silently disappeared down the stairs.

Elise grabbed a vase from the nightstand and threw it at the closed door. The glass shattered with a loud crash, then fell silently onto the thick, gray carpet. "Have it your way then! For now," Elise yelled. *Benjamin, I am, and always will be, stronger than you. I will prevail. I will deal with you when and if I have to. And—if necessary—I will kill you!* She sat for several minutes, listening to the quiet, then she got up. She had other things to do.

Elise lifted one of the two bags onto the bed and took out one of maybe a dozen books. She giggled when she read the first page. "Property of Sara Lawson." She had Sara's diaries in her possession. Hugging the book to her chest, she picked up another and another. After taking all the books from both bags, she put them in chronological order. Elise took the first two books downstairs to the living room. She found a bottle of cherry liqueur, poured herself a small glass and curled up on the sofa. She read all night, until she began to see the first signs of light. She left the house to sit on the bluff over the ocean. She watched the sunrise, a ritual she would repeat every morning. Again Elise thought of Benjamin and the increasing threat she felt from him.

Chapter 139

"Joe, did you talk to Mandy at the realty firm about the beach house?" Tom stood on his balcony, looking down the beach while he talked with Joe on the phone.

"I did. She's out of town, said she'd get over there and check when she gets back. She wasn't too concerned though. She said her son wasn't staying there. But I got the impression she might have been covering up for him. She said she'll drive over this weekend. What's up?"

"Last night someone was in my house again. I chased him out."

"What the hell! Did you call the sheriff? "

"No. I'm pretty sure it was that transient. I don't want to make a big deal out of it. I don't think there's anything of value missing here. What I want to do is to get it across to this guy I've had enough. I'm going to pay a visit to the beach house. I'm pretty sure the guy's staying there. A little fear should do the trick. A few carefully worded threats."

"Yeah, well, I'm going with you, then. We can give it a try. I'll be there in an hour," Joe said. "But if the guy gives us any shit, I think we better call Sheriff Jamison."

"I agree. See you in a while."

A few hours later, Tom and Joe found the back door of the beach house broken in, the remnants of a fire still burning and Cassie's stolen earring on the floor. Outside, a few yards down the path, Tom spotted a cloth bag with Cassie's other jewelry in it. They called the sheriff to report the break-in.

Later that evening Cassie sorted through the bag. All her jewelry was there, nothing was missing. "I can't believe I didn't notice my jewelry was been gone. God! Those earrings were an anniversary gift from Michael. There's been so much going on lately that I never bothered to check."

Sara burst into tears when she learned her personal diaries had been stolen—and apparently used for fuel in the fireplace at the house down the beach. "It feels so personal. I wrote in my journals for years. What a nasty thing to do!" Sara pounded her fist on the table. "That bastard!" She wiped her tears with her knuckles. "Thank God I've got a backup of the books on my computer. I've been entering them in for months—just in case. A premonition I guess." Sara reached out and took Tom's hand. "You're sure they have the right guy?"

"Yeah, Sheriff Jamison picked him up late last night. Name's John Darby. Jamison found him passed out down on the side of the highway. Matched our description to a 'T'. The sheriff ran a background check. The guy was violating his parole. He'd skipped town, so there was a warrant out. Jamison's sending him back to Rawlinson this afternoon. So the guy's locked up, will be for some time, I imagine," Joe explained. "When Jamison questioned Darby about the break-ins, he denied them of course, but that's a scumbag thief for you."

"Thank God it's over. Maybe we can have some normalcy around here!" Cassie said, gently patting Tom on his shoulder.

"Maybe." Tom smiled at Cassie. Putting his arm around Sara, he said, "I'm sorry I got you into this. How can I make it up to you?"

"It's not anyone's fault. It's over. The thief got caught. That's some consolation," Sara said sadly. "Let's go fix something to eat, you guys must be starving."

Chapter 140

Benjamin stayed away for five days. Elise hoped he would not come back. Everything was much simpler with him gone. Although she hated being alone again, she recognized and feared the changes in Benjamin. She knew she had to be extremely wary of him.

She spent hours each day reading Sara's diaries and journals. When she finished, she reread the last book and felt she knew everything she could possibly need to know about Sara Lawson.

Benjamin returned on the sixth day. She found him on the doorstep after dusk, waiting for her to return from her ritual of watching the sunset. "Where have you been?" she asked. She motioned him to follow her into the house.

"It doesn't matter. I needed to be alone. I had decisions to make." Benjamin turned his back to Elise. "I wasn't sure what I wanted. Now I know. I want to stay with you." He turned to face her. "As you know, at one time I was involved with the demonic Gathering. The Lindemans initiated me many years ago. But I have found the satanic cult gives me no peace and no satisfaction."

Elise listened, nodded her head.

"Nor, judging from your reaction to the ceremony we participated in, does it appear to be your chosen path." Benjamin began pacing the floor of the living room. "If I am to wander these shores for eternity, I do not want to be one with the dark underworld." He wrung his hands, then stopped and pounded his fists against the doorframe. "I will not promise my soul to them. I will belong to no one!"

Elise listened but still said nothing.

Suddenly, Benjamin spun around and grabbed her. He effortlessly lifted her off the ground, then set her down before him. "Say something!" he yelled.

She shook his hands off her and spoke in a loud, angry voice, "Let me be very clear, Benjamin. I have only one purpose right now and that is to cause the downfall of Thomas Gardner. I have waited a very long time to make that happen. Neither you nor anyone else will interfere with my plans." Elise took a quick breath, then continued. "If you are completely clear about that, then stay. But it will be on my terms." Elise put her hands on Benjamin's shoulders. "And if you don't like my terms, leave!" Dropping her hands to her sides, she backed away.

Benjamin shook his fists at Elise and shouted, "I will not be treated like a servant as I was by the Lindemans. Never again! I am a man! Do you understand that?" He took a step toward her. "Look at me!"

Elise stepped back, lifted her face to look into his eyes. She recognized the fury in his soul, saw the man he must have been, in a life before the Lindemans had trapped his soul and diminished him to be their slave. With her right hand she reached out and touched Benjamin's cheek. "I can see that, Benjamin. But if you stay here, you will not interfere with my plans. That is how it has to be. Do you understand?"

He took her hands into his. "I do. But, tell me, Elise, can you understand my needs?"

"I will treat you with respect, Benjamin. Nothing more. I cannot allow myself to become involved with you. If you will accept that, stay. Otherwise, you must leave."

Benjamin dropped her hands and turned away. "All right then. We have an understanding. I will ask nothing more of you. For now!" He laughed, the loud, booming reverberation shook the floor under Elise's feet. He disappeared down the hallway. Elise heard the door to the basement slam.

Shaking, Elise ascended the stairs to her room and lay swathed in the warmth of the blankets on the soft, feather-topped bed. She slept for several hours, waking at sunset. It was four thirty. The darkness of the coming evening closed in on her. Feeling trapped, Elise ran to the attic where she could look out the unshuttered window at the surrounding landscape. She dared to open the window a crack. A gentle breeze stirred the curtain before her. Elise inhaled the pungent, salty ocean air into her lungs.

Someone was walking on the beach below her. Elise focused the telescope. It was Sara. Sara had her cell phone in her hand and was talking animatedly to someone. She laughed and then seemed to scold the person on the other end of the line, her left hand flailing into empty air. Then she began running, sliding her phone closed as she did. She was laughing. Then Elise saw him.

Tom stood, arms outstretched toward Sara. Elise could see Sara mouth his name as she ran to him. He laughed and yelled something to her. Elise watched as Sara doubled over in laughter and collapsed onto the sandy beach. Tom ran to her, falling down to sit beside her, grabbing and pulling her closer to him. After several minutes they got up, arms entwined, and walked down the beach toward the cliff stairs to Remington House.

Elise jumped. Benjamin had come up silently behind her and laid his hand on her shoulder. She looked at him and said, "It's almost time. Tomorrow we begin. Are you ready?"

"I am," Benjamin said.

Benjamin was again altered in appearance. Elise had to look up at him. He was at least six inches taller than she was. He was no longer old or stooped. He had a full head of dark brown hair, with no traces of gray, no signs of his former balding.

Elise touched his hair, then let her fingers trace his forehead. She looked into his eyes, no longer faded or myopic but vibrant and alive, his dark pupils reflecting her own eyes. "What have you done, Benjamin? How did you do this?" she asked, her eyes wide and alert, her hand cautiously brushing the smooth skin of his cheek.

"It is because I am free. I am no longer a slave to anyone. I am reborn! At last!"

"I'm happy for you." She took her hand from his face. "Come on, we have much to discuss." Elise led him downstairs and out of the house. On the cliff edge, above the pounding ocean, she began sharing her plans with Benjamin. All night they talked. As the sun rose in the morning, the two lay back and let the warmth of the rising sun warm their chilled bones.

Chapter 141

"Tom, I'm going into town. Do you want to come with me?" Sara asked.

Laura V. Keegan

"No, I have a lot of financials to go over. Isn't Cassie going with you?" Tom looked up from his papers, frowned as he found a discrepancy with the Harrison account. "Shit," he muttered under his breath.

"No, she's got plans with Terese today. I have to get some Christmas shopping done. I need to send the gifts to Boston this week—for Viv, William and the boys."

"Any idea when they might come back here?" asked Tom. He put his pencil down, watched Sara as she zipped up her leather boots.

"Not any time soon. Viv's still not doing well. William said maybe they'd come in the spring." Sara slipped her arms into her ski coat. "I sure miss the boys. Especially Jimmy."

"Bet you do. But if Vivian isn't doing well, we certainly don't want her here wreaking havoc again. She needs to be close to her doctors. Right?"

"Absolutely. William is taking some time off, too. That's such a good step. For all of them. Anyway, off I go. I won't be back till late afternoon. Think I'll have lunch with Mary. If she can get away." She gave Tom a kiss and left. Tom heard her tires crunching in the gravel as she drove down the drive. A log rolled in the fireplace, burst into flames and sent sparks shooting. Tom took out his calculator and got back to work.

Sara was halfway down the beach highway when she saw a man standing on the side of the road. He was tall with wavy blonde hair; he wore a black parka and had a dark red scarf wrapped around his neck against the frigid cold. Behind him, an older, silver sedan was parked on the shoulder of the road, the hood open. He waved, flagging Sara down.

Making sure her doors were locked, she pulled over and rolled her passenger window halfway down. "Hi. Looks like you've got car trouble. Want me to call a tow truck for you?"

"I don't need a tow. You wouldn't have jumper cables by chance? Battery ran down. I walked down to the beach to take some pictures, forgot I'd turned the headlights on when I drove through a bank of fog," he explained. He was bending down and talking to Sara through the crack in the window. "Need a jump is all."

Sara popped the trunk and opened her car door. "I'm sure I have a set. Let me get them." She walked to the back of the car, keeping an eye on the pleasant looking man. He kept his distance, obviously aware of Sara's discomfort. She pulled the cables out and handed them to him.

"Can you pull you car closer to mine?"

Sara nodded and got back in her car.

Once she was stopped in front of his car, he said, "Go ahead and shut your car off. Pop the hood latch, and I'll hook the cables up." Sara did as he asked, then waited while he attached the heavy cables. He signaled for her to start her car. She did and, after several attempts, his car started. He got out and undid the cables. Sara met him at the back of her car.

Too late, Sara saw the woman. In her hand was a handkerchief that she forced against Sara's face. The strong smell of ether assaulted Sara. Though she struggled, she was out in seconds.

"Benjamin, help me!" Elise called before realizing he was already by her side, carefully lifting Sara into the trunk. Benjamin looked around, then slammed the trunk. Making sure no one was about, he climbed into the stolen sedan and pulled it off the road. The car belonged to the young man he was inhabiting, a possession that was essential so he could perform the physical activities necessary to kidnap Sara. Benjamin drove Sara's car a mile down the highway to the back road leading to the Harrison house, then turned up the long drive. He parked the car in the garage and carried Sara's limp body into the house to a small, spare bedroom. Benjamin laid her gently on the twin bed. When Sara began to wake up, Elise injected her with a small dose of Demerol. "There, she'll sleep now. Are you ready, Benjamin?"

"Go ahead. The effects of the Demerol won't last more than a few minutes."

Before Elise slipped into Sara's body, before she entered into her psyche, she stared into Benjamin's eyes, fleetingly grabbed his hand. Then she was gone. Sara was in a deep sleep. Elise concentrated and, very slowly was able to open Sara's eyes. She smiled at Benjamin. "I've done it!" She struggled to get up. "Help me sit up."

Supporting her back, Benjamin gently pushed her into a sitting position. "How do you feel?"

Elise leaned back against the headboard. After steadying herself, she swung her legs over the edge of the bed. "Like I weigh a ton. Sara's still heavily drugged. I didn't think we gave her that strong of a dose. I don't know if I can fight the Demerol." Elise leaned sideways resting her shoulder and head against Benjamin.

"Elise! Damnit!" Benjamin slapped her roughly on her cheek. "You haven't worked this hard to give up so easily."

Elise focused. She lifted her hand and grabbed Benjamin before he could slap her again.

"There you go. Fight! That's it!" Benjamin stood up, pulling Elise off the bed. "Walk!" He held her up. She began moving Sara's legs, slowly at first, then with more strength and determination.

"You can let go of me now." Elise walked back and forth, then began going in circles around Benjamin.

Benjamin stopped her when he realized she was taunting him. "Enough! We have no time for your foolishness. You need some strong coffee. Then we better get moving. We need to get into town before anyone misses Sara."

Elise drove Sara's car. Benjamin sat beside her and listened as she explained that now that she was inside Sara's body, she could read her thoughts. "Her will is strong. I can't let my mind wander for a second. She's not easily controllable like Vivian was." Elise concentrated as she maneuvered the road. "Sara was on her way to do some Christmas shopping. Won't that be fun!"

Sara's cell phone rang. Benjamin grabbed it from her purse, hit the speakerphone button and handed it to Elise, mouthing, "It's Tom."

"Hi, Tom." Elise smiled at Benjamin.

"Hi. You in town yet?" Tom asked.

"Almost. What's up?"

"I'm heading into Brewster with Joe to look at some equipment for the gym. Wanted to let you know I'll be gone for most of the afternoon. And, Nate called. He's wrapping up everything in Jamestown and plans to take the train here next Monday."

"That's wonderful news. I know you'll be relieved to have him here. Don't worry about me this afternoon. I have plenty of shopping to do. And I still plan on having lunch with Linda."

"Who?" Tom asked. "I thought you were meeting Mary."

"That's what I said, Tom. Lunch with Mary." Elise frowned at Benjamin who watched her carefully as she talked to Tom. Benjamin reached his hand out, gently laying it on Elise's shoulder. "I'll see you later tonight."

"Okay. Say hi to Mary. Bye."

Elise pulled the car off the road and down the dirt road out of sight of the highway where the stolen car was parked. "I can't believe that happened. I forgot Mary's name! Sara did that! I can feel her fighting me for control."

"Look at me, Elise," Benjamin said.

Elise stared into his eyes as he held her face, his gaze fixed on her.

"Concentrate. You're stronger than Sara. That's never been more evident. Look at me." He held her face as she tried to turn away. "You are in control. Not Sara."

"I need to rest, Benjamin. I need to go back home. Now!"

"All right, but we need to deal with Sara and her memories of what we have done to her." Benjamin held Elise's face in his hands and watched her struggle to maintain control. "We have to, Elise."

"Okay. Help me." She grabbed his wrists. "Please."

Chapter 142

Without further hesitation, Benjamin inhabited Sara's body. He felt Sara's strong spirit fight his own. "Sara, relax. You can trust me. I will take care of you." As he talked to her, she began to give up her control. "You are tired, Sara. You need to rest. I will help you do that." She leaned her head against the headrest. "That's it. Now take some deep breaths. You're fine. Listen to my voice, Sara. I'm going to count to five. As I count, you will be more and more relaxed. When you hear me say 'five', you will sleep and hear nothing but my voice.

"That's it. One. You are so tired. Two. Three. You are ready to sleep, Sara. Close your eyes. Relax. Four. You hear the sound of my voice. Your breaths are deeper and slower. You can't keep your eyes open. That's it. Five. You will sleep now. You are safe. I will not let anything harm you." Her head lolled forward to rest on her chest.

"Sara, when I wake you up, you will remember nothing about the man you saw on the side of the road. You will remember that you were on your way to Ravenswood to go Christmas shopping and to have lunch with Mary. You will remember that Tom called you. He told you Nate is coming on Monday. Tom is going with Joe to Brewster this afternoon. On your way into Ravenswood, you stopped when you saw a lost dog running along the beach. You hunted for him, but never found him. That's why it took you so long to get to town. You will remember these things and nothing more about your drive into Ravenswood. When I tell you to awaken, you will be relaxed and refreshed. Do you understand?"

Sara whispered, "Yes."

Benjamin released her body and watched as she slept, her head now resting comfortably against the headrest of the car. "Good. Sara, listen very carefully. In the future, when you hear Elise or me say 'the ocean is red' you will go into a hypnotic trance. You will hear only Elise or me. You will do exactly what we tell you to do. You will not fight us. We will not harm you. You will be safe. You will have no memory of what we do when you are hypnotized. We will tell you what to remember, and you will be fine with that. Do you understand?"

"I do," Sara whispered, nodding her head.

"Good. I want you to let me talk to Elise. All right?"

"Yes."

"Elise, can you hear me?"

"I can."

"Good. Be patient, I'm going to talk with Sara again." Benjamin spoke softly, taking Sara's hand into his. "Sara, listen carefully. You will now be able to hear Elise's voice as well as mine. You will always do as she says. You will listen to both Elise and me. Open your eyes, please. Do you understand?"

Sara said, "Yes."

Benjamin rubbed Sara's cheek very gently, pushed away the soft, brown curls that had fallen over her face and gazed into her violet-blue eyes. "Elise, tell Sara that she must listen to you. She must be able to recognize your voice so we can hypnotize her when we need to. Talk to her now." For several minutes Elise spoke to Sara.

"Good," Benjamin said. "Sara, do you understand what Elise and I have told you?"

"I do," she answered. A single tear fell from the corner of her eye. Benjamin wiped it away.

"Elise, it's time to say goodbye to Sara. Leave her peacefully. She must not be afraid of you."

Sara continued to sleep, her head rolling sideways on the back of the seat. Elise now sat beside Benjamin. "That bitch! How I long to make her fear me!"

"In time. Not today. Elise, let me handle this." Elise nodded. Benjamin spoke softly to Sara. "You will remember nothing that has happened since you left Remington this morning except what I have told you to remember. Soon I will count backwards from five to one. When I say 'one' you will be fully awake and feel wonderfully calm. You will have only the memories that Elise and I have given you. I need you to continue sleeping right now. Do you understand everything I have told you?"

Sara nodded. "Good. Rest now." Benjamin got out of the car. Walking to the sedan parked down the dirt road out of site, he climbed into the driver's seat. Pulling a syringe from the man's coat pocket, Benjamin injected the man's arm, then threw the syringe over the edge of the bluff. The man would sleep, never knowing what had transpired.

Benjamin, now a dark mist too tired to manifest himself, returned to Sara's car. "Sara, I will begin counting backwards now," Benjamin whispered soothingly. "You will remain relaxed. Five. Four. You feel very relaxed still. Three. Two. You are beginning to wake."

Sara nodded.

"You will be completely alert and go on with your day. You will drive to Ravenswood and do your shopping. One. Wake up."

Benjamin and Elise disappeared as Sara opened her eyes. Momentarily, a gray mist settled in the backseat of Sara's car. Elise and Benjamin hovered in this mist and watched Sara awaken.

Chapter 143

For perhaps two seconds Sara remained confused and then she said out loud, "I hope that dog finds its way home. Well, I better get to Ravenswood." She pulled the car onto the winding road. A wave of nausea took her by surprise. She pulled the car to the side of the highway. Opening her door, she heaved up her breakfast. When her stomach was empty, she laid her head back against the seat and closed her eyes. Breathing in slow shallow breaths, she let the cold, salty sea-air soothe her. In minutes she felt calm and her stomach settled. She rinsed her mouth with her bottled water and sat back. She stayed parked until she felt more like herself, then she pulled onto the road and headed to Ravenswood. "That was strange."

As Sara drove, a nagging memory tried to force its way through. She felt afraid and almost in a panic. Her head hurt, her arm ached. Her phone rang. Again she pulled over. "Hello?" She smiled when she heard the voice on the line. "Jimmy, I'm so glad you called." She forgot her fears as she talked to Jimmy. He called to tell her he missed her and to tell her what he wanted for Christmas.

When Sara reached town, she parked in the busy lot across from the café. She decided not to call Mary, nor to have lunch. She'd pick up a few things for the boys and then go home. She didn't feel well.

When Tom returned from Brewster, he found Sara in bed, shivering and running a slight fever. Pale and withdrawn, she stayed in bed the rest of the day, letting Tom and Cassie take care of her.

The next morning, Tom puzzled over Sara's unnecessary worry about a dog she saw on her way to town. "Sara, Mary told you no one reported a lost dog and no dog was picked up." As they walked along the hard packed beach, arm in arm, he asked her, "Why are you so worried about it? It's not like you to get upset over something so trivial. Most likely its owner was close by. They were probably taking a walk."

Sara shrugged. She bent over, picked up a shell and threw it far out into the water. By late morning, the dog seemed to be a non-issue—or so Sara said. Tom drove her and Cassie into Ravenswood. They spent most of the afternoon shopping, then stopped by the post office to mail the packages back to the Harrisons in Boston.

Chapter 144

On Sunday, the weather again turned cold. Black clouds blew in early in the afternoon. By four o'clock snowflakes the size of dimes fell, quickly accumulating and covering the landscape. Cassie, Sara and Tom loaded into the van and drove to town. At five o'clock they were meeting the train at Ravenswood station. Michael and Lizzie were arriving to spend the next few weeks at Remington. After Christmas, Cassie, Michael, and Lizzie would return to New York.

"Mama!" Lizzie shouted, hopping down the two metal steps to the platform. She ran to Cassie, who swept her up and hugged her. Michael, burdened with bags, almost fell down the steps. Tom grabbed his arm to steady him and took some of the bags.

"Toys," Michael said smiling. "Lizzie got a new doll from her grandma. The doll has more clothes than I do!" He ruffled Lizzie's head and hugged her and Cassie.

Lizzie squirmed to get out of his embrace and ran to Tom. "Uncle Tom, I have a present for you!" She reached into one of the cloth bags and pulled out a package wrapped in velvet-flocked paper. "Here, open it now!" she held it toward him. Then she saw Sara. "What are you doing here?"

"Lizzie!" Cassie said sternly. "For heaven's sake! You mind your manners, young lady." Cassie looked at Sara and shrugged. "I'm so embarrassed. I can't imagine what got into her."

"Not to worry. She's tired and wants you to herself. It's okay," Sara said, forcing a smile.

Snowflakes piled on Sara's hair and clothes. Tom took her arm."We need to get out of this cold. Come on everyone. Let's get back to the house."

Cassie lagged behind with Lizzie. "Lizzie, don't be rude. You hurt Sara's feelings."

"She doesn't belong here. The sooner she realizes that, the better!"

"What did you just say?" Cassie whispered so no one else would hear.

Lizzie closed her eyes for minute. Cassie grabbed her as she started to teeter. Then, just as suddenly, Lizzie stood up straight. "Mommie! I'm so happy to see you." She gave Cassie a big grin. "I missed you so much. Look, I have a new baby doll. I named her Cassandra—after you." Lizzie looked around. "Where is everyone?" She bolted when she saw her father and uncle walking ahead of her with Sara. "Wait for us!" she yelled. "Sara, give me a big hug!" She grabbed Sara around her waist and walked beside her to the car.

In the hustle and bustle of getting everyone into the car, Tom's package from Lizzie lay in the back of the jeep, hidden underneath an old blanket. It would lie there forgotten until spring. No one, not even Lizzie, would remember it. It contained Tom's wedding ring, carefully wrapped in one of Elise's lace handkerchiefs.

***

When Lizzie and Michael arrived on the train, Benjamin and Elise were there. In the shadows of darkness, as the setting sun glimmered with a faint peach glow along the horizon, the train pulled into the station. The roar of the engines diminished as it rolled to a stop. Elise and Benjamin were as excited as the rest of the platform crowd.

As snow sparkled in diamond patterns and glittered in the bright lights on the platform, Elise thought she'd never felt more radiant or alive. There, not a foot from her, stood Tom. She longed to tear into his skin with her teeth, to see blood run in rivulets on his hands and neck, to bite his lips and feel his horror as he realized she was still here. She relished these thoughts but remained still. She was patient. She would savor these encounters. They were enough. For now.

Elise's frail, translucent body was perched in the bare branch of a tree that stood sentry beside the track. Twinkling Christmas lights sparkled in her golden hair. Benjamin sat beside her, a striking figure of a man. She smiled at him as she watched Lizzie descend the steps of the train. For several minutes Elise controlled Lizzie. She giggled with joy when Lizzie handed Tom Elise's package. She did not control Lizzie for long, released her in only minutes. Elise loved the child and did not want to frighten her. The child never knew what had transpired. Cassie, though puzzled, never suspected. *I am here!* It was all Elise could do to keep from shouting out loud.

Chapter 145

Nate arrived the next day. Joe braved ice packed highways to
pick him up at the train station. Nate and Joe, close in age and
demeanor, hit it off right away. When Joe's taxi slid off the
highway at the hairpin curve halfway to Remington, Joe
pushed the car while Nate steered it back onto the slick
pavement. Then Joe took over, driving them safely to the
house.

A pattern of normalcy reigned at Remington. Food was
served, eaten, dishes washed, laughter and loud conversation
prevailed. The family was together, the warmth of the
Christmas season brought calm and joy.

Wednesday morning everyone bundled up in their winter coats,
donned gloves and scarves, and climbed the hill behind the
house. Half a mile above the last stand of beech trees, in a
grove of pines, they found the perfect Christmas tree. By
evening it stood in the corner of the living room by the window
overlooking the ocean. Everyone strung popcorn and
cranberries, made silver angels from cardboard they covered
with aluminum foil. Tom and Joe rummaged around the
basement storage room and found several boxes filled with
vintage glass bells and strings of bubble lights. By midnight,
the tree was beautifully adorned and adored.

***

At the Harrison house, far from the noise and joyous hubbub at
Remington, Elise and Benjamin waited patiently and prepared
themselves. Soon they would once again visit the Gardner
home. Elise, with Benjamin constantly by her side, had been
practicing inhabitation. Discouraged after her last encounter
with Sara, Elise inhabited anything and anyone who happened
to come within earshot of the Harrison house. Several stunned
deer, a young couple out for a hike along the bluff, a moose
and numerous ravens and rabbits, all gave Elise a chance to

practice, sometimes for hours at a time. At each encounter Benjamin too possessed the creatures. If there was only one available body, he followed Elise and watched in amazement as she soared over the ocean or bounded through the woods.

Elise and Benjamin were more confident with each passing day. With all the practice, transferring their spirit into the animals became easier, now taking only seconds. Several times, when they were inside ravens, they landed on the window ledges at Remington to observe Tom's household.

Benjamin became more enamored with Elise, though she seemed not to notice. He did his best to ensure she did not. Every day Elise became more focused and joyous at the thought of Tom's demise. When the holidays were past and Cassie, Michael and their daughter were gone, Elise's plans would begin in earnest.

Tonight, as the Gardner family and friends enjoyed an evening at home, Elise wanted more. Now. She opened the attic window. Summoned by Elise, two ravens landed on the sill. She glanced at Benjamin. He followed her out the window and into the crisp winter air. Soaring and somersaulting in the cold night was invigorating. They chased a lone, great-horned owl back into the stand of trees behind Tom's house, then flew to the porch outside the living room of Remington to watch the tree-decorating festivities.

Tom and Sara, arm in arm, came out of the house and stood on the terrace. Benjamin nodded to Elise who left the raven. Silently she went to Sara and whispered in her ear. Sara closed her eyes. As her body started to go limp, Tom reached to grab her. She opened her eyes and smiled. Elise said nothing, simply put her hand on Tom's hand and squeezed gently. Then, as quickly as she had come into Sara, she retreated.

"Tom, I'm cold. Let's go back inside." Sara said, turning and opening the french doors.

Elise and Benjamin watched a puzzled Tom shrug his shoulders and follow Sara into the house.

"Let's go home," Benjamin said. He flew away into the dark night. Elise did not follow.

Elise returned to the raven, lingering outside. Through the window she watched the family gather around the piano. Tom ceremoniously pulled his sleeves up and began to play something with a very fast tempo, his fingers dancing on the keys. Everyone laughed and sang, though Elise could not hear what song they were singing. Angry, she flew at the window, glanced off the cold, solid pane of glass. No one except Sara noticed. Shuddering, Sara looked at the raven—stared into its black eyes, then turned away to watch the others, obviously having fun. Tom glanced at Sara, smiled warmly, licked his finger and flipped the page of the songbook.

Elise lifted her wings and flew into the winter sky glistening with diamond-bright stars. Glowing hues of gray-rimmed clouds were visible as the moon crossed the ink-black sky. Elise did not return to the Harrison house, but instead flew to the edge of the bluff. She released the bird and sat shivering on the rocky edge to watch the lights from a passing ship. Hours later, as the morning twilight grew near, Benjamin joined her. Together they watched the sun rise.

Benjamin wrapped his arm around Elise's shoulder. They sat for perhaps an hour, then hand in hand, began the short walk to the Harrison home.

It was beginning to snow. A blast of arctic air howled through the trees. Snowflakes swirled, fell and coated the rocky ground. Benjamin stopped halfway up the path to the house and turned Elise to face him. "What will you do to Sara? Do you know?"

Elise laughed. "Yes, I know what I will do. I will make Tom love her as he once loved me. And then, well . . . never mind. I'll tell you more—in time." Elise threw her head back and laughed. Snowflakes covered her ghostly form. They melted, dripped and froze into tiny icicles around her chin and fingertips as her temperature dropped. She was tired. "I'm freezing!" She laughed, her voice reaching an hysterical crescendo. "Build me a roaring fire, Benjamin. Make me warm again!" She floated down the path and into the house, a peal of laughter echoing eerily behind her.

Chapter 146

Construction was just about wrapped up at Remington. The basement gym, steam room, sauna, bathroom, and boxing ring neared completion. From the new billiard room at the west end could be heard the clacking of billiard balls as Tom leveled the table and rolled balls back and forth. It was three days before Christmas. Joe's crew carried the last of the equipment through the long basement hallway and into the gym. The city inspector had been by a few days earlier and approved the plumbing and wiring. The last of the ceiling tiles had been installed, a final coat of paint sprayed on the walls, a top coat of spar varnish sealed the heavy wooden plank flooring.

Two days before Christmas, the small bedroom that had been the last sanctuary for the Lindemans was emptied out. The doors of the closet were taken off and shelves installed for storage. The cement floor, once the final resting place of dear Harold, was covered with dark walnut flooring. The remaining pieces of furniture, boxes of old clothing, a few remaining dishes, linens, knick-knacks and books were packed and loaded into Joe's truck, then hauled to town to Amy's Thrift Store. There remained nothing of the old couple. All traces of Helen and Gabe were gone from Remington. At last!

On this eve of Christmas Eve, Terese, Mary, Cassie, Lizzie, Sara, Tom and a hobbling Nate, went downstairs to the basement to wait for Joe. He'd gone to deliver the truckload of goods to the thrift store. After that he drove to a small studio to pick up a piece of artwork. At six thirty he returned. With Tom's help he carried the six by ten foot painting downstairs. Tom had the piece commissioned by a local artist. It was a collage done in oil of Muhammad Ali, Joe Frazier, Larry Holmes, Sugar Ray Leonard, and Wilfred Benitez. As the men hung the painting on the wall opposite the boxing ring, the ladies clapped, delighted with the work of art.

"Tom, it's magnificent!" Sara stood back and admired the painting. "Wow! You must have paid a fortune for it. It's a Hagerman! I *am* impressed." She smiled at Tom.

"Yeah, a few bucks. But well worth it, don't you think?"

"It's great," Cassie said, adding, "Joe, your crew did an amazing job down here. The basement is awesome."

"To think just a few weeks ago we were afraid to come down here!" Mary cupped her hand over her mouth. "Sorry, I shouldn't have said that."

A look of sadness, quickly changing to anger, flashed across Tom's face. Mary blushed.

"It's all right." Terese spoke up in her lilting, melodic voice. In the soft, colorful glow of light from Tiffany lamps and numerous hanging colored-glass fixtures, she looked like an elf. Her hair sparkled with glitter, her short fingernails were each painted a different color. She wore a black velvet pantsuit with red and gold buttons shaped like Christmas ornaments. A pendant with a huge, ruby-red stone, surrounded by seed pearls, hung from her neck. The heavy gold chain glistened as she bent over and took an amber glass vial from her tapestry bag. "I want to bless this basement, Tom. Is that all right?"

"Oh, for Pete's sake . . . " Tom started to say. Terese pulled the stopper from the bottle. Bright, glittering confetti and foot long streamers spewed out.

"Priceless! How festive, Terese!" Cassie yelled. "What a hoot."

"All right! Everyone into the poolroom. Let's have some fun! Who can I destroy in a game of eight-ball?" Tom laughed and led the way.

***

At the Harrison house, Elise paced the attic. She made no sound that mortals could hear, not that there were any mortals at the house to disturb. But two floors down, in the basement, Benjamin lay on his bed and felt the vibrations of air rushing through the house as Elise walked back and forth.

What's got her so upset? After listening to her pace for an hour, Benjamin went upstairs.

Elise was in one of her dark moods, angry and vile. She pounded and kicked the walls. There was nothing to throw in the dark, dusty attic room. The only thing in the room was the telescope Elise used to watch Tom's house. She shrieked, "Damn it! The witch is there. We can't even go close to the house now. Why is she there?"

"The psychic is friends with the girls. Tonight they're celebrating. Don't worry. She'll leave soon. The house disturbs her."

"Why would you say that, Benjamin? What do you know that I don't?" Elise snarled, flying over to stand in front of him. "Tell me!"

"I've seen her walking along the beach. She watches the house. But she never comes any closer. Not until tonight."

"Do you think she knows about us? Do you!" Elise flailed her fists into the air.

"How could she?" Benjamin stepped toward her, taking several blows to his chest. He grabbed her hands and pushed them to her sides. "No!" he said with conviction. "There is no way she could know we're here. We've been too careful." He released Elise's arms.

"Have we? Are you so sure?" Elise focused the telescope at the house. She lamented, "The lights are on in the basement. Damn! What are they doing?"

Chapter 147

After playing several games of pool, Tom, his family and guests went upstairs to the dining room. The table was laden with trays of sliced ham and turkey, rye and oat-nut bread, a huge bowl of spinach and artichoke salad and a tray of brownies and iced shortbread cookies. Nate added kindling to the fires. The pop and snap of cinders provided a warm, toasty atmosphere while holiday music played softly on the stereo. Everyone loaded their plates, then sat in the living room to eat and celebrate their first Christmas season at Remington. After feasting, they played several rounds of charades and drank hot-spiced cider.

At ten o'clock, Joe stood up and stretched his long limbs. "I'm bushed. I'm heading home before I get too comfortable and fall asleep. Great evening. Thank you for making me a part of your celebration."

"We couldn't celebrate without you!" Cassie gave him a hug. Everyone smiled.

Joe buttoned his parka. "Nite, all." The solitary red taillights of his truck were visible in the clear night as he drove down the long drive, finally disappearing around the curve.

***

Terese left a few minutes later. A mile ahead she saw Joe's headlights flash through the trees, his brake lights glowed red as he slowed to take the curves on the beach highway. *I'm relieved to be leaving. I'm bone tired. I'm going home, taking a hot bath and reading myself to sleep.*

Over the past weeks, Terese had several nightmares about Remington. Everything was not right at her friends' home. She'd driven over there on several sleepless nights to see if she could detect the cause of her angst. But she knew. Without even going there. Her senses were never wrong. Evil had coiled its tendrils around Remington House. There were spirits about. Again. Still. But different souls. Not the Lindemans.

One day last week, before Cassie's husband and child arrived, before Nate came to stay, Terese walked along the beach below Remington. A murder of ravens circled the bluff behind her, finally landing several yards down the beach. The large birds sat in the cold sand, waves lapping at their long, scaly legs. They were joined by another flock of ravens, until the beach was a solid mass of black feathers and gunmetal-black beaks. For several minutes the birds did nothing but stare at Terese. Then, one by one and two by two, they cawed until the cacophony of noise was deafening.

Terese knew she could show no fear, though she wanted to scream. She reached inside her coat, grasping the silver talisman she always wore. Holding it out before her, she began chanting a prayer to protect herself from their evil. She'd taken a deep breath and walked slowly and steadily toward the mass of birds. Sleek, black bodies bobbed up and down, in and out on the waves. Several ran as she neared them, raising their wings in flight. Terese chanted louder and louder, her voice strong and clear. A dozen more ravens rose from the beach, flying in unison to disappear behind the rocky cliff.

Finally there was one bird left. The largest of the ravens. As Terese neared it, the bird rose up and flew in a circle around her. Suddenly Terese was thrown to the ground. A black cloud surrounded her as she lay on her back in the sand. Grabbing her talisman she thrust it into the mist—the mist vanished, the bird with it.

Trembling, Terese got to her feet. She glanced around. She couldn't see the birds, but heard their eerie calls from where they had landed in the trees behind the cliff. She felt the force of an entity. Strong. Virile. And confusingly benign. She felt no malice from it, but rather sensed it was only demonstrating its potential strength. And, God in heaven, this spirit was strong! She felt its desire to survive. She recognized it had gone through a recent renewal. Strongest of all, she recognized its passions, recognized its desperate need for love and companionship.

Deeply disturbed and uncertain, Terese went home and read her Tarot cards. She did three readings. Each time the spirit was represented as The Emperor. *I'm indeed facing a male spirit with immeasurable determination and intelligence. At least he is not malevolent. But very strong. I'll need time to prepare before I dare meet him again.*

Terese had taken a steaming shower when she returned home, letting the water pour over her head, massaging her neck and back until she used up all the hot water. Climbing into bed, she cuddled into the soft downy comforter, and picked up her book. Reading always helped her relax. She read for an hour, then slipped into a dreamless sleep, her chin resting awkwardly on her chest. At two in the morning she woke with a crick in her neck and trepidation in her heart. She prayed she would be up to the task before her.

Terese slept no more that night, instead spent the rest of the night reading her books of incantations. She would not go back to sleep.

That had been a week ago. This evening, the celebration with her friends at Remington should have been a joyous occasion. Tom was so proud of the work the men did in his basement; his excitement was genuine and heartfelt. Everyone had expectations of joyous times ahead. But Terese also had sensed an underlying fear in Sara and Tom. Both tried to hide it, maybe to deny it, but it was a clear and dark presence in their minds. From the moment Terese arrived at the turnoff to Remington House that evening, she knew something was wrong.

Now, as Terese drove the lonely beach highway on her way home, she cursed the ancestors who had passed this ability on to her. She was so tired, not fully recovered from the séances nor the encounter with the birds and spirit of the man. She needed more time to prepare. She may not have it.

Ahead, she saw the lights of the little town of Ravenswood. She was almost home. In an hour, she was reading, tucked in her warm bed, a glass of hot cocoa steaming on her nightstand. For several hours she read, trying to clear her mind. Finally she gave up and took a sleeping pill. She needed sleep. The coming events would require she be rested and strong.

Terese slept hard for a few hours, then gasping for breath, she grabbed for her phone to dial 911. She was having horrible, mind-numbing chest pains. As she reached for the phone, she bumped the cocoa, now icy cold. It poured over her hand, the coldness jarred her awake. It was only a dream. She sat for a minute trying to still her racing heart.

After cleaning up the spill, Terese fluffed her pillow and immediately fell asleep. Her dreams were troubling but clear in their meaning. She must find the spirit and send him on. She recognized she needed to be the aggressor. It was imperative she show him she was much stronger than he was.

Terese got up at nine and called her best friend and lover, Sheriff Vince Jamison. "Hi, are you coming over tonight?"

"It's Christmas Eve, sweetheart. Of course. You already invited me for dinner. You okay?" he asked.

"Rough night, that's all. I need you here with me. So I can rest."

"You went to Gardner's house last night. What happened?"

"Nothing. I had a lovely time. But I had a dream last night —a revelation actually. For weeks I've felt the presence of spirits." She imagined Vince's frown. "I know you don't want to hear this, Vince, but I will be summoned. Soon. There is a spirit, maybe two, that I must send to the other side." Vince said nothing. He didn't have to. Terese knew he was irritated. He didn't like her involvement in the spirit world. He thought it was too dangerous. "Vince, don't worry." She paused and waited for him to say something. He didn't take the cue. "Okay, have it your way then. We'll talk about it later. I'll see you tonight."

"Tonight—with bells on. I can't be mad at you, Terese," he laughed. "I love you. Can't help myself. You take it easy today. Okay? I worry about you."

"Promise. I plan to spend the day cooking and cleaning. That will cure what ails me!" Terese laughed.

"Good. I'll be over as soon as I get off shift. You, my sweet, are in for a very special night. See you at eight."

Terese spent the morning dusting and vacuuming her already pristine house. Cleaning was her therapy. By early afternoon her house was almost immaculate. Next she made chocolate chip cookies and a spinach salad. She sat at the kitchen table and drank a glass of hard pear cider. Too anxious to sit still, she got up and peeled and sliced potatoes. It was only three o'clock. She put a pork roast in the oven. Still it was only three thirty.

She had another glass of cider and absently munched on a limp celery stalk. She decided to run to the store. Carrots, celery, grape tomatoes, maybe some brie, and a small wheel of gruyere. Hmm, what else did she need? She wrote a list, checked her cupboard for crackers. Yep, need crackers. Oh! Olives.

The street was packed with cars filled with people on their way home for Christmas Eve or making last minute trips to the stores before they closed.

It took half an hour to get all the food items and then Terese waited patiently in the checkout line. By the time she got her bags in the car and headed home, it was still only five o'clock. She prepared the tray of cheese and crackers, took a hot shower, and set the table. She put the potatoes in the oven and had another glass of cider.

It was then that Terese decided to go for a drive. She could drive to the Gardner house and back in just over an hour. Still plenty of time before Vince would get here. She'd be back by seven maybe seven thirty at the latest. Terese took the highway, speeding the whole way there. The roads were clear and there was no traffic once she was outside the city limits. In thirty minutes she'd parked at the road along the beach and was walking the half mile to the beachfront below Remington House. She sat on a smooth rock below the cliff wall so no one could see her. Sheltered from the cold wind and light snow that was beginning to fall, Terese closed her eyes and chanted softly.

In minutes Terese was in a deep trance. She traveled out of her body and along the shoreline searching for the spirit she desperately wanted to help crossover.

Panic! Almost too late Terese detected them—two spirits—in a black mist rolling down the beach toward her helpless body, now completely vulnerable to their attack. But she was faster than they were; her spirit got to her body just before the black mist surrounded her.

She slipped in quickly, forced her eyes open and chanted. "Tueri me ex hoc entitatem. Amplecti puram lucem me in." (Protect me from this entity. Envelop me in your pure light.) The mist was cold as it wrapped around her. "I'm not afraid of you. Spirits, let me help you. You are lost. I can guide you to the light. Don't be afraid."

A force like a fist hit Terese, throwing her backward off the rock. She landed in the hard-packed sand, hitting hard enough to knock the wind out of her. She gathered her wits and sat up, then jumped to her feet. Again she was thrown backwards, falling full force onto the beach. She hit her head on a rock half-buried in the sand. A trickle of blood ran into her ear. Shocked, Terese struggled to sit up. Cautiously she touched the side of her head. The wound was not deep but was bleeding profusely. Taking her scarf off, she covered the wound and put pressure on the cut. She yelled. "I am not afraid of you!"

Booming laughter echoed in the air. The black mist formed into a man. Tall and strong. He was almost too human to be a spirit. He was much stronger than Terese had prepared for. If she had to battle both spirits, she may not be able to escape. *Please let me be ready.* Terese glanced around. The second spirit had not materialized, was retreating down the beach. She breathed a sigh of relief. "I am stronger than you. I will send you on. Have no doubt about that!" she yelled. "You don't belong here. I will help you see that. The other side is your salvation."

Terese took her small vial of holy water from her pocket. Well practiced, she–pulled the stopper from the tiny bottle. Holding the bottle carefully, she flung several drops at the male spirit. The droplets sizzled as they hit his arm and cheek. He did not react, seemingly unaware of the burns. Terese chanted, "Valeo, me secura nequitia!" (I am strong, I am safe from your evil!) In an unwavering voice, she continued, "You will not harm me. Understand that!" Terese smiled at Benjamin. "For you see, I am calling upon all my guardians to help me." Only feet from Terese, Benjamin stood his ground.

"Come to me, my dear guardians. Guide this lost spirit to the light! Help me show him the purity and safety of the other side. Come to me, guardians. Now!" she yelled. A white mist rolled in from the ocean. Waves pounded the shore throwing cold droplets of water high into the air. The heavy, white cloud settled behind Benjamin. Suddenly a raven swooped down from the cliff, hovered above the spirit, then flew into the darkening sky. Benjamin was gone.

Alone on the shore, Terese let the white mist surround and protect her. She gathered her bloody scarf and rinsed it in the cold ocean. As she limped to her car, Terese indeed felt blessed. And very foolish. She shouldn't have come today. She was not ready. How had she misjudged their strength and intentions? She had to be more careful. Tomorrow she must begin her preparations. There was much she had to do.

Deeply disturbed but confident in her abilities, Terese drove on and was home long before Vince arrived. She took a quick shower, and tended to her cut, covering it with a well-placed silk poinsettia. When Vince arrived, Terese was calm. She felt better now that she knew what she was up against. She wondered if the spirit might be Harold, the man who'd stolen from Tom and then driven his car off the highway. But who was the other spirit? She wondered if he had someone in the car with him when he died. Maybe the body was never recovered; maybe it washed out to sea. She'd find out if anyone had filed a missing persons report, she would ask Vince tonight. He would know.

Later in the evening, filled with good food and lots of wine and wearing a diamond engagement ring, her Christmas gift from Vince, Terese forgot to ask about a missing girl. Nor would she ask for some time. Vince had plane tickets—the other part of her Christmas gift. In the morning they were flying to Las Vegas.

Terese selfishly forgot about the spirits on the beach below Remington, perhaps deluding herself they had no reason to bother Tom. He and his family should be fine without her for a while. After all, she'd been at the Gardner home only last night and hadn't felt their presence inside the house. These spirits she'd encountered seemed to be confined to the beach and bluff area. She believed that her friends were safe. Unfortunately, she'd be gone when they needed her most.

Chapter 148

Elise was furious with Benjamin for revealing himself to the medium. "You know how *powerful* Terese is! How could you do this to us? To me! Damn you! Now what will we do? You may have ruined everything." She snarled, then attacked Benjamin, biting and scratching his arms, already painful from the burns Terese had inflicted with the holy water. He easily pushed her away, but let her continue to rant and curse him.

Elise stopped and fell onto the couch at the Harrison house. Nearly out of control she yelled at Benjamin, "You will pay for this! I don't want you here. I never want to see you again. Do you understand? You put everything I—we—have worked for in jeopardy tonight. Why? How could you!" She jumped up, flailing her arms at him. "Terese could have destroyed us both!"

"No!" Benjamin snapped. "I'm stronger than she is. Trust me, Elise. I'm not afraid of her. I won't let her do anything to harm you. Or me." He held his hand out to her.

"Get out of here! Before *I* destroy *you*, Benjamin! Don't think for a second I can't." Elise stood up, flew above Benjamin, and landed on his back. She pressed her tiny fingers into his temple as hard as she could. Within seconds Benjamin started to fade. Reaching for her hands, he pulled them away and spun around. Elise opened her arms wide and hugged Benjamin to her, squeezing harder and harder until once again Benjamin began to lose his human appearance.

Benjamin lifted his arms with a force Elise wasn't prepared for, breaking her hold. She screamed, backed away, and ran at him. She passed through his body as he let himself become a cold mist. Elise screamed again, then turned to face him. Her eyes glared, her lips rounded as if she were going to whistle. Instead she blew and blew scattering the mist into a million minute droplets that dissipated throughout the room. As she stopped to take another breath, Benjamin gathered himself and materialized before her.

"Stop!" Benjamin commanded. "Enough! Until you calm down and realize how much you need me, I will go. For now. But you *will* miss me. You can't bear to be alone. You need me. You'll see." Benjamin reached out and stroked her hair. "In time, you'll understand that I was protecting you today. I had to stop the psychic from finding out where we're staying. We can't let her come here, to this house. Don't you see that?" Benjamin didn't wait for her to answer. He went to the basement, gathered his books in his bag and left. Later, in the darkness of his cave, he lay staring at the rock ceiling above his head. He began to form a plan.

At sunrise, he left to find Terese. He did not find her. Terese and Vince left town before dawn, taking the train to Concord, from there catching a flight to Vegas. On the desk, Benjamin found a note Terese had penned for her neighbor about her travel itinerary. She would be gone for two weeks.

Chapter 149

Cassie choked back tears. Tom hugged her, then turned to Lizzie and said, "Little princess, I'm going to miss you. I'm glad you guys were here with me for Christmas. Promise you'll call me whenever you want to. Okay?"

Lizzie nodded.

"Before you know it, you'll be back to visit me." Tom tousled Lizzie's hair, then gave her a big hug. "Young lady, you take care of your mom for me. She may be your mother, but she's still my little sister." Tom took her tiny, gloved hand.

"I will." Lizzie swung her uncle's hand back and forth. "Uncle Tommy, will you come visit us?"

"I might just do that." The train whistle blew; it was time for the family to board. "Cassie, call me when you get home."

"I will. Tom, it's been wonderful to be able to spend all this time with you. I hate to leave you. You sure you'll be all right?"

"I'll be fine. You need to get on with your life. I have Sara and Nate to keep me going. Don't worry. You better get on the train. It's ready to roll. Love you." He turned to his brother-in-law. "Michael, it's been great having you here. Take good care of Lizzie and Cassie." Tom reached his hand out, thought better of it and pulled Michael to him for a brotherly hug.

Sara kissed Cassie and Lizzie, hugged Michael and wiped away the tears running down her cheeks. "Bye! I'll miss you. Call me soon," she yelled as the family climbed up the metal steps and onto the train. "Have a good trip!"

Standing arm in arm, Tom and Sara watched the train pull out of Ravenswood Station. Lizzie held her doll to the glass and waved its hand at them. Then they were gone.

There was no sunshine on this bleak winter day. A freezing drizzle coated a landscape already caked with grime and soot. The train, slowly picking up speed, disappeared into a heavy fog. "Let's go have lunch at the café before we go home." Tom hugged Sara to his side.

"Sure. I wonder if Joanie is working today. Poor kid must be in terrible shape after all she went through with Harold."

"Joe said she left town. Went to live with her mom in New Haven," Tom said. "Harold certainly left a lot of people heartbroken."

"Yeah, though Nate seems to be handling Harold's death well. Time is a great healer," Sara said thoughtfully. "Nate's a great guy. I'm glad he's here."

"Me, too. He and Joe seemed to have hit it off. That's a relief, since they'll be together a lot." Tom took Sara's hand. "Come on. I'm starving!"

Chapter 150

Nate and Joe were setting up a temporary office. Until Joe had the attic remodeled, Nate was using the bedroom across the hall from the library for his room and the library as an office. "That's the last box," Nate said as he slipped the blade of his pocketknife under the packing tape. Joe helped Nate lift the printer out of the box, then put it on the floor. "Think I'll set it up over there. Help me move the desk against that wall."

Joe lifted one side of the oak desk, accidentally bumping Nate's cast. "Shit! Sorry. You all right?"

"Damn!" Nate hobbled over to the chair and sat down. "Not sure my leg is ever going to heal," he said rubbing his leg above the cast. "Guess I'll find out next week. I'm taking the train to Jamestown. Time to get another x-ray and see if my leg's mending okay. Seems to be taking forever. I hope I don't need another cast. This is getting old."

"Well, it was a pretty nasty break. Give it time, it'll heal." Joe dragged the desk the rest of the way across the room. "When are you going?"

"Wednesday. I'll stay with my sister, Rosa. I need to spend some time with her. She's doing pretty well, but still . . ." Nate paused for a second and then went on. "There are some papers we need to go over. I'll come back the following Monday."

"I could drive you. There's a contractor there I did some work for a few years ago. Tom wants to move a few walls and add a large office in the attic. I'd like this guy to check the schematics before I get in over my head. There's going to be some major electrical work that'll need to be done. Not sure I want to take it on myself."

"Yeah. Sure, that'd work. Need somewhere to stay? You can stay at Rosa's. Plenty of room," Nate said.

"Nah. I have a good friend there—she'll be happy to put me up." Joe lifted the computer onto the desk. "It'll be good to get away for a few days." He put the printer on the stand beside the desk.

"I know what you mean. This house has an odd, even oppressive atmosphere. Maybe it's because it was closed up so long." Nate said.

"Could be. I think most old houses have their own character. The old couple who lived here before Tom was very reclusive—never opened the curtains, let alone the windows. It always smelled like a sick room. I did what work I had to do and got out. Takes a while for a house to learn to breathe again. Get rid of its former occupants." Joe laughed. "Geez, that sounded lame!" He plugged the computer and printer into a power strip. "There. Did everything come on?"

"Yep. All right! Maybe I can get some work done now. Thanks for the help."

"Sure." Joe moved a small, oak filing cabinet next to the desk. "If you don't need help with anything else, I'm gonna head back to town."

"I'm fine. I have plenty to do to keep busy while Tom and Sara are gone. See you tomorrow, Joe."

***

Elise sat quietly on the couch. She was finally warm. A small fire burned in the white, polished-stone fireplace. The room was toasty, the atmosphere cozy. Nate, busy at the computer, was completely oblivious of her presence.

Tom had moved all of Elise's poetry books to this room. The shelves were filled with her collections—Whitman, Poe, Plath, McKuen, e e cummings, Ginsberg—oh, how she wished she could pick one of them up right now. It was all she could to do keep her hands off of her books. Resisting the urge, she lay back, rested her head on the sofa arm and closed her eyes.

She was incredibly lonely since she'd made Benjamin leave. She needed companionship. The Harrison house was so big and so empty. She'd stay here today, until Tom and Sara came home. Her mind drifted, her thoughts traveled far away from this lonely existence. She remembered herself as she had been ten years ago—in love, her life thrilling and full. She became involved with—and finally married Tom. A dream come true. Those few years were the only time in her life that she'd found contentment. Her life had been perfect. Until Tom changed. She opened her eyes, wiped a tear from her cheek. How foolish she had been. She thought she'd found happiness. Damn Tom to hell for ruining her dreams! She slammed her fist against the sofa.

Nate whirled around. Elise heard his quick intake of breath. He stared right at her. She froze.

"What the hell!" Nate got up and walked toward her. Elise didn't move, waiting to see if she would need to fight him. Puzzled, he circled the room, his cast dragging and leaving a trail behind him in the plush carpet. "Is there someone here?" he called.

He can't see me. Good! Elise sighed. Nate looked around again. Elise pulled her knees up to her chest, wrapping her arms around them. Amused, she watched Nate.

Nate walked across the room, peered into the hallway. "Joe? Did you forget something?" he yelled. When there was no answer, he walked out onto the balcony. Elise crept up behind him as he paced up and down, looking down into the yard. "Huh. . . . Nobody's here. I swear I heard someone." He closed the balcony doors. "Creepy old house!"

Not wanting to risk exposure, Elise slipped out of the room. She floated down the stairs and toured the empty house. She had to be so careful now. Though he was not extremely sensitive to her, Nate seemed to sense her presence. Damn! She hated being alone.

In the basement, Elise wandered around taking in all the changes made since she'd last been here. Entering what had been the Lindemans' room, she was relieved to find all of their belongings gone. *May they rot in hell!*

Elise sat down on the floor in the middle of the room that had been Helen and Gabe's last sanctuary. Touching her fingertips to the wooden floor, she closed her eyes. With a jolt, her head jerked up. She felt the presence of another spirit. "Who's here?" she whispered. There was no response.

Almost too late, Benjamin saw Elise and vanished.

Elise strained to identify the entity. After sitting motionless for five minutes, she gave up. *Maybe it was only the last discharge of energy from Harold.*

Overhead, the slamming of a door and the sound of footsteps going up the stairs jarred her into motion. Tom was home. She had to leave though she wished she could stay and see if Nate said anything to him.

***

"Nate, we're back," Tom hollered walking up the stairs.

"In the library," Nate answered. "Cassie get off okay? You were gone a long time, train must have been late."

"No. The train was on time. Everyone got off just fine." Tom looked over Nate's shoulder at the computer screen. "Sara and I stayed in town and had lunch. Looks like you and Joe pretty much have the office set up. Good. I have some papers I need you to go over. Got a few minutes?"

"Sure. I just got the internet working. We're ready to roll!"

Chapter 151

While Nate and Tom discussed business, Sara went for a walk along the beach. Wiggins trailed behind her pouncing on the water bugs and small fish that washed ashore. Sara laughed. "Come here, kitty." She threw a stone at the water's edge. The cat raced to spring on it, then disgustedly shook the water from his paws. Finding a piece of driftwood, Sara threw it as far in to the waves as she could, then watched it toss and tumble back to shore. She picked it up and threw it again. The waves caught it, washing it further down the beach. Sara chased it, Wiggins bounding after her. They played in the water, moving farther and farther down the beach until Sara realized she was below her cousin Vivian's house.

She hasn't been there for weeks. She decided to check the house. She climbed the beach stairs, then followed the steep path to the house. Slightly winded, Sara sat down on the porch to catch her breath. Wiggins hissed, jumped off the landing and raced into the trees. "That was odd. He must have spotted a mouse or something," she said out loud to no one. Her voice sounded unnaturally loud in the cold, still air.

Inside the house, on the other side of the door, Elise waited. When Sara didn't come in, Elise passed through the door, crawling on her knees to kneel behind Sara. Elise whispered softly in her ear. Sara slumped over backwards, falling hard onto the stone porch floor. "You deserved that." Elise laughed as she watched a trickle of blood pool on the stones under Sara's head. Sara moaned, began to stir.

Tom ran up the steps. "Sara! God! You're bleeding!" Elise slithered unseen into the house.

"What happened?" Sara gasped, touching her hand to her head.

"Don't get up, Sara. Let me see." Tom knelt beside her, turned her head gently to examine the wound. "It's a small cut; it's just bleeding a lot. You're okay. Sit still for a minute" He pulled his wool scarf off, handed it to her. "Hold this on your head; we need to apply pressure. I wish we could get in the house."

"We can. There's a spare key." Sara pointed across the porch. "There, under the planter."

Tom retrieved the key and unlocked the front door. He lifted Sara, carried her inside to the kitchen. With his foot he pulled a chair away from the table. "Sit here, honey." When the bleeding stopped, Tom cleaned the blood out of Sara's hair as best he could. "You need to stay quiet for a while; make sure the bleeding doesn't start again. What happened? Did you trip coming up the stairs?"

"No. I sat down to catch my breath. That's the last I remember. I think something hit me in the head. Go look around, Tom."

Tom found nothing. "If you were winded, maybe your blood pressure dropped or something, and you got dizzy."

"Maybe," Sara sighed. "I just don't remember."

Tom stroked her cheek. "We should get you home." He gave her a quick kiss on her forehead. "You want me to walk home and get the car?"

"No." Sara stood up. Tom reached out to steady her. "I'm okay. I can walk. Let's take the upper path though. I don't think I can handle the beach stairs." She didn't wait for Tom but walked down the hallway to the front door. "How did you know I was here?"

"I was looking for you. I saw you from the beach, when you were climbing the stairs. What are you doing here?"

Sara answered, "Being curious. I don't know. I thought I should look around Viv's house, make sure everything was okay. The house's been empty for a month."

"You want me to take a quick look around?"

"This house is too big for a quick look," Sara grinned. "You better come back tomorrow."

"Okay. Let's get you back to Remington."

Chapter 152

Fishing the key from his pocket, Tom unlocked the front door to the Harrison house. He'd hoped Joe could come with him. But no such luck. Joe was in town working on the plans for the attic remodel with a local architect. Having told Sara he would check out her cousin's house today, he knew he needed to keep his promise.

His footsteps echoed in the empty hallways. He wandered down the corridor and into the living room, then into the dining room. Nothing was amiss. The first floor was an endless maze of rooms. All were elaborately and expensively decorated. Vivian had impeccable taste. She loved being surrounded in luxury, that was obvious. Tom picked up a delicately sculpted figurine of a ballerina, laughed when he saw the face was a likeness of a much younger Vivian. He hoped she was getting better. He would call William later today, see how everything was going. Maybe he and Vivian will bring the boys back here pretty soon. It was a lonely place with everyone gone. Tom never imagined he'd miss those boys, well certainly not Billy. He even missed Viv, her presence brought a lot of life to this beach front.

In the kitchen, Tom checked the windows and back doors. Everything seemed fine. On the second floor, he checked all five bedrooms and baths, the office and a sewing room. The hall light to the upstairs attic was burned out, so Tom decided not to go up there. Really no need to. Back on the main floor, as he passed through the hallway, he glanced into the family room. There was a bottle of liquor on the coffee table. "How did I miss that?" he asked out loud.

Disturbed, Tom picked up the bottle. Pulling the glass stopper, he brought the bottle to his nose and sniffed. His mouth went dry. Elise's favorite liqueur. He glanced around the room. Nothing else was disturbed or out of place. Ahh. So sweet. Cherry and almonds. Memories of Elise flooded his mind. Tom sank down into the soft cushion of the sofa and took a drink, then another. Hot and smooth. It hit his empty stomach, felt so good. He tipped the bottle, draining it. Warmth ran though his body. He felt it first in his belly, then his arms, his neck. He sat back on the sofa and thought for a minute.

The gentle emotion brought on by old memories quickly faded into anger. Tom threw the etched crystal-bottle, watched as it smashed into tiny shards against the back wall of the fireplace. Getting up, he kicked a few pieces of stray glass that lay on the hearth into the fireplace. He turned and stormed out of the room.

Seeing the basement stairs, Tom flipped the light on and walked slowly down into the basement. He stepped on something hard in the carpet. Bending over, he found a polished stone. He picked it up and put it in his pocket. He'd seen many like this one only weeks ago in the basement of Remington. He walked farther into the room. Melted into the carpet in a circle were large drops of black candle wax.

"Shit!" Tom took several deep breaths, gave himself a minute to think. His imagination. Nothing to any of this. He'd finish looking around, then he was out of there. He'd walk along the beach, and throw the fucking stone as far out into the water as he could. Then he'd go home. Sara would be waiting for him. She's who he needed to get Elise out of his mind. Being with Sara would make him forget.

The walk did little to settle his angst. Tom stopped and watched the waves, kicked sand into the air, studied the swirling black clouds on the horizon as a storm moved in. A dozen ravens flew circles around him. Tom threw the stone far out into the ocean. The birds chased the stone as it flipped and cartwheeled through the air. The second the stone hit the surface, the largest of the birds dove into the water, grabbing the stone in its beak. The other birds cawed and flew excitedly in a circle, then swooped down at Tom. One of the ravens pecked and tore Tom's cheek. In a cacophony of caws, the birds flew behind the bluff above the beach. Tom wrapped his scarf around his cheek, ran up the beach stairs and up the path to Remington. When he opened the door, the house was cold and dark. No one was home. Tom found a note taped to the banister:

> Tom, You left your cell phone here. A package from John Atwood is waiting for a signature at the post office. It's the contracts we've been waiting for. Knew you wanted them ASAP. Sara offered to drive me into town. Back in a few hours. –Nate

Tom climbed the stairs, shut the door to his room and went into his bathroom to tend to the gash on his cheek. "Nasty cut! It'll leave a scar no doubt. Good thing I'm not vain. One more cut on this mug. Adds character, so I'm told," he said to his reflection in the mirror. He cleaned the cut, dabbed some antibiotic ointment on it and covered it with a band-aid. He opened the cabinet, putting the band-aids and ointment away. When he closed the mirrored door, he froze.

Behind Tom, in the shadows, was a man. Dark hair, brown eyes, several inches taller than Tom, the man was muscular, his stance menacing. His deep-set eyes glowed like black diamonds in the mirror. The man took a step forward. Tom whirled around. There was no one there. Tom turned back, staring into the mirror. The man stood beside him. Tom turned his head. No one there. But again, in the mirror, the man appeared clear and distinct. He stood perhaps a foot away, was now facing Tom. Tom looked to his side. No one was there. Except . . . Tom saw a vague outline, nothing more than an obscurity of the air, a slight transparency, so subtle as to be nearly undetectable. His fingers touched the air. He felt an icy-cold chill.

"What do you want?" Tom yelled at the profile in the mirror.

"To warn you."

"What?" Tom stammered. "Who are you?" Tom pivoted, tried to grab the intruder. His hands passed through icy air. Facing the mirror, Tom turned toward the man, plainly visible beside him. "Wait! I get it. I'm dreaming. This is a nightmare!" Tom laughed at his own stupidity. "I'm sleepwalking!"

"Perhaps. But know that dreams often foretell the future, Tom." The man leaned over and whispered threateningly into his ear. "You *will* hear me out!"

Droplets of salty sweat ran down Tom's brows and into his eyes. He wiped them away with the back of his hand. His upper lip was damp, his lips and tongue were dry.

The man cupped his hand menacingly on Tom's shoulder. His strong fingers dug painfully into his collarbone. Tom stood paralyzed—not by fear—but by some unseen force holding him immobile. "I can't move because I'm asleep. I'm paralyzed, so I can't hurt myself while I sleep."

"Then how can you be sleep walking?" the man asked.

"This is a dream. Dreams make no sense. That's how!" Tom tried to laugh. His voice sounded unreal as it echoed hollowly in the small room. He watched the man in the mirror while trying to figure out how to wake himself up. He couldn't seem to, remained trapped in his nightmare. "I want you to get out of here right . . . "

"Be quiet! Listen to me. I don't care anything about you, Tom Gardner. You are nothing more than a dead-man-walking. Like me!" Benjamin laughed. "If it were my choice, I would kill you now. But it's not. I'm bound by my loyalty to Elise. She wants you to live. For now."

"What! What the hell are you talking about? Elise is dead! God let me wake up!" In the mirror Tom watched the man place his hands around his neck.

"I could choke the life out of you right now," Benjamin shrieked. His voice cut through the night, sent shivers down Tom's spine. Suddenly the man dropped his hands to his sides. "I will not kill you. You will live. Because Elise desires it. Elise, though, is to be mine. The only reason I am here is to see that she does not get what she wants. She wants to take Sara. To punish you. You cannot let Elise do that!"

"Sara? Leave Sara out of this! She has nothing to do with Elise!"

"Shut up!" Benjamin hissed. "Listen to me. You will tell Sara about Elise. Elise has possessed her mind many times. You will make Sara understand that."

Tom's face went ashen.

"Ahh, now you see what has been happening. Don't you?" Benjamin sneered.

"How could she do that? It's not possible."

"I helped her. But I won't help her again. Elise will be mine. It is *my* time to be her love. So, Tom Gardner," Benjamin pointed menacingly at Tom, "you will stop Elise. If she finds herself powerless over Sara, she will give up and come to me. She will see that I will keep her safe, that I cherish her. And—I'll make her stay away from you."

"This is crazy. Wake up!" Still unable to move, Tom could do nothing more than stare at the man beside him. Then his eyes widened. He knew. "You! You're the one who keeps breaking in here. Get out of here." Tom turned his head—there was no one beside him. Looking again into the mirror, he watched Benjamin's lips curl in sinister laughter.

"Shut up, man! Heed my warning. Elise intends to destroy both of you. Do you understand?" Benjamin put both hands on Tom's shoulders turning him away from the mirror. "Do you see me now?" Benjamin stood before Tom—as real and as solid as any man. "Do you know what you have to do? Answer me!" Benjamin screamed. An icy waft of air smelling of mildew and must, brushed Tom's cheek.

He was not dreaming. This was real. "What can I do to stop her?"

"Ahh. You finally believe." Benjamin smiled, releasing his painful hold on Tom's shoulders. "You will tell Sara the truth about Elise. That her spirit lives, that she intends to possess her. Sara will believe you. She will know that her 'spells' were Elise forcing her will on her. She knows about spirits, knows they were in this house. You have only to ask her. She and a medium, along with your sister and a young friend, cast the Lindemans souls from this house. From this earth."

"The Lindemans! What are you talking about?"

"It doesn't matter now. The old ones are gone. What matters is that you tell Sara she must let me come to her. I will tell her what she must do to stop Elise. You have to trust me. Or you will lose Sara."

Benjamin began to fade. Although Tom clearly heard his voice, once again there was no one in the room with him. Tom stared into the mirror. The man stood beside him. His hands reached toward Tom, settling on his shoulders. Benjamin squeezed his fingers into Tom's shoulders. Tom fell to his knees. "Will you do as I tell you?" he snarled.

"Yes." Tom fell over, writhing in pain.

"Good. I will come tonight. At midnight. To this room."

Tom was shaking. He crawled on all fours to the bed, then pulled himself up. Elise. . . . He had to destroy her. And her minion.

Chapter 153

"Tom! We're back," Sara called as she and Nate came into the house, slamming the front door. "Oh my gosh it's cold in here. Tom! Where are you?" She threw her coat over the banister and walked across the entry to the thermostat. "Sixty four. Brrr." She turned the dial, listening for the *whoof* of the gas igniting. "There. I'm going to find Tom. Nate, throw some wood in the fireplace would you?"

Sara finally found Tom upstairs in his room, sitting at the table staring out the window.

"Hi, we got the papers John sent." Walking over to Tom she put her hands on his shoulders. He winced. "Wow! Did that hurt? Sorry." When Tom didn't answer, she walked around the table. "What happened to your cheek? Tom?"

"We need to talk, Sara."

"Is something wrong? Wait. I smell booze. You're drunk, aren't you?"

"No. Sit down, Sara."

"What's wrong?"

Tom got up, pulled out another chair. Sitting beside Sara, his gaze focused intently into her violet-blue eyes, he took her hands in his. "I have some rather disturbing events to share with you."

Chapter 154

"Mary? Hi, it's Sara. I need to talk to you. Do you have a few minutes?"

"You sound serious. What's up?"

"I'm in town. Can you meet me in the courtyard at St. James?"

"Sure. Give me ten minutes. I'm at work. I have to finish changing an IV on a puppy. Sara, something's wrong, isn't it?"

"I'll tell you when you get here." Sara started to hang up then added, "Mary! Don't tell anyone where you're going. Or that you're meeting me. Promise?"

"Of course."

"Okay. Bye."

Sara parked her car at the lot on Maine Street, looking around before she got out, making sure no one was following her. *Like I would see them anyway. God, when will this end?* She walked briskly down the near-empty street to the church. It was another frigid winter day, no snow but the wind was brutal, at times unleashing bone-chilling gusts. Sara nodded at a priest as he passed her. He hesitated, but when she didn't stop to talk, he continued on into the rectory. Finding a bench sheltered from the wind, Sara waited for Mary.

"Hey! There you are." Mary hurried up the sidewalk and dropped onto the bench beside Sara. She'd brought steaming cups of hot cocoa for them. "Here."

"Hi, sorry to get you out in this awful cold." Sara took the cardboard cup from Mary. "We have to be very discreet. We need to keep our voices low. No one can hear us."

"You're scaring me." Mary shivered. She put her cup down on the cement and pulled the fur collar on her coat up around her neck. "The spirits are back. We didn't get rid of them, did we?"

"We did. Kind of. The séances worked—for the spirits that were in the house." Sara paused, watched her breath form clouds that wafted like smoke into the freezing air. She put her cup down, reached out and took Mary's gloved hands in hers. "There are more spirits. Two of them."

Mary's face paled. "Two?"

"I know it's crazy." Sara stared into the clear, blue sky, took a long shallow breath. "One of them is Tom's wife, Elise."

"What?"

"And there's a man—I mean the spirit of a man. I have seen him. I have talked with him."

"Oh, God!" Tears spilled down Mary's cheeks. She wiped them away. Across the yard the chapel door opened, then slammed shut. Its loud report echoed off the courtyard walls as if half a dozen doors had been slammed, one after the other. Both women whirled around to see who came out. There was no one there.

"The wind? Or . . .? Maybe we better go inside the church," Sara said in a whisper.

"It might be safer. Come on," Mary said, standing up. She was hit by a heavy gust of wind that threatened to knock her over. She grabbed the back of the bench to steady herself, then grasped Sara's arm, pulling her up. They ran across the yard.

Hanging on the stone wall inside the cathedral's small, wrought iron fenced yard was a sculpted rendering of *St. Michael's Victory Over the Devil.* The devil's evil face glared at them, his eyes glowing red. Winking, he turned his head to watch them as they ran past. "Don't look at him!" Sara threw her body against the wooden door as a strong force shoved against it. "We're in the church, we're safe now."

A priest appeared in the hallway. He made the sign of the cross in the air as he hurried over to Sara and Mary. "Mother of God! What was that?"

Risking a glance at the sculpture, Sara relaxed. "It's all right. It was the wind."

"Don't lie, child." He reached his hands out to Mary and Sara. "You need my help. Come with me."

Ten minutes later, after blessing them and anointing their foreheads with holy water, Father Gabriel told them he would pray for their protection, then left Sara and Mary in the back of the church.

Huddled together, Sara and Mary sat in the last pew at the back of the church. From there they could see anyone coming into the building. They whispered animatedly for an hour, then left. Father Gabriel met them at the door and walked with them to the edge of the church yard. Both women were pale, deep furrows etched their foreheads. They hugged and said their goodbyes, going in two different directions to their cars. Atop the church spire, high in the gray clouded sky, a single raven perched.

Chapter 155

Mary's heart sank. Terese's voicemail picked up on the first ring. *She has her phone turned off. Damn! Not that I blame her —it is her honeymoon. God I hope we can do this without her. I guess we have no choice.* Mary left a voice mail asking Terese to call her as soon as possible. "The situation at Remington is 'code red.'" Last night Mary had received an email from Terese. She and Vince were married yesterday afternoon in a simple ceremony at The Wedding Bell Chapel in Vegas.

Grabbing her heavy parka out of the closet, Mary yelled to her mom, "I have some errands to run. Back in a while." The car was freezing inside, however, she didn't notice. Sweat trickled down the center of her back. *Nerves! Get a grip, girl!*

Pulling her red sedan as far into Terese's driveway as she could, Mary glanced around then got out. Underneath a flat, oval stone in the rabbit flowerpot was a spare key to Terese's house. She unlocked the door and let herself in. After switching on a table lamp, Mary went straight to Terese's bedroom. It took her twenty minutes to find the tapestry bag—she'd almost given up. Sitting on the edge of Terese's bed, she'd shone her flashlight around the room one last time and saw the faint outline of a small door in the back of the clothes closet. After taking the cloth bag out, she shone the light into the cubicle. The box with all the other implements she needed was there as well. *All right—I can get out of here now. I hate sneaking around like this, but it's for a good cause. Terese will understand.*

After locking the house, Mary drove to work. She took Terese's book on banishment and cleansing ceremonies out, putting it under her seat. In the employee's room, she put the bag and boxes in a small storage locker and clicked the padlock shut. Once she was back in her car, she called Terese again and left a message explaining what she had taken and why. Mary drove home, stopping twice to gather her wits.

"Mary, you look awful! What's wrong?" her mother asked, passing her in the hallway.

"Gee thanks, Mom. Nothing's wrong except I almost fell on the ice. You should make Tony get off his little butt and shovel the sidewalk before one of us breaks our neck."

"I'll try, but don't hold your breath! You know your brother! I'll have your dad talk to him when he gets home."

"Yeah, all right. Anyway, . . . I'm going to my room to study. I have a test in English lit tomorrow," Mary lied. "Lots of reading to do. Don't let Tony or Evie bother me okay?"

"I'll do my best. Can I bring you a sandwich and some soup?"

"Sure, Mom. Thanks." Mary closed her door. From her backpack she pulled Terese's well-worn leather-bound book of spiritual cleansing rituals. Mary studied them all evening and into the night, stopping only when her mother knocked on the door and handed her a tray. "Mom, you're the best. Thanks. See you in the morning."

"Get some sleep. You look beat."

"I will. Oh, and I'll be gone most of the day tomorrow. I have an early class, then I promised Sara I'd spend the afternoon with her. I might even stay the night at Remington."

"Okay. Seems like you and Sara are becoming really close friends. Isn't she a little old for you?"

"Not really. She's like a big sister. She's very cool. We get along really well."

"As long as you aren't neglecting your studies and can fit in your job at the vet clinic. Sure wish she lived closer."

"You worry too much. Goodnight." Mary smiled and shut her door.

Chapter 156

It was six the next morning when Joe and Nate drove off, headed for Jamestown. "You guys take it easy," Tom said. "No need to hurry. If the roads are bad, stop and stay the night somewhere,"

"Yes, Dad!" Nate laughed. "It's not a long drive, Tom. We'll be in Jamestown by dinnertime. I'll send you a text when we get there."

Tom watched them for a minute. It was still dark, an hour till sunrise. Tired, Tom lay down on the couch in front of the warm fire and slept for a few more hours.

At eight, he woke with Sara nudging his shoulder. "Morning. What're you doing down here?"

Tom pulled her onto the couch beside him. "Hi, there. Didn't want to wake you."

"Well, you could have. I mean, . . . " She smiled as Tom began unbuttoning her robe. They made love on the chenille blanket in front of the fire. Afterwards, they lay quietly for a few minutes watching the burning embers. Sara lay on her belly. Tom traced the slight curve of her spine with his fingers, then he gently rolled her over onto her back. She wrapped her legs around him as he entered her in one gentle thrust. Neither one closed their eyes as they made love again, looking deep into each other's soul, committing without words to each other. A while later, entwined in each other's arms, they drifted into a light sleep.

When they woke at nine, Tom and Sara took a long, hot shower, then ate breakfast at the bedroom table overlooking the ocean. The day was bright, not a cloud marred the crystal-blue sky; waves broke in glistening splashes on the beach below. Tom brought up a tray of Belgium coffee and bagels with cream cheese, a plate of sliced blood oranges and black grapes. The two remained silent, not speaking of the day before them —a day both knew would be the most difficult they had yet faced together.

"She's here!" Sara pointed as Mary's sedan rounded the curve at the lower end of the lane. They hurried downstairs to meet her.

"Morning!" Sara called as Mary got out of her car.

Tom unloaded the tapestry bag and boxes, then parked Mary's car in the garage beside Sara's. His own car was parked in the circular driveway by the front porch, ready—if they needed it.

When Tom returned, Mary and Sara had gone to the dining room. They'd taken the bags and boxes and pushed them under the dining table.

"There. That's good for now. Do you have the book?" Sara asked.

"Here," Mary took it out of her backpack. "I studied it most of the night. I think I'm ready. Sit down with me, and we can go over everything."

"You sure we can do this?" asked Tom, frowning and rubbing the telltale stubble of beard on his chin.

"No, but what choice do we have? I can't get hold of Terese, and if we wait any longer, who knows what Elise will be capable of doing. The real question is—are *you* ready, Sara?" Mary took Sara's hands into her own cold, sweaty hands. "Can you do this?"

"Yes. Absolutely." Sara smiled weakly. "Like you said, what choice is there?"

"This is going to be extremely intense," Tom said. "We have a lot to do to get ready for tonight." He abruptly shoved his chair back and stood up. "Before we get started, I need more coffee. I have to be alert. You two relax a minute. I'll be back" He left them studying the worn, leather book, undoubtedly belonging to Terese, and went to the kitchen to make more coffee. Wiggins was curled up on the braided rug in front of the fire. Tom poured him a saucer of milk and stroked his soft fur while he waited for the coffee to finish brewing. "What have we gotten into?" Wiggins stared sedately at Tom, then began licking his paws, fastidiously cleaning his whiskers and chin. "What in God's name have we gotten ourselves into?"

Chapter 157

Mary positioned ten lead-crystal vases filled with ten white roses around the dining room, carefully centering one on the table in the triangle of Terese's ceremonial lace tablecloth. "Ten—the all-encompassing number. Perfection, order, law. The return to unity. Ten candles. Ten white roses," Mary whispered. In three ceramic burners, she placed the cinnamon, frankincense, and sandalwood, just as Terese had in their earlier séances. She felt empowered having done that. And much calmer. At nine o'clock that evening, the ceremony would begin. *Nine—the number of completion: attainment, the beginning, the end.* She nodded to Sara and Tom, who looked up from studying Terese's book—the banishment ceremony in particular. "We're ready for tonight."

It was early afternoon. Tom, Mary, and Sara sat on the couch huddled around the book. For several more hours they read and practiced until they had memorized all the chants and knew what each one of their roles would be. At five, they tried to eat a dinner of lean turkey sandwiches with avocado slices and spinach greens on grain bread. They drank oolong tea and chewed dried apricots dipped in dark chocolate.

At eight, Mary put her heavy winter coat on, wrapped her woolen scarf around her neck and walked out the side door of the living room onto the front porch. Hugging the wall, she slipped over the banister and dropped soundlessly to the ground. From tree to bush, she made her way to a stand of juniper trees, thick of limb, pungent with berries. The strong smell of the berries would cover her own scent. She crouched down to wait, her view of the beach clear.

Watching Mary through binoculars, Tom stood on the balcony outside his bedroom, waiting until she was in place, safely hidden in the trees. He took his cell phone from his pocket and dialed the number that had been Billy's—one of the phones Elise now had with her at the Harrison house—

Benjamin had given him this information. No one answered, of course—Billy now had a new phone and a new number. When the "Please leave a message," came on, Tom spoke slowly and clearly, "Billy, it's Tom Gardner. I found a credit card with your name on it down by the bluff. Not sure if you've replaced it already, but just in case, please call me. Guess your family is having a good holiday season. Sara says 'Hi' and says she'll write your name in the sand—she's about to go for a stroll on the beach. Anyway, call me one way or the other about the card. 'Bye."

The raven sitting on the balcony railing cawed and flew in a giant circle around Tom, then disappeared into the night. Benjamin would stay out of sight now, so Elise could not detect his presence.

Curious, lonely and bored, Elise picked up the cell phone and retrieved the message from Tom. "At last!" She smiled into the dark room, her white teeth glistening as a ray of moonlight sliced the darkness.

Chapter 158

Moonlight sparkled, shimmering on frothy waves breaking far out on the Atlantic. The haunting blast of a ship's horn rode the breeze, lulling Sara as she walked. Her heavy winter boots left deep prints that filled with water as the tide rolled in. Surprisingly calm, she moved slowly, wrapped in the warmth of a down-filled parka, the hood tied loosely around her head. Then it began. Behind her she heard a whisper as Elise quietly spoke the words that only a day ago would have put Sara into a trance. Sara dropped her head, let her body gently fall to the sand.

Clearing her mind, Sara allowed Elise to possess her, though she never gave up her mind to Elise. Benjamin has removed most of Elise's power over her. Sara took several deep breaths as she allowed Elise's thoughts to fill her head.

She performed her own form of disassociation to keep from reacting to the almost unbearable, dark hatred that was the essence of Elise. She concentrated on the breaking waves and the gentle sound of water slapping the shore. Sara knew her body was being moved, felt herself lifted up from the cold sand. Stars twinkled above, waves lapped soothingly. She let Elise take control of her. She climbed the beach steps up to the bluff and raced up the steep path to Remington.

Mary texted Tom telling him, "Sara's coming." Mary waited for five minutes, then retraced her steps to the house, this time entering from the back door. Once in the kitchen, she pulled her coat off and silently opened the door into the dining room. From the box sitting on a dining room chair, she took the large, glass jar filled to the top with Celtic sea salt.

Next Mary took the sage from the tapestry bag, leaving it carefully wrapped in three layers of plastic wrap so not even a small odor could escape. Taking the vial of holy water from Terese's bag, she carefully dropped it into her pocket next to several small boxes of matches.

And then Mary sat down to wait.

***

"Sara! You look like you're freezing!" Tom hugged Sara to him, felt the subtle difference in body language as Elise tried to respond lovingly to him—whom she despised. Tom smiled—he couldn't help himself. "Give me your coat, and come sit by the fire. I'll get you a cup of hot tea. Come on." He led her to the couch, threw another log onto the fire. On the table he had a tray of hot tea and two cups. He poured the steaming liquid into the cups, dropped a lump of sugar into one, and handed it to Sara. The clock struck the quarter hour; it was eight forty-five.

Sitting close to her on the couch, Tom took her free hand and held it to his lips. Gently blowing on her fingers, he felt her fight not to pull away. Again he smiled. "Darling, let me hold you and warm you up. He wrapped his arms around her, her body tense and resistant. "I know what will get your blood flowing." He laughed. "Play for me. Come on." He pulled her to her feet, led her to the Steinway.

For five minutes Tom played Bach's *Toccata and Fugue in D Minor* expecting Elise to join in and play along with him, even though he knew Elise hated his choice.

Finally, frustrated and angry, Elise began to play—but not the song Tom played. A song of her own choosing. *Für Elise.* She leaned forward, concentrating, her fingers dancing off the keys.

Tom asked, "Why would you play that? You know it reminds me of Elise! Stop, Sara! Play something else. Play *Moonlight Sonata*. You play that so well." Tom began to play the soothing sonata. Elise did not join him. Instead she placed her hands in her lap and stared out the window into the star-filled black sky.

From the dining room, Mary heard the refrains of *Moonlight Sonata*—her cue. She went on to her next task. Removing the lid from the heavy, glass jar, she circled the room, pouring the crystals of sea-salt into a heavy line all around the perimeters of the room, leaving only a small opening by the door into the living room. She took her place beside the door, waiting.

***

From far away, Sara heard the reverberating chords of the rhapsodic melody as Tom played. The sonata soothed her, awakened her. She began to prepare.

Tom finished the sonata. Elise sat rigidly beside him. He smiled and reached for her hand. "Sara, darling, come with me to the dining room. I fixed a tray of fruits and cheese for us. Let's have something to eat, then we can go upstairs. Tonight is our night. We have the house to ourselves. I have wonderful plans for you, my love." Tom turned to Elise, took her face gently into his two hands, and whispered, "Sara, dear, dear Sara. I love you. Do you hear me?"

Elise glared, then turned away to hide her obvious contempt. Sara heard Tom's voice, felt him touch her face and firmly take the hand that was hers—but was also Elise's. Tom led her across the room. Sara faded in and out. But she knew she was Sara. *I am stronger than Elise. And—I'm alive!*

***

Tom led Elise into the dining room, gently closing the door behind them, leading her across the room to the dining table.

Mary poured the final line of salt across the doorway.

Elise sat down, unaware of Mary's presence. Next, Mary unwrapped the sage and lit a match. The dried herb caught quickly. Smoke curled up toward the ceiling. Caught by a draft, it drifted toward Elise. She jumped up, hands grabbing at her throat as the tendrils of smoke wafted and encircled her. She struggled desperately for breath. "What are you doing?" she screamed, her voice strangled and frantic.

Mary laid the sage in a white china plate on the table, then ignited another match. She lit one of the candles. Hot wax dripped on her fingers, burning her skin. She winced, but didn't stop. She ran around the room lighting the other nine candles.

Elise's hands flew up to her face. Tom was much faster than she was. He managed to grab her hands to keep her from shielding her nose from the smoke. "Sara," he yelled, "it's time!"

Elise snarled at him. Her spittle, like a fine mist, settled on Tom's lips. She tried to push her face to his to bite his lips, but he was too strong and Sara was holding her back.

Grabbing Tom's arm, Sara shrieked, "I'm ready!"

As Tom and Mary chanted the incantations they had memorized from Terese's book, the spirit of Elise was expelled from Sara and into the glowing firelight. Elise was in a total panic, unable to cross through the salt and flee the room. The smoky curtain of burning sage engulfed her as she flew helplessly around the room. Suddenly she stopped, her ghostly image becoming more and more solid. She stood before Tom, Mary and Sara and in a show of amazing strength, Elise sucked the power from the room, from the fire, and from Mary, who bravely managed to show nothing more than a hint of fear. She stared at Elise, now standing directly before her. Elise laughed as Mary fell to her knees. Elise fought to gain control over Mary's soul.

Tom and Sara's voices cut through the silence. "We are not afraid of you, Elise!"

Mary joined the chanting. Calmly and loudly she said, "I'm not afraid of you. You will leave us. You, the spirit of Elise, who has chosen to stay on this earth, are not welcome here. You do not belong here. You will leave us. You must go into the light."

Tom, Mary, and Sara chanted together, "Go to the light, Elise Gardner. You will find peace there. You will be safe. Go to the light." Tom helped Mary to her feet. Mary reached into her pocket, pulled out the crystal vial of holy water, quickly handing it to Tom.

Tom fumbled, almost dropping the tiny bottle. He caught it before it hit the floor and pulled the cork stopper out.

Elise snarled, ran frantically around the room trying to find a way to escape. She could not. She was trapped behind the veil of smoke from the sage and the line of salt encompassing the room. Her pale skin glimmered with sweat, her eyes glowed with fear. And hatred. She spat at Tom.

"Elise Gardner, you must find your peace. We will help you find the safety of the next world. Elise, go to the light," they chanted. Tom raised the bottle. Elise shrieked and dove behind the table, crouching behind a chair. Desperate, she began to scream obscenities at Tom.

The electrifying sound of splintering window-glass interrupted the chanting. Everyone whirled toward the sound, watched shards of glass fly through the air, bouncing and glittering like a spray of diamonds in the radiant amber and golden firelight. All the candle flames extinguished at once, leaving plumes of pungent smoke that permeated their nostrils and choked their senses. A brittle, cold wind filled the room, blowing the curtain inward. The heavy material flapped eerily against the wall, its shadow writhing in grotesque patterns on the floor and ceiling.

"Damn you!" Benjamin boomed. He stood outside the window. His eyes wide and livid, sparked with flames. "You will pay for this. Damn you all!"

"Benjamin!" Elise screamed, her eyes wild with fear. "Help me!" she pleaded, her body writhing on the floor as she crawled toward him.

A dozen ravens, huge and menacing, flew into the room. Their wings beat at the line of salt below the shattered window and cleared a path in the salt. As the sage, dispersed by the wind and beating wings, cleared, Elise flew out the window and into the dark sky. The murder of ravens, beaks filled with bits of cheese and fruit followed, leaving not a morsel behind.

Benjamin snarled, "You were going to kill her! You lied to me." Shards of glass lifted from the floor, flew at Tom, narrowly missing him as he ducked.

Tom, shaking his fist and lunging toward Benjamin, yelled, "We're not afraid of either of you. Not anymore. Now get out of my house!"

Benjamin laughed. "Elise is mine now. For that I am grateful. But damn you for deceiving me!" A dark, vaporous mist swirled around him, and he disappeared into the night.

Stunned, Tom, Sara and Mary stared out the window into the blackness as a single raven crossed the moon. It's *caw, caw* echoed hauntingly into the room.

"How did Benjamin find out?" Mary asked. "We were so careful to keep our plans secret." Her face was pale, her blonde hair almost white in the soft moonlight filtering into the room. Yet she looked strong, showed no signs of fear or defeat.

"It doesn't matter," Tom said. "The important thing is he knows Elise has no power here. We showed her we are stronger than she is." Tom turned a light on, pulled the curtain closed against the chill air. "I don't believe she'll be back. You saw how she depended on Benjamin to get her away from us. I think she knows next time we won't hesitate to destroy her. Benjamin won't take that chance again."

"Do you really believe that?" Sara stared at Tom. "When I let her control me, I felt her hatred. It was horrifying."

"Trust me," Tom said, forcing a smile. He mopped the sweat from his forehead. "Come on, I feel like celebrating. I put a bottle of vodka in the freezer. One drink. Then we should all get some rest." Tom pushed the kitchen door open, stepping across the thick line of salt.

They heard a muffled ringing. "It's my cell phone," Mary said.

"Go on, answer it," Tom said, flipping the light on.

Chapter 159

"Hello?"

"Mary, thank God! I've been desperate to reach you."

"Terese! God! You won't believe what happened! Just minutes ago! We did it! We got rid of Elise."

"You did what?" Terese's shrill voice resonated in Mary's ear. "*Who* got rid of Elise?"

"Sara, Tom and I. We couldn't wait for you. We had to act quickly. I'll explain it all to you later."

"Oh, my heavens! Is everyone all right?"

"We are. We tricked Elise." Mary paused, then added, "And Benjamin. They're the spirits I told you about in the voice mail. They're gone now."

"You sent them to the other side?"

"Not exactly. But they won't be back. They know they can't come here anymore. Benjamin knows we're too strong and that next time we'll send Elise away—permanently," Mary said with total conviction.

"I wish I were with you right now. I'll get there as soon as I can. Vince and I are at the airport, waiting on stand-by. I'm so proud of you." Terese took a quick breath and added, "I knew you were strong."

"I went to your house; I found your book of incantations. And all the other things you had hidden in your closet. We used them to perform a banishment ceremony."

"Oh, child. Bless your bravery. Mary, I have to go. They're paging Vince and me. We've gotten seats on the next flight. We're on our way! Please, please be careful. Love to you all."

"Don't worry. Everything's fine now. See you tomorrow." Mary closed her phone. She smiled at Sara and Tom, both visibly exhausted as they leaned against the counter.

Tom handed Mary her drink and raised his glass. "To us!" They clinked their glasses together.

"I'm going outside to close the shutter on the dining room window. It'll keep the weather out until I can have the pane replaced. You two go on upstairs. I'll sweep up the glass and be up in a few minutes."

"Mary, are you okay to stay alone in Cassie's room?" Sara asked.

"Yeah, I'm so tired, I really think I could sleep anywhere."

"You're not afraid?" Sara asked, leading Mary up the back staircase.

"Not anymore. What about you?"

"No. I know, without a doubt, I—we—are stronger than Elise." Sara turned the hall light on, adding, "Or Benjamin." She hugged Mary, then watched her walk down the hall and into the bedroom. "Goodnight." The door closed with a gentle whisper of wood on wood, a quiet end to the harrowing night.

Mary would sleep soundly all night, not waking until late morning. Tom and Sara would sleep fitfully, entwined in each other's arms, waking at every creak and groan as the house settled into the night. All would wake to a chilling, dark morning filled with swirling fog, wind and heavy rain.

Chapter 160

Vince held her hand as Terese shared what Mary had told her. When she was silent, staring off into the dark sky, he asked her a simple question, "Do you think those spirits, Elise and Benjamin, are gone?"

"I honestly can't tell. When we get home, as soon as it's light out, I'll go to Remington."

Vince squeezed her hand. "I know you will. But, Terese, I don't want you to go."

"I have to. You know that. I need to know if the spirits are truly gone. They can't hide from me." Tracing her finger against the cold, glass window of the plane, Terese whispered sadly," I think Sara may still be in trouble. I have to help her."

Hours later, as the sun struggled to brighten a horizon heavy with clouds, Terese kissed Vince gently on his cheek and left him sleeping soundly. By the time she reached the beach highway a thick fog had rolled over the coast. Pounding rain beat against her windshield, the wiper blades unable to keep the window clear.

Chapter 161

Elise was curled in a fetal position, arms covering her head, when Benjamin found her at the outlook above the ocean. He said nothing as he took his place beside her.

"Benjamin, how did you know I needed your help?" Elise sat up, placed her pale hand on Benjamin's. "I would not have survived their attack."

"We have a strong bond, you and I," Benjamin said softly to Elise, who shivered uncontrollably beside him. "I sensed your danger." Benjamin pulled Elise close to him, enclosed her body in his. "That you were—are—safe, is my only desire."

"I am so relieved you didn't give up on me, Benjamin. After all the things I said to you. We will stay together now. You and I. If you are willing, that is." Softly she stroked his cheek and traced the line of his jawbone. "Benjamin, where will we go now?"

"We won't be leaving, Elise. We'll stay here, close to Remington House. Why would we leave? We still have much to accomplish. Eventually. There is no hurry."

"What? You saw what they did to me! When the medium comes back, she will search us out and destroy both of us. We have to leave."

"We don't. Come with me." Benjamin stood up. "I was still at Remington when Terese called Mary. I listened to their conversation. Terese is the only person who can detect us. She's on her way. We will stop her."

Benjamin helped Elise off the ground and led her down the bluff. They fought the torrential rain and wind—Elise and Benjamin found no ravens to transport them that stormy morning.

Chapter 162

Terese couldn't see a thing! She pulled over onto the shoulder of the road, now soft and unstable from the torrents of hard-driving rain. The car began slipping sideways. Terese gunned the engine, but the tires found no traction in the wet, sand-laden dirt. Panicked, she undid her seatbelt and grabbed the door handle. The door wouldn't open. The car slid faster now, beginning to descend the steep, rocky embankment above the ocean. Frantically she pushed the unlock button. Nothing. She slammed her shoulder against the door. It wouldn't budge. As the car began to tumble, she rolled the window down. When the driver's side was facing skyward, Terese clawed at the window frame, pulled herself up and jumped.

Her chances of survival may have been better had she stayed in the car. After rolling three times, Terese's black sedan came to rest, right side up, against a one-hundred-year-old white pine, its roots firmly embedded in the rocky hillside. Terese, free flying, bounced off an outcrop of rocks, striking her head. Her body was brutally slammed again and again against the cliff as she tumbled. Briefly, her body landed on a precipice of sandy earth, now sodden with rain. The earth crumbed and slid downward. Terese, unconscious and unable to grab onto the deeply rooted shrubs that surely could have held her weight, never felt the final impact as her body was hurled head first into the wall of rocks that served to break the ocean waves violently pounding the shore.

On a boulder, whipped with ocean spray, a man and woman, ghostly and pale, stood watching as Terese's body repeatedly slammed the rocks.

Minutes earlier, as Terese pulled off the highway, Benjamin and Elise saw her car and flew down to the shoulder of the road behind her. Hidden in the heavy fog, Benjamin had taken his physical form—powerful and strong. He pushed and shoved the car as Terese helplessly fought to get back onto solid pavement.

When Terese managed to escape the car, Benjamin and Elise readied themselves to attack. It proved unnecessary. Watching from above, satisfied that their task was complete, they returned to the Harrison's house to find shelter from the storm.

Days later, curled up in front of a warm fire, Benjamin twisted a lock of Elise's golden hair between his fingers. "Elise, I've been thinking. There's a small, hidden room in the attic at Remington. We'll go there, no one will know. We should be there. Close to Tom. And Sara."

Smiling, Elise turned her face to him. Her velvet-brown eyes glistened as a single tear balanced precariously at the corner, then spilled. Benjamin gently wiped it away with his thumb. He brought his thumb to his mouth, savored the salty taste with his tongue, acknowledged the essence of his love.

Chapter 163

On a cold, winter's day in mid-January, the town of Ravenswood laid Terese Montagna-Jamison to rest. The sun shone brightly, warming the ground as her casket, covered in a blanket of white roses, disappeared into the earth.

Most of the town turned out to say their farewells. Tom, Cassie, Mary and Sara knew, without a doubt, that Terese had died trying to make certain they were safe.

Cassie, who had arrived earlier that morning from New York, lagged behind at the grave to talk to Mary and her parents. Mary's mother patted Cassie on the back, finally drew her close and hugged her. Cassie's sobs echoed in the still morning.

Sara said, "I should go to Cassie." As Sara turned, Sheriff Vince Jamison, Terese's newly widowed husband, grabbed her arm.

"Terese died because of you! She was the love of my life. This is your fault. Damn you!"

"Vince, I'm so sorry." Sara struggled to pull her arm from Vince's strong hold. "If only she'd called one of us, we would have told her not to drive in the storm."

Tom put an arm around Vince's shoulder, disengaging his hold on Sara. He said, "It was an accident. You know that, Vince. We would never have let her drive in the storm. Come on. I'll walk you to your car."

Vince's daughter, Lisa, came up from behind. "Dad! Come on, let's go home." To Tom and Sara she said, "I'm sorry. Dad's beside himself. Forgive him."

"There's nothing to forgive. We understand." Tom smiled at Lisa. "Vince, Lisa, please accept our deepest sympathy."

Vince nodded, extending his hand to Tom. "I'm sorry. I miss her so much. I can't understand how this could happen. She knew better than to drive that highway in a storm."

"The storm probably rolled in quickly and caught her off guard. The beach highway is a dangerous stretch of road, even in the best of conditions," Tom said.

Vince nodded again and turned away.

Lisa asked, "Mr. Gardner, will you and your family come to Dad's house for the funeral reception? It would mean a lot to both of us."

"We'd like that very much. Thank you."

Lisa ran to catch up with her dad, wrapping her arm around his drooping shoulders.

"Is Vince all right?" Cassie asked, walking across the rocky ground to Tom and Sara. She dabbed at her red, puffy eyes with a delicately embroidered handkerchief.

"No. He's not. He's had his heart torn out. He may never get over it," Tom said solemnly. He opened the door of the Jeep and motioned Cassie to get into the back seat. When she was in, he closed her door. "Sara, get in the front. We'll follow Vince's car. I have no idea where he lives."

"We're going to Vince's house? We barely know him," Cassie said.

"Terese would like it. She'll know we're there," Sara said, watching the rows of gravestones pass by her window as they followed the line of cars out of the cemetery.

"You're right, of course," Cassie said. "She *will* know we're there. She may even try to contact us."

"That's a sobering thought," Sara said. "One more haunted spirit to add to our menagerie at Remington. Terese, if you're listening, go to the other side. Rest and find your peace. We'll be fine." Sara tried to sound clever, hoping to make the others laugh. They did not.

***

On the hillside overlooking Terese's grave, Elise and Benjamin sat high up on the thick branch of a barren, beech tree. No one had been aware of their presence, even though they'd been there for the entire service. "This would be a good time to settle into Remington House. Tom and his *ladies* won't be back for hours," Benjamin said, grabbing Elise's arm and pulling her to the ground. They floated downward in a heavy, gray mist, landing silently and gently—not a single leaf disturbed, not a single pebble dislodged. In the distance the last car driving down the twisting, cemetery road took the final curve and entered the highway back to town.

Chapter 164

Hours later, as the late afternoon twilight burned the sky orange and crimson, Tom, Sara and Cassie drove up the long winding road to Remington House, slipping and sliding on the snow-covered driveway in yet another winter storm.

Elise and Benjamin had just finished dragging the last of their belongings into the narrow attic room carefully hidden behind a false wall in a bedroom closet at the western end of the house. Benjamin slid the panel closed in the back of the bedroom closet. They were safe.

The room was warm; Elise had been pleased. The chimney from the lower floors, as well as a furnace vent, heated the room well. There was one small octagonal, double-paned window, unnoticeable from outside, tucked in behind the chimney wall. The thick glass afforded a soft peach glow from the setting sun to filter into the room.

Elise and Benjamin, worn out from their long day, curled up on the feather mattress that Benjamin had hauled into the room many years ago. To make certain the Lindemans never found out about the room's existence, Benjamin had rarely stayed there—it had been his only sanctuary.

Sighing, Elise pulled the heavy, down comforter around her chin and immediately fell asleep, safe and secure with Benjamin beside her. Benjamin watched her for a few minutes, stroking her pale cheeks and golden hair.

Elise did not awaken when he got out of bed. Leaving the tiny room, he walked down the hall to the room facing east, the room above Tom's bedroom. Benjamin paced back and forth waiting for the morning twilight.

As the sun cast shimmers of light on the tumultuous ocean, dozens of ravens gathered on bare branches at the bluff's edge to greet the coming of morning. Benjamin laughed. *In time this will all be Elise's and mine.* In the mirrored surface of the window glass, his eyes glowed orange, reflecting the rising sun.

***

Tom too watched his woman sleep. Beside him, Sara dreamed fitfully, mumbling words Tom couldn't understand. He stroked her hair and cheeks, finally pulled her closer, trying to soothe her and banish her nightmares. She relaxed, sighed softly and snuggled into Tom's arms.

From outside, on the balcony, the faint fluttering of wings, the soft, eerie caws of one raven, then another and another, kept Tom awake. Shadows of the birds, huge and encompassing, undulated across the floor, onto the bed, the walls, the ceiling. Tom held Sara closer, listened to her strained breathing. As her nightmare started anew, she whispered, "They're here." Tom cradled her, gently kissed the top of her head. Sara moaned softly and turned over.

Tom got quietly out of bed. For hours he sat, a blanket wrapped around his shoulders, listening to the lonely calls of the ravens echoing through the frigid, night air. He waited for the sun to rise over the night-blackened ocean. Overhead, the attic floor creaked. The faint sound of laughter reached Tom's ears.

Epilog

We are not alone. At Remington House, someone always waits. We hear their soft, hushed footsteps behind us, see gray mist swirl and materialize into shapes of those we hoped and prayed had departed this world. We hear whispers and laughter. Sometimes these ghosting spirits steal into our dreams. We cannot escape them.

They hide behind half-closed doors, under beds shrouded with dust ruffles, in dark closets, around shadowy corners. They crouch at the top of the stairs, hidden in night's shadows. As we climb, we see them waiting. As we near, they vanish.

Darkness deceives us. Is it them or merely a shadow? Sometimes we think we cannot bear it any longer. But we know we have no choice. They live among us. Or is it that we live among them? We know they will follow us, no matter *where* we go. We cannot rid ourselves of them, though we have tried again and again.

No. We are not alone. With a shot of vodka, and another and another, we try to banish these demons. We do not succeed.

And yet . . . we are drawn to them. Even as we fear them. For some perverse reason, we savor their undying devotion. They cannot, or will not, leave us. They are as bound to us as we are to them. These demons, our own dark side.

Some mornings, if we wake before dawn, we see them on the bluff. As the sun rises in glowing shades of peaches and grays, they are visible as misty shadows, reflecting the soft hues of dawn. This rising and setting of the sun seems to give them power. We, mere mortals, are helpless to stop the cycle of day and night that feeds them.

The ones we thought lost forever are here. They creep about the halls and down the stairs at Remington House. Reflected in mirrors, they stand behind us, arms drawn around our shoulders. Hidden in the dark shadows, they follow us. Always there. Always waiting.

No. We are not alone.

∞ Finis ∞

THE HAUNTING TIME OF TWILIGHT   Laura Keegan

Hopes, dreams, loves, desires.
Have they faded into eternity with the day's last breath,
as dusk cloaks the landscape
with its first glimmers of twilight,
when colors explode and radiate
before succumbing to the night?

Twilight bursts with colors
like vibrant shards of glass,
glimmering dangerously,
sharp as razorblades.

Passion and desire wane.
Defeated they surrender to the black night,
somehow remaining miraculously entwined
with glistening fragments of unrealized expectations
and visions of dreams to come.

At this haunting time of twilight,
when day yields to night,
and everything is shrouded in suffocating hopelessness,
we envision ourselves lost in an eternal desolation,
dejected and abandoned.

Yet—won't we see the ominous midnight hours
give way to faint glimmers of first light?
Will the sun not rise again in splinters of radiance?

As dawn breaks,
golden red spears and flaming orange spikes
will slice and cut the horizon,
suggesting the possibility—
we have yet another chance to pursue
our hopes, dreams, loves, desires.

Acknowledgement

I could never have written this novel without the mentoring and encouragement of my special friends: Judy, Jamie, Mary, Barb, Beth, Heidi, Sherri, Pat, Laurie and John. I am forever grateful to them for their faith in me.

About the Author

Haunting at Remington House is Laura V. Keegan's debut novel. Laura is an award winning author, speaker, President of the Poetry Society of Colorado and is active in local government.

She has written numerous poems and short stories. A collection of her poetry, *Dark Side of My Soul*, is scheduled for release soon. She's currently working on a sequel to *Haunting at Remington House*. Laura resides with her family in Edgewater, Colorado.

Visit Laura's website at: www.lauravkeegan.com

www.ingramcontent.com/pod-product-compliance
Lightning Source LLC
Chambersburg PA
CBHW022203030726
47494CB00019B/19